C0-ARW-564

Music Education

A GUIDE TO INFORMATION SOURCES

Volume 1 in the Education Information Guide Series

Ernest E. Harris

Professor of Music Education
Director of Instructional Support Services
Teachers College, Columbia University

Gale Research Company
Book Tower, Detroit, Michigan 48226

Library of Congress Cataloging in Publication Data

Harris, Ernest E
Music education.

(Education information guide series; v.1) (Gale information guide library)
Includes indexes.
1. Music—Instruction and study—Directories. 2. School music—Instruction and study—Directories. 3. Music—Bibliography. I. Title. II. Series: Education information guide series; v. 1.
ML19.H37 780'.7 74-11560
ISBN 0-8103-1309-X

VITA

Ernest E. Harris is currently professor of music education and director of Instructional Support Services at Teachers College, Columbia University. He received his B.A. from Catawba College; his M.A. and Ed.D. from Teachers College, Columbia University; and his Litt. D. from Catawba College. Professor Harris's former positions include the Executive Board of the National Music Council; National Chairman of the Committee on Instrumental Music in the Schools, Music Educators National Conference; National President of the American String Teachers Association; and Province Governor of Phi Mu Alpha Sinfonia Fraternity. He makes numerous appearances as festival conductor, adjudicator, lecturer, clinician, and director of workshops for music educators.

While serving as consultant to the Department of Education, State of Hawaii, Dr. Harris received commendation for his contribution to the artistic and aesthetic development of youth in a resolution by the House of Representatives, State of Hawaii, in 1965.

He is coauthor of LEARNING TO TEACH THROUGH PLAYING and YOUNG AMERICA AT THE VIOLIN (three volumes). Professor Harris is the author of THE SOLO DRUMMER and arranger of numerous compositions for school bands and orchestras as well as a contributor of articles to professional journals.

CONTENTS

Foreword xi

Acknowledgments xiii

Introduction xv

Part I General Reference Sources
- Section 1 Guides to Special Libraries and Collections 3
- Section 2 Directories--Comprehensive 7
- Section 3 Directories--Organizations and Institutions 9
- Section 4 Directories--Performing Arts and Festivals 13
- Section 5 Comprehensive Guides to Books and Literature 15
- Section 6 Guides to Book Reviews 19
- Section 7 Guides to Periodicals and Professional Journals 21
- Section 8 Indexing Journals 23
- Section 9 Abstracting Journals 27
- Section 10 Thematic Indexes and Catalogs 29
- Section 11 Selected Guides to Bibliographic Sources 33
- Section 12 Research Journals--Music Education 37
- Section 13 Research Journals--Allied Fields 39
- Section 14 State Journals 41
- Section 15 Dissertations 43
- Section 16 Masters' Theses 47
- Section 17 Research Techniques 49
- Section 18 Information Services and Systems 53
- Section 19 Guides to Grant Support Programs, Funding Agencies, and Proposal Writing 57
- Section 20 Business Aspects of Music and Music Education 61
- Section 21 National Music Fraternities, Sororities, and Honor Society 69
- Section 22 Dictionaries and Encyclopedias--Music 71
- Section 23 Dictionaries and Encyclopedias--Education 79

Part II Music in Education
- Section 24 Philosophical Foundations, Principles, and Practices . . . 83
- Section 25 Psychological and Physiological Aspects of Music 99

Contents

Section 26 Music in Early Childhood Education 107
Section 27 Music in the Elementary School 109
Section 28 Music in Junior High and Middle Schools 125
Section 29 Music in Secondary Schools. 127
Section 30 Music in Higher Education and Teacher Education. 131
Section 31 Urban Education and the Culturally Disadvantaged 141
Section 32 Administration and Supervision of Music Education 149

Part III Subject Matter Areas
Section 33 Aesthetics and Music 161
Section 34 Appreciation and Understanding of Music. 167
Section 35 History of Music 179
Section 36 Musicology 191
Section 37 Ethnomusicology. 199
Section 38 Folk Music and Folklore 203
Section 39 American Music. 213
Section 40 Contemporary Music 221
Section 41 Electronic Music, Musique Concrète, and Computer Music 233
Section 42 Opera, Ballet, and Dance 237
Section 43 Popular Music--Jazz--Rock 255
Section 44 Music and the Black Culture 265
Section 45 Jewish Music 271
Section 46 Religious Music 275
Section 47 Choral and Vocal Music 281
Section 48 Instrumental Music 295
Section 49 Musical Instruments--Historical References 331
Section 50 Keyboard Music, Instruments, and Pedagogy. 339
Section 51 Music Structure, Theory, and Composition 349
Section 52 Conducting 369
Section 53 Acoustics 377

Part IV Special Uses of Music
Section 54 Music and the Physically and Mentally Handicapped . . . 383
Section 55 Music in Therapy. 393
Section 56 Music and the Gifted. 397
Section 57 Music and Recreation 399

Part V Technology, Multimedia Resources, and Equipment
Section 58 Technology in Music Education 405
Section 59 Computer Applications 409
Section 60 Comprehensive Guides to Audiovisual Materials and Services 411
Section 61 Phonograph Records and Audio Tapes. 413
Section 62 Guides to Films and Filmstrips (General) 425
Section 63 Companies or Services Specializing in Music Education Films 427
Section 64 8mm Cartridge Film Producers and Distributors 429
Section 65 Filmstrip Producers and Distributors 431
Section 66 Video Tapes 433

Section 67 Slides 435
Section 68 Overhead Transparencies 437
Section 69 Sources for Easy-to-Play Instruments and Music Teaching Aids--Partial List 439
Section 70 Musical Instrument Manufacturers 441
Section 71 Audiovisual Equipment 445
Section 72 Platforms, Shells, Storage and Sound Modules 447
Section 73 Nonprint Media--Journals 449
Section 74 Nonprint Media--Associations 451

Appendixes
Appendix A Supplemental Listing of Holdings in Certain Libraries as Revealed in a Recent Survey 455
Appendix B Periodicals 475

Indexes
Author Index 495
Title Index 517
Subject Index 553

FOREWORD

To deal with the realm of music education implies a recognition of the fact that we are dealing with human values and with aesthetic experience. And if we think that music education is important there is also an assumption that the tonal and temporal dimensions of sound in interaction with composer, performer, and listener are important, even necessary, to human life.

This particular bibliography with its annotations exemplifies a concern with the importance of music education, with the values of a democratic, pluralistic society, and with the maximum development of each individual's powers of aesthetic-musical discrimination. These ends could be accomplished only by an explicit effort to present the complex considerations involved in the whole range of music education. At present an unevaluated comprehensive bibliography of music education would be enormous--beyond the capabilities of human or mechanical control. Only by a selective sifting and organization of the vast mass of available materials, utilizing the judgment of a master musician, master educator, and master bibliographer--Ernest Harris, professor of music education and director of Instructional Support Services in association with the Teachers College Library in New York City--could this be accomplished.

Sidney Forman
Professor of Education
Librarian
Teachers College
Columbia University
New York, New York

ACKNOWLEDGMENTS

It would be difficult, indeed impossible, to properly express my gratitude to the numerous people who contributed in one way or another to the preparation of this book. Friends, colleagues, and many other experienced music educators were generous in expressing judgments concerning content, and in many instances contributed specific suggestions. I owe a special debt of gratitude to those individuals in the national offices of the Music Educators National Conference; the MENC Historical Center; the National Education Association; the Music Division of the Library of Congress; the U.S. Office of Education; the Department of Health, Education and Welfare; the National Archives; the Music Division of the New York Public Library at Lincoln Center; and the librarians at Columbia University and Teachers College. These last not only consulted with me personally, but also provided generous assistance in the use of the holdings in their institutions. There were many other people associated with major music and music education libraries, associations, publishers, colleges, and universities who, by means of correspondence, rendered valuable assistance. Deep appreciation is also expressed to those several individuals who assisted in the preparation of the manuscript.

I can only hope that the work will prove useful to expedite and enhance the effort of music educators to beautify man's existence through music.

INTRODUCTION

The goal of any music education program is human betterment through music. The variety of ways in which this takes place is infinite. All teaching, learning, and research, however, should focus directly or indirectly on this aim. This book of information sources is intended to assist music educators in their never-ending efforts to enhance the quality of life through music.

Because music becomes human experience and influences human behavior in many ways, the field of music education is highly complex. In considering the total field of music education it is helpful to view it as a community of disciplines. The worker, commonly referred to as a music educator, is expected to be a musician, an educator, a researcher, a musicologist, a philosopher, a curriculum specialist, a psychologist, a physiologist, a scientist, a guidance counselor, a conductor, a composer, and an administrator. It is folly, of course, to suggest that any individual should be equally skilled in all of these areas. However, the good music educator will realize the necessity of constantly seeking to enlarge and develop those insights and facts which enhance competency.

In bringing together this guide an effort has been made to represent both works which reflect current thought and those older sources whose content remains pertinent and useful to today's practitioner. Some users will consider the result more extensive than they would like, preferring a limited list of highly recommended materials. The author feels that there is merit in having a broad range--yet always selective--from which intelligent choices can be made in the interest of meeting the special or unique needs of any given situation.

THE BROAD FIELD OF MUSIC EDUCATION

Music education encompasses most aspects of music and is associated with many fundamentals of education. It includes the social and philosophical foundations, the total curriculum, guidance, and administration of education as well as allied educational fields such as psychology, the humanities, and science. It is important to note also that the manner in which music is taught is both unique and relatively young in the field of education. All of these facts make it understandable that a truly comprehensive, well-organized bibliographic source covering the field of music in education is late in development. The present bibliographic tools available to the music educator are, too often, fragmentary and scattered. This situation is changing rapidly, however, because of progress being made in the development of information services and systems. We are no longer waiting for new technology to be developed. This is already available, and now research, programming, and implementation must catch up to it. Several significant systems have already been launched and are now being used. Some of the more practical ones are cited in this volume.

GENERAL REFERENCES

General references, which include certain indexing and abstracting journals, and the research journals in some allied fields, are a rich source of information for the conscientious music educator. All too often music educators ignore references which do not contain the words "music" or "music education" in the title. These reference sources should be considered essential for in-depth researching in this field.

MUSIC HISTORY AND UNDERSTANDING

Some of the bibliographies cited are of a musicological nature. This is inevitable, as one of the major points of this guide is that the basic goal of music education is human betterment. The music educator, then, must be cognizant of the role music has played in other cultures, ethnic groups, and the aesthetic development of mankind in general. That music teaching and learning be enriched--directly or indirectly--in this respect is essential if music education is to be good music education. The present list of references in this area would by no means meet the needs of the serious musicologist, but it should be adequate for the purposes intended. Sections 36 and 37, Musicology and Ethnomusicology, extend this list for teachers of music history and music understanding.

PEDAGOGY AND MUSIC

In locating bibliographies which focus primarily on the pedagogical aspects of music in the schools, one will need to examine carefully the various textbooks on the subject. Nearly all such sources contain bibliographies or reference lists. Some are broad and "all-inclusive" while others are highly selective. In any case, the searcher will, at all times, want to be observant and sensitive to the quality of the selection and the chronological coverage.

No attempt has been made to provide comprehensive coverage of textbooks on any given aspect of music or music education. The texts that are cited were selected for their coverage of the subject and/or for the bibliographic material which they contain.

RESEARCH TECHNIQUES

The meaning and place of research in any of the arts is always a controversial issue. The sources presented here have been selected on the belief that all music educators should inculcate scholarly research interest of an appropriate kind. The extent and level of the research interest is, of course, the critical issue. The determining factors include the type of professional work in which the individual is engaged, or expects to be engaged, and other personal interests. The sources listed, therefore, provide a wide range of information concerning fundamental techniques for conducting and interpreting both musical research and educational research.

DISSERTATIONS

Except for a few rare cases, dissertations have not been cited as separate entries. The section devoted to guides, indexes, and abstracts for dissertations--including computer searching--should be quite adequate for the utilization of this rich resource of information.

ANNOTATIONS

Almost all entries carry an annotation. The length of the annotation does not reflect the possible usefulness of the source. In some instances the title is quite self-explanatory. In other cases, the title, or the nature of the subject--or both--may justify a more lengthy comment. The annotations indicate the content in a general way, letting the reader decide if further investigation is desirable.

SOURCES AND CATEGORIES

Many sources belong in more than one category, and the "See also" list of references at the end of each section covers most of these instances. In a few cases duplication is permitted when it is considered essential to the category. In all cases the principal placement of an entry is based on the nature of the content and the style of presentation rather than on title alone.

No section can be considered complete or exhaustive. The works that are listed are those considered to be pertinent to the subject and which also provide references or bibliographies which will lead the searcher to still other works. By combining the sources listed with the additional sources contained in their references, a comprehensive coverage of the subject will result.

Part I

GENERAL REFERENCE SOURCES

Section 1
GUIDES TO SPECIAL LIBRARIES AND COLLECTIONS

One of the hallmarks of a competent researcher is his facility in locating the material he wishes to examine. An important first step is a visit to the reference section of a library to consult one or more of the guides to special libraries listed below. Two outcomes are likely. It is almost certain that a number of libraries, institutions, organizations, or information centers will be found which contain holdings of the type being sought. Secondly, the investigator will probably be surprised to learn of the rich research resources which are located near his own geographical area.

Since travel and study abroad is commonplace today, this section also contains guides to special library resources for the entire world.

Benton, Rita, comp. DIRECTORY OF MUSIC RESEARCH LIBRARIES. 3 vols. Iowa City: University of Iowa, 1967-72.

A most useful tool for the serious researcher in the field of music. Part I: CANADA AND THE UNITED STATES (1967); part II: THIRTEEN EUROPEAN COUNTRIES (1970); part III: SPAIN, FRANCE, ITALY AND PORTUGAL (1972).

Brummel, Leendert, and Egger, E. GUIDE TO UNION CATALOGUES AND INTERNATIONAL LOAN CENTERS. The Hague: Nijhoff, 1961. 89 p.

Lists approximately 200 union catalogs, including printed ones, in approximately 50 countries. Text also in French.

Cudworth, Charles L. "Libraries and Collections." In GROVE'S DICTIONARY OF MUSIC AND MUSICIANS, 5th ed., edited by Eric Blom, vol. 5, pp. 160-223. London: Macmillan, 1954.

Includes U.S. and foreign libraries and collections. Bibliography.

Dove, Jack. McCOLVIN AND REEVES' MUSIC LIBRARIES. Rev. ed. 2 vols. London: Andre Deutsch, 1965.

Volume I: GENERAL ORGANIZATION AND CONTENTS, 172 p. Discusses the contemporary music scene and its impact on libraries; the collection of municipal, university, cathedral, college, and other libraries both British and foreign; the Code of Cataloguing by the International Association of Music Libraries.

Volume II: LITERATURE AND SCORES: BIBLIOGRAPHY, 744 p. A bibliography of music literature covering more than 6,000 British and foreign books published to the end of 1962. Also a selected bibliography of musical compositions since 1957.

Langwill, Lyndesay Graham. "Collections of Instruments in Europe and America." In GROVE'S DICTIONARY OF MUSIC AND MUSICIANS, 5th ed., edited by Eric Blom, vol. 4, pp. 509-15. London: Macmillan, 1954.

Lewanski, Richard C. SUBJECT COLLECTIONS IN EUROPEAN LIBRARIES, A DIRECTORY AND BIBLIOGRAPHICAL GUIDE. New York: R.R. Bowker Co., 1965. 789 p.

Special music section, pages 499-514.

Library of Congress, comp. THE NATIONAL UNION CATALOG OF MANUSCRIPT COLLECTION, 1959-1962, INDEX. 2 vols. Hamden, Conn.: Shoe String Press, 1964. 732 p.

Alphabetized catalog of manuscript collections--includes extensive listings on music, music education, scores, societies, instruments, musicians.

Long, Maureen W. MUSICIANS AND LIBRARIES IN THE UNITED KINGDOM. London: Library Association, 1972. 152 p.

MacKeigan, Helaine, comp. 1973-1974 AMERICAN LIBRARY DIRECTORY, 29TH EDITION: A CLASSIFIED LIST OF LIBRARIES IN THE UNITED STATES AND CANADA WITH PERSONNEL AND STATISTICAL DATA. New York and London: R.R. Bowker Co., 1973.

A descriptive listing of libraries in the United States and Canada. Includes public, university, college, junior college, and special libraries. This serial has been compiled biennially since 1908.

Seaton, Douglass. "Important Library Holdings at Forty-one North American Universities." CURRENT MUSICOLOGY 17 (1974): 7-68.

SUBJECT COLLECTIONS. 3d ed., rev. and comp. by Lee Ash and Denis Lorenz. New York and London: R.R. Bowker Co., 1974. 908 p.

A guide to special book collections and subject emphases as reported by university, college, public, and special libraries in the United States and Canada.

UNESCO. GUIDE TO NATIONAL BIBLIOGRAPHIC INFORMATION CENTERS. 2d ed. Paris: 1962. 74 p.

Addresses, aims, resources, publications, and so forth, of centers in seventy-seven countries.

Veinstein, Andre, ed. PERFORMING ARTS LIBRARIES AND MUSEUMS OF THE WORLD. 2d ed., rev. by Cecile Giteau. Paris: Editions du Centre National de la Recherche Scientifique, 1967. 801 p.

This edition lists all the known performing art collections, libraries, and museums throughout the world. The general characteristics of the collection, the nature of the documents, hours, admission procedures, and assistance given to the reader are notes. Name and subject indexes.

Young, Margaret Labash; Young, Harold Chester; and Kruzas, Anthony T., eds. DIRECTORY OF SPECIAL LIBRARIES AND INFORMATION CENTERS. 4th ed. 3 vols. Detroit: Gale Research Co., 1977.

A guide to special libraries, research libraries, information centers, archives, and data centers maintained by government agencies, business, industry, newspapers, educational institutions, nonprofit organizations, and societies in the fields of science, technology, medicine, law, art, religion, history, social sciences, and humanistic studies.

Volume 1 covers over 13,000 special libraries in 2,000 fields. It includes a subject index. Volume 2 is a geographic-personnel index. Volume 3 is a periodic supplement including cumulative indexes.

_____. SUBJECT DIRECTORY OF SPECIAL LIBRARIES. 4th ed. 5 vols. Detroit: Gale Research Co., 1977.

This directory contains the same information found in volume 1 of DIRECTORY OF SPECIAL LIBRARIES (see above), arranged according to subject. Volume 4, SOCIAL SCIENCES AND HUMANITIES LIBRARIES, has a section on music libraries.

ASSOCIATIONS

Music Library Association (MLA), 343 South Main Street, Rm. 205; Ann Arbor, Mich. 48108.

Publications: NOTES. Quarterly. One of the most reliable and scholarly reference journals in the field of serious music. Provides bibliographies and various lists, reviews books and records, and surveys musical literature.

Index Series. Irregular.

MUSIC CATALOGING BULLETIN. Monthly.

Newsletter. Quarterly.

TECHNICAL REPORTS. Irregular.

International Association of Music Libraries, United States Branch, Northwestern University Music Library, Evanston, Ill. 60201.

Publication: FONTES ARTIS MUSICAE.

Section 2
DIRECTORIES—COMPREHENSIVE

This group of directories is limited to those which are both comprehensive and diversified. If the source being sought is not included in one of the directories listed below, it is likely that it will be found in one of the directories which follow, or, in the appropriate subject matter section of this book.

EDUCATOR'S WORLD (EW). Englewood, Colo.: Fisher Publishing Co., 1971. 685 p.

Contains detailed information on educational associations, including descriptions of their memberships and purposes, their periodicals, and their conventions. Sections on educational research centers and educational foundations contain information on their activities and fields of concentration, their facilities, and their publications. A separate section--Publications--lists essential information on more than 2,000 educational journals, magazines, newsletters, and proceedings reports published either by organizations or by independent publishing companies. Also included is a calendar of meetings and conventions in chronological order. A section--The Area of Interest--groups the associations, research centers, foundations, publications, and conventions into sixty-seven different fields of interest, enabling the reader to locate information dealing with specific aspects of the educational field.

Field, Gladys S., ed. in chief. THE MUSICIANS' GUIDE: DIRECTORY OF THE WORLD OF MUSIC. 5th ed. New York: Music Information Service, 1972. 1,013 p.

Listing of associations, competitions, awards, grants, educational facilities, libraries, publications, recordings, performances, professions, trade, and industry. One of the most comprehensive music directories available. New edition scheduled for 1977.

Klein, Bernard, ed. GUIDE TO AMERICAN EDUCATIONAL DIRECTORIES. 3d ed. New York: B. Klein and Co., 1969. 235 p.

Includes eighteen listings in the field of music, ranging from encyclopedias to guides to music industries, manufacturers, and publishers.

Pavlakis, Christopher. THE AMERICAN MUSIC HANDBOOK. New York: Free Press; London: Collier-Macmillan Publishers, 1974. 836 p.

A valuable resource book that attempts to bring together information on all areas of organized musical activity in the United States. Emphasis is on "serious" music. More than 5,000 entries are included, covering associations and organizations of all kinds; performing groups; individual musicians; composers; music festivals and competitions; institutions that teach music; communications media (periodicals, radio, television) that are related to music; awards, grants, and fellowships in music; music industries; publishers; and concert managers. In addition, there is a foreign supplement which lists music festivals, international competitions and awards, and music publishers.

Section 3

DIRECTORIES—ORGANIZATIONS AND INSTITUTIONS

Associated Councils of the Arts. DIRECTORY OF NATIONAL ARTS ORGANIZATIONS. New York: 1972. 60 p. Paper.

Provides names, addresses, and chief executive officers for ninety-seven national arts organizations and complete details of membership, services, programs, and publications for twenty-six of these.

EDUCATION ASSOCIATIONS 1974. Washington, D.C.: Superintendent of Documents, Government Printing Office, 1974. 107 p.

Lists names and addresses of educational and professional organizations related to schools in each state. Includes publications.

EDUCATION DIRECTORY--ELEMENTARY AND SECONDARY EDUCATION--PUBLIC SCHOOL SYSTEMS. Washington, D.C.: Government Printing Office, 1969/70-- .

An annual directory of all agencies providing free public elementary and secondary education in the United States and its outlying areas.

EDUCATION DIRECTORY--HIGHER EDUCATION. Washington, D.C.: Government Printing Office, 1969/70-- .

Lists institutions in the United States and its outlying areas that offer at least a two-year program. Provides considerable amount of information concerning each institution, including names of principal officers by functional areas of responsibility.

ENCYCLOPEDIA OF ASSOCIATIONS. 12th ed. Edited by Mary Wilson Pair. 3 vols. Detroit: Gale Research Co., 1978. 1,450 p.

A major reference source for information concerning nonprofit American membership organizations. Provides detailed information regarding all important associations in the fields of music, music education, and allied fields.

Macmillan-Information Division. THE COLLEGE BLUE BOOK. 14th ed. 5 vols. New York: Macmillan, 1972.

List and description of U.S. colleges; degrees offered; accreditation; scholarships, fellowships, and grants available; specialized programs, etc.

Music Educators National Conference. "Official Directory--Registry of Music Education Leadership." MUSIC EDUCATORS JOURNAL.

The directory is published annually in the September issue and includes the following: MENC National Executive Board officers and division presidents, Secretariat, MENC division boards, MENC National Assembly, Joint Committee for the MENC Historical Center, auxiliary organizations, associated organizations, MENC official bodies, state music educators associations, state music education periodicals and editors, Council of State Supervisors of Music, Council of Student Member Chairmen, division chairmen, state chairmen, MENC Student Chapter roster, calendar of activities, MENC constitution and bylaws.

Short, Craig R., ed. and comp. DIRECTORY OF MUSIC FACULTIES IN COLLEGES AND UNIVERSITIES, UNITED STATES AND CANADA, 1974-76. 5th ed. Binghamton, N.Y.: College Music Society, 1974. 607 p.

This listing of more than 17,000 names is organized according to departments and schools, by state, degrees offered, ranks of faculty members, and teaching specializations. Includes national alphabetical list.

STANDARD EDUCATION ALMANAC, 1973-74. Edited by John S. Greene. Orange, N.J.: Academic Media, 1974. 506 p.

A comprehensive guide to educational facts and statistics. Covers all school levels.

UNESCO. International Society for Music Education. INTERNATIONAL DIRECTORY OF MUSIC EDUCATION INSTITUTIONS. New York: UNESCO Publications Center, 1968. 115 p.

Published at the request of UNESCO to meet the demand of students, teachers, and members of the general public throughout the world who plan to visit or study in countries other than their own, and who would like information concerning available educational programs and events in the field of music. Contains information collected from seventy-one countries concerning major educational institutions devoted to music and music education.

Materials arranged by country, alphabetically in ten categories: (1) conservatories and academies; (2) music and music education schools or faculties in universities; (3) other music institutions; (4) international music or music education workshops, summer courses, teacher training; (5) international competition; (6) international music festivals; (7) music libraries, archives; (8) collections of music instruments; (9) national and international organization and societies of music and music education; (10) national and international music periodicals.

WORLD OF LEARNING, 1972-73. 23d ed. 2 vols. London: Europa Publications, 1973. (Distr. by Gale Research Co., Detroit.)

Comprehensive guide to educational, scientific, and cultural organizations all over the world. The first part lists almost 500 international organizations together with their addresses, publications, officials, and a brief statement of their aims and activities. The second part includes universities, colleges, libraries, research institutions, museums, art galleries, and learned societies, together with an outline of their functions, principal officials, and periodical publications. Also listed are professors of major universities with the subjects they teach.

See also Section 30: Music in Higher Education and Teacher Education for additional directories.

Section 4
DIRECTORIES—PERFORMING ARTS AND FESTIVALS

Barish, Mort, and Mole, Michaela M. MORT'S GUIDE TO FESTIVALS, FEASTS, FAIRS AND FIESTAS. 2 vols. Princeton, N.J.: CMG Publishing Co., 1974. 176 p.

Describes numerous music festivals and sources for further information. Subject and location indexes.

Chicorel, Marietta, ed. CHICOREL BIBLIOGRAPHY TO THE PERFORMING ARTS. Chicorel Index Series, vol. 3A. New York: Chicorel Library Publishing Corp., 1972. 498 p.

A guide with over 8,000 entries arranged under more than 300 subject headings, such as dance, opera, staging, recording, etc.

Jacobs, Arthur, ed. THE MUSIC YEARBOOK, 1973-74. New York: St. Martin's Press; London: Macmillan, 1973. 841 p.

Statistics and directory pertaining to musicians and music activities in the United Kingdom.

MUSICAL AMERICA: ANNUAL DIRECTORY OF THE PERFORMING ARTS. Cincinnati, Ohio: High Fidelity/Musical America, 1976. 448 p.

Provides recent information concerning music and musicians, including entries for North America and foreign music publishers, orchestras, opera companies, artist managers, festivals, music magazines, service and professional music organizations, and a variety of other subjects. This is the most recent edition of this annual.

THE NATIONAL DIRECTORY FOR THE PERFORMING ARTS AND CIVIC CENTERS. Momence, Ill.: Handel & Company--The Baker & Taylor Companies, 1975. 982 p.

A listing of all important performing arts organizations and facilities by state, city, and category.

THE NATIONAL DIRECTORY FOR THE PERFORMING ARTS/EDUCATIONAL. Momence, Ill.: Handel & Company--The Baker & Taylor Companies, 1975. 824 p.

Detailed information concerning educational institutions with performing arts facilities. Includes courses, term lengths, degrees offered, and financial assistance.

Rachow, Louis, and Hartley, Katherine. GUIDE TO THE PERFORMING ARTS--1968. Metuchen, N.J.: Scarecrow Press, 1972. 407 p.

An index to selected periodicals in the performing arts. This volume indexes forty-eight publications.

Schoolcraft, Ralph Newman, ed. ANNOTATED BIBLIOGRAPHY OF NEW PUBLICATIONS IN THE PERFORMING ARTS. New York: Drama Book Shop, 1972. 52 p. Paper.

Stoll, Dennis Gray. MUSIC FESTIVALS OF THE WORLD: A GUIDE TO LEADING FESTIVALS OF MUSIC, OPERA AND BALLET. New York: Pergamon Press, 1963. 310 p. Photos.

Lists about one hundred festivals, giving detailed descriptions for about seventy.

UNESCO. INTERNATIONAL DIRECTORY OF MUSIC EDUCATION INSTITUTIONS. New York: UNESCO Publications Center, 1968. 115 p.

Includes festivals, competitions, music and music education workshops, summer courses, and so on, thoughout the world.

See also Section 2: Directories--Comprehensive.

Section 5

COMPREHENSIVE GUIDES TO BOOKS AND LITERATURE

GENERAL

BOOKS IN PRINT 1977-1978. 4 vols. New York and London: R.R. Bowker Co., 1977.

A highly useful bibliographic tool for educational research. Contains details on all books available from more than 3,500 publishers. Includes author, title, editor, price, publisher, publication date, series, translator, number of volumes, whether or not illustrated, binding, language, order number, edition, grade range, Library of Congress number, and ISBN. For a listing of titles by subject, see next entry.

Chicorel, Marietta, ed. CHICOREL BIBLIOGRAPHY TO BOOKS ON MUSIC AND MUSICIANS. Chicorel Index Series, vol. 10. New York: Chicorel Library Publishing Corp., 1974. 487 p.

Lists over 8,000 entries under more than 460 subject headings such as composers, musicians, folk music, instrumental music, religious music, music for young people, and so forth.

CHILDREN'S BOOKS IN PRINT. New York: R.R. Bowker Co., 1969-- . Annual.

See Section 27: Music in the Elementary School.

CUMULATIVE BOOK INDEX. New York: H.W. Wilson Co., 1928-- . Monthly, with annual cumulations.

Author-subject-title international bibliography of books published in the English language. Does not include government documents.

EL-HI TEXTBOOKS IN PRINT. 6th ed. New York: R.R. Bowker Co., 1976. 597 p.

Main emphasis is on textbooks for the classroom, appropriate reference books for use in elementary and high schools, pedagogical books, and teaching aids and programmed learning materials in book form. Includes various music series for use in general music programs.

GUIDE TO REFERENCE MATERIALS. 2d ed. Vol. 3. London: The Library Association, 1970.

Lists wide range of music reference works. Annotated.

SUBJECT GUIDE TO BOOKS IN PRINT 1976. 2 vols. New York and London: R.R. Bowker Co., 1976.

Classifies approximately 371,500 titles by subject. A companion volume to BOOKS IN PRINT 1976 (see above).

U.S. Department of Health, Education, and Welfare. SUBJECT CATALOG OF THE DEPARTMENT LIBRARY. Boston: G.K. Hall & Co., 1965.

Volume 11 contains music references, listings of courses of study, texts, and so forth.

Winchell, Constance M., ed. GUIDE TO REFERENCE BOOKS. 8th ed. Chicago: American Library Association. 1967. 741 p.

Annotated listing of reference books which are basic to research--general and special. See also the following supplements:

FIRST SUPPLEMENT 1965-1966. Compiled by Eugene Sheehy. Chicago: American Library Association, 1968. 122 p.

SECOND SUPPLEMENT 1967-1968. Compiled by Eugene Sheehy. Chicago: American Library Association, 1970. 165 p.

THIRD SUPPLEMENT 1969-1970. Compiled by Eugene Sheehy. Chicago: American Library Association, 1972. 190 p.

Wynar, Bohdan S., ed. AMERICAN REFERENCE BOOKS ANNUAL. Littleton, Colo.: Libraries Unlimited, 1970-- . Annual.

Especially useful to music librarians as a guide to the selection and evaluation of new reference books in the field of music. Entries are not duplicated from year to year.

OTHER GUIDES TO MUSICAL LITERATURE

Blom, Eric. A GENERAL INDEX TO MODERN MUSICAL LITERATURE IN THE ENGLISH LANGUAGE. 1927. Reprint. New York: Da Capo Press, 1970. 129 p.

A reference guide to the literature of every facet of music published up until 1927.

Charles, Sydney R. A HANDBOOK OF MUSIC AND MUSIC LITERATURE IN SETS AND SERIES. New York: Free Press, 1972. 497 p.

A selective listing of multivolume collections (sets and series) of music and musical literature available to today's musicologist-researcher and teacher.

Davies, J.H. MUSICALIA: SOURCES OF INFORMATION IN MUSIC. 2d ed. New York: Pergamon Press, 1969. 184 p. Music, illus., paper.

Contains a variety of approaches to the exploration of musical repertory.

Gerboth, Walter. AN INDEX TO MUSICAL FESTSCHRIFTEN AND SIMILAR PUBLICATIONS. New York: W.W. Norton and Co., 1969. 188 p.

A guide to the literature about music. Part I, a master list of books indexed; part II, a comprehensive list of articles arranged by subject area; and part III, a cross-index by author and subject.

Marco, Guy A. INFORMATION ON MUSIC: A HANDBOOK OF REFERENCE SOURCES IN EUROPEAN LANGUAGES. Vol. 1. Littleton, Colo.: Libraries Unlimited, 1975. 164 p.

Each source is annotated. Includes various kinds of dictionaries, encyclopedias, bibliographies, lists of music, and discographies. Highly useful for the serious researcher in music and musicology.

Westinghouse Learning Corp. LEARNING DIRECTORY. 7 vols. New York: 1970-72. SUPPLEMENT, 1972-73.

A categorized compendium of educational materials sources, listing instructional items under topic headings. Each listing is broken down into topic, grade level, medium, title, size, date, price, and source. A special source index lists names, addresses, and telephone numbers of all sources listed. Revised and reissued annually.

Whalon, Marion K., comp. PERFORMING ARTS RESEARCH: A GUIDE TO INFORMATION SOURCES. Detroit: Gale Research Co., 1975. 240 p.

Contains guides, dictionaries, encyclopedias, and handbooks. Also has directories, bibliographical indexes, and abstracts.

MUSIC ON MICROFICHE

Comprehensive collections of music scores, anthologies, and various historical editions are available in microfiche from the following sources:

MICROFICHE REPRINT SERIES. New York: University Music Editions, 1972. 54 p.

Collected editions of significant composers, monuments of music, and historical anthologies.

MUSICACHE. Wooster, Ohio: Bell and Howell, Micro Photo Division, 1970.

A collection of more than 1,000 complete music scores of important works on microfiche.

Section 6

GUIDES TO BOOK REVIEWS

Most of the professional journals in the fields of music and music education publish reviews of books in their respective fields. Many journals also review music teaching materials and compositions. In addition to consulting the indexes which appear below, the cumulative indexes of the appropriate music and music education journals should also be consulted for reviews.

AMERICAN REFERENCE BOOKS ANNUAL. Littleton, Colo.: Libraries Unlimited, 1970-- . Annual.

A reviewing service covering reference books in numerous fields, including music. Includes all important types of reference materials.

BOOK REVIEW DIGEST. Bronx, N.Y.: H.W. Wilson Co., 1905-- . Monthly with annual cumulations.

Contains condensed reports of book reviews. Describes scope of book and location of review.

BOOK REVIEW INDEX. Detroit: Gale Research Co., 1965-- . Bimonthly with annual cumulations.

Index to book reviews in periodicals, arranged alphabetically by author. Title of book reviewed is given as well as name of periodical, date, and page number.

EDUCATION INDEX. New York: H.W. Wilson Co., 1929-- . 10/year.

Reviews of books pertaining to music education, the teaching of music, and so forth, are located under heading "Book Reviews."

AN INDEX TO BOOK REVIEWS IN THE HUMANITIES. Williamston, Mich.: Phillip Thomson, 1960-- . Quarterly.

Indexes book reviews in humanities periodicals. Includes author, title, reviewer, and identification of periodical.

Guides to Book Reviews

THE LIBRARY JOURNAL BOOK REVIEW. New York: R.R. Bowker Co., 1967-74.

Excellent for music book reviews. Well indexed.

Music Library Association. NOTES. Ann Arbor, Mich.: Music Library Association, 1943-- . Quarterly.

A most important research tool. Contains bibliographic references, book reviews, music reviews, index to record reviews, various music lists, and catalogs. Back issues available from AMS Reprint Co.

NEW YORK TIMES INDEX. New York: New York Times Co., 1913-- . 2/month with annual cumulations.

Under the heading book reviews there are two listings. The first includes edited works, anthologies, and collaborations. The second is a listing by author for works by a single author.

Wolf, Arthur S. SPECULUM: AN INDEX OF MUSICALLY RELATED ARTICLES AND BOOK REVIEWS. MLA Index Series 9. Ann Arbor, Mich.: Music Library Association, 1970. 31 p. Paper.

A guide to locating material related to music contained in SPECULUM, A JOURNAL OF MEDIEVAL STUDIES, from volume 1 (1926) through volume 93 (1968). Contains both articles and reviews of books and music.

See also Section 7: Guides to Periodicals and Professional Journals.

Section 7

GUIDES TO PERIODICALS AND PROFESSIONAL JOURNALS

BOWKER SERIALS BIBLIOGRAPHY SUPPLEMENT. 1974. New York: R.R. Bowker Co., 1974. 358 p.

Contains bibliographic and buying information for more than 7,200 current serials published throughout the world. Expands the coverage of ULRICH'S INTERNATIONAL PERIODICALS DIRECTORY (see below).

Duckles, Vincent [Harris]. "Lists of Music Periodicals." In MUSIC REFERENCE AND RESEARCH MATERIALS: AN ANNOTATED BIBLIOGRAPHY, 3d ed., pp. 149-54. New York: Free Press, 1974.

Field, Gladys, ed. in chief. THE MUSICIANS' GUIDE: DIRECTORY OF THE WORLD OF MUSIC. 5th ed. New York: Music Information Service, 1972. 1,013 p.

See Section 2: Directories--Comprehensive.

Keller, Michael A. "Music Serials in Microform and Reprint Editions." MUSIC LIBRARY NOTES 29 (June 1973): 675-93.

This valuable checklist of serials includes 394 separate entries. Formats listed include reprint, microfilm, microcard, and microfiche. Most titles, except those in the Library of Congress, are available from U.S. commercial firms. The New York Public Library collections are available from Kraus Reprint, Microform Division.

King, A. Hyatt. "Periodicals." In GROVE'S DICTIONARY OF MUSIC AND MUSICIANS, 5th ed., edited by Eric Blom, vol. 6, pp. 637-72. New York: St. Martin's Press, 1954.

Extensive coverage including sources and bibliographical notes, list of periodicals arranged in alphabetical and chronological order from first date of appearance, selective subject index, and historical and critical summary. See SUPPLEMENT, volume 10, 1961, for additions.

Pavlakis, Christopher. THE AMERICAN MUSIC HANDBOOK. New York: Free Press; London: Collier-Macmillan Publishers, 1974. 836 p.

See Section 2: Directories--Comprehensive.

ULRICH'S INTERNATIONAL PERIODICALS DIRECTORY, SIXTEENTH EDITION 1975-1976: A CLASSIFIED GUIDE TO CURRENT PERIODICALS, FOREIGN AND DOMESTIC. New York and London: R.R. Bowker Co., 1932-- . Annual.

Comprehensive information about magazines and newsletters published throughout the world. There are approximately 57,000 periodicals listed. Entries for each periodical include, where applicable and available, full title, former title, editor's name, circulation figures, subscription rates, frequency of issue, year of initial publication, name and address of publisher, languages used in the text, names of services which index or abstract the periodical, and whether it carries advertising, book reviews, bibliographies, or illustrations. There are notations on the availability of back issues and from whom microfilm is available. Of special importance is a listing of abstracting and indexing services. This serial began publication in 1932.

Weichlein, William J. A CHECKLIST OF AMERICAN MUSIC PERIODICALS, 1850-1900. Detroit Studies in Music Bibliography no. 16. Detroit: Information Coordinators, 1970. 103 p.

Earlier studies are coordinated with much new bibliographic data, such as lengths of runs, names of editors and publishers, and other publication information. Does not include periodicals which published only music, or program notes, or proceedings of associations.

Section 8

INDEXING JOURNALS

BIBLIOGRAPHIC INDEX. New York: H.W. Wilson Co., 1937-- . 3/year.

Indexes bibliographies in books, parts of books, pamphlets, and selected periodicals. Arranged by subject. A major reference source.

BIOGRAPHY INDEX. New York: H.W. Wilson Co., 1947-- . Quarterly.

A comprehensive guide to biographical materials which have appeared in books, periodicals, and the NEW YORK TIMES.

BRITISH HUMANITIES INDEX. New York: International Publications Service, 1966-- . Annual.

CURRENT INDEX TO JOURNALS IN EDUCATION (CIJE). Washington, D.C.: U.S. Office of Education, Educational Resources Information Center (ERIC), 1966-- . Monthly.

A guide to major educational and education-related periodical literature. Includes a main entry section with annotations. Indexed by subject and author. Semiannual cumulative indexes are available. Computer searching available via Dialog Information Retrieval Service. For details see Section 18: Information Services and Systems.

EDUCATION INDEX. New York: H.W. Wilson Co., 1932-- . Annual.

One of the most important guides to the contents of periodicals in the educational field. It includes many educational books, monographs, government documents, important yearbooks, courses of study, tests, book reviews, bibliographies, and various reports. In addition, it contains the publications of the Office of Education and the National Education Association. Coverage begins with 1929.

Indexing Journals

HUMANITIES INDEX. New York: H.W. Wilson Co., 1974-- . Quarterly.

INDEX MEDICUS. Bethesda, Md.: National Library of Medicine, 1960-- . Monthly.

A compilation of citations to journal articles from the world's periodical biomedical literature. Includes medical research involving music and music therapy.

MUSIC ARTICLE GUIDE. Philadelphia: Music Article Guide, 1966-- . Quarterly with annual cumulations.

An annotated reference guide to significant feature articles in American music periodicals.

MUSIC EDUCATORS JOURNAL INDEX. Vienna, Va.: Music Educators National Conference, 1959-- . Annual.

Since 1959 the MUSIC EDUCATORS JOURNAL has been indexed in the final issue of each volume year. In recent years this has been the May issue. Two cumulative indexes are available as follows:

Volumes 46-51: September 1959 to July 1965.

Volumes 52-56: September 1966 to May 1970.

THE MUSIC INDEX. Detroit: Information Coordinators, 1949-- . Monthly with annual cumulations.

A comprehensive subject-author guide to current music periodical literature. It is a dictionary-catalog compiled directly from almost 200 periodicals representing twenty countries. The complete list of subject headings with their cross references, published annually, facilitates the full use of the index, and serves as a tool for all concerned with the filing and indexing of music materials. Subjects include music personalities, past and present; the history of music; forms and types of music; musical instruments from the earliest times to the electronic instruments of today; reviews of books, music, recordings, and performances.

READERS GUIDE TO PERIODICAL LITERATURE. New York: H.W. Wilson Co., 1900-- . 7/year with annual cumulations.

Emphasis is on popular general magazines. An author and subject list. Coverage begins with 1900.

SOCIAL SCIENCE INDEX, 1974-- . New York: H.W. Wilson Co., 1974-- . Quarterly.

STATE EDUCATION JOURNAL INDEX. Westminster, Colo.: State Education Journal Index, 1963-- . Semiannual.

An annotated index to the state education association journals.

Section 9
ABSTRACTING JOURNALS

ABSTRACTS IN ANTHROPOLOGY. Westport, Conn.: Greenwood Press, 1970-- . Quarterly.

ACOUSTICAL SOCIETY OF AMERICA JOURNAL. New York: American Institute of Physics, 1929-- . Monthly.

CHILD DEVELOPMENT ABSTRACTS AND BIBLIOGRAPHY. Chicago, Ill.: University of Chicago Press, 1927-- . 3/year.

DISSERTATION ABSTRACTS INTERNATIONAL. Ann Arbor, Mich.: Xerox University Microfilms, 1938-- . Monthly, with annual cumulations.

See Section 15: Dissertations.

EDUCATIONAL ADMINISTRATION ABSTRACTS. Columbus, Ohio: Educational Administration Publications, 1966-- . 3/year.

EXCEPTIONAL CHILD EDUCATION ABSTRACTS. Arlington, Va.: The Council for Exceptional Children, 1969-- . 4/year.

For abstracts via computer, see Dialog Information Retrieval Service in Section 18: Information Services and Systems.

PSYCHOLOGICAL ABSTRACTS. Washington, D.C.: American Psychological Association, 1927-- . Monthly.

Also available via computer. See Dialog Information Retrieval Service in Section 18: Information Services and Systems.

RESOURCES IN EDUCATION (RIE). Washington, D.C.: U.S. Office of Education, Educational Resources Information Center (ERIC), 1966-- . Monthly.

An abstract journal which reports and describes documents of educational significance. Includes music education. Indexed by subject, author or investigator, and institution. Semiannual and annual cumulative indexes are available. Full texts of documents are available in either microfiche form or papercopy from the ERIC Document Reproduction Service (EDRS). Many colleges and university libraries and other educational centers now maintain the entire ERIC microfiche collection. For a list of ERIC materials locations contact the ERIC office. Computer access to all holdings in RESOURCES IN EDUCATION is available through the Dialog Information Retrieval Service. For details see Section 18: Information Services and Systems. (Prior to January 1975, this publication was known as RESEARCH IN EDUCATION.)

RILM ABSTRACTS (Repertoire Internationale de la Litterature Musicale [International repertory of musical literature]). New York: International RILM Center, The City University of New York, 1967-- . Quarterly.

Publishes abstracts of significant literature in music that has appeared since January 1967. The fourth issue each year is a cumulative index. Included are abstracts of books, articles, essays, reviews, dissertations, catalogs, iconographies, and so forth.

RILM ABSTRACTS is published with the support and sponsorship of the American Council of Learned Societies National Committee in forty-two countries.

SOCIOLOGICAL ABSTRACTS. Brooklyn, N.Y.: Sociological Abstracts, 1953-- . 5/year.

See also Section 12: Research Journals--Music Education, and Section 13: Research Journals--Allied Fields.

Section 10

THEMATIC INDEXES AND CATALOGS

Albrecht, Otto E. A CENSUS OF AUTOGRAPH MUSIC MANUSCRIPTS OF EUROPEAN COMPOSERS IN AMERICAN LIBRARIES. Philadelphia: University of Pennsylvania Press, 1953. 331 p.

Lists 2,017 manuscripts by 571 composers. Contains bibliography which serves as a convenient reference to those works referred to in the text--complete editions, thematic and other catalogs of composers and collections, and studies bearing on specific manuscripts.

Barlow, Howard, and Morgenstern, Sam, eds. A DICTIONARYOF MUSICAL THEMES. New York: Crown, 1948. 642 p. Music.

Contains more than 10,000 themes from instrumental repertory--symphonies, concertos, other orchestral works, chamber music, sonatas, and other concert music. Important is a "Notation Index Key" that lists all themes alphabetically according to notation (transposed to key of C).

______. A DICTIONARY OF OPERA AND SONG THEMES. New York: Crown, 1966. 547 p. Music.

Includes more than 8,000 themes from operas, cantatas, oratorios, art songs, and miscellaneous others. Contains notation of the music as well as the words. The book is arranged according to the composer, and indexed according to title and first line. Note: This is a reprint of the original work, A DICTIONARY OF VOCAL THEMES (New York: Crown, 1950).

Berkowitz, Freda Pastor. POPULAR TITLES AND SUBTITLES OF MUSICAL COMPOSITIONS. New York: Scarecrow Press, 1962. 182 p.

Useful for dealing with confusing similarity in the names of musical compositions; especially helpful with nicknames.

Brook, Barry S., ed. THE BREITKOPF THEMATIC CATALOGUE: THE SIX PARTS AND SIXTEEN SUPPLEMENTS, 1762-1787. New York: Dover Publications, 1966. 445 p.

The first thematic catalog ever printed. It is the only source for many "lost" compositions and serves as an index to eighteenth-century musical taste. Includes 15,000 incipits by 1,000 composers, plus dates, text underlays, position of composer, instrumentation, etc.

_____. THEMATIC CATALOGUES IN MUSIC: AN ANNOTATED BIBLIOGRAPHY. Hillsdale, N.Y.: Pendragon Press, 1972. 347 p.

Includes printed, manuscript, and in-preparation catalogs; related literature and reviews; an essay on the definitions, history, functions, historiography, and future of the thematic catalog. A highly useful reference tool.

Bryden, John R., and Hughes, David G., comps. AN INDEX OF GREGORIAN CHANT. Vol. 2. Cambridge, Mass.: Harvard University Press, 1969.

A thematic index.

Burrows, Raymond M., and Redmond, Bessie C. CONCERTO THEMES. New York: Simon and Schuster, 1951. 296 p. Music.

Themes are given as they appear in the first complete form. Includes instrumentation of the first entry and expression markings. In addition there is a listing of scores, program notes, and articles in books and magazines.

_____. SYMPHONY THEMES. New York: Simon and Schuster, 1942. 295 p.

This book not only contains the principal thematic material of one hundred symphonies, but also provides a useful reference list of scores, analyses, and program notes.

Charles, Sydney R. A HANDBOOK OF MUSIC AND MUSIC LITERATURE IN SETS AND SERIES. New York: Free Press; London: Collier-Macmillan, 1972. 497 p.

Divisions include: (a) monuments--principally sets of music by several composers; (b) complete works--a single composer in more than one volume; (c) monographs--series of volumes on a single subject by a single author; (d) periodicals--those with general musical coverage and a scholarly approach. Intended to supplement the works by Anna Harriet Heyer on monuments and complete works, and Fred Blum on monograph series (see Section 11: Selected Guides to Bibliographic Sources).

Köchel, Ludwig Ritter von. CHRONOLOGISCH-THEMATISCHES VERZEICHNIS SAMTLICHER-TONWERKE WOLFGANG AMADE MOZARTS [Chronological thematic catalog of works by Wolfgang Amadeus Mozart]. 6th ed. Edited by Franz Giegling et al. Wiesbaden: Breitkopf and Härtel, 1964. 1,024 p. (Distr. by C.F. Peters Corp., New York.) Music.

Section 11

SELECTED GUIDES TO BIBLIOGRAPHIC SOURCES

While this guide is concerned throughout with bibliographic sources, this section intends to draw attention to a few works which serve as bibliographies of bibliographies or as guides to bibliographies. More specific bibliographic sources dealing with the educational aspects of music are found in the sections concerned with philosophy, principles, and practices in music education; the subject matter areas; and research techniques.

GENERAL

Besterman, Theodore. MUSIC AND DRAMA: A BIBLIOGRAPHY OF BIBLIOGRAPHIES. Totowa, N.J.: Rowman and Littlefield, 1971. 365 p.

Contains all the titles in music and drama found in A WORLD BIBLIOGRAPHY OF BIBLIOGRAPHIES, 4th ed. (Lausanne: Societas Bibliographica, 1965-66).

BIBLIOGRAPHIC INDEX. New York: H.W. Wilson Co., 1937-- . 3/year.

Indexes bibliographies in books, parts of books, pamphlets, and selected periodicals. Arranged by subject. A major reference source.

Blum, Fred. MUSIC MONOGRAPHS IN SERIES. New York: Scarecrow Press, 1964. 197 p.

A bibliography of numbered monograph series in the field of music, current since 1945.

Downs, Robert B. AMERICAN LIBRARY RESOURCES: A BIBLIOGRAPHICAL GUIDE, SUPPLEMENT 1961-1970. Chicago: American Library Association, 1972. 256 p.

An annotated listing of more than 3,400 bibliographical finding aids. Arranged by subject. Includes music.

Duckles, Vincent Harris, comp. MUSIC REFERENCE AND RESEARCH MATERIALS: AN ANNOTATED BIBLIOGRAPHY. 3d ed. New York: Free Press, 1974. 526 p.

One of the most useful anthologies and practical guides to music bibliographies available to musicologists and music educators. Includes listings of music dictionaries, encyclopedias, histories (including histories of music printing and publishing), chronologies, discographies, yearbooks, periodicals, and library collection catalogs, as well as bibliographies of music literature, musical works, and other music bibliographies. New sections on jazz and popular music have been added to this edition.

Heyer, Anna Harriet, comp. HISTORICAL SETS, COLLECTED EDITIONS, AND MONUMENTS OF MUSIC--A GUIDE TO THEIR CONTENTS. 2d ed. Chicago: American Library Association, 1969. 573 p.

Lists publications and contents, with bibliographical information.

Hill, George R. A PRELIMINARY CHECKLIST OF RESEARCH ON THE CLASSIC SYMPHONY AND CONCERTO TO THE TIME OF BEETHOVEN (EXCLUDING HAYDN AND MOZART). Hackensack, N.J.: Joseph Boonin, 1970. 58 p.

Mixter, Keith E. GENERAL BIBLIOGRAPHY FOR MUSIC RESEARCH. 2d ed. Detroit Studies in Music Bibliography. Detroit: Information Coordinators, 1975. 135 p.

A guide to references to bibliographic tools for research in music.

RILM ABSTRACTS. (Repertoire Internationale de la Litterature Musicale [International repertory of musical literature]).

A computer-indexed bibliography of literature of music in the form of abstracts. See Section 9: Abstracting Journals.

Solow, Linda, comp. A CHECKLIST OF MUSIC BIBLIOGRAPHIES AND INDEXES IN PROGRESS AND UNPUBLISHED. 3d ed. Ann Arbor, Mich.: Music Library Association, 1974. 40 p. Paper.

For purposes of this work the term "unpublished" refers to items that were not available to the general trade as of December 31, 1972. Included are card files, mimeographed material, and computer printouts. Revisions of published works are included in the term "in progress." In cases where plans for publication have already been made, the term "to be published" is used. This is a highly useful work for the music educator involved in doctoral study.

UNESCO. GUIDE TO NATIONAL BIBLIOGRAPHIC INFORMATION CENTERS. 2d ed. Paris: 1962. 74 p.

Describes resources and publications, and provides names and addresses of centers in seventy-seven countries.

Watanabe, Ruth T. INTRODUCTION TO MUSIC RESEARCH. Englewood Cliffs, N.J.: Prentice-Hall, 1967. 237 p.

Excellent bibliographic sources are described in chapters 9-12: "Bibliography: Books"; "Bibliography: Periodicals"; "Bibliography: Music"; and "Discography."

RISM (REPERTOIRE INTERNATIONAL DES SOURCES MUSICALES [INTERNATIONAL INVENTORY OF MUSICAL SOURCES])

It has been estimated that when completed, the RISM (Repertoire International des Sources Musicales) will be the major tool for locating primary source material in the field of music. RISM provides a catalog of many available bibliographical music works, writings about music, and textbooks from all countries of the world, including monodic music, liturgical sources, song books, treatises and methods, and books and periodicals on music, from the earliest times to the year 1800. The work includes two series, one alphabetic and the other systematic. Those titles which can be cataloged according to the names of editors and which are available in individual sources appear in the alphabetical catalog. Included in the systematic catalog are the titles of collections, anonymous works, or other music works and writings which lend themselves to systematic rather than alphabetical cataloging. The following volumes have been issued.

See also Section 17: Research Techniques.

Lesure, Francais, ed. ECRITS IMPRIMES CONCERNANT LA MUSIQUE. 2 vols. München-Duisburg, Germany: G. Henle Verlag, 1971.

A variety of published works about music--includes theoretical, historical, aesthetic, and technical aspects.

______. RISM--RECUEILS IMPRIMES XVI-XVII SIECLES. München-Duisburg, Germany: G. Henle Verlag, 1960. 639 p.

This work comprises more than 2,700 printed collections of the sixteenth and seventeenth centuries.

______. RISM--RECUEILS IMPRIMES, XVIII SIECLE. München-Duisburg, Germany: G. Henle Verlag, 1964. 461 p.

Details about 1,800 collections printed between 1701 and 1801. Included are works of theory.

Reaney, Gilbert, ed. MANUSCRIPTS OF POLYPHONIC MUSIC:

11TH-EARLY 14TH CENTURIES. München-Duisburg, Germany: G. Henle Verlag, 1966. 876 p. Illus., tables, music.

Provides descriptions, bibliography, and thematic incipits for all the known polyphonic manuscripts up to the beginning of the Ars Nova period.

_____. MANUSCRIPTS OF POLYPHONIC MUSIC (C 1320-1400). München-Duisburg, Germany: G. Henle Verlag, 1969. 427 p. Illus., music.

Provides description, bibliography, and thematic incipits for all the known polyphonic manuscripts between ca. 1320 and ca. 1400.

Schlager, Karlheinz, ed. EINGELDRUKE VOR 1800. 3 vols. Kassel, Germany: Bärenreiter Verlag, 1971-72.

Lists the location of single printed editions of works by individual composers. Entries include title, additions to title, imprint, location, information about parts, and authors of special lists. Three volumes available at this printing.

Von Waesberghe, Joseph Smits, ed. RISM--THE THEORY OF MUSIC. 2 vols. München-Duisburg, Germany: G. Henle Verlag, 1961 and 1968.

Volume 1 (1961): Describes all manuscripts in which are preserved Latin treatises dealing with the theory of music which was in use from the Carolingian era to 1400.
Volume 2 (1968): A continuation of volume 1--covering Italian sources.

Von Fischer, Kurt, and Lutolf, Max, eds. HANDSCHRIFTEN MIT MEHRSTIMMIGER MUSIK, DES 14., 15. UND 16. JAHRHUNDERTS. 2 vols. München-Duisberg, Germany: G. Henle Verlag, 1972.

A continuation of the two volumes by G. Reaney--MANUSCRIPTS OF POLYPHONIC MUSIC: 11TH-EARLY 14TH CENTURIES, and C 1320-1400. Volume 1 covers Austria and Yugoslavia. Text in German.

Von Husmann, Heinrich, ed. TROPEN-UND SEQUENZENHANDSCHRIFTEN. München-Duisburg, Germany: G. Henle Verlag, 1964. 236 p.

Treats manuscripts dealing with tropes and sequences.

Section 12
RESEARCH JOURNALS—MUSIC EDUCATION

GENERAL

COUNCIL FOR RESEARCH IN MUSIC EDUCATION. BULLETIN. Champaign: University of Illinois, Division of University Extension in Music, College of Education, 1963-- . Quarterly.

An important journal devoted to the dissemination of research information in the field of music education.

Hilton, Lewis B., ed. MISSOURI JOURNAL OF RESEARCH IN MUSIC EDUCATION. Jefferson City, Mo.: State Department of Education, 1967-- . Annual.

Publishes articles of a philosophical, historical, or scientific nature, which report the results of research pertinent to instruction in music as carried on in the educational institutions of Missouri.

INTERNATIONAL SOCIETY FOR MUSIC EDUCATION. YEARBOOK. Oldenburg, Germany: I.S.M.E., 1973-- .

Contains important contributions on problems encountered in the various fields of music education. The articles are worldwide in scope and are published in English with short summaries in French and German. This journal replaces THE INTERNATIONAL MUSIC EDUCATOR, which ceased publication in Spring 1973.

JOURNAL OF RESEARCH IN MUSIC EDUCATION. Vienna, Va.: Music Educators National Conference, Society for Research in Music Education, 1953-- . Quarterly.

A major source of information concerning selected research studies in the area of music education. Rich in bibliographic references covering a wide range of music education topics. Beginning with the Spring 1974 issue, each article is preceded by an abstract. Keyword listings are included after every abstract to facilitate referencing and accessibility. The keywords are taken from a music education thesaurus and the THESAURUS OF ERIC DESCRIPTORS.

OTHER RESEARCH SOURCES

1. The journals of major organizations and some commercial periodicals, representing various interests in music education, occasionally publish research studies or articles based on research studies. Notable among those of a general nature are the following:

THE AMERICAN MUSIC TEACHER (Music Teachers National Association)
THE MUSIC EDUCATORS JOURNAL (Music Educators National Conference)
MUSIC JOURNAL
MUSICAL QUARTERLY
THE SCHOOL MUSICIAN, DIRECTOR AND TEACHER

Addresses of these journals are available in appendix B.

2. In addition to the above, there are many organizations and associations devoted to specialized areas of music and music education. Their journals are of particular importance to the researcher. A list of these organizations and their respective journals can be found at the conclusion of each major section of this book.

3. The various trade journals in the music industry are also useful sources of information.

CONN CHORD
MUSIC TEMPO
MUSIC TRADES MAGAZINE
MUSIC WORLD
MUSICAL MERCHANDISE REVIEW
ORCHESTRA NEWS
PIANO TECHNICIANS JOURNAL
PTM MAGAZINE: THE BUSINESS AND FINANCIAL JOURNAL OF THE MUSIC INDUSTRY.
SELMER BANDWAGON

Addresses available in appendix B.

NOTE: For research journals in the field of musicology see Section 36: Musicology.

Section 13

RESEARCH JOURNALS—ALLIED FIELDS

The music educator is concerned not only with his immediate field of specialization but also with the relationship of music to other areas of human experience. To learn how music serves mankind through other disciplines it is necessary to examine the literature in other fields. Some of the sources most useful to music educators are listed in this section.

ACOUSTICAL SOCIETY OF AMERICA JOURNAL. New York: American Institute of Physics, 1929-- . Monthly.

> A valuable source of information concerning psychology of hearing, musical acoustics, characteristics of instruments, concert halls, etc. Cumulative.

AMERICAN EDUCATIONAL RESEARCH JOURNAL. Washington, D.C.: American Educational Research Association, National Educational Association, 1964-- . 4/year.

CALIFORNIA JOURNAL OF EDUCATION RESEARCH. Burlingame: California Teachers Association, 1950-- . 5/year.

CHILD DEVELOPMENT (Journal). Lafayette, Ind.: The Society for Research in Child Development, 1930-- . Quarterly.

JOURNAL OF ABNORMAL PSYCHOLOGY. Washington, D.C.: American Psychological Association, 1965-- . Bimonthly.

JOURNAL OF EDUCATIONAL PSYCHOLOGY. Washington, D.C.: American Psychological Association, 1910-- . 3/year.

JOURNAL OF EDUCATIONAL RESEARCH. Madison, Wis.: Dembar Publications, 1920-- . 9/year.

Research Journals—Allied Fields

JOURNAL OF EXPERIMENTAL EDUCATION. Madison, Wis.: Dembar Publications, 1932-- . Quarterly.

JOURNAL OF EXPERIMENTAL PSYCHOLOGY. Washington, D.C.: American Psychological Association, 1916-- . Monthly.

JOURNAL OF PERSONALITY AND SOCIAL PSYCHOLOGY. Washington, D.C.: American Psychological Association, 1965-- . Monthly.

JOURNAL OF TEACHER EDUCATION. Washington, D.C.: National Commission on Teacher Education and Professional Standards, National Education Association, 1950-- . Quarterly.

PSYCHOLOGICAL REVIEW. Washington, D.C.: American Psychological Association, 1894-- . Bimonthly.

REVIEW OF EDUCATIONAL RESEARCH. Washington, D.C.: American Educational Research Association, National Education Association, 1931-- . Quarterly.

Section 14
STATE JOURNALS

STATE MUSIC JOURNALS

Each state has a music education association which is affiliated with the Music Educators National Conference (MENC) and publishes its own state journal. A list of the state associations may be found in each issue of the MUSIC EDUCATORS JOURNAL. A complete listing of state music education periodicals and editors is contained in the following directory:

> Music Educators National Conference. "Official Directory--Registry of Music Education Leadership." MUSIC EDUCATORS JOURNAL 60 (September 1974): 63-102.

OTHER STATE PUBLICATIONS

All state education departments publish and distribute materials which are designed to meet the administrative and instructional needs of workers in the state educational systems. Such materials are frequently in the form of curriculum studies, guides, handbooks, resource lists, survey findings, courses of study by subjects and grades, and so forth. Included are many music education materials. Inquiries concerning these publications should be made to the appropriate state education department.

Hernon, Peter. "State Publications: A Bibliographic Guide for Reference Collections." LIBRARY JOURNAL 99 (November 1, 1974): 2810-19.

> Updates and expands the author's "State Publications," LIBRARY JOURNAL 97 (April 15, 1972): 1393-98. The bibliography lists bluebooks or manuals, checklists, state statistical abstracts, and other revelant publications. A concise and useful bibliography.

STATE EDUCATION JOURNAL INDEX. Westminster, Colo.: State Education Journal Index, 1964-- . Semiannual.

> An annotated index to state education association journals.

State Journals

See also MONTHLY CHECKLIST OF STATE PUBLICATIONS. Washington, D.C.: Library of Congress, 1910-- .

Section 15
DISSERTATIONS

GENERAL

ACTA MUSICOLOGICA. Basel, Switzerland: Societé Internationale de Musicologie, 1928-- . Biannual.

> All non-American dissertations of historical interest are listed, beginning with the Fall 1972 issue. The compilation is supplemented annually. Text in English, French, and German.

Adkins, Cecil, comp. DOCTORAL DISSERTATIONS IN MUSICOLOGY. 5th ed. Philadelphia: American Musicological Society, 1971. 203 p.

> This fifth cumulative edition contains 1,917 titles, representing fifty-six American and two Canadian universities through July 1970. Classified by category (Renaissance, Baroque, and so forth). Subject and author index. New edition in preparation.

COMPREHENSIVE DISSERTATION INDEX. 37 vols. Ann Arbor, Mich.: Xerox University Microfilms, 1973.

> Prior to the publication of this index, locating doctoral dissertations was made difficult by their sheer number and the various well-meaning, but inadequate, attempts to index them. This index, covering the period 1861-1972, is an effort to provide comprehensive and orderly coverage. Volumes 20-24 are the indexes for dissertations written on education, and volumes 15-19 cover psychology (including psychological aspects of music). Approximately 320 pages of volume 31, COMMUNICATION AND THE ARTS, are devoted to music dissertations, arranged by subject area. It should be noted that this is simply a listing of dissertations and the researcher must still consult DISSERTATION ABSTRACTS INTERNATIONAL (see below) for abstracts of dissertations. The volume number, issue number, page number, and the order number are given for those dissertations also appearing in DISSERTATION ABSTRACTS INTERNATIONAL. To obtain a copy of these dissertations one must purchase either a xerox copy or microfilm from Xerox University

Microfilms. Ordering information can be found in the prefatory section of each volume of the index.

In the entries for dissertations that are not abstracted in DISSERTATION ABSTRACTS INTERNATIONAL, the letters "L," "W," and "X," followed by a year number, are used to indicate that this information was derived from AMERICAN DOCTORAL DISSERTATIONS. (There is no need to consult that source since it does not contain any additional information, nor an abstract.) Some dissertations are available on interlibrary loan. (For computer services see DATRIX II below.)

DISSERTATION ABSTRACTS INTERNATIONAL. Ann Arbor, Mich.: Xerox University Microfilms, 1938-- . Monthly, with annual cumulations.

A key source to dissertation information. Provides condensed reports describing research completed in partial fulfillment of the requirements for a doctoral degree. All listed are available on either microfilm or xerox from Xerox University Microfilms, Inc. Since 1955/56 DISSERTATION ABSTRACTS INTERNATIONAL includes as the last issue each year an author list called INDEX TO AMERICAN DOCTORAL DISSERTATIONS. This includes all dissertations completed each year whether microfilmed or not. The latter is also issued separately. (For computer service see DATRIX II below.)

DOCTORAL DISSERTATIONS--MENC LISTINGS:

BIBLIOGRAPHY OF RESEARCH STUDIES IN MUSIC EDUCATION, 1932-1948, compiled by William S. Larson. Chicago: Music Educators National Conference, Music Education Research Council, 1949. 119 p.

BIBLIOGRAPHY OF RESEARCH STUDIES IN MUSIC EDUCATION, 1949-1956, compiled by William S. Larson. Washington, D.C. Music Educators National Conference, Music Education Research Council, Fall 1957 issue of JOURNAL OF RESEARCH IN MUSIC EDUCATION. 225 p.

DOCTORAL DISSERTATIONS IN MUSIC AND MUSIC EDUCATION, 1957-1963, compiled by Roderick Dean Gordon. Washington, D.C.: Music Educators National Conference, Music Education Research Council, Spring 1964 issue of JOURNAL OF RESEARCH IN MUSIC EDUCATION. 119 p.

DOCTORAL DISSERTATIONS IN MUSIC AND MUSIC EDUCATION, 1963-1967, compiled by Roderick Dean Gordon. Vienna, Va.: Music Educators National Conference, Society for Research in Music Education, Summer 1968 issue of JOURNAL OF RESEARCH IN MUSIC EDUCATION. 144 p.

DOCTORAL DISSERTATIONS IN MUSIC AND MUSIC EDUCATION, 1968-1971, compiled by Roderick Dean Gordon. Vienna, Va.: Music Educators National Conference, Society for Research in Music Education, Spring 1972 issue of JOURNAL OF RESEARCH IN MUSIC EDUCATION, 208 p.

A supplementary listing for the 1968-71 period:

DOCTORAL DISSERTATIONS IN MUSIC AND MUSIC EDUCATION, compiled by Roderick Dean Gordon. Summer 1974 issue of JOURNAL OF RESEARCH IN MUSIC EDUCATION, 67-111.

Gillis, Frank, and Merriam, Alan P., comps. and eds. ETHNOMUSICOLOGY AND FOLK MUSIC: AN INTERNATIONAL BIBLIOGRAPHY OF DISSERTATIONS AND THESES. Middletown, Conn.: Wesleyan University Press, 1966. 148 p.

A bibliography which includes related topics such as Negro music, jazz, the education of youth and children in non-Western music, the sociology and psychology of music, and the computer in music research. Some items are annotated.

INDEX TO AMERICAN DOCTORAL DISSERTATIONS. Ann Arbor, Mich.: University Microfilms, 1956-- . Annual.

A comprehensive author list of dissertations. Published as the final yearly issue of DISSERTATION ABSTRACTS INTERNATIONAL (see above).

Schneider, Erwin H. and Cady, Henry L. EVALUATION AND SYNTHESIS OF RESEARCH STUDIES RELATING TO MUSIC EDUCATION. Cooperative Research Project E-016. Item ED 010 298 in ERIC Document Reproduction Service. Cleveland, Ohio: Bell and Howell Co., 1965. 652 p. Hard copy and microfiche.

A major reference source for those involved in graduate study--whether as students or graduate study advisors--and for people in the teaching field itself, regardless of school level. The report covers the period 1930-62. From 9,150 titles, 1,818 were selected for either review or abstracting. Of those, 273 were considered relevant and competent, were microfilmed in their entirety, and placed in the ERIC storage system. Abstracts appear in appendix A. For retrieval purposes, there are 182 doctoral dissertations, 40 masters' theses, and 51 published documents. Because of the significance of this project covering the period 1930-62, one can hope that it will be continued. In using the current work, the user should inquire as to whether later issues (since 1962) have become available.

COMPUTER SERVICES

DATRIX II. Ann Arbor, Mich.: Xerox University Microfilms.

Datrix II is the acronym for "Direct Access to Reference Information: A Xerox Service.: A comprehensive and up-to-date computer service for doctoral dissertations." The service offers three distinct advantages over the human hunt system: (1) It can reveal new dissertations which are not yet published in the usual indexes. (2) It can compile an interdisciplinary listing more efficiently than a manual search. (3) It is fast and accurate.

Contains practically all dissertations since 1861. The service can compile a list of dissertations on any subject. Printout lists are arranged in chronological order, beginning with the most recent title. Includes author's name, degree, degree year, and institution. Cites appropriate references in DISSERTATION ABTRACTS INTERNATIONAL (see above) or other sources, and gives order number for those dissertations which are available in microfilm or xerographic copy. Requests are submitted by way of a special order form which is based on keyword indexing technique. Service is rapid and relatively inexpensive. For special order forms and a keyword list, contact Xerox University Microfilms, 300 North Zeeb Road, Ann Arbor, Michigan 48106.

OTHER SOURCES

Many colleges, universities, and schools of music publish lists, digests, or abstracts of their own doctoral dissertations and masters' theses.

Section 16

MASTERS' THESES

De Lerma, Dominique-René, comp. A SELECTIVE LIST OF MASTER'S THESES IN MUSICOLOGY. Bloomington, Ind.: Denia Press, 1970. 42 p.

A listing of 257 titles contributed by 36 major universities. Includes author's name, subject matter, and year.

MASTERS' ABSTRACTS. Ann Arbor, Mich.: University Microfilms, 1962-- . Quarterly.

Abstracts of selected masters' theses. Includes brief summaries in journal form and is accompanied by the publication of the complete theses as positive microfilm or as xerographic enlargements in book form.

Silvey, H.M., ed. MASTERS' THESES IN EDUCATION. Cedar Falls, Iowa: Research Publications, 1951-- . Annual.

Lists masters' theses in education (including music). Provides name of author, title of thesis, and name of institution. Does not contain digests.

Section 17
RESEARCH TECHNIQUES

Alexander, Carter. HOW TO LOCATE EDUCATIONAL INFORMATION AND DATA. New York: Teachers College, Columbia University, 1962. 419 p. Illus.

A well-known and valuable guide to procedures for locating information.

Barzun, Jacques, and Graff, Henry F. THE MODERN RESEARCHER. New York: Harcourt, Brace and Co., 1957. 386 p. Illus.

Describes the art of researching. Emphasis is on thought processes and attitudes as well as technical skills. Bibliography.

Benton, Rita. DIRECTORY OF MUSIC RESEARCH LIBRARIES. 3 vols. Iowa City: University of Iowa, 1967-72.

One of the most useful of all tools for the serious researcher in the field of music. Part I: CANADA AND THE UNITED STATES (1967); part II: THIRTEEN EUROPEAN COUNTRIES (1970); part III: SPAIN, FRANCE, ITALY, AND PORTUGAL (1972).

Best, John W. RESEARCH IN EDUCATION. Englewood Cliffs, N.J.: Prentice-Hall, 1959. 320 p.

Presents the theory and application of educational research in a clear and concise manner. Written primarily for the graduate student. Bibliography.

Borg, Walter R. EDUCATIONAL RESEARCH: AN INTRODUCTION. New York: David McKay Co., 1963. 418 p.

Provides insights and information essential to planning and conducting educational research. Presented in a manner that conveys different and abstract concepts in clear and simple language. Numerous annotated references.

Corey, Stephen. ACTION RESEARCH TO IMPROVE SCHOOL PRACTICES. New York: Bureau of Publications, Teachers College, Columbia University, 1953. 161 p.

Describes and illustrates the principles of "action research" as a means by which teachers, supervisors, and administrators can study current practices for the purpose of effecting changes.

Goldman, Bernard. READING AND WRITING IN THE ARTS: A HANDBOOK. Detroit: Wayne State University Press, 1972. 163 p.

Annotated references concentrating on sources accessible to researchers in America. Offers guidelines for research.

Madson, Clifford K., and Madson, Charles H. EXPERIMENTAL RESEARCH IN MUSIC. Englewood Cliffs, N.J.: Prentice-Hall, 1970. 116 p.

Organizes, clarifies, and stimulates topics of experimental interest and provides the rationale, terminology, and processes necessary to conduct and interpret experimental research in music.

Madson, Clifford K., and Moore, Randall S. EXPERIMENTAL RESEARCH IN MUSIC--WORKBOOK IN DESIGN AND STATISTICAL TESTS. Dubuque, Iowa: Kendall-Hunt Publishing Co., 1974. 172 p.

A guide to closed systems, research designs, and statistical tests. A programmed workbook designed to accompany EXPERIMENTAL RESEARCH IN MUSIC (see above).

Mixter, Keith E. AN INTRODUCTION TO LIBRARY RESOURCES FOR MUSIC RESEARCH. Columbus: School of Music, College of Education, Ohio State University, 1963. 61 p. Paper.

Although this work was designed for use in music bibliography courses, it is a guide to much musical literature useful in music education.

Morgan, Hazel B., and Burmeister, Clifton A. MUSIC RESEARCH HANDBOOK. Evanston, Ill.: Instrumentalist Co., 1962. 111 p. Paper.

A useful manual that includes general information and specific directions for graduate advisors and students majoring in music and music education.

Phelps, Roger P. A GUIDE TO RESEARCH IN MUSIC EDUCATION. Dubuque, Iowa: William C. Brown Co., 1969. 239 p.

One of the few research guides designed specifically for the music educator. Good orientation manual.

Sax, Gilbert. EMPIRICAL FOUNDATIONS OF EDUCATIONAL RESEARCH. Englewood Cliffs, N.J.: Prentice-Hall, 1968. 443 p.

A detailed presentation of the organization and handling of research informational materials. Principles and practices are readily applicable to research in the fields of music and music education.

Schneider, Edwin H., and Sedoris, Robert D., eds. RESEARCH IN MUSIC EDUCATION. Volume III: CURRENT ISSUES IN MUSIC EDUCATION. Columbus: Ohio State University, 1967. 53 p.

A collection of the papers presented as a symposium dealing with current issues in music education. Authorities in the field review existing conditions in the music education research area and offer suggestions for improvement.

Shumsky, Abraham. THE ACTION RESEARCH WAY OF LEARNING. New York: Bureau of Publications, Teachers College, Columbia University, 1958. 210 p.

Van Dalen, Deobold. UNDERSTANDING EDUCATIONAL RESEARCH. 3d ed. New York: McGraw-Hill Book Co., 1973. 512 p.

A step-by-step introduction to the logical and theoretical foundations of scientific investigation.

Watanabe, Ruth T. INTRODUCTION TO MUSIC RESEARCH. Englewood Cliffs, N.J.: Prentice-Hall, 1967. 237 p.

A practical handbook for the serious graduate student or music researcher. Deals primarily with basic elements of music research. Includes numerous bibliographic references.

See also Section 59: Computer Applications, and Section 11: Selected Guides to Bibliographic Sources.

Section 18

INFORMATION SERVICES AND SYSTEMS

Computer information retrieval and data processing are now available to educators. Many colleges, universities, school systems, and state education departments provide these services. This section describes those services and systems which are especially useful to music educators.

DATRIX II. Ann Arbor, Mich.: Xerox University Microfilms.

A computerized service for compiling a list of doctoral dissertations on any subject. (See DATRIX II in Section 15: Dissertations.)

DIALOG INFORMATION RETRIEVAL SERVICE. Palo Alto, Calif.: Lockheed Information Systems.

A computer retrieval system for searching certain data bases. Those data banks available through this system and most useful to the work of music education include the complete file of educational material from the Educational Resources Information Center known as ERIC (described below). The two principal subfiles of ERIC are:

RESOURCES IN EDUCATION (RIE). Washington, D.C.: Educational Resources Information Center, National Institute of Education, 1966-- . Monthly. (Formerly called RESEARCH IN EDUCATION.)

Abstracts of educational research reports, descriptions of innovative programs, curriculum guides.

CURRENT INDEX TO JOURNALS IN EDUCATION (CIJE). New York: Macmillan Information, Division of Macmillan Publishing Co., 1969-- . Monthly.

Selected periodical articles are indexed and annotated.

Two other data banks available through this service are:

EXCEPTIONAL CHILD EDUCATION ABSTRACTS. Reston, Va.: The Council for Exceptional Children, 1969-- . Quarterly.

Abstracts of materials of particular interest to workers in this field. Documents selected by the Council for Exceptional Children.

PSYCHOLOGICAL ABSTRACTS. Washington, D.C.: American Psychological Association, 1967-- . Monthly.

More than 150,000 abstracts to journal articles in psychology.

EDUCATIONAL RESOURCES INFORMATION CENTER (ERIC). Washington, D.C.: U.S. Office of Education.

A national information system. It gathers, evaluates, reproduces, and disseminates to the educational community documents pertaining to recent or current educational research and developments in specialized areas. Its resources provide access to reports of innovative programs and selective efforts in educational research, both current and historical. Included are reports, journal articles, curricular guides, and other related materials. The principal reference tools for locating ERIC materials are as follows:

RESOURCES IN EDUCATION (RIE). (Prior to January 1975, known as RESEARCH IN EDUCATION). 1966-- . Monthly.

An abstract journal reporting recently completed research, descriptions of outstanding programs, and other documents of educational significance. Indexed by subject, author or investigator, and institution. Semiannual and annual indexes are available.

CURRENT INDEX TO JOURNALS IN EDUCATION (CIJE).

A monthly guide to periodical literature. Articles are indexed and annotated. Semiannual indexes.

Libraries subscribing to ERIC have immediate access to these materials by means of microfiche, which can be used with mechanical readers. Paper copy of the reports can be acquired at once where reader-printer machines are available. Copy of the full text of the documents may also be obtained from the ERIC Document Reproduction Service (EDRS), P.O. Box 190, Arlington, Virginia 22210. Computer searching in ERIC materials is also available (for details see DIALOG INFORMATION RETRIEVAL SERVICE, above).

DEVELOPMENT OF OTHER SYSTEMS

In addition to commercially developed computer retrieval systems already available, significant progress in applying modern technology to research is being made in colleges and universities. A notable example is the School of Music

Information System at Ohio State University. This information center collects bibliographic references and processes documents relating to music, including acoustics, psychology (especially perception), sociology, and aesthetics. Music history is not included except as it pertains to music analysis. By means of a coordinate indexing system and optical scanning equipment, these materials are made available to the university faculty and students.

Such efforts will undoubtedly spread rapidly. Interlibrary exchange of research findings among institutions of higher learning via computer is likely in the near future. The technology is already available; it is the implementation that must be forthcoming.

Section 19

GUIDES TO GRANT SUPPORT PROGRAMS, FUNDING AGENCIES, AND PROPOSAL WRITING

ANNUAL REGISTER OF GRANT SUPPORT. Los Angeles: Academic Media, 1969-- . Annual.

The most recent edition of an annually revised source of detailed information, including subject, geographic, organizational, and personnel indexes. Identifies more than one million current grants, fellowships, travel and construction grants, scholarships, awards, and prizes.

Daetz, Helen, et al., eds. SOURCES OF INFORMATION ON FUNDS FOR EDUCATION: AN ANNOTATED BIBLIOGRAPHY. 2d ed. Corvallis: Oregon State System of Higher Education, 1971. 96 p.

A bibliography of sources of support for educational purposes.

GUIDE TO GRANTS, LOANS, AND OTHER TYPES OF GOVERNMENT ASSISTANCE AVAILABLE TO STUDENTS AND EDUCATIONAL INSTITUTIONS. Washington, D.C.: Public Affairs Press, 1967. 92 p.

A comprehensive guide to various types of government assistance available to college students and educational institutions of higher education.

Hall, Mary. DEVELOPING SKILLS IN PROPOSAL WRITING. Corvallis: Oregon State System of Higher Education, 1971. 194 p.

Excellent treatment of proposal writing. Describes different types of funding agencies. Includes sample of covering letters, budget statements, and application forms used by the Department of Health, Education, and Welfare.

HANDBOOK OF INTERNATIONAL STUDY FOR U.S. NATIONALS. New York: Institute of International Education, 1970. 293 p.

A guide to undergraduate and graduate study abroad. Includes programs sponsored by U.S. institutions and summer programs.

Horn, Robert, ed. THE GUIDE TO FEDERAL ASSISTANCE FOR EDUCATION. 2 vols. Des Moines, Iowa: Meredith Corp., 1966-- . Updated monthly.

A listing of federal aid programs for individuals and schools for research and training.

Kruger, Chaddie B., comp. POST-BACCALAUREATE GRANTS AND AWARDS IN MUSIC. 4th ed. Vienna, Va.: Music Educators National Conference, 1974. Paper.

Offers information about financial aid and awards available to outstanding musicians who seek financial backing for additional schooling, study, composition, or recognition. Lists graduate schools with brief information concerning their fellowship and scholarship programs in music.

Lewis, Marianna, ed. THE FOUNDATION DIRECTORY. 4th ed. New York: The Foundation Center, 1971. 642 p.

Describes more than 5,000 foundations giving grants to educational, social, and charitable agencies. Restricted to nongovernmental, nonprofit organizations which make grants of $25,000 or more per year.

Millsaps, Daniel. GRANTS AND AID TO INDIVIDUALS IN THE ARTS. 2d ed. Washington, D.C.: Washington International Arts Letter, 1972. 155 p.

Listing of colleges, universities, professional schools, and societies which offer financial assistance to individuals in the arts.

______. PRIVATE FOUNDATIONS AND BUSINESS CORPORATIONS ACTIVE IN ARTS/HUMANITIES/EDUCATION. Vol. 2. Washington, D.C.: Washington International Arts Letter, 1974. 264 p.

An alphabetical listing and description of grants offered by private foundations to institutions in the arts and humanities.

______, ed. MILLIONS FOR THE ARTS: FEDERAL AND STATE CULTURAL PROGRAMS. AN EXHAUSTIVE SENATE REPORT. Washington, D.C.: Washington International Arts Letter, 1972. 58 p.

Sources of assistance in the arts from federal and state sources for institutions and individuals.

New York City Foundation Center. THE FOUNDATIONS GRANTS INDEX. New York: Columbia University Press, 1972. 292 p.

A cumulative record of foundation grants indexed by field of interest. Includes music.

Pavlakis, Christopher. THE AMERICAN MUSIC HANDBOOK. New York: Free Press, 1974. 836 p.

Part 8: "U.S. Musical Contests, Awards Grants, Fellowships and Honors" describes in detail a wide variety of grant-supported opportunities.

Phelps, Roger P. "Subsidization of Research in Music." In his A GUIDE TO RESEARCH IN MUSIC EDUCATION, pp. 207-17. Dubuque, Iowa: William C. Brown Co., 1969. 239 p.

A good description of the considerations and procedures necessary for seeking support for research.

Rich, Maria F., ed. AWARDS FOR SINGERS. New York: Central Opera Service, 1969-- . 16 p. Biannual supplements.

Awards for study offered by private foundations, societies, and U.S. colleges and universities. Also includes information on vocal competitions in the United States and abroad.

SCHOLARSHIPS, FELLOWSHIPS AND LOANS NEWS SERVICE. Arlington, Mass.: Bellman Publishing Co., 1955-- . Bimonthly.

A newsletter containing announcements of research grants and student aid.

Turner, Roland, ed. THE GRANTS REGISTER 1973-1975. New York: St. Martin's Press, 1973. 685 p.

Describes grants, scholarships, and professional awards for many types of academic and artistic activities. Primarily for graduate students.

WASHINGTON INTERNATIONAL ARTS LETTER. Washington, D.C.: 1962-- . 10/year.

Covers grants, awards, and support programs. Includes arts and government; humanities and education; books and publications.

FUNDING SOURCE

NATIONAL ENDOWMENT FOR THE ARTS: OFFICE OF MUSIC PROGRAMS. 806 Fifteenth Street, N.W., Washington, D.C. 20506.

Grants money to individuals and organizations under programs prescribed by Public Law 89-209 and those developed by the endowment. An extensive support program for worthy music causes. Its main advisory body is the National Council for the Arts.

Section 20

BUSINESS ASPECTS OF MUSIC AND MUSIC EDUCATION

COPYRIGHT REFERENCES

Berk, Lee. LEGAL PROTECTION FOR THE CREATIVE MUSICIAN. Boston: Berklee Press Publications, 1970. 371 p. Biblio. SUPPLEMENT. 1973. 28 p.

Bogsch, Arpad. THE LAW OF COPYRIGHT UNDER THE UNIVERSAL CONVENTION. New York: R.R. Bowker Co., 1968. 696 p.

Jass Enterprises. JASS GUIDE TO PUBLIC DOMAIN MUSIC. New York: 1966. 232 p.

A convenient listing of music in the public domain. Alphabetical by title and category in original published form in the United States.

Library of Congress. Copyright Office. COPYRIGHT FOR MUSICAL COMPOSITIONS. Washington, D.C.: Library of Congress, 1966.

Music Publishers' Association of the United States, Inc., and Music Publishers' Protective Association, Inc., comps. CLEARANCE OF RIGHTS IN MUSICAL COMPOSITIONS: A GUIDE AND DIRECTORY. New York: 1966. 16 p. Paper.

A list of the leading music publishers of the world, showing the proper source for clearance of various rights. Includes a description of the various rights.

Pilpel, Harriet, and Goldberg, Morton. A COPYRIGHT GUIDE. New York: R.R. Bowker Co., 1968.

Rothenberg, Stanley. LEGAL PROTECTION OF LITERATURE, ART AND MUSIC. New York: Clark Boardman Co., 1960. 367 p.

An introductory reference to the law of literary, artistic, and musical property. Covers in detail the major questions which the legal practictioner and layman will encounter and refers them to the proper sources for answers. Bibliography.

Taubman, Joseph. PERFORMING ARTS MANAGEMENT AND LAW. 2 vols. New York: Law-Arts Publishers, 1972. 1,417 p.

Focuses primarily on the copyright law as it relates to creators and performers. Bibliography.

______, ed. THE BUSINESS AND LAW OF MUSIC. New York: Federal Legal Publications, 1965. 111 p.

A collection of essays presented at the Symposium of the Committee on the Law of the Theatre of the Federal Bar Associations of New York, New Jersey, and Connecticut. Includes information on copyright for music publishing, recording, theatre, and movie and television music. Also discusses practices of performing rights societies. Bibliography.

Wager, Willis [Joseph]. A MUSICIAN'S GUIDE TO COPYRIGHT AND PUBLISHING. Brighton, Mass.: Carousel Publishing Corp., 1975. 22 p. Illus., biblio.

A practical guide with step-by-step procedures for securing or renewing copyright.

Walls, Howard. COPYRIGHT HANDBOOK FOR FINE AND APPLIED ARTS. New York: Watson-Guptill Publications, 1963. 125 p.

A broad, succinct perspective of copyright for artists and composers.

BUSINESS AND INDUSTRY

Ackerman, Paul, and Zhito, Lee. THE COMPLETE REPORT OF THE FIRST INTERNATIONAL MUSIC INDUSTRY CONFERENCE. New York: Billboard Publishing Co., 1969. 335 p.

A compilation of speeches and discussion resulting from the 1969 meeting of the First International Music Industry Conference. Examines many segments of the music business.

Cutler, Bruce, ed. THE ARTS AT THE GRASS ROOTS. Lawrence: University Press of Kansas, 1968. 270 p. Paper.

A practical guide providing all types of information on the arts. One section deals with music. Reports how arts organizations and concerned leaders produced a statewide program of action in the arts. Bibliography.

DIRECTORY OF PUBLISHING OPPORTUNITIES. 2d ed. Orange, N.J.: Academic Media, 1973. 722 p.

A comprehensive guide to publishing opportunities in every major academic, research, scholarly, and technical field. Formerly entitled THE DIRECTORY OF SCHOLARLY AND RESEARCH PUBLISHING OPPORTUNITIES.

Greyser, Stephen A., ed. CULTURAL POLICY AND ARTS ADMINISTRATION. Cambridge, Mass.: Harvard Summer School Institute in Arts Administration, 1973. (Distr. by Harvard University Press.) 173 p. Paper.

A collection of articles discussing cultural policy and objectives as related to the management of arts organizations. Includes bibliographic references.

Huntley, Leston. THE LANGUAGE OF THE MUSIC BUSINESS, A HANDBOOK OF ITS CUSTOMS, PRACTICES, AND PROCEDURES. Nashville, Tenn.: Del Capo Publications, 1965. 465 p.

Lins, L. Joseph, and Rees, Robert A. SCHOLAR'S GUIDE TO JOURNAL OF EDUCATION AND EDUCATIONAL PSYCHOLOGY. Madison, Wis.: Dembar Educational Research Services, 1960. 150 p.

Useful guide to writers of articles for publication. Lists 134 leading professional journals. Information includes addresses, publication facts, types of material used, remuneration policies, and editorial practices.

Music Educators National Conference. MUSIC CODE OF ETHICS. Washington, D.C.: 1947. 3 p. Pamphlet.

As adopted by the American Federation of Musicians, Music Educators National Conference, and American Association of School Administrators.

Music Industry Council. THE MUSIC INDUSTRY COUNCIL GUIDE FOR MUSIC EDUCATORS. Reston, Va.: Music Educators National Conference, 1976. 32 p. Paper.

Provides numerous suggestions for guidance in the business contacts that are an essential part of any music education program.

Reiss, Alvin H. THE ARTS MANAGEMENT HANDBOOK. New York: Law-Arts Publishers, 1974. 802 p. Illus.

Contains articles which appeared in ARTS MANAGEMENT between February 1962 and February 1973. Covers the practical aspects of arts administration and the social aspects of the arts.

Ross, Ted. THE ART OF MUSIC ENGRAVING AND PROCESSING. Miami Beach, Fla., and New York: Hansen Books, 1970. 278 p. Music, illus.

A manual, reference, and textbook on preparing music for reproduction and print.

Shemel, Sidney, and Krasilovsky, M. William. THE BUSINESS OF MUSIC. Edited by Paul Ackerman. New York: Billboard Publishing Co., 1964. 420 p.

A comprehensive guide to the music and recording industries. Presents facts for decision making and covers informally the legal and accounting aspects of the music business. See also MORE ABOUT THIS MUSIC BUSINESS, below.

_____. MORE ABOUT THIS MUSIC BUSINESS. Rev. ed. Edited by Lee Zhito. New York: Billboard Publishing Co., 1974. 204 p.

Additional topics and materials not contained in THIS BUSINESS OF MUSIC, above.

Worrel, John W. DIRECTORY OF THE MUSIC INDUSTRY. Evanston, Ill.: Instrumentalist Co., 1970. 48 p. Paper.

Alphabetical listing with addresses and cross-references: music publishers, textbook publishers, manufacturers and distributors of instruments, instrumental accessories, cases, uniforms, choir robes, recordings, teaching aids, awards, storage equipment, etc.

CAREERS IN MUSIC

Csida, Joseph. THE MUSIC/RECORD CAREER HANDBOOK. Studio City, Calif.: First Place Music Publishers, 1973. 374 p.

A valuable reference for individuals considering music as a career. Covers the creative aspects, the commentary careers, business, and education. Includes historical background and prognosis for the new developments.

Curtis, Robert E. YOUR FUTURE IN MUSIC. New York: Richard Rosen Press, 1962. 160 p.

A realistic look at all the fields of professional endeavor in music.

DIRECTORY OF PUBLISHING OPPORTUNITIES. 2d ed. Orange, N.J.: Academic Media, 1975. 722 p.

A comprehensive guide to publishing opportunities in every major academic, research, scholarly, and technical field. Formerly entitled THE DIRECTORY OF SCHOLARLY AND RESEARCH PUBLISHING OPPORTUNITIES.

Institute of International Education. SCHOLARSHIPS AND FELLOWSHIPS FOR FOREIGN STUDY--A SELECTED BIBLIOGRAPHY. New York: 1975. 6 p.

Provides lists of important sources of information about opportunities for scholarship aid for Americans planning to study abroad.

Music Educators National Conference. CAREERS IN MUSIC. Washington, D.C.: 1973. 24 p. Paper.

Foldout brochure of facts on opportunities, earnings, qualifications, and training needed for careers in the field of music. Designed for students.

Newman, Bernard. YOUR FUTURE IN THE HIGH FIDELITY INDUSTRY. New York: Richard Rosen Press, 1966. 128 p.

A guide to the career opportunities and requirements in a rapidly growing industry.

Richey, Robert W. PREPARING FOR A CAREER IN EDUCATION: CHALLENGES, CHANGES, AND ISSUES. New York: McGraw-Hill Book Co., 1974. 288 p.

Presents basic considerations concerning the teaching profession as a career.

Ward, John Owen. CAREERS IN MUSIC. New York: H.Z. Walck, 1968. 127 p.

ASSOCIATIONS

American Federation of Musicians of the United States and Canada, 1500 Broadway, New York, N.Y. 10036.

Publication: INTERNATIONAL MUSICIAN. Monthly.

American Guild of Authors and Composers (AGAC), 40 West 57th Street, New York, N.Y. 10019.

Publication: NEWS. Quarterly.

American Society of Composers, Authors and Publishers (ASCAP), One Lincoln Plaza, New York, N.Y. 10023.

Publications: TODAY. 3-4/year.

Membership list. Annual.

BIOGRAPHICAL DICTIONARY. Every 10 years.

Association of College, University and Community Arts Administrators, P.O. Box 2137, Madison, Wis. 53701.

Publications: Bulletin. Monthly.

Bulletin Supplement. Monthly.

Membership List. 3/year.

Broadcast Music, Inc., 40 West 57th Street, New York, N.Y. 10019.

Administers performance rights for writers and publishers. Makes music available to all parts of the world by reciprocal contracts with foreign organizations of the same type.

Guitar and Accessory Manufacturers Association of America (GAMA), 111 East Chestnut Street, Chicago, Ill. 60611.

International Society of Performing Arts Administrators, c/o James Bernhard, 615 Louisiana Street, Houston, Tex. 77002.

Major Symphony Managers Association (MSMA), c/o American Symphony Orchestra League, 1551 Trap Road, Vienna, Va. 22180.

Metropolitan Symphony Managers Association (MSMA), c/o American Symphony League, P.O. Box 66, Vienna, Va. 22180.

Music Industry Council (MIC), c/o J.W. Pepper and Son, Inc., Box 850, Valley Forge, Pa. 19482.

Music Performance Trust Funds, 1501 Broadway, New York, N.Y. 10036.

Music Publishers Association of the United States (MPA), 810 Seventh Avenue, New York, N.Y. 10019.

National Association of Accordion Wholesalers (NAAW), 5820 North Nagle Avenue, Chicago, Ill. 60646.

National Association of Band Instrument Manufacturers, c/o G. LeBlanc Corporation, 30th Avenue, 71st Street, Kenosha, Wis. 53141.

National Association of Electronic Organ Manufacturers (NAEOM), c/o The Wurlitzer Co., 1700 Pleasant Street, DeKalb, Ill. 60115.

National Association of Musical Merchandise Wholesalers (NAMMW), c/o Smith, Bucklin and Associates, 111 East Wacker Drive, Chicago, Ill. 60601.

Publication: Newsletter. Monthly.

National Association of Music Merchants (NAMM), 35 East Wacker Drive, Suite 3320, Chicago, Ill. 60601.

Publication: NAMM MUSIC RETAILER NEWS. Monthly.

National Association of School Music Dealers (NASMD), 1121 Broadway Plaza, Tacoma, Wash. 98402.

Publications: Newsletter. Quarterly.

Membership directory. Annual.

National Council of Music Importers and Exporters (NCMIE), 51 West 21st Street, New York, N.Y. 10010.

National Music Publishers Association (NMPA), 110 East 59th Street, New York, N.Y. 10022.

National Piano Manufacturers Association of America (NMPA), c/o George M. Otto Associates, Inc., 435 North Michigan Avenue, Chicago, Ill. 60611.

Publication: Monthly unit shipment and dollar volume reports.

National Piano Travelers Association (NPTA), c/o Charles Ramsey Corporation, 15 Gage Street, Kingston, N.Y. 12401.

New York State Educational Communication Association, Inc., 555 Warren Road, Ithaca, N.Y. 14850.

Piano Technicians Guild (PTG), P.O. Box 1813, Seattle, Wash. 98111.

Publications: PIANO TECHNICIANS JOURNAL. 12/year.

Members bulletin. Monthly.

PTG OFFICIAL DIRECTORY. Annual.

Section 21

NATIONAL MUSIC FRATERNITIES, SORORITIES, AND HONOR SOCIETY

FRATERNITIES

Kappa Kappa Psi Fraternity, 122 Center for the Performing Arts, Oklahoma State University, Stillwater, Okla. 74074.

Publication: THE PODIUM.

Mu Beta Psi National Honorary Musical Fraternity, 3401 Hickory Crest Drive, Marietta, Ga. 30064.

Publication: THE CLEF.

Phi Beta Mu, Drawer 2127, University Post Office, Enid, Okla. 73701.

Publication: SCHOOL MUSICIAN.

Phi Mu Alpha-Sinfonia, "Lyrecrest," 10600 Old State Road, Evansville, Ind. 47711.

Publication: SINFONIAN NEWSLETTER.

SORORITIES

Delta Omicron International Music Fraternity, 18518 Cherrylawn, Detroit, Mich. 48221.

Publication: THE WHEEL OF DELTA OMICRON.

Mu Phi Epsilon, 1097 Arnott Way, Campbell, Calif. 95008.

Publication: THE TRIANGLE.

Phi Beta, 1397 Maetzel Drive, Columbus, Ohio 43227.

Publication: THE BATON.

Sigma Alpha Iota, 4119 Rollins Avenue, Des Moines, Iowa 50312.

Publication: PAN PIPES.

Tau Beta Sigma Sorority, 122 Center for the Performing Arts, Oklahoma State University, Stillwater, Okla. 74074.

Publication: THE PODIUM MAGAZINE.

HONOR SOCIETY

Pi Kappa Lambda, P.O. Box 6222, University, Ala. 35486.

Publication: Newsletter.

Section 22

DICTIONARIES AND ENCYCLOPEDIAS—MUSIC

Recognizing the fact that music educators select music dictionaries and encyclopedias according to their own research needs and/or according to the needs of students whose requirements may vary in light of their age levels, experience, and purposes, the list here is extensive and allows a wide range of selection both as to depth of treatment and scope of coverage. It should also be noted that some older publications have been included because they frequently contain information which was considered important in a particular period of music history but the information is no longer available in more recent issues. This is particularly true in the case of musical personalities.

Ammer, Christine. HARPER'S DICTIONARY OF MUSIC. New York: Harper and Row, 1972. 414 p.

> Included are the most commonly used terms, information concerning musical works, styles, and periods ranging from the Renaissance to the twentieth century. Many foreign language terms. Pronunciations are included. Many helpful tables. The articles on musical instruments generally indicate some repertory for each instrument.

______. MUSICIAN'S HANDBOOK OF FOREIGN TERMS. New York: G. Schirmer, 1971. 71 p. Music, paper.

> Contains the English equivalents of approximately 2,700 foreign expression marks and directions taken from French, German, Italian, Latin, Portuguese, and Spanish scores.

Apel, Willi. HARVARD DICTIONARY OF MUSIC. 2d ed., rev. and enl. Cambridge, Mass.: Belknap Press of Harvard University Press, 1969. 935 p. Illus.

> A standard work. This edition includes entries for rarely performed major works, electronic music, film music, music education, and the music of minor nations. Lacking is information concerning certain newer developments in American popular music.

Apel, Willi, and Daniel, Ralph T. THE HARVARD BRIEF DICTIONARY OF MUSIC. Cambridge, Mass.: Harvard University Press, 1960. 341 p. Illus.

Somewhat similar in character to the HARVARD DICTIONARY OF MUSIC, but more limited in scope and much simpler in style of presentation.

THE ASCAP BIOGRAPHICAL DICTIONARY OF COMPOSERS, AUTHORS AND PUBLISHERS. 3d ed. Compiled by Lynn Farnol Group. New York: American Society for Composers, Authors and Publishers, 1966. 845 p.

Contains an entry for each of more than 5,000 members of the society with biographical sketches, date and place of birth, education, sketch of career, with emphasis on music, residence, and selection of best-known works.

Baker, Theodore. BAKER'S BIOGRAPHICAL DICTIONARY OF MUSICIANS. 5th ed. Rev. and enl. by Nicolas Slonimsky. New York: G. Schirmer, 1971. 2,117 p.

A standard reference work, revised by Nicolas Slonimsky. Includes supplement.

_____. DICTIONARY OF MUSICAL TERMS. 1933. Reprint. New York: AMS, 1970. 257 p.

An old but useful dictionary consisting of terms gleaned from standard works of reference.

_____. PRONOUNCING POCKET MANUAL FOR MUSICAL TERMS. Rev. ed. New York: G. Schirmer, 1933. 256 p. Paper.

A convenient pocket-sized dictionary of musical terms. Limited in scope.

Blom, Eric, comp. EVERYMAN'S DICTIONARY OF MUSIC. Rev. by Sir Jack [A.] Westrup. New York: St. Martin's Press, 1971. 793 p. Music.

An excellent one-volume dictionary. Musical examples included to illustrate technical terms.

Bryant, E.T. MUSIC. New York: Philosophical Library, 1965. 84 p.

This British annotated guide surveys major dictionaries, encyclopedias, and 250 music texts.

Carter, Henry H. A DICTIONARY OF MIDDLE ENGLISH MUSICAL TERMS. Indiana University Humanities Series, no. 45. Bloomington: Indiana University Press, 1961. 655 p.

A definitive study of Middle English musical terms. Terms included in this work refer to the theory, performance, materials, and forms of Middle English music.

Cooper, Martin, ed. THE CONCISE ENCYCLOPEDIA OF MUSIC AND MUSICIANS. 2d rev. ed. London: Hutchinson, 1971. 481 p.

An easily digestible reference work, especially suitable for the "average music lover." Treats various historical and technical aspects of music.

Coover, James B. MUSIC LEXICOGRAPHY: INCLUDING A STUDY OF LACUNAE IN MUSIC LEXICOGRAPHY AND A BIBLIOGRAPHY OF MUSIC DICTIONARIES. 3d ed. Carlisle, Pa.: Carlisle Books, 1971. 175 p.

Deals with the problems encountered in writing music dictionaries. Includes an extensive listing, with some annotations, of music dictionaries and encyclopedias.

Cross, Milton, and Ewen, David. THE MILTON CROSS NEW ENCYCLOPEDIA OF THE GREAT COMPOSERS AND THEIR MUSIC. Rev. ed. 2 vols. Garden City, N.Y.: Doubleday and Co., 1969. 1,910 p.

The lives, music, and impact of sixty-seven of the world's foremost composers. Discography.

De Becker, L.J. BLACK'S DICTIONARY OF MUSIC AND MUSICIANS. London: A. & C. Black, 1924. 758 p.

Covers the period of musical history from the earliest times to 1924. It was intended to serve as a bridge between the large works of musical reference (such as Grove's) and the smaller works which provide only a mere outline of the subject. Basically English, but with a reasonable account of American musical activities for the period covered.

Dunstan, Ralph. A CYCLOPAEDIC DICTIONARY OF MUSIC. 1925. Reprint. New York: Da Capo Press, 1973. 632 p.

Eaglefield-Hull, A. DICTIONARY OF MODERN MUSIC AND MUSICIANS. 1924. Reprint. New York: Da Capo Press, 1971. 544 p.

Ewen, David. ENCYCLOPEDIA OF CONCERT MUSIC. New York: Hill and Wang, 1959. 566 p.

Grant, W. Parks. HANDBOOK OF MUSIC TERMS. Metuchen, N.J.: Scarecrow Press, 1967. 476 p. Music, illus.

Employs numerous features in the interest of practicality. Many cross-references and simplified definitions which include synonyms, antonyms, pronunciations, and variant spellings.

GROVE'S DICTIONARY OF MUSIC AND MUSICIANS. 5th ed. 9 vols. Edited by Eric Blom. New York: St. Martin's Press, 1954. SUPPLEMENT, 1961. Vol. 10. Edited by Eric Blom, assoc. ed. Denis Stevens. Also available in paper.

This ten-volume work is undoubtedly the most widely used, all-inclusive English language reference tool for information pertaining to musical matters. It does not deal with pedagogical information as such. While its principal function is that of a dictionary, it also provides copious bibliographies which serve as references to further reading, increasing tremendously its value as a source of information.

Illing, Robert. PERGAMON DICTIONARY OF MUSICIANS AND MUSIC. 2 vols. New York: Macmillan, 1963, 1964. 175 p., 260 p. Illus., tables, music.

A revision of the dictionary published by Penguin Books in 1950. Volume 1: MUSICIANS is biographical and includes primarily composers. Volume 2: MUSIC is concerned with musical terms and information about music.

Jacobs, Arthur. A NEW DICTIONARY OF MUSIC. Chicago, Ill.: Aldine Publishing Co., 1962. 416 p.

A useful reference for the amateur music lover.

Karp, Theodore. DICTIONARY OF MUSIC. New York: Dell Publishing Co., 1973. 448 p.

Katayen, Lelia, and Telberg, Val. RUSSIAN-ENGLISH DICTIONARY OF MUSICAL TERMS. New York: Telberg Book Corp., 1965. 125 p.

LAROUSSE ENCYCLOPEDIA OF MUSIC. Edited by Geoffrey Hindley. New York: World Publishing Co., 1971. 576 p. Photos.

Based on LA MUSIQUE, LES HOMMES, LES INSTRUMENTS, LES OEUVRES, edited by Norbert Dufourcq (Paris: Augi, Gillon, Hollier-Larousse Moreauet Cie, Librarie Larousse, 1965). A nontechnical source of information. Bibliography.

Lloyd, Norman. THE GOLDEN ENCYCLOPEDIA OF MUSIC. New York: Golden Press, 1968. 720 p. Photos, music, illus.

A highly readable and attractive encyclopedia especially suited to school use at the secondary level. Includes a special section about instruments by E(manuel) Winternitz.

Pratt, Waldo Selden, ed. THE NEW ENCYCLOPEDIA OF MUSIC AND MUSICIANS. Rev. ed. New York: Macmillan, 1929. 969 p.

A large and comprehensive volume covering a wide range of information concerning music, musicians, organizations, and institutions.

Pulver, Jeffrey. A BIOGRAPHICAL DICTIONARY OF ENGLISH MUSIC. 1927. Reprint. New York: Da Capo Press, 1973. 537 p.

Includes musical biographies from thirteenth through seventeenth centuries--primarily composers, theorists, printers, performers, and instrument makers, and brief coverage of foreign artists who have had some impact on English music and musicians.

Read, Sir Herbert Edward, ed. ENCYCLOPEDIA OF THE ARTS. New York: Meredith, 1966. 966 p.

Runes, Dagobert, and Schrickel, Harry G., eds. ENCYCLOPEDIA OF THE ARTS. New York: Philosophical Library, 1946. 1,064 p.

A concise source of information dealing with the various aspects of the several arts--including music.

Sacher, Jack, et al., trans. and eds. MUSIC A. TO Z. New York: Grosset and Dunlap, 1957. 432 p. Music, illus., photos.

An adaptation and expansion of Rudolf Stephan's music encyclopedia, FISCHER LEXIKON (Frankfort, Germany: Fisher Bucherer, 1957). Includes a biographical dictionary, a glossary of technical terms and articles on various musical topics. Especially useful is the bibliography of works in English related to the topics discussed in the text.

Sainsbury, John S., ed. A DICTIONARY OF MUSICIANS FROM THE EARLIEST TIMES. 2 vols. 1825. Reprint. New York: Da Capo Press, 1966. 962 p. Music.

Sandved, K.B., ed. THE WORLD OF MUSIC: AN ILLUSTRATED ENCYCLOPEDIA. Rev. ed. 4 vols. New York: Abradale Press, 1963. 1,516 p. Illus.

Originally published in Norway and later translated into other languages. Revised and enlarged for American readers.

Scholes, Percy A. THE CONCISE OXFORD DICTIONARY OF MUSIC. 2d ed. Edited by John Owen Ward. London: Oxford University Press, 1964. 636 p.

A reduction of the author's OXFORD COMPANION TO MUSIC. It does have some features not included in the COMPANION: hundreds of brief biographical listings of vocal and instrumental performers and conductors (as distinct from composers); and hundreds of entries on individual compositions (i.e., operas, symphonic poems, song cycles, etc.).

_____. OXFORD COMPANION TO MUSIC. 10th ed. Revised and edited by John Owen Ward. New York: Oxford University Press, 1970. 1,189 p. Illus., music, photos.

Probably the best-known British one-volume encyclopedia of music. A standard reference work.

Slocum, Robert B. BIOGRAPHICAL DICTIONARIES AND RELATED WORKS: AN INTERNATIONAL BIBLIOGRAPHY OF COLLECTIVE BIOGRAPHIES. Detroit: Gale Research Co., 1967. 1,056 p.

Smith, William James. A DICTIONARY OF MUSICAL TERMS IN FOUR LANGUAGES--ENGLISH, FRANCAIS, ITALIANO, DEUTSCH. London: Hutchinson, 1961. 195 p.

Thompson, Oscar, ed. in chief. THE INTERNATIONAL CYCLOPEDIA OF MUSIC AND MUSICIANS. 10th ed. Edited by Bruce Bohle. New York: Dodd, Mead and Co., 1975. 2,510 p.

Thompson's first edition in 1939 was recognized as the outstanding single-volume work in its field. Changes in the latest edition were not intended to change the body of material which is concerned with historical and classical material, but rather to focus on the new generation of music and musicians. Full listing of works of important composers, with dates of composition, first performance, and publication wherever possible. There is an attempt at being international in scope, with particular emphasis on American music, musicians, and the American scene.

Tinctores, Johannes. DICTIONARY OF MUSICAL TERMS. Translated and edited by Carl Parrish. New York: Free Press of Glencoe, 1963.

A Latin-English edition.

Watson, Jack M., and Watson, Corine. A CONCISE DICTIONARY OF MUSIC. New York: Dodd, Mead and Co., 1965. 332 p. Illus., music, paper.

An introductory reference book designed mainly for beginning students of music.

WEBSTER'S BIOGRAPHICAL DICTIONARY: A DICTIONARY OF NAMES OF NOTEWORTHY PERSONS WITH PRONUNCIATION AND CONCISE BIOGRAPHIES. Springfield, Mass.: G. and C. Merriam Co., 1969. 1,697 p.

Westrup, [Sir] Jack A., and Harrison, F[rank].L. THE NEW COLLEGE ENCYCLOPEDIA OF MUSIC. New York: W.W. Norton and Co., 1960. 739 p.

A good, practical, one-volume source. Many articles contain brief bibliographies.

WHO'S WHO

INTERNATIONAL WHO'S WHO 1973-74. 37th ed. Europa Publications, 1973. 1,900 p. (Distr. by Gale Research Co., Detroit.)

This work is not only the standard source of biographical information about eminent personalities in every country of the world today, but it is also the only place to find details on persons from the many countries having no national "Who's Who."

INTERNATIONAL WHO'S WHO IN MUSIC AND MUSICIANS' DIRECTORY. 7th ed. Edited by Ernest Kay. Cambridge, Engl.: International Biographical Centre, 1975. 1,348 p.

Contains 12,000 biographies. In addition, the appendixes list the names and addresses of orchestras, music organizations, competitions and awards, festivals, concert halls and opera houses, conservatories, colleges and universities where music is taught, and masters of the king's or queen's music.

Lann, Jack H. WHO'S WHO IN THE ARTS. 2d ed. Portland, Oreg.: International Scholarly Book Service, 1974.

WHO'S WHO IN AMERICA. Chicago: Marquis Who's Who, 1908-- . Biennial.

WHO'S WHO IN THE WORLD, 1974-1975. 2d ed. Chicago: Marquis Who's Who, 1974.

Yates, J.V. WHO'S WHO IN MUSIC AND MUSICIANS INTERNATIONAL. 6th ed. New York: Hafner Press, 1972.

Section 23

DICTIONARIES AND ENCYCLOPEDIAS—EDUCATION

Deighton, Lee C., ed. THE ENCYCLOPEDIA OF EDUCATION. 10 vols. New York: Macmillan and Free Press, 1971.

Contains more than 1,000 articles dealing with the history, theory, research, and philosophy of education.

Ebel, Robert L., ed. ENCYCLOPEDIA OF EDUCATIONAL RESEARCH. 4th ed. New York: Macmillan, 1969. 1,500 p.

A project of the American Educational Research Association. Provides concise summaries of research and many references for further study. Covers education at all levels and in most fields of specialization, including music education.

Good, Carter V., ed. DICTIONARY OF EDUCATION. 3d ed. New York: McGraw-Hill Book Co., 1973. 681 p.

Prepared under the auspices of Phi Delta Kappa. Defines terms used in education according to commonly accepted meanings.

Wolman, Benjamin B., et al., comps. and eds. DICTIONARY OF BEHAVIORAL SCIENCE. New York: Van Nostrand Reinhold Co., 1973. 487 p.

Covers all areas of psychology such as experimental and developmental psychology, personality, learning, perception, motivation, and intelligence. Excellent reference tool for music educators concerned with music learning and human behavior.

Part II

MUSIC IN EDUCATION

Section 24
PHILOSOPHICAL FOUNDATIONS, PRINCIPLES, AND PRACTICES

GENERAL

Anderson, Warren D. ETHOS AND EDUCATION IN GREEK MUSIC: THE EVIDENCE OF POETRY AND PHILOSOPHY. Cambridge, Mass.: Harvard University Press, 1966. 306 p.

Deals mainly with the Hellenic poets and philosophers and their views of the moral and educational values of music. Bibliography.

Benner, Charles L. TEACHING PERFORMING GROUPS. From Research to the Music Classroom, no. 2. Washington, D.C.: Music Educators National Conference, 1972. 32 p. Paper.

Interprets research on the performing student, the teacher, rehearsal techniques, and conditions of performance.

Birge, Edward Bailey. HISTORY OF PUBLIC SCHOOL MUSIC IN THE UNITED STATES. 1939. Reprint. Washington, D.C.: Music Educators National Conference, 1966. 323 p.

An important work which documents early developments of music education in the United States up to 1939.

Boyle, David, comp. INSTRUCTIONAL OBJECTIVES IN MUSIC: RESOURCES FOR PLANNING INSTRUCTION AND EVALUATING ACHIEVEMENT. Vienna, Va.: Music Educators National Conference, 1974. 265 p.

A collection of materials from various sources useful for the planning of instructional objectives. The sourcebook is organized into four sections: Philosophical and Theoretical Foundations; Selecting, Implementing, and Evaluating Instructional Objectives; Writing Instructional Objectives; Examples of Instructional Objectives.

Brocklehurst, J. Brian. RESPONSE TO MUSIC: PRINCIPLES OF MUSIC EDUCATION. London: Routledge & Kegan Paul, 1971. 141 p.

A British view of the place of music in education, its values, and how teaching can reflect these principles effectively in a changing society. Bibliography.

Bruner, Jerome S. THE PROCESS OF EDUCATION. Cambridge, Mass.: Harvard University Press, 1960. 97 p.

A challenging statement concerning intellectual development. Provides basic concepts for a new philosophy of education.

Buttleman, Clifford V., ed. WILL EARHART: A STEADFAST PHILOSOPHY. Washington, D.C.: Music Educators National Conference, 1962. 143 p.

A selection of papers written by Will Earhart dating from 1914, including his last writings, previously unpublished. Includes personal reflections of his followers and students. An important resource for the study of philosophic trends in music education in America. Bibliography.

Choate, Robert A., ed. DOCUMENTARY REPORT OF THE TANGLEWOOD SYMPOSIUM. Washington, D.C.: Music Educators National Conference, 1968. 154 p.

Significant for the researcher concerned with music in American society. The Tanglewood Symposium brought together musicians; sociologists; scientists; labor leaders; educators; representatives of corporations, foundations, communications, and government; and others concerned with the many facets of music. The symposium sought to reappraise and evaluate basic assumptions about music in the educative forces and institutions of our society. Bibliography.

Colwell, Richard. THE EVALUATION OF MUSIC TEACHING AND LEARNING. Englewood Cliffs, N.J.: Prentice-Hall, 1970. 182 p.

A sound presentation of the principles of measurement and evaluation as related to the instructional processes in music education. Bibliographical references.

Colwell, Richard, and Colwell, Ruth. CONCEPTS FOR A MUSICAL FOUNDATION. Englewood Cliffs, N.J.: Prentice-Hall, 1974. 320 p.

A self-instructional basic music book for beginners, particularly for the potential school teacher. This programmed book includes two recordings to be used with the application sections of the book.

Council for Research in Music Education. "Accountability." BULLETIN OF THE COUNCIL FOR RESEARCH IN MUSIC EDUCATION 36 (Spring 1974): entire issue.

Discusses the status of accountability as it affects music education. The report is based on a study which included all fifty states.

Davis, Hazel, and Webb, Lois N., eds. MUSIC AND ART IN THE PUBLIC SCHOOLS. Washington, D.C.: National Education Association, 1963. 88 p.

A research report based on two questionnaire surveys. Describes the status of music education and art education as of 1962. Highly useful for educators involved in tracing developments and trends in music education.

Dykema, Peter W., and Cundiff, Hannah M. SCHOOL MUSIC HANDBOOK: A GUIDE FOR MUSIC EDUCATORS. 3d ed. Boston: C.C. Birchard and Co., 1955. 669 p. Photos, music, illus.

This publication served well as a standard reference work for many years. The wealth of practical suggestions which it contains continues to make it useful.

Earhart, Will. THE MEANING AND TEACHING OF MUSIC. New York: M. Whitmark and Sons, 1935. 250 p. Illus., music.

Treats music philosophically, with implications for music teaching. A work of importance from the earlier days of music education. Bibliography.

Ernst, Carl D., and Gary, Charles L. MUSIC IN GENERAL EDUCATION. Washington, D.C.: Music Educators National Conference, 1965. 223 p. Tables, music, paper.

Basic considerations concerning the role of music experiences in general education. Special attention given to philosophy, objectives, and implementation of programs. Excellent bibliography.

Farnsworth, Paul R. THE SOCIAL PSYCHOLOGY OF MUSIC. 2d ed. Ames: Iowa State University Press, 1969. 298 p.

Treats the sociopsychological variables associated with music. Extensive notes and references cited at end of each section.

Gardner, Howard. THE ARTS AND HUMAN DEVELOPMENT. New York: Wiley-Interscience, 1973. 395 p. Music, illus.

A comprehensive discussion of development, accomplishment, and problem solving in the arts and sciences.

Gary, Charles L., and Landis, Beth. COMPREHENSIVE MUSIC PROGRAMS. Washington, D.C.: Music Educators National Conference, 1972. 12 p. Paper.

An overview of the ideal modern curriculum.

Giannaris, George. MIKIS THEODORAKIS: MUSIC AND SOCIAL CHANGE. New York: Praeger, 1972. 322 p.

A discussion of music as a political force, and the involvement of the artist in social and political problems. Includes Theodorakis's views on music education. The appendix gives a list of Theodorakis's works from 1939 to 1971, including dates and places of first performances. Bibliography and discography.

Horner, V. MUSIC EDUCATION: THE BACKGROUND OF RESEARCH AND OPINION. Victoria, Australia: Council for Educative Research, 1965. 226 p.

A comprehensive survey of research and opinion in music education. Stresses basic differences in views held by British and American music educators. Serious attention given to the nature of musical abilities, the learning process, measurement, and prognosis in music education. Excellent bibliography.

International Society for Music Education. MUSIC EDUCATION IN THE MODERN WORLD. Moscow: Progress Publishers, 1974. 378 p. Photos. (Distr. by Imported Publications, Chicago.)

A report of the proceedings of the Ninth Conference of the International Society for Music Education, held in Moscow in 1970. All of the papers presented at the conference have been translated and printed in this book.

Jaques-Dalcroze, Emile. RHYTHM, MUSIC AND EDUCATION. New York: Benjamin Blom, 1921. 351 p. Illus.

An evaluation of rhythm as the basis of all learning activity.

Jones, Archie N., ed. MUSIC EDUCATION IN ACTION: BASIC PRINCIPLES AND PRACTICAL METHODS. Boston: Allyn and Bacon, 1960. 571 p.

A collection of articles by professional musicians and music educators which deals primarily with teaching problems and solutions. Bibliographies.

Kaplan, Max. FOUNDATIONS AND FRONTIERS OF MUSIC EDUCATION. New York: Holt, Rinehart and Winston, 1966. 261 p.

Basic concepts and critical issues concerning the role of music in education. Develops the sociological aspects of music. Contains a bibliography which is especially useful for the development of a social philosophy of music education.

Kowall, Bonnie C. PERSPECTIVES IN MUSIC EDUCATION: SOURCE BOOK III. Washington, D.C.: Music Educators National Conference, 1966. 575 p.

Contains 92 carefully selected articles (from a collection of approximately 500) which deal not only with the major areas and levels of music education, but include theoretical and philosophical aspects of the subject. Bibliography.

Kraus, Egon. THE PRESENT STATE OF MUSIC EDUCATION IN THE WORLD. Washington, D.C.: International Society for Music Education, 1960. 184 p.

Under the sponsorship of UNESCO, the International Society for Music Education prepared and published this collection of reports on the current status of music education and its organization and methods in different countries as of 1960.

Landor, R.A. THE EDUCATION OF EVERYCHILD: ON THE TEACHING AND LEARNING OF LIBERAL ARTS. Berea, Ohio: Liberal Arts Publishing Co., 1974. 150 p.

Emphasizes the arts as instructional media for a liberal education. Bibliography.

Leonhard, Charles, and House, Robert W. FOUNDATIONS AND PRINCIPLES OF MUSIC EDUCATION. 2d ed. New York: McGraw-Hill Book Co., 1972. 432 p.

Treats comprehensively the total music program, including discussions of the historical, philosophical, and psychological foundations as well as the interrelated processes of curriculum instruction, administration, supervision, and evaluation. Bibliography.

Livingston, James A., et al. ACCOUNTABILITY AND OBJECTIVES FOR MUSIC EDUCATION. Costa Mesa, Calif.: Educational Media Press, 1972. 29 p. Paper.

A guide prepared for use in California but equally useful elsewhere. Provides examples of objectives for the various program areas.

McMullen, Roy. ART, AFFLUENCE AND ALIENATION: THE FINE ARTS TODAY. New York: Praeger, 1968. 272 p.

An examination of the link between contemporary artistic development and the social, economic, political, and technological changes of the twentieth century.

Markel, Roberta. PARENTS' AND TEACHERS' GUIDE TO MUSIC EDUCATION. New York: Macmillan, 1972. 208 p. Illus., music.

An informal description of music study for children--primarily for parents. Provides advice and suggestions.

Morgan, Hazel B., ed. MUSIC IN AMERICAN EDUCATION: MUSIC EDUCATION SOURCE BOOK NUMBER TWO. Washington, D.C.: Music Educators

National Conference, 1955. 365 p.

A compendium of data, opinions, and recommendations compiled from the reports of investigations, studies, and discussions conducted by the Music in American Education Committees of the Music Educators National Conference during the period 1951-54. Also includes selected material from other sources.

JAMES L. MURSELL

The writings of James L. Mursell served the music teaching profession for many years as one of the principal sources of authority. His books have strongly influenced the quality and type of music education that has developed in America. In spite of the fact that most were written some years ago, they continue to be a stimulating and useful source of information.

Mursell, James L. EDUCATION FOR MUSICAL GROWTH. Boston: Ginn and Co., 1948. 342 p.

Develops the concept of growth as it relates to music education. Bibliography.

_____. HUMAN VALUES IN MUSIC EDUCATION. New York: Silver Burdett Co., 1934. 388 p.

Outlines the values of music education and shows how a social educational philosophy can be applied to music teaching. Bibliography.

_____. MUSIC AND THE CLASSROOM TEACHER. New York: Silver Burdett Co., 1951. 304 p.

Designed to aid the classroom teacher to teach music adequately. Bibliography and discography.

_____. MUSIC EDUCATION PRINCIPLES AND PROGRAMS. Morristown, N.J.: Silver Burdett Co., 1956. 386 p.

An authoritative treatment of the school music program. Concentrates on three areas: the foundations of the music program, the special areas of the program, and the coordination of the program. Includes suggested readings.

_____. MUSIC IN AMERICAN SCHOOLS. New York: Silver Burdett Co., 1943. 312 p. Photos.

Analysis of music education practices in the schools with suggestions for improvement.

_____. PRINCIPLES OF MUSICAL EDUCATION. New York: Macmillan, 1937. 300 p.

This work had considerable influence on the development of music education in American public schools in the late 1930s and 1940s. Emphasizes psychological principles as they relate to music education. Bibliography.

_____. THE PSYCHOLOGY OF MUSIC. 1937. Reprint. New York: Johnson Reprint Corp., 1970. 389 p. Illus., music.

Brings together much research relating to the psychology of music. Extensive bibliography.

Mursell, James L., and Glenn, Mabelle. THE PSYCHOLOGY OF SCHOOL MUSIC TEACHING. New York: Silver Burdett Co., 1938. 386 p.

Discusses psychological investigations in the fields of music and education as related to music teaching. Bibliography.

MUSIC, AN OVERVIEW. Washington, D.C.: Superintendent of Documents, Government Printing Office, 1974. 42 p. (Order no. 1780-01340.)

Discusses a survey that attempted to measure the effectiveness of music education among children and young adults.

Music Educators National Conference. THE SCHOOL MUSIC PROGRAM: DESCRIPTION AND STANDARDS. Vienna, Va.: 1974. 66 p.

For description, see Section 32: Administration and Supervision of Music Education.

_____. TANGLEWOOD SYMPOSIUM: MUSIC IN AMERICAN SOCIETY. Washington, D.C.: 1967. 32 p.

Reprint of the MUSIC EDUCATORS JOURNAL insert on the symposium. Presents highlights from the special Summer 1967 seminar held in Lenox, Massachusetts.

Mussulman, Joseph A. THE USES OF MUSIC. Englewood Cliffs, N.J.: Prentice-Hall, 1974. 258 p. Illus.

A discussion of the status of music in American life. Includes coverage of music in the schools, religious music, ceremonial music, etc.

National Society for the Study of Education. BASIC CONCEPTS IN MUSIC EDUCATION. Edited by Nelson B. Henry. The Fifty-seventh Yearbook of the National Society for the Study of Education, Part I. Chicago: 1958. 362 p. (Distr. by the University of Chicago Press.)

A series of statements prepared by authorities in music education and related disciplines. Section I interprets the implications of fundamental concepts of major disciplines for current issues regarding educational theory and practice. Section II describes music instruction relating to various features of accredited school programs.

Pitts, Lilla Belle. THE MUSIC CURRICULUM IN A CHANGING WORLD. New York: Silver Burdett Co., 1944. 165 p.

Implications for developing the music curriculum with emphasis on creativity.

Regelski, Thomas A. PRINCIPLES AND PROBLEMS OF MUSIC EDUCATION. Englewood Cliffs, N.J.: Prentice-Hall, 1975. 330 p. Paper.

Sets forth a sound philosophical basis upon which learning experiences may be designed. Presents principles of teaching music in such a way that the learner is led to develop his own conceptualizations. Bibliography.

Reimer, Bennett. A PHILOSOPHY OF MUSIC EDUCATION. Englewood Cliffs, N.J.: Prentice-Hall, 1970. 173 p.

Reveals how each major aspect of aesthetics gives tangible implications for teaching music, and explains the available aesthetic and educational alternatives and the implications of each. Contains diagrams and models for a comprehensive curriculum in the combined arts.

Rogers, A. Robert. THE HUMANITIES: A SELECTIVE GUIDE TO INFORMATION SOURCES. Littleton, Colo.: Libraries Unlimited, 1974. 400 p.

Squire, Russell N. INTRODUCTION TO MUSIC EDUCATION. New York: Ronald Press, 1952. 185 p.

Deals with the philosophical, psychological, and sociological bases of music education from kindergarten through college. Bibliography.

Sunderman, Lloyd F. NEW DIMENSIONS IN MUSIC EDUCATION. Metuchen, N.J.: Scarecrow Press, 1972. 305 p.

A revised edition of the author's previous book, SCHOOL MUSIC TEACHING: ITS THEORY AND PRACTICE (New York: Scarecrow Press, 1965). Includes courses of study from various sections of the United States. A useful source of reference concerning the growth of music education in America even though many important developments and personalities are absent. Extensive bibliography.

Suzuki, Schinichi. NURTURED BY LOVE: A NEW APPROACH TO EDUCATION. Translated by Waltraud Suzuki. Jericho, N.Y.: Exposition Press, 1969. 121 p. Photos, music.

Presents the underlying philosophy and principles of the teaching methods of this noted Japanese music educator.

Tellstrom, A. Theodore. MUSIC IN AMERICAN EDUCATION: PAST AND PRESENT. New York: Holt, Rinehart and Winston, 1971. 358 p. Illus., music.

Principles and practices of music education. Bibliography.

UNESCO. MUSIC IN EDUCATION: INTERNATIONAL CONFERENCE ON THE ROLE AND PLACE OF MUSIC IN THE EDUCATION OF YOUTH AND ADULTS, BRUSSELS, (29 JUNE TO 9 JULY) 1953. Paris: 1955. 335 p.

Despite its date, this document retains importance as a survey of music education internationally. The individual reports describe the philosophy and the status of music education in each country.

U.S. Department of Health, Education, and Welfare. Arts and Humanities Program, Harold [W.] Arberg, Chief. SCHOOLS AND SYMPHONY ORCHESTRAS. Washington, D.C.: Government Printing Office, 1971. 99 p. Paper.

Based on a comprehensive study of youth concert activities in twenty cities, this report outlines the history and purpose of youth concerts in the cities surveyed; discusses the ways in which youth concerts are financed; and summarizes the operating practices of youth concert activities.

YEARBOOKS AND SOURCEBOOKS

The yearbooks and books called "Proceedings of Meetings" held by the major national education associations are rich in information concerning trends, changing philosophies, and practices in the growth and development of music education in the United States. Among the most important are those listed below.

The Music Educators National Conference (and its predecessor the Music Supervisors' National Conference) published yearbooks from 1910 to 1940. Many of these are to be found in college and university libraries. All volumes, with the exception of the 1911 edition, are located in the MENC Historical Center in the McKeldin Library at the University of Maryland. Since 1940 three "source" books have been issued.

MUSIC EDUCATION SOURCE BOOK I. Edited by Hazel [B.] Morgan. Chicago: MENC, 1947. 256 p.

MUSIC IN AMERICAN EDUCATION: SOURCE BOOK NUMBER TWO. Edited by Hazel [B.] Morgan. Chicago: MENC, 1955. 365 p.

PERSPECTIVES IN MUSIC EDUCATION: SOURCE BOOK THREE. Edited by Bonnie C. Kowall. Washington, D.C.: MENC, 1966. 575 p.

The Music Teachers National Association published yearbooks called PROCEEDINGS OF THE MUSIC TEACHERS NATIONAL ASSOCIATION from 1907 to 1949 (Hartford, Conn.: MTNA).

In addition to the above, The National Society for Study in Education published two important yearbooks which were devoted entirely to music education.

THE THIRTY-FIFTH YEARBOOK. Part II. Edited by Guy M. Whipple. Bloomington, Ill.: NSSE, 1936. 260 p.

THE FIFTY-SEVENTH YEARBOOK. Part I. Edited by Nelson B. Henry. Chicago: NSSE, 1958. 362 p.

See also Section 33: Aesthetics and Music.

ASSOCIATIONS—GENERAL

American Guild of Music, P.O. Box 3, Downers Grove, Ill. 60515.

Sets standards for studio teachers.

Publication: ASSOCIATE NEWS. Bimonthly.

American Music Conference (AMC), 150 East Huron Street, Chicago, Ill. 60611.

Provides literature and motion pictures on school music. Develops and promotes many services to stimulate greater interest in the use of music for educational, recreational, and cultural purposes for public benefit. Surveys and researches the kinds and quality of amateur musical activities.

Publications: MUSIC USA-INDUSTRY STATISTICS. Annual.

Organizational manuals, survey findings, and a wide range of promotional materials.

American Orff-Schulwerk Association, Executive Headquarters, P.O. Box 18495, Cleveland Heights, Ohio 44118.

Publications: ORFF ECHO. 3/year.

Directory. Annual.

Inter-American Institute of Music Education (Instituto Inter-Americano de Educacion Musical) Intem, Casilla No. 2100, Santiago, Chile.

Inter-American Music Council (CIDEM), Technical Unit of Music & Folklore, Pan American Union Bldg., Washington, D.C. 20006.

Intercollegiate Musical Council, Box 4303, Grand Central Station, New York, N.Y. 10017.

Publications: NEWS. Monthly.

Yearbook.

International Federation of Youth and Music, Palais des Beaux Arts, 10 Rue Royale, B-1000 Brussels, Belgium.

Publications: REPORT OF GENERAL ASSEMBLY. Annual.

INFORMATION BULLETIN. Irregular.

International Institute for Comparative Music Studies and Documentation (IICMSD), Winklerstrasse 20, D-1033 Berlin, West Germany.

Publications: THE WORLD OF MUSIC. Quarterly.

CONGRESS REPORTS.

Series of records and books.

International Music Council (UNESCO), 1 Rue Miollis, F-75015, Paris, France.

Publication: THE WORLD OF MUSIC. Quarterly.

International Society for Music Education (ISME), Secretary-General: Henning Bro Rasmussen, 133 Carinaparken, DK-3460 Birkerod, Denmark.

Publication: ISME YEARBOOK--Reports important contributions from different countries on problems in music education. Published in English with short version in French and German. Publications available in the United States from Belwin-Mills Publishing Corp., Melville, N.Y. 11746.

Modern Music Masters Honor Society, P.O. Box 347, Park Ridge, Ill. 60068.

Designed for faculty and students in junior and senior high schools. Aims to maintain high standards of performance.

Publication: TRI-M NOTES. Quarterly.

Music Educators National Conference MENC), Center for Educational Associations, 1902 Association Drive, Reston, Va. 22091.

The Music Educators National Conference, affiliate of the National Education Association, is composed of professional workers in all areas of music education and at all institutional levels. Since its inception in 1907 it has come to be considered the national spokesman for music education in the United States.

The organization conducts national, divisional, and state conventions, and provides a comprehensive program of commissions, workshops, and special projects for its members. All members receive the MUSIC EDUCATORS JOURNAL. Those enrolled as research members also receive the JOURNAL OF RESEARCH IN MUSIC EDUCATION. The MENC publishes a wide range of materials which are designed to assist the profession in its work. These materials--some of which are important sources of information--appear in this guide under the appropriate subject headings.

STATE ORGANIZATIONS: Persons joining the Music Educators National Conference also join a federated state music educators association (both the national and state dues are combined). This membership includes a subscription to the MUSIC EDUCATORS JOURNAL and to the state association magazine. A list of the state organizations may be found in each issue of the MUSIC EDUCATORS JOURNAL.

STUDENT MEMBERSHIP: Well over six hundred college campus chapters of the MENC are available for students with a special interest in music education as a profession.

ASSOCIATED ORGANIZATIONS: A wide range of other national musical interests and organizations are associated with the work of the MENC. Some of these are officially affiliated with the conference and share in the national and state meetings.

THE MENC HISTORICAL CENTER: This is the official archival repository of the MENC, which is located at the McKeldin Library, University of Maryland. The center collects and preserves materials which document the broad scope of historical as well as current developments in music education. The collection lends itself to scholarly research in this field. Documents of conference activities range from minutes of the early board meetings and the first Research Council to reports and background material on current topics such as youth music and music in urban education. Conventions are represented by program booklets of national and divisional meetings from 1928 through the present, all yearbooks except 1911, a collection of scrapbooks, and numerous other items.

Books, pamphlets, and magazines are regular acquisitions of the center. Along with extensive holdings of periodicals published by state music education associations, the center has nearly complete files of out-of-print historical magazines such as EASTERN SCHOOL MUSIC HERALD, MUSIC BULLETIN, SCHOOL MUSIC, and SUPERVISORS SERVICE BULLETIN. In addition to more than 500 school music textbooks, the collection contains many titles in methodology, philosophy, music appreciation, and related subjects.

A large percentage of the center's collection consists of papers and records of distinguished individuals and music education organizations. The biographical files, which receive frequent additions, preserve information on many prominent music educators, past and present. Other materials include curriculum guides, photographs, instructional films, disc recordings, tape-recorded speeches and performances, and the oral history collection of taped interviews with seven past presidents.

The historical center is a reference library as well as a repository. Located on the University of Maryland campus at College Park, near Washington, D.C., the collection is housed in separate facilities in the university's McKeldin Library, where there is room for visiting scholars to work. Although the collection does not circulate, every effort is made to assist those who are not able to come to College Park. A few materials can be loaned to cooperating institutions through interlibrary loan, and photo duplication service is available for those materials which can be reproduced. The curator invites inquiries about the content and use of the collection. For information concerning the center, write to:

Curator, MENC Historical Center, McKeldin Library, University of Maryland, College Park, Md. 20742.

In addition to the MENC Historical Center, the following collections of historical and research materials are maintained at the McKeldin Library at the University of Maryland: The American Bandmasters Association Research Center; The American String Teachers Association; The National Association of College Wind and Percussion Instructors Research Center; and the Wallenstein Collection of Music.

COUNCILS: Council of State Editors, Council of State Supervisors of Music, Music Education Research Council, Council of Associated Organization Presidents.

Publications: MUSIC EDUCATORS JOURNAL. 9/year. Back issues of the MEJ are now available both in printed editions and on microfilm. Reprints are available from Kraus Reprint Corp., Route 100, Millwood, N.Y. Microfilms are available from University Microfilms, 313 North First Street, Ann Arbor, Mich. 48107.

JOURNAL OF RESEARCH IN MUSIC EDUCATION. Quarterly.

OFFICIAL DIRECTORY OF MENC AND ASSOCIATED ORGANIZATIONS. Biennial. For description, see Section 3.

DIRECTORIES--ORGANIZATIONS AND INSTITUTIONS.

Curriculum and teaching guides, various music education materials, and career information.

Music Library Association, 343 South Main Street, Room 205, Ann Arbor, Mich. 48108.

Publications: NOTES. Quarterly.

MUSIC CATALOGING BULLETIN. Monthly.

Newsletter. Quarterly.

TECHNICAL REPORTS. Irregular.

Index series. Irregular.

Music Publisher's Association of the United States, 810 Seventh Avenue, New York, N.Y. 10019.

Music Teachers National Association, 408 Carew Tower, Cincinnati, Ohio 45202.

The oldest major music teachers' association in America. Its purpose is to serve the interests of music teachers. By means of its conferences and publications, it seeks to raise standards of music teaching and also the status of the profession. The association has done much to establish and implement certification methods and standards for private studio teachers.

Publications: THE AMERICAN MUSIC TEACHER. 6/year.

DIRECTORY OF NATIONALLY CERTIFIED TEACHERS. Annual.

National Association of Pastoral Musicians, P.O. Box 28373, Washington, D.C. 20005.

Publication: PASTORAL MUSIC. 6/year.

National Association of Schools of Music (NASM), 11250 Roger Bacon Drive, No. 5, Reston, Va. 22090.

For description and publications see Section 30: Music in Higher Education and Teacher Education.

National Federation of Music Clubs, 310 South Michigan Avenue, Suite 1936, Chicago, Ill. 60605.

A major organization dedicated to fostering young musical talent. Sponsors National Music Week. Provides extensive program of scholarships and other awards.

Publications: MUSIC CLUBS MAGAZINE. 5/year.

JUNIOR KEYNOTES. Quarterly.

National Fraternity of Student Musicians (NFSM), 808 Rio Grande, Box 1807, Austin, Tex. 78767.

Publication: PIANO GUILD NOTES.

National Guild of Community Schools of the Arts. 200 West 57th Street, Suite 707, New York, N.Y. 10019.

Provides conferences, seminars and consulting services.

Publications: GUILD LETTER. Occasional.

COMMUNITY SCHOOL ORGANIZATIONAL MANUAL.

National Music Council (NMC), 50 West 57th Street, Suite 626, New York, N.Y. 10019.

The NMC is composed of representations of national music organizations in the United States. Among its purposes is to provide a forum for free discussion of problems affecting the national musical life of this country.

Publication: NMC BULLETIN. 2/year.

People-to-People Music Committee, John F. Kennedy Center, Washington, D.C. 20566.

Promotes international cooperation through music by presenting American music materials to countries desiring such, and arranges concert tours for young American artists who desire to present concerts abroad.

Young Audiences, Inc., 115 East 92d Street, New York, N.Y. 10028.

A national performing arts education organization which presents music, dance, and theatre programs principally in elementary schools.

Publication: Newsletter. 3/year.

For other associations, see section under appropriate specialization.

Section 25

PSYCHOLOGICAL AND PHYSIOLOGICAL ASPECTS OF MUSIC

Bailey, Ben Edward. CONSTRUCTING CLASSROOM TESTS IN MUSIC. Northbrook, Ill.: Whitehall, 1971. 93 p.

Bentley, Arnold. MUSICAL ABILITY IN CHILDREN AND ITS MEASUREMENT. London: George G. Harrap & Co., 1966. 151 p.

Based on growth sequences for musical development, this book serves primarily as a manual for a musical ability test battery intended for children ages seven through fourteen.

_____, comp. PAPERS OF THE INTERNATIONAL SEMINAR ON EXPERIMENTAL RESEARCH IN MUSIC EDUCATION. Washington, D.C.: Music Educators National Conference, 1969. 176 p.

A compilation of reports of experimental research in the field of music education. Focus is on psychological and physiological areas of investigation. A reprint of the Spring 1969 issue of JOURNAL OF RESEARCH IN MUSIC EDUCATION.

Buck, Percy C. PSYCHOLOGY OF MUSICIANS. New York and London: Oxford University Press, 1944. 115 p. Music, illus.

Deals with psychological principles that are applicable to music performance and teaching. Bibliography.

Buros, Oscar Krisen, ed. TESTS IN PRINT: A COMPREHENSIVE BIBLIOGRAPHY OF TESTS FOR USE IN EDUCATION, PSYCHOLOGY AND INDUSTRY. Highland Park, N.J.: Gryphon Press, 1961. 479 p.

Includes section on music tests, with brief descriptions, indication of age level, and areas of music covered in the tests.

Farnsworth, Paul R. THE SOCIAL PSYCHOLOGY OF MUSIC. 2d ed. Ames: Iowa State University Press, 1969. 298 p.

Treats the sociopsychological variables associated with music. Extensive notes and references cited at end of each section.

Franklin, Erik. MUSIC EDUCATION: PSYCHOLOGY AND METHOD. London: George G. Harrap & Co., 1972. 142 p. Illus.

A discussion of the interrelationship of general psychology and music psychology; general method and music methods. Bibliography.

Glasford, Irene S. BIO-MECHANICS: RHYTHM, REASON AND RESPONSE. New York: Exposition Press, 1970. 154 p.

Gordon, Edwin. THE PSYCHOLOGY OF MUSIC TEACHING. Englewood Cliffs, N.J.: Prentice-Hall, 1971. 138 p.

Subject matter is divided into two major parts: musical aptitude and musical achievement. Emphasis is on the learning process. Bibliography.

STUDIES IN THE PSYCHOLOGY OF MUSIC

This series was initiated by Carl E. Seashore nearly half a century ago at the University of Iowa. The series provided the impetus for the relatively new discipline of the psychology of music at that time. Under the general editorship of Edwin Gordon, the following interdisciplinary books present experimental research studies in music, education, psychology, measurement, and/or acoustics. A current bibliography is included beginning in volume 7.

Gordon, Edwin, ed. EXPERIMENTAL RESEARCH IN THE PSYCHOLOGY OF MUSIC: 9. Studies in the Psychology of Music, vol. 9. Iowa City: University of Iowa Press, 1974. 234 p.

Research reports include "A Study of Ability in Spontaneous and Prepared Jazz Improvisation among Students Who Possess Different Levels of Musical Aptitude," by Joseph J. Briscuso; "An Investigation of the Effect of the Provision of the 'In Doubt' Response Option of the Reliability and Validity of Certain Subtests of the Iowa Tests of Music Literacy," by Roger V. Foss; "Toward the Development of a Taxonomy of Tonal Patterns and Rhythm Patterns: Evidence of Difficulty Level and Growth Rate," by Edwin Gordon.

_____. EXPERIMENTAL RESEARCH IN THE PSYCHOLOGY OF MUSIC: 8. Studies in the Psychology of Music, vol. 8. Iowa City: University of Iowa Press, 1972. 142 p.

Research reports include "An Experimental Analysis of the Development of Rhythmic and Tonal Capabilities of Kindergarten and First Grade Children," by Robert M. De Yarman; "The Third-Year Results of a Five-Year Longitudinal Study of the Musical Achievement of Culturally Disadvantaged Students," by Edwin Gordon; "An Investigation of the Inter-relation of Personality Traits, Musical Aptitude, and Musical Achievement," by Stanley L. Schleuter; "The Nature of Absolute Pitch," by Jane A. Siegel; "The Interrelation of Personality Traits, Musical Achievement, and Different Measures of Musical Aptitude," by Robert W. Thayer; and "Are Steady State Musical Sounds as Identifiable as Steady State Vowels?" by John C. Webster.

_____. EXPERIMENTAL RESEARCH IN THE PSYCHOLOGY OF MUSIC: 7. Studies in the Psychology of Music, vol. 7. Iowa City: University of Iowa Press, 1971. 216 p.

Research reports include "A Computer Simulation of Musical Performance Adjudication," by Warren C. Campbell; "The Rhythmic Perception of Micro-Melodies; Detectability by Human Observers of a Time Increment between Simusoidal Pulses of Two Different, Successive Frequencies," by Pierre L. Divenyi; "The Second-Year Results of a Five-Year Longitudinal Study of the Musical Achievement of Culturally Disadvantaged Students," by Edwin Gordon; "An Investigation of the Criterion Related Validity of the Iowa Tests of Music Literacy," by James L. Mohatt; and "Bibliography: 1937-1970," by Edwin Gordon.

_____. EXPERIMENTAL RESEARCH IN THE PSYCHOLOGY OF MUSIC. 6. Studies in the Psychology of Music, vol. 6. Iowa City: University of Iowa Press, 1970. 120 p.

Research reports include "An Investigation of Some Musical Capabilities of Elementary School Students," by Edgar E. Dittmore; "Taking into Account Musical Aptitude Differences among Beginning Instrumental Students," by Edwin Gordon; "The Effect of Timbre on Brass-Wind Intonation," by R. Douglas Greer; and "A Study of the Musical Achievement of Culturally Deprived Children and Culturally Advantaged Children at the Elementary School Level," by John D. Hill.

_____. A THREE-YEAR LONGITUDINAL PREDICTIVE VALIDITY STUDY OF THE MUSICAL APTITUDE PROFILE. Studies in the Psychology of Music, vol. 5. Iowa City: University of Iowa Press, 1967. 78 p.

Seashore, Carl E. PSYCHOLOGY OF THE VIBRATO IN VOICE AND INSTRUMENT. Studies in the Psychology of Music, vol. 3. Iowa City: University of Iowa Press, 1936. 159 p.

Stanton, Hazel Martha. MEASUREMENT OF MUSICAL TALENT. Studies in the Psychology of Music, vol. 2. Iowa City: University of Iowa Press, 1935. 140 p.

Gutsch, Kenneth U. OBJECTIVE MEASUREMENT IN INSTRUMENTAL MUSIC PERFORMANCE. U.S. Department of Health, Education and Welfare, Cooperative Research Program, Project 5-1372. ED003 305. Hattiesburg: University of Southern Mississippi, 1964. 135 p.

Kreitler, Hans, and Kreitler, Shulamith. PSYCHOLOGY OF THE ARTS. Durham, N.C.: Duke University Press, 1972. 514 p.

A discussion of the similar psychological bases on which the various art forms are based. Three chapters focus on music.

Lehman, Paul R. A SELECTIVE BIBLIOGRAPHY OF WORKS ON MUSIC TESTING. Washington, D.C.: National Education Association Publications, 1969. 16 p. Paper.

Reprinted from the Winter 1969 issue of the JOURNAL OF RESEARCH IN MUSIC EDUCATION.

______. TESTS AND MEASUREMENT IN MUSIC. Englewood Cliffs, N.J.: Prentice-Hall, 1968. 128 p.

Presents the underlying principles of written tests of aptitude and achievement. Subjective evaluation in music also discussed. A well-organized and authoritative introductory text. Reference list.

Luchsinger, Richard, and Arnold, Godfrey [E.]. VOICE-SPEECH-LANGUAGE: CLINICAL COMMUNICOLOGY: ITS PHYSIOLOGY AND PATHOLOGY. Translated by Godfrey E. Arnold and Evelyn Robe Finkbeiner. Belmont, Calif.: Wadsworth Publishing Co., 1965. 812 p. Photos, illus., music.

An authoritative and comprehensive work based on psychology, neuropsychiatry, otolaryngology, pediatrics, oral surgery, dentistry, internal medicine, and endocrinology as well as the basic sciences. A valuable source book for professionals, including those in the field of voice training. One section deals with music. Bibliography.

Ludin, Robert W. AN OBJECTIVE PSYCHOLOGY OF MUSIC. 2d ed. New York: Ronald Press, 1967. 345 p.

Deals with psychological aspects of musical behavior. Provides a scientific basis for understanding human responses to musical stimuli. Also covers programmed learning, musical therapy, and tests for the measurement of musical abilities. Bibliography.

Madson, Clifford K.; Greer, [R.] Douglas; and Madsen, Charles A., Jr. RESEARCH IN MUSIC BEHAVIOR. New York: Teachers College Press, 1975. 277 p.

Deals with issues relevant to music instruction as behavior modification and with issues relevant to research methodology; procedures and techniques intended to serve as models for researchers and educators. Extensive bibliography and glossary.

Mursell, James. THE PSYCHOLOGY OF MUSIC. 1937. Reprint. New York: Johnson Reprint Corp., 1970. 389 p. Music, illus.

Brings together much research having bearing on the psychology of music. Extensive bibliography.

Music Educators National Conference. PAPERS OF THE INTERNATIONAL SEMINAR ON EXPERIMENTAL RESEARCH IN MUSIC EDUCATION. Washington, D.C.: 1969. 176 p.

Originally published as the Spring 1969 JOURNAL OF RESEARCH IN MUSIC EDUCATION. Papers from the 1968 meeting in Reading, England. An overview of current developments. Emphasis is on predictive measurement of musical success and psychological learning theories.

Music Research Foundation. MUSIC AND YOUR EMOTIONS: A PRACTICAL GUIDE TO MUSIC SELECTION ASSOCIATED WITH DESIRED EMOTIONAL RESPONSES. New York: Liveright, 1952. 128 p. Illus.

Reports on scientific investigations of the effect of music on human emotions.

Osborn, Wendell L. A STUDY TO EXPLORE NEW METHODS OF IDENTIFYING AND MEASURING MUSICAL TALENT. Austin: University of Texas, 1966. 120 p.

This study, supported by the Cooperative Research Program of the Office of Education, sought to "explore characteristics not usually considered musical, and yet which might combine in persons in such a way that results may lead to a clearer understanding and more accurate measurement and prediction of musical talent." Bibliography.

Polnauer, Frederick F. "Bio-mechanics, a New Approach to Music Education." JOURNAL OF THE FRANKLIN INSTITUTE 254 (October 1954): 297-316.

Polnauer, Frederick F., and Marks, Martin. SENSO-MOTOR STUDY AND ITS APPLICATION TO VIOLIN PLAYING. 2d ed. Urbana, Ill.: American String Teachers Association, 1964. 211 p. Illus., photos.

A pioneer work that explores violin playing in depth based on the latest findings in physiological matters and Gestalt psychology. Bibliography at the end of each section.

Schoen, Max. THE PSYCHOLOGY OF MUSIC: A SURVEY FOR TEACHER AND MUSICIAN. New York: Ronald Press, 1940. 258 p.

A survey of research studies that bear directly on musical art, musical artistry, and music education. Bibliography.

SCHOOL PERSONNEL RESEARCH AND EVALUATION SERVICES: COMMON EXAMINATIONS; MUSIC EDUCATION EXAMINATION. Princeton, N.J.: Educational Testing Service, 1972.

This test battery includes twenty specialty examinations of 120 minutes each, one of which is on music education. The music education examination contains items dealing with music history and literature, theory, curriculum and instruction, and professional information.

Seashore, Carl E. PSYCHOLOGY OF MUSIC. New York and London: McGraw-Hill Book Co., 1938. 408 p. Music, tables.

Seashore was one of America's pioneers in developing and exploring theories pertaining to musical experience, musical talent, and musical behavior in general. This work surveys what was known about the psychology of music up to the year 1938. Bibliography.

______. THE PSYCHOLOGY OF MUSICAL TALENT. New York: Silver Burdett Co., 1919. 288 p. Photos, music.

An appraisal of the psychological components of musical talent and development. Important as a pioneer effort in this field.

Shuter, Rosamund. THE PSYCHOLOGY OF MUSICAL ABILITY. Rome and London: Butler and Tanner, 1968. 347 p. (Distr. by Barnes and Noble, New York.)

Contains a considerable amount of information important to people concerned with educating children of varying degrees of talent. While the work grows out of the author's British environment and experience, the American music educator will, nevertheless, find much of value. Bibliography.

Wallace, William. THE MUSIC FACULTY: ITS ORIGINS AND PROCESSES. London: Macmillan, 1914. 228 p.

A discussion of the mental processes concerned with creating and performing music. Focus is on psychology. Bibliography.

Whybrew, William E. MEASUREMENT AND EVALUATION IN MUSIC. 2d ed. Dubuque, Iowa: William C. Brown Co., 1971. 210 p. Tables.

Covers testing principles and concepts. Explains existing measures in music with instructions for construction of evaluative instruments.

JOURNALS—THE PSYCHOLOGY OF MUSIC

The following journals are important sources of information concerning music and human behavior. While some of these carry such reports only occasionally, they are, nevertheless, of sufficient significance that they should not be overlooked.

ACOUSTICAL SOCIETY OF AMERICA, JOURNAL
335 East 45th Street
New York, N.Y. 10017
Monthly

AUDIO ENGINEERING SOCIETY, JOURNAL
124 East 40th Street
New York, N.Y. 10016
Monthly

BEHAVIORAL SCIENCE
Health Science Center Library
University of Louisville
P.O. Box 1055
Louisville, Ky. 40201
Bimonthly

BRITISH JOURNAL OF EDUCATIONAL PSYCHOLOGY
Scottish Academic Press
25 Perth Street
Edinburgh EH 3 3DW, Scotland
3/year

COUNCIL FOR RESEARCH IN MUSIC EDUCATION, BULLETIN
University of Illinois, College of Education
School of Music
Urbana, Ill. 61801
Quarterly

GROUP PSYCHOTHERAPY AND PSYCHODRAMA
Beacon House, Inc.
259 Wolcott Avenue
Beacon, N.Y. 12508
Quarterly

JOURNAL OF EXPERIMENTAL PSYCHOLOGY
1200 Seventeenth Street, N.W.
Washington, D.C. 20036
5/year

JOURNAL OF PSYCHOLOGY
Journal Press
2 Commercial Street
Provincetown, Mass. 02657
3/year

JOURNAL OF RESEARCH IN MUSIC EDUCATION
8150 Leesburg Pike
Vienna, Va. 22810
Quarterly

PSYCHOLOGICAL REPORTS
Box 1441
Missoula, Mont. 59801
2/year

Section 26

MUSIC IN EARLY CHILDHOOD EDUCATION

Aronoff, Frances W. MUSIC AND YOUNG CHILDREN. New York: Holt, Rinehart and Winston, 1969. 144 p.

A guide for the implementation of music experience programs for very young children. Interprets educational theory as applied at this level. Includes an appendix on Dalcroze, a bibliography, and a list of kindergarten music textbooks.

Bailey, Eunice. DISCOVERING MUSIC WITH YOUNG CHILDREN. New York: Philosophical Library, 1958. 119 p. Photos.

Describes young children and their experiences with music.

Biasini, Americole, et al. MMCP INTERACTION: EARLY CHILDHOOD CURRICULUM. 2d ed. Bardonia, N.Y.: Media Materials, 1971. 119 p.

A comprehensive plan for early childhood music learning produced by the Manhattanville Music Curriculum Program and sponsored by the Arts and Humanities Program of the Office of Education. Bibliography and discography.

Central Midwest Regional Education Laboratory. THE FIVE SENSE STORE: THE AESTHETIC EDUCATION PROGRAM. New York: Viking Press, 1973.

A set of multimedia curriculum materials designed by CEMREL of St. Louis, Missouri. The series is designed to acquaint children with various aspects of the arts and the creative process. Twelve of the forty components are now available. Music is the focus of some of the sets.

Landeck, Beatrice. CHILDREN AND MUSIC: AN INFORMAL GUIDE FOR PARENTS AND TEACHERS. New York: Sloane, 1952. 279 p. Music.

A discussion of the ways in which music can enrich the child's life and aid in his general educational development. Bibliography and discography.

Music Educators National Conference. National Commission on Instruction, Barbara L. Andress, Chairman Early Childhood Committee. MUSIC IN EARLY CHILDHOOD. Washington, D.C.: MENC, 1973. 80 p. Paper.

Helps educators identify and understand the behaviors of preschool children. Describes the developmental growth of the young child and contributes new insights about how music can become an integral part of that sequence.

Young, William T. A STUDY OF REMEDIAL PROCEDURES FOR IMPROVING THE LEVEL OF MUSICAL ATTAINMENT AMONG PRESCHOOL DISADVANTAGED. Final Report. ED 051 252. Washington, D.C.: Office of Education, U.S. Department of Health, Education, and Welfare, 1971. 122 p.

A study of the effect of musical training on the musical abilities of preschool children from disadvantaged environments.

NONPRINT MATERIALS AND EQUIPMENT

For indexes, guides, and sources for nonprint materials and equipment see Part V: Technology, Multimedia Resources and Equipment.

See also Section 27: Music in the Elementary School.

Section 27

MUSIC IN THE ELEMENTARY SCHOOL

Andrews, Gladys. CREATIVE RHYTHMIC MOVEMENT FOR CHILDREN. Englewood Cliffs, N.J.: Prentice-Hall, 1954. 198 p.

The focus of this work is on creative expression through physical movement. Includes suggestions for relating music to other areas of the curriculum. Bibliography and discography.

Association for Childhood Education International. BIBLIOGRAPHY OF BOOKS FOR CHILDREN. Washington, D.C.: 1937-- . Biennial.

Contains more than 1,500 annotated listings giving price, age level, publisher, and author.

Baird, Peggy Flanagan. MUSIC BOOKS FOR THE ELEMENTARY SCHOOL LIBRARY. Washington, D.C.: Music Educators National Conference, 1972. 48 p. Paper.

Annotated and topical listings of selected books currently available for elementary school children. Includes suggested grade level. The author's choice of outstanding books is indicated.

Beer, Alice S., and Hoffman, Mary E. TEACHING MUSIC: WHAT, HOW, WHY. Morristown, N.J.: General Learning Press, 1973. 169 p. Illus.

Keyed to the Silver Burdett series. Includes two phonodiscs. Bibliography.

Bergethon, Bjornar, and Boardman, Eunice. MUSICAL GROWTH IN THE ELEMENTARY SCHOOL. 3d ed. New York: Holt, Rinehart and Winston, 1975. 352 p. Music, photos.

Provides sound guidelines and principles for planning and implementing desirable musical learning experiences. Presents structured lesson plans. Bibliography.

Biasini, Americole, and Pogonowski, Lee. DEVELOPMENT OF A MUSIC CURRICULUM FOR YOUNG CHILDREN. Washington, D.C.: Central Atlantic Regional Educational Laboratory, 1969. 90 p. Paper.

A report of the two-year program which developed and tested new music programs for primary school children. Includes innovative approaches. Bibliography and discographies.

Brooks, B. Marian, and Brown, Harry A. MUSIC EDUCATION IN THE ELEMENTARY SCHOOL. New York: American Book Co., 1946. 376 p. Music, photos.

A textbook which deals with principles and practices of music education in the elementary school. Bibliography.

Cheyette, Irving, and Cheyette, Herbert. TEACHING MUSIC CREATIVELY IN THE ELEMENTARY SCHOOL. New York: McGraw-Hill Book Co., 1969. 418 p.

A valuable sourcebook for the music specialist and the regular classroom teacher. Includes bibliography for the education of the music teacher, and a research bibliography of basic music series of the last hundred years.

CHILDREN'S BOOKS IN PRINT. New York: R.R. Bowker Co., 1969-- . Annual.

An annual author, title, and illustrator index of children's books.

Crook, Elizabeth, et al. MUSIC: MATERIALS FOR TEACHING. Morristown, N.J.: Silver Burdett Co., 1976. 320 p.

Serves as a teacher-training text for SILVER BURDETT MUSIC (Crook, Elizabeth, et al. Morristown, N.J.: Silver Burdett, 1974-76), a series providing material from early childhood through junior high level. Includes recordings, illustrations, and bibliography.

Cutts, Norma E., and Moseley, Nicholas, eds. PROVIDING FOR INDIVIDUAL DIFFERENCES IN THE ELEMENTARY SCHOOL. Englewood Cliffs, N.J.: Prentice-Hall, 1960. 273 p.

Contains a chapter on music by Robert E. Nye and Vernice T. Nye which considers how pupils can and must be treated as individuals with special qualities and personalities. Includes general references and lists of films, instruments, and recordings. Bibliography.

Dimondstein, Geraldine. EXPLORING THE ARTS WITH CHILDREN. New York: Macmillan, 1974. 320 p. Illus.

Presents methods and materials for creating an environment conducive to understanding the deeper meaning of the arts.

Driver, Ann. MUSIC AND MOVEMENT. 1936. Reprint. New York: Oxford University Press, 1966. Illus., paper.

A discussion of the use of rhythm in the child's musical education.

Ellison, Alfred. MUSIC WITH CHILDREN. New York: McGraw-Hill Book Co., 1959. 294 p.

Written for classroom teachers in the elementary school. Offers specific suggestions for implementing many music activities appropriate to the typical classroom situation. Bibliography and discography.

Evans, Ken. CREATIVE SINGING: THE STORY OF AN EXPERIMENT IN MUSIC CREATIVITY IN THE PRIMARY CLASSROOM. New York: Oxford University Press, 1971. 95 p. Illus., music.

Suggestions for using creative and experimental approaches in the classroom. Focuses on the vocal program.

Garretson, Robert L. MUSIC IN CHILDHOOD EDUCATION. Englewood Cliffs, N.J.: Prentice-Hall, 1976. 320 p.

Focuses primarily on musical concepts with suggested activities designed to lead to their comprehension.

Gelineau, R. Phyllis. SONGS IN ACTION. New York: McGraw-Hill Book Co., 1974. 315 p.

A book of suggested activities related to the songs presented. Many areas of the elementary curriculum are included as well as music. Includes a highly useful section on resource materials--song collections, discographies, film and filmstrip listings, and bibliography.

Gray, Vera, and Percival, Rachel. MUSIC, MOVEMENT AND MIME FOR CHILDREN. 1962. Reprint. New York: Oxford University Press, 1969. Photos, music.

A manual for teaching music and dance to children.

Greenberg, Marvin, and MacGregor, Beatrix. MUSIC HANDBOOK FOR THE ELEMENTARY SCHOOL. West Nyack, N.Y.: Parker Publishing Co., 1972. 253 p.

Presents a variety of activities specifically designed to arouse curiosity, and stresses independent inquiry in solving musical problems. Bibliography.

Hertzberg, Alvin, and Stone, Edward F. SCHOOLS ARE FOR CHILDREN:

AN AMERICAN APPROACH TO THE OPEN CLASSROOM. New York: Schocken Books, 1971. 232 p. Illus., paper.

A practical guide for teachers. Includes section on the arts.

Hess, Robert P., and Croft, Doreen J. TEACHERS OF YOUNG CHILDREN. Boston: Houghton Mifflin Co., 1972. 337 p.

A textbook designed primarily for the preschool teacher. Developmental and educational theories are applied to practical situations, including music. Bibliographic references for each chapter.

Hickok, Dorothy, and Smith, James A. CREATIVE TEACHING OF MUSIC IN THE ELEMENTARY SCHOOL. Rockleigh, N.J.: Allyn and Bacon, 1974. 333 p.

Deals with the principles and theories of creativity and shows how they can be applied in the elementary music curriculum. Includes bibliographies after each chapter and resource lists.

Hood, Marguerite V. TEACHING RHYTHM AND USING CLASSROOM INSTRUMENTS. Englewood Cliffs, N.J.: Prentice-Hall, 1970. 142 p. Music, paper.

Instruction in basic rhythmic skills for using instruments in the general classroom. Focus is on traditional folk and rhythm instruments, small wind instruments, tuned bar instruments, and stringed instruments. Bibliography.

Hood, Marguerite V., and Schultz, E.J. LEARNING MUSIC THROUGH RHYTHM. Boston: Ginn and Co., 1949. 180 p. Music.

An activities-based approach to develop rhythmic sense and the ability to read rhythmic notation. Bibliography.

Horton, John. MUSIC. Informal Schools in Britain. New York: Citation Press, 1972. 27 p. Music, photos, paper.

Describes the music curriculum in the British primary schools, specifically the informal situation. Bibliography.

Humphreys, Louise, and Ross, Jerrold. INTERPRETING MUSIC THROUGH MOVEMENT. Englewood Cliffs, N.J.: Prentice-Hall, 1964. 149 p.

Intended for the classroom teacher. Useful to the music specialist as it presents expected outcomes of tested procedures. Bibliography after each chapter.

Jensen, Clayne R., and Jensen, Mary Bee. BEGINNING FOLK DANCING. Belmont, Calif.: Wadsworth Publishing Co., 1966. 60 p. Photos, paper.

This handbook discusses the values, history, and basic procedures of folk dancing. Twenty-four selected dances are illustrated with photographs. Bibliography.

John, Robert [W.], and Douglas, Charles H. PLAYING SOCIAL AND RECREATIONAL INSTRUMENTS.

See Section 48: Instrumental Music.

The Juilliard School [of Music]. JUILLIARD REPERTORY LIBRARY. Cincinnati, Ohio: Canyon Press, 1970. 384 p.

The Juilliard Repertory Project began through a grant from the Office of Education to the Juilliard School of Music to research and collect music suitable for use in grades K-6. The research consultants collected works that were generally unavailable to the classroom teacher. The purpose was to enrich existing material and provide works of greater variety relative to historical era, ethnic validity, and musical scope. The library consists of a 384-page Reference-Library Edition containing all vocal and instrumental music with text; eight Vocal Performances Editions; and four Instrumental Performance Editions. Includes scores and parts.

Land, Lois Rhea, and Vaughan, Mary Ann. MUSIC IN TODAY'S CLASSROOM: CREATING, LISTENING, PERFORMING. New York: Harcourt Brace Jovanovich, 1973. 200 p.

Designed as a text with the elementary education major in mind. Bibliography.

Landon, Joseph W. HOW TO WRITE LEARNING ACTIVITY PACKAGES FOR MUSIC EDUCATION. Costa Mesa, Calif.: Educational Media Press, 1973. 109 p.

A valuable manual for music educators interested in individualizing music instruction. Includes rationale and step-by-step procedures. Bibliography.

Marsh, Mary Val. EXPLORE AND DISCOVER MUSIC: CREATIVE APPROACHES TO MUSIC EDUCATION IN ELEMENTARY, MIDDLE, AND JUNIOR HIGH SCHOOL. New York: Macmillan, 1970. 202 p. Photos, music.

Designed to extend the music teacher's dimensions with regard to the development of ideas and use of materials. Bibliography.

Marvel, Lorene M. MUSIC RESOURCE GUIDE FOR PRIMARY GRADES. Minneapolis, Minn.: Schmitt, Hall, and McCreary, 1961. 272 p.

A handbook listing the available materials for teaching music to children from kindergarten through the third grade. Bibliography.

Maynard, Olga. CHILDREN AND DANCE AND MUSIC. New York: Scribner, 1968. 311 p. Illus.

Outlines specific approaches to developing musical creativity in children. Includes suggestions for integrating the arts in the classroom.

Monsour, Sally, ed. CLASSROOM MUSIC ENRICHMENT UNITS. 9 vols. New York: Center for Applied Research in Education, 1975. Paper.

Palmer, Mary. Vol. 1: SOUND EXPLORATION AND DISCOVERY. 64 p.

Ways to develop children's musical sensitivity and literacy. Attention given to environmental sounds.

Mulligan, Mary Ann. Vol. 2: INTEGRATING MUSIC WITH OTHER STUDIES. 64 p.

Techniques for integrating music with mathematics, science, social studies, and the language arts. Film listings, discographies, and bibliographies.

Daniels, Elva S. Vol. 3: PERFORMING FOR OTHERS. 64 p.

Suggestions for helping children share musical achievements in both creative and structured situations. Examples of festivals for special days and occasions.

Baird, Jo Ann. Vol. 4: USING MEDIA IN THE MUSIC PROGRAM. 64 p.

New processes and procedures for using multimedia resources in music.

Crews, Katherine. Vol. 5: MUSIC AND PERCEPTUAL-MOTOR DEVELOPMENT. 64 p.

Activities involving sound and rhythmic movement are presented as means of increasing children's temporal and spatial awareness.

Gingrich, Donald. Vol. 6: RELATING THE ARTS. 64 p.

A series of lessons combining music with pictures, poems, plays, and dances for the intermediate grades.

Willman, Fred. Vol. 7: ELECTRONIC MUSIC FOR YOUNG PEOPLE. 64 p.

Five lesson units from the very simple to the complex. Discography.

Monsour, Sally. Vol. 8: MUSIC IN OPEN EDUCATION. 64 p.

Deals with problems in the nontraditional use of space.

Batcheller, John M. Vol. 9: MUSIC IN EARLY CHILDHOOD. 64 p.

Activities for exploring basic musical concepts with young children.

Murray, Ruth Lovell. DANCE IN ELEMENTARY EDUCATION: A PROGRAM FOR BOYS AND GIRLS. New York: Harper and Row, 1963. 451 p. Illus., music, photos.

A valuable dance guide which includes suggestions for creative uses of songs, poetry, music, and dance. Appropriate for elementary through junior high school. Bibliography.

Music Educators National Conference. MUSIC IN OPEN EDUCATION. Vienna, Va.: 1974. 62 p. Paper.

Originally published as the April 1974 issue of the MUSIC EDUCATORS JOURNAL. Contains articles relating to the background and philosophy of open education, teaching techniques, source materials, evaluation, and case studies. Extensive bibliography.

Music Educators National Conference. Elementary Commission, Flavis Evenson, Chairman. STUDY OF MUSIC IN THE ELEMENTARY SCHOOL: A CONCEPTUAL APPROACH. Edited by Charles Gary. Washington, D.C.: MENC, 1967. 182 p. Paper.

Guide for teaching music through the conceptual approach in the areas of rhythm, melody, harmony, form in music, forms of music, tempo, dynamics, and tone color. Student activities and musical materials suggested.

Myers, Louise Kifer. TEACHING CHILDREN MUSIC IN THE ELEMENTARY SCHOOL. Englewood Cliffs, N.J.: Prentice-Hall, 1961. 368 p.

Provides step-by-step suggestions for teaching each of the areas of music usually required in the elementary school program. Extensive bibliography and section on sources of materials.

Mynatt, Constance V., and Kaiman, Bernard D. FOLK DANCING FOR STUDENTS AND TEACHERS. Dubuque, Iowa: William C. Brown Co., 1968. 113 p. Illus.

A handbook which gives instructions for teaching folk dance, including facilities and equipment needed, and suggestions for planning the lesson. Sixty-five dances are illustrated.

Newman, Elizabeth. HOW TO TEACH MUSIC TO BEGINNERS. New York: Carl Fischer, 1957. 152 p. Music.

Suggestions for teaching the concepts of music to young children through games and then through more advanced methods. Bibliographic references.

Nye, Robert E. MUSIC FOR ELEMENTARY SCHOOL CHILDREN. Washington, D.C.: The Center for Applied Research in Education, 1963. 113 p.

Provides basic considerations for the development of the music curriculum, with special attention to teacher preparation. Bibliography.

Nye, Robert E., and Nye, Vernice T. ESSENTIALS OF TEACHING ELEMENTARY SCHOOL MUSIC. Englewood Cliffs, N.J.: Prentice-Hall, 1974. 576 p.

Establishes conditions for learning music. Considers objectives, concepts, cognitive process skills, lesson plans, and evaluation. Also describes music learning experiences. Discussions of Dalcroze, Orff, and Kodaly.

______. MUSIC IN THE ELEMENTARY SCHOOL: AN ACTIVITIES APPROACH TO MUSIC METHODS AND MATERIALS. 3d ed. Englewood Cliffs, N.J.: Prentice-Hall, 1970. 660 p. Music.

Treats a broad spectrum of trends, teaching techniques, media, and other aspects of music teaching by means of activities approach. Includes a section of music for the disadvantaged and handicapped. Bibliography.

Paynter, John, and Aston, Peter. SOUND AND SILENCE: CLASSROOM PROJECTS IN CREATIVE MUSIC. London: Cambridge University Press, 1970. 365 p. Music, illus., photos.

The central idea throughout this book is the importance of children having direct experience in making music. Details practical projects through which young people compose music themselves. Discography.

Porter, Evelyn. MUSIC THROUGH THE DANCE: A HANDBOOK FOR TEACHERS AND STUDENTS, SHOWING HOW MUSICAL GROWTH HAS BEEN INFLUENCED BY THE DANCE THROUGHOUT THE AGES. London: B.T. Batsford, 1937. 155 p. Photos, illus., music.

Describes methods of developing musical understanding through the medium of dance. Bibliography.

Raebeck, Lois, and Wheeler, Lawrence. NEW APPROACHES TO MUSIC IN THE ELEMENTARY SCHOOL. Dubuque, Iowa: William C. Brown Co., 1974. 329 p. Music, illus., paper.

Presents a philosophy for elementary music education. Includes a wide range of suggestions for implementing the viewpoints expressed. Serves as a guide for evaluating activities and approaches. Suggests desirable attitudes and skills needed by the teacher. Bibliography.

Rainbow, Bernard. HANDBOOK FOR MUSIC TEACHERS. London: Novello, 1968. 653 p.

One of a series of handbooks compiled for teachers by London University's Institute of Education. Numerous articles, lists of reference books, reviews of materials for school use, and bibliographic sources (primarily British).

Rathbone, Charles H., ed. OPEN EDUCATION: THE INFORMAL CLASSROOM. New York: Citation Press, 1971. 207 p.

A collection of articles dealing with teacher preparation and rationale of the British informal schools and their American counterparts. Includes list of recommended music materials.

Rinderer, Leo, et al. MUSIC EDUCATION: A HANDBOOK FOR MUSIC TEACHING IN THE ELEMENTARY GRADES. Park Ridge, Ill.: Neil A. Kjos Music Co., 1961. 48 p.

Practical procedures for teaching music at the elementary school level.

Runkle, Aleta, and Eriksen, Mary Le Bow. MUSIC FOR TODAY: ELEMENTARY SCHOOL METHODS. 3d ed. Boston: Allyn and Bacon, 1976. 400 p. Music, photos.

Main content of book is the explanation of numerous music activities with possible methods for presenting each activity. Bibliography.

Schubert, Inez. THE CRAFT OF MUSIC TEACHING IN THE ELEMENTARY SCHOOL. Rev. ed. Morristown, N.J.: Silver Burdett Co., 1976. 302 p. Music, photos, illus.

Useful for regular classroom teachers or specialists in music education. Contains structured lessons for use in the elementary school music curriculum.

Sheehy, Emma D. CHILDREN DISCOVER MUSIC AND DANCE. New York: Teachers College Press, 1968. 207 p.

An experience-based guide for classroom teachers and music consultants.

_____. THERE'S MUSIC IN CHILDREN. New York: Henry Holt & Co., 1946. 120 p.

Describes ways in which parents and teachers may bring out the natural love for music which every child possesses. Bibliography and discography.

Silberman, Charles E., ed. THE OPEN CLASSROOM READER. New York: Random House, 1973. 789 p.

A basic reference which includes articles relating to all aspects of this type of educational practice.

Swanson, Bessie R. MUSIC IN THE EDUCATION OF CHILDREN. 3d ed. Belmont, Calif.: Wadsworth Publishing Co., 1974. 384 p.

A somewhat comprehensive guide to the organization and implementation of music experiences for elementary school music.

Thackray, R. CREATIVE MUSIC IN EDUCATION. London: Novello, 1965. 142 p.

A discussion of creativity with specific suggestions for vocal and instrumental improvisation as well as music composition. Appropriate for elementary school through college. Bibliography.

Wadsworth, Barry J. PIAGET'S THEORY OF COGNITIVE DEVELOPMENT: AN INTRODUCTION FOR STUDENTS OF PSYCHOLOGY AND EDUCATION. New York: David McKay Co., 1971. 160 p.

The basic elements of Piaget's theory with implications for education.

Weidemann, Charles Conrad. MUSIC IN THE STICKS AND STONES: HOW TO CONSTRUCT AND PLAY SIMPLE INSTRUMENTS. New York: Exposition Press, 1967. 91 p. Paper.

Willis, Vera G., and Manners, Ande. A PARENT'S GUIDE TO MUSIC LESSONS. New York: Harper and Row, 1967. 274 p.

This book describes musicianship and how it is developed. The techniques of the various instruments are discussed with suggestions for guidance in choosing a particular area of performance and a teacher. Includes a music camp directory, lists of publishers, and youth symphony orchestras in the United States. Bibliography and discography.

Zimmerman, Marilyn P. MUSICAL CHARACTERISTICS IN CHILDREN. From Research to the Music Classroom, no. 1. Washington, D.C.: Music Educators National Conference, 1971. 32 p. Paper.

Presents research results for use by music teachers. Studies reported here concern the perceptual, conceptual, affective, vocal, and manipulative development of children.

PEDAGOGICAL AND MUSICAL PRINCIPLES OF DALCROZE, KODALY, AND ORFF

Chosky, Lois. THE KODALY METHOD: COMPREHENSIVE MUSIC EDUCATION

FROM INFANT TO ADULT. Englewood Cliffs, N.J.: Prentice-Hall, 1974. 224 p.

A practical guide to the Kodaly method--its development in Hungary and application in American schools.

Findlay, Elsa. RHYTHM AND MOVEMENT: APPLICATIONS OF DALCROZE EURHYTHMICS. Evanston, Ill.: Summy-Birchard, 1971. 89 p. Music, illus., photos, paper.

Contains detailed directions for developing rhythmic response and rhythmic concepts in children, based on the Dalcroze method.

Hall, Doreen. TEACHERS' MANUAL, ORFF-SCHULWERK FOR CHILDREN. New York: Associated Music Publishers, 1960. 32 p. Paper.

A basic handbook for the Orff teacher. Covers the instruments, body instruments, rhythm and speech, rondo, canon, and other aspects of this method.

Jaques-Dalcroze, E[mile]. EURHYTHMICS, ART AND EDUCATION. Translated by F. Rothwell. Edited by Cynthia Cox. 1931. Reprint. New York: Benjamin Blom, 1972. 265 p. Illus.

This book, which is a collection of articles written by the master of eurhythmics, provides much insight into his theories and system. The Jaques-Dalcroze system of eurhythmics is explained as a pedagogical tool for guiding the young to a better understanding of music and dance.

Landis, Beth, and Carder, Polly. THE ECLECTIC CURRICULUM IN AMERICAN MUSIC EDUCATION: CONTRIBUTIONS OF DALCROZE, KODALY, AND ORFF. Washington, D.C.: Music Educators National Conference, 1972. 247 p.

Delineates well the plan devised by each of these music educators. Each method is developed in terms of its potential for the enrichment of music teaching and learning in American schools. Of considerable value is the list of books, articles, and studies pertaining to the work of each authority.

Liess, Andreas. CARL ORFF: HIS LIFE AND HIS MUSIC. London: Calder and Boyars, 1966. 184 p. Music.

This book traces the medieval, classical, and Bavarian sources of Orff's dramatic world; his approach to rhythm, language, and gesture; and the nature of his unique and unmistakeable style. Includes an examination of his Schulwerk and other contributions to music education. Bibliography.

Nye, Robert E., and Nye, Vernice T. ESSENTIALS OF TEACHING ELEMENTARY SCHOOL MUSIC. Englewood Cliffs, N.J.: Prentice-Hall, 1974. 576 p.

Broad in scope and highly practical. Includes discussions of Dalcroze, Orff, and Kodaly methods.

Richards, Mary Helen. THRESHOLD TO MUSIC. San Francisco: Fearon Publishers, 1964. 142 p. Illus., music.

Techniques of adapting the Kodaly pedagogical and musical principles to elementary school programs.

Szabo, Helga. THE KODALY CONCEPT OF MUSIC EDUCATION. Revised by Geoffry Russel-Smith. Oceanside, N.Y.: Boosey and Hawkes, 1969. 36 p. Music, illus.

A detailed description of the Kodaly method of music education. Three long-playing records are included which illustrate the techniques described in the text.

Wheeler, Lawrence, and Raebeck, Lois. ORFF AND KODALY ADAPTED FOR THE ELEMENTARY SCHOOL. Dubuque, Iowa: William C. Brown Co., 1972. 320 p. Illus., tables, music.

Describes the educational bases upon which the concepts of the Orff and Kodaly methods are founded. Proposes types of activities and experiences for implementation in the elementary school. Bibliography.

MUSIC FOR THE ELEMENTARY CLASSROOM TEACHER AND THE NONMUSIC MAJOR

Beckwith, Mary. SO YOU HAVE TO TEACH YOUR OWN MUSIC? West Nyack, N.Y.: Parker Publishing Co., 1970. 223 p.

Designed to help the classroom teacher become more effective in the teaching of music. Many approaches are proposed.

Darnell, Josiah. CHILDREN'S MUSIC. Dubuque, Iowa: William C. Brown Co., 1969. 203 p.

A text or handbook which describes objectives, principles, and methods of classroom music for elementary school teachers.

Elliott, Raymond. LEARNING AND TEACHING MUSIC: SKILLS, METHODS AND MATERIALS FOR THE ELEMENTARY SCHOOL TEACHER. 2d ed. Columbus, Ohio: Charles E. Merrill Books, 1966. 390 p.

A presentation of the rudiments of music with application through voice and keyboard and methods of presenting music to children in the elementary grades. Keyed to music in elementary song series. Bibliography.

Gelineau, [R.] Phyllis. EXPERIENCES IN MUSIC. 2d ed. New York: McGraw-Hill Book Co., 1970. 480 p.

A book of practical suggestions and procedures for elementary school teachers who need both encouragement and skills for teaching music. Provides lists of supplies and materials. Discography and film listings.

Hughes, William O. A CONCISE INTRODUCTION TO TEACHING ELEMENTARY MUSIC. Belmont, Calif.: Wadsworth Publishing Co., 1973. 122 p.

A handbook containing the basic information needed by a beginning teacher.

Kaplan, Max, and Steiner, Frances. MUSICIANSHIP FOR THE CLASSROOM TEACHER. Chicago: Rand McNally, 1966. 147 p.

Beginning with a brief overview of current philosophies of music education, the book provides the classroom teacher with information and materials necessary for teaching music reading, theory, and listening skills.

Mathews, Paul W. YOU CAN TEACH MUSIC: A HANDBOOK FOR THE CLASSROOM TEACHER. Rev. ed. New York: E.P. Dutton, 1960. 196 p. Music, photos.

Designed for the teacher with limited musical background, but who wants to include music in the curriculum. Practical suggestions are given for using music effectively in the classroom. Bibliography.

Mursell, James L. MUSIC AND THE CLASSROOM TEACHER. New York: Silver Burdett Co., 1951. 304 p.

Designed to aid the classroom teacher in dealing with music adequately. Bibliography and discography.

Nordholm, Harriet, and John, Robert W. LEARNING MUSIC: MUSICIANSHIP FOR THE ELEMENTARY CLASSROOM TEACHER. Englewood Cliffs, N.J.: Prentice-Hall, 1970. 150 p.

Provides an understanding of those facets of music which will be most useful to a classroom teacher in the elementary school.

Nye, Robert E., and Bergethon, Bjornar. BASIC MUSIC: FUNCTIONAL MUSICIANSHIP FOR THE NON-MUSIC MAJOR. 4th ed. Englewood Cliffs, N.J.: Prentice-Hall, 1973. 214 p.

A popular textbook in music fundamentals for the nonmusic major. Features an integrated approach to developing functional musicianship through singing and listening, playing instruments, reading and writing musical notation, analyzing, and creating music.

Pace, Robert L. MUSIC ESSENTIALS. Belmont, Calif.: Wadsworth Publishing Co., 1969. 222 p. Paper.

Designed expressly for the person with little or no knowledge of music fundamentals. Presents the basic tools for understanding musical structure and performance.

Pierce, Anne E., and Glenn, Neal E. MUSICIANSHIP FOR THE ELEMENTARY TEACHER: THEORY AND SKILLS THROUGH SONGS. New York: McGraw-Hill Book Co., 1967. 224 p. Music, illus.

Basic musical information and skills necessary for teaching music to children. A text for elementary education students.

Reynolds, Jane L. MUSIC LESSONS YOU CAN TEACH. West Nyack, N.Y.: Parker Publishing Co., 1970. 202 p.

A step-by-step guide for the elementary school teacher, grades one to six.

Smith, Robert B. MUSIC IN THE CHILD'S EDUCATION. New York: Ronald Press, 1970. 358 p. Music.

Describes the development of the musical capacities of children in a sequential program of musical activities through classroom instruction. Highly useful for the practicing general classroom teacher.

Whitlock, John B. MUSIC HANDBOOK. New York: MSS Information Corp., 1972. 183 p.

Designed for the nonspecialist in music. Explains the various aspects of the music program and gives suggestions for implementation.

Wisler, Gene C. MUSIC FUNDAMENTALS FOR THE CLASSROOM TEACHER. 2d ed. Boston: Allyn and Bacon, 1965. 255 p. Music, illus.

A college text dealing with basic music skills for the elementary school teacher.

MUSIC BOOKS SERIES AND GENERAL MUSIC

Some of the more recent music book series for elementary and junior high school general music programs are listed below.

DISCOVERING MUSIC TOGETHER. 8 vols. Edited by Charles Leonhard, Beatrice Perham Krone, Irving Wolfe, and Margaret Fullerton. Chicago: Follett Publishing Co., 1970. Grade levels K-8.

Includes recordings.

EXPLORING MUSIC. Rev. ed. 8 vols. Edited by Eunice Boardman, Beth Landis, and Lara Hoggard. New York: Holt, Rinehart and Winston, 1971. Grade levels K-8.

Includes teachers' editions, recordings, and instrumental parts.

GROWING WITH MUSIC. 2d ed. 8 vols. Edited by Harry R[obert]. Wilson, Walter Ehret, Alice M. Snyder, Edward J. Hermann, and Albert A. Renna. Englewood Cliffs, N.J.: Prentice-Hall, 1966. Grade levels K-8.

Includes teachers' editions, special charts, and recordings.

THE MAGIC OF MUSIC. 6 vols. Edited by Lorrain E. Watters, Louis G. Wersen, William C. Hartshorn, L. Eileen McMillan, Alice Gallup, and Frederick Beckman. Boston, Mass.: Ginn and Co., 1965-68. Grade levels K-6.

Includes teachers' editions and recordings.

MAKING MUSIC YOUR OWN. 8 vols. Edited by Beatrice Landeck, Elizabeth Crook, Harold Youngsberg, and Otto Luening. Morristown, N.J.: Silver Burdett Co., 1971. Grade levels K-6.

Includes teachers' editions and recordings.

MUSIC IN OUR LIFE and MUSIC IN OUR TIMES. Enl. ed. Edited by Irvin Cooper, Roy E. Freeburg, Warner Imig, Harriet Nordholm, Raymond Rhea, and Emile H. Serposs. Morristown, N.J.: Silver Burdett Co., 1967. Grade levels 7-8.

Includes teachers' editions and recordings.

NEW DIMENSIONS IN MUSIC. 7 vols. Edited by Robert A. Choate, Lee Kjelson, Richard C. Berg, and Eugene W. Troth. New York: American Book Co., 1970. Grade levels K-6.

Stresses ethnic music and related arts. Includes teachers' editions and recordings.

NEW DIMENSIONS IN MUSIC: SOUND, BEAT, AND FEELING. Edited by Robert A. Choate, Barbara Kaplan, and James Standifer. New York: American Book Co., 1972. Grade 7.

Includes teacher's edition and recordings.

NEW DIMENSIONS IN MUSIC: SOUND, SHAPE, AND SYMBOL. Edited by Robert A. Choate, Barbara Kaplan, and James Standifer. Grade 8.

Includes teacher's edition and recordings.

SILVER BURDETT MUSIC. 9 vols. Edited by Elizabeth Crook, Bennett Reimer, and David S. Walker. Morristown, N.J.: Silver Burdett Co., 1974-76. Grade levels early childhood-8.

Includes teachers' editions, discs and cassettes, sound/color filmstrips, and spirit masters.

SPECTRUM OF MUSIC. 5 vols. Edited by Mary Val Marsh, Carroll Rinehart, Edith Savage, Ralph Beelke, and Ronald Silverman. New York: Macmillan, 1974. Grade levels 1-6.

Includes recordings.

THIS IS MUSIC. 2d ed. 8 vols. Edited by William R[aymond]. Sur, Adeline McCall, Mary R. Tolbert, William R. Fisher, and Charlotte DuBois. Rockleigh, N.J.: Allyn and Bacon, 1973. Grade levels K-8.

Includes teachers' editions, accompaniment books, charts, and recordings.

NONPRINT MATERIALS AND EQUIPMENT

For indexes, guides, and sources for nonprint materials and equipment, see Part V: Technology, Multimedia Resources, and Equipment. See also Folk Dancing in Section 42: Opera, Ballet, and Dance.

Section 28

MUSIC IN JUNIOR HIGH AND MIDDLE SCHOOLS

Allen, Larry D. BEGINNING ELECTRONIC MUSIC IN THE CLASSROOM: A PRE-SYNTHESIZER CURRICULUM USING THE TAPE RECORDER. Southington, Conn.: Larry D. Allen, 1974. 32 p. Photos, paper.

A set of thirty-six lesson plans for use in teaching an electronic music course. Designed for junior high school students.

Andrews, Frances M. JUNIOR HIGH SCHOOL GENERAL MUSIC. Englewood Cliffs, N.J.: Prentice-Hall, 1971. 107 p.

Details the aims, goals, and techniques for developing an effective general music program in the junior high school.

Berger, Melvin, and Clark, Frank. SCIENCE AND MUSIC. New York: Whittlesay House, McGraw-Hill Book Co., 1961. 176 p.

A book about musical acoustics especially suited to the junior high student.

Cooper, Irwin, and Kuernsteiner, Karl. TEACHING JUNIOR HIGH SCHOOL MUSIC. 2d ed. Boston: Allyn and Bacon, 1970. 466 p. Music, illus., paper.

Primarily a lesson-by-lesson plan for dealing with the various aspects of the general music program in the junior high school. Bibliographic references.

Hughes, William O. PLANNING FOR JUNIOR HIGH SCHOOL GENERAL MUSIC. Belmont, Calif.: Wadsworth Publishing Co., 1967. 115 p. Music, illus.

Designed as a college textbook for music methods at the seventh and eighth grade levels. Concentrates on those procedures and steps needed for effective planning. Includes sample lesson plans with directions for presentation. Bibliography.

John, Malcolm, ed. MUSIC DRAMA IN SCHOOLS. Cambridge: University Press, 1971. 176 p.

A collection of articles exploring the relationship of drama and music in the public schools. Includes descriptions of five projects, focusing on students' creative efforts in this field. Bibliography.

McKenzie, Duncan. TRAINING THE BOY'S CHANGING VOICE. New Brunswick, N.J.: Rutgers University Press, 1956. 146 p. Music, illus.

The focus of this work is the alto-tenor plan of training the boy's changing voice. Other methods are also described.

Marple, Hugo D. BACKGROUNDS AND APPROACHES TO JUNIOR HIGH MUSIC. Dubuque, Iowa: William C. Brown Co., 1975. 494 p. Illus., music.

Contains a wealth of ideas and suggestions for the general music program in the junior high school. Includes teaching plans and describes various trends in general music teaching. Does not stress any single pedagogical method or system. Bibliography.

Marsh, Mary Val. EXPLORE AND DISCOVER MUSIC: CREATIVE APPROACHES TO MUSIC EDUCATION IN ELEMENTARY, MIDDLE, AND JUNIOR HIGH SCHOOL. New York: Macmillan, 1970. 202 p. Photos, music.

Designed to extend the music teacher's dimensions with regard to the development of ideas and use of materials. Bibliography.

Monsour, Sally, and Perry, Margaret. A JUNIOR HIGH SCHOOL MUSIC HANDBOOK. 2d ed. Englewood Cliffs, N.J.: Prentice-Hall, 1970. 147 p.

Provides considerable information concerning organizational plans, improvement, lesson plans, references, and sources of supply.

Swanson, Frederick J. MUSIC TEACHING IN THE JUNIOR HIGH AND MIDDLE SCHOOL. New York: Meredith Corp., 1973. 307 p. Music, illus.

A college text covering principles and practices in music education at the school levels indicated.

NONPRINT MATERIALS AND EQUIPMENT

For indexes, guides, and sources for nonprint materials and equipment, see Part V: Technology, Multimedia Resources, and Equipment. For additional junior high school references, see Section 29: Music in Secondary Schools.

Section 29

MUSIC IN SECONDARY SCHOOLS

Bessom, Malcolm E., et al. TEACHING MUSIC IN TODAY'S SECONDARY SCHOOLS. New York: Holt, Rinehart and Winston, 1974. 448 p. Illus., music.

The authors' definition of secondary education includes the curriculum from the fifth grade through high school. Nongraded schools and the open classroom are also discussed. The focus of the work is the development of conceptual understanding of music through a varied program of activities in performance and nonperformance classes. Individualized instruction and special education are included.

COLLEGE PROGRAMS FOR HIGH SCHOOL STUDENTS--SUMMER 1975. Hillsdale, N.J.: Directory Publishing Co., 1975.

Describes approximately 350 summer programs held in 1975 at approximately 350 institutions. Music is one of the areas covered.

Dykema, Peter W., and Gehrkens, Karl L. THE TEACHING AND ADMINISTRATION OF HIGH SCHOOL MUSIC. Boston: C.C. Birchard and Co., 1941. 614 p. Photos, music.

The two authors of this book were men who had a profound influence on the early growth and development of music education in this country. This large work describes their views of music education and also details methods of implementing a total secondary school music program. Bibliography.

Edelson, Edward. THE SECONDARY SCHOOL MUSIC PROGRAM FROM CLASSROOM TO CONCERT HALL. West Nyack, N.Y.: Parker Publishing Co., 1972. 224 p.

Describes a variety of music activities suitable for grades nine to twelve. Bibliography.

Glenn, Neal E., et al. SECONDARY SCHOOL MUSIC: PHILOSOPHY,

THEORY, AND PRACTICE. Englewood Cliffs, N.J.: Prentice-Hall, 1970. 275 p.

Relates the American educational system--the historical and philosophical foundations from which it grew--to help the student teacher understand contemporary educational milieu.

Hartshorn, William C., et al., eds. MUSIC FOR THE ACADEMICALLY TALENTED STUDENT IN THE SECONDARY SCHOOL. National Education Association Project on the Academically Talented Student and Music Educators National Conference, a Department of the National Education Association. Washington, D.C.: NEA, 1960. 127 p.

Discusses the basic functions of secondary music education, particularly for the academically talented student as distinguished from the musically talented student. Bibliography.

Hayes, Elizabeth. DANCE COMPOSITION AND PRODUCTION FOR HIGH SCHOOLS AND COLLEGES. New York: Ronald Press, 1955. 210 p.

A source book designed to help the inexperienced teacher. Includes suggestions and teaching procedures, with a focus on the aesthetic approach. Considerable attention is given to music accompaniment. Assumes a background in dance technique. Bibliography.

Hill, Thomas H., and Thompson, Helen M. THE ORGANIZATION, ADMINISTRATION, AND PRESENTATION OF SYMPHONY ORCHESTRA YOUTH CONCERT ACTIVITIES FOR MUSIC EDUCATIONAL PURPOSES IN SELECTED CITIES. ERIC no. ED 025 532. Washington, D.C.: U.S. Office of Education, Department of Health, Education and Welfare, Bureau of Research, 1968. 826 p.

The complete 826-page report, which includes case studies in twenty cities and extensive statistical data, may be obtained in hard copy and microfiche from the ERIC Document Reproduction Service, P.O. Drawer O, Bethesda, Maryland 20014. Orders must include the full title of the report and the ERIC number.

Hoffer, Charles R. TEACHING MUSIC IN THE SECONDARY SCHOOL. 2d ed. Belmont, Calif.: Wadsworth Publishing Co., 1973. 544 p. Illus., music.

A practical guide to the teaching of music in the secondary schools. Gives some attention to the aesthetic, philosophical, and psychological aspects of music education. Deals with many of the day-to-day teaching problems.

Jipson, Wayne R. THE SECONDARY SCHOOL VOCAL MUSIC PROGRAM. West Nyack, N.Y.: Parker Publishing Co., 1972. 224 p. Music, tables, illus.

A four-year sequential music program based on the choral class. Includes discussion of vocal techniques and repertoire, production of the school musical, choral facilities, and administrative procedures.

Lasker, Henry. TEACHING CREATIVE MUSIC IN TODAY'S SECONDARY SCHOOL. Boston: Allyn and Bacon, 1971. 385 p.

Techniques and procedures for the encouragement of student composition, including contemporary idioms.

Moses, Harry E. DEVELOPING AND ADMINISTERING A COMPREHENSIVE HIGH SCHOOL MUSIC PROGRAM. West Nyack, N.Y.: Parker Publishing Co., 1970. 221 p. Illus., photos.

An all-inclusive type of book which deals with the total music curriculum. Offers many practical suggestions for the solution of everyday problems met in high school.

Music Educators National Conference. YOUTH MUSIC. Edited by Charles B. Fowler. Washington, D.C.: 1970. 32 p. Illus., paper.

Special booklet originally published in the November 1969 MUSIC EDUCATORS JOURNAL. Reports the Wisconsin Youth Music Symposium. Articles discuss rock and other youth music, their import to youth, and their place in the school curriculum. Bibliography and discography.

Music Educators National Conference. Committee on Contemporary Music. CONTEMPORARY MUSIC: A SUGGESTED LIST FOR HIGH SCHOOLS AND COLLEGES. Washington, D.C.: 1964. 32 p. Paper.

A recommended graded list of materials for band, orchestra, and choir.

Music Educators National Conference. Music in American Life Commission on Music in the Senior High School. MUSIC IN THE SENIOR HIGH SCHOOL. Washington, D.C.: 1959. 112 p. Paper.

A comprehensive statement which provides a sound basis for the development of a music program in the high school. All important elements of the music offerings are described.

MUSIC IN SECONDARY EDUCATION, RESOURCE BOOK: SENIOR HIGH, JUNIOR HIGH, AND INTERMEDIATE SCHOOLS. Richmond, Va.: State Department of Education, Division of Secondary Education, Music Education Service, 1970. 75 p. Paper.

A resource book for administrators, supervisors, and teachers for the development of effective music offerings for secondary schools.

National Association of Secondary School Principals. EDUCATION BOOKS AND AUDIOVISUALS CATALOG. Washington, D.C.: 1974.

An annotated catalog containing curriculum reports, administrative internship publications, and a variety of other studies. Films and filmstrips are included. Available from the National Association of Secondary School Principals (NASSP), Dulles International Airport, P.O. Box 17430, Washington, D.C. 20041.

Singleton, Ira C., and Anderson, Simon V. MUSIC IN SECONDARY SCHOOLS. 2d ed. Boston: Allyn and Bacon, 1969. 200 p.

Provides outlines for goals to be achieved and procedures for developing lesson plans. Includes both vocal and instrumental programs.

Sur, William R[aymond]., and Schuller, Charles F. MUSIC EDUCATION FOR TEENAGERS. New York: Harper and Row, 1966. 603 p. Photos.

Presents a functional approach to music education and curriculum development in junior and senior high school. Classified listings of new educational media, instruments, music books, and films (with addresses).

Swan, Alfred J. THE MUSICAL DIRECTOR'S GUIDE TO MUSICAL LITERATURE (FOR VOICES AND INSTRUMENTS). New York: Prentice-Hall, 1941. 164 p. Illus., music.

A survey and discussion of musical literature suitable for amateur performers. Suggestions for rehearsal and performance are given. Includes bibliography for each chapter.

U.S. Department of Health, Education, and Welfare. Arts and Humanities Program, Harold [W.] Arberg, Chief. SCHOOLS AND SYMPHONY ORCHESTRAS. Washington, D.C.: Government Printing Office, 1971. 99 p. Paper.

This is a summary of youth concert activities (covering the 1966-67 school year) from the research report THE ORGANIZATION, ADMINISTRATION, AND PRESENTATION OF SYMPHONY ORCHESTRA YOUTH CONCERT ACTIVITIES FOR MUSIC EDUCATIONAL PURPOSES IN SELECTED CITIES, by Thomas H. Hill and Helen M. Thompson (see above).

NONPRINT MATERIALS AND EQUIPMENT

For indexes, guides, and sources for nonprint materials and equipment, see Part V: Technology, Multimedia Resources, and Equipment. See also Section 28: Music In Junior High and Middle Schools.

Section 30
MUSIC IN HIGHER EDUCATION AND TEACHER EDUCATION

INSTITUTIONAL INFORMATION

American Council on Education. AMERICAN COLLEGES AND UNIVERSITIES. 11th ed. Washington, D.C.: 1973. 1,879 p.

THE COLLEGE BLUE BOOK. 14th ed. 5 vols. New York: Macmillan, 1972.

> List and description of U.S. colleges; degrees offered; accreditation; scholarships, fellowships, and grants available; specialized programs; and so forth.

COLLEGE CATALOG COLLECTION (MICROFICHE). La Jolla, Calif.: National Microfilm Library, 1974.

> A highly useful tool for researching in higher education. Provides complete catalog content for more than 3,000 institutions. Approximately six updates issued per year.

Lincoln, Harry B., ed. and comp. DIRECTORY OF MUSIC FACULTIES IN COLLEGES AND UNIVERSITIES, UNITED STATES AND CANADA, 1974-76. 5th ed. Binghamton, N.Y.: College Music Society, 1974. 790 p.

> This listing of more than 17,000 names is organized according to departments and schools, state, degrees offered, ranks of faculty members, and teaching specializations. Includes national alphabetical list. The present edition incorporates material previously published separately as the INDEX TO GRADUATE DEGREES IN MUSIC, U.S. AND CANADA (see below).

______, ed. INDEX TO GRADUATE DEGREES IN MUSIC, U.S. AND CANADA. Binghamton, N.Y.: College Music Society, 1971. 168 p.

NATIONAL FACULTY DIRECTORY 1978. 2 vols. Detroit: Gale Research Co., 1977.

Alphabetical listing of faculty and administrative personnel at U.S. and selected Canadian junior colleges, colleges, and universities. Covers about 449,000 faculty members including the individual's name, name of the institution, department designation, street address, city, state, and zip code. Useful for the development of survey lists.

THE NEW YORK TIMES GUIDE TO CONTINUING EDUCATION IN AMERICA. Prepared by the College Entrance Examination Board, edited by Francis Coombs Thomson. New York: Quadrangle Books, 1972. 811 p.

The major part of the book (625 pages) consists of specific course listings by 2,098 accredited institutions that offer adult classroom instruction. Included is each institution's size, location, student body, class meeting hours, acceptance of transfer students, and general admissions requirements. There is a separate listing of 183 accredited correspondence schools with similar details.

Pavlakis, Christopher. THE AMERICAN MUSIC HANDBOOK. New York: Free Press, 1974. 836 p.

Part 9: Music and Education lists 863 institutions of higher education in the United States that teach music in some form. Pertinent information concerning each school is provided.

U.S. Department of Health, Education, and Welfare, comp. EDUCATION DIRECTORY-HIGHER EDUCATION: 1973-74. Washington, D.C.: Government Printing Office, 1974. 570 p.

A listing of institutions in the United States offering at least a two-year program of college-level studies in residence. Includes address, telephone number, Fall 1972 enrollment, undergraduate tuition and fees, calendar system, highest level of offering, type of program, accreditation, and principal administrative officers.

Willingham, Warren W., and Associates. THE SOURCE BOOK FOR HIGHER EDUCATION: A CRITICAL GUIDE TO LITERATURE AND INFORMATION ON ACCESS TO HIGHER EDUCATION. New York: College Entrance Examination Board, 1973. 550 p.

Identifies critically important writings and sources of information on all aspects of access to higher education. Organizes and describes 1,500 major publications, important programs, and influential organizations.

YEARBOOK OF HIGHER EDUCATION. Chicago, Ill.: Marquis Academic Media, 1969-- .

An annual compilation of essential data about U.S., Canadian, and Mexican colleges and universities. Lists the names, addresses, phone numbers, and key faculty members and administrators for more than 3,000 accredited junior colleges, colleges, and universities; also, important facts about enrollment, earned degrees, expenditures, staff, research, federal support, and related topics.

GENERAL INFORMATION

Association for Student Teaching. INTERNSHIPS IN TEACHER EDUCATION. Washington, D.C.: National Education Association, 1968. 220 p.

Includes bibliography.

Boney, Joan, and Thea, Lois. A GUIDE TO STUDENT TEACHING IN MUSIC. Englewood Cliffs, N.J.: Prentice-Hall, 1970. 372 p.

Examines the procedures involved in teaching music from a practical point of view. Suitable for use in music methods courses or by graduate students who expect to supervise student teachers.

Carpenter, Nan Cooke. MUSIC IN THE MEDIEVAL AND RENAISSANCE UNIVERSITIES. Norman: University of Oklahoma Press, 1958. 394 p.

Deals primarily with the teaching of music in the universities of Medieval and Renaissance Europe. Also covers the philosophy and influence of the universities on the development of music in the major European countries. Bibliographic references.

COLLEGE MUSIC SYMPOSIUM. New Brunswick, N.J.: College Music Society, Rutgers University College of Arts and Sciences, 1961-- . Annual.

A journal devoted to topics of interest to college music teachers.

Elam, Stanley. "Performance-based Teacher Education: What is the State of the Art?" AMERICAN ASSOCIATION OF COLLEGES FOR TEACHER EDUCATION BULLETIN 24 (December 1971): 3-6.

Glenn, Neal E., and Turrentine, Edgar M. INTRODUCTION TO ADVANCED STUDY IN MUSIC EDUCATION. Dubuque, Iowa: William C. Brown Co., 1968. 133 p. Tables.

An overview of the music teacher's continuing needs in the areas of historical and philosophical foundations of music teaching, research, and skills. Bibliography.

Halls, W.D. INTERNATIONAL EQUIVALENCES IN ACCESS TO HIGHER EDUCATION: A STUDY OF PROBLEMS WITH SPECIAL REFERENCE TO SELECTED COUNTRIES. New York: UNESCO Publications Center, 1971. 137 p. Illus., tables.

Analyzes present methods used to establish agreements on equivalences in access to higher education and indicates special factors which may affect a student's academic career abroad. Presents a methodology for comparing different upper secondary school programs in eight countries in order to discover the degree of pedagogical objectives in the final examinations.

International Association of Universities. UNESCO. METHODS OF ESTABLISHING EQUIVALENCE BETWEEN DEGREES AND DIPLOMAS. New York: UNESCO Publications Center, 1970. 143 p.

The first part of this study brings together the results of an investigation into the methods and practices followed in six countries--the United States, Czechoslovakia, France, Federal Republic of Germany, United Kingdom, and USSR. The second part is a comparative appraisal of the methods of establishing these equivalences.

Jeffers, Edmund V. MUSIC FOR THE GENERAL COLLEGE STUDENT. New York: King's Crown Press, 1944. 213 p.

While written some years ago as a research study, this work is one of the few attempts to trace historically the place of music in a liberal arts education. Extensive bibliography and reference notes.

Kragen, Kenneth, and Fritz, Kenneth. SUCCESSFUL COLLEGE CONCERTS. New York: Billboard Publications, 1967. 87 p.

A guide to effective concert planning.

Lindsey, Margaret, et al. ANNOTATED BIBLIOGRAPHY OF THE PROFESSIONAL EDUCATION OF TEACHERS. Washington, D.C.: National Education Association, 1969. 176 p.

MacKenzie, Norman, et al. TEACHING AND LEARNING: AN INTRODUCTION TO NEW METHODS AND RESOURCES IN HIGHER EDUCATION. New York: UNESCO Publications Center, 1970. 209 p. Illus., tables.

A discussion of innovations, the impact of new media, teaching suggestions, and the administration of resources. Bibliographic references.

Mahoney, Margaret, and Moore, Isabel, eds. THE ARTS ON CAMPUS: THE NECESSITY FOR CHANGE. Greenwich, Conn.: New York Graphic Society, 1970. 143 p.

Focuses on the need for change in teaching the arts to undergraduates. Contains a chapter on music. Bibliography.

Music Educators National Conference. Commission on Teacher Education.

RECOMMENDED STANDARDS AND EVALUATIVE CRITERIA FOR THE IDENTIFICATION OF MUSIC TEACHERS. Washington, D.C.: 1972. 16 p. Paper.

Final report of the Task Group V of the Commission on Teacher Education of the MENC. For use as a self-evaluative tool.

_____. TEACHER EDUCATION AND MUSIC. Washington, D.C.: 1970. 16 p. Paper.

Originally published in the October 1970 MUSIC EDUCATOR'S JOURNAL as the interim report of the MENC Commission on Teacher Education. Of importance to music teachers, administrators, and college and university faculty involved with teacher education.

_____. TEACHER EDUCATION IN MUSIC: FINAL REPORT. Robert Klotman, Committee Chairman. Washington, D.C.: 1973. 53 p. Illus., paper.

Complete report from the commission. Lists qualities and competencies for educators, describes needed changes in teacher education, identifies innovative programs, and presents criteria for self-evaluation. Appendices contain supplementary materials. Bibliography.

Music Educators National Conference. Committee on Contemporary Music. CONTEMPORARY MUSIC: A SUGGESTED LIST FOR HIGH SCHOOLS AND COLLEGES. Washington, D.C.: 1964. 32 p. Paper.

A recommended graded list of materials for band, orchestra, and choir.

Music Educators National Conference. Contemporary Music Project. COMPREHENSIVE MUSICIANSHIP: THE FOUNDATION OF COLLEGE EDUCATION IN MUSIC--A REPORT. Washington, D.C.: 1965. 88 p. Paper.

A report of a seminar sponsored by the Contemporary Music Project of the MENC in 1965. Forty music educators--including composers, theorists, musicologists, and performers--examined the state of musical training in American universities and colleges.

National Association of State Directors of Teacher Education and Certification. PROPOSED STANDARDS FOR STATE APPROVAL OF TEACHER EDUCATION-CIRCULAR 351. Washington, D.C.: U.S. Department of Health, Education, and Welfare, U.S. Office of Education, 1968. 43 p.

Includes standards being applied in the field of music education.

Ruth, Diane. POST-BACCALAUREATE GRANTS AND AWARDS IN MUSIC. Washington, D.C.: Music Educators National Conference, 1969. 40 p. Paper.

For annotation see Section 19: Guides to Grant Support Programs, Funding Agencies, and Proposal Writing.

SCHOOL PERSONNEL RESEARCH AND EVALUATION SERVICES: COMMON EXAMINATIONS; MUSIC EDUCATION EXAMINATION. Princeton, N.J.: Educational Testing Service, 1972.

This test battery includes twenty specialty examinations of 120 minutes each, one of which is on music education. The music education examination contains items dealing with music history and literature, theory, curriculum and instruction, and professional information.

Stover, Edwin L., comp. MUSIC IN THE JUNIOR COLLEGE. Washington, D.C.: Music Educators National Conference, 1970. 54 p. Tables.

Describes types of music programs offered in junior colleges. Presents guidelines for junior college administrators and music faculty in developing performing groups and in planning the music curriculum, music major program, and staff and administration. Bibliography.

Swift, Frederic Fay. PRACTICAL SUGGESTIONS FOR YOUNG TEACHERS. Oneonta, N.Y.: Swift-Dorr Publications, 1974. 66 p. Paper.

A handbook for beginning teachers. Includes career choice, applications, interviews, contracts, etc.

Thompson, Randall. COLLEGE MUSIC. New York: Macmillan, 1935. 279 p. Illus.

While based on an investigative study of music in American colleges (1932-33), this work is useful to individuals researching the historical aspects of the development of music offerings in the colleges.

Tuthill, Burnet Corwin. NASM, THE FIRST FORTY YEARS; A PERSONAL HISTORY OF THE NATIONAL ASSOCIATION OF SCHOOLS OF MUSIC. Washington, D.C.: National Association of Schools of Music, 1973. 66 p.

Wager, Willis Joseph, and McGrath, Earl J. LIBERAL EDUCATION AND MUSIC. New York: Published for the Institute of Higher Education by the Bureau of Publications, Teachers College, Columbia University, 1962. 209 p.

A critical examination of undergraduate programs in the various fields of music. The analysis and recommendations are intended to serve as guidelines for needed improvements.

Westervelt, Esther Manning, and Fixter, Deborah A. WOMEN'S HIGHER

AND CONTINUING EDUCATION; AN ANNOTATED BIBLIOGRAPHY WITH SELECTED REFERENCES ON RELATED ASPECTS OF WOMEN'S LIVES. New York: College Entrance Examination Board, 1971. 78 p.

An annotated listing of more than 300 books, articles, and research monographs.

Wolfe, Irving. STATE CERTIFICATION OF MUSIC TEACHERS--1972. Washington, D.C.: Music Educators National Conference, 1972. 168 p.

A state-by-state history of requirements for music teacher certification, and analytical information concerning present practices in certification and their history. Includes the preliminary report of the MENC Teacher Evaluation Commission task group on Standards and Evaluative Criteria for the Accreditation of Teacher Evaluation in Music.

NONPRINT MATERIALS AND EQUIPMENT

For indexes, guides, and sources for nonprint materials and equipment, see Part V: Technology, Multimedia Resources, and Equipment. See also Section 32: Administration and Supervision of Music Education.

ASSOCIATIONS

American Association of Colleges for Teacher Education (AACTE), One Dupont Circle, Washington, D.C. 20036.

Publications: Bulletin. 12-14/year.

JOURNAL OF TEACHER EDUCATION. Quarterly.

Books, reports, and monographs concerning teacher education.

Directory. Annual.

Association of College, University, and Community Arts Administrators, Inc., P.O. Box 2137, Madison, Wis. 53701.

Publications: Bulletin. Monthly.

Bulletin supplement. Monthly.

Membership list. 3/year.

Association of Independent Conservatories of Music (AICM), 162 West 56th Street, Suite 406, New York, N.Y. 10019.

Canadian Association of University Schools of Music, University of British Columbia, Department of Music, Vancouver, British Columbia, Canada.

Publication: JOURNAL.

College Music Society (CMS), Department of Music, SUNY, Binghamton, N.Y. 13901.

Publications: COLLEGE MUSIC SYMPOSIUM. Annual.

Newsletter. 3/year.

DIRECTORY OF MUSIC FACULTIES IN COLLEGES AND UNIVERSITIES--U.S. AND CANADA.

Intercollegiate Musical Council (IMC), 4303 Grand Central Station, New York, N.Y. 10017.

Publications: IMC NEWS. Monthly (Oct.-June).

Yearbook.

National Association of Music Executives in State Universities (NAMESU), Chairman, School of Music, University of Washington, Seattle, Wash. 98195.

The NASM was founded to promote a better understanding among institutions of higher education, establish uniform methods of granting credit, and set minimum standards for the granting of degrees. The services of the NASM are available to all types of institutions in higher education, and membership is on a voluntary basis. The NASM has been designated by the National Commission on Accrediting as the responsible agency for the accreditation of all collegiate programs in music except music education.

The National Council for the Accreditation of Teacher Education (NCATE) has been assigned primary responsibility for the accreditation of all programs in teacher education including music education, by the National Commission on Accrediting. In the field of music education NCATE cooperates closely with NASM, relying on it for the development and maintaining of standards relating to the education and preparation of music teachers and for a panel of competent evaluators in the field of music education. NASM also cooperates with the six regional associations and with the National Association for Music Therapy in the processes of accreditation.

Publications: DIRECTORY--published annually, lists accredited schools and departments of music, name of music executive, and each institution's music degree offerings.

CAREERS IN MUSIC--a pamphlet outlining fields, employment opportunities, approximate earnings, and personal qualifications and education required.

MUSIC IN HIGHER EDUCATION, 1973-74--a compendium of statistical information from NASM annual reports, including faculty salaries, budgets, enrollments, and so forth.

HANDBOOK (1974)--curricular and membership standards, by-laws, constitutions.

GUIDELINES FOR JUNIOR COLLEGE MUSIC PROGRAMS--recommendations for general enrichment and music major transfer curricula, faculty, and so forth.

PROCEEDINGS OF THE ANNUAL MEETINGS--available each year since 1959, except for 1968.

MONOGRAPHS ON MUSIC IN HIGHER EDUCATION, NO. 1--PAPERS AND REPORTS FROM CONFERENCES SPONSORED BY THE CONTEMPORARY MUSIC PROJECT; NO. 2--REPORTS OF FORUM ON "THE EDUCATION OF MUSIC CONSUMERS."

National Association of State Directors of Teacher Education and Certification, c/o Dr. Vere A. McHenry, State Bd. of Educ., Dir. of Staff Development, 250 East Fifth Street South, Salt Lake City, Utah 84111.

National Council for Accreditation of Teacher Education (NCATE), 1750 Pennsylvania Avenue, N.W., Room 411, Washington, D.C. 20006.

Works closely with the National Association of Schools of Music in conjunction with the preparation of teachers of music.

Publication: Annual List of Accredited Institutions.

See also Section 24: Philosophical Foundations, Principles, and Practices.

Section 31

URBAN EDUCATION AND THE CULTURALLY DISADVANTAGED

American Institute for Research in Behavioral Sciences. AFTERNOON REMEDIAL AND ENRICHMENT PROGRAM, BUFFALO, NEW YORK. ELEMENTARY PROGRAM IN COMPENSATORY EDUCATION, 2. ERIC No. ED 038 468. Washington, D.C.: Government Printing Office, 1969. 13 p.

A description and analysis of an afternoon remedial and enrichment program for inner city, low-income children. Music is included.

Bonilla, Frank. RATIONALE FOR A CULTURALLY BASED PROGRAM OF ACTION AGAINST POVERTY AMONG NEW YORK PUERTO RICANS. ERIC No. ED 011 543. Cleveland, Ohio: ERIC Document Reproduction Service, 1964. 24 p.

Music activities are included in this description of the cultural life of the Puerto Ricans in New York City.

Booth, Robert, et al., comps. CULTURALLY DISADVANTAGED: A BIBLIOGRAPHY AND KEY-WORD-OUT-OF-CONTEXT INDEX. (KWOC). Detroit: Wayne State University College of Education, Library-Science Dept., 1967. 803 p.

This publication is a variant form of a keyword-in-context index (KWIC) to a bibliography of the literature relating to the culturally disadvantaged. Approximately 1,200 items important to the field of the culturally disadvantaged appear in this bibliography. While music education is not treated specifically, this work provides a wealth of background material on the subject.

Bowman, David L., et al. QUANTITATIVE AND QUALITATIVE EFFECTS OF REVISED SELECTION AND TRAINING PROCEDURES IN THE EDUCATION OF TEACHERS OF THE CULTURALLY DISADVANTAGED. VOL. II, FINAL REPORT. ERIC No. ED 041 853. Oshkosh: Wisconsin State University, 1970. 147 p.

Appendix C of this study is a structured curriculum for a preservice course entitled Elementary Music Practicum, designed to identify behavioral objectives in terms of the learner's musical abilities and to identify the types of musical experiences to be used to achieve each behavioral objective.

Camden City Schools, New Jersey. TITLE I ESEA 1966-67 PROJECTS OF THE CAMDEN CITY BOARD OF EDUCATION: EVALUATION REPORT. ERIC No. ED 018 473. Camden, N.J.: Board of Education, 1967. 86 p.

This report includes evaluation of an expanded fine arts instructional program for grades K-6, involving more than 12,000 students in special work in art and music and a summer music program.

Carabo-Cone, Madeleine. NEW OBJECTIVES FOR CULTURAL ENRICHMENT PROGRAMS: INTELLECTUAL STIMULATION FOR DISADVANTAGED PRE-SCHOOL CHILDREN. New York: Carabo-Cone, 1969. 32 p. Paper.

A summary of a lecture for Headstart teachers. The philosophical bases for slum area culture centers are discussed. Included is a classroom diary, describing the special activities at a Harlem day care center.

Cohen, Harold L., et al. MEASURING THE CONTRIBUTION OF THE ARTS IN THE EDUCATION OF DISADVANTAGED CHILDREN: FINAL REPORT. ERIC No. ED 024 746. Silver Spring, Md.: Institute for Behavioral Research, 1968. 192 p.

A description and evaluation of a project concerned with behavior changes in urban Negro children and underachieving, middle-class white children who participated in a six-week demonstration program in the arts.

Collier, Nina P. TITLE I PROJECTS AND OTHERS, ESPANOLA VALLEY PILOT PROGRAM RESEARCH, 1966-67: PRELIMINARY REPORT. ERIC No. ED 012 643. Alcade: Youth Concerts of New Mexico, 1967. 91 p.

A comprehensive report of youth concerts which brought artists to public schools. A comparison of the effects on urban and rural school children is included.

Denisoff, R. Serge. GREAT DAY COMING: FOLK MUSIC AND THE AMERICAN LEFT. Urbana: University of Illinois Press, 1971. 219 p.

Chapter 3 examines the use of folk music by the American Left, especially the Communist Party, during the '30s and '40s.

East Chicago City School District, Indiana. EAST CHICAGO JUNIOR POLICE: AN EFFECTIVE PROJECT IN THE NON-ACADEMIC AREA OF THE SCHOOL'S TOTAL EDUCATIONAL ATTACK ON THE DISADVANTAGEMENT OF YOUTH. ERIC No. ED 053 241. East Chicago, Ind.: City School

District, 1970. 65 p. Paper.

A description of a program utilizing nonacademic youth interests, including music.

Fox, David J., et al. SUMMER 1967 ELEMENTARY SCHOOL PROGRAMS FOR DISADVANTAGED PUPILS IN POVERTY AREAS IN NEW YORK CITY: EVALUATION OF NEW YORK CITY TITLE I EDUCATIONAL PROJECTS, 1966-67. ERIC No. ED 034 011. New York: Center for Urban Education, 1967. 323 p.

An evaluation of a summer program involving 40,000 disadvantaged children who were retarded in reading. Several of the schools provided for cultural enrichment through music.

Fox, David J., and Ward, Eric. SUMMER MUSICAL TALENT SHOWCASE FOR DISADVANTAGED HIGH SCHOOL STUDENTS. EVALUATION OF NEW YORK CITY TITLE I EDUCATIONAL PROJECTS, 1966-67. ERIC No. ED 029 922. New York: Center for Urban Education, Committee on Field Research and Evaluation, 1967. 17 p. Paper.

Evaluation of a summer project in New York City involving musically talented high school students from poverty areas who presented concerts at elementary school assemblies. The concerts focused on the musical contributions of minority groups.

Golin, Sanford. THE SELF-ESTEEM AND GOALS OF INDIGENT CHILDREN: PROGRESS REPORT. ERIC No. ED 036 586. Pittsburgh, Pa.: Pittsburgh University, Department of Psychology, 1969. 14 p. Paper.

A discussion of summer and full-year programs in black history and culture, including African and Afro-American music and dance, which were offered to elementary and junior high students.

Great Cities Program for School Improvement. GREAT CITIES RESEARCH COUNCIL EDUCATIONAL COMMUNICATIONS PROJECT. FINAL REPORT. APPENDICES: EXHIBIT A, DATA PROCESSING IN THE GREAT CITIES, MARCH 1967; EXHIBIT C, CREATIVITY IN URBAN EDUCATION; EXHIBIT D, THE CENTRAL CITIES CONFERENCE. ERIC No. ED 031 087. Chicago: The Research Council of the Great Cities Program for School Improvement, 1969. 410 p.

Exhibit C of this report inventories more than 900 kindergarten-through-adult education programs, locally developed materials, programs, and projects. It describes level, audience, medium, place of development, and availability.

Griffin, Louise. USING MUSIC WITH HEADSTART CHILDREN. Washington, D.C.: Office of Economic Opportunity, 1968. 25 p.

Deals with the role of music in the Headstart program. Includes teaching suggestions, lists of discographies, resource and song books, music publishers, and addresses.

Hartley, Ruth E. DEMONSTRATION AND TEACHER TRAINING PROGRAMS FOR TEACHERS OF DISADVANTAGED PUPILS IN NON-PUBLIC SCHOOLS. ERIC No. ED 011 275. New York: Center for Urban Education, 1966. 154 p.

An interim evaluation of a project which includes offerings in music training.

Hartog, John F., and Modlinger, Roy. IMPROVEMENT OF SELF-IMAGE; PUBLIC LAW 89-10, TITLE I--PROJECT 1939N, EVALUATION. ERIC No. ED 022 812. Freeport, Ill.: School District #145, 1967. 17 p. Paper.

A description of a three-week camping program for disadvantaged children from two institutions for neglected children. Activities included music. Student attitudes and behavior and the program itself are critically reviewed.

Harvard University. Graduate School of Education. AFTER SCHOOL CENTERS PROJECT. FINAL REPORT: WINTER 1968-69; SUMMER 1969. ERIC No. ED 034 013. Cambridge, Mass.: Harvard University, Graduate School of Education, 1969. 53 p.

A description of the Cambridge school department's programs for disadvantaged and foreign-born children. Music and drama are included.

Hill, John D. "A Study of the Musical Achievement of Culturally Deprived Children and Culturally Advantaged Children at the Elementary School Level." In EXPERIMENTAL RESEARCH IN THE PSYCHOLOGY OF MUSIC: 6. Studies in the Psychology of Music, vol. 6, edited by Edwin Gordon, pp. 95-123. Iowa City: University of Iowa Press, 1970.

Hinz, Marian C. RESUME OF MATERIALS, SUGGESTIONS, AND REFERENCES GATHERED DURING THE SHIPPENSBURG CONFERENCE ON THE EDUCATION OF THE MIGRANT CHILD. ERIC No. ED 029 722. Shippensburg, Pa.: State College, 1969. 145 p.

Contains abstracts of speeches relating to the teaching of predominantly rural, migrant, and disadvantaged children. Several units of study are suggested, with materials needed and references. Music activities are included.

Hymovitz, Leon. DISCOVERY IN THE URBAN SPRAWL. ERIC No. ED 011 896. Cleveland, Ohio: ERIC Document Reproduction Service, 1966. 6 p.

A discussion of a cultural enrichment project in a disadvantaged Philadelphia high school. Music events were included.

Kofsky, Frank. BLACK NATIONALISM AND THE REVOLUTION IN MUSIC. New York: Pathfinder Press, 1970. 280 p. Photos, illus.

A description of the revolution in jazz, its dynamics, and the innovations of individual revolutionists. It is also a cultural and sociological study of the developments both in music and the urban ghetto which go under the names of black nationalism, the return to African roots, and the new militancy. Bibliography and discography.

Kohanski, Dorothy D. PASSAIC, N.J. REPORT ON ESEA TITLE I SUMMER PROGRAM, JULY 1970. ERIC No. ED 053 467. Paterson, N.J.: Board of Education, 1970. 32 p. Paper.

An evaluation of a summer program which included vocal and instrumental music for non-English-speaking children.

Lohman, Maurice A. AFTER-SCHOOL TUTORIAL AND SPECIAL POTENTIAL DEVELOPMENT IN I.S. 201--MANHATTAN. ERIC No. ED 019 336. New York: Center for Urban Education, 1967. 23 p. Paper.

Detailed reports on the art, music, and tutorial programs offered in this project.

_____. THE EXPANSION OF THE AFTER SCHOOL STUDY CENTERS FOR DISADVANTAGED PUBLIC AND NON-PUBLIC SCHOOL PUPILS. New York: Center for Urban Education, 1967. 122 p.

Evaluation of a program that included music as an enrichment factor.

Long, Charles M. A PROJECT TO DEVELOP A CURRICULUM FOR DISADVANTAGED STUDENTS IN THE INTERMEDIATE SCHOOL. ERIC No. ED 011 534. New York: Center for Urban Education, 1966. 114 p.

A report on the development of curriculums, including music programs, for middle schools.

Music Educators National Conference. FACING THE MUSIC IN URBAN EDUCATION. Washington, D.C.: 1970. 96 p. Paper.

Originally published as the January 1970 MUSIC EDUCATORS JOURNAL. Intended to help the music educator cope with the severe educational problems created by poor housing, unemployment, poverty, and other conditions that exist in cities throughout the United States. Bibliography and film listing.

Neckritz, Benjamin, and Forlano, George. PROGRAM TO EXCITE POTENTIAL, WINTER PROGRAM 1968-1969. ERIC No. ED 036 593. New York: New York Bureau of Educational Research, Board of Education, 1969. 33 p. Paper.

This project, funded by the New York State Urban Education Program, was a second follow-through of a project held the previous summer involving forty-five ninth and tenth grade New York City students who were disadvantaged underachievers, but musically talented. Results of the efforts are indicated.

New York State Education Department. EDUCATING THE DISADVANTAGED CHILD: AN ANNOTATED BIBLIOGRAPHY. Albany, N.Y.: 1968. 95 p. Paper.

This bibliography covers a wide range of facets of the education of the disadvantaged. Music education is included.

Nye, Robert E., and Nye, Vernice T. MUSIC IN THE ELEMENTARY SCHOOL: AN ACTIVITIES APPROACH TO MUSIC METHODS AND MATERIALS. 3d ed. Englewood Cliffs, N.J.: Prentice-Hall, 1970. 660 p.

Treats a broad spectrum of trends, teaching techniques, media, and other aspects of music teaching by means of an activities approach. Includes a section on music for the disadvantaged and handicapped. Bibliography.

Pittsburgh Public Schools, Pennsylvania. ESEA TITLE I PROJECTS EVALUATION REPORT, 1967. ERIC No. ED 026 430. Vol. I. Pittsburgh, Pa.: Board of Education, 1967. 698 p.

Seventeen programs in various areas, including music, are discussed. The focus of this project was on reduced class size, use of television and library resources, and special teachers.

Rose, Hanna Toby. A SEMINAR ON THE ROLE OF THE ARTS IN MEETING THE SOCIAL AND EDUCATIONAL NEEDS OF THE DISADVANTAGED. Brooklyn, N.Y.: Brooklyn Museum, 1967. 285 p. Illus.

A report of lectures on the place of the arts in urban areas. Philosophical and practical applications are discussed. The appendixes include reports of projects. Bibliography.

Steinhoff, Carl R. IMPROVED EDUCATIONAL SERVICES IN SELECTED SPECIAL SERVICE ELEMENTARY AND JUNIOR HIGH SCHOOLS. ERIC No. ED 019 338. New York: Center for Urban Education, 1967. 92 p. Paper.

An evaluation of a program which placed supplementary personnel, supplies, and equipment in selected elementary and junior high schools to upgrade education in disadvantaged areas. Music programs are discussed.

_____. SUMMER PROGRAM IN MUSIC AND ART FOR DISADVANTAGED PUPILS IN PUBLIC AND NON-PUBLIC SCHOOLS. ERIC No. ED 011 025. New York: Center for Urban Education, 1966. 39 p. Paper.

A description of eighty-seven summer music and art programs for disadvantaged children, grades one to six.

"Upward Bound--War on Talent Waste at Indiana University." TEACHERS COLLEGE JOURNAL 38 (January 1967): 1-66. Special issue.

A description of a precollege program for underachieving, disadvantaged high school students recruited from metropolitan areas. The theoretical framework, counseling services, activities, and programs are discussed by participating teachers. Music is included. Extensive bibliography.

Wichita Unified School District #259, Kansas. ESEA TITLE I, EVALUATION REPORT, WICHITA PROGRAM FOR EDUCATIONALLY DEPRIVED CHILDREN, SEPTEMBER 1968-AUGUST 1969. ERIC No. ED 034 818. Wichita, Kans.: 1969. 293 p.

Although designed for correcting reading problems, this program for elementary and junior high school students included music activities. The report includes description and evaluation of the music projects.

_____. WICHITA PROGRAM FOR EDUCATIONALLY DEPRIVED CHILDREN: ESEA TITLE I EVALUATION REPORT, 1966-67. ERIC No. ED 020 286. Wichita, Kans.: 1967. 292 p.

A discussion of the objectives, procedures, evaluation strategies, and results of each activity or service in the program. Music activities are included.

Wrightstone, J. Wayne. "Discovering and Stimulating Culturally Deprived Talented Youth." TEACHERS COLLEGE RECORD 60 (October 1958): 23-27.

Young, William T. A STUDY OF REMEDIAL PROCEDURES FOR IMPROVING THE LEVEL OF MUSICAL ATTAINMENT AMONG PRESCHOOL DISADVANTAGED: FINAL REPORT. ERIC No. ED 051 252. Washington, D.C.: Bureau of Research, Department of Health, Education and Welfare, 1971. 122 p.

A description of a structured program in music and an analysis of its effects on preschool, disadvantaged children.

Zumbrunn, Karen Lee Fanta. EFFECTS OF A LISTENING PROGRAM IN CONTEMPORARY MUSIC UPON THE APPRECIATION BY JUNIOR HIGH SCHOOL STUDENTS OF REPRESENTATIVE LITERATURE OF OTHER PERIODS. FINAL REPORT. ERIC No. ED 033 968. Los Angeles and Berkeley: University of California Press, 1968. 128 p.

Discussion of a taped, guided listening program for junior high school students, showing the success of using twentieth-century music in inner city "deprived" schools.

INFORMATION SERVICE

ERIC CLEARINGHOUSE ON URBAN EDUCATION (ERIC-CUE). Teachers College, Columbia University, New York.

This is part of ERIC (Educational Resources Information Center), a national information system designed and supported by the National Institute of Education of the Department of Health, Education and Welfare to provide ready access to results of exemplary programs, research, and development efforts. (For a description of the ERIC system as well as procedures for gaining access to its materials via printed journals, microfiche, and computer, see Section 18: Information Services and Systems.)

The ERIC Clearinghouse on Urban Education collects, evaluates, and disseminates published and unpublished materials concerning the education of urban children and youth. Resumés of accepted documents--including bibliographic information, abstracts, and index terms--are available in RESOURCES IN EDUCATION (RIE), ERIC's monthly abstract journal. The clearinghouse also monitors prominent journals which contain articles relating to urban education. These articles are indexed and annotated in monthly issues of CURRENT INDEX TO JOURNALS IN EDUCATION (CIJE).

In addition, the ERIC/CUE publishes the following serial publications:

THE IRCD BULLETIN. 1965-- . Quarterly. Features an analytic or review article and bibliography devoted to a single subject and aimed to synthesize and formulate concepts and practices which will improve the development and educational achievement of urban children and youth, especially black, Puerto Rican, and Asian Americans.

THE URBAN DISADVANTAGED SERIES. 1969-- . Irregular. Consists of state-of-the-art papers, brief reviews, and annotated bibliographies.

THE DOCTORAL RESEARCH SERIES. 1973-- . Irregular. Consists of annotated bibliographies of doctoral dissertations dealing with various aspects of the education of minority groups.

THE EQUAL OPPORTUNITY REVIEW. 1975-- . Irregular. Presents brief overviews of research and practice relating to the education of diverse urban populations.

See also Section 44: Music and the Black Culture, and Section 57: Music and Recreation.

Section 32
ADMINISTRATION AND SUPERVISION OF MUSIC EDUCATION

American Association of School Administrators. MUSIC IN THE SCHOOL CURRICULUM. Arlington, Va.: 1965. 10 p.

Joint statement issued by the American Association of School Administrators and the Music Educators National Conference.

American Music Conference. THE MUSIC REVOLUTION. Chicago: 1974. 64 p. Photos, illus., paper.

A description of fourteen innovative school music programs in elementary, junior high, and high schools.

Arberg, Harold [W.], and Wood, Sarah P., comps. MUSIC CURRICULUM GUIDES. Washington, D.C.: U.S. Department of Health, Education and Welfare, 1964. 48 p. (Distr. by the Government Printing Office.)

A comprehensive bibliography of 491 entries, prepared in cooperation with state departments of education and numerous cities and countries. Each entry is annotated. A subject index is provided. The work was intended to encourage an exchange of curriculum ideas, materials, and philosophy in music education at all levels. The list was complete as of September 15, 1963.

Bessom, Malcolm E. SUPERVISING THE SUCCESSFUL SCHOOL MUSIC PROGRAM. West Nyack, N.Y.: Parker Publishing Co., 1969. 214 p.

A practical guide for either prospective or in-service music supervisors. Covers the development of curriculum content, selection of materials, and suggestions for working with teachers, administrators, and the community.

Bloom, Benjamin S., ed. TAXONOMY OF EDUCATIONAL OBJECTIVES. 2 vols. HANDBOOK I: COGNITIVE DOMAIN; HANDBOOK II: AFFECTIVE DOMAIN. New York: David McKay Co., 1971. 207 and 196 p. Illus.

Campbell, Ronald F., et al. INTRODUCTION TO EDUCATIONAL ADMINISTRATION. 4th ed. Boston: Allyn and Bacon, 1971. 461 p.

Includes bibliography.

Cox, Richard C., and Unks, N. A SELECTED AND ANNOTATED BIBLIOGRAPHY OF STUDIES CONCERNING THE TAXONOMY OF EDUCATIONAL OBJECTIVES: COGNITIVE DOMAIN. Pittsburgh: University of Pittsburgh Learning Research and Development Center, 1967.

"Directory of Summer Music Camps, Clinics, and Workshops." THE INSTRUMENTALIST 30 (March 1976): 25-56.

A convenient directory arranged alphabetically by states. Information includes location, name of director, opening and closing dates, age limits of participants, costs, courses offered, and availability of college credit.

Doll, Ronald C. CURRICULUM IMPROVEMENT: DECISION MAKING AND PROCESS. 2d ed. Boston: Allyn and Bacon, 1970. 440 p.

Includes bibliography.

EDUCATIONAL ADMINISTRATION ABSTRACTS. Columbus, Ohio: Educational Administration Publications, 1966-- . 3/year.

EL-HI TEXTBOOKS IN PRINT. New York: R.R. Bowker Co., 1956-- . Annual.

List of textbooks by subject, author, title, and series.

Gaines, Joan. APPROACHES TO PUBLIC RELATIONS FOR THE MUSIC EDUCATOR. Washington, D.C.: Music Educators National Conference, 1968. 44 p.

Geerdes, Harold P. PLANNING AND EQUIPPING EDUCATIONAL MUSIC FACILITIES. Reston, Va.: Music Educators National Conference, 1975. 96 p. Illus., biblio.

Practical guidelines for designing, constructing, or remodeling music facilities at all school levels.

Graham, Floyd Freeman. PUBLIC RELATIONS IN MUSIC EDUCATION. New York: Exposition Press, 1954. 241 p.

Techniques for building good public relations. Useful for musicians, teachers, and administrators. Bibliography.

Hartley, Harry J. EDUCATIONAL PLANNING--PROGRAMMING--BUDGETING: A SYSTEMS APPROACH. Englewood Cliffs, N.J.: Prentice-Hall, 1968. 290 p.

Hermann, Edward J. SUPERVISING MUSIC IN THE ELEMENTARY SCHOOL. Englewood Cliffs, N.J.: Prentice-Hall, 1965. 210 p.

Focuses on the role of the elementary school music specialist. Bibliography.

House, Robert W. ADMINISTRATION IN MUSIC EDUCATION. Englewood Cliffs, N.J.: Prentice-Hall, 1973. 192 p.

Clear description of basic administrative functions. The subject is treated broadly and in sufficient depth. Serves well as either a text or reference source. Suggested readings are included.

Klotman, Robert H. THE SCHOOL MUSIC ADMINISTRATOR AND SUPERVISOR: CATALYSTS FOR CHANGE IN MUSIC EDUCATION. Englewood Cliffs, N.J.: Prentice-Hall, 1973. 248 p.

Describes procedures necessary for development and management of an elementary or high school music program. Includes evaluation and the process of change. Bibliography.

______, ed. SCHEDULING MUSIC CLASSES. Washington, D.C.: Music Educators National Conference, 1968. 72 p. Paper.

Contains reports of many current scheduling practices in music, elementary through high school. Also discusses data processing and computer scheduling for teacher and administrator.

Kraus, Egon, ed. INTERNATIONAL LISTING OF TEACHING AIDS IN MUSIC. Cologne, Germany: International Society for Music Education, 1959. 52 p. (Distr. by Moseler Verlag, Wolfenbuttel, Germany.)

Although this publication is not recent, the fact that it provides information concerning teaching aids from thirty-one countries justifies its continued use as a reference.

Labuta, Joseph A. GUIDE TO ACCOUNTABILITY IN MUSIC INSTRUCTION. West Nyack, N.Y.: Parker Publishing Co., 1974. 216 p.

Provides guidelines and workshop material for in-service training programs through which music administrators and teachers work toward "accountability." A how-to approach. Bibliography.

Landon, Joseph W. LEADERSHIP FOR LEARNING IN MUSIC EDUCATION. Costa Mesa, Calif.: Educational Media Press, 1975. 306 p. Music, charts, biblio., paper.

Discusses various philosophical views. Examines the forces of society and their effect on American education. Provides considerable material for the development of the music curriculum. Intended for all levels of music education.

McDonald, William F. FEDERAL RELIEF ADMINISTRATION AND THE ARTS. Columbus: Ohio State University Press, 1969. 896 p.

Included in this work is a description of the Works Progress Administration (WPA) program of extensive music activities which operated intensively between 1935 and 1939. Bibliographical references.

Meske, Eunice Boardman, et al., comps. INDIVIDUALIZED INSTRUCTION IN MUSIC. Vienna, Va.: Music Educators National Conference, 1975. 160 p.

The principles of individualized instruction are presented with suggestions for implementing programs in elementary, junior high, and secondary schools. Includes description of programs being used throughout the country.

Music Educators National Conference. NIMAC MANUAL--MANAGING INTERSCHOLASTIC MUSIC ACTIVITIES. Washington, D.C.: 1963. 160 p.

Administrative guide on how to organize and manage interscholastic music activities. Standards of adjudication, sight reading contests, and so forth.

Music Educators National Conference. National Commission on Instruction and the National Council of State Supervisors of Music. THE SCHOOL MUSIC PROGRAM: DESCRIPTION AND STANDARDS. Vienna, Va.: 1974. 66 p.

Includes a rationale for music in the schools; outline for the curriculum for all age levels from early childhood education through high school; indigenous needs and community resources; guidelines for support. Bibliography.

Music Library Association. MANUAL OF MUSIC LIBRARIANSHIP. Edited by Carol June Bradley. Ann Arbor, Mich.: Music Library Association, 1966. 140 p.

While intended as a handbook for the American music librarian, this work is highly useful as a source of information to administrators and others responsible for the organization and development of a music library.

National Association of Secondary School Principals. EDUCATION BOOKS AND AUDIOVISUALS CATALOG. Washington, D.C.: 1974.

An annotated catalog containing curriculum reports, administrative internship publications and a variety of other studies. Films and filmstrips are included.

National Council of State Supervisors of Music. GUIDELINES IN MUSIC EDUCATION: SUPPORTIVE REQUIREMENTS. Washington, D.C.: Music Educators National Conference, 1972. 46 p. Paper.

A service book prepared by the National Council of State Supervisors of Music. Supportive requirements for the development of a comprehensive program of music education include considerations of staffing, facilities, scheduling, and materials and equipment.

National Education Association, Research Division. MUSIC AND ART IN THE PUBLIC SCHOOLS. Washington, D.C.: National Education Association, 1963. 88 p. Paper.

A report of the status of music and art in the public schools as of 1962. Covers curriculum, scheduling, teaching, enrollment, facilities, and other related topics.

Neidig, Kenneth L. MUSIC DIRECTOR'S COMPLETE HANDBOOK OF FORMS. West Nyack, N.Y.: Parker Publishing Co., 1974. 350 p.

A wide variety of forms suitable for use in administering a music program.

New York State Commission on Cultural Resources. ARTS AND THE SCHOOLS: PATTERNS FOR BETTER EDUCATION. Albany, N.Y.: 1972. 100 p. Table, paper.

A valuable guide for those interested in providing aesthetic experiences in the schools. Various programs are described and evaluated.

Palisca, Claude V. MUSIC IN OUR SCHOOLS: A SEARCH FOR IMPROVEMENT. Washington, D.C.: Government Printing Office, 1964. 61 p. Paper.

This is a report of the Yale seminar on music education held under the auspices of the Office of Education for the purpose of helping to extend and improve education in the arts and humanities at all levels.

Robertson, J.M., comp. COURSES OF STUDY. Folcroft, Pa.: Folcroft Library Editions, 1973. 526 p.

Available in most education libraries and state education department libraries.

Schmidt, Lloyd. A TAXONOMY FOR BEHAVIORAL OBJECTIVES IN MUSIC. Hartford, Conn.: State Department of Education, Bureau of Secondary Education, 1971. 28 p. Paper.

A guide for developing objectives for instructional programs in music. Bibliography.

Sidnell, Robert. BUILDING INSTRUCTIONAL PROGRAMS IN MUSIC EDUCATION. Englewood Cliffs, N.J.: Prentice-Hall, 1973. 149 p.

Principles for developing the music education curriculum. Stresses systematic instructional planning. Bibliography.

Snyder, Keith D. SCHOOL MUSIC ADMINISTRATION AND SUPERVISION. 2d ed. Boston: Allyn and Bacon, 1965. 352 p. Illus.

An effective guide for dealing with administration and supervision problems normally encountered by music educators.

U.S. Department of Health, Education, and Welfare. SUBJECT CATALOG OF THE DEPARTMENT LIBRARY. 20 vols. Boston: G.K. Hall and Co., 1965.

Volume 11 contains music references, listings of courses of study, texts, etc.

Weyland, Rudolph H. A GUIDE TO EFFECTIVE MUSIC SUPERVISION. 2d ed. Dubuque, Iowa: William C. Brown Co., 1968. 352 p.

Discusses and provides directions for the implementation of current theories related to music supervision. Bibliography.

NONPRINT MATERIALS AND EQUIPMENT

For indexes, guides, and sources for nonprint materials and equipment, see Part V: Technology, Multimedia Resources, and Equipment.

Note: The administrative and supervisory aspects of music education are also treated as chapters or portions of textbooks. See other sections according to school levels.

ASSOCIATIONS

American Association of Colleges for Teacher Education (AACTE), One Dupont Circle, Washington, D.C. 20036.

Publications: Bulletin. 12-14/year.

JOURNAL OF TEACHER EDUCATION. Quarterly.

Directory. Annual.

Books, reports, and micrographs concerning teacher education.

American Association of School administrators, 1801 North Moore Street, Arlington, Va. 22209.

Publications: THE SCHOOL ADMINISTRATOR. 11/year.

Membership roster. Annual.

Report. Annual.

Books, pamphlets, special reports, and filmstrips.

Association for Supervision and Curriculum Development (ASCD), 1701 K Street, N.W., Suite 1100, Washington, D.C. 20006.

Publications: EDUCATIONAL LEADERSHIP. 8/year.

Yearbook.

NEWS EXCHANGES.

Booklets.

Association of College, University and Community Arts Administrators. (ACUCAA), P.O. Box 2137, Madison, Wis. 53701.

Publications: Bulletin. Monthly.

Bulletin supplement. Monthly.

Membership list. 3/year.

College Music Society (CMS), Department of Music, SUNY, Binghamton, N.Y. 13901.

Publications: Newsletter. 3/year.

COLLEGE MUSIC SYMPOSIUM. Annual.

DIRECTORY OF MUSIC FACULTIES IN COLLEGES AND UNIVERSITIES--UNITED STATES AND CANADA.

Also plans to publish CMS MUSIC BOOK LIST, a guide for librarians in purchasing books on music, and BIBLIOGRAPHIES IN AMERICAN MUSIC.

International Society for Music Education (ISME), Carinaparken 133, DK--3460 Birkerod, Denmark.

Publication: Yearbook.

Music Educators National Conference (MENC), 1902 Association Drive, Reston, Va. 22091.

Publications: MUSIC EDUCATORS JOURNAL. Monthly.

JOURNAL OF RESEARCH IN MUSIC EDUCATION. Quarterly.

MUSIC POWER. Quarterly newsletter.

OFFICIAL DIRECTORY OF MUSIC EDUCATION LEADERSHIP. Annual.

Administration, supervision, and teacher education materials; piano and string instrument teaching materials; bibliography; competition materials; career information; and music lists.

Music Teachers National Association (MTNA), 408 Carew Tower, Cincinnati, Ohio 45202.

Publications: AMERICAN MUSIC TEACHER MAGAZINE. 6/year.

DIRECTORY OF NATIONALLY CERTIFIED TEACHERS. Annual.

National Association of Music Executives in State Universities (NAMESU), Chairman, School of Music, University of Washington, Seattle, Wash. 98195.

National Association of Schools of Music (NASM), 11250 Roger Bacon Drive, Number 5, Reston, Va. 22090.

Publications: Directory. Annual.

MUSIC IN HIGHER EDUCATION. Annual.

Proceedings. Annual.

Bulletins on theory and history of music, careers in music, bibliographies.

National Association of Secondary School Principals (NASSP), 1904 Association Drive, Reston, Va. 22091.

Publications: CURRICULUM REPORT. 5/year.

NEWSLETTER/SPOTLIGHT. 10/year.

STUDENT ADVOCATE. 10/year.

Bulletin. 9/year.

CITY CURRENTS. 5/year.

LEGAL MEMORANDA. 5/year.

National Association of Pastoral Musicians (NAPM), P.O. Box 28373, Washington, D.C. 20005.

Publications: PASTORAL MUSIC. 6/year.

Handbooks, syllabi, and curriculum guides for all levels.

National Council of State Supervisors of Music, c/o George R. Neaderhiser, Kansas Dept. of Education, 120 East Tenth Street, Topeka, Kans. 66612.

Publication: STATE SUPERVISION OF MUSIC.

National Guild of Community Schools of the Arts, 200 West 57th Street, Suite 707, New York, N.Y. 10019.

Publications: GUILD LETTER. Occasional.

COMMUNITY SCHOOL ORGANIZATION MANUAL.

Provides conferences, seminars, and consulting services.

National Society for the Study of Education, 5835 Kimbark Avenue, Chicago: 60637.

Publications: Yearbook. Annual.

Paperback series on contemporary educational issues.

Part III

SUBJECT MATTER AREAS

Section 33

AESTHETICS AND MUSIC

Beardsley, Monroe C. AESTHETICS: PROBLEMS IN THE PHILOSOPHY OF CRITICISM. New York: Harcourt, Brace, and Co., 1958. 614 p.

An introduction to the philosophical theories of aesthetics, and the nature and value of the arts. Bibliographies.

Berlyne, D.E. STUDIES IN THE NEW EXPERIMENTAL AESTHETICS: TOWARD AN OBJECTIVE PSYCHOLOGY OF AESTHETIC APPRECIATION. Washington, D.C.: Hemisphere Publishing Corp., 1974. 350 p.

An in-depth study of the influence of the stimulus properties of art and the impact of those properties on attentional behavior.

Coker, Wilson. MUSIC AND MEANING: A THEORETICAL INTRODUCTION TO MUSICAL AESTHETICS. New York: Free Press, 1972. 256 p.

Presents the author's theories on aesthetics. Excellent and definitive bibliography of works in English on musical aesthetics.

Coleman, Mina P. MUSIC AND AESTHETICS. Rev. ed. Dubuque, Iowa: William C. Brown Co., 1967. 110 p. Paper.

Cooke, Deryck. THE LANGUAGE OF MUSIC. New York and London: Oxford University Press, 1959. 289 p. Music.

An examination of the expressive functions in music. Provides considerable material for reasoning in the field of musical aesthetics.

Debussy, Claude, et al. THREE CLASSICS IN THE AESTHETICS OF MUSIC. New York: Dover Publications, 1962. 188 p.

An unabridged reprint of MONSIEUR CROCHE THE DILETTANTE HATER by Claude Debussy, translated by B.N. Langdon Davies (New York: Viking Press, 1928); SKETCH OF A NEW ESTHETIC OF MUSIC by Ferrucio Busoni, translated by Dr. Th[eodore]. Baker (New York: G. Schirmer, 1911); and ESSAYS BEFORE A SONATA by Charles Ives (New York: Knickerbocker Press, 1920).

Dewey, John. ART AS EXPERIENCE. New York: Minton, Balch and Co., 1934. 355 p.

Based on a series of lectures given at Harvard University, this classic work focuses on the philosophy of aesthetics. Bibliographic references.

Einstein, Alfred. GREATNESS IN MUSIC. Translated by César Saerchinger. New York and London: Oxford University Press, 1941. 287 p.

A critical analysis of the great masters of music, based on the author's definition and standards for "greatness."

Epperson, Gordon. THE MUSICAL SYMBOL: A STUDY OF THE PHILOSOPHIC THEORY OF MUSIC. Ames: Iowa State University Press, 1967. 323 p.

Probes the problems of meaning in music. Draws heavily on opinions of music held by such philosophers and musical theorists as Schopenhauer, Nietzsche, Hanslick, Gruner, and Langer.

Ferguson, Donald N. MUSIC AS METAPHOR: THE ELEMENTS OF EXPRESSION. Minneapolis: University of Minnesota Press, 1960. 198 p. Music.

A personal exposition of the author's theories of musical expression and the philosophical and psychological questions they raise. Bibliographic references.

Fink, Robert. THE UNIVERSALITY OF MUSIC. Detroit: Greenwich Meridian Co., 1970. 293 p. Paper.

An explanation of the phenomenon of music according to natural laws and cultural forces. Includes discussion of acoustics and an evaluation of modern music based on the author's theories.

Hall, James B., and Ulanov, Barry. MODERN CULTURE AND THE ARTS. 2d ed. New York: McGraw-Hill Book Co., 1972. 574 p. Photos.

Issues relevant to the arts of our time are discussed by leaders in the various areas. One section deals with music. Bibliography.

Howes, Frank. MAN, MIND AND MUSIC. 1948. Reprint. Freeport, N.Y.: Books for Libraries Press, 1970. 184 p. Music.

A discussion of music as a part of culture and education, relating it to anthropology, psychology, and philosophy. Bibliographic references.

Kreitler, Hans, and Kreitler, Shumalith. PSYCHOLOGY OF THE ARTS.

Durham, N.C.: Duke University Press, 1972. 514 p. Illus.

Integrates basic psychological theories with structural and aesthetic analyses of music, dance, painting, sculpture, and literature. Bibliography.

Moles, Abraham. INFORMATION THEORY AND ESTHETIC PERCEPTION. Urbana: University of Illinois Press, 1966. 217 p.

A serious approach to the role of information theory as it relates to aesthetics and the psychology of perception. Includes important bibliographic references.

Parker, De Witt H. THE PRINCIPLES OF AESTHETICS. New York: Silver Burdett Co., 1920. 374 p.

This standard text expresses the nature and meaning of all aspects of art, including music. Bibliography.

Prall, D.W. AESTHETIC ANALYSIS. 1936. Reprint. New York: Thomas Y. Crowell Co., 1967. 211 p. Paper.

A well-known, standard study of aesthetics.

Rader, Melvin. A MODERN BOOK OF ESTHETICS: AN ANTHOLOGY. 3d ed. New York: Holt, Rinehart and Winston, 1960. 540 p.

A collection of writings by recognized aestheticians. Treats seriously the principal problems, ideas, and trends concerned with aesthetics.

Reimer, Bennett, et al. TOWARD AN AESTHETIC EDUCATION. Washington, D.C.: Music Educators National Conference, 1971. 190 p. Tables, photos.

Defines aesthetic education, explores its development, and lists resources. Derived from papers presented at the 1970 MENC Biennial Convention, in cooperation with the Central Midwestern Regional Educational Laboratory, Inc. Bibliography.

Schnabel, Arthur. MUSIC AND THE LINE OF MOST RESISTANCE. Princeton, N.J.: Princeton University Press, 1942. 90 p.

Consists of the text of three lectures delivered at the University of Chicago in 1940. Expresses the author's personal views on the aesthetics and philosophy of music. His views are those of a performer.

Schwadron, Abraham A. AESTHETICS: DIMENSIONS FOR MUSIC EDUCATION. Washington, D.C.: Music Educators National Conference, 1967. 130 p. Paper.

A study of the theoretical components of musical aesthetics and educational philosophy. Bibliography.

Smith, Charles T. MUSIC AND REASON: THE BASIS OF LISTENING, COMPOSING, AND ASSESSING. London: Watts and Co., 1947. 158 p.

An explanation of music as related to art, literature, and religion.

Sorell, Walter. THE DUALITY OF VISION: GENIUS AND VERSATILITY IN THE ARTS. New York: Bobbs-Merrill Co., 1970. 360 p.

Focuses on artistic geniuses with more than one talent, illustrating the various manifestations of creativity. One section deals with music. Bibliography.

Stravinsky, Igor. POETICS OF MUSIC IN THE FORM OF SIX LESSONS. Bilingual ed. Translated by Arthur Knodel and Ingolf Dahl. Cambridge, Mass.: Harvard University Press, 1970. 187 p.

An English translation of six lectures by Stravinsky given at Harvard University. Includes personal views on the phenomenon of music, composing, typology, performance, and political influences on Russian music.

Torossian, Aram. A GUIDE TO AESTHETICS. Stanford, Calif.: Stanford University Press; London: H. Milford and Oxford University Press, 1937. 343 p. Photos.

A comprehensive work discussing the functional and expressive values of all areas of artistic endeavor. Designed as an introduction to this field. Extensive bibliography.

Van Loon, Hendrick Willem. THE ARTS. New York: Simon and Schuster, 1937. 677 p. Illus.

A discussion of the nature of art and its development from prehistoric times to the early twentieth century. Discography.

Zuckerkandl, Victor. SOUND AND SYMBOL. Vol. 1: MUSIC AND THE EXTERNAL WORLD. New York: Pantheon Books, 1956. 399 p.

Provides a series of concepts--some highly provocative--concerning music and the external world.

_____. SOUND AND SYMBOL. Vol. II: MAN THE MUSICIAN. Translated by Norbert Guterman. Princeton, N.J.: Princeton University Press, 1973. 450 p.

An analysis of the various ways man perceives music.

See also Section 34: Appreciation and Understanding of Music, and Section 24: Philosophical Foundations, Principles, and Practices.

JOURNALS

BRITISH JOURNAL OF AESTHETICS
Thames and Hudson, Ltd.
44 Clockhouse Road
Farnborough, Hants, Engl.

INTERNATIONAL REVIEW OF THE AESTHETICS AND SOCIOLOGY OF MUSIC
Izdavacki zavod JAZU
Gundjliceva 24
41000 Zagreb, Yugoslavia

JOURNAL OF AESTHETIC EDUCATION
Bureau of Educational Research
College of Education
University of Illinois
Urbana, Ill. 61801

JOURNAL OF AESTHETICS AND ART CRITICISM
Wayne State University
Detroit, Mich. 48202

JOURNAL OF THE AMERICAN MUSICOLOGICAL SOCIETY
William Byrd Press
2901 Byrdhill Road
Richmond, Va. 33228

MUSICAL QUARTERLY
G. Schirmer, Inc.
609 Fifth Avenue
New York, N.Y. 10017

ASSOCIATIONS

American Society for Aesthetics (ASA), Cleveland Museum of Art, Cleveland, Ohio 44106.

Publication: JOURNAL OF AESTHETICS AND ART CRITICISM. Quarterly.

Section 34

APPRECIATION AND UNDERSTANDING OF MUSIC

Barlow, Wayne. FOUNDATIONS OF MUSIC. New York: Appleton-Century-Crofts, 1953. 274 p. Music.

A text for teaching music appreciation to the layman. Knowledge of the basic elements of music as form or design is stressed and considered vital to intelligent listening.

Bekker, Paul. THE ORCHESTRA. New York: W.W. Norton and Co., 1963. 320 p. Photos.

Discusses the various types of orchestras from the beginning of the classical orchestra to the modern orchestra.

Bernstein, Martin, and Picker, Martin. AN INTRODUCTION TO MUSIC. 4th ed. Englewood Cliffs, N.J.: Prentice-Hall, 1972. 682 p.

A long-time popular text which has been updated. A considerable amount of material for the development of intelligent listening to music. Reading lists and bibliography.

Blacking, John. HOW MUSICAL IS MAN? Seattle: University of Washington Press, 1973. 116 p. Photos.

A provocative presentation of views concerning the humanistic aspects of music. Suggests various new approaches to music understanding and music teaching.

Blume, Friederich. RENAISSANCE AND BAROQUE MUSIC: A COMPREHENSIVE SURVEY. Translated by M.D. Herter Norton. New York: W.W. Norton and Co., 1967. 180 p.

Two essays written by a distinguished German musicologist. Especially valuable for its discussion of related nonmusical developments of the period, in particular those pertaining to the social structure and the arts. Bibliography.

Bockman, Guy Alan, and Starr, William J. SCORED FOR LISTENING: A GUIDE TO MUSIC. 2d ed. New York: Harcourt Brace Jovanovich, 1972. 213 p.

An introduction to the history and elements of music. Covers representative musical works from Gregorian chant to twentieth-century music. A set of six records is available.

Bornoff, Jack. MUSIC AND THE TWENTIETH CENTURY MEDIA. Florence, Italy: L.S. Olschki, 1972. 219 p.

Brown, Calvin S. MUSIC AND LITERATURE: A COMPARISON OF THE ARTS. Athens: University of Georgia Press, 1948. 287 p. Illus.

An attempt to systematically explore the relationship existing between these two arts.

Buggert, Robert W., and Fowler, Charles B. THE SEARCH FOR MUSICAL UNDERSTANDING. Belmont, Calif.: Wadsworth Publishing Co., 1973. 448 p.

An introduction to perceptive music listening. Covers classical, popular, electronic, and ethnic music.

Chavez, Carlos. MUSICAL THOUGHT. Cambridge, Mass.: Harvard University Press, 1961. 126 p. Music, illus.

Presents this composer's personal views of the arts as they relate to musical composition and music audiences. Bibliography.

Cooke, Deryck. THE LANGUAGE OF MUSIC. London and New York: Oxford University Press, 1959. 289 p.

An attempt to analyze music as a language. Includes discussion of the technical and expressive elements.

Cott, Jonathan. HE DREAMS WHAT IS GOING ON INSIDE HIS HEAD. San Francisco: Straight Arrow Books, 1973. 349 p. Illus., paper. (Distr. by Quick Fox, New York.)

Describes changes taking place in the relationships between art and politics in the 1960s and 1970s. Includes suggested listening.

Crocker, Richard L., and Basart, Ann P[hillips]. LISTENING TO MUSIC. New York: McGraw-Hill Book Co., 1970. 420 p.

A core text designed for the one-quarter or one-semester course in appreciation. Totally oriented toward a listening approach. Includes four LP records.

Cullen, Marion E., comp. MEMORABLE DAYS IN MUSIC. Metuchen, N.J.: Scarecrow Press, 1970. 233 p.

Yearbook, compilation of popular quotations pertaining to music--primarily significant dates, arranged by month and day. Includes, for example, world premieres, debuts (world and national), births and deaths. Dates go back to 1500s.

Cuyler, Louise. THE SYMPHONY. New York: Harcourt Brace Jovanovich, 1973. 236 p. Paper.

Traces the development of the symphony from its beginning through the contemporary era. Detailed analyses of selected works, including all the symphonies of Beethoven and Brahms. Bibliographies.

Dallin, Leon. LISTENER'S GUIDE TO MUSICAL UNDERSTANDING. Dubuque, Iowa: William C. Brown Co., 1959. 306 p. Photos, illus.

Designed as a text for college music appreciation classes. Emphasis is on guided listening. Discography.

Daniels, Arthur, and Wagner, Lavern, eds. MUSIC. New York: Holt, Rinehart and Winston, 1975. 512 p. Illus., glossary, soundsheet.

For use in an introductory, college-level course. Broad coverage. Includes recent and current musical idioms.

De Long, Patrick D., et al. ART AND MUSIC IN THE HUMANITIES. Englewood Cliffs, N.J.: Prentice-Hall, 1966. 244 p.

A textbook for use in humanities courses.

Dent, Frank L. THE LECTURE-PERFORMANCE: AN INSTRUMENT FOR AUDIENCE EDUCATION. Technical Report no. 7, Harvard Project Zero. Cambridge, Mass.: Harvard Graduate School of Education, 1972. 31 p. Paper.

A description of the approaches used by various artists to increase the audience's understanding of the music performed. Includes discussion of the psychological factors of discrimination, perception of time, space, memory, emotion, etc. No evaluation is included.

Dwyer, Terence. TEACHING MUSICAL APPRECIATION. New York and London: Oxford University Press, 1967. 135 p.

A discussion of the process of listening to music and practical procedures for teaching young children and adults. Bibliography.

Ewen, David. THE COMPLETE BOOK OF CLASSICAL MUSIC. Englewood Cliffs, N.J.: Prentice-Hall, 1965. 946 p.

Biographies and critical evaluations of both major and minor composers from 1300 to 1900, and detailed notes on more than 1,000 musical works.

_____. DAVID EWEN INTRODUCES MODERN MUSIC: A HISTORY AND APPRECIATION FROM WAGNER TO WEBERN. Philadelphia and New York: Chilton Book Co., 1962. 303 p. Photos.

Designed to acquaint the layman with twentieth-century music. A nontechnical approach.

_____. GREAT COMPOSERS, 1300-1900: A BIOGRAPHICAL AND CRITICAL GUIDE. New York: H.W. Wilson Co., 1966. 429 p. Photos.

A replacement for COMPOSERS OF YESTERDAY, which was published in 1937. Includes almost 200 composers. Includes the principal works with a bibliography; appendixes provide a chronological listing of composers in the period 1300-1900.

_____. ORCHESTRAL MUSIC: ITS STORY TOLD THROUGH THE LIVES AND WORKS OF ITS FOREMOST COMPOSERS. New York: Franklin Watts, 1973. 312 p. Illus., photos.

Covers orchestral music from the sixteenth century to the present. Geared for young people. Glossary.

Ferguson, Donald N. MASTERWORKS OF THE ORCHESTRAL REPERTOIRE: A GUIDE FOR LISTENERS. 1954. Reprint. Minneapolis: University of Minnesota Press, 1968. 662 p. Illus.

Analyses and descriptions of the principal symphonies, overtures, and concertos from classical and selected modern composers.

Finkelstein, Sidney. COMPOSER AND NATION: THE FOLK HERITAGE OF MUSIC. New York: International Publishers, 1960. 333 p.

This work explores the ideas expressed in music and traces the popular and folk melodies of the great composers from its sources. The influence of social change on the music is discussed. Coverage is from the Renaissance to the twentieth century. Bibliographical references.

Foster, Donald L. THE MODERN ARTS: AN OUTLINE FOR THE LIBRARIAN, EDUCATOR, AND GENERAL READER. Champaign: Illinois University Bookstore, 1963. 78 p. Paper.

Discusses modern trends and styles in the arts. Includes annotated lists of books and recordings.

Frankenstein, Alfred. A MODERN GUIDE TO SYMPHONIC MUSIC. New York: Meredith Press, 1967. 667 p. Photos, music.

A guide which provides analytical and historical information on each major opus of sixty-two symphonic composers from the baroque period to the twentieth century--246 pieces in all. Principal and secondary themes are quoted in their entirety.

Gillespie, John. THE MUSICAL EXPERIENCE. 2d ed. Belmont, Calif.: Wadsworth Publishing Co., 1972. 475 p. Photos, music.

A music appreciation text designed to permit considerable flexibility in the use of material. The teaching format can progress either in chronological order, or by forms, etc. Bibliography included after each chapter. Special record album available which includes representative selections of great music from the ninth to the twentieth century.

Haggin, Bernard H. A DECADE OF MUSIC. New York: Horizon, 1973. 256 p. Music.

A critical evaluation of musical events--vocal and instrumental concerts, operas, ballets, and books--from 1963 to the spring of 1973.

Hartnoll, Phyllis, ed. SHAKESPEARE IN MUSIC: ESSAYS BY JOHN STEVENS, CHARLES CUDWORTH, WINTON DEAN, ROGER FISHER. New York: St. Martin's Press, 1964. 333 p.

After four essays, this work contains two excellent chapters entitled "Catalogue of Musical Works Based on the Plays and Poetry of Shakespeare" and "Checklist of Composers."

Hemming, Roy. DISCOVERING MUSIC, WHERE TO START ON RECORDS AND TAPES, THE GREAT COMPOSERS AND THEIR WORKS, TODAY'S MAJOR RECORDING ARTISTS. New York: Four Winds Press, 1974. 379 p. Photos.

A guide to the selection of music recordings (discs and tapes). Considers the opinions of fifty outstanding musicians.

Hoffer, Charles R. A CONCISE INTRODUCTION TO MUSIC LISTENING. Belmont, Calif.: Wadsworth Publishing Co., 1974. 304 p.

A listening oriented text in music appreciation. Covers the elements of music, various forms, musical types, and styles. Includes baroque, American, twentieth century, jazz, and rock. Supplementary record album and student workbook available.

______. THE UNDERSTANDING OF MUSIC. 3d ed. Belmont, Calif.: Wadsworth Publishing Co., 1976. 350 p. Photos, music.

An introduction to the technical and aesthetic aspects of music and its relationship to culture. Surveys music in chronological order from the gothic motet to rock and jazz. Extensive coverage of ethnic music. An accompanying instructor's manual student study guide, and record album is available.

Janson, H.W., and Kerman, Joseph. A HISTORY OF ART AND MUSIC. New York: Harry N. Abrams, 1968. 318 p.

Combines the history of music and art for use as a text in a general humanities course. Bibliography.

Kerman, Joseph. LISTEN. New York: Worth Publishers, 1972. 392 p. Illus., music, photos.

A series of discussions concerning the aesthetic content of various musical works.

Lockspeiser, Edward. MUSIC AND PAINTING: A STUDY IN COMPARATIVE IDEAS FROM TURNER TO SCHOENBERG. New York: Harper and Row, 1973. 197 p. Photos.

An interpretation of the interaction of ideas in music and painting. Bibliographic references.

Long, John H. SHAKESPEARE'S USE OF MUSIC. 3 vols. Gainesville: University of Florida Press, 1955-71.

An examination of the function of music in the works of Shakespeare. Contains an annotated bibliography.

Vol. 1: SHAKESPEARE'S USE OF MUSIC: A STUDY OF THE MUSIC AND ITS PERFORMANCE IN THE ORIGINAL PRODUCTION OF SEVEN COMEDIES. 1955. 213 p.

Vol. 2: SHAKESPEARE'S USE OF MUSIC: THE FINAL COMEDIES. 1961. 159 p.

Vol. 3: SHAKESPEARE'S USE OF MUSIC: THE HISTORIES AND TRAGEDIES. 1971. 306 p.

McGehee, Thomasine C. PEOPLE AND MUSIC. Revised by Alice D. Nelson. Boston: Allyn and Bacon, 1963. 451 p.

The development of music from its earliest beginnings to the present. Written for teenage readers.

Machlis, Joseph. THE ENJOYMENT OF MUSIC. 3d ed. New York: W.W. Norton and Co., 1970. Photos, music, illus.

Presents the ingredients of music from the listener's point of view. Relates music to the other arts and to the social and historical background. Bibliography.

Marple, Hugo D. THE WORLD OF MUSIC. Boston: Allyn and Bacon, 1974. 600 p.

A nontechnical introductory text for courses in music appreciation. Recording lists are provided at the end of each chapter.

Martin, F. David, and Jacobus, Lee A. THE HUMANITIES THROUGH THE ARTS. New York: McGraw-Hill Book Co., 1975. 416 p. Illus.

A self-contained exploratory approach to connecting each art form with the humanistic values it reveals. Music section includes a glossary of styles with suggestions for listening.

Mason, Daniel Gregory. THE QUARTETS OF BEETHOVEN. New York: Oxford University Press, 1947. 294 p. Music.

Primarily a guide for the listener. Deals with the background and technical aspects of the works. Bibliography.

Mellers, Wilfrid [Howard]. MUSIC AND SOCIETY: ENGLAND AND THE EUROPEAN TRADITION. 2d ed. London: Dennis Dobson, 1968. 230 p. Photos.

An account of the evolution of English musical styles in relation to the European tradition. Bibliography.

Meyer, Leonard B. EXPLAINING MUSIC: ESSAYS AND EXPLORATIONS. Los Angeles and Berkeley: University of California Press, 1973. 284 p.

A serious work which seeks to explain, by critical analysis, how the structure and process of a particular composition are related to the competent listener's comprehension of it.

_____. MUSIC, THE ARTS, AND IDEAS: PATTERNS AND PREDICTIONS IN TWENTIETH-CENTURY CULTURE. Chicago: University of Chicago Press, 1967. 342 p.

A thought-provoking work which explores music as an agent in understanding today's culture.

Miller, William Hugh. INTRODUCTION TO MUSIC APPRECIATION: AN OBJECTIVE APPROACH TO LISTENING. Philadelphia and New York: Chilton Book Co., 1961. 329 p. Photos, music.

Deals extensively with the aesthetics of music and the related arts as comprehended through listening. Covers in detail the fundamentals of music. Bibliography and discography.

Nadeau, Roland, and Tesson, William. LISTEN: A GUIDE TO THE PLEASURES OF MUSIC. 2d ed. Boston: Allyn and Bacon, 1976. 544 p. Music, photos, illus., paper.

Contains sections on music fundamentals, music history, and listening. Focus is on perceptive listening. Includes a companion workbook.

Nallin, Walter E. THE MUSICAL FORM: A CONSIDERATION OF MUSIC AND ITS WAYS. New York: Macmillan, 1968. 650 p.

Describes music, its materials, lore, stylistic evaluation, and traditions. Much background detail intended to enrich the listening experience of the nonmusician. Bibliography.

Nettl, Paul. BEETHOVEN ENCYCLOPEDIA. New York: Philosophical Library, 1956. 325 p.

A chronological listing of events, personalities, compositions, and other items related to Beethoven.

_____. NATIONAL ANTHEMS. 2d ed. Translated by Alexander Gode. New York: Frederick Ungar Publishing Co., 1967. 261 p.

The origins, evolution, and cultural meaning of the world's national anthems. Bibliography. (See also Shaw and Coleman's NATIONAL ANTHEMS OF THE WORLD, below.)

Ratner, Leonard [G.]. MUSIC: THE LISTENER'S ART. 2d ed. New York: McGraw-Hill Book Co., 1957. 463 p. Music, illus., photos.

Written to stimulate the listener to learn more about music. Considerable material provided to show the relationship between musical techniques and expressive values in music. Bibliography.

Rauchhaupt, Ursula von, ed. THE SYMPHONY. Translated by Eugene Horzoll. London: Thames and Hudson, 1973. 324 p.

Reimer, Bennett, and Evans, Edward G., Jr. THE EXPERIENCE OF MUSIC. Englewood Cliffs, N.J.: Prentice-Hall, 1972. 434 p. Music, photos, illus.

A teaching program designed to aid teachers in directing students to more active and perceptive listening. A unique format for the development of music appreciation. Additional materials include: (1) library for developing the experience of music (a fourteen-record set); (2) developing the experience of music: listening charts; (3) listening for the experience of music (a seven-record set); and (4) teaching the experience of music (a guide). Bibliographies.

Sacher, Jack, and Eversole, James. THE ART OF SOUND: AN INTRODUCTION TO MUSIC. Englewood Cliffs, N.J.: Prentice-Hall, 1971. 332 p.

Discusses the conventions, traditions, and characteristics of the media and genres of music to give the potential listener a conception and understanding of each through which he can develop a viable system for appreciating music more completely. Includes a basic record library listing and a bibliography.

Schoen, Max, ed. EFFECTS OF MUSIC: A SERIES OF ESSAYS. 1927. Reprint. Freeport, N.Y.: Books for Libraries Press, 1968. 273 p. Photos, illus.

An examination of a variety of factors that bear on problems of appreciation, taste, and artistic creation.

Schwartz, Paul. HEARING MUSIC WITH UNDERSTANDING. Chicago: Educational Methods, 1968. 170 p.

A self-instructional basic theory course with accompanying tape recordings.

Shaw, Martin, and Coleman, Henry, eds. NATIONAL ANTHEMS OF THE WORLD. New York: Pitman Publishing Corp., 1963. 408 p.

Useful references for the understanding of national anthems of various countries. (See also Paul Nettl's NATIONAL ANTHEMS, cited above.)

Slonimsky, Nicolas. LEXICON OF MUSICAL INVECTIVE. New York: Coleman-Ross Co., 1965. 325 p.

Collection of critical attacks on many composers since Beethoven.

Stringham, Edwin John. LISTENING TO MUSIC CREATIVELY. 2d ed. Englewood Cliffs, N.J.: Prentice-Hall, 1959. 624 p. Illus., photos, music.

A guide for perceptive listening. Designed for the layman and the general college student. Focus is on the interrelationships of music and the other arts. Bibliography.

Swan, Alfred J. RUSSIAN MUSIC AND ITS SOURCES IN CHANT AND FOLK SONG. London: John Baker, 1973. 234 p. Music, photos.

A narrative discussion of the uses of original cultural sources in the music of Russian composers from the eighteenth to the twentieth century. The appendix includes a listing of Russian folk song collection and a discussion of early notation. Bibliography.

Taubman, Howard, ed. THE NEW YORK TIMES GUIDE TO LISTENING PLEASURE. New York: Macmillan, 1968. 328 p.

A compilation of articles dealing with the various forms of music from opera and classical music to jazz, folk, and music of the theatre. Discography.

Thomas, Edrie. TEACHING MUSIC APPRECIATION THROUGH LISTENING SKILL TRAINING. West Nyack, N.Y.: Parker Publishing Co., 1972. 212 p.

Develops specific skill activities for increased enjoyment of music listening.

Ulrich, Homer. MUSIC: A DESIGN FOR LISTENING. 3d ed. New York: Harcourt Brace Jovanovich, 1970. 476 p. Music, illus., photos.

A nontechnical introduction to the elements of music as perceived through listening. Includes discussion of modern music, including electronic, jazz, and rock music. A set of twelve records is available.

_____. SYMPHONIC MUSIC: ITS EVOLUTION SINCE THE RENAISSANCE. New York and London: Columbia University Press, 1952. 352 p.

A cohesive and reliable account of symphonic music, covering form and style along with appropriate historical commentary.

Voorhees, Anna Tipton. INDEX TO SYMPHONIC PROGRAM NOTES IN BOOKS. Kent, Ohio: Kent State University School of Library Science, 1970. 136 p.

A list of books containing program notes. Also provides an index to annotations of orchestral compositions included in the books on the list.

Walker, Alan. AN ANATOMY OF MUSICAL CRITICISM. New York: Chilton Book Co., 1968. 114 p.

Discusses principles and theories pertaining to musical criticism. Bibliography.

Walter, Don C. MEN AND MUSIC IN WESTERN CULTURE. New York: Appleton-Century-Crofts, 1969. 244 p.

Treats the role music has played in Western culture.

Weber, Max. THE RATIONAL AND SOCIAL FOUNDATIONS OF MUSIC. Translated and edited by Don Martindale et al. Carbondale: Southern Illinois University Press, 1958. 148 p.

An analysis of tone systems, scales, chords, systems of notation, and the development of instruments as related to the social needs of the society and the technical resources available. Bibliography.

Wink, Richard L., and Williams, Lois G. INVITATION TO LISTENING: AN INTRODUCTION TO MUSIC. 2d ed. Boston: Houghton Mifflin Co., 1976. 352 p. Illus., music.

A music appreciation text designed to develop listening skills. Also provided is set of related records and an instructor's manual containing numerous practical suggestions.

Winold, Allen. ELEMENTS OF MUSICAL UNDERSTANDING. Englewood Cliffs, N.J.: Prentice-Hall, 1966. 404 p. Photos, music, illus.

Designed to build an understanding of the nature and meaning of music through active musical experience.

Zuckerkandl, Victor. THE SENSE OF MUSIC. Princeton, N.J.: Princeton University Press, 1959. 246 p. Illus., music.

A text designed with the liberal arts student in mind. Covers the basic elements of music.

Section 35
HISTORY OF MUSIC

Abraham, Gerald, general ed. THE HISTORY OF MUSIC IN SOUND. 10 vols. New York: Oxford University Press, 1953-59.

Designed as a companion reference to the NEW OXFORD HISTORY OF MUSIC. These ten handbooks list recordings with annotations.

Vol. I: ANCIENT AND ORIENTAL MUSIC. Edited by Egon Wellesz. 1957. 41 p.
Vol. II: EARLY MEDIEVAL MUSIC UP TO 1300. 2d ed. Edited by Dom Anselm Hughes. 1960. 69 p.
Vol. III: ARS NOVA AND THE RENAISSANCE. 2d ed. Edited by Dom Anselm Hughes. 1960. 83 p.
Vol. IV: THE AGE OF HUMANISM. Edited by [Sir] J[ack]. A. Westrup. 1954. 71 p.
Vol. V: OPERA AND CHURCH MUSIC. Edited by [Sir] J[ack]. A. Westrup. 1954. 55 p.
Vol. VI: THE GROWTH OF INSTRUMENTAL MUSIC. Edited by [Sir] J[ack].A. Westrup. 1954. 51 p.
Vol. VII: THE SYMPHONIC OUTLOOK. Edited by Egon Wellesz. 1957. 63 p.
Vol. VIII: THE AGE OF BEETHOVEN. Edited by Gerald Abraham. 1958. 65 p.
Vol. IX: ROMANTICISM. Edited by Gerald Abraham. 1958. 67 p.
Vol. X: MODERN MUSIC. Edited by Gerald Abraham. 1959. 63 p.

Bauer, Marion, and Peyser, Ethel. MUSIC THROUGH THE AGES: AN INTRODUCTION TO MUSIC HISTORY. 3d ed. Revised by Elizabeth E. Rogers. New York: Putnam, 1967. 748 p.

A long-time favorite for layman and student. This edition includes some new material. Major genres have been expanded, and technicalities are at a minimum.

Blume, Friederich. RENAISSANCE AND BAROQUE MUSIC: A COMPREHENSIVE SURVEY. Translated by M.D. Herter. New York: W.W. Norton and Co., 1967. 180 p.

Two essays written by a distinguished German musicologist.

Boelza, Igor Fedorovich. HANDBOOK OF SOVIET MUSICIANS. Edited by Alan Bush. 1943. Reprint. St. Clair Shores, Mich.: Scholarly Press, 1972. 101 p.

A survey of Soviet concert, operatic, and ballet music. Forty selected composers are listed, with brief biographical details and a complete catalog of their works. Bibliography.

Borroff, Edith. MUSIC IN EUROPE AND THE UNITED STATES: A HISTORY. Englewood Cliffs, N.J.: Prentice-Hall, 1971. 752 p.

Views music from six major eras and for each concentrates on representative forms and central stylistic definitions.

Brown, Howard Mayer. INSTRUMENTAL MUSIC PRINTED BEFORE 1600: A BIBLIOGRAPHY. Cambridge, Mass.: Harvard University Press, 1965. 559 p. Illus.

Designed to make easily accessible to the investigators of this music all of the pertinent data.

Bukofzer, Manfred F. MUSIC IN THE BAROQUE ERA: FROM MONTEVERDI TO BACH. New York: W.W. Norton and Co., 1947. 489 p. Music.

An in-depth coverage of the music of this period. Bibliography.

_____. STUDIES IN MEDIEVAL AND RENAISSANCE MUSIC. New York: W.W. Norton and Co., 1950. 324 p. Music.

A series of essays which investigates compositions which have not hitherto been understood in their historical and musical importance. Bibliography.

Burney, Charles. A GENERAL HISTORY OF MUSIC. 2 vols. Edited by Frank Mercer. 1935. Reprint. New York: Dover Publications, 1957.

Detailed historical coverage of all aspects of music from earliest times to the 1780s. Still basically sound. Especially valuable for coverage of Burney's contemporaries, for which it is an important primary source.

Cannon, Beekman, et al. THE ART OF MUSIC. New York: Thomas Y. Crowell Co., 1960. 484 p. Illus., music, photos.

A history of musical styles and ideas. Covers early Greek and Roman foundations to the twentieth century.

Carse, Adam. THE ORCHESTRA FROM BEETHOVEN TO BERLIOZ. New York:

Brande Bros., 1949. 514 p.

A history of the orchestra from the first half of the nineteenth century. Includes development of orchestral conducting.

Clendenin, William R. MUSIC: HISTORY AND THEORY. 1964. Reprint. Totowa, N.J.: Littlefield Adams and Co., 1974. 468 p. Paper.

Designed for use as a college course guide in the history of music. The forms of music are traced from primitive beginnings to the modern era.

Cook, Harold E. SHAKER MUSIC: A MANIFESTATION OF AMERICAN FOLK CULTURE. Lewisburg, Pa.: Bucknell University Press, 1973. 312 p.

A description of the social and historical background of the Shaker movement, their hymnody, notation, and theory; technical aspects of musical practice and performance; song types and analysis. Includes descriptive lists of Shaker music holdings at various museums and libraries throughout the United States. Especially valuable are the chronological bibliography of printed Shaker hymnals and the general bibliography.

Danielou, Alain. NORTHERN INDIAN MUSIC. New York: Praeger, 1968. 403 p. Illus., tables, music.

Information based on research on a considerable amount of Sanskrit literature of music. Extensive analytic treatment with many musical examples. Bibliography.

Davidson, Ake. RARE MUSIC WORKS ON MICROFICHE. Zug, Switzerland: Inter-Documentation Co., 1971.

This catalog of rare music works available on manuscript (by individual editions) can be obtained from Inter Documentation Company AG, Poststrasse 4, Zug, Switzerland.

De Lafontaine, Henry Cart. THE KING'S MUSICK: A TRANSCRIPT OF RECORDS RELATING TO MUSIC AND MUSICIANS (1460-1700). 1709. Reprint. New York: Da Capo Press, 1974. 522 p.

A primary source of information on the lives and performances of court musicians during the Tudor and Stuart reigns. Includes definitions of archaic terms and brief biographies of the most important musicians.

Einstein, Alfred. MUSIC IN THE ROMANTIC ERA. New York: W.W. Norton and Co., 1947. 371 p.

An in-depth analysis of the role of music and its relationship to the romantic period.

______. A SHORT HISTORY OF MUSIC. 4th ed. Translated by Eric Blom et al. New York: Alfred A. Knopf Co., 1954. 438 p.

A narrative presentation of the development of music from the ancient Greeks to the present. Assumes some musical background.

Eisler, Paul E., comp. WORLD CHRONOLOGY OF MUSIC HISTORY. 10 vols. projected. Dobbs Ferry, N.Y.: Oceana Publications, 1972-- .

Vol. I: 1972. 547 p. Covers 30,000 BC-1954 AD.
Vol. II: 1973. 523 p. Covers 1594-1684.
Vol. III: 1974. 512 p. Covers 1685-1735.
Vol. IV: Scheduled for 1976.
An interim index for volumes I, II, and III. Remaining volumes scheduled to follow.

Elliott, Kenneth, and Rimmer, Frederick. A HISTORY OF SCOTTISH MUSIC. London: British Broadcasting Co., 1973. 84 p.

Engel, Carl. THE MUSIC OF THE MOST ANCIENT NATIONS: PARTICULARLY OF THE ASSYRIANS, EGYPTIANS, AND HEBREWS, WITH SPECIAL REFERENCE TO DISCOVERIES IN WESTERN ASIA AND IN EGYPT. London: William Reeves Co., 1929. 380 p.

Includes bibliography.

Ferguson, Donald N. A HISTORY OF MUSICAL THOUGHT. 3d ed. New York: Appleton-Century-Crofts, 1950. 675 p. Illus., music.

Designed as a college text in music history. Focuses on the numerous forces that helped shape music development. Bibliography.

Ford, Wyn K. MUSIC IN ENGLAND BEFORE 1800: A SELECT BIBLIOGRAPHY. London: The Library Association, 1967. 128 p.

Covers well those works which deal specifically with music, composition, and performance up to the year 1800. Includes works on the theory of music.

Fuld, James J. THE BOOK OF WORLD-FAMOUS MUSIC: CLASSICAL, POPULAR, AND FOLK. Rev. ed. New York: Crown, 1971. 688 p.

Provides much valuable information concerning well-known melodies, many of which have not been previously treated historically. Particularly useful to music educators.

Gerboth, Walter. MUSIC OF EAST AND SOUTHEAST ASIA. Albany: University of the State of New York, State Education Department, 1963. 23 p. Paper.

A selected bibliography of books, pamphlets, and articles.

Gregory, Julia, and Bartlett, Hazel. CATALOGUE OF EARLY BOOKS ON MUSIC. Reprint of the 1913 ed. with its 1944 supplement. New York: Da Capo Press, 1969. 455 p.

This catalog, with its supplement, lists and describes the Library of Congress holdings in the field of early theory and history.

Grout, Donald Jay. A HISTORY OF WESTERN MUSIC. Rev. ed. New York: W.W. Norton and Co., 1973. 818 p. Illus., music.

Long recognized as one of the leading one-volume histories of music in the English language. A high level of scholarship combined with lucid, yet elegant style. Excellent bibliography.

_____. A HISTORY OF WESTERN MUSIC: SHORT EDITION. New York: W.W. Norton and Co., 1973. 540 p. Illus., music.

A brief, alternative version of A HISTORY OF WESTERN MUSIC, see above. A complete work, but less detailed.

Hagopian, Viola L. ITALIAN ARS NOVA MUSIC: A GUIDE TO MODERN EDITIONS AND RELATED LITERATURE. 2d rev. ed. Los Angeles and Berkeley: University of California Press, 1973. 175 p.

Hansen, Peter S. AN INTRODUCTION TO TWENTIETH CENTURY MUSIC. 3d ed. Boston: Allyn and Bacon, 1971. 464 p.

Surveys the main lines of the development of twentieth-century music through a study of selected compositions by its most influential composers. Bibliography.

Harman, Alec, et al. MAN AND HIS MUSIC: THE STORY OF MUSICAL EXPERIENCE IN THE WEST. London: Barrie and Jenkins, 1962. 1,204 p.

This one-volume history of music (originally four volumes) was written for use in the British higher education system. Bibliography and discography.

Hawkins, Sir John. A GENERAL HISTORY OF THE SCIENCE AND PRACTICE OF MUSIC. 2 vols. 1853. Reprint. New York: Dover Publications, 1963. Music, photos.

A reference work of importance for music historians.

Hays, William, ed. TWENTIETH-CENTURY VIEWS OF MUSIC HISTORY. New York: Charles Scribner's Sons, 1972. 471 p.

An anthology of modern writings concerning some of the major points in the development of Western art music from medieval to modern times. Bibliography after each chapter.

Heger, Theodore E. MUSIC OF THE CLASSIC PERIOD. Dubuque, Iowa: William C. Brown Co., 1969. 116 p. Illus., music.

An informative, though limited, account of eighteenth-century music. Especially written for the person with little knowledge of music.

Hitchcock, H. Wiley, ed. THE PRENTICE-HALL HISTORY OF MUSIC SERIES. 8 vols. Englewood Cliffs, N.J.: Prentice-Hall, 1965-74.

The series is planned as foundation texts for the periods they encompass.

Seay, Albert. MUSIC IN THE MEDIEVAL WORLD. 1965. 182 p. Bibliog.

Palisca, Claude V. BAROQUE MUSIC. 1970. 230 p. Bibliog.

Pauly, Reinhard G. MUSIC IN THE CLASSIC PERIOD. 2d ed. 1973. 206 p. Bibliog.

Longyear, Rey M. NINETEENTH-CENTURY ROMANTICISM IN MUSIC. Rev. ed. 1973. 289 p. Bibliog.

Salzman, Eric. TWENTIETH-CENTURY MUSIC: AN INTRODUCTION. 3d ed. 1974. 240 p. Bibliog.

Hitchcock, H. Wiley. MUSIC IN THE UNITED STATES. 2d ed. 1974. 288 p. Bibliog.

Malm, William P. MUSIC CULTURES OF THE PACIFIC, THE NEAR EAST, AND ASIA. 1967. 169 p. Bibliog., discog.

Nettl, Bruno. FOLK AND TRADITIONAL MUSIC OF THE WESTERN CONTINENT. 1965. 213 p. Bibliog., discog.

Hughes, David G. A HISTORY OF EUROPEAN MUSIC: THE ART MUSIC TRADITION OF WESTERN CULTURE. New York: McGraw-Hill Book Co., 1974. 512 p.

A survey of Western art music from Gregorian chant to the present, covering all significant forms and styles.

Hutchings, Arthur J. THE BAROQUE CONCERTO. New York: W.W. Norton and Co., 1961. 363 p. Music.

Traces the history of the concerto. Bibliography.

Jacobs, Arthur. A SHORT HISTORY OF WESTERN MUSIC. Harmondsworth, Engl.: Penguin Books, 1972. 363 p.

The development of music from the medieval troubadours and the Ars Nova musical of the fourteenth century to jazz and the music of Stravinsky, Britten, and Stockhausen.

Janson, H.W., and Kerman, Joseph. A HISTORY OF ART AND MUSIC.

Englewood Cliffs, N.J.: Prentice-Hall, 1968. 317 p. Illus., music, photos.

A useful reference book for the integration of these fields in the area of the humanities. Bibliography.

Kaufmann, Walter. THE RAGAS OF NORTH INDIA. Bloomington: Indiana University Press, 1968. 625 p. Music, photos.

Bibliography.

Klaus, Kenneth B. THE ROMANTIC PERIOD IN MUSIC. Boston: Allyn and Bacon, 1970. 563 p. Illus., music, photos.

An in-depth study of this period with emphasis on comparison of the composers. Bibliography.

Krohn, Ernst C. THE HISTORY OF MUSIC: AN INDEX TO THE LITERATURE AVAILABLE IN A SELECTED GROUP OF MUSICOLOGICAL PUBLICATIONS. Rev. ed. St. Louis, Mo.: Baton Music Co., 1958. 488 p.

Krummel, D.W. BIBLIOTHECA BOLDUANIANA: A RENAISSANCE MUSIC BIBLIOGRAPHY. Detroit Studies in Music Bibliography, no. 22. Detroit: Information Coordinators, 1972. 191 p.

Especially useful to the serious researcher in Renaissance music. Facsimile reprint of Paulus Bolduanus's seventeenth-century bibliography of music, with annotations and corrections.

Lang, Paul Henry. MUSIC IN WESTERN CIVILIZATION. New York: W.W. Norton and Co., 1941. 1,107 p.

One of the most thorough and reliable sources concerning music in the making of Western civilization. Extensive bibliography.

Leichtentritt, Hugo. MUSIC, HISTORY, AND IDEAS. Cambridge, Mass.: Harvard University Press, 1939. 292 p.

A study of the relationship of music to social, political, and spiritual values. Traces these concepts from early Greece to the twentieth century. Bibliography.

_____. MUSIC OF THE WESTERN NATIONS. Edited by Nicholas Slonimsky. Cambridge, Mass.: Harvard University Press, 1956. 324 p.

A discussion of music as an expression of national culture. Traces the early Greek roots to twentieth-century Western music.

Linker, Robert White. MUSIC OF THE MINNESINGER AND EARLY MEISTERSINGER; A BIBLIOGRAPHY. 1962. Reprint. New York: AMS Press, 1970. 79 p.

Original edition issued as number 32 of the University of North Carolina Studies in the Germanic languages and literature.

McKinney, Howard D., and Anderson, W.R. MUSIC IN HISTORY: THE EVOLUTION OF AN ART. 3d ed. New York: American Book Co., 1966. 820 p. Illus., photos.

A presentation of music history as related to other arts of the various periods. Covers primitive civilizations to twentieth-century developments. Bibliography.

Nathan, M. Montagu. A HISTORY OF RUSSIAN MUSIC: BEING AN ACCOUNT OF THE RISE AND PROGRESS OF THE RUSSIAN SCHOOL OF COMPOSERS, WITH A SURVEY OF THEIR LIVES AND A DESCRIPTION OF THEIR WORKS. 1914. Reprint. Boston: Milford House, 1973. 346 p.

Covers the history from the prenationalist period to Stravinsky.

Nettl, Paul. THE STORY OF DANCE MUSIC. New York: Philosophical Library, 1947. 370 p. Music, photos.

This work is of particular value to music educators in revealing the influence of the dance on the development of music.

Parry, C. Hubert H. THE EVOLUTION OF THE ART OF MUSIC. Edited by H.C. Colles. New York: D. Appleton-Century Co., 1938. 483 p. Music.

This book, first published in 1893, has been considered by some as one of the foundations of English musical literature. It is not so much a history but rather a theory of evolution founded on historical facts as interpreted by Sir Hubert Parry.

Pearsall, Ronald. VICTORIAN POPULAR MUSIC. Detroit: Gale Research Co., 1973. 240 p. Illus.

Explores not only music room and drawing room song, but also ballet, opera, oratorio, and the wide variety of outdoor music. Brings the whole field of music of the era into focus, and includes the related field of dancing. Bibliography.

Raynor, Henry. A SOCIAL HISTORY OF MUSIC: FROM THE MIDDLE AGES TO BEETHOVEN. New York: Schocken Books, 1972. 373 p.

This book is an effort to fill part of the gap between the history of music which deals with the development of musical styles and the general history of the world in which the composers carried out their function. Bibliography.

Reese, Gustave. MUSIC IN THE MIDDLE AGES. New York: W.W. Norton and Co., 1940. 502 p. Music, photos.

One of the most reliable sources available concerning medieval music. Bibliography and discography.

_____. MUSIC IN THE RENAISSANCE. Rev. ed. New York: W.W. Norton and Co., 1959. 1,022 p. Music, photos.

A complete and authoritative account of the music produced in the fifteenth and sixteenth centuries. Bibliography.

Robertson, Alec, and Stevens, Denise, eds. A HISTORY OF MUSIC. 2 vols. Vol. I: ANCIENT FORMS TO POLYPHONY. London: Cassell, 1962. 341 p. Vol. II: RENAISSANCE AND BAROQUE. New York: Barnes and Noble, 1965. 355 p.

A historical treatment of music as it relates to its social, aesthetic, and religious backgrounds.

Rossi, Nick, and Rafferty, Sadie. MUSIC THROUGH THE CENTURIES. Boston: Bruce Humphries, 1963. 744 p. Music, photos.

Designed to aid the music listener to acquire perceptivity. An in-depth study of music from early to contemporary periods. Bibliography.

Sachs, Curt. RHYTHM AND TEMPO: A STUDY IN MUSIC HISTORY. New York: W.W. Norton and Co., 1953. 391 p. Illus., music.

An in-depth history of rhythm and tempo in music from primitive beginnings to the twentieth century.

_____. THE RISE OF MUSIC IN THE ANCIENT WORLD EAST AND WEST. New York: W.W. Norton and Co., 1943. 324 p. Illus., music.

An in-depth study of music from ancient times to the Middle Ages.

Sargent, Sir Malcolm, and Cooper, Martin, eds. THE OUTLINE OF MUSIC. New York: Arco Press, 1962. 506 p. Photos.

A nontechnical account of the evolution of Western music from its origins to its most recent developments.

Scholl, Sharon, and White, Sylvia. MUSIC AND THE CULTURE OF MAN. New York: Holt, Rinehart and Winston, 1970. 307 p.

A broad view of music as part of the cultural processes of the Western world. Considers music as an integral part of the corporate life of man, rather than as the isolated activity of remarkable individuals. Bibliography.

Sternfeld, Frederick William, ed. MUSIC FROM THE MIDDLE AGES TO THE

RENAISSANCE. Praeger History of Western Music, vol. 1. New York: Praeger, 1973. 524 p. Music.

Traces the history of music from its roots in ancient Greece to 1600. Discussion focuses on the major trends, rather than on biographical details. Bibliography and discography.

_____. MUSIC IN THE MODERN AGE. Praeger History of Western Music, vol. 5. New York: Praeger, 1973. 515 p. Music.

Covers the development of Western music from Debussy to the more recent techniques of Boulez. Representative composers are presented to illustrate significant trends. Extensive bibliography and discography.

Stevenson, Robert [Murrell]. MUSIC BEFORE THE CLASSIC ERA: AN INTRODUCTORY GUIDE. London: Macmillan, 1958. Reprint. Westport, Conn.: Greenwood Press, 1973. 215 p. Music.

Covers the development of music from Biblical times to the middle of the eighteenth century. A nontechnical approach. Bibliography.

Stevenson, Ronald. WESTERN MUSIC: AN INTRODUCTION. New York: St. Martin's Press, 1972. 216 p.

The social and historical aspects of music are developed. Bibliography.

Strunk, Oliver. SOURCE READINGS IN MUSIC HISTORY: FROM CLASSICAL ANTIQUITY THROUGH THE ROMANTIC ERA. New York: W.W. Norton and Co., 1950. 919 p. Music.

Contains representative selections from many great writings on music from Plato and Aristotle to Liszt and Wagner. Bibliography.

Thompson, Verne W., and Selhorst, Eugene J. STUDIES IN MUSIC LITERATURE: CLASSICAL PERIOD TO PRESENT DAY. Dubuque, Iowa: William C. Brown Co., 1968. 95 p.

A survey of the literature of music from the mid-eighteenth century to the mid-twentieth century. Lists the main developments and representative compositions. Grouped according to style periods and countries. Bibliography.

Ulrich, Homer, and Pisk, Paul A. A HISTORY OF MUSIC AND MUSICAL STYLE. New York: Harcourt, Brace, and World, 1963. 696 p. Music.

A history of music that places emphasis on musical style rather than on the composers. Bibliography.

Wachsmann, Klaus P., ed. ESSAYS ON MUSIC AND HISTORY IN AFRICA. Evanston, Ill.: Northwestern University Press, 1971. 268 p. Illus., music.

A collection of essays describing the history and organization of music, musical instruments, and the interrelation of African and Arabian musics. Bibliographical references.

Wallaschek, Richard. PRIMITIVE MUSIC: AN INQUIRY INTO THE ORIGINS AND DEVELOPMENT OF MUSIC, SONGS, INSTRUMENTS, DANCES AND PANTOMIMES OF SAVAGE RACES. 1893. Reprint. New York: Da Capo Press, 1970. 326 p.

An investigation of the music of savage races and its relationship to the comparatively advanced culture of ancient civilization. Bibliography.

Westrup, Sir Jack A. AN INTRODUCTION TO MUSICAL HISTORY. New York: Harper and Row, 1964. 174 p.

Valuable for its discussion of problems and conditions inherent in music history writing.

_____. THE NEW OXFORD HISTORY OF MUSIC. New York: Oxford University Press, 1954-- .

Planned as a replacement of the OXFORD HISTORY OF MUSIC. A complete survey of music from the earliest times down to the present day, including the contributions of the Western world, Eastern civilizations, and primitive societies. Of the eleven volumes scheduled for publication, the following volumes are presently available:

I. ANCIENT AND ORIENTAL MUSIC. Edited by Egon Wellesz. 1957. 530 p.

II. EARLY MEDIEVAL MUSIC UP TO 1300. Edited by Dom Anselm Hughes. 1954. 434 p.

III. ARS NOVA AND THE RENAISSANCE (c. 1300-1540). Edited by Dom Anselm Hughes and Gerald Abraham. 1960. 565 p.

IV. THE AGE OF HUMANISM (1540-1630). Edited by Gerald Abraham. 1968. 978 p.

VII. THE AGE OF ENLIGHTENMENT (1745-1970). Edited by Wellesz and Sternfeld, 1973. 724 p.

X. THE MODERN AGE (1890-1960). Edited by Martin Cooper. 1975. 764 p.

Wiora, Walter. THE FOUR AGES OF MUSIC. Translated by M.D. Herter. New York: W.W. Norton and Co., 1965. 233 p.

Departs from the traditional approach of presenting music history by periods. Instead, the author employs a procedure of historical synthesis which demonstrates the common trends, styles, and techniques found in all eras, societies, and cultures. Bibliography.

Worner, Karl H. HISTORY OF MUSIC. 5th ed. Translated and supplemented by Willis [Joseph] Wager. New York: Macmillan, 1973. 608 p.

The scope of this broadly conceived book includes music from the earliest times (Stone Age), to ancient high civilizations such as Egypt and China, to Europe from the Middle Ages to the present. Special effort has been made to relate developments to America.

ASSOCIATIONS

American Institute of Musicology (AIM), C.P. 515, San Silvestro, Rome, Italy.

Publications: CORPUS MENSURABILIS MUSICAE.

CORPUS SCRIPTORUM DE MUSICA.

MUSICOLOGICAL STUDIES AND DOCUMENTS.

MISCELLANEA.

CORPUS OF EARLY KEYBOARD MUSIC.

MUSICA DISCIPLINA.

American Musicological Society (AMS), University of Pennsylvania, 201 South 34th Street, Philadelphia, Pa. 19174.

The society is primarily concerned with the advancement of scholarly research in the various aspects of music, musical history, and science.

Publications: AMERICAN MUSICOLOGICAL SOCIETY JOURNAL. 3/year.

Newsletter. Semiannual.

Abstracts of papers read at annual meetings.

Lists of doctoral dissertations and masters' theses.

International Musicological Society, P.O. Box 588, CH-4001 Basel, Switzerland.

Publications: ACTA MUSICOLOGICA. Semiannual.

Reports on musical data, documents, literature, and sources.

Society for Ethnomusicology (SEM), Room 513, 201 South Main, Ann Arbor, Mich. 48108.

Publications: Newsletter. 6/year.

ETHNOMUSICOLOGY. 3/year.

Section 36
MUSICOLOGY

The references cited here are representative guides to the literature, also serving to describe the nature of the discipline itself. The coverage does not attempt to be exhaustive but rather is intended to be suitable to the work of the American music educator.

Allen, Warren D. PHILOSOPHIES OF MUSIC HISTORY: A STUDY OF GENERAL HISTORIES OF MUSIC 1600-1960. New York: Dover Publications, 1962. 382 p. Illus., photos.

A document which has had much influence on the establishment of foundational philosophy and methodology of the science of musicology in America. Penetrating analysis of historical musicological studies, covering both individual works and philosophical questions. Bibliography.

American Musicological Society, Greater New York Chapter. MUSICOLOGY AND THE COMPUTER, MUSICOLOGY 1966-2000: A PRACTICAL PROGRAM. (THREE SYMPOSIA.) Edited by Barry S. Brook. New York: City University of New York Press, 1970. 275 p. Illus., music.

A compilation of papers by leading musicologists on the subject of computer applications to various aspects of music. In addition, the volume contains one of the finest bibliographies on the subject.

Brook, Barry S., et al., eds. PERSPECTIVES IN MUSICOLOGY. New York: W.W. Norton and Co., 1972. 363 p.

The state and growth of musical scholarship as viewed by fifteen leading musicologists. Bibliography.

Bukofzer, Manfred [F.]. THE PLACE OF MUSICOLOGY IN AMERICAN INSTITUTIONS OF HIGHER LEARNING. New York: Liberal Arts Press, 1957. 52 p.

A description of musicology and the frame of reference within which it should be studied. Describes European and American plans of instruction.

Daugherty, D.H., et al. A BIBLIOGRAPHY OF PERIODICAL LITERATURE IN MUSICOLOGY AND ALLIED FIELDS, NUMBER 1 AND 2, OCTOBER, 1938--SEPTEMBER, 1940 WITH A RECORD OF GRADUATE THESES ACCEPTED, OCTOBER, 1938--SEPTEMBER, 1939. 2 vols. in 1. Reprint of 1940 and 1943 eds. New York: Da Capo Press, 1972. 150 p.

Includes musicians; history; theory; pedagogy; ethnology; psychology and aesthetics; physics, including acoustics.

Duckles, Vincent Harris, comp. MUSIC REFERENCE AND RESEARCH MATERIALS: AN ANNOTATED BIBLIOGRAPHY. 3d ed. New York: Free Press, 1974. 526 p.

One of the most useful anthologies and practical guides to music bibliographies available to musicologists and music educators. For additional information see Section 11: Selected Guides to Bibliographic Sources.

Harrison, Frank L., et al. MUSICOLOGY. Englewood Cliffs, N.J.: Prentice-Hall, 1963. 337 p. Illus., photos.

An overview of musicology as an acknowledged science. Defines and discusses the difficulties involved in studying unfamiliar musical cultures. Suggests ways of linking musicology and other areas of the humanities.

Haydon, Glen. INTRODUCTION TO MUSICOLOGY: A SURVEY OF THE FIELDS, SYSTEMATIC AND HISTORICAL, OF MUSICAL KNOWLEDGE AND RESEARCH. Englewood Cliffs, N.J.: Prentice-Hall, 1941. Reprint. Chapel Hill: University of North Carolina Press, 1959. 329 p.

An early and important work defining musicology as a research subject. Bibliography.

Krohn, Ernst C., comp. THE HISTORY OF MUSIC: AN INDEX TO THE LITERATURE AVAILABLE IN A SELECTED GROUP OF MUSICOLOGICAL PUBLICATIONS. Rev. ed. St. Louis, Mo.: Baton Music Co., 1958. 488 p.

An index of special value to the serious researcher in music history and musicological matters.

Mixter, Keith E. GENERAL BIBLIOGRAPHY FOR MUSIC RESEARCH. 2d ed. Detroit Studies in Music Bibliography, no. 4. Detroit: Information Coordinators, 1975. 135 p.

A guide to references to bibliographic tools for research in music. Highly useful to the serious researcher.

Parrish, Carl. THE NOTATION OF MEDIEVAL MUSIC. New York: W.W. Norton and Co., 1957. 234 p. Illus., music, photos.

Describes the development of notation from the late ninth century, when the first written musical notation of western Europe appeared, to the beginning of the fifteenth century, including the Ars Nova.

Pruett, James W., ed. STUDIES IN MUSICOLOGY: ESSAYS IN THE HISTORY, STYLE, AND BIBLIOGRAPHY OF MUSIC IN MEMORY OF GLEN HAYDON. Chapel Hill: University of North Carolina Press, 1969. 286 p.

A collection of stimulating musicological essays written by Haydon's contemporaries in the United States and Europe.

RILM ABSTRACTS. (Repertoire Internationale de la Litterature Musicale--[International repertory of musical literature]). New York: International RILM Center--The City University of New York, 1967-- . Quarterly.

For description see Section 9: Abstracting Journals.

RISM (International Inventory of Musical Sources).

This series of publications of catalogs of available bibliographical music works is a major tool for locating primary source material. For description see Section 11: Selected Guides to Bibliographic Sources.

Schnapper, Edith B., ed. BRITISH UNION CATALOGUE OF EARLY MUSIC PRINTED BEFORE THE YEAR 1801. 2 vols. Hamden, Conn.: Shoe String Press, 1957.

This is a catalog of printed music published before the end of 1800 now preserved in more than one hundred libraries throughout the British Isles. Most European countries are represented.

Spiess, Lincoln Bruce. HISTORICAL MUSICOLOGY: A REFERENCE MANUAL FOR RESEARCH IN MUSIC. New York: Institute of Medieval Music, 1963. 294 p.

Details sources for researching in the fields of music history and musicology. A significant tool.

Stevenson, Robert Murrell. RENAISSANCE AND BAROQUE MUSICAL SOURCES IN THE AMERICAS. Washington, D.C.: General Secretariat, Organization of American States, 1970. 346 p. Music.

Watanabe, Ruth T. INTRODUCTION TO MUSIC RESEARCH. Englewood Cliffs, N.J.: Prentice-Hall, 1967. 237 p.

While the book is designed as a handbook for the serious graduate student or researcher, the chapters "Bibliography: Music," and "Survey of Contemporary Music Periodicals" are particularly useful as guides to musicological literature.

For dissertations in the field of musicology see Section 15: Dissertations, and Section 16: Masters' Theses. For other related sources see the following sections: Section 37: Ethnomusicology, Section 38: Folk Music and Folklore, Section 35: History of Music, Section 49: Musical Instruments--Historical References, Section 10: Thematic Indexes and Catalogs, Section 1: Guides to Special Libraries and Collections, Section 11: Selected Guides to Bibliographic Sources.

JOURNALS

Since so much of the important musicological literature appears in periodicals and journals, the following additional sources are suggested.

ACTA MUSICOLOGICA, Societé International de Musicologie, Basel, Switzerland.

The official journal of the International Musicological Society. Includes a listing of all non-American dissertations of historical interest, beginning with the Fall 1972 issue. The compilation is supplemented annually. Text in English, French, and German.

AMERICAN MUSICOLOGICAL SOCIETY JOURNAL, American Musicological Society, William Byrd Press, 2901 Byrdhill Road, Richmond, Va. 23205.

One of the most important journals on this subject in the English language. It makes available articles, speeches, and research reports concerning various aspects of musicology.

ARTI MUSICES, Institute of Musicology, Music Academy in Zagreb, Gunduliceva 6, Zagreb, Yugoslavia.

BACH, Riemenschneider Bach Institute, Baldwin-Wallace College, Berea, Ohio 44017.

THE BRITISH CATALOGUE OF MUSIC, Council of the British National Bibliography, London, England.

CHORD AND DISCORD, Bruckner Society of America, P.O. Box 1171, Iowa City, Iowa 52240.

Irregular.

COLLEGE MUSIC SYMPOSIUM, College Music Society, Inc., c/o College of Arts and Sciences, Rutgers University, New Brunswick, N.J. 08903.

CURRENT MUSICOLOGY, Columbia University, Department of Music, New York, N.Y. 10027. Semiannual.

Provides news of current activities in musicology. Includes information about domestic and foreign scholarships and fellowships available to North American students of music. Also wide range of articles dealing with history of music, criticism, pedagogy, methodology, psychology and music, physiology and music, and so forth.

DISSERTATION ABSTRACTS INTERNATIONAL, Xerox University Microfilms, Ann Arbor, Mich. 48106.

See Section 15: Dissertations.

EARLY MUSIC, Oxford University Press, 200 Madison Avenue, New York, N.Y. 11216.

ETHNOMUSICOLOGY, Society for Ethnomusicology, Wesleyan University Press, Middletown, Conn. 06457.

INSTITUTE OF ETHNOMUSICOLOGY, SELECTED REPORTS, Institute of Ethnomusicology, University of California at Los Angeles, Los Angeles, Calif. 90024.

JOURNAL OF AESTHETICS AND ART CRITICISM, Wayne State University, Detroit, Mich. 48202. Quarterly.

The summer issue contains a current bibliography of fields covered by the journal, with a section on music and musicology.

MISCELLANEA MUSICOLOGICA: ADELAIDE STUDIES IN MUSICOLOGY, Libraries Board of South Australia, Adelaide, Australia.

MUSICA DISCIPLINA: A YEARBOOK OF THE HISTORY OF MUSIC, American Institute of Musicology, P.O. Box 33655, Dallas, Tex. 75230.

THE MUSICAL QUARTERLY, c/o G. Schirmer, Inc., 609 Fifth Avenue, New York, N.Y. 10017.

Contains articles by experts in every field of musical knowledge; current reports on musical events from all areas in the United States and in foreign countries; reviews of new books and recordings.

MUSIC AND LETTERS, Oxford University Press, 44 Conduit Street, London W1R ODE Engl. Quarterly.

THE MUSIC FORUM, Columbia University Press, Irvington, N.Y. 10533. Annual.

A scholarly journal devoted to many areas of music, especially musicology.

NOTES, Music Library Association, School of Music, University of Michigan, Ann Arbor, Mich. 48105.

One of the most reliable and scholarly reference journals in the field of serious music. Provides bibliographies and various lists, reviews books and records, and surveys musical literature.

QUARTERLY CHECKLIST OF MUSICOLOGY, American Bibliographic Service, P.O. Box 1141, Darien, Conn. 06820.

RENAISSANCE QUARTERLY (formerly RENAISSANCE NEWS), 1161 Amsterdam Avenue, New York, N.Y. 10027.

REVISTA ITALIANA DI MUSICOLOGIA, Societa Italiana di Musicologia, Viuzzo del Pozzetto (Viale Europa), 50126 Florence, Italy.

REVUE DE MUSICOLOGIE, Societe Francaise de Musicologie, 28 F. Heugel, Depositaire Exclusif, 2 Bix rue Vivienne, Paris (2e) France.

SEM NEWSLETTER, Society for Ethnomusicology, Trent University, Peterborough, Ontario, Canada.

SPECULUM, 1430 Massachusetts Avenue, Cambridge, Mass. 02138.

STUDIA MUSICOLOGICA, Publishing House of the Hungarian Academy of Sciences, Alkotmany U. 21, Budapest 5, Hungary.

Text in English, French, German, Italian, or Russian.

STUDIES IN MUSIC, University Bookshop, Nedlands, Western Australia.

STUDIES IN THE RENAISSANCE, 1161 Amsterdam Avenue, New York, N.Y. 10027. Annual.

ASSOCIATIONS

American Institute of Musicology (AIM), C.P. 515, San Silvestro, Rome, Italy.

Publications: CORPUS MENSURABILIS MUSICAE.

CORPUS SCRIPTORUM DE MUSICA.

MUSICOLOGICAL STUDIES AND DOCUMENTS.

MISCELLANEA.

CORPUS OF EARLY KEYBOARD MUSIC.

MUSICA DISCIPLINA.

American Musical Instrument Society (AMIS), Seventeen Lincoln Avenue, Massapequa Park, N.Y. 11762.

Publications: Newsletter. 3/year.

Journal. Annual.

Membership Roster. Annual.

AMERICAN MUSICAL INSTRUMENT MAKERS DIRECTORY.

American Musicological Society (AMS), University of Pennsylvania, 201 South 34th Street, Philadelphia, Pa. 19174.

The society is primarily concerned with the advancement of scholarly research in the various aspects of music, musical history, and science.

Publications: AMERICAN MUSICOLOGICAL SOCIETY JOURNAL. 3/year.

Newsletter. Semiannual.

Abstracts of papers read at annual meetings.

Lists of doctoral dissertations and masters' theses.

Bruckner Society of America, P.O. Box 2570, Iowa City, Iowa 52240.

Publication: CHORD AND DISCORD. Irregular.

International Bach Society, Institute for Bach Studies, 165 West 57th Street, New York, N.Y. 10019.

Perpetuates high standards of performance, provides study grants, and has created a Bach repertory group.

Publication: REPORT TO MEMBERS. 3/year.

International Gustav Mahler Gesellschaft (IGMG), (also known as International Gustav Mahler Society), 6/2 Wiedner Gurtel, A-1040, Vienna, Austria.

Publications: NEWS ABOUT MAHLER RESEARCH. Semiannual.

HERAUSGABE DER KRITISHEN GESAMTAUSGABE DER WERKE GUSTAV MAHLERS. Irregular.

International Heinrich Schutz Society, 35 Kassel-Wilhelmshohe, Heinrich Schutz-Allee 35, Hessen, West Germany.

Publications: ACTA SAGITTARIANE. Irregular.

SAGITTARIUS. Annual.

Musicology

International Musicological Society, P.O. Box 588, CH-4001 Basel, Switzerland.

Publications: ACTA MUSICOLOGICA. Semiannual.

Reports on musical data, documents, literature, and sources.

See also Section 37: Ethnomusicology.

Section 37
ETHNOMUSICOLOGY

The literature pertaining to various ethnic musics is considerable. Since this guide seeks to meet the usual research needs of music educators, the references presented here are those which describe ethnomusicological methods, materials, and bibliographical resources. Works concerning specific ethnic musics may be found in bibliographies contained in the materials cited.

ABSTRACTS IN ANTHROPOLOGY. Westport, Conn.: Greenwood Press, 1970-- . 4/year.

Boulton, Laura. MUSICAL INSTRUMENTS OF WORLD CULTURES. New York: Intercultural Arts Press, 1972. 89 p. Illus., photos, paper.

Selected examples of instruments as related to various cultures.

Brandel, Rose. THE MUSIC OF CENTRAL AFRICA: AN ETHNOMUSICOLOGICAL STUDY. The Hague: Nijhoff, 1961. 272 p. Illus., music, photos.

A scholarly report of research in the music of Central Africa. Deals with all aspects of the music and compares the various elements. Bibliography.

Briegleb, Ann. DIRECTORY OF ETHNOMUSICOLOGICAL SOUND RECORDING COLLECTIONS IN THE UNITED STATES AND CANADA. Ann Arbor, Mich.: Society for Enthnomusicology, 1971. 45 p.

A useful guide to the location of ethnomusicological recordings. Includes descriptions of technical facilities, collection content, and geographical index.

Chao-Mei-Pa. THE YELLOW BELL: A BRIEF SKETCH OF THE HISTORY OF CHINESE MUSIC. Baldwin, Md.: Barbery Hill, 1934. 61 p.

An introduction to Chinese music. Bibliography.

Collaer, Paul. MUSIC OF THE AMERICAS: AN ILLUSTRATED MUSIC ETHNOLOGY OF THE ESKIMO AND AMERICAN INDIAN PEOPLES. Translated by Irene Gibbons. New York: Praeger, 1970. 207 p. Music, photos.

A comprehensive coverage of the development of Eskimo and American Indian music. Includes a brief account of the anthropology and culture of the pre-European settlers and their influences. Bibliography.

Deva, Bigamundre Chaitanya. AN INTRODUCTION TO INDIAN MUSIC. New Delhi: Ministry of Information, Publications Division, 1973. 130 p. Photos.

A comprehensive, analytical coverage which describes the structure, sociohistorical background, and aesthetics of Indian music. Bibliography and discography.

Gillis, Frank, and Merriam, Alan P., comps. and eds. ETHNOMUSICOLOGY AND FOLK MUSIC: AN INTERNATIONAL BIBLIOGRAPHY OF DISSERTATIONS AND THESES. Middletown, Conn.: Wesleyan University Press, 1966. 148 p.

A partially annotated bibliography which includes Negro music, jazz, the education of youth and children in non-Western music, the sociology and psychology of music, and the computer in music research.

Hood, Mantle. THE ETHNOMUSICOLOGIST. New York: McGraw-Hill Book Co., 1971. 386 p. Illus.

While intended for ethnomusicologists, this work is of value to music educators with need for information related to Asian, African, and numerous other ethnic musics.

Jenkins, Jean, ed. ETHNIC MUSICAL INSTRUMENTS: IDENTIFICATION-CONSERVATION. London: H. Evelyn for the International Council of Museums. New York: Unipub, 1970. 59 p. Illus.

Suggestions for identifying, cataloging, conserving, and restoring ethnic musical instruments.

Kunst, Jaap. ETHNOMUSICOLOGY. 3d ed. The Hague: Nijhoff, 1959. 303 p. Illus., music. SUPPLEMENT. The Hague: Nijhoff, 1960. 45 p.

Provides one of the largest and most useful bibliographies on the subject.

Merriam, Alan P. THE ANTHROPOLOGY OF MUSIC. Evanston, Ill.: Northwestern University Press, 1964. 358 p.

A serious and important attempt to change the traditional manner of viewing music. Demonstrates through the findings of ethnomusicological research that many concepts held by Westerners regarding music are culture-bound and not reflective of a universal pattern of musical behavior.

Music Educators National Conference. MUSIC IN WORLD CULTURES. Introduction by Margaret Mead. Washington, D.C.: 1972. 138 p. Paper.

An exact reprinting of all articles, photographs, recordings, and references from the October 1972 MUSIC EDUCATORS JOURNAL. Identifies the music of eight global areas, and describes implementation at all levels of education.

Nettl, Bruno. REFERENCE MATERIALS IN ETHNOMUSICOLOGY. 2d rev. ed. Detroit: Information Coordinators, 1969. 40 p.

Bibliographic essay which succinctly evaluates books and articles on primitive, oriental, and folk music.

_____. THEORY AND METHOD IN ETHNOMUSICOLOGY. Riverside, N.J.: Free Press, 1964. 305 p.

A most practical and useful resource for the study of non-Western and folk cultures, individually or in groups. Chapter entitled "Bibliographical Resources of Ethnomusicology," pp. 27-61, is especially useful for additional sources.

UNESCO. AFRICAN MUSIC. New York: Unipub, 1973. 154 p. Illus.

A discussion of historical influences and current trends in African music as viewed by African musical experts.

A considerable number of additional references related to ethnic music are to be found in the following sections: Section 36: Musicology; Section 35: History of Music; Section 38: Folk Music and Folklore; Section 34: Appreciation and Understanding of Music; and Section 49: Musical Instruments--Historical References.

ASSOCIATIONS

African Music Society, P.O. Box 138, Roodeport, Transvaal, South Africa.

Publication: AFRICAN MUSIC.

Afro-American Music Opportunities Association, 2909 Wayzata Boulevard, Minneapolis, Minn. 55405.

Publications: AAMOA REPORTS. Bimonthly.

Resource Papers. Irregular.

Black Music Center, Black Culture Center, 109 North Jordan Street, Bloomington, Ind. 47401.

Institute of Ethnomusicology, UCLA, 045 Hilgard Avenue, Los Angeles, Calif. 90024.

Society for Asian Music, Asia House, 112 East 64th Street, New York, N.Y. 10021.

Publication: ASIAN MUSIC. Semiannual.

Society for Ethnomusicology (SEM), Room 513, 201 South Main, Ann Arbor, Mich. 48108.

Publications: Newsletter. 6/year.

ETHNOMUSICOLOGY. 3/year.

See also Section 36: Musicology.

Section 38

FOLK MUSIC AND FOLKLORE

GENERAL

Buchner, Alexander. FOLK MUSIC INSTRUMENTS OF THE WORLD. New York: Crown, 1972. 292 p. Illus.

A study of the most primitive to more recent folk music instruments from around the world.

CATALOG OF FOLKLORE AND FOLK SONGS. 2 vols. Boston, Mass.: G.K. Hall & Co., 1964.

Catalog of the John G. White Department, Cleveland Public Library.

Dean-Smith, Margaret. A GUIDE TO ENGLISH FOLK SONG COLLECTIONS 1826-1952. Liverpool: University Press of Liverpool in association with The English Folk Dance and Song Society, 1954. 120 p.

Includes index to contents of songs and historical annotations.

Gillis, Frank, and Merriam, Alan P., comps. and eds. ETHNOMUSICOLOGY AND FOLK MUSIC: AN INTERNATIONAL BIBLIOGRAPHY OF DISSERTATIONS AND THESES. Middletown, Conn.: Wesleyan University Press, 1966. 148 p.

A partially annotated bibliography which includes such topics as Negro music, jazz, the education of youth and children in non-Western music, the sociology and psychology of music, and the computer in music research.

Haywood, Charles, ed. FOLK SONGS OF THE WORLD. New York: John Day Co., 1966. 320 p.

Contains original texts, English translations, and notes on each of 180 songs from 119 countries. Bibliographies and lists of recordings.

Hickerson, Joseph C., comp. A LIST OF AMERICAN RECORD COMPANIES SPECIALIZING IN FOLK MUSIC. Washington, D.C.: Library of Congress, 1972. 5 p. Paper.

Library of Congress. Music Division. A BIBLIOGRAPHY OF PUBLICATIONS RELATING TO THE ARCHIVE OF FOLK SONG. Washington, D.C.: 1971. 5 p. Paper.

Lloyd, A.L. FOLK SONG IN ENGLAND. New York: International Publishers, 1967. 433 p. Music.

Traces the development of folk song style with the evolution of English society.

Lomax, Alan. FOLK SONG STYLE AND CULTURE. Washington, D.C.: American Association for the Advancement of Science, 1968. 363 p. Illus., music.

A scholarly report of the research activities of a group of skilled musicologists, linguists, anthropologists, statisticians, programmers, and movement analysts. Deals with the universal relationships of folk music and culture. Bibliography and film source listing.

Nettl, Bruno. FOLK AND TRADITIONAL MUSIC OF THE WESTERN CONTINENT. 2d ed. Englewood Cliffs, N.J.: Prentice-Hall, 1973. 258 p. Music, illus.

A comprehensive survey of traditional and folk music of Europe, Africa, and America. Excellent bibliography and discography at the end of each section.

Vetterl, Karel, ed. in chief. A SELECT BIBLIOGRAPHY OF EUROPEAN FOLK MUSIC. Prague: Institute for Ethnography and Folklore of the Czechoslovak Academy of Sciences (in cooperation with the International Folk Music Council), 1966. 144 p.

Lists many useful publications, especially those of a scholarly nature, that bear on the folk music of particular European countries.

White, Rev. Edward A., comp. AN INDEX OF ENGLISH SONGS. Edited by Margaret Dean-Smith. London: The English Folk Dance and Song Society, 1951. 58 p.

An index of those songs contributed to the JOURNAL OF THE FOLK SONG SOCIETY between 1899 and 1931, and its continuation, the JOURNAL OF THE ENGLISH FOLK DANCE AND SONG SOCIETY to 1950. Indexed according to titles and first lines as well as special categories, such as carols, chanties, game-songs, and so forth.

AMERICAN MUSIC (INCLUDING COUNTRY AND WESTERN)

Barry, Phillips, ed. BULLETIN OF THE FOLK-SONG SOCIETY OF THE NORTHEAST #1-12. Cambridge, Mass.: Powell Printing Co., 1930-37.

Traces the traditional history of the ballads, songs, conte-fables, and music of the regions mentioned.

Brown, Len, and Friedrich, Gary. THE ENCYCLOPEDIA OF COUNTRY AND WESTERN MUSIC. New York: Tower Publishers, 1971. 191 p. Photos.

An informal but highly useful directory which includes brief biographies of outstanding performers and indications of record successes.

Combs, Josiah. FOLK SONGS OF THE SOUTHERN UNITED STATES. Edited by D.K. Wilgus. Austin: University of Texas Press, 1967. 254 p.

FOLK SONGS DU MIDI DES ETATS-UNIS, published as a doctoral dissertation at the University of Paris in 1925, was an introduction to the study of the folk songs of the Southern Appalachians, together with a selection of folk song texts selected by Combs. FOLK SONGS OF THE SOUTHERN UNITED STATES, the first publication of that work in English, is based on the French text and Combs's English draft. To this is appended an annotated history of all songs in the Josiah H. Combs Collection in the Western Kentucky Folklore Archive at the University of California, Los Angeles.

Cox, John Harrington. FOLK SONGS OF THE SOUTH. Cambridge, Mass.: Harvard University Press, 1925. 545 p. Music.

A collection of the texts of indigenous southern folk songs.

Davis, Arthur Kyle, Jr. FOLK-SONGS OF VIRGINIA. Durham, N.C.: Duke University Press, 1949. 389 p.

A descriptive index and classification of folk songs, all types that are seemingly traditionally known in Virginia, with their variants.

Denisoff, R. Serge. GREAT DAY COMING: FOLK MUSIC AND THE AMERICAN LEFT. Urbana: University of Illinois Press, 1971. 219 p. Photos.

An examination of the use of folk music by the American Left, especially the Communist Party during the 1930s and 1940s, to achieve sociopolitical results. Bibliography and discography.

Gentry, Linnell. A HISTORY AND ENCYCLOPEDIA OF COUNTRY, WESTERN, AND GOSPEL MUSIC. St. Clair Shores, Mich.: Scholarly Press, 1972. 380 p.

Haywood, Charles. A BIBLIOGRAPHY OF NORTH AMERICAN FOLKLORE AND FOLKSONG. 2d rev. ed. 2 vols. New York: Dover Publications, 1961. 1,301 p.

Indispensible bibliography of books, articles, periodicals, music, records, etc. First volume covers American social and occupational groups, blues, Negro material, and so on; second volume covers general and Indian materials.

Hemphill, Paul. THE NASHVILLE SOUND: BRIGHT LIGHTS AND COUNTRY MUSIC. New York: Simon and Schuster, 1970. 289 p.

A description of country and western music, its background, and aspects of the culture in which it flourishes.

Herzog, George. RESEARCH IN PRIMITIVE AND FOLK MUSIC IN THE UNITED STATES: A SURVEY. Bulletin no. 24. Washington, D.C.: American Council of Learned Societies, April 1936. 97 p.

The serious researcher in the field of primitive and folk music in the United States will continue to find this scholarly survey useful in spite of the fact that it was first issued more than thirty years ago.

Hickerson, Joseph C., comp. AMERICAN FOLKLORE: A BIBLIOGRAPHY OF MAJOR WORKS. Washington, D.C.: Music Educators National Conference, 1973. 22 p. Paper.

Includes: General Works; Regional and Occupational Collections; American Indian Folklore; Negro Folklore; Specific Genres; Folk Arts and Crafts; Folk Architecture; Folk Belief and Custom; Proverb and Riddle; Folk Speech; Folk Song and Rhyme; Play/Party/Dance/Games; plus an addendum.

______. A BIBLIOGRAPHY OF HAMMERED AND PLUCKED (APPALACHIAN OR MOUNTAIN) DULCIMERS AND RELATED INSTRUMENTS. Washington, D.C.: Library of Congress, 1973. 9 p. Paper.

______. A LIST OF FOLKLORE AND FOLK MUSIC ARCHIVES AND RELATED COLLECTIONS IN THE UNITED STATES AND CANADA. Washington, D.C.: Library of Congress, 1972. 9 p. Paper.

______. 1973 FOLK MUSIC FESTIVALS, FIDDLERS' CONVENTIONS, AND RELATED EVENTS IN THE UNITED STATES AND CANADA. Washington, D.C.: Library of Congress, 1973. 40 p.

A comprehensive list, organized according to states, useful as an indicator of the range of activities of this type in the United States and Canada.

_____. NORTH AMERICAN FOLKLORE AND FOLK MUSIC SERIAL PUBLICATIONS. Washington, D.C.: Library of Congress, 1973. 8 p. Paper.

A listing of names and addresses of 123 serial folk music publications.

_____. NORTH AMERICAN FOLKLORE AND FOLKSONG SOCIETIES AND FIDDLERS' ASSOCIATIONS. Washington, D.C.: Library of Congress, n.d. 13 p. Paper.

A listing of 116 folklore societies located in the United States and Canada. Contains names and addresses with names of some executive officers.

Lawless, Ray M. FOLKSINGERS AND FOLKSONGS IN AMERICA. New York: Duell, Sloan, and Pearce, 1965. 750 p. Photos.

A handbook of biography, bibliography, and discography. Comprehensive and highly useful.

Library of Congress. Music Division. Archive of American Folk Song. CHECK-LIST OF RECORDED SONGS IN THE ENGLISH LANGUAGE IN THE ARCHIVE OF AMERICAN FOLK SONG TO JULY, 1940. 3 vols. Washington, D.C.: 1942.

_____. FOLK MUSIC: A CATALOG OF FOLK SONGS, BALLADS, DANCES, INSTRUMENTAL PIECES, AND FOLK TALES OF THE UNITED STATES AND LATIN AMERICA ON PHONOGRAPH RECORDS. Washington, D.C.: Government Printing Office, 1965. 107 p.

A sampling of folk music, most of which was recorded in its native environment and is available for purchase from the Library of Congress.

_____. RECENT PUBLICATIONS ON FOLKLORE ARCHIVES AND ARCHIVING IN NORTH AMERICA, 1969-1971. Washington, D.C.: 1971. 3 p. Paper.

Lomax, Alan, and Cowell, Sidney Robertson. AMERICAN FOLKSONG AND FOLK LORE, A REGIONAL BIBLIOGRAPHY. P.E.A. Service Center Pamphlet no. 8. New York: Progressive Education Association, 1942. 59 p.

A selected regional listing of American folk songs of the North, the white South, the black South, and the West. Annotated.

Lomax, John, and Lomax, Alan. COWBOY SONGS AND OTHER FRONTIER BALLADS. Rev. ed. New York: Macmillan, 1938. 431 p.

A popular reference work for this folk art.

Malone, Bill C. COUNTRY MUSIC U.S.A.: A FIFTY YEAR HISTORY. Austin: University of Texas Press, 1968. 422 p. Photos.

A general, chronological history of the development of American country music from its folk background to its more recent commercial status. Extensive bibliography and discography.

Mangler, Joyce Ellen. RHODE ISLAND MUSIC AND MUSICIANS 1733-1850. Detroit: Information Coordinators, 1965. 90 p.

Includes directory of persons active in the music community, and listings by profession.

Moore, Ethel, and Moore, Chauncey O. BALLADS AND FOLKSONGS OF THE SOUTHWEST. Norman: University of Oklahoma Press, 1964. 414 p. Music.

Detailed references tracing folk song origins in the area. Excellent bibliography.

Nettl, Bruno. AN INTRODUCTION TO FOLK MUSIC IN THE UNITED STATES. Detroit: Wayne State University Press, 1960. 122 p.

An informal yet important treatment of the various aspects of American folk music.

Pichierri, Louis. MUSIC IN NEW HAMPSHIRE. New York: Columbia University Press, 1960. 297 p.

A survey of music and music instruction in New Hampshire as it developed from the earliest settlement of the colony to the beginning of the nineteenth century.

Price, Steven D. OLD AS THE HILLS: THE STORY OF BLUEGRASS MUSIC. New York: Viking Press, 1975. 256 p.

Useful as a historical reference to the origins and development of bluegrass music. Includes bluegrass clubs and magazines. Discography.

Rosenberg, Bruce A. THE FOLKSONGS OF VIRGINIA: A CHECKLIST. Charlottesville: University Press of Virginia, 1969. 145 p.

A list of the Works Progress Administration holdings of the Alderman Library, University of Virginia.

Sharp, Cecil. ENGLISH FOLK SONGS FROM THE SOUTHERN APPALACHIANS. 2 vols. London and New York: Oxford University Press, 1932. 845 p.

A collection of songs which reveals the culture of the remote mountain people of this area.

Stambler, Irwin. GUITAR YEARS: POP MUSIC FROM COUNTRY AND WESTERN TO HARD ROCK. Garden City, N.Y.: Doubleday and Co., 1970. 137 p. Photos.

A narrative account of the role of the guitar and its players in different styles of music--from country and western, rhythm and blues, rock, folk-rock, and so forth. The relationships of the different musics are also discussed.

Stambler, Irwin, and Landon, Grelun. ENCYCLOPEDIA OF FOLK, COUNTRY, AND WESTERN MUSIC. New York: St. Martin's Press, 1969. 396 p. Illus.

A significant landmark in the field of folk, country, and western music.

_____. GOLDEN GUITARS: THE STORY OF COUNTRY MUSIC. New York: Four Winds Press, 1971. 186 p. Photos, illus.

A narrative, historical account of the origin and development of country and western music. Includes recent innovations. Bibliographic references.

White, Newman I. THE FRANK C. BROWN COLLECTION OF NORTH CAROLINA FOLKLORE. 7 vols. Durham, N.C.: Duke University Press, 1952-64. Illus., music.

Contents are indicated by volume titles: I: GAMES AND RHYMES, BELIEFS, AND CUSTOMS, RIDDLES, PROVERBS, SPEECH, TALES, AND LEGENDS; II: FOLK BALLADS; III: FOLK SONGS; IV: THE MUSIC OF THE FOLK BALLAD; V: THE MUSIC OF THE FOLK SONGS; VI: POPULAR BELIEFS AND SUPERSTITIONS, part 1; VII: POPULAR BELIEFS AND SUPERSTITIONS, part 2. Bibliography.

Wilgus, D.K. ANGLO-AMERICAN FOLKSONG SCHOLARSHIP SINCE 1898. New Brunswick, N.J.: Rutgers University Press, 1959. 466 p.

Particularly useful for researching material for integrating music in general education. Bibliography.

See also Section 37: Ethnomusicology, and appendix A: "Library of Congress--The Music Division," under District of Columbia.

ASSOCIATIONS

The British Folk Music Journals and the publications of the International Folk Music Council which are described below are of particular interest to the serious researcher in this field.

American Folklore Society, Folklore Center, Speech Bldg., 203, University of Texas, Austin, Tex. 78712.

Publications: JOURNAL OF AMERICAN FOLKLORE. Quarterly.

THE MEMOIR SERIES. Irregular.

THE BIBLIOGRAPHICAL AND SPECIAL SERIES. Irregular.

British Folk Music Journals.

The journals which follow (covering the years from 1899 to 1969) constitute a rich resource of folk music collected within the British Isles. All are available from Kraus Reprint, a division of Kraus-Thompson Organization, Ltd. FL-9491 Nendeln, Liechtenstein.

a. Folk Song Society, London. JOURNAL. 1899-1931.

b. English Folk Dance Society, London. JOURNAL. 1914-31.

Bound in one volume

The two journals merged and continued as:

c. English Folk Dance and Song Society, London. JOURNAL. 1932-64.

Continued as:

d. FOLK MUSIC JOURNAL. London: 1965-69.

Country Music Association (CMA), Seven Music Circle North, Nashville, Tenn. 37203.

Publication: CLOSE-UP. Monthly.

Folklore Center, Archives of Traditional Music, 013 Maxwell Hall, Indiana University, Bloomington, Ind. 47401.

Friends of Old-Time Music (FOTM), c/o Folklore Center, 321 Sixth Avenue, New York, N.Y. 10014.

International Folk Music Council (IFMC), Department of Music, Queen's University, Kingston, Ontario, Canada.

A worldwide organization affiliated with UNESCO through its membership in the International Music Council and the International Union of Anthropological and Ethnological Sciences. Holds conferences and publishes materials in the interest of preserving and disseminating information concerning folk music.

Publications: DIRECTORY OF INSTITUTIONS AND ORGANIZATIONS CONCERNED WHOLLY OR IN PART WITH FOLK MUSIC. Edited by R.W.I. Bond. Kingston, Ont.: IFMC, 1964. 40 p.

INTERNATIONAL CATALOGUE OF RECORDED FOLK MUSIC. Edited by Norman Fraser. Kingston, Ont.: Prepared and Published for UNESCO by the IFMC, Oxford University Press, 1954. 210 p.

INTERNATIONAL CATALOGUE OF PUBLISHED RECORDS OF FOLK MUSIC. Edited by Klaus [P.] Wachsmann. Kingston, Ont.: IFMC, 1961.

A sequel to the preceding. Kingston, Canada: IFMC, 1961.

FOLK SONGS OF EUROPE. Edited by Maud Karpeles. London: Novello & Co., 1956.

FOLK SONGS OF THE AMERICAS. Edited by A.L. Lloyd and I. Aretz de Ramon y Rivera. London: Novello & Co., 1965.

THE COLLECTING OF FOLK MUSIC AND OTHER ETHNOMUSICOLOGICAL MATERIAL. Edited by Maud Karpeles. Kingston, Ont.: IFMC, 1958. 44 p.

A SELECT BIBLIOGRAPHY OF EUROPEAN FOLK MUSIC. Edited by Karel Vetterl, Erik Dal, Laurence Picken, and Erich Stockmann. Prague: Published by the Institute for Ethnography and Folklore of the Czechoslovak Academy of Science in cooperation with the IFMC, 1966. 144 p.

ANNUAL BIBLIOGRAPHY OF EUROPEAN ETHNOMUSICOLOGY. Edited by Oskar Elschek, Erich Stockmann, and Ivan Macak. Bratislava, Czechoslovakia: Published by the Slovak Academy of Science, and the German Academy of Science, Berlin, in cooperation with the IFMC, 1967. Annual.

FILMS ON TRADITIONAL MUSIC. A FIRST INTERNATIONAL CATALOGUE. Compiled by the IFMC. Edited by Peter Kennedy. Paris: UNESCO, 1970. 261 p.

This catalog lists films showing performances by traditional exponents of authentic folk dance, song, and instrumental music, together with associated customs and ceremonies in ninety-nine counties.

Also publishes a journal, yearbook, and bulletin.

National Folk Festival Association, 1346 Connecticut Avenue, N.W., Washington, D.C. 20036.

Publication: Newsletter. Quarterly.

For additional sources related to folk music see also Section 37: Ethnomusicology; Section 44: Music and the Black Culture; Section 27: Music in the Elementary School; Section 34: Appreciation and Understanding of Music; Section 35: History of Music; Section 49: Musical Instruments--Historical References.

Section 39

AMERICAN MUSIC

Barzun, Jacques. MUSIC IN AMERICAN LIFE. Bloomington: Indiana University Press, 1965. 126 p.

A major essay in which Professor Barzun expresses his views on the music situation in America. Bibliography.

Buttleman, Clifford V. MUSIC EDUCATORS NATIONAL CONFERENCE AND THE STAR SPANGLED BANNER. Washington, D.C.: Music Educators National Conference, 1964. 13 p. Paper.

Chase, Gilbert. AMERICA'S MUSIC: FROM THE PILGRIMS TO THE PRESENT. 2d rev. ed. New York: McGraw-Hill Book Co., 1967. 759 p.

A chronicle of American music. Includes developments in electronic and computer-produced music.

Claghorn, Charles Eugene. BIOGRAPHICAL DICTIONARY OF AMERICAN MUSIC. West Nyack, N.Y.: Parker Publishing Co., 1974. 491 p.

A comprehensive reference work. More than 5,000 entries are listed, covering all kinds of American music and musicians--from the hymns of the seventeenth century to hard rock of the twentieth century.

Cowell, Henry, ed. AMERICAN COMPOSERS ON AMERICAN MUSIC. Stanford, Calif.: Stanford University Press, 1933. 226 p.

A collection of articles by well-known American composers. Discussions of the direction of the twentieth-century music as well as critical reviews of compositions.

De Lerma, Dominique-René, comp. CHARLES EDWARD IVES, 1874-1954: A BIBLIOGRAPHY OF HIS MUSIC. Kent, Ohio: Kent State University Press, 1970. 212 p.

In addition to the bibliography of music by Ives, this volume includes a publication index; a medium index; a chronological index; an index of arrangers, facts, and librettists; a phonorecord index; and a performer index.

Densmore, Frances. THE MUSIC OF THE NORTH AMERICAN INDIAN. 13 vols. New York: Da Capo Press, 1972. Original publication dates are shown below.

This is a series of reprints of important monographs by the ethnomusicologist, Dr. Frances Densmore.

CHIPPEWA MUSIC. 2 vols. 1910. 557 p.

CHOCTAW MUSIC. 1943. 87 p.

MANDAN AND HIDATSU MUSIC. 1923. 192 p.

MENOMINEE MUSIC. 1932. 230 p.

MUSIC OF ACOMA, ISLETA, COCHITI, AND ZUNI PUEBLOS. 1957. 117 p.

MUSIC OF THE INDIANS OF BRITISH COLUMBIA. 1943. 99 p.

NOOTKA AND QUILEUTE MUSIC. 1939. 358 p.

NORTHERN UTE MUSIC. 1922. 213 p.

PAPAGO MUSIC. 1929. 229 p.

PAWNEE MUSIC. 1929. 129 p.

SEMINOLE MUSIC. 1956. 223 p.

TETON SIOUX MUSIC. 1918. 561 p.

YUMAN AND YAQUI MUSIC. 1932. 216 p.

Dichter, Harry, and Shapiro, Elliot. EARLY AMERICAN SHEET MUSIC, ITS LURE AND ITS LORE, 1768-1889. New York: R.R. Bowker Co., 1941. 287 p. 32 facsim., including music.

Arranged in four parts: I: classified history of early American sheet music; II: directory of early American music publishers; III: lithographers and artists working on American sheet music before 1870; IV: illustrations.

Eagon, Angelo. CATALOG OF PUBLISHED CONCERT MUSIC BY AMERICAN COMPOSERS. 2d ed. Metuchen, N.J.: Scarecrow Press, 1969. 348 p. SUPPLEMENT. Metuchen, N.J.: Scarecrow Press, 1971. 150 p.

Intended as an up-to-date reference for the large repertory of concert music by American composers. Included are works generally available in some printed form, and appropriate for professional and amateur organizations. Listings are for voice (solo or chorus), instrumental (solo or ensemble), concert jazz, percussion, orchestra, opera, and band.

Edmunds, John, and Gordon, Boelzner. SOME TWENTIETH CENTURY AMERICAN COMPOSERS: A SELECTIVE BIBLIOGRAPHY. 2 vols. New York: New York Public Library, 1957.

A bibliography of published writings by and about a representative group of twentieth-century American composers of various tendencies--conservative, dodecaphonic, moderate, and experimental.

Edwards, Arthur C., and Marrocco, W. Thomas. MUSIC IN THE UNITED STATES. Dubuque, Iowa: William C. Brown Co., 1968. 179 p.

A historical survey of music in the United States from the days of the psalters to contemporary electronic music. Bibliography and discography.

Ellinwood, Leonard, and Porter, Keyes, comps. BIO-BIBLIOGRAPHIC INDEX OF MUSICIANS IN THE UNITED STATES OF AMERICA SINCE COLONIAL TIMES. 1941. Reprint. New York: Da Capo Press, 1956. 440 p.

Lists the names of persons who have contributed to the history of music in the United States with references to books which contain information about them.

Ewen, David, comp. and ed. LIVING MUSICIANS. New York. H.W. Wilson Co., 1940. 390 p. SUPPLEMENT. New York: H.W. Wilson Co., 1957. 178 p.

Gives biographical sketches of composers active in today's musical world. Deals primarily with Americans.

Ewen, David, comp. POPULAR AMERICAN COMPOSERS FROM REVOLUTIONARY TIMES TO THE PRESENT: A BIOGRAPHICAL AND CRITICAL GUIDE. New York: H.W. Wilson Co., 1962. 217 p. Photos.

Guide to 130 foremost American popular composers from William Billings to Andre Previn.

Hausman, Ruth L. HAWAII--MUSIC IN ITS HISTORY. Rutland, Vt: Charles E. Tuttle Co., 1968. 112 p. Illus., music.

A historical commentary on the music of the fiftieth state. Many indigenous songs included. Bibliography.

Helbig, Otto H. A HISTORY OF MUSIC IN U.S. ARMED FORCES DURING WORLD WAR II. Philadelphia: M.W. Lads, 1966. 247 p. Illus.

An account of music in the military services during World War II. Includes a considerable amount of documentary evidence to support the material presented.

Historical Records Survey, District of Columbia. BIOGRAPHICAL INDEX OF MUSICIANS IN THE UNITED STATES OF AMERICA SINCE COLONIAL TIMES. 2d ed. Washington, D.C.: Pan American Union, Music Section, 1956. 439 p.

Hitchcock, H. Wiley. MUSIC IN THE UNITED STATES: A HISTORICAL INTRODUCTION. 2d ed. Englewood Cliffs, N.J.: Prentice-Hall, 1974. 288 p.

Gives particular attention to principal composers in whose works the major themes of twentieth-century American music have been expressed most clearly and with the most influence.

Hixon, Donald L. MUSIC IN EARLY AMERICA: A BIBLIOGRAPHY OF MUSIC IN EVANS. Metuchen, N.J.: Scarecrow Press, 1970. 607 p.

An index to the music published in seventeenth-and eighteenth-century America as represented by Charles Evans's AMERICAN BIBLIOGRAPHY and the Readex Corporation's microprint edition of EARLY AMERICAN IMPRINTS, 1639-1800.

Howard, John Tasker. OUR AMERICAN MUSIC: A COMPREHENSIVE HISTORY FROM 1620 TO THE PRESENT. 4th ed. New York: Thomas Y. Crowell Co., 1965. 944 p. Photos.

While the first edition appeared in 1929, this version has been updated considerably. Revised and extended bibliography.

Howard, John Tasker, and Bellows, George Kent. A SHORT HISTORY OF MUSIC IN AMERICA. New York: Thomas Y. Crowell Co., 1967. 496 p.

For more extensive treatment and an extensive bibliography, see John Tasker Howard's comprehensive book, OUR AMERICAN MUSIC, cited above. This volume is primarily for general reference.

Jackson, Richard. UNITED STATES MUSIC: SOURCES OF BIBLIOGRAPHY AND COLLECTIVE BIOGRAPHY. Brooklyn, N.Y.: City University of New York, Brooklyn College, Institute for Studies in American Music, 1973. 80 p.

A concise list with commentaries on sources of information about music and musicians in the United States.

Lang, Paul Henry. ONE HUNDRED YEARS OF MUSIC IN AMERICA. New York: G. Schirmer, 1961. 322 p.

A comprehensive coverage of important aspects of American musical life.

Library of Congress. General Reference and Bibliography Division. A GUIDE TO THE STUDY OF THE UNITED STATES OF AMERICA. 1960. Reprint. Washington, D.C.: Government Printing Office, 1971. 1,193 p.

A description of approximately 10,000 books that reflect the development of life and thought in the United States. Provides extensive treatment of many fields, including music.

Lowens, Irving. MUSIC AND MUSICIANS IN EARLY AMERICA. New York: W.W. Norton and Co., 1964. 328 p. Illus., music.

Describes some of the significant musical publications issued in this country from colonial times to the middle of the nineteenth century. Includes biographical portraits of some of the outstanding American composers of that period. Bibliography.

Marrocco, W. Thomas, and Gleason, Harold. MUSIC IN AMERICA. New York: W.W. Norton and Co., 1964. 371 p.

A volume of importance for researching American music for the years 1620-1865.

Mussulman, Joseph A. MUSIC IN THE CULTURED GENERATION: A SOCIAL HISTORY OF MUSIC IN AMERICA, 1870-1900. Evanston, Ill.: Northwestern University Press, 1971. 298 p. Illus., music.

For the investigator of music in American society for the period covered, this work offers a considerable amount of data. Bibliography.

Ritter, Frederic Louis. MUSIC IN AMERICA. 1895. Reprint. New York: B. Franklin, 1972. 521 p.

Detailed analysis of the early developments of American music.

Rockefeller Brothers' Fund, Special Studies Project. THE PERFORMING ARTS: PROBLEMS AND PROSPECTS. New York: McGraw-Hill Book Co., 1965. 272 p.

This effort by the thirty-member Rockefeller Fund Panel attempts to survey the state of the performing arts in America, identify problems and issues, and suggest further steps.

Sablosky, Irving L. AMERICAN MUSIC. Chicago: University of Chicago Press, 1969. 228 p.

A cultural approach to the development of music in America. Bibliography.

Sonneck, Oscar G. A BIBLIOGRAPHY OF EARLY SECULAR AMERICAN MUSIC. Revised and enlarged by William T. Upton. 1945. Reprint. New York: Da Capo Press, 1964. 617 p.

A complete collection of titles of secular music and books, pamphlets, essays, and so forth, relating to secular music issued by the American press prior to the nineteenth century and extant in certain libraries; issued but not extant in these libraries; written by native or naturalized Americans and extant in manuscript; written by the same, but apparently not published.

_____. EARLY CONCERT-LIFE IN AMERICA, 1731-1800. Leipzig: Breithopf & Hartel, 1907. 338 p.

Traces the introduction of public concerts in America.

Stoutamire, Albert. MUSIC OF THE OLD SOUTH: COLONY TO CONFEDERACY. Teaneck, N.J.: Fairleigh Dickinson University Press, 1972. 349 p. Illus., photos.

Provides research findings which reveal musical happenings in the southern colonies and in the southern part of the United States for the period cited. Bibliography.

U.S. Congress. House. Committee on the Judiciary. THE STAR-SPANGLED BANNER: HEARINGS BEFORE SUBCOMMITTEE NO. 4 ON H.J. RES. 17, H.J. RES. 517, H.R. 10542, H.J. RES. 558, AND H.R. 12231. 85th Cong., 2d sess., 21, 22, 28 May 1958. Serial 18. 174 p.

These hearings concerned a number of bills to provide a standardized version of "The Star-Spangled Banner." The 174 pages of hearings provide statements by many leading authorities and scholars concerning the origin and history of our national anthem.

Wilder, Alec. AMERICAN POPULAR SONG: THE GREAT INNOVATORS, 1900-1950. Edited by James T. Maher. New York: Oxford University Press, 1972. 536 p.

Wolfe, Richard J. SECULAR MUSIC IN AMERICA 1801-1825: A BIBLIOGRAPHY. 3 vols. New York: New York Public Library, 1964.

Extensive encyclopedia of the nearly 10,000 musical works published in the United States from 1801 to 1825. Indicates the library in which the piece may be located, along with detailed annotation. More complete than Sonneck-Upton's A BIBLIOGRAPHY OF EARLY SECULAR AMERICAN MUSIC, cited above.

Yerbury, Grace D. SONG IN AMERICA FROM EARLY TIMES TO ABOUT 1850. Metuchen, N.J.: Scarecrow Press, 1971. 305 p.

An attempt to extend the standard Sonneck-Upton A BIBLIOGRAPHY OF EARLY AMERICAN SECULAR MUSIC, cited above.

See also Section 40: Contemporary Music; Section 41: Electronic Music, Musique Concrète, and Computer Music; Section 35: History of Music; Section 42: Opera, Ballet, and Dance; Section 43: Popular Music--Jazz--Rock.

ASSOCIATIONS

American Music Center, 250 West 57th Street, Suite 626-7, New York, N.Y. 10019.

An information center concerning American composers and their work. Maintains a library of the works of composer-members.

Publications: Newsletter. 6/year.

DIRECTORY OF PERFORMING ENSEMBLES.

CATALOG OF CHORAL AND VOCAL HOLDINGS OF LIBRARY.

Section 40
CONTEMPORARY MUSIC

DICTIONARIES, BIBLIOGRAPHIES, AND SPECIAL REPORTS

Basart, Ann Phillips. SERIAL MUSIC: A CLASSIFIED BIBLIOGRAPHY OF WRITINGS ON TWELVE-TONE AND ELECTRONIC MUSIC. Los Angeles and Berkeley: University of California Press, 1971. 151 p.

An annotated bibliography of significant writings--philosophical, historical, and analytical--which have appeared on serial music.

Bull, Storm. INDEX TO BIOGRAPHIES OF CONTEMPORARY COMPOSERS. New York: Scarecrow Press, 1964. 405 p.

A listing of composers with vital statistics. Sources are noted in which biographical material can be found. Limited to composers whose works can be found in reference sources and to those still living or who were born in 1900 or later.

Carlson, Effie B. A BIO-BIBLIOGRAPHICAL DICTIONARY OF TWELVE-TONE AND SERIAL COMPOSERS. Metuchen, N.J.: Scarecrow Press, 1970. 233 p.

Features eighty representative composers and their contributions to the development of twelve-tone and serial composition through piano music.

Cohn, Arthur. TWENTIETH-CENTURY MUSIC IN WESTERN EUROPE: THE COMPOSITION AND THE RECORDINGS. Philadelphia: J.B. Lippincott Co., 1965. 510 p.

An encyclopedic treatment of recorded twentieth-century music.

THE CONTEMPORARY MUSIC PROJECT (CMP). Washington, D.C.: Music Educators National Conference.

The Contemporary Music Project (CMP) for Creativity in Music Education was originally administered by the Music Educators National Conference under a grant from the Ford Foundation. Its general aim was to bring about conditions favorable to the creation, study, and performance of contemporary music. The various activities of this project focused primarily on the field of composition and music education in the belief that a close working relationship between the two will, in time, provide the standards and values needed in a contemporary musical life. The publications which follow are outgrowths of the CMP.

CMP--COMPREHENSIVE MUSICIANSHIP: AN ANTHOLOGY OF EVOLVING THOUGHT. Washington, D.C.: MENC, 1971. 119 p.

A discussion of the first ten years (1959-69) of the Contemporary Music Project, particularly as they relate to the development of comprehensive musicianship. Derived from articles and speeches by those closely associated with the project.

CMP--COMPREHENSIVE MUSICIANSHIP: THE FOUNDATION FOR COLLEGE EDUCATION IN MUSIC. Washington, D.C.: MENC, 1965. 88 p.

Summary of the recommendations for the improvement of music curriculums, formulated at the CMP Seminar on Comprehensive Musicianship held at Northwestern University, April 1965.

CMP--COMPREHENSIVE MUSICIANSHIP AND UNDERGRADUATE MUSIC CURRICULA. By David Willowby. Washington, D.C.: MENC, 1971. 116 p.

A discussion of curricular implications of comprehensive musicianship as derived from thirty-two experimental college programs sponsored by the Contemporary Music Project under its Institutes for Music in Contemporary Education.

CMP--CONTEMPORARY MUSIC FOR SCHOOLS. Washington, D.C.: MENC, 1966. 88 p.

A catalog of works written by composers participating in the Young Composers Project, 1959-64.

CMP--CREATIVE PROJECTS IN MUSICIANSHIP. By Warren Benson. Washington, D.C.: MENC, 1967. 55 p.

A report of CMP pilot projects in teaching contemporary music at Ithaca College and Interlochen Arts Academy.

CMP--EXPERIMENTS IN MUSICAL CREATIVITY. Washington, D.C.: MENC, 1966. 88 p.

A report of the CMP pilot projects in elementary music education in Baltimore, San Diego, and Farmingdale.

CMP--SOURCE BOOK OF AFRICAN AND AFRO-AMERICAN MATERIALS FOR MUSIC EDUCATORS. By James A. Standifer and Barbara Reeder. Washington, D.C.: MENC, 1972. 147 p.

A reference source for students, teachers, and librarians. Provides lists of books, articles, recordings, and other materials dealing with African and Afro-American music traditions. Many titles are annotated.

MUSIC PROJECT LIBRARY. 3 vols. Washington, D.C.: MENC, 1976-69. Unpaged.

Vol. I: WORKS FOR BRASS, WINDS AND PERCUSSION/SOLOS. Vol. II: WORKS FOR ORCHESTRA AND STRING INSTRUMENTS. Vol. III: WORKS FOR CHORUS AND VOICE.

This catalog supercedes CONTEMPORARY MUSIC FOR SCHOOLS (see above) and includes lists of all works written for the Composers in Public Schools Program during its ten-year period. Each work described provides name of composer, historical and technical data, and two representative score pages.

Crystal Record Co. COMPOSIUM ANNUAL INDEX TO CONTEMPORARY COMPOSITIONS 1975. Los Angeles: 1976. 64 p.

A list of works by living composers, composed or published within the last two years (and not listed previously). Includes listing by instrumentation and composer, addresses for ordering purposes, composers' biographies, and grade difficulty.

Finell, Judith G., comp. THE CONTEMPORARY MUSIC PERFORMANCE DIRECTORY. New York: American Music Center, 1976. 254 p.

A comprehensive listing of performing ensembles, sponsoring agencies, performing facilities, concert series, and festivals of contemporary music. Also includes index of musicians, administrators, and organizations.

Music Educators National Conference. Committee on Contemporary Music. CONTEMPORARY MUSIC: A SUGGESTED LIST FOR HIGH SCHOOLS AND COLLEGES. Washington, D.C.: 1964. 32 p. Paper.

A recommended graded list of materials for band, orchestra, and choir.

Thompson, Kenneth. A DICTIONARY OF TWENTIETH-CENTURY COMPOSERS: 1911-1971. New York: St. Martin's Press, 1973. 666 p.

Contains much factual information concerning the works of each composer. Its usefulness is enhanced by the inclusion of a bibliography for each composer.

UNESCO. MUSIC AND TECHNOLOGY. Paris: La Revue Musicale, 1971. 208 p. Illus.

A collection of reports and papers presented at the meeting on music and technology organized by UNESCO in collaboration with the Fylkingen Society for Contemporary Composers in 1970 in Stockholm. The reports deal mainly with trends and developments in the creation of new music. Bibliographic references.

Vinton, John, ed. DICTIONARY OF CONTEMPORARY MUSIC. New York: E.P. Dutton, 1974. 834 p. Music, illus.

A reference work of considerable significance. Useful to anyone with a need to know the works a particular composer has written. Includes performance requirements. Contains articles about prominent contemporary composers, technical and interdisciplinary subjects, and musical developments in many countries. Bibliographies.

OTHER SOURCES

Adorno, Theodor W. PHILOSOPHY OF MODERN MUSIC. Translated by Anne G. Mitchell and Wesley V. Blomster. New York: Seabury Press, 1973. 220 p.

Focuses on the techniques of Stravinsky and Schoenberg. Bibliography.

Austin, William W. MUSIC IN THE 20TH CENTURY: FROM DEBUSSY THROUGH STRAVINSKY. New York: W.W. Norton and Co., 1966. 708 p. Music, photos.

A definitive work covering the era from Debussy to 1966. Contains one of the most comprehensive and useful bibliographies available on the subject.

Boretz, Benjamin, and Cone, Edward T., eds. PERSPECTIVES ON CONTEMPORARY MUSIC THEORY. New York: W.W. Norton and Co., 1972. 285 p. Music.

A collection of essays dealing with theoretical principles of contemporary music.

Bornoff, Jack. MUSIC AND THE TWENTIETH CENTURY MEDIA. Florence, Italy: L.S. Olschki, 1972. 219 p.

Boulez, Pierre. BOULEZ ON MUSIC TODAY. Translated by Susan Bradshaw and

Richard Rodney Bennett. Cambridge, Mass.: Harvard University Press, 1971. Music, illus.

An analytical study of twentieth-century music in terms of its structure and function.

Collaer, Paul. A HISTORY OF MODERN MUSIC. Translated by Sally Abeles. New York: Grosset and Dunlap, 1961. 414 p. Music, paper.

A history of the new music of the twentieth century and the men who composed it.

Cope, David. NEW DIRECTIONS IN MUSIC. Dubuque, Iowa: William C. Brown Co., 1971. 140 p. Illus., paper.

An introduction and survey of avant-garde and post-avant-garde music in the twentieth century to 1970. Bibliography and discography.

Czigany, Gyula, ed. CONTEMPORARY HUNGARIAN COMPOSERS. Budapest: Edito Musica, 1970. 156 p.

Contains biographical information on seventy-three composers, including birth/death dates; stage and choral works; orchestral music; chamber music; and other musical works.

Dallin, Leon. TECHNIQUES OF TWENTIETH CENTURY COMPOSITION: A GUIDE TO THE MATERIALS OF MODERN MUSIC. 3d ed. Dubuque, Iowa: William C. Brown Co., 1974. 260 p. Music.

Covers the major styles in twentieth-century composition. Special emphasis on developments since 1950, including avant-garde techniques and electronic music.

Dennis, Brian. EXPERIMENTAL MUSIC IN SCHOOLS: TOWARD A NEW WORLD OF SOUND. London: Oxford University Press, 1970. 76 p. Illus., music.

Presents a variety of experimental techniques for the development of an understanding of contemporary music.

Deri, Otto. EXPLORING TWENTIETH-CENTURY MUSIC. New York: Holt, Rinehart and Winston, 1968. 546 p. Music, photos.

Provides much material for the reorientation of listening habits and aesthetic attitudes for the comprehension of twentieth-century music. Bibliography and discography.

Dolan, Robert Emmett. MUSIC IN MODERN MEDIA: TECHNIQUES IN TAPE, DISC, AND FILM RECORDING, MOTION PICTURE AND TELEVISION SCORING, AND ELECTRONIC MUSIC. New York: G. Schirmer, 1967. 181 p. Illus., music.

Details and explains the processes that produce the new sounds on disc, tape, and film recording; the techniques used in scoring music for documentary, cartoon, and feature motion pictures; music production methods in live, taped, and filmed television; and the relation of electronic music to these media.

Eschman, Karl. CHANGING FORMS FOR MODERN MUSIC. 2d ed. Boston: E.C. Schirmer Music Co., 1968. 213 p.

A detailed account of the various aspects of form analysis as it relates to modern music.

Ewen, David. COMPOSERS TO TOMORROW'S MUSIC. New York: Dodd, Mead and Co., 1971. 176 p.

A nontechnical introduction to the musical avant-garde movement.

______, ed. COMPOSERS SINCE 1900: A BIOGRAPHICAL AND CRITICAL GUIDE. New York: H.W. Wilson Co., 1969. 639 p.

______. DAVID EWEN INTRODUCES MODERN MUSIC: A HISTORY AND APPRECIATION FROM WAGNER TO WEBERN. Philadelphia and New York: Chilton Book Co., 1962. 303 p. Photos.

Designed to acquaint the layman with aspects of twentieth-century music. A nontechnical approach.

______. EUROPEAN COMPOSERS TODAY: A BIOGRAPHICAL AND CRITICAL GUIDE. New York: H.W. Wilson Co., 1954. 200 p. Photos.

Biographical and critical guide to more than one hundred European composers who have exerted major influence on music of the twentieth century.

______. THE WORLD OF TWENTIETH-CENTURY MUSIC. Englewood Cliffs, N.J.: Prentice-Hall, 1968. 989 p.

Contains biographies and critical evaluations of both major and minor twentieth-century composers with detailed notes on more than 1,500 musical works. Bibliography.

Forte, Allen. CONTEMPORARY TONE STRUCTURE. New York: Bureau of Publications, Teachers College, Columbia University, 1955. 194 p.

Describes procedures and techniques for the analysis of contemporary tone-structures. Applications are illustrated.

______. THE STRUCTURE OF ATONAL MUSIC. New Haven, Conn.: Yale University Press, 1973. 224 p.

The presentation of a theoretical framework for the systematic study of the processes underlying atonal music. Does not include twelve-tone or paratonal music as such. Bibliography.

Hamm, Charles, et al. CONTEMPORARY MUSIC AND MUSIC CULTURES. Englewood Cliffs, N.J.: Prentice-Hall, 1975. 270 p. Music.

Covers well the recent and current scenes in music, mirrored against today's society and culture. Music in the United States receives ample treatment. Considers the influence of developing technologies on music practices. Bibliography and discography.

Hansen, Peter S. AN INTRODUCTION TO TWENTIETH CENTURY MUSIC. 3d ed. Boston: Allyn and Bacon, 1971. 464 p.

Surveys the main lines of the development of twentieth-century music through a study of selected compositions by its most influential composers. Bibliography.

Harder, Paul O. BRIDGE TO 20TH CENTURY MUSIC. Boston: Allyn and Bacon, 1973. 322 p.

An introduction to twentieth-century music for classes where a theoretical emphasis is desired.

Lang, Paul Henry, and Broder, Nathan. CONTEMPORARY MUSIC IN EUROPE: A COMPREHENSIVE SURVEY. New York: G. Schirmer, 1965. 308 p. Photos, music.

Principal composers and their works, representing twenty-two countries, are covered. Contemporary styles and terms are described.

Marquis, George Welton. TWENTIETH-CENTURY MUSIC IDIOMS. Englewood Cliffs, N.J.: Prentice-Hall, 1964. 269 p. Music.

The rules inherent in compositional devices of major composers of the first half of the twentieth century are presented with music examples. Directed toward the novice in contemporary music--composer, performer, teacher, student and/or layman. Assumes a basic background in music theory. Bibliography.

Mitchell, Donald. THE LANGUAGE OF MODERN MUSIC. 3d rev. ed. New York: St. Martin's Press, 1969. 185 p. Music, illus., paper.

Using the serial method of Schoenberg as a point of departure, the author develops stimulating theories concerning contemporary music with particular stress on the interrelationships of music, painting, and architecture.

Myers, Rollo. MODERN FRENCH MUSIC: FROM FAURE TO BOULEZ. New York: Praeger, 1971. 210 p.

A study of seventeen composers from Fauré to Boulez.

______, ed. TWENTIETH CENTURY MUSIC. New York: Orion Press, 1968. 289 p. Illus., music.

An attempt to bridge the gap between the composer and his audience. This collection of articles, written by experts, focuses on the more abstract aspects of contemporary music. One section surveys contemporary music activities in Europe, the United States, and Latin America. Bibliographic references.

Partch, Harry. GENESIS OF A MUSIC. 2d ed. 1949. Reprint. New York: Da Capo Press, 1974. 517 p. Illus., music, photos.

Treats monophony as related to historic and current trends. Includes philosophy and principles.

Perle, George. SERIAL COMPOSITION AND ATONALITY: AN INTRODUCTION TO THE MUSIC OF SCHOENBERG, BERG, AND WEBERN. 2d ed. Los Angeles and Berkeley: University of California Press, 1968. 166 p. Illus., music.

A detailed and evaluative examination of the technical aspects of atonal and twelve-tone compositions as represented by three composers. Bibliography.

Persichetti, Vincent. TWENTIETH-CENTURY HARMONY: CREATIVE ASPECTS AND PRACTICE. New York: W.W. Norton and Co., 1961. 287 p.

A detailed examination of the harmonic devices found in music of the first half of the twentieth century.

Peyser, Joan. THE NEW MUSIC: THE SENSE BEHIND THE SOUND. New York: Delacorte Press, 1971. 204 p.

An analytical history of trends and transitions as reflected in the achievements of Schoenberg, Stravinsky, and Varese. Bibliography.

Rossi, Nick, and Choate, Robert A. MUSIC OF OUR TIME. Boston: Crescendo Publishing Co., 1969. 406 p.

An anthology of works by selected twentieth-century composers. Bibliography.

Rostand, Claude. FRENCH MUSIC TODAY. Translated by Henry Marx. 1955. Reprint. New York: Da Capo Press, 1973. 147 p.

A comprehensive survey of modern music, focusing on the role of France as the center of twentieth-century composition.

Routley, Erik. TWENTIETH-CENTURY CHURCH MUSIC. New York: Oxford University Press, 1964. 244 p. Music.

Deals with new approaches to church music and shows the relationships to social developments of the time. Bibliography and discography.

Salzman, Eric. TWENTIETH-CENTURY MUSIC: AN INTRODUCTION. 2d ed. Englewood Cliffs, N.J.: Prentice-Hall, 1974. 242 p.

Designed to enable the reader to develop tools for understanding music of this era. Treats musical idioms and materials against a background of social and artistic change.

Schwartz, Elliott [S.], and Childs, Barney, eds. CONTEMPORARY COMPOSERS ON CONTEMPORARY MUSIC. New York: Holt, Rinehart and Winston, 1967. 375 p.

The nature and status of contemporary music as viewed by thirty-four distinguished modern composers.

Searle, Humphrey, and Layton, Robert. TWENTIETH CENTURY COMPOSERS, VOLUME III: BRITAIN, SCANDINAVIA, AND THE NETHERLANDS. Edited by Anna Kallin and Nicolas Nabokov. New York: Holt, Rinehart and Winston, 1972. 200 p. Photos.

A survey of twentieth-century music as represented by composers of Northern Europe. The cultural background of the time is discussed, as well as the lives of selected composers. Bibliography.

Slonimsky, Nicolas. MUSIC SINCE 1900. 4th ed. New York: Charles Scribner's Sons, 1971. 1,595 p.

Especially useful for tracing important musical events and developments that influence the future of music.

Strobel, Heinrich. STRAVINSKY: CLASSIC HUMANIST. Translated by Hans Rosenwald. 1955. Reprint. New York: Da Capo Press, 1974. 184 p.

Includes detailed structural analysis of Stravinsky's musical compositions as well as discussion of the creative principles of his work.

Stuckenschmidt, H.H. TWENTIETH CENTURY COMPOSERS, VOLUME II: GERMANY AND CENTRAL EUROPE. Edited by Anna Kallin and Nicolas Nabokov. New York: Holt, Rinehart and Winston, 1971. 256 p. Photos, illus.

A discussion of the lives and compositions of leading composers of this geographical area.

______. TWENTIETH CENTURY MUSIC. Translated by Richard Deveson. New York: McGraw-Hill Book Co., 1969. 256 p. Music, illus., photos, paper.

Discusses the elements of musical form and expression as inherited by modern composers and proceeds through the period to include recent innovations. Includes an effective presentation of music's place among other arts.

Thomson, Virgil. TWENTIETH-CENTURY COMPOSERS: VOLUME I--AMERICAN MUSIC SINCE 1910. Edited by Anna Kallin and Nicolas Nabokov. New York: Holt, Rinehart and Winston, 1970. 204 p. Photos, music.

A nontechnical, highly readable account of the major composers of this century. Bibliography.

Ulehla, Ludmila. CONTEMPORARY HARMONY: ROMANTICISM THROUGH THE TWELVE-TONE ROW. New York: Free Press, 1966. 534 p. Music.

Links chromatic harmony to contemporary musical structure. Highly detailed treatment.

Vincent, John. THE DIATONIC MODES IN MODERN MUSIC. New York: Mills Music, 1951. 298 p. Illus., music.

A thorough treatment of modal theory and its development. Especially useful for the music theorist and practicing composers. Bibliography.

Webern, Anton. THE PATH TO NEW MUSIC. Translated by Willi Reich. Bryn Mawr, Pa.: Theodore Presser Co., 1963. 67 p. Music.

Comprised of a series of lectures given by Webern in 1932 and 1933 in Vienna. Deals specifically with twelve-tone composition.

Wilder, Robert D. TWENTIETH-CENTURY MUSIC. Dubuque, Iowa: William C. Brown Co., 1969. 133 p. Paper.

Reviews the significant musical developments since 1900. The discussion focuses primarily on the music rather than facts about music. Bibliography.

Yates, Peter. TWENTIETH-CENTURY MUSIC. New York: Pantheon Books--Random House, 1967. 367 p. Tables.

Describes developments in contemporary music from the last half of the nineteenth century to the present.

See also Section 39: American Music; Section 41: Electronic Music, Musique Concrète, and Computer Music; Section 35: History of Music; Section 42: Opera, Ballet, and Dance; and Section 43: Popular Music--Jazz--Rock.

ASSOCIATIONS

American Music Center, 250 West 57th Street, Suite 626-27, New York, N.Y. 10019.

An information center concerning American composers and their work. Maintains a library of the works of composer-members.

Publications: Newsletter. 6/year.

DIRECTORY OF PERFORMING ENSEMBLES.

CATALOG OF CHORAL AND VOCAL HOLDINGS OF THE LIBRARY.

International Society for Contemporary Music (ISCM), 7, Boulevard Jacques Dalcroze, Ch-1204, Geneva, Switzerland.

Society for Commissioning New Music, P.O. Box 67, Valley Lee, Md. 20692.

Publication: Newsletter. 4-6/year.

Section 41

ELECTRONIC MUSIC, MUSIQUE CONCRETE, AND COMPUTER MUSIC

Allen, Larry D. BEGINNING ELECTRONIC MUSIC IN THE CLASSROOM: A PRE-SYNTHESIZER CURRICULUM USING THE TAPE RECORDER. Southington, Conn.: Larry D. Allen, 1974. 32 p. Photos, paper.

A set of thirty-six lesson plans for use in teaching an electronic music course. Designed for junior high school students.

Appleton, Jon H., and Perera, Ronald C., eds. THE DEVELOPMENT AND PRACTICE OF ELECTRONIC MUSIC. Englewood Cliffs, N.J.: Prentice-Hall, 1975. 400 p. Illus., photos, music.

A collection of articles by specialists in electronic music. Contains computer application.

Brace, Michele, et al., comps. "Selected Readings on Electronic Music." MUSIC EDUCATORS JOURNAL, November 1968, pp. 174-79.

Includes books, periodicals, essays, encyclopedia articles, and recordings.

Cross, Lowell M., comp. A BIBLIOGRAPHY OF ELECTRONIC MUSIC. Toronto: University of Toronto Press, 1967. 126 p.

The books, articles, monographs, and abstracts cited here represent an attempt to compile as exhaustive a bibliography as possible for "musique concrète," "elektronische musik," "tape music," "computer music," and the closely related fields in experimental music.

Crowhurst, Norman H. ELECTRONIC MUSICAL INSTRUMENTS. Blue Ridge Summit, Pa.: Tab Books, 1971. 168 p. Illus., photos.

A technical account of the working principles of these instruments.

Davies, Hugh, comp. REPERTOIRE INTERNATIONAL DES MUSIQUES ELECTROACOUSTIQUES [International electronic music catalog]. Paris: Cooperative publication of Le Groupe de Recherches Musicales de l'O.R.T.F., Paris, France, and The Independent Electronic Music Center, Inc., Trumansburg, N.Y., 1968. 330 p. (Distr. by M.I.T. Press, Cambridge, Mass.)

This survey covers the first twenty years of electronic music and is intended to be a complete source of information on the subject.

Dorf, Richard H. ELECTRONIC MUSICAL INSTRUMENTS. 3d ed. New York: Radiofile, 1968. 393 p.

Douglas, Alan L.M. THE ELECTRONIC MUSICAL INSTRUMENT MANUAL: A GUIDE TO THEORY AND DESIGN. 5th ed. London: Pitman, 1968. 372 p.

Dwyer, Terence. COMPOSING WITH TAPE RECORDERS: MUSIC CONCRETE FOR BEGINNERS. New York: Oxford University Press, 1971. 74 p. Photos.

A handbook for the amateur composer of tape recorder music. Bibliography and discography.

ELECTRONIC MUSIC FOR THE SEVENTIES. Morristown, N.J.: Ionic Industries, 1971. 44 p.

A combination introduction to electronic music and an operating manual for equipment.

Ernst, David. MUSIQUE CONCRETE. Boston: Crescendo Publishing Co., 1972. 37 p.

Basic concepts and procedures for composition in this medium. Bibliography.

Hiller, Lejaren A., Jr., and Isaacson, Leonard M. EXPERIMENTAL MUSIC: COMPOSITION WITH AN ELECTRONIC COMPUTER. New York: McGraw-Hill Book Co., 1959. 197 p. Illus.

Details experimental work which was done to explore the capabilities of the computer as a generator of musical composition.

Howe, Hubert S. ELECTRONIC MUSIC SYNTHESIS: CONCEPTS, FACILITIES, TECHNIQUES. New York: W.W. Norton and Co., 1975. 272 p. Illus.

Describes basic information about acoustics and psychoacoustics, equipment, and methods of synthesis in terms of the three primary techniques: studio work, integrated synthesizers, and computer generation. Bibliography.

Judd, F.C. ELECTRONIC MUSIC AND MUSIQUE CONCRETE. Letchworth,

Hertfordshire, Engl.: Garden City Press, 1961. 92 p. Illus., tables, photos.

Deals with musique concrète, electronic music, radiophonics, and abstract sound reproduction with magnetic tape as the recording and composing media.

Lincoln, Harry B. THE COMPUTER AND MUSIC. Ithaca, N.Y.: Cornell University Press, n.d. 372 p. Tables, figures.

Documents the efforts of composers and music researchers using the computer in their work, and illustrates the wide range of possibilities for its use in the future. Provides a bibliography of composers and their works.

Luening, Otto, et al. ELECTRONIC MUSIC. Washington, D.C.: Music Educators National Conference, 1968. 97 p. Illus., photos, music.

A manual dealing with electronic music for musicians and educators. Bibliography and discography. Originally published as the November 1968 issue of the MUSIC EDUCATORS JOURNAL.

Mathews, Max V., et al. THE TECHNOLOGY OF COMPUTER MUSIC. Cambridge, Mass.: M.I.T. Press, 1969. 188 p. Illus., tables.

Especially useful for musicians concerned with sound synthesis and perception. Intended primarily for people who plan to use computers for sound processing. Mathematical background desirable.

Pellegrino, Ronald. AN ELECTRONIC MUSIC STUDIO MANUAL. 2 vols. Columbus: Ohio State University College of the Arts, 1969. 235 p.

A useful and practical guide. Especially worthwhile for effective use of the now popular Moog synthesizers. Includes audio tape.

Russcol, Herbert. THE LIBERATION OF SOUND: AN INTRODUCTION TO ELECTRONIC MUSIC. Englewood Cliffs, N.J.: Prentice-Hall, 1972. 315 p.

The development and experimentation in electronic music and the advantages and problems of computer-assisted compositions. Chronologies of electronic music, reviews of recorded selections, and a glossary of terms are provided in addition to a reprint of a partial discography compiled by Peter Frank and essays by Jacques Barzun, Otto Luening, and others.

Schwartz, Elliott S. ELECTRONIC MUSIC: A LISTENER'S GUIDE. New York: Praeger, 1973. 306 p.

Describes the basic facts of electronic music in a clear and nontechnical fashion. Useful bibliography and discography.

Sear, Walter. THE NEW WORLD OF ELECTRONIC MUSIC. New York: Alfred Publishing Co., 1972. 131 p. Illus., paper.

A practical book that gives the basic principles of sound, acoustics, electricity, magnetism, and recording techniques necessary to understand the concepts and functions of the synthesizer.

Strange, Allen. ELECTRONIC MUSIC: SYSTEMS, TECHNIQUES, AND CONTROLS. Dubuque, Iowa: William C. Brown Co., 1972. 160 p. Illus.

Describes the processes and production of electronic music, including available techniques and methods.

KNOW YOUR SYNTHESIZER. Newton Highland, Mass.: Tonus, Inc., 1971. 116 p.

A text or reference book for electronic music courses.

Trythall, Gilbert. PRINCIPLES AND PRACTICES OF ELECTRONIC MUSIC. New York: Grosset and Dunlap, 1973. 214 p. Illus., photos.

Designed as a text for secondary- or introductory college-level courses. Proceeds from a description of basic acoustics and electronics to the actual equipment and techniques of electronic music. Includes a recording. Bibliography.

Wells, Thomas, and Vogel, Eric S. THE TECHNIQUE OF ELECTRONIC MUSIC. Austin, Tex.: University Stores, n.d. 250 p. Illus.

While it was intended as a text, this book serves well as a reference manual regarding technical matters related to the production of electronic music.

See also Section 59: Computer Applications; Section 39: American Music; Section 40: Contemporary Music; Section 35: History of Music.

Section 42

OPERA, BALLET, AND DANCE

Schoolcraft, Ralph Newman. PERFORMING ARTS BOOKS IN PRINT: AN ANNOTATED BIBLIOGRAPHY. New York: Drama Book Specialists, 1973. 761 p.

This work is a revised, updated version of THEATRE BOOKS IN PRINT, originally published in 1963 and revised in 1966. Descriptive information is given for books concerned with the performing arts, including the literature of the theatre, drama, motion pictures, television, radio, and the mass media. Limited to books that are now available in the United States. Musical theatre is included, but music theory and composition, and books related to the playing of musical instruments are excluded.

OPERA

General References

Barlow, Harold, and Morgenstern, Sam, eds. A DICTIONARY OF OPERA AND SONG THEMES. New York: Crown, 1966. 547 p. Music.

For annotation, see Section 10: Thematic Indexes and Catalogs.

Belknap, Sara Yancey, comp. GUIDE TO THE PERFORMING ARTS, 1967. New York: Scarecrow Press, 1969. 514 p.

A guide to articles on theatre, drama, dance, and music that appeared in American and foreign periodicals during 1967.

Brockway, Wallace, and Weinstock, Herbert. THE WORLD OF OPERA. New York: Random House, 1966. 723 p.

A huge collection of reliable information about all aspects of opera. Well indexed for quick reference.

Cross, Milton, and Kohrs, Karl. MORE STORIES OF THE GREAT OPERAS. Garden City, N.Y.: Doubleday and Co., 1971. 752 p.

The interpretation of forty-five operas that are in active production. Includes brief histories of 700 leading singers (past and present), a glossary of operatic terms, a survey of opera, and a listing of opera associations in America. Bibliography.

Eaton, Quaintance. THE MIRACLE OF THE MET: AN INFORMAL HISTORY OF THE METROPOLITAN OPERA, 1883-1967. New York: Meredith Press, 1968. 490 p. Photos.

A narrative account of the historical development of the Metropolitan Opera, based on newspaper and periodical files, personal interviews, and the Metropolitan archives. Bibliography.

England, Paul. FAVORITE OPERAS BY GERMAN AND RUSSIAN COMPOSERS. New York: Dover Publications, 1973. 288 p. Paper.

Discussion of twenty-two operas and their composers. Formerly published as part of FIFTY FAVORITE OPERAS (London: George G. Harrap & Co., 1925.

______. FAVORITE OPERAS BY ITALIAN AND FRENCH COMPOSERS. New York: Dover Publications, 1973. 313 p. Paper.

A discussion of twenty-nine operas and their composers. Formerly published as part of FIFTY FAVORITE OPERAS (London: George G. Harrap & Co., 1925).

Ewen, David. THE NEW ENCYCLOPEDIA OF THE OPERA. New York: Hill and Wang, 1971. 759 p.

Comprehensive. Highly detailed descriptions of more than one hundred important operas.

Fellner, Rudolph. OPERA THEMES AND PLOTS. New York: Simon and Schuster, 1958. 354 p. Music.

Includes summaries of plots as well as musical motives and themes in their original keys.

Graf, Herbert. THE OPERA AND ITS FUTURE IN AMERICA. Port Washington, N.Y.: Kennikat Press, 1973. 305 p.

Harewood, George Henry [Earl of Harewood]. KOBBE'S COMPLETE OPERA BOOK. Rev. ed. New York: G.P. Putnam's Sons, 1972. 1,262 p.

One of the standard reference works on the subject. Arranged by centuries and subdivided into countries.

Harris, Kenn. OPERA RECORDINGS: A CRITICAL GUIDE. New York: Drake, 1973. 328 p.

Surveys the available complete recordings of seventy-six operas with comments and the author's evaluations.

Hurd, Michael. YOUNG PERSON'S GUIDE TO THE OPERA. New York: Roy Publishers, 1966. 119 p.

Surveys the historical development of opera from the seventeenth to the twentieth century.

Jacobs, Arthur, and Sadie, Stanley. OPERA: A MODERN GUIDE. New York: Drake, 1972. 492 p. Music. Reprinted from THE PAN BOOK OF OPERA. London: Pan Books, 1964.

Gives pertinent background and synopses of representative operas from Purcell to Bernstein. Bibliography.

Knapp, J. Merrill. THE MAGIC OF OPERA. New York: Harper and Row, 1972. 371 p. Music, photos, illus.

This text is designed for the layman and/or college student. Includes a brief historical survey and a discussion of the forms of opera with concentration on a few of the great classics.

Mitchell, Ronald E. OPERA: DEAD OR ALIVE--PRODUCTION, PERFORMANCE AND ENJOYMENT OF MUSICAL THEATRE. Madison: University of Wisconsin Press, 1970. 322 p.

A broad coverage of musical theatre from classical Greece to the twentieth century. Seventeen representative musical dramas are analyzed. Bibliography.

Moore, Frank Ledlie, ed. CROWELL'S HANDBOOK OF WORLD OPERA. New York: Thomas Y. Crowell Co., 1961. 683 p.

An encyclopedic guide to more than 500 operas with entries on singers and composers. Discography and dictionary.

Pauly, Reinhard G. MUSIC AND THE THEATER: AN INTRODUCTION TO OPERA. Englewood Cliffs, N.J.: Prentice-Hall, 1970. 462 p.

Stresses opera's dramatic aspects and how music can enhance its impact. Examines opera's literary origins, social history, principal characters, and conventions of performance.

Pleasants, Henry. THE GREAT SINGERS FROM THE DAWN OF OPERA TO OUR OWN TIME. New York: Simon and Schuster, 1966. 382 p. Illus.

Highlights the careers of singers representative of each age of opera from its beginnings to the present time.

Rich, Maria F., ed. DIRECTORY OF FOREIGN CONTEMPORARY OPERA. New York: Central Opera Service, 1969. 66 p.

This directory is limited to those foreign contemporary operas which were premiered after January 1, 1950. Information includes composer, nationality, length, and premiere data and place. The listing includes a total of 1,564 operas by 581 composers from forty foreign countries.

Rosenthal, Harold, and Warnack, John. CONCISE OXFORD DICTIONARY OF OPERA. London: Oxford University Press, 1964. 446 p.

A concise but comprehensive reference work. Presents summaries of composers' works, rather than a chronicle of their lives.

Ross, Anne. THE OPERA DIRECTORY. New York: Sterling, 1961. 566 p. Illus.

Extensive factual information concerning opera and operetta singers, conductors, musical staff, producers and designers, administrative and technical staff, theatres and opera-producing organizations, festivals, works by living composers, librettists, colleges and schools of music. Includes casting index and glossary (English, French, German, Italian, Russian, and Spanish).

Towers, John. DICTIONARY-CATALOG OF OPERAS AND OPERETTAS. 2 vols. 1910. Reprint. New York: Da Capo Press, 1967. 1,045 p.

Part I--Alphabetical listing of the work, followed by composer, nationality, and date of birth. Part II--Alphabetical listing of the composer, followed by the work; also an alphabetical list of libretti with the number of times they have been set to music for the stage.

THE VICTOR BOOK OF THE OPERA. 13th ed., rev. by Henry W. Simon. New York: Simon and Schuster, 1968. 475 p. Illus., photos.

See also Section 35: History of Music, and Section 34: Appreciation and Understanding of Music.

Opera History

Berges, Ruth. THE BACKGROUNDS AND TRADITIONS OF OPERA. 2d ed. South Brunswick, N.J.: A.S. Barnes, 1970. 269 p. Illus., photos.

A new edition of OPERA: ORIGINS AND SIDELIGHTS. Discusses

the "behind-the-scenes" activities in opera. Explains opera as a part of life. Covers composers, librettists and catalogers. Bibliography.

Bornoff, Jack, ed. MUSIC THEATRE IN A CHANGING SOCIETY: THE INFLUENCE OF THE TECHNICAL MEDIA. Paris: UNESCO, 1968. 144 p.

Brody, Elaine. MUSIC IN OPERA: A HISTORICAL ANTHOLOGY. Englewood Cliffs, N.J.: Prentice-Hall, 1970. 604 p.

A historical and geographical survey of the development of opera during the past four centuries.

Ewen, David. OPERA: ITS STORY TOLD THROUGH THE LIVES AND WORKS OF ITS FOREMOST COMPOSERS. New York: Franklin Watts, 1972. 264 p. Photos.

A historical account with musical description and plots of the standard works. Includes basic technical aspects with a glossary of operatic terms. Written for the young opera lover as well as the layman.

Grout, Donald J[ay]. A SHORT HISTORY OF OPERA. 2d ed. 2 vols. New York: Columbia University Press, 1965. 1,226 p.

A comprehensive account of the history of opera. Contains extensive bibliographies covering guides, histories, lexicons, collected essays, etc.

Loewenberg, Alfred. ANNALS OF OPERA, 1597-1940. 2d ed., rev. 2 vols. Geneva: Societas Bibliographica, 1955.

An outline of the history of opera in dates and facts. Highly informative. Arranged chronologically, with no descriptions of plots, no analyses of the music, and no personal critical comments.

Orrey, Leslie. A CONCISE HISTORY OF OPERA. New York: Scribners; London: Thames and Hudson, 1972. 252 p. Photos.

Treats opera mainly as drama and dialogue, intensified by music. Surveys the musical evolution, changing theatrical conditions, theatre architecture, and the influence of the producer. Includes operetta, musical comedy, and the musical as well as twentieth-century developments. Bibliography.

Surian, Elvidio. A CHECKLIST OF WRITINGS ON 18TH CENTURY FRENCH AND ITALIAN OPERA (EXCLUDING MOZART). Hackensack, N.J.: Joseph Boonin, 1970. 121 p.

THE VICTOR BOOK OF THE OPERA. 13th ed., rev. by Henry W. Simon. New York: Simon and Schuster, 1968. 475 p. Illus., photos.

The historical background and act-by-act summaries of 120 operatic works, outline history of opera, and complete listings of the best available recordings.

Von Westerman, Gerhart. OPERA GUIDE. Edited by Harold Rosenthal. Translated by Anne Ross. New York: E.P. Dutton, 1965. 584 p.

A reference work that deals with the development of opera from the late eighteenth century to the present. Includes synopses and musical examples from major works.

Opera in America

Drummond, Andrew H. AMERICAN OPERA LIBRETTOS. Metuchen, N.J.: Scarecrow Press, 1973. 277 p.

An investigative survey of the development of the American opera libretto from the late nineteenth century to 1948, followed by an examination of the dramatic elements in the librettos of American operas performed at the New York City Opera from 1948 to 1971. Selected bibliography.

Graf, Herbert. OPERA FOR THE PEOPLE. Minneapolis: University of Minnesota Press, 1951. 289 p. Illus., music, photos.

Deals with the status of opera in all areas of American life. Includes factual information on the elements of opera production. Bibliography.

_____. PRODUCING OPERA FOR AMERICA. 2d ed. New York and Zurich: Atlantis Books, 1963. 211 p. Photos.

A comprehensive survey of the status of opera in the United States and Europe, with recommendations for the future.

Johnson, Harold Earle. OPERAS ON AMERICAN SUBJECTS. New York: Coleman-Ross, 1964. 125 p.

Alphabetized by author-composer, this work presents an extensive listing of operas based on American themes (not necessarily by American authors). Provides historical and musical information on each work cited.

Kolodin, Irving. THE METROPOLITAN OPERA 1883-1966: A CANDID HISTORY. New York: Alfred A. Knopf Co., 1966. 762 p. Illus.

A thorough historical account of the Metropolitan Opera Company.

Mattfeld, Julius. A HANDBOOK OF AMERICAN OPERATIC PREMIERES, 1731-1962. Detroit: Information Coordinators, 1963. 142 p.

A guide to first American performances of operas. Includes date, place, and language, and a composer index.

Rich, Maria F., ed. DIRECTORY OF AMERICAN CONTEMPORARY OPERA. New York: Central Opera Service, 1967. 79 p. Paper.

Lists American contemporary operas, both published and nonpublished from 1930 to 1967. Provides names of composer and librettist, title of opera, general information, premiere date and place, length, cast, and orchestration.

_____. DIRECTORY OF OPERA COMPANIES AND WORKSHOPS IN THE U.S. AND CANADA. New York: Central Opera Service, 1971. 42 p. Paper.

This directory is updated through its supplement: Central Opera Service. ADDRESS LIST OF OPERA COMPANIES AND WORKSHOPS IN THE U.S. AND CANADA. New York: 1974-- . Irregular.

_____. DIRECTORY OF OPERA PRODUCING ORGANIZATIONS IN THE UNITED STATES AND CANADA. New York: Central Opera Service, 1975. 42 p.

_____. OPERA REPERTORY U.S.A., 1966-1972. New York: Central Opera Service Bulletin, 1972. 60 p. Paper.

A reference guide to operatic repertory in the United States from 1966 to 1972. The operas are listed in order of total number of performances showing popularity of the works. The second section lists opera for children, identifying those for public school audiences and those for public school performers.

Seltsam, William H., comp. METROPOLITAN OPERA ANNALS. New York: H.W. Wilson Co., 1947. 751 p. Illus. FIRST SUPPLEMENT, 1947-1957; SECOND SUPPLEMENT, 1957-1966.

A chronicle of artists and performances.

Sonneck, Oscar G. EARLY OPERA IN AMERICA. 1915. Reprint. New York: Benjamin Blom, 1964. 230 p. Illus.

Historical account from pre-Revolutionary times to 1800.

Light Opera and Musicals

Burton, Jack. THE BLUE BOOK OF BROADWAY MUSICALS. Watkins Glen, N.Y.: Century House, 1952. 320 p.

Drinkrow, John. THE OPERETTA BOOK. New York: Drake, 1973. 124 p. Photos.

An alphabetical listing which includes brief details of the origins, plots, and principal numbers of over fifty works of French, Austrian, and German origin. A companion volume of English and American works is in preparation. International discography.

Ewen, David. COMPLETE BOOK OF THE AMERICAN MUSICAL THEATER. New York: Holt, Rinehart and Winston, 1959. 447 p. Illus., photos.

Broad coverage of the American musical theater, past and present, including many plots, production histories, stars, songs, composers, and writers.

______. COMPOSERS FOR THE AMERICAN MUSICAL THEATRE. New York: Dodd, Mead and Co., 1968. 270 p. Photos.

Detailed biographical sketches of fourteen men--from Victor Herbert to Leonard Bernstein--commentary on their impact and lasting influence in American theatre.

Green, Stanley. THE WORLD OF MUSICAL COMEDY. New York: Ziff-Davis, 1960. 391 p. Illus.

Hughes, Gervase. COMPOSERS OF OPERETTA. London: Macmillan; New York: St. Martin's Press, 1962. 283 p. Music, illus.

Traces the origin and development of the various European schools of operetta.

Laufe, Abe. BROADWAY'S GREATEST MUSICALS. New York: Funk & Wagnalls, 1973. 502 p.

Comprehensive coverage of the subject. Bibliography.

Lubbock, Mark H. COMPLETE BOOK OF LIGHT OPERA. Des Moines, Iowa: Appleton-Century-Crofts, 1963. 953 p. Illus.

Richards, Stanley, ed. TEN GREAT MUSICALS OF THE AMERICAN THEATRE. New York: Chilton Book Co., 1973. 594 p. Illus.

A discussion of ten recent Broadway productions. Includes librettos.

Tumbusch, Tom. GUIDE TO BROADWAY MUSICAL THEATRE. New York: R. Rosen Press, 1972. 224 p.

Gilbert and Sullivan

Ayre, Leslie. THE GILBERT AND SULLIVAN COMPANION. New York:

Dodd, Mead and Co., 1972. 485 p.

This work is written as an encyclopedia of Gilbert and Sullivan's words, phrases, and characters, with summaries of each of the operas and names of those who played the various parts. An excellent, easy-to-use reference work.

Baily, Leslie. THE GILBERT AND SULLIVAN BOOK. Rev. ed. New York: Coward-McCann, 1957. 475 p. Photos, illus., music.

A comprehensive account of the Gilbert and Sullivan operas and the period in which they were written. Bibliographical references.

Cellier, Francois Arsene. GILBERT AND SULLIVAN AND THEIR OPERAS. 1914. Reprint. New York: Benjamin Blom, 1970. 443 p.

Hardwick, John Michael Drinkrow. THE DRAKE GUIDE TO GILBERT AND SULLIVAN. New York: Drake, 1973. 284 p.

A handbook which gives the historical background, plot summary, and quotations from each comic opera. Includes an index of first lines, a who's who description of every character, short biographies of Gilbert, Sullivan, and D'Oyly Carte, their producer, and a glossary of obscure allusions and terms. Bibliography and discography.

Kline, Peter. THE THEATRE STUDENT: GILBERT AND SULLIVAN PRODUCTION. New York: Richards Rosen Press, 1972. 299 p. Music, photos.

An extensive and detailed guide to the production of these operas. Bibliography and discography.

Moore, Frank Ledlie. CROWELL'S HANDBOOK OF GILBERT AND SULLIVAN. New York: Thomas Y. Crowell Co., 1962. 264 p. Music.

A comprehensive work listing characters, settings, arias, ensembles and choruses, detailed synopses of plots, and historical background. Bibliography.

Poladian, Sirvart, comp. SIR ARTHUR SULLIVAN: AN INDEX TO THE TEXTS OF HIS VOCAL WORKS. Detroit: Information Coordinators, 1961. 93 p.

An index, in strict word-by-word alphabetical order, of titles, first lines, repeated refrains, and important musical sections in the operettas and other larger vocal works of Sir Arthur Sullivan.

Searle, Townley. A BIBLIOGRAPHY OF SIR WILLIAM SCHWENCK GILBERT WITH BIBLIOGRAPHICAL ADVENTURES IN THE GILBERT AND SULLIVAN OPERAS. Burt Franklin Bibliographical and Reference Series, no. 192. 1931. Reprint. New York: Burt Franklin, 1968. 107 p.

An extensive bibliography of Gilbert's works, with notes and comments by Gilbert himself in some instances. Notes are lengthy concerning the circumstances surrounding the compositions, and their place in Gilbert's writings.

Williamson, Audrey. GILBERT AND SULLIVAN OPERA: A NEW ASSESSMENT. 2d ed. London: Rockliff, 1955. 292 p. Photos, music.

A critical examination of each work. Practical suggestions for diction, acting, and styles of singing.

Opera Production

Dwyer, Terence. OPERA IN YOUR SCHOOL. New York and London: Oxford University Press, 1964. 139 p.

A guide for producing operas in schools. Includes suggestions for all phases of the production as well as an annotated list of recommended operas.

Eaton, Quaintance. OPERA PRODUCTION. 2 vols. Minneapolis: University of Minnesota Press, 1961, 1974. 266 p., 347 p.

Details the production requirements for each opera. Volume 1 treats the more familiar operas. Volume 2 covers the lesser known operas, both old and new.

Engel, Lehman. PLANNING AND PRODUCING THE MUSICAL SHOW. Rev. ed. New York: Crown, 1966. 148 p.

A practical handbook for amateur producers. Includes detailed instructions for every phase of production. Annotated checklist for seventy-six popular shows. Bibliography.

Gibson, Gordon, and Philips, Thomas. A MANUAL OF TELEVISION OPERA PRODUCTION. Albuquerque: University of New Mexico Press, 1973. 98 p. Paper.

Prepared under the sponsorship of the National Opera Association to outline procedures for the production of theatrical and musical programming. Covers all facets of television production from management of the studio to the refined techniques of special effects. Although the focus of the work is opera production, all of the techniques discussed are applicable to other areas.

Goldovsky, Boris. BRINGING OPERA TO LIFE: OPERATIC ACTING AND STAGE DIRECTION. Englewood Cliffs, N.J.: Prentice-Hall, 1968. 424 p. Illus., music.

A comprehensive discussion of the dramatic aspects of opera as they relate to the music and stage production. Bibliography of background texts.

Huber, Louis H. PRODUCING OPERA IN THE COLLEGE. New York: Bureau of Publications, Teachers College, Columbia University, 1956. 115 p.

Deals with the function, organization, and administration of opera workshops. Includes a list of ten recommended operas in English with performance details. Bibliography.

Rich, Maria F., ed. DIRECTORY OF SETS AND COSTUMES FOR RENT, OPERA COMPANIES AND OTHER SOURCES. New York: Central Opera Service Bulletin, 1970.

Sharp, Harold S., and Sharp, Marjorie Z., comps. INDEX TO CHARACTERS IN THE PERFORMING ARTS, PART II--OPERAS AND MUSICAL PRODUCTIONS. New York: Scarecrow Press, 1969. 1,253 p.

This work identifies characters in opera, operetta, musical comedy, and plays in which music is introduced. Brief details are given about the character, author of the material is given, and information about the composer and first production. Coverage is from the thirteenth-century folk plays to the 1965/66 Broadway season. Identifies 2,542 productions and 20,000 characters.

SIMON'S DIRECTORY OF THEATRICAL MATERIALS, SERVICES AND INFORMATION. 4th ed. New York: Package Publicity Services, 1970. 320 p.

A classified listing of firms specializing in staging materials and equipment. Includes more than 13,000 U.S. and Canadian sources. Also contains more than 600 recent and standard books and other miscellaneous information.

Turfery, Cossar, and Palmer, King. THE MUSICAL PRODUCTION: A COMPLETE GUIDE FOR AMATEURS. London: Pitman, 1953. 226 p. Photos, illus.

Covers all of the principal details involved in producing musical theatre.

Volbach, Walther R[ichard]. PROBLEMS OF OPERA PRODUCTION. 2d ed. New York: Archon Books, 1967. 218 p. Photos, illus.

A comprehensive work covering the various aspects of opera production, including the singing, conducting, staging, designing, rehearsing, and performing. The organization behind the production is also described in detail. A valuable listing of publishers, rental agencies, associations, and councils is given. Bibliography.

BALLET

Balanchine, George. BALANCHINE'S NEW COMPLETE STORIES OF THE GREAT BALLETS. Edited by Francis Mason. Garden City, N.Y.: Doubleday and Co., 1968. 626 p. Illus., photos.

Describes 231 of the most significant ballets in performance. Bibliography.

Beaumont, Cyril W. COMPLETE BOOK OF BALLETS: A GUIDE TO THE PRINCIPAL BALLETS OF THE 19TH AND 20TH CENTURIES. Rev. ed. London: Putnam, 1956. 1,106 p. Illus., photos.

A comprehensive work dealing with the stories of the principal ballets of the nineteenth and twentieth centuries, grouped together in chronological order under their choreographers.

Clarke, Mary, and Crisp, Clement. THE BALLET: AN ILLUSTRATED HISTORY. New York: Universe Books, 1973. 245 p. Illus., photos.

Traces the development of ballet from the royal courts in Italy to twentieth-century practices. Important leaders in the field are discussed. Bibliography.

Cohen, Selma Jeanne. STRAVINSKY AND THE DANCE. New York: New York Public Library, 1962. 60 p. Paper.

A survey of the ballets choreographed to Stravinsky's music from 1910 to 1962.

Fiske, Roger. BALLET MUSIC. London: George G. Harrap & Co., 1958. 88 p. Music, photos.

One of the few available books which focus on music composed especially for the ballet. Contains many musical quotations and details of published scores. Discography.

Gadan, Francis, and Maillard, Robert, eds. DICTIONARY OF MODERN BALLET. New York: Tudor, 1959. 360 p.

A comprehensive, annotated, alphabetical listing of performers, terms, ballet companies, stories of ballets, and other related information.

Grant, Gail. TECHNICAL MANUAL AND DICTIONARY OF CLASSICAL BALLET. 2d ed. New York: Dover Publications, 1967. 127 p. Photos.

A description and definition of more than 800 ballet steps, movements, and poses. A pictorial supplement of diagrams illustrating proper execution of the more common ballet steps and movements. Bibliography.

Lawrence, Robert. THE VICTOR BOOK OF BALLETS AND BALLET MUSIC. New York: Simon and Schuster, 1950. 531 p. Illus., music.

Serves well as a quick reference guide to the stories of the ballets.

Mara, Thalia. THE LANGUAGE OF BALLET: AN INFORMAL DICTIONARY. Brooklyn, N.Y.: Dance Horizons, 1966. 120 p. Illus., paper.

A simple and easy-to-understand glossary for the layman and student.

Percival, John. MODERN BALLET. New York: E.P. Dutton, 1970. 159 p. Photos, paper.

An explanation of the more recent changes that have taken place in ballet. Fifty companies in Europe, Russia, and the United States are discussed.

Searle, Humphrey. BALLET MUSIC: AN INTRODUCTION. 2d rev. ed. New York: Dover Publications, 1973. 256 p.

Terry, Walter. THE BALLET COMPANION: A POPULAR GUIDE FOR THE BALLET-GOER. New York: Dodd, Mead and Co., 1968. 236 p. Illus.

A comprehensive coverage of the field of ballet. Includes techniques of the dance, historical development, and discussion of the music itself. A glossary of terms and a list of ballets with historical data is found in the appendixes.

UNESCO. CATALOGUE: TEN YEARS OF FILMS ON BALLET AND CLASSICAL DANCE, 1956-1965. Paris: 1968. 105 p.

A representative listing of films on ballet, classical, and modern dance. Covers the important stylistic movements in these three fields. Does not include videotapes.

Wilson, G.B.L. A DICTIONARY OF BALLET. 3d ed. London: A. & C. Black, 1974. 539 p.

A standard reference work. Includes recent developments in ballet and modern dance.

DANCE

Arvey, Verna. CHOREOGRAPHIC MUSIC: MUSIC FOR THE DANCE. New York: E.P. Dutton, 1941. 523 p. Music, photos.

A study of the musical literature for the dance from primitive dance ceremonials to modern times. Bibliography.

Bruce, Violet Rose. DANCE AND DANCE DRAMA IN EDUCATION. New York: Pergamon Press, 1965. 118 p. Photos, illus., paper.

Based on the work of Rudolf Laban, this text illustrates how the language of movement can be used in the curriculum of the public schools. Bibliography.

Chujoy, Anatole, and Manchester, P.W., eds. THE DANCE ENCYCLOPEDIA. Rev. ed. New York: Simon and Schuster, 1967. 992 p. Illus.

Gilbert, Pia, and Lockhart, Aileene. MUSIC FOR THE MODERN DANCE. Dubuque, Iowa: William C. Brown Co., 1961. 120 p. Music, illus.

Develops understanding of the relationship between dance and music, the teacher and accompanist, and the composer and choreographer. Bibliography and discography.

Haberman, Martin, and Meisel, Tobie Garth, eds. DANCE: AN ART IN ACADEME. New York: Teachers College Press, 1970. 172 p.

A discussion of the nature of dance and its place in the curriculum. Specific problems are analyzed with guiding principles and model programs suggested. Bibliography.

Horst, Louis, and Russell, Carroll. MODERN DANCE FORMS IN RELATION TO THE OTHER MODERN ARTS. 1961. Reprint. Brooklyn, N.Y.: Dance Horizons, 1967. Illus., music, photos, paper.

A study of dance as an art form. The elements of dance are discussed with suggested musical accompaniments.

Humphrey, Doris. THE ART OF MAKING DANCES. Edited by Barbara Pollack. New York: Rinehart and Co., 1959. 189 p. Illus.

Highly useful as a practical guide. Features a special chapter explaining the use and interpretation of music in the dance.

Joyce, Mary. FIRST STEPS IN TEACHING CREATIVE DANCE. Palo Alto, Calif.: National Press Books, 1973. 191 p. Illus.

A source book for classroom teachers interested in giving students a creative dance experience. Includes definitive lesson plans. Bibliography.

Nettl, Paul. THE DANCE IN CLASSICAL MUSIC. New York: Philosophical Library, 1963. 168 p.

Describes the philosophical and artistic place of dance in musical expression.

_____. THE STORY OF DANCE MUSIC. New York: Philosophical Library, 1947. 370 p. Music, photos.

This work is of particular value to music educators in revealing the influence of the dance on the development of music.

Percival, John. EXPERIMENTAL DANCE. New York: Universe Books, 1971. 160 p. Photos.

An analysis of the novel uses of dance in theatrical and similar activities in the 1970s. Includes background and the general ideas underlying experimental dance. Discusses individual artists and their contributions. Bibliography.

Porter, Evelyn. MUSIC THROUGH THE DANCE: A HANDBOOK FOR TEACHERS AND STUDENTS, SHOWING HOW MUSICAL GROWTH HAS BEEN INFLUENCED BY THE DANCE THROUGHOUT THE AGES. London: B.T. Batsford, 1937. 155 p. Photos, illus., music.

Describes methods of developing musical understanding through the medium of dance. Bibliography.

Raffe, W.G. DICTIONARY OF THE DANCE. New York: A.S. Barnes and Co., 1964. 583 p.

Not only a dictionary, this includes a bibliography of works from the fifteenth century to the present, a geographical index, and a subject index.

Russell, Joan. MODERN DANCE IN EDUCATION. New York: Praeger, 1968. 99 p. Photos.

Designed as an aid to beginning teachers of the dance. A practical guide describing methods of integrating dance in the school curriculum. Bibliography and discography.

Sachs, Curt. WORLD HISTORY OF THE DANCE. Translated by Bessie Schonberg. 1937. Reprint. New York: W.W. Norton and Co., 1963. 469 p. Illus., photos.

A comprehensive history which discusses the general types and characteristics of the dance and deals specifically with its many forms and symbols, ranging from the Stone Age to the twentieth century. Bibliography.

Stearns, Marshall [W.], and Stearns, Jean. JAZZ DANCE: THE STORY OF AMERICAN VERNACULAR DANCE. New York: Macmillan, 1968. 464 p. Photos, illus.

A unique work which traces the history of American jazz dance. Includes two important appendices. One is an extensive list of films--documentaries, television productions, and full-length motion pictures. The other is an analysis, in labanotation, of basic African, popular American, and jazz dance movements.

Terry, Walter. THE DANCE IN AMERICA. Rev. ed. New York: Harper and Row, 1971. 272 p. Illus., photos.

A history of the varieties of dance in America from the colonial times to the 1950s. The influence of traditional and romantic ballet on the development of the dance is discussed. Includes biographies of leading dancers.

Turner, Margery J., et al. NEW DANCE: APPROACHES TO NONLITERAL CHOREOGRAPHY. Pittsburgh: University of Pittsburgh Press, 1971. 128 p. Photos.

Deals with the new forms of modern dance, specifically the developments since 1951. Suggestions for implementing innovative forms are given. Bibliography and discography.

Willis, John. DANCE WORLD. New York: Crown, 1975. 220 p. Photos.

Provides broad coverage of information pertaining to the dance. Includes activities of regional professional companies, summer festivals, and biographies of choreographers and leading dancers.

See also Section 26: Music in Early Childhood Education, and Section 27: Music in the Elementary School.

Folk Dancing

Czarnowski, Lucile K. FOLK DANCE TEACHING CUES. 3d ed. Palo Alto, Calif.: National Press, 1963. 93 p. Illus., music.

Basic problems encountered in teaching folk dance are discussed and practical ideas and methods suggested.

English Folk Dance and Song Society. FOLK DIRECTORY, 1971. London: 1971. Paper.

Listing of English folk artists and services. Includes books, events, federations, international associations and clubs, record companies, and speakers.

Gilbert, Cecile. INTERNATIONAL FOLK DANCE AT A GLANCE. Minneapolis: Burgess Publishing Co., 1969. 171 p. Illus., paper.

A handbook which gives step-by-step instructions for sixty-seven folk dances. Discography and bibliography.

Jensen, Clayne R., and Jensen, Mary Bee. BEGINNING FOLK DANCING. Belmont, Calif.: Wadsworth Publishing Co., 1966. 60 p. Photos, paper.

This handbook discusses the values, history, and basic procedures for folk dancing. Twenty-four selected dances are illustrated with photographs. Bibliography.

Mason, Bernard S. DANCES AND STORIES OF THE AMERICAN INDIAN. New York: Ronald Press, 1944. 269 p. Photos, illus.

A description of American Indian dances with instructions for performance.

Mynatt, Constance V., and Kaiman, Bernard D. FOLK DANCING FOR STUDENTS AND TEACHERS. Dubuque, Iowa: William C. Brown Co., 1968. 113 p. Illus.

A handbook which gives instructions for teaching folk dance, including facilities and equipment needed, and suggestions for planning the lesson. Sixty-five dances are illustrated.

ASSOCIATIONS

American Dance Guild, 1619 Broadway, Room 603, New York, N.Y. 10019.

Publications: DANCE SCOPE. 2/year.

Newsletter. Quarterly.

Various manuscripts.

Membership list.

Central Opera Service (COS), Metropolitan Opera, Lincoln Center Plaza, New York, N.Y. 10023.

Publications: CENTRAL OPERA SERVICE BULLETIN. Quarterly.

Various directories and special listings.

Chinese Musical and Theatrical Association, 181 Canal Street, New York, N.Y. 10013.

Metropolitan Opera Guild (MOG), 1865 Broadway, New York, N.Y. 10023.

Publication: OPERA NEWS. Weekly during opera broadcast season (December-April), monthly May-December.

Musical Theatres Association (MTA), Five Westland Road, Hamden, Conn. 06517.

Publication: Bulletin. Irregular.

National Opera Association (NOA), c/o Constance Eberhart, 823 Hotel Wellington, Seventh & 55th Streets, New York, N.Y. 10019.

Publications: NOA OPERA JOURNAL. Quarterly.

Membership directory. Annual.

Addresses, papers, lists of translations, technical reports.

Section 43
POPULAR MUSIC—JAZZ—ROCK

POPULAR MUSIC

American Society of Composers, Authors and Publishers. HIT TUNES. New York: n.d. 120 p.

A listing of some of the great hit tunes from 1892 through 1970. Includes a list of motion picture Academy Award songs from 1934 through 1969.

Burton, Jack. THE BLUE BOOK OF TIN PAN ALLEY: A HUMAN INTEREST ENCYCLOPEDIA OF AMERICAN POPULAR MUSIC. Vol. 1: 1776-1860-1910. Watkins Glen, N.Y.: Century House, 1962. 304 p.

Chipman, John H. INDEX TO TOP-HIT TUNES, 1900-1950. Boston: Bruce Humphries, 1962. 249 p.

An alphabetical and chronological listing of more than 3,000 titles of the most popular songs Americans enjoyed during the first half of the twentieth century.

Denisoff, R. Serge. SING A SONG OF SOCIAL SIGNIFICANCE. Bowling Green, Ohio: Bowling Green University Popular Press, 1972. 229 p. Illus., photos.

A serious study and discussion of the protest song. Special attention is given to the role music plays in a period of political polarization and turmoil. Bibliography.

Ewen, David, ed. AMERICAN POPULAR SONGS FROM THE REVOLUTIONARY WAR TO THE PRESENT. New York: Random House, 1966. 507 p.

A comprehensive, factual guide to songs from 1765 to 1966.

Gammond, Peter, and Clayton, Peter. DICTIONARY OF POPULAR MUSIC. New York: Philosophical Library, 1961. 274 p.

Kinkle, Roger D. THE COMPLETE ENCYCLOPEDIA OF POPULAR MUSIC AND JAZZ 1900-1950. 4 vols. New Rochelle, N.Y.: Arlington House, 1974.

A rather exhaustive coverage of these two important streams of American music.

Lewine, Richard, and Simon, Alfred, comps. ENCYCLOPEDIA OF THEATRE MUSIC. New York: Random House, 1961. 2,481 p.

A comprehensive listing of more than 4,000 songs from Broadway to Hollywood during 1900 to 1960. Cross-referenced, alphabetical lists contain basic information--composers, lyricists, show, dates of play productions--on all the published songs from Broadway shows between 1925 and 1960. Includes many songs of pre-1925 era written by theatre composers for the movies.

Mattfeld, Julius. VARIETY: MUSIC CAVALCADE 1620-1969. 3d ed. Englewood Cliffs, N.J.: Prentice-Hall, 1971. 766 p.

A chronological checklist of music which was popular in the United States from the time of the Pilgrims to the present day.

Mellers, Wilfrid Howard. TWILIGHT OF THE GODS: THE MUSIC OF THE BEATLES. New York: Viking Press, 1973. 215 p. Music, photos.

An analytical study of the text and music of representative Beatle songs. Focus is on songs readily available on extant recordings. Discography.

Melly, George. REVOLT INTO STYLE: THE POP ARTS. Garden City, N.Y.: Anchor Books, 1971. 270 p. Paper.

A discussion of British pop culture and its music, literature, film, television, radio, and theatre productions.

Shapiro, Nat, ed. POPULAR MUSIC: AN ANNOTATED INDEX OF AMERICAN POPULAR SONGS. 5 vols. New York: Adrian Press, 1964-69.

Volume 1: 1950-59 (1964); volume 2: 1940-49 (1965); volume 3: 1960-64 (1967); volume 4: 1930-39 (1968); volume 5: 1920-29 (1969).

Simon, George T. THE BIG BANDS. Rev. ed. New York: Macmillan, 1975. 594 p. Photos.

The men and the music that made 400 bands famous. Seventy-two of the top-ranking organizations are profiled at length. Discography.

Stambler, Irwin. ENCYCLOPEDIA OF POPULAR MUSIC. New York: St. Martin's Press, 1965. 359 p. Illus.

Covers the breadth and depth of popular music: the people responsible for it, its various forms, and its effects on modern life.

Whitburn, Joel, comp. TOP POP RECORDS 1955-1970. Detroit: Gale Research Co., 1972. Unpaged.

This book lists every record that achieved Billboard's "Top 100" and "Hot 100" ratings from November 1955 through December 1969. The 1970 supplement lists top hits from January through December 1970. More than 2,500 artists and 9,800 records are included. Each selection is listed by artist with the date that the record was first listed on the chart; highest position reached; number of weeks on the chart; and record title, label, and number.

JAZZ

Blesh, Rudi. SHINING TRUMPETS: A HISTORY OF JAZZ. New York: Alfred A. Knopf Co., 1953. 365 p. Music, photos.

Traces the development of jazz from its roots in Africa to the present. Analysis, evaluation, and comparison with other types of music are included. Bibliography.

Chilton, John. WHO'S WHO OF JAZZ: STORYVILLE TO SWING STREET. New York: Chilton Book Co., 1972. 419 p. Photos.

An anthology of biographies detailing the careers of more than 1,000 musicians whose names are part of jazz history.

Collier, Graham. INSIDE JAZZ. London: Quartet Books, 1973. 144 p. Photos.

An informal discussion of the art. Includes sections on performance, instruments, performers, musical forms, and recording problems.

Feather, Leonard G. ENCYCLOPEDIA OF JAZZ. Rev. and enl. ed. New York: Horizon Press, 1960. 527 p. Illus., music.

_____. THE ENCYCLOPEDIA OF JAZZ IN THE SIXTIES. New York: Horizon Press, 1966. Unpaged.

A supplement to the author's ENCYCLOPEDIA OF JAZZ (see above).

Gold, Robert S. A JAZZ LEXICON. New York: Alfred A. Knopf Co., 1964. 363 p.

Terms from the field of jazz are defined. Bibliography.

Gregor, Carl. INTERNATIONAL JAZZ BIBLIOGRAPHY: JAZZ BOOKS FROM 1919-1968. Strasbourg: Editions P.H. Heitz, 1969. 198 p.

Survey of the jazz literature published in independent form during the fifty-year period, 1919-68. Limited to jazz as a separate form of music.

Henthoff, Nat, and McCarthy, Albert. JAZZ: NEW PERSPECTIVES ON THE HISTORY OF JAZZ BY TWELVE OF THE WORLD'S FOREMOST JAZZ CRITICS AND SCHOLARS. 1959. Reprint. New York: Da Capo Press, 1974. 387 p.

A compilation of essays relating to the historical development of jazz. Discography.

Hickerson, Joseph C., comp. A BIBLIOGRAPHY OF THE BLUES. Washington, D.C.: Library of Congress, 1971. 16 p.

An excellent bibliography for the subject. Includes a list of Blues periodicals with addresses.

Hodeir, André. THE WORLDS OF JAZZ. Translated by Nöel Burch. New York: Grove Press, 1972. 279 p. Illus.

A scholarly, analytical work which discusses performers and composers in the field of jazz. One section is a compilation of lectures on history and aesthetics.

Jasen, David A. RECORDED RAGTIME, 1897-1958. Hamden, Conn.: Shoe String Press, 1973. 155 p. Illus.

Bibliography.

Kennington, Donald. THE LITERATURE OF JAZZ: A CRITICAL GUIDE. Chicago: American Library Association, 1971. 142 p.

Lists books on every aspect of jazz--its sociology, performers, history, and impact on other arts. Reference sources include discographies and annotated record guides.

Leonard, Neil. JAZZ AND THE WHITE AMERICANS. Chicago: University of Chicago Press, 1962. 216 p.

Deals with the social and intellectual implications of the adoption by white Americans of an art form associated primarily with the black.

Longstreet, Stephen. THE REAL JAZZ OLD AND NEW. Baton Rouge: Louisiana State University Press, 1956. 202 p. Illus.

A report of the jazz life of New Orleans, New York, Chicago, and Los Angeles, as told by the performers themselves.

Markewich, Reese. THE NEW EXPANDED BIBLIOGRAPHY OF JAZZ COMPOSITIONS BASED ON THE CHORD PROGRESSIONS OF STANDARD TUNES. New York: Markewich, 1974. 44 p. Paper.

An expanded revision of BIBLIOGRAPHY OF JAZZ AND POP TUNES SHARING THE CHORD PROGRESSIONS OF OTHER COMPOSITIONS (New York: Markewich, 1970). Presents groups of compositions that share the chord progressions of standard popular songs and other jazz compositions. Information includes title, author, publisher, recording labels, and shows or movies. A list of publishers' addresses is also given.

Merriam, Alan P. A BIBLIOGRAPHY OF JAZZ. 1954. Reprint. New York: Da Capo Press, 1970. 145 p.

Covers jazz since its origin as an identifiable musical system in the last decade of the nineteenth century.

Nanry, Charles, ed. AMERICAN MUSIC: FROM STORYVILLE TO WOODSTOCK. New Brunswick, N.J.: Transaction Books, 1972. 290 p.

A set of sociological studies of the jazz phenomenon in America.

Oliver, Paul. THE STORY OF THE BLUES. New York: Chilton Book Co., 1969. 176 p. Illus., music, photos.

A comprehensive coverage of the blues from the music of the African slaves in America to the blues in modern rock. Bibliography and discography.

Rose, Al, and Souchon, Edmond. NEW ORLEANS JAZZ: A FAMILY ALBUM. Baton Rouge: Louisiana State University Press, 1967. 304 p. Photos.

A comprehensive pictorial and textual coverage of jazz in New Orleans from the 1880s to the middle of the twentieth century. Includes more than 1,000 biographical sketches of jazz artists who started in New Orleans, a list of jazz bands and brass bands of New Orleans, and the places where jazz was played.

Russo, William. JAZZ COMPOSITION AND ORCHESTRATION. Chicago: University of Chicago Press, 1968. 826 p. Illus.

Basic procedures for writing in the jazz idiom.

Schafer, William J., and Riedel, Johannes. THE ART OF RAGTIME: FORM AND MEANING OF AN ORIGINAL BLACK AMERICAN ART. Baton Rouge: Louisiana State University Press, 1973. 249 p. Illus., music.

An extensive, musicological analysis of ragtime as an American musical form. Coverage is from the 1890s through 1915. Ragtime is presented as it relates to jazz and other black musical forms. Selected major ragtime composers are discussed in depth. Bibliography.

Schuller, Gunther. THE HISTORY OF JAZZ--VOLUME I: EARLY JAZZ: ITS ROOTS AND MUSICAL DEVELOPMENT. New York: Oxford University Press, 1968. 401 p. Illus., music.

A serious study of jazz. Important is the author's account of the genesis of jazz in African musical forms. Discography.

Seidel, Richard, ed. THE BASIC RECORD LIBRARY OF JAZZ. Boston: W. Schwann, 1974. 20 p. Paper.

Contains listing of more than 250 jazz recordings with annotations. One section lists recommended jazz books and major jazz periodicals.

Stearns, Marshall W. THE STORY OF JAZZ. 1958. Reprint. London and New York: Oxford University Press, 1972. 379 p. Illus., photos.

A systematic description of the evolution of the unique American musical phenomenon. Bibliography.

Stewart, Rex. JAZZ MASTERS OF THE 30'S. The Macmillan Jazz Masters Series. Martin Williams, general ed. New York: Macmillan, 1972. 224 p.

Tanner, Paul O.W. A STUDY OF JAZZ. 2d ed. Dubuque, Iowa: William C. Brown Co., 1973. 208 p.

A broad coverage of the field of jazz--historical roots and development, including modern trends. An accompanying disc recording gives aural examples of the styles discussed. Bibliography and discography.

Ulanov, Barry. A HANDBOOK OF JAZZ. New York: Viking Press, 1960. 248 p.

An introduction to jazz and its makers. Bibliography.

Williams, Martin. THE SMITHSONIAN COLLECTION OF CLASSIC JAZZ. New York: W.W. Norton and Co., 1973. 48 p. and six 12" stereo records. Illus.

The material provides a concise history of jazz, a jazz bibliography, and factual information concerning each of the recorded selections. Included is a guide to obtaining jazz records.

ROCK

Belz, Carl. THE STORY OF ROCK. New York: Oxford University Press, 1969. 256 p. Photos.

Describes the history of rock music as a folk expression. Seeks to define its origin, its essential nature, and its musical significance. Discography.

Eisen, Jonathan, ed. THE AGE OF ROCK: SOUNDS OF THE AMERICAN CULTURAL REVOLUTION. A READER. New York: Random House, 1969. 388 p. Illus.

Essays on rock music and its performers.

_____. THE AGE OF ROCK--2: SIGHTS AND SOUNDS OF THE AMERICAN CULTURAL REVOLUTION. New York: Random House, 1970. 339 p. Photos, illus.

A compilation of articles dealing with prominent rock groups and their music.

Hall, Douglas Kent, comp. ROCK: A WORLD BOLD AS LOVE. New York: Cowles Book Co., 1970. 192 p. Illus., photos.

A photographic and interview account of some of the leading rock performers. Includes their views of music, themselves, and other performers.

Hopkins, Jerry. THE ROCK STORY. New York: New American Library, 1970. 222 p. Photos.

A history of rock and roll music with a description of the performers' life styles. Discography.

Meltzer, Richard. THE AESTHETICS OF ROCK. New York: Something Else Press, 1970. 346 p. Photos.

A philosophical discussion of rock and roll music by one of its performers.

Nite, Norman N. ROCK ON: THE ILLUSTRATED ENCYCLOPEDIA OF ROCK, THE GOLDEN YEARS. New York: Thomas Y. Crowell Co., 1974. 676 p. Photos, tables.

A comprehensive work with data on more than 1,000 artists. Includes biographical and other pertinent information, including top recordings.

Roxon, Lillian. ROCK ENCYCLOPEDIA. New York: Grosset and Dunlap, 1969. 61 p. Illus.

An alphabetical listing of groups and single artists, their development, their top albums and singles. Also contains a chronological listing of top singles and albums, week by week, from 1950 through 1967.

ASSOCIATIONS

Country Music Association, Seven Music Circle North, Nashville, Tenn. 37203.

Publication: CLOSE-UP. Monthly.

Country Music Foundation, Four Music Square East, Nashville, Tenn. 37203.

Publication: THE JOURNAL OF COUNTRY MUSIC. Quarterly.

Duke Ellington Society, Box 31, Church Street Station, New York, N.Y. 10008.

Publication: Newsletter.

Jazz-Lift, 194 North Union Street, Battle Creek, Mich. 49011.

Publications: Distributes jazz literature, magazines, and musical scores.

Jazzmobile, Inc., 361 West 125th Street, New York, N.Y. 10027.

National Association of Jazz Educators (NAJE), Box 724, Manhattan, Kans. 66502.

Publication: EDUCATOR. 4/year.

New Orleans Jazz Club (NOJC), 833 Conti Street, New Orleans, La. 70130.

Publication: SECOND LINE. Quarterly.

Ragtime Society, P.O. Box 520, Weston, Ontario, Canada.

Publication: THE RAGTIMER (newsletter). 6/year.

Southern California Hot Jazz Society (SCHJS), Los Angeles, California.

Publication: SCHJS FANFARE. Monthly.

Transaction Periodicals Consortium, Rutgers University, New Brunswick, N.J. 08903.

Publication: JOURNAL OF JAZZ STUDIES. Semiannual.

Section 44

MUSIC AND THE BLACK CULTURE

This section presents useful sources of information concerning African and Afro-American music traditions, the essence and development of black folk music, black music in the cultural matrix of American life, black nationalism, and curriculum materials for teaching black music in the American culture.

BIBLIOGRAPHIC AND RESEARCH SOURCES

Curriculum Consultation Service. THE NEGRO IN THE U.S.: A LIST OF SIGNIFICANT BOOKS SELECTED FROM A COMPILATION BY THE N.Y. PUBLIC LIBRARY. ERIC No. ED 019 339. New York: 1965. 5 p.

Several books on Negro music and musicians are cited in this bibliography.

De Lerma, Dominique-René. AAMOA RESOURCE PAPERS. Minneapolis, Minn.: Afro-American Music Opportunities Association.

This monograph series, intended for researchers, performers, and teachers of black music, has been initiated by the Afro-American Music Opportunities Association. For details on forthcoming monographs, write to the association, Box 662, Minneapolis, Minnesota 55440.

______. "Black Music: A Bibliographic Essay." LIBRARY TRENDS 23 (January 1975): 517-32.

Excellent bibliographic coverage of the black music field. All items well chosen and organized by categories.

______. REFLECTIONS ON AFRO-AMERICAN MUSIC. Kent, Ohio: Kent State University Press, 1973. 271 p.

A series of articles pertaining to the black music curriculum, jazz, and related topics. Contains chapter on information sources which discusses various sources of Afro-American music--scores, recordings, publishers, and bibliographies. Also includes a chapter "Black Music in College Music History Texts."

Johnson, Harry A. MULTIMEDIA MATERIALS FOR AFRO-AMERICAN STUDIES: A CURRICULUM ORIENTATION AND ANNOTATED BIBLIOGRAPHY OF RESOURCES. New York: R.R. Bowker Co., 1971. 353 p.

Music Educators National Conference. "Bibliography of Negro and African Music." MUSIC EDUCATORS JOURNAL 56 (January 1970): 113-20.

A highly useful bibliography listing books and films dealing with black and African music.

Standifer, James A., and Reeder, Barbara. SOURCE BOOK OF AFRICAN AND AFRO-AMERICAN MATERIALS FOR MUSIC EDUCATORS. Washington, D.C.: Music Educators National Conference, Contemporary Music Project, 1972. 147 p. Illus., music.

Includes lists of books, articles, recordings, and other materials dealing with African and Afro-American music traditions. Many titles are annotated.

Tracey, Hugh, et al. CODIFICATION OF AFRICAN MUSIC AND TEXTBOOK PROJECT: A PRIMER OF PRACTICAL SUGGESTIONS FOR FIELD RESEARCH. Roodepoort, South Africa: International Library of African Music, 1969. 54 p. Paper.

White, Davidson. SELECTED BIBLIOGRAPHY OF PUBLISHED CHORAL MUSIC BY BLACK COMPOSERS. Washington, D.C.: Howard University Bookstore, 1975. 87 p.

Describes more than 700 compositions by sixty-three black composers and arrangers.

OTHER SOURCES

Brandel, Rose. THE MUSIC OF CENTRAL AFRICA: AN ETHNOMUSCOLOGICAL STUDY. The Hague: Nijhoff, 1961. 272 p. Illus., music, photos.

A scholarly report of research in the music of Central Africa. Deals with all aspects of the music and compares the various elements. Bibliography.

Butcher, Vada E., et al. DEVELOPMENT OF MATERIALS FOR A ONE-YEAR COURSE IN AFRICAN MUSIC FOR THE GENERAL UNDERGRADUATE STUDENT. Washington, D.C.: U.S. Office of Education, Project in African Music, 1970. 281 p.

Courlander, Harold. NEGRO FOLK MUSIC, U.S.A. New York: Columbia University Press, 1963. 324 p. Music.

Explores the essence and development of Negro folk music, both vocal and instrumental, in terms of its historical and organic development, relating it to social settings and to traditions out of which it took shape. Included are musical examples, bibliography, discography, sources or notated songs, and an index.

Cuney-Hare, Maude. NEGRO MUSICIANS AND THEIR MUSIC. 1936. Reprint. New York: Da Capo Press, 1974. 439 p.

A comprehensive survey of the origins and development of Negro music from its roots in African song and dance to its inclusion in twentieth-century works for the concert hall.

D'Azevedo, Warren L., ed. THE TRADITIONAL ARTIST IN AFRICAN SOCIETIES. Bloomington: Indiana University Press, 1973. 454 p. Illus., photos.

A compilation of articles written by ten Africanists for a conference on "The Traditional Artist in African Society" held in 1964. The discussions focus on the role, status, and social funtion of the African artists; definition of art as it is expressed in different kinds of societies; and relating the art to western society. Bibliography.

De Lerma, Dominique-René. BLACK MUSIC IN OUR CULTURE: CURRICULUM IDEAS ON THE SUBJECTS, MATERIALS, AND PROBLEMS. Kent, Ohio: Kent State University Press, 1970. 263 p.

Defines black music, its sources and materials, and its role not only in education, but also in the total cultural matrix of American life. Appendixes include lists of scores, recordings, films, books, and sample curricular syllabi.

Fisher, Miles Mark. NEGRO SLAVE SONGS. New York: Russell and Russell, 1968. 233 p.

Discusses the origin of the melodies, their functional use, and their personal value. Bibliography.

Garland, Phyl. THE SOUND OF SOUL. Chicago: Henry Regnery, 1969. 246 p.

An informal account of the influence of soul music on the culture of the United States. Also traces its ethnic roots. Discography.

Gayle, Addison, Jr., ed. THE BLACK AESTHETIC. Garden City, N.Y.: Doubleday and Co., 1971. 432 p.

An anthology of thirty-four articles by twenty-nine writers. Seven articles are about music and the black humanities.

Golin, Sanford. THE SELF-ESTEEM AND GOALS OF INDIGENT CHILDREN: PROGRESS REPORT. ERIC No. ED 036 586. Pittsburgh: Pittsburgh University Department of Psychology, 1969. 14 p.

A discussion of summer and full-year programs in black history and culture, including African and Afro-American music and dance, which were offered to elementary and junior high students.

Jones, Le Roi. BLUES PEOPLE. 1963. Reprint. New York: William Morrow, 1970. 244 p. Paper.

A discussion of Negro music as it relates to American social history.

Katz, Bernard, ed. THE SOCIAL IMPLICATIONS OF EARLY NEGRO MUSIC IN THE UNITED STATES. New York: Arno Press, 1969. 250 p. Illus.

Pioneering writings on the history of early Afro-American music. Bibliography.

Keil, Charles. URBAN BLUES. Chicago: University of Chicago Press, 1966. 231 p.

A description of Negro-American culture and its music. Bibliographical references.

Kofsky, Frank. BLACK NATIONALISM AND THE REVOLUTION IN MUSIC. New York: Pathfinder Press, 1970. 280 p. Photos, illus.

A description of the revolution in jazz, its dynamics, and the innovations of individual revolutionists. It is also a cultural and sociological study of the developments both in music and the urban ghetto which go under the names of black nationalism, the return to African roots, and the new militancy. Bibliography and discography.

Krehbiel, Henry Edward. AFRO-AMERICAN FOLKSONGS: A STUDY IN RACIAL AND NATIONAL MUSIC. 1913. Reprint. New York: Frederick Ungar Publishing Co., 1962. 176 p. Music.

An analysis of folk songs to discover distinctive idioms and a comparison of them in relation to other folk melodies.

Locke, Alain. THE NEGRO AND HIS MUSIC: NEGRO ART: PAST AND PRESENT. 1936. Reprint. New York: Arno Press and the New York Times, 1969. 122 p.

An account of the Negro's contribution to American culture and art as viewed by a literary and art critic of the early part of this century. Bibliography.

Lovell, John R. BLACK SONG: THE FORGE AND THE FLAME. New York: Macmillan, 1972. 686 p. Illus.

An excellent source of authentic information concerning the origin, development, and influence of the spiritual.

Nketia, J.H. Kwabena. THE MUSIC OF AFRICA. New York: W.W. Norton and Co., 1974. 278 p. Music, illus., photos.

A broad and useful survey of African music stressing the social and cultural aspects. Bibliography.

Roach, Hildred. BLACK AMERICAN MUSIC: PAST AND PRESENT. Boston: Crescendo Publishing Co., 1973. 199 p. Illus., music.

Surveys Afro-American composers and their music. Bibliography.

Roberts, John Storm. BLACK MUSIC OF TWO WORLDS. New York: Praeger, 1972. 286 p. Illus., music, photos.

An in-depth study of neo-African music, Afro-American styles, and the blending of African and European music. Bibliography and discography.

Rublowsky, John. BLACK MUSIC IN AMERICA. New York and London: Basic Books, 1971. 150 p.

Traces the history of black music and its cultural influence in America. Bibliography.

Southern, Eileen. THE MUSIC OF BLACK AMERICANS: A HISTORY. New York: W.W. Norton and Co., 1972. 552 p. Illus.

One of the first books to reach into the colonial period for information about the music of black Americans and to carry forward the story of its development to the present. Features a comprehensive chronology listing important events in four categories: Negro history, general American history, history of black American music, and history of American music.

______, comp. READINGS IN BLACK AMERICAN MUSIC. New York: W.W. Norton and Co., 1971. 302 p. Music.

A representative selection of authentic, contemporary documents illustrating the history of black American music from the seventeenth century to the present.

Tracey, Hugh. THE EVOLUTION OF AFRICAN MUSIC AND ITS FUNCTION IN THE PRESENT DAY. Johannesburg: Institute for the Study of Man in Africa, 1961. 24 p. Paper.

Discusses the definition of African music and deals with the problems of preserving indigenous music in a modern Africa. Discography.

Walton, Ortez. MUSIC: BLACK, WHITE, AND BLUE: A SOCIOLOGICAL SURVEY OF THE USE AND MISUSE OF AFRO-AMERICAN MUSIC. New York: William Morrow, 1972. 180 p. Illus.

Deals with the place of Afro-American music in American culture. Special attention is given to the structure of music industry as related to black music. Bibliography.

ASSOCIATIONS

African Music Society, P.O. Box 138, Roodeport, Transvaal, South Africa.

Publication: AFRICAN MUSIC.

Afro-American Music Opportunities Association, 2909 Wayzata Boulevard, Minneapolis, Minn. 55405.

Publications: AAMOA REPORTS. Bimonthly.

Resource Papers. Irregular.

Issues the Columbia Black Composers Series of record albums of symphonies, concertos, string quartets, and so forth. Composers include Chevalier de Saint-George, Ulysses S. Kay, George Theophilus, William Grant Still, Samuel Coleridge-Taylor, and Roque Cordero.

Black Music Center, Black Culture, 109 North Jordan Street, Indiana University, Bloomington, Ind. 47401.

The Society of Black Composers, c/o Carman L. Moore, 148 Columbus Avenue, New York, N.Y. 10023.

Section 45
JEWISH MUSIC

Appleton, Lewis. BIBLIOGRAPHY OF JEWISH VOCAL MUSIC. Rev. ed. New York: National Jewish Music Council, 1968. 128 p.

A comprehensive catalog of Jewish vocal music resources.

Benzoor, N. BIBLIOGRAPHY OF JEWISH PERIODICALS. Amli Studies in Music Bibliography. Haifa, Israel: The Haifa Music Museum and Amli Library, 1970. 34 p. Paper.

Music periodicals in Hebrew, Yiddish, and other languages, including English.

Eisenstein, Judith Kaplan. HERITAGE OF MUSIC: THE MUSIC OF THE JEWISH PEOPLE. New York: Union of American Hebrew Congregations, 1972. 340 p. Music.

Recounts the development of Jewish music from 2000-year-old Semitic melodies to contemporary works.

Goldberg, Ira S., comp. BIBLIOGRAPHY OF INSTRUMENTAL MUSIC OF JEWISH INTEREST. 3 parts. New York: Jewish Music Council of the National Jewish Welfare Board, 1970-71.

Part 1: ORCHESTRA AND BAND, 1970. 80 p.; part 2: ENSEMBLE AND SOLO, 1970. 181 p.; part 3: VOICE WITH INSTRUMENTS, 1971. 120 p.

Gradenwitz, Peter. THE MUSIC OF ISRAEL: ITS RISE AND GROWTH THROUGH 5,000 YEARS. New York: W.W. Norton and Co., 1949. 334 p. Illus., music, photos.

A survey of the music of Israel from the ancient Hebrew period to the music of modern Palestine. Stresses the functional aspects of the art. Bibliography.

Heskes, Irene, comp. JEWISH MUSIC PROGRAMS. New York: Jewish

Music Council of the National Jewish Welfare Board, 1973. 82 p.

A sampling of festivals from 1970-73 including concerts, liturgical services, and special events.

Heskes, Irene, and Wolfson, Arthur M., eds. THE HISTORIC CONTRIBUTION OF RUSSIAN JEWRY TO JEWISH MUSIC. New York: Jewish Music Council of the National Jewish Welfare Board, 1967. 80 p. SUPPLEMENT: THE HISTORICAL CONTRIBUTION OF RUSSIAN JEWRY TO JEWISH MUSIC. 1968. 30 p.

Nulman, Macy. CONCISE ENCYCLOPEDIA OF JEWISH MUSIC. New York: McGraw-Hill Book Co., 1974. 256 p.

Covers biographical, musicological, and historic facts. Includes a chronological listing of highlights in Jewish music history.

Rothmüller, Aron Marks. THE MUSIC OF THE JEWS: AN HISTORICAL APPRECIATION. Rev. ed. Translated by H.S. Stevens. South Brunswick, N.J.: Thomas Yoseloff, Publisher, 1967. 320 p.

A nontechnical, historical presentation of all music that can be attributed to a recognized Jewish tradition. Bibliography.

Sendrey, Alfred. BIBLIOGRAPHY OF JEWISH MUSIC. New York: Columbia University Press, 1951. Reprint. New York: Kraus, 1969. 404 p.

Includes almost 10,000 titles of literary works and musical pieces, together with an introductory historical survey of bibliography of Jewish music. All entries are carefully classified according to field of study. Annotations are provided for most items which are not made clear by title.

______. MUSIC IN ANCIENT ISRAEL. New York: Philosophical Library, 1969. 674 p.

A comprehensive study of ancient Hebrew music. Includes historical primary sources of Jewish music and a listing of direct and indirect references to music in the Bible. Bibliographic references.

ASSOCIATIONS

Hebrew Arts School for Music and Dance, 15 West 65th Street, New York, N.Y. 10023.

Jewish Music Alliance, One Union Square West, New York, N.Y. 10023.

Publications: TWO BROTHERS. Biennial.

POETS IN SONG. Quadriennial.

National Jewish Music Council (NJMC), 15 East 26th Street, New York, N.Y. 10010.

Publications: JEWISH MUSIC NOTES. Semiannual.

Program aids.

Section 46

RELIGIOUS MUSIC

Blume, Friederich. PROTESTANT CHURCH MUSIC: A HISTORY. New York: W.W. Norton and Co., 1975. 848 p. Photos, music.

A comprehensive and definitive study of Protestant church music. This newly translated edition has also been updated since it was originally published in 1964. An authoritative work.

Bryden, John R., and Hughes, David G., comps. AN INDEX OF GREGORIAN CHANT. 2 vols. Cambridge, Mass.: Harvard University Press, 1969.

A practical work dealing primarily with what is usually referred to as Gregorian chant (Ambrosian and the local Roman dialect of Gregorian chant have been omitted). A comprehensive work covering that portion of the chant that was in general use for a considerable period of time.

Volume I: ALPHABETICAL INDEX--entries presented in alphabetical order of the textual incipits. Useful for finding sources for known liturgical texts, and finding sources for different settings of the same text or category.

Volume II: THEMATIC INDEX--same information as volume 1, but entries are arranged in numberical order of melodic incipits. Useful for bringing together in one place melodies having same incipit, and identification of a melody that has been transmitted without a text.

Davies, J.G., ed. A DICTIONARY OF CHRISTIAN WORSHIP. New York: Macmillan, 1972. 385 p.

Treats the principal aspects of liturgy and worship, but the important ancillaries of worship (i.e., architecture, music, vestments, and so forth) are also discussed.

Diehl, Katharine S. HYMNS AND TUNES: AN INDEX. Metuchen, N.J.: Scarecrow Press, 1966. 1,242 p.

Conveniently locates hymns by first line, author, composer, tune names, and other variants.

Ellinwood, Leonard. THE HISTORY OF AMERICAN CHURCH MUSIC. 1953. Reprint. New York: Da Capo Press, 1970. 274 p. Photos.

A comprehensive coverage of the development of church music from 1500 to the twentieth century. Includes selective music lists and biographies of American church musicians. Bibliography.

Foote, Henry Wilder. THREE CENTURIES OF AMERICAN HYMNODY. 1940. Reprint. New York: Archon Books, 1968. 441 p.

This work traces the development of hymns and their writers from early colonial times to the twentieth century. Includes indexes of names, subjects, psalm and hymn books, and first lines.

Gombosi, Marilyn, ed. CATALOG OF THE JOHANNES HERBST COLLECTION. Chapel Hill: University of North Carolina Press, 1970. 755 p.

First in a series of thematic catalogs being prepared under the auspices of the Moravian Music Foundation. Herbst Collection originally contained 464 manuscripts containing scores of about 1,000 anthems and arias for use in Moravian worship services. Compiled as a reference library rather than a practical working collection, the range covers the whole Moravian sacred music tradition through sixty years of its most vigorous growth--from its inception in the mid-eighteenth century to its maturity in the first decade of the nineteenth century.

Hartley, Kenneth R. BIBLIOGRAPHY OF THESES AND DISSERTATIONS IN SACRED MUSIC. Detroit: Information Coordinators, 1967. 127 p.

More than 1,500 dissertations are listed geographically by state and alphabetically by conferring university. Author, composer, and subject indexes are included.

Hughes, [Dom] Anselm. LITURGICAL TERMS FOR MUSIC STUDENTS: A DICTIONARY. 1940. Reprint. St. Clair Shores, Mich.: Scholarly Press, 1972. 40 p.

Not intended to be exhaustive. Concise definitions of those terms in the literature of ancient ecclesiastical music of the West. Most refer to the mass and the Catholic liturgy.

Julian, John. A DICTIONARY OF HYMNOLOGY. Rev. ed. London: J. Murray, 1908. 1,768 p.

The origin and history of Christian hymns of all ages and nations. More than 30,000 alphabetical entries (title, author, historical period, and so forth) provide data on authors, dates, textual variants, and denominational and ritual usages.

Le Huray, Peter. MUSIC AND THE REFORMATION IN ENGLAND: 1549-1660. Studies in Church Music. New York: Oxford University Press, 1967. 454 p. Illus., music, photos.

Traces the development of English liturgical and devotional music through one of the most fruitful periods in the history of English music. Bibliography.

Other volumes in the series include 20TH CENTURY CHURCH MUSIC, by Erik Routley; ENGLISH CHURCH MUSIC, 1650-1750, by Christopher Dearnley; CHURCH MUSIC IN THE NINETEENTH CENTURY, by Arthur Hutchings; and THE MUSICAL WESLEYS, by Erik Routley.

Mason, Henry L., comp. HYMM TUNES OF LOWELL MASON: A BIBLIOGRAPHY. Cambridge, Mass.: University Press, 1944. 118 p.

A listing of the 1,697 hymn tunes either composed or arranged by Mason, along with the dates of their creation. Includes bibliography of books containing Mason's works.

Morrison, Theodore. CHAUTAUQUA: A CENTER FOR EDUCATION, RELIGION, AND THE ARTS IN AMERICA. Chicago: University of Chicago Press, 1974. 351 p. Photos, illus.

A review of the contribution of this important institution to the cultural and religious life of America.

Parks, Edna D. EARLY ENGLISH HYMNS: AN INDEX. Metuchen, N.J.: Scarecrow Press, 1972. 168 p.

Compilation of hymns, primarily from the seventeenth and eighteenth centuries, many of which are not listed in JULIAN'S DICTIONARY OF HYMNOLOGY. Includes first line, meter, number of stanzas, and name of author.

Reynolds, William Jensen. A SURVEY OF CHRISTIAN HYMNOLOGY. New York: Holt, Rinehart and Winston, 1963. 320 p.

An historical overview. A bibliography of suggested supplementary readings and three indexes are included.

Routley, Erik. TWENTIETH-CENTURY CHURCH MUSIC. New York: Oxford University Press, 1964. 244 p. Music.

Deals with new approaches to church music and shows the relationships with social developments of the time. Bibliography and discography.

Sparks, Edgar H. CANTUS FIRMUS IN MASS AND MOTET. Los Angeles and Berkeley: University of California Press, 1963. 504 p.

A discussion of the development and use of the Cantus Firmus in mass and motet writing from 1420 to Obrecht and Josquin. Bibliographical references.

Stainer, Sir John. THE MUSIC OF THE BIBLE WITH SOME ACCOUNT OF THE DEVELOPMENT OF MODERN MUSICAL INSTRUMENTS FROM ANCIENT TYPES. 1914. Reprint. New York: Da Capo Press, 1970. 230 p.

An account of every musical instrument mentioned in the Bible, with discussions on what is known about their construction, origin, and uses.

Stevens, Denis W. TUDOR CHURCH MUSIC. 1955. Reprint. New York: Da Capo Press, 1974. 144 p.

Covers the history of the liturgy, mass, and motet. Includes the role of instrumental music in this area. Bibliography.

Stevenson, Robert [Murrell]. PROTESTANT CHURCH MUSIC IN AMERICA: A SHORT SURVEY OF MEN AND MOVEMENTS FROM 1564 TO THE PRESENT. New York: W.W. Norton and Co., 1966. 168 p. Music.

Includes selective bibliography.

Wienandt, Elwyn A. CHORAL MUSIC OF THE CHURCH. New York: Free Press, 1965. 494 p. Illus., music.

An overview of the choral styles and practices of three principal liturgical streams that developed in Europe: the Roman Catholic, the Anglican, and the Lutheran.

Wienandt, Elwyn A., and Young, Robert H. THE ANTHEM IN ENGLAND AND AMERICA. Riverside, N.J.: Free Press, 1970. 495 p.

Defines the main trends and developments throughout the history of the form from the English Reformation to the present. Comprehensive bibliography.

ASSOCIATIONS

Church Music Association of America (CMAA), 548 Lafond Avenue, St. Paul, Minn. 55103.

Publication: SACRED MUSIC. Quarterly.

Church Music Publishers Association (CMPA), 501 East Third Street, Dayton, Ohio 45401.

Fellowship of Christian Musicians, Wheaton College Conservatory of Music, Wheaton, Ill. 60187.

Sponsors clinics and conferences and sets up student chapters in high schools and colleges.

The Fellowship of United Methodist Musicians (FUMM), Box 40, Nashville, Tenn. 37202.

Publication: NEWS NOTES. Monthly.

Gregorian Institute of America (GIA), 7404 South Mason, Chicago, Ill. 60638.

Publication: THE QUARTERLY.

Hymm Society of America (HSA), 475 Riverside Drive, New York, N.Y. 10027.

Publications: THE HYMM. Quarterly.

PAPERS OF THE SOCIETY. Irregular.

Lutheran Society for Worship, Music and the Arts (LSWMA), Valparaiso University, Valparaiso, Ind. 46383.

Publications: RESPONSE. Quarterly.

ACCENT ON WORSHIP, MUSIC, THE ARTS. 5/year.

Moravian Music Foundation (MMF), 20 Cascade Avenue, Salem Station, Winston-Salem, N.C. 27108.

Publications: Bulletin. Semiannual.

Bibliographical-historical reprints on the music of American Moravians.

National Church Music Fellowship (NCMF), 916 Walter, Des Plaines, Ill. 60016.

Publication: Newsletter. Quarterly.

National Convention of Gospel Choirs and Choruses, 4154 South Ellis Avenue, Chicago, Ill. 60635.

Publication: MINUTES. Biennial.

Plainsong and Medieval Music Society (PMMS), c/o D.H. Turner, Kiddell, The Church Lodge, Wimborne Street, Giles, Wimborne, Dorset, England.

Publication: Sponsors publication of choir texts, facsimile volumes of original manuscripts of Gregorian Chant, reference books, and so forth.

Religious Music

Standing Commission on Church Music, 865 Madison Avenue, New York, N.Y. 10021.

Section 47

CHORAL AND VOCAL MUSIC

The entries cited in this section are limited to those which are devoted primarily to choral and vocal music matters. Numerous other sources are to be found as chapters or portions of books listed in Section 24: Philosophical Foundations, Principles, and Practices; Section 27: Music in the Elementary School; Section 28: Music in Junior High and Middle Schools; and Section 29: Music in Secondary Schools.

INDEXES AND CATALOGS

British Broadcasting Co. Music Library. SONG CATALOGUE. 4 vols. London: BBC, 1966.

Extensive index of songs. First two volumes indexed by composers, last two volumes indexed by titles. Includes basically solo songs with keyboard accompaniment, but also duets with piano, unaccompanied songs and duets, recitations with piano, popular song annuals, and folk, national, and patriotic songs.

Campbell, Frank G. A CRITICAL ANNOTATED BIBLIOGRAPHY OF PERIODICALS. American Choral Foundation, memo no. 33. New York: American Choral Foundation, 1962. 14 p. Paper.

An annotated list of more than forty periodicals dealing with choral music and other resources.

Charbon, Marie H. THE HAGUE GEMEENTEMUSEUM CATALOGUE OF THE MUSIC LIBRARY. Vol. 2: VOCAL MUSIC 1500–c1650. New York: Da Capo Press, 1974. 243 p.

Deals exclusively with vocal works from 1500 to c1650, including a cappella works as well as vocal compositions with instrumental accompaniment.

Cushing, Helen Grant. CHILDREN'S SONG INDEX. New York: H.W. Wilson Co., 1936. 798 p.

DeCharms, Desiree, and Breed, Paul F. SONGS IN COLLECTIONS: AN INDEX. Detroit: Information Services, 1966. 588 p.

Primarily an index of solo songs with piano accompaniment; emphasis is on art songs and operatic arias. Includes all of the collections published between 1940 and 1957. Also contains a select number of folk songs, anthologies, Christmas carols, and sacred songs. Totals 411 collections, 9,493 songs.

Dwyer, Edward J. SINGERS IN NEW YORK: A DIRECTORY OF OPPORTUNITIES AND SERVICES. New York: William-Frederick Press, 1972. 95 p.

Heaton, Wallace, and Hargens, C.W., eds. AN INTERDISCIPLINARY INDEX OF STUDIES IN PHYSICS, MEDICINE, AND MUSIC RELATED TO THE HUMAN VOICE. Bryn Mawr, Pa.: Theodore Presser Co., 1968. 61 p. Illus.

A reference guide to information in print about vocal research. Includes abstracts and brief critiques of studies conducted by physical scientists, physicians, and musicians.

Kutsch, K.J., and Riemens, Leo. A CONCISE BIOGRAPHICAL DICTIONARY OF SINGERS. Translated by Harry Earl Jones. Philadelphia: Chilton Book Co., 1969. 487 p.

Lists roles, recordings, and professional and personal information for approximately 1,500 singers whose works are recorded.

Leigh, Robert. INDEX TO SONG BOOKS. 1964. Reprint. New York: Da Capo Press, 1973. 242 p.

Music Educators National Conference. Contemporary Music Project. THE CONTEMPORARY MUSIC PROJECT LIBRARY. 3 vols. Washington, D.C.: MENC, 1967-69. Unpaged.

Volume 3 of this series lists all works written for chorus and voice for the Composers in Public Schools Program during its ten-year period. Each work described provides name of composer, historical and technical data, and two representative score pages. For additional details of this project, see CONTEMPORARY MUSIC PROJECT (CMP) in Section 40: Contemporary Music.

Nardone, Thomas R., et al., eds. CHORAL MUSIC IN PRINT. 2 vols. Vol. 1: SACRED MUSIC. Vol. 2: SECULAR MUSIC. Philadelphia: Musicdata, 1974. 656 p. and 614 p.

This work represents a unique effort to use modern technology for the production of a comprehensive listing of music in print. A new company recently computerized the catalogs of more than 300 domestic and foreign publishers. Each composition is listed by title and cross-referenced to the composer, where it is listed again with additional information. Each volume will be updated yearly with a second edition following in three years. A special retrieval service for special lists of editions (based on voicing, seasonal usage, publisher, and so forth) is available by special arrangement with the company. For further information, contact Musicdata, Department D, 18 West Chelten Avenue, Philadelphia, Pennsylvania 19144.

Sears, M.E. SONG INDEX: AN INDEX TO MORE THAN 12,000 SONGS, AND SUPPLEMENT. 2 vols. in 1. Hamden, Conn.: Shoe String Press, 1966. 1,014 p.

Indexes 177 collections comprising 262 volumes. It is not to be considered a comprehensive dictionary of songs.

Steane, J.B. THE GRAND TRADITION: SEVENTY YEARS OF SINGING ON RECORD, 1900-70. New York: Charles Scribner's Sons, 1974. 628 p. Photos.

Analyzes outstanding operatic performances since the turn of the century. Describes well the evolution of recording techniques: pre electrical (1900-1925), the seventy-eight (1925-50), and the long-playing disc (1950-70). Contains appendix which compares interpretations of various artists.

Taylor, Jed H. VOCAL AND INSTRUMENTAL MUSIC IN PRINT. New York: Scarecrow Press, 1965. 166 p.

Information is neither complete nor up-to-date, since it was based on publisher's catalogs for 1963 through 1964. The list is useful, however, because the entries are graded into four levels of difficulty.

PEDAGOGY

Ades, Hawley. CHORAL ARRANGING. Delaware Water Gap, Pa.: Shawnee Press, 1966. 246 p.

A practical manual and text for the development of skill in writing music for chorus.

Adler, Kurt. PHONETICS AND DICTION IN SINGING: ITALIAN, FRENCH, SPANISH, GERMAN. Minneapolis: University of Minnesota Press, 1967. 161 p. Illus.

A manual for teachers, coaches, and students of singing by the Metropolitan Opera conductor and chorus master.

American Academy of Teachers of Singing. TERMINOLOGY IN THE FIELD OF SINGING. New York: G. Schirmer, 1969. 26 p. Paper.

This dictionary, arranged alphabetically, is an attempt to clarify the meanings of terms used by teachers of singing and to provide a uniform guide to vocal terminology. Includes the fields of physics, anatomy, psychology, and music. Does not include terms of vocal methodology.

American Choral Directors Association. GUIDE FOR THE BEGINNING CHORAL DIRECTOR. Tampa, Fla.: 1972. 41 p.

A practical manual prepared by the National Committee on High School Choral Music. Bibliography.

Appleman, D. Ralph. THE SCIENCE OF VOCAL PEDAGOGY. Bloomington: Indiana University Press, 1967. 434 p.

Develops theories based on reliable experimentation and scientific evidence. Considerable attention to the interrelationship of the International Alphabet phonemes, and formats. The supplementary recordings are of considerable value.

Bacilly, Benigne de. A COMMENTARY UPON THE ART OF PROPER SINGING. Translated and edited by Austin B. Caswell. Brooklyn, N.Y.: Institute of Medieval Music, 1968. 224 p. Music.

A significant work by one of the most important writers on the French vocal style. Based on the 1668 edition. Includes discussion of general vocal style, ornamentation, and French pronunciation as applied to vocal music.

Boyd, Jack. REHEARSAL GUIDE FOR THE CHORAL CONDUCTOR. West Nyack, N.Y.: Parker Publishing Co., 1970. 254 p.

Detailed information on methods of planning rehearsals along logical and specific lines. Bibliography.

Brodnitz, Friederich S. KEEP YOUR VOICE HEALTHY: A GUIDE TO THE INTELLIGENT USE AND CARE OF THE SPEAKING AND SINGING VOICE. New York: Harper and Bros., 1953. 234 p.

A guide to the prevention, treatment, and understanding of voice difficulties. Bibliography.

Browne, Lennox, and Behnke, Emile. VOICE, SONG AND SPEECH. 6th ed. New York: G.P. Putnam's Sons, 1887. 248 p.

A work of historical interest for researching pioneer efforts to establish physiological principles for vocal productions.

Burgin, John Carroll. TEACHING SINGING. Metuchen, N.J.: Scarecrow Press, 1973. 290 p. Illus.

The author has patterned this text after the standard work by Victor Fields, TRAINING THE SINGING VOICE (New York: King's Crown Press, 1942. 337 p.). Using literature published since that time, sources of information concerning vocal pedagogy are discussed and critically analyzed. Extensive annotated bibliography.

Colorni, Evelina. SINGER'S ITALIAN: A MANUAL OF DICTION AND PHONETICS. New York: G. Schirmer, 1970. 157 p.

Although designed for singers, this handbook is useful for accompanists, conductors, editors, and composers. Bibliography.

Cox, Richard G. THE SINGER'S MANUAL OF GERMAN AND FRENCH DICTION. New York: G. Schirmer, 1970. 63 p. Illus., paper.

A guide to the pronunication of French and German as applied to the performance of vocal works. Bibliography.

Darrow, Gerald F. FOUR DECADES OF CHORAL TRAINING. Metuchen, N.J.: Scarecrow Press, 1975. 223 p. Biblio.

Presents seven phases of choral instruction which have been analyzed in a way that choral directors may compare their methods with those of others. An overview of trends in choral training between 1930 and 1970. Annotated bibliography contains 475 titles.

Davison, Archibald. THE TECHNIQUE OF CHORAL COMPOSITION. Cambridge, Mass.: Harvard University Press, 1960. 206 p.

A practical guide for the beginning choral composer.

De Young, Richard. THE SINGER'S ART: AN ANALYSIS OF VOCAL PRINCIPLES. Chicago: De Paul University, 1958. 174 p. (Distr. by North Shore Press, Waukegan, Ill.)

A description and analysis of the physical and psychological principles as applied to vocal training.

Duey, Philip A. BEL CANTO IN ITS GOLDEN AGE--A STUDY OF ITS CONCEPTS. New York: King's Crown Press, Columbia University, 1951. 222 p.

Analyzes the Bel Canto style of singing. Bibliography.

Fields, Victor Alexander. TRAINING THE SINGING VOICE, AN ANALYSIS

OF THE WORKING CONCEPTS CONTAINED IN RECENT CONTRIBUTIONS OF VOCAL PEDAGOGY. New York: Columbia University Press, 1947. 337 p.

Its general aims are threefold: to survey and correlate available sources of bibliographic information on methods of training the singing voice, to provide a core of organized information for the use of all teachers of singing, and to provide an orientation and background for research in this and related fields.

Fuhr, Hayes M. FUNDAMENTALS OF CHORAL EXPRESSION. Lincoln: University of Nebraska Press, 1944. 103 p.

A discussion of the organization and administration of the choral program in the secondary school. Includes section on vocal technique.

Gardiner, Julian. A GUIDE TO GOOD SINGING AND SPEECH. Boston: Crescendo Publishing Co., 1972. 300 p. Illus., music, photos.

A practical guide for singers and speakers. Focus is on the physiological aspects of vocal production. Bibliographical references.

Gilliland, Dale V. GUIDANCE IN VOICE EDUCATION. Columbus, Ohio: Typographic Printing Co., 1970. 174 p. Illus., photos.

A text specifically written for the teacher of voice. In addition to explaining the principles of singing as viewed by this author, there is information concerning the application of the principles in the voice class situation.

Hale, Leslie William. VOCAL PEDAGOGY: A SUMMARY OF COURSES OFFERED IN TWENTY-ONE SELECTED UNIVERSITIES. Ann Arbor, Mich.: Xerox University Microfilms, 1973. 206 p.

Heaton, Wallace, and Hargens, C.W., eds. AN INTERDISCIPLINARY INDEX OF STUDIES IN PHYSICS, MEDICINE, AND MUSIC RELATED TO THE HUMAN VOICE. Bryn Mawr, Pa.: Theodore Presser Co., 1968. 61 p.

An extensive annotated bibliography covering twelve classifications of vocal research. References include investigations of the vocal tract and certain pertinent observations by physical scientists, physicians, and musicians.

Herbert-Caesari, Edgar F. THE SCIENCE AND SENSATIONS OF VOCAL TONE: A NATURAL VOCAL MECHANISM. 2d rev. ed. Boston: Crescendo Publishing Co., 1968. 199 p. Music, illus.

An attempt to describe the exact sensations which the singer experiences during the formation and production of vocal tone in accordance with the author's concept of certain physiological and acoustical laws. Many diagrams are used.

Howerton, George. TECHNIQUE AND STYLE IN CHORAL SINGING. New York: Carl Fischer, 1957. 201 p.

A practical handbook which provides procedures and suggestions for training amateur singers for performance. Bibliography.

Ingram, Madeline D., and Rice, William C. VOCAL TECHNIQUE FOR CHILDREN AND YOUTH. New York: Abingdon Press, 1962. 175 p.

Traces the development of the human vocal mechanism from early childhood through adolescence to near maturity. Organized by grade levels. Bibliography and film listing.

Kjelson, Lee, and McCray, James. THE CONDUCTOR'S MANUAL OF CHORAL LITERATURE. New York: Belwin-Mills Publishing Corp., 1973. 270 p. Music, paper.

Designed as a textbook for choral conducting, choral literature, or choral techniques classes. A comprehensive overview of choral music is presented, arranged by historical periods. Representative works are preceded by biographical information, musical analysis, and performance suggestions.

Krone, Max T. THE CHORUS AND ITS CONDUCTOR (FROM ORGANIZATION TO PERFORMANCE). Park Ridge, Ill.: Neil A. Kjos Co., 1945. 134 p. Illus., music, paper.

A practical guide for developing and conducting choral groups. Assumes a musical background. Bibliographical references.

Lamb, Gordon H. CHORAL TECHNIQUES. Dubuque, Iowa: William C. Brown Co., 1974. 285 p. Music.

Stresses methods and techniques of building choral programs. Includes rehearsal techniques. Bibliography.

Lehmann, Lotte. MORE THAN SINGING: THE INTERPRETATION OF SONGS. Translated by Frances Holden. London: Boosey and Hawkes, 1946. 192 p. Music.

This work focuses on the German Lieder, with the inclusion of a few French, Old English, Italian, and Russian songs which have become classics and were used in this artist's repertoire.

Luchsinger, Richard, and Arnold, Godfrey E. VOICE-SPEECH-LANGUAGE: CLINICAL COMMUNICOLOGY: ITS PHYSIOLOGY AND PATHOLOGY. Translated by Godfrey E. Arnold and Evelyn Robe Finkbeiner. Belmont, Calif.:

Wadsworth Publishing Co., 1965. 812 p. Photos, illus., music.

An authoritative and comprehensive work based on psychology, neuropsychiatry, otolaryngology, pediatrics, oral surgery, dentistry, internal medicine, and endocrinology as well as the basic sciences. A valuable source book for professionals, including those in the field of voice training. One section deals with music. Bibliography.

Moe, Daniel. BASIC CHORAL CONCEPTS. Minneapolis, Minn.: Augsburg, 1972. 31 p. Paper.

Basic techniques for beginning choral conductors. Bibliographical references.

Neidig, Kenneth L., and Jennings, John W. CHORAL DIRECTORS GUIDE. West Nyack, N.Y.: Parker Publishing Co., 1967. 308 p.

A collection of writings dealing with a variety of choral activities and responsibilities which normally constitute the choral director's job.

Peterson, Paul W. NATURAL SINGING AND EXPRESSIVE CONDUCTING. Winston-Salem, N.C.: John F. Blair, 1966. 181 p.

Basic vocal techniques for the singer, teacher, and choral conductor. Includes a selective list of repertoire. Bibliography.

Pfautsch, Lloyd. MENTAL WARMUPS FOR THE CHORAL DIRECTOR. New York: Lawson-Gould, 1969. 46 p.

A description of the qualifications needed for effective choral directing, and the preparation that precedes good performances.

Potter, Ralph K., et al. VISIBLE SPEECH. 1947. Reprint. New York: Dover Publications, 1966. 439 p. Illus., photos.

A nontechnical discussion of the analysis of speech through the use of the sound spectograph and direct translator. Information is included with possible application in the field of vocal music. Bibliography.

Reid, Cornelius. BEL CANTO: PRINCIPLES AND PRACTICES. New York: Coleman-Ross, 1950. 211 p.

A detailed study of this particular style of singing. Considerable attention given to basic procedures for training the voice. Bibliography.

_____. THE FREE VOICE. New York: Coleman-Ross, 1965. 225 p. Illus., music.

An attempt to employ scientific knowledge to refute a mechanistic approach to singing.

Roe, Paul F. CHORAL MUSIC EDUCATION. Englewood Cliffs, N.J.: Prentice-Hall, 1970. 400 p.

Presents methods of developing and administering choral music activities. Deals with practical problems.

Rose, Arnold. THE SINGER AND THE VOICE: VOCAL PHYSIOLOGY AND TECHNIQUE FOR SINGERS. New York: St. Martin's Press, 1971. 267 p.

A textbook covering the basic scientific and anatomical knowledge required by the vocal teacher. Includes techniques of training voices. Bibliography.

Rosewall, Richard. HANDBOOK OF SINGING. Evanston, Ill.: Summy-Birchard, 1961. 114 p.

This work is designed as a guide for the beginning voice class teacher. Includes helpful teaching suggestions for a year of study of basic vocal techniques. Bibliography.

Rushmore, Robert. THE SINGING VOICE. New York: Dodd, Mead and Co., 1971. 332 p.

Surveys a wide range of matters of major importance pertaining to the singing voice. Scope of discourse varies from bel canto to "pop" singing. Bibliography.

Sample, Mabel Warkentin. LEADING CHILDREN'S CHOIRS. Nashville, Tenn.: Broadman Press, 1966. 127 p.

Principles and practices for the guidance of the leader of singing groups composed of children with unchanged voices. Selected list of repertoire and bibliography.

Schiotz, Askel. THE SINGER AND HIS ART. New York: Harper and Row, 1970. 214 p.

A guide for the vocal performer. The focus is on the interpretation of the various types of literature. It does not deal with singing methods as such, but rather describes the author's personal vocal technique. Bibliography and discography.

Stanley, Douglas. THE SCIENCE OF VOICE. 4th ed. New York: Carl Fischer, 1948. 384 p. Illus., music, photos.

A classic in the field of vocal performance and vocal pedagogy. Presents theories based on scientific research. Bibliography.

Steane, J.B. THE GRAND TRADITION: SEVENTY YEARS OF SINGING ON RECORD, 1900-1970. New York: Charles Scribner's Sons, 1974. 628 p. Photos.

Analyzes outstanding operatic performances since the turn of the century. Describes well the evolution of recording techniques: preelectrical (1900-1925), the seventy-eight (1925-50), and the long-playing disc (1950-70). Contains appendix which compares interpretations of various artists.

Sunderman, Lloyd F. ARTISTIC SINGING: ITS TONE PRODUCTION AND BASIC UNDERSTANDINGS. Metuchen, N.J.: Scarecrow Press, 1970. 159 p. Illus., music.

This text is addressed to choral directors and vocal soloists. Discussion of tone production as related to register, resonance, and diction. Bibliography.

Tosi, Pietro Francesco. OBSERVATIONS ON THE FLORID SONG. 2d ed. Translated by J.E. Galliard. 1743. Reprint. New York: Johnson Reprint Corp., 1968. 184 p. Music.

This well-known work is still useful in the study of ornamentation as related to vocal style.

Uris, Dorothy. TO SING IN ENGLISH: A GUIDE TO IMPROVED DICTION. New York: Boosey and Hawkes, 1971. 317 p. Music, illus.

A detailed study of English pronunciation as applied to vocal performance. Bibliography.

Whitlock, Weldon. BEL CANTO FOR THE TWENTIETH CENTURY. Champaign, Ill.: Pro Musica Press, 1968. 109 p. Music.

A discussion of the traditional bel canto method of singing, with suggestions for achieving this style. Selected vocalists are included for teaching purposes.

Wilson, Harry Robert. ARTISTIC CHORAL SINGING. New York: G. Schirmer, 1959. 374 p.

Encompasses a wide range of choral singing activities, techniques, and practical suggestions.

Winsel, Regnier. THE ANATOMY OF VOICE: AN ILLUSTRATED MANUAL OF VOCAL TRAINING. New York: Exposition Press, 1966. 96 p.

A discussion of the physical, psychological, and acoustical aspects of vocal training with exercises to illustrate the author's premises.

REPERTORY

Burnsworth, Charles C. CHORAL MUSIC FOR WOMEN'S VOICES: AN ANNOTATED BIBLIOGRAPHY OF RECOMMENDED WORKS. Metuchen, N.J.: Scarecrow Press, 1968. 179 p.

An annotated bibliography describing general content of musical elements and styles; catalog-type information which includes number of parts, range, publisher, grade of difficulty, and type of accompaniment, with a system of cross-references.

Coffin, Berton. SINGER'S REPERTOIRE. 2d ed. 5 vols. New York: Scarecrow Press, 1960-62.

Part I: COLORATURA SOPRANO, LYRIC SOPRANO, DRAMATIC SOPRANO. 1960. 321 p.; part II: MEZZO SOPRANO, CONTRALTO. 1960. 222 p.; part III: LYRIC TENOR, DRAMATIC TENOR. 1960. 223 p.; part IV: BARITONE, BASS. 1960. 210 p.; part V: PROGRAM NOTES OF THE SINGER'S REPERTOIRE. 1962. 217 p.

Based on preselection of songs sung by noteworthy or accepted singers--distribution of some 8,000 songs into 818 lists for the nine voices--not a complete bibliography. Aid for program building, training repertoire, specific or seasonal occasions, and sacred repertoires.

_____, et al. WORD-BY-WORD TRANSLATIONS OF SONGS AND ARIAS, PART I: GERMAN AND FRENCH. Metuchen, N.J.: Scarecrow Press, 1966. 620 p.

Drinker, Henry S. TEXTS OF THE CHORAL WORKS OF JOHANN SEBASTIAN BACH IN ENGLISH TRANSLATION. 4 vols. (in 2 books). New York: Association of American Colleges, Arts Programs, 1942-43.

Volume 1: CANTATAS 1-100. 1942. 200 p. (Includes a lengthy essay on the translation of Bach texts); volume 2: CANTATAS 101-199. 1942. 378 p.; volume 3: PASSIONS, ORATORIOS, MOTETS, SECULAR AND UNPUBLISHED CANTATAS AND SONGS. 1943. 567 p.; volume 4: INDEX AND CONCORDANCE TO THE ENGLISH TEXTS OF THE COMPLETE CHORAL WORKS OF JOHANN SEBASTIAN BACH. 1942. 81 p.

DRINKER LIBRARY OF CHORAL MUSIC. Free Library of Philadelphia.

See description under Pennsylvania in appendix A.

Jacobs, Arthur, ed. CHORAL MUSIC: A SYMPOSIUM. Baltimore: Penguin Books, 1963. 444 p. Music.

A collection of essays on various aspects of choral music. Deals with the historical periods and their related styles. Bibliography and discography.

Kagen, Sergius. MUSIC FOR THE VOICE: A DESCRIPTIVE LIST OF CONCERT AND TEACHING MATERIAL. Rev. ed. Bloomington: Indiana University Press, 1968. 780 p.

A practical guide with critical notes and performance suggestions for solo vocal music. Entries include composer, song title, general style and form, type of voice best suited, compass and tessitura, problems of execution for singer and accompanist, available editions, and recommended translations and transpositions.

Music Educators National Conference and the American Choral Directors Association, comps. SELECTIVE MUSIC LISTS-1974. VOCAL SOLOS AND ENSEMBLES. Washington, D.C.: 1974.

Sacred and secular listings of vocal solos, small vocal ensembles, large choral groups, and junior high choruses. Titles rated according to level of difficulty. Includes catalog numbers and directory of publishers.

Roberts, Kenneth. A CHECKLIST OF TWENTIETH CENTURY CHORAL MUSIC FOR MALE VOICES. Detroit: Information Coordinators, 1970. 32 p.

This attempts to update the traditional list by Merrill Knapp (SELECTED LIST OF MUSIC FOR MEN'S VOICES. Princeton, N.J.: Princeton University Press, 1952--now out of print, but available from University Microfilms, Ann Arbor, Michigan, 1967). The two works together constitute a useful catalog of music for this category.

Schoep, Arthur, and Harris, Daniel. WORD-BY-WORD TRANSLATIONS OF SONGS AND ARIAS, PART II: ITALIAN. Metuchen, N.J.: Scarecrow Press, 1972. 575 p.

A companion to SINGER'S REPERTOIRE by Berton Coffin, cited above.

Tortolano, William. ORIGINAL MUSIC FOR MEN'S VOICES: A SELECTED BIBLIOGRAPHY. Metuchen, N.J.: Scarecrow Press, 1973. 123 p.

A listing of more than 500 items organized according to historical periods. Only music in print is included, or that which is fairly accessible in libraries, etc. Includes titles, composers, scoring for voices, soloists, accompaniment, instruments, language, text sources, publishers, catalog numbers, and other pertinent information.

Ulrich, Homer. A SURVEY OF CHORAL MUSIC. New York: Harcourt Brace Jovanovich, 1973. 245 p. Illus., music.

Contains many principal sources concerning choral music and the development of choral forms. A compact reference work. Bibliography.

Young, Percy M. THE CHORAL TRADITION: AN HISTORICAL AND ANALYTICAL SURVEY FROM THE SIXTEENTH CENTURY TO THE PRESENT DAY. London: Hutchinson, 1962. 371 p. Illus., music.

A history of choral music since the sixteenth century. Major works which are in the general repertoire are discussed in detail. Bibliography.

For choral composition and arranging see "Composition" in Section 51: Music Structure, Theory, and Composition. For choral conducting see Section 52: Conducting.

ASSOCIATIONS

American Academy of Teachers of Singing (AATS), c/o William Gephart, 75 Bank Street, New York, N.Y. 10014.

Publications: Song lists, various materials on auditions, etc.

American Choral Directors Association (ACDA), c/o R. Wayne Hugoboom, 10616 Coquita Lane, Tampa, Fla. 33618.

Publications: CHORAL JOURNAL. Monthly.

American Choral Foundation (ACF), 130 West 56th Street, New York, N.Y. 10019.

Publications: AMERICAN CHORAL REVIEW. Monthly.

Research memorandum. 9/year.

American Concert Choir, 130 West 56th Street, New York, N.Y. 10019.

American Union of Swedish Singers (AUSS), c/o Ragnar Nelson Travel Bureau, Inc., 333 North Michigan Avenue, Chicago, Ill. 60601.

Publication: MUSIKTIDNING. 10/year.

Associated Male Choruses of America (AMCA), 1338 Oakcrest Drive, Appleton, Wis. 54911.

Publication: AMCA NEWSLETTER. Monthly (September-May).

Association of Choral Conductors (ACC), 130 West 56th Street, New York, N.Y. 10019.

Publications: AMERICAN CHORAL REVIEW. Quarterly.

Research bulletins. 9/year.

Federation of Workers' Singing Societies of the U.S.A., 1832 Hillsdale Avenue, Dayton, Ohio 45414.

Publication: SAENGER-ZEITUNG. 10/year.

Intercollegiate Musical Council, P.O. Box 4303, Grand Central Station, New York, N.Y. 10017.

Serves secondary schools, colleges, and universities for the encouragement of male choruses.

National Association of Teachers of Singing (NATS), 250 West 57th Street, New York, N.Y. 10019.

Publications: Bulletin. Quarterly.

INTER NOS. Quarterly.

Membership directory. Biennial.

Norwegian Singers Association of America (NSAA), 3316 Xenwood Avenue, South, Minneapolis, Minn. 55416.

Publication: SANGER-HILSEN (Singers Greetings). Bimonthly.

Society for the Preservation and Encouragement of Barber Shop Quartet Singing in America (SPEBSQSA), 6315 Third Avenue, Kenosha, Wis. 53141.

Publication: HARMONIZER. Bimonthly.

Sweet Adelines, P.O. Box 45168, Tulsa, Okla. 74145.

Publication: PITCH PIPE. Quarterly.

United Choral Conductors Club of America, c/o Mozart Hall, 328 East 86th Street, New York, N.Y. 10028.

See also various subsections on associations in part II: Music in Education.

Section 48

INSTRUMENTAL MUSIC

The sources listed here are limited to those which are devoted primarily to the administrative or the teaching and learning aspects of instrumental music. A considerable number of additional sources concerning instrumental music are to be found as portions of other books listed in the following sections: Section 24: Philosophical Foundations, Principles, and Practices; Section 27: Music in the Elementary School; Section 28: Music in Junior High and Middle Schools; and Section 29: Music in Secondary Schools.

PEDAGOGICAL GUIDES AND REFERENCE BOOKS

General

"Buyer's Guide." INSTRUMENTALIST (August). 1946-- . Annual.

A comprehensive listing of the companies supplying the needs of instrumental music. Published annually in the August issue of the INSTRUMENTALIST magazine.

Caimi, Florentino, et al. LITERATURE AND MATERIALS GUIDE FOR INSTRUMENTAL MUSIC. Montgomery, Pa.: Intrada Publishing Co., 1974. 449 p. Illus., photos.

A mixture of many kinds of information pertaining to the teaching of instrumental music (stringed instruments omitted). Caution is advised concerning the validity of portions of material.

Diehl, Ned C. DEVELOPMENT OF COMPUTER-ASSISTED INSTRUCTION IN INSTRUMENTAL MUSIC. Washington, D.C.: U.S. Office of Education, 1969.

Duerksen, George L. TEACHING INSTRUMENTAL MUSIC. From Research to the Music Classroom. Washington, D.C.: Music Educators National Conference, 1972. 32 p. Paper.

Reports research on instrumental music programs, instructional methods, educational technology, and outcomes of instruction.

Heim, Norman, comp. MUSIC AND TAPE RECORDINGS FILED IN THE NACWPI RESEARCH LIBRARY. College Park: University of Maryland, McKeldin Library, 1972. Unpaged.

Alphabetical listing by composer of cataloged published and unpublished music and tapes in the National Association of College Wind and Percussion Instructors Library (about 1000 items). Supplemental lists are issued periodically. This collection of music and tape recordings forms part of the NACWPI Research Center maintained at the University of Maryland. It includes a considerable amount of music and tapes for woodwind, brass, and percussion. For information concerning availability of these materials, contact the curator, NACWPI Research Library, McKeldin Library, University of Maryland, College Park, Maryland.

Hendrickson, Clarence V., comp. INSTRUMENTALISTS' HANDY REFERENCE MANUAL. New York: Carl Fischer, 1957. 96 p. Illus., photos, tables.

In addition to fingering charts for all the regular instruments of the band and orchestra, this manual includes position charts for string instruments, drum rudiments, transposition charts, and ranges of instruments.

House, Robert W. INSTRUMENTAL MUSIC FOR TODAY'S SCHOOLS. Englewood Cliffs, N.J.: Prentice-Hall, 1965. 282 p. Illus.

A guide to the establishment of a coherent instrumental music program. Includes beginning instruction to more advanced activities. A practical handbook for instrumental directors. Bibliography.

John, Robert [W.], and Douglas, Charles H. PLAYING SOCIAL AND RECREATIONAL INSTRUMENTS. Englewood Cliffs, N.J.: Prentice-Hall, 1972. 112 p.

A nontechnical manual on how to play and teach instruments such as the guitar, the autoharp, the recorder, and other nonorchestral instruments. Written for the person with little or no previous musical training.

Kuhn, Wolfgang E. INSTRUMENTAL MUSIC: PRINCIPLES AND METHODS OF INSTRUCTION. 2d ed. Boston: Allyn and Bacon, 1970. 256 p.

Discusses the role of instrumental music in the school curriculum. Stresses ways of achieving a sensible balance between music subject matter and instructional method. Contains practical suggestions for dealing with organizational and teaching problems. Bibliography.

Leblanc, Albert. ORGANIZING THE INSTRUMENTAL MUSIC LIBRARY. Evanston, Ill.: Instrumentalist Co., n.d. 44 p.

A practical handbook for the instrumental music librarian. Suggestions for library storage, record keeping, purchasing, and cataloging.

Music Educators National Conference, comp. SELECTIVE MUSIC LISTS, 1971: BAND, ORCHESTRA, AND STRING ORCHESTRA. Washington, D.C.: 1971. 64 p.

_____. SELECTIVE MUSIC LISTS, 1972: INSTRUMENTAL SOLOS AND ENSEMBLES. Washington, D.C.: 1972. 176 p.

Pottle, Ralph R. TUNING THE SCHOOL BAND AND ORCHESTRA: WITH WIND INSTRUMENT GUIDES BY MARK H. HINDSLEY AND PERCUSSION AND STRING GUIDES BY RALPH R. POTTLE. 3d ed. Hammond, La.: Ralph R. Pottle, 1970. 84 p.

Analyses and description of tuning procedures for instruments of the band and orchestra.

Weidensee, Victor. INSTRUMENTAL MUSIC IN THE PUBLIC SCHOOLS. Boston: Crescendo Publishing Co., 1969. 103 p.

A college-level text for the instrumental music teacher. Bibliography after each chapter.

Orchestra

Dalby, John B. SCHOOL AND AMATEUR ORCHESTRAS. New York: Pergamon Press, 1966. 225 p. Illus., photos.

Guidelines for the development of an effective orchestral program. Bibliography.

Daniels, David. ORCHESTRAL MUSIC: A SOURCE BOOK. Metuchen, N.J.: Scarecrow Press, 1972. 319 p.

Diverse information about orchestral works. Includes instrumentation, duration, and publisher for each work. Useful for program planning, rehearsals, etc.

Hart, Philip. ORPHEUS IN THE NEW WORLD: THE SYMPHONY ORCHESTRA AS AN AMERICAN CULTURAL INSTITUTION. New York: W.W. Norton and Co., 1973. 562 p. Tables, photos.

Traces the background of 100 orchestras in the United States through the careers of important figures who helped shape them. Six major orchestras are studied in depth. Includes management, economics, and the role of the audience. Bibliography.

International Music Council. SYMPHONIC MUSIC, 1880-1954. Frankfurt, Germany: C.F. Peters, 1957. 63 p.

Foreword and preface in English and German. An international listing of orchestral works in print written for groups of the standard orchestra size, of high artistic value, and not exceeding the capacities of the amateur performer.

Lacy, Gene M. ORGANIZING AND DEVELOPING THE HIGH SCHOOL ORCHESTRA. West Nyack, N.Y.: Parker Publishing Co., 1971. 205 p.

Offers practical ideas and suggestions for dealing with the day-to-day problems of developing a school orchestra.

Moore, June. IMPROVING AND EXTENDING THE JUNIOR HIGH SCHOOL ORCHESTRA REPERTORY. Washington, D.C.: U.S. Office of Education, Bureau of Research, 1967.

Mueller, John H. THE AMERICAN SYMPHONY ORCHESTRA: A SOCIAL HISTORY OF MUSICAL TASTE. Bloomington: Indiana University Press, 1951. 437 p. Illus., photos.

The development of the American Symphony Orchestra from its beginnings in European tradition. Treats repertory and the problems of aesthetic taste. Bibliography.

Mueller, Kate. TWENTY-SEVEN MAJOR AMERICAN SYMPHONY ORCHESTRAS: A HISTORY AND ANALYSIS OF THEIR REPERTOIRES, SEASONS 1842-43 THROUGH 1969-70. Bloomington: Indiana University Press, 1973. 398 p.

Provides much hard data. Discusses the relationships of the performing arts to society and its culture.

Murphy, O.J. "Measurements of Orchestral Pitch." JOURNAL OF THE ACOUSTICAL SOCIETY OF AMERICA 12 (January 1941): 395-98. Also published as Monograph B-1282 of the Bell Telephone System Technical Publications. New York: 1941. 8 p.

The results of 750 observations to determine if the standard frequency of 440 cycles for note "A" in the treble clef is being adhered to in musical concerts.

Music Educators National Conference. Contemporary Music Project. THE CONTEMPORARY MUSIC PROJECT LIBRARY. Vol. 2. Washington, D.C.: MENC, 1967-69. Unpaged.

Volume 2 of this series lists all works written for orchestra and string instruments for the Composers in Public Schools Program during its ten-year period. Each work described provides name of composer, historical and technical data, and two representative score pages. For additional details of this project, see Contemporary Music Project (CMP) in Section 40: Contemporary Music.

Rothrock, Carson. TRAINING THE HIGH SCHOOL ORCHESTRA. West Nyack, N.Y.: Parker Publishing Co., 1972. 224 p.

A compilation of many procedures and suggestions for the development of the high school orchestra.

Saltonstall, Cecilia Drinker, and Smith, Hannah Coffin, comps. CATALOGUE OF MUSIC FOR SMALL ORCHESTRA. Edited by Otto E. Albrecht. Washington, D.C.: Music Library Association, 1947. 267 p.

A catalog of music especially suitable for performance by small orchestras.

Seltzer, George. THE PROFESSIONAL SYMPHONY ORCHESTRA IN THE UNITED STATES. Metuchen, N.J.: Scarecrow Press, 1975. 486 p.

A group of selections describing the development of the orchestra in this country. Also discusses the role of the conductor, the musician, and the audience. Bibliography.

Smith, G. Jean. "Directory of Known Youth Orchestras (In the U.S.)." AMERICAN STRING TEACHER 23 (Winter 1973): 29A-34A.

A list of 252 known youth orchestras in the United States as reported in a 1971-72 survey made by the American String Teachers Association project YORD (Youth Orchestra Research and Development).

U.S. Department of Health, Education, and Welfare. Arts and Humanities Program, Harold [W.] Arberg, Chief. SCHOOLS AND SYMPHONY ORCHESTRAS. Washington, D.C.: Government Printing Office, 1971. 99 p. Paper.

Based on a comprehensive study of youth concert activities in twenty cities, this report outlines the history and purpose of youth concerts in the cities surveyed; discusses the ways in which youth concerts are financed; and summarizes the operating practices of youth concert activities.

Band

American School Band Directors Association, comp. THE ASBDA CURRICULUM GUIDE: A REFERENCE FOR SCHOOL BAND DIRECTORS. Pittsburgh, Pa.: Volkwein Bros., 1973. 357 p. Illus., photos.

A resource book for band directors. Provides many examples of organizational patterns and teaching procedures.

Berger, Kenneth. BAND ENCYCLOPEDIA. Evansville, Ind.: Band Associates, 1960. 612 p.

Covers a wide range of band matters, such as various terms peculiar to the band, biographical sketches of bandsmen, band bibliography.

Bierley, Paul E. JOHN PHILIP SOUSA: A DESCRIPTIVE CATALOGUE OF HIS WORKS. Urbana: University of Illinois Press, 1973. 177 p.

A highly informative reference work pertaining to the many and varied compositions of this composer. Concludes with a convenient chronology of works and a list of his publishers. Bibliography.

______. JOHN PHILIP SOUSA: AMERICAN PHENOMENON. New York: Appleton-Century-Crofts, 1973. 261 p. Illus.

A comprehensive source book on the life and work of Sousa, based on thousands of documents relating to his private and professional life. Bibliography.

Duvall, W. Clyde. THE HIGH SCHOOL BAND DIRECTOR'S HANDBOOK. Englewood Cliffs, N.J.: Prentice-Hall, 1960. 256 p.

A book of practical suggestions.

Goldman, Richard Franko. THE WIND BAND: ITS LITERATURE AND TECHNIQUE. Boston: Allyn and Bacon, 1961. 286 p.

Covers the history of band music in the United States from European origins to the contemporary era. Instrumentation, scoring, and repertoire are also discussed. Bibliography.

Holz, Emil A., and Jacobi, Roger E. TEACHING BAND INSTRUMENTS TO BEGINNERS. Englewood Cliffs, N.J.: Prentice-Hall, 1966. 118 p.

Detailed suggestions for class teaching of each family of instruments. Bibliography.

The Instrumentalist Co. BAND MUSIC GUIDE. 6th ed. Evanston, Ill.: 1975. 375 p.

A directory of U.S. published band music, arranged alphabetically by titles, composers-arrangers, and publishers. Listed according to five catagories: concert and marching music, collections, solos and ensembles with band, band method books, and marching routines.

Intravaia, Lawrence J. BUILDING A SUPERIOR SCHOOL BAND LIBRARY. West Nyack, N.Y.: Parker Publishing Co., 1972. 272 p. Illus.

Practical suggestions for selecting, acquiring, cataloging, and maintaining a band music library. Bibliography.

Labuta, Joseph A. TEACHING MUSICIANSHIP IN THE HIGH SCHOOL BAND. West Nyack, N.Y.: Parker Publishing Co., 1972. 232 p.

Presents practical suggestions for the development of musicianship through participation in the school band. Bibliography.

Mercer, Jack. BAND DIRECTOR'S BRAIN BANK. Evanston, Ill.: Instrumentalist Co., 1973. 94 p. Charts, graphs, paper.

A compendium of teaching techniques based on interviews with band directors. Covers all aspects of the band program.

Music Educators National Conference. Contemporary Music Project. THE CONTEMPORARY MUSIC PROJECT LIBRARY. Vol. 1. Washington, D.C.: MENC, 1967-69. Unpaged.

Volume 1 of this series lists all works written for band, winds, and percussion/solos for the Composers in Public Schools Program during its ten-year period. Each work described provides name of composer, historical and technical data, and two representative score pages. For additional details of this project, see Contemporary Music Project (CMP) in Section 40: Contemporary Music.

Otto, Richard A. EFFECTIVE METHODS FOR BUILDING THE HIGH SCHOOL BAND. West Nyack, N.Y.: Parker Publishing Co., 1971. 256 p.

Contains ideas, suggestions, and techniques for developing the high school band program.

Pegram, Wayne F. PRACTICAL GUIDELINES FOR DEVELOPING THE HIGH SCHOOL BAND. West Nyack, N.Y.: Parker Publishing Co., 1973. 224 p.

Covers a variety of topics related to the organization and maintenance of the high school band. Special attention is given to the role of the elementary and junior high school instrumental programs as an important part of the curriculum.

Pizer, Russell A. ADMINISTERING THE ELEMENTARY BAND; TEACHING BEGINNING INSTRUMENTALISTS AND DEVELOPING A BAND SUPPORT PROGRAM. West Nyack, N.Y.: Parker Publishing Co., 1971. 227 p.

Suggestions and aids for teaching beginning instrumentalists.

Schwartz, H.W. BANDS OF AMERICA. Garden City, N.Y.: Doubleday and Co., 1957. 320 p. Music, photos.

A historical account of the band era from the mid-nineteenth century to the mid-twentieth century.

Weerts, Richard. DEVELOPING INDIVIDUAL SKILLS FOR THE HIGH SCHOOL BAND. West Nyack, N.Y.: Parker Publishing Co., 1969. 235 p. Illus., music, photos.

A practical reference source for high school band directors.

Whitwell, David. A NEW HISTORY OF WIND MUSIC. Evanston, Ill.: Instrumentalist Co., 1972. 80 p.

Historical material. Bibliography.

Wright, Al G., and Newcomb, Stanley. BANDS OF THE WORLD. Evanston, Ill.: Instrumentalist Co., 1970. 112 p. Photos.

A pictorial reference source of more than 200 bands, including selected bands of the United States. Includes instrumentation, types of instruments, uniforms, marching formations, and concert seating arrangements.

Marching Band

Binion, W.T., Jr. THE HIGH SCHOOL MARCHING BAND. West Nyack, N.Y.: Parker Publishing Co., 1973. 273 p. Diagrams, photos.

Methods and procedures for developing a marching band.

Butts, Carrol M. HOW TO ARRANGE AND REHEARSE FOOTBALL BAND SHOWS. West Nyack, N.Y.: Parker Publishing Co., 1974. 204 p.

Foster, William. BAND PAGEANTRY. Winona, Minn.: Hal Leonard Music, 1968. 174 p.

A source book including programs, drills, formations, and schedules for half-time pageantry.

Lee, Jack. MODERN MARCHING BAND TECHNIQUES. Winona, Minn.: Hal Leonard Music, 1955. 267 p. Illus., photos.

Discusses the educational and artistic values of the marching band and its function. Practical suggestions for organizing and administering an effective show band.

Marcouiller, Don R. MARCHING FOR MARCHING BANDS. Dubuque, Iowa: William C. Brown Co., 1958. 131 p.

Presents many marching drills and sequences which may be used with equal effect by bands, drum and bugle corps, and drill teams of all varieties. Bibliography.

Opsahl, Julian E. PRECISION MARCHING. Evanston, Ill.: Instrumentalist Co., 1961. 54 p. Illus., paper.

Contains ideas for steps, maneuvers, and precision marching with directions and explanatory drawings.

Spohn, Charles L., and Heine, Richard W. THE MARCHING BAND: COMPARATIVE TECHNIQUES IN MOVEMENT AND MUSIC. Boston: Allyn and Bacon, 1969. 176 p.

Wright, Al G. SHOW BAND. Evanston, Ill.: Instrumentalist Co., 1971. 135 p. Illus., photos, paper.

Contains 114 complete shows with suggested music for each; 324 field formations, designing and materials. Bibliography.

Instrument Maintenance

Brand, Erick D. BAND INSTRUMENT REPAIR MANUAL. Elkhart, Ind.: Erick Brand, 1946. 198 p. Photos, illus., paper.

Extensive source book for tools and repair supplies. Includes illustrated instructions for woodwind and brass repair.

Burgan, Arthur. BASIC STRING REPAIRS: A GUIDE FOR STRING CLASS TEACHERS. New York: Oxford University Press, 1974. 59 p. Illus.

A useful handbook for the classroom string teacher. Contains general suggestions for care, maintenance, and minor repairs.

Sloane, Irving. GUITAR REPAIR. New York: E.P. Dutton, 1973. 95 p. Photos.

All common guitar repairs are discussed. One section deals with restoration techniques for antique instruments. Includes a list of sources for repair supplies and tools. Assumes a basic knowledge of woodworking.

Springer, George H. MAINTENANCE AND REPAIR OF BAND INSTRUMENTS. Boston: Allyn and Bacon, 1970. 176 p. Illus., photos.

A practical manual covering repair procedures for woodwind, brass, and percussion instruments.

Tiede, Clayton H. THE PRACTICAL BAND INSTRUMENT REPAIR MANUAL. 3d ed. Dubuque, Iowa: William C. Brown Co., 1976. 160 p.

Weisshaar, Otto H. PREVENTIVE MAINTENANCE OF MUSICAL INSTRUMENTS. Rockville Centre, N.Y.: Belwin, 1966. 108 p. Photos.

A handbook which includes instrument specifications and suggestions for cleaning, maintenance, and minor repairs.

INSTRUMENTAL TECHNIQUES

Literature for the development of instrumental techniques is divided into four parts--strings, woodwinds, brasses, and percussion. There are, of course, literally hundreds of method books for the various instruments of the band and orchestra written for private or class teaching purposes. There is no attempt to list such publications here. This guide does include those books primarily designed to serve either as college textbooks for future teachers or as reference works. Most, in addition to providing both text and exemplary musical material for the development of techniques, also include a bibliography and list of recommended materials--such as solo and ensemble music at various levels of advancement, and supplementary study materials. The list is confined primarily to those books issued in recent years.

Strings

Applebaum, Samuel, and Applebaum, Sada. WITH THE ARTISTS: WORLD FAMOUS STRING PLAYERS DISCUSS THEIR ART. New York: John Markert, 1955. 318 p. Photos, music.

A discussion of performance problems and other aspects of string playing from the artist's point of view. Useful for students and teachers. Based on personal interviews with most of the world's leading string players.

Bachmann, Werner. THE ORGINS OF BOWING AND THE DEVELOPMENT OF BOWED INSTRUMENTS UP TO THE THIRTEENTH CENTURY. Translated by Norma Deane. New York: Oxford University Press, 1969. 178 p.

Traces the history and development of string instrument bowing techniques throughout the European and Asian world up to the thirteenth century. Extensive bibliography.

Barrett, Henry. THE VIOLA: COMPLETE GUIDE FOR TEACHERS AND STUDENTS. University: University of Alabama Press, 1972. 165 p. Music.

Text is based on problems submitted to the author through a survey of more than 250 viola teachers who are members of the American String Teachers Association. Covers literature and teaching procedures. Bibliography.

Bobri, Vladimir. THE SEGOVIA TECHNIQUE. New York: Macmillan, 1972. 94 p. Illus.

Includes historical survey of the classical guitar, virtuosi of the instrument, Segovia technique, pedagogy, and selected lists of guitar methods and instruction books.

Bone, Philip James. THE GUITAR AND MANDOLIN: BIOGRAPHIES OF CELEBRATED PLAYERS AND COMPOSERS. 2d ed. London and New York: Schott, 1954. 388 p.

Boyden, David D. THE HISTORY OF VIOLIN PLAYING FROM ITS ORIGINS TO 1761 AND ITS RELATIONSHIP TO THE VIOLIN AND VIOLIN MUSIC. London: Oxford University Press, 1965. 569 p. Photos.

Useful as an historical record and a reference tool concerning performance practice for the teacher and performer.

Clarke, A. Mason. A BIOGRAPHICAL DICTIONARY OF FIDDLERS. 1895. Reprint. St. Clair Shores, Mich.: Scholarly Press, 1972. 360 p.

Includes performers on the violoncello and double bass, containing a sketch of their artistic career, together with notes of their compositions, and so forth.

Collins, Gertrude. VIOLIN TEACHING IN CLASS: A HANDBOOK FOR TEACHERS. New York and London: Oxford University Press, 1962. 183 p. Illus., music.

A detailed analysis of string class pedagogy. Bibliography.

Creighton, James. THE DISOPAEDIA OF THE VIOLIN. Toronto: University of Toronto Press, 1974. 988 p.

This unique volume lists all of the known recorded performances of more than 1,600 violinists, covering a period of more than eight years. It includes all known commercial disc recordings and cylinders.

De Smet, Robin, comp. PUBLISHED MUSIC FOR THE VIOLA DA GAMBA AND OTHER VIOLS. Detroit: Information Coordinators, 1971. 105 p.

Edwards, Arthur C. STRING ENSEMBLE METHOD. 2d ed. Dubuque, Iowa: William C. Brown Co., 1973. 103 p. Music.

Elgar, Raymond. LOOKING AT THE DOUBLE BASS. St. Leonards-on-Sea, Sussex, Engl.: Raymond Elgar, 1967. 44 p. Illus.

Farga, Franz. VIOLINS AND VIOLINISTS. Translated by Egon Larsen and Bruno Raikin. New York: Praeger; London: Barrie and Rockliff, The Cresset Press, 1969. 247 p.

Farish, Margaret K. STRING MUSIC IN PRINT. 2d ed. New York: R.R. Bowker Co., 1973. 464 p.

> A comprehensive English-language guide to available music for stringed instruments. A listing of more than 25,000 pieces representing 350 U.S. and foreign publishers. Entries include solos, duos, trios, etc., chamber music scores, solo instruments with orchestra, study materials, composer index, and list of publishers (including U.S. agents for foreign publishers).

Green, Elizabeth [A.H.]. TEACHING STRINGED INSTRUMENTS IN CLASSES. Englewood Cliffs, N.J.: Prentice-Hall, 1966. 106 p.

Grodner, Murray. COMPREHENSIVE CATALOG OF AVAILABLE LITERATURE FOR THE DOUBLE BASS. 2d ed. Bloomington, Ill.: Lemur Musical Research, 1964. 84 p.

> A graded listing of methods, etudes, and solo and ensemble works for the string bass.

Grunfeld, Frederic V. THE ART AND TIMES OF THE GUITAR: AN ILLUSTRATED HISTORY OF GUITARS AND GUITARISTS. New York: Macmillan, 1969. 340 p.

Hodgson, Percival. MOTION STUDY AND VIOLIN BOWING. 1934. Reprint. Bryn Mawr, Pa.: Theodore Presser Co., 1958. 106 p. Illus., photos.

> This work is an extension of the ideas presented in F.G. Steinhausen's book, DIE PHYSIOLOGIE DES BOGENFÜHRUNG, published in 1903. The anatomical, acoustical, mechanical, and geometrical aspects of bowing are discussed with actual movements portrayed and classified with diagrams, cyclegraphs, and photographs.

Hutchins, Carleen M., ed. MUSICAL ACOUSTICS. Part I: VIOLIN FAMILY COMPONENTS. Stroudsburg, Pa.: Dowden, Hutchinson and Ross, 1975. 478 p.

> Contains twenty-seven papers dealing with various aspects of violin acoustics. A companion work is MUSICAL ACOUSTICS. Part II: VIOLIN FAMILY FUNCTIONS, by the same author and publisher.

Jalovec, Karel. GERMAN AND AUSTRIAN VIOLIN-MAKERS. Translated by George Theiner. Edited by Patrick Hanks. London: Hamlyn, 1967. 439 p.

Klotman, Robert H., and Harris, Ernest E. LEARNING TO TEACH THROUGH PLAYING: STRING TECHNIQUES AND PEDAGOGY. Reading, Mass.: Addison-Wesley, 1971. 180 p. Music, photos.

Kuhn, Wolfgang E. THE STRINGS, PERFORMANCE AND INSTRUCTIONAL TECHNIQUES. Boston: Allyn and Bacon, 1967. 171 p.

Lamb, Norman. A GUIDE TO TEACHING STRINGS. Dubuque, Iowa: William C. Brown Co., 1971. 165 p.

Landsman, Jerome. ANNOTATED CATALOG OF AMERICAN VIOLIN MUSIC COMPOSED BETWEEN 1947-1961. Bryn Mawr, Pa.: Theodore Presser, 1968. 55 p.

Attempts to continue the account of American composition started by Clare Reis in the book COMPOSERS IN AMERICA, specifically in the field of violin music. Includes only works by American citizens, sonatas and suites for violin, and music available in American editions. Bibliography.

Leipp, Emile. THE VIOLIN: HISTORY, AESTHETICS, MANUFACTURE, AND ACOUSTICS. Translated by Hildegarde W. Parry. Toronto: University of Toronto Press, 1969. 126 p. Illus., photos.

Letz, Hans, comp. MUSIC FOR THE VIOLIN AND VIOLA. New York: Rinehart, 1948. 107 p.

Bibliography and graded lists.

Loft, Abraham. VIOLIN AND KEYBOARD: THE DUO REPERTOIRE. 2 vols. New York: Grossman Publishers, 1973. Music.

Volume I: FROM THE SEVENTEENTH CENTURY TO MOZART. 360 p.; volume II: FROM BEETHOVEN TO THE PRESENT. 417 p. A historical survey of sonatas for piano (or harpsichord) and violin. Analyses range from sonatas of the early 1600s to the 1960s, with separate sections devoted to specific composers. Bibliography.

Matesky, Ralph, and Rush, Ralph E. PLAYING AND TEACHING STRINGED INSTRUMENTS, PART I. Englewood Cliffs, N.J.: Prentice-Hall, 1963. 152 p.

Mozart, Leopold. A TREATISE ON THE FUNDAMENTAL PRINCIPLES OF VIOLIN PLAYING. 2d ed. Translated by Edith Knocker. New York: Oxford University Press, 1951. 235 p. Music.

A translation of VERSUCH EINER GRUNDLICHEN VIOLINSCHULE, published in Augsburg in 1756. A work of great historical and educational interest.

Nelson, Sheila M. THE VIOLIN AND VIOLA. London: E. Benn; New York: W.W. Norton and Co., 1972. 277 p.

Covers the history and construction of these instruments. Discusses performers, teachers, and composers as well. Extensive bibliography.

Neumann, Frederick. VIOLIN LEFT HAND TECHNIQUE: A SURVEY OF RELATED LITERATURE. Urbana, Ill.: American String Teachers Association, 1968. 141 p.

An extensive survey and appraisal of the main writings of the past. Bibliography.

Polnauer, Frederick F. "Bio-mechanics, A New Approach to Music Education." JOURNAL OF THE FRANKLIN INSTITUTE 254 (October 1952): 297-316.

Proposes and describes the application of the principles of physiology to the development of violin skills.

_____. TOTAL BODY TECHNIQUE OF VIOLIN PLAYING. Bryn Mawr, Pa.: Theodore Presser Co., 1974. 51 p. Photos, illus., paper.

One of the few works based on scientific fundamentals of motion physiology which imply that violin playing must be conceived as a Motion-Gestalt applied to the body and its parts as a whole. Through numerous photographs and text this work illustrates the interaction of all parts of the body and shows how to control these varied interactions in such a way as to optimize the "total body technique."

Polnauer, Frederick F., and Marks, Martin. SENSO-MOTOR STUDY AND ITS APPLICATION TO VIOLIN PLAYING. 2d ed. Urbana, Ill.: American String Teachers Association, 1964. 211 p. Illus., photos.

An analysis of violin playing and teaching based on scientific principles. A pioneer work that explores violin playing in depth with the latest physiological findings and Gestalt psychology. Bibliography at the end of each section.

Rensch, Roslyn. THE HARP: ITS HISTORY, TECHNIQUE, AND REPERTOIRE. London: Duckworth; New York: Praeger, 1969. 246 p.

Rolland, Paul, and Mutschler, Marla. THE TEACHING OF ACTION IN STRING PLAYING. Bryn Mawr, Pa.: Theodore Presser Co., 1974. 214 p. Music, photos, illus.

A comprehensive guide for teaching basic violin and viola skills. There is also a series of fifteen films of the same title. Both the book and the film series consist of the principal results of the five-year study by the University of Illinois String Research Project.

Sloane, Irving. CLASSIC GUITAR CONSTRUCTION. New York: E.P. Dutton, 1966. 95 p. Diagrams, illus., photos.

Step-by-step instructions for making classic guitars.

Sollinger, Charles. STRING CLASS PUBLICATIONS IN THE UNITED STATES, 1851-1951. Detroit: Information Coordinators, 1974. 71 p.

Straeten, Edmund Sebastian Joseph van der. THE HISTORY OF THE VIOLIN: ITS ANCESTORS AND COLLATERAL INSTRUMENTS FROM EARLIEST TIMES. 2 vols. 1933. Reprint. New York: Da Capo Press, 1968.

Swalin, Benjamin F. THE VIOLIN CONCERTO: A STUDY IN GERMAN ROMANTICISM. Chapel Hill: University of North Carolina Press, 1941. 172 p.

Considers the stylistic and technical aspects of concertos in German Romanticism from Spohr to Brahms. Bibliography.

Szende, Otto, and Nemussurei, Mihaly. THE PHYSIOLOGY OF VIOLIN PLAYING. Translated by I. Szmodis. London: Collet's; Bryn Mawr, Pa: Theodore Presser Co., 1971. 202 p.

Timmerman, Maurine, and Griffith, Celeste. GUITAR IN THE CLASSROOM. Dubuque, Iowa: William C. Brown Co., 1971. 128 p.

Turetzky, Bertram. THE CONTEMPORARY CONTRABASS. Los Angeles and Berkeley: University of California Press, 1974. 128 p. Paper.

Many new techniques are described in this work and are illustrated with music examples from solo bass literature. Focus is on twentieth-century repertoire, but eighteenth- and nineteenth-century literature is also represented. A seven-inch disc recording is included.

Wasielewski, Wilhelm Joseph von. THE VIOLONCELLO AND ITS HISTORY. Translated by Isobella S.E. Stigand. 1894. Reprint. New York: Da Capo Press, 1968. 225 p.

Wassell, Albert W., and Wertmán, Charles H. BIBLIOGRAPHY FOR STRING TEACHERS. Rev. ed. Washington, D.C.: Music Educators National Conference, 1964. 39 p. Paper.

A selective listing especially useful for college string class instructors. Deals with history, pedagogy, literature, and instrument care.

Wechsberg, Joseph. THE GLORY OF THE VIOLIN. New York: Viking

Press, 1973. 314 p. Photos.

A narrative account of the origins and development of the violin, its makers, performers, dealers, and collectors. Sections on performance and pedagogy.

Wilkins, Wayne. INDEX OF VIOLIN MUSIC (STRINGS). Magnolia, Ark.: Music Register, 1972. 246 p. SUPPLEMENT. 1973. 33 p.

Includes index of baroque trio-sonatas.

THE SUZUKI METHOD

Cook, Clifford. SUZUKI EDUCATION IN ACTION. Jericho, N.Y.: Exposition Press, 1970. 144 p.

Provides insights to the Japanese culture as related to this approach to teaching the violin.

Kendall, John D. THE SUZUKI VIOLIN METHOD IN AMERICAN MUSIC EDUCATION: WHAT THE AMERICAN MUSIC EDUCATOR SHOULD KNOW ABOUT SCHINICHI SUZUKI. Washington, D.C.: Music Educators National Conference, 1973. 31 p. Paper.

Revised and updated from TALENT, EDUCATION AND SUZUKI (Washington, D.C.: MENC, 1966), this booklet concentrates on recent developments in Suzuki's method in American music education. Lists all Suzuki materials currently published in America.

Mills, Elizabeth, and Murphy, Sister Therese Cecile, eds. THE SUZUKI CONCEPT. Berkeley, Calif.: Diablo Press, 1973. 216 p.

A description of the Suzuki concepts and methods as viewed by different authors, including Suzuki.

Suzuki, Schinichi. NURTURED BY LOVE; A NEW APPROACH TO EDUCATION. Translated by Waltraud Suzuki. Jericho, N.Y.: Exposition Press, 1969. 21 p.

The philosophy of the Talent Education program as the author believes, lives, and teaches it.

See also "Chamber Music," below, this section.

Woodwinds

BAGPIPE MUSIC INDEX. Glen Ridge, N.J.: Bagpipe Music Index, 1966.

Bartolozzi, Bruno. NEW SOUNDS FOR WOODWIND. Translated by Reginald S[mith]. Brindle. New York and London: Oxford University Press, 1967. 78 p. Illus., music.

Proposes and explores new and different sounds which can be generated with conventional instruments and thereby extend tonal possibilities for composition.

Cooper, Lewis H., and Toplansky, Howard. ESSENTIALS OF BASSOON TECHNIQUES. Union, N.J.: Howard Toplansky, 1968. 384 p.

Errante, F. Gerard. A SELECTIVE CLARINET BIBLIOGRAPHY. Oneonta, N.Y.: Swift-Dorr Publications, 1973. 82 p.

Gilbert, Richard. THE CLARINETISTS' SOLO REPERTOIRE: A DISCOGRAPHY. New York: Grenadilla Society, 1972. 100 p.

Gillespie, James E., Jr., comp. THE REED TRIO: AN ANNOTATED BIBLIOGRAPHY OF ORIGINAL PUBLISHED WORKS. Detroit: Information Coordinators, 1971.

_____. SOLOS FOR UNACCOMPANIED CLARINET: AN ANNOTATED BIBLIOGRAPHY OF PUBLISHED WORKS. Detroit: Information Coordinators, 1973. 79 p.

Globus, Rodo S., ed. THE WOODWIND ANTHOLOGY. New York: Woodwind Magazine, 1952. 94 p.

Gold, Cecil V., comp. CLARINET PERFORMING PRACTICES AND TEACHING IN THE UNITED STATES AND CANADA. 2d ed. Moscow: University of Idaho School of Music Publication, 1973. 90 p.

Heim, Norman, comp. MUSIC AND TAPE RECORDINGS FILED IN THE NACWPI RESEARCH LIBRARY. College Park: University of Maryland, McKeldin Library, 1972. Unpaged. Paper.

Alphabetical listing by composer of cataloged published and unpublished music and tapes in the National Association of College Wind and Percussion Instructors Library (about 1,000 items). Supplemental lists are issued periodically. For further details see "Pedagogical Guides and Reference Books," above, this section.

Heller, George N. ENSEMBLE MUSIC FOR WIND AND PERCUSSION INSTRUMENTS: A CATALOG. Washington, D.C.: Music Educators National Conference, 1970. 142 p.

Hilton, Louis B. LEARNING TO TEACH THROUGH PLAYING, A WOODWIND METHOD. Reading, Mass.: Addison-Wesley, 1970. 184 p.

Hotteterre, Jacques. PRINCIPLES OF THE FLUTE, RECORDER, AND OBOE. Translated and edited by David Lasocki. London: Barrie and Rockliff; New York: Praeger, 1968. 88 p.

______. RUDIMENTS OF THE FLUTE, RECORDER, AND OBOE. Translated by Paul Marshall Douglas. New York: Dover Publications, 1968. 73 p.

The Instrumentalist Co., comp. WOODWIND ANTHOLOGY. Evanston, Ill.: 1972. 704 p.

Kroll, Oscar. THE CLARINET: ITS HISTORY, LITERATURE, AND GREAT MASTERS. Revised by Diethard Riehm. New York: Taplinger, 1968. 183 p.

Langwill, Lyndesay [Graham]. THE BASSOON AND CONTRABASSOON. New York: W.W. Norton and Co., 1965. 269 p. Illus., music.

Lehman, Paul R. THE HARMONIC STRUCTURE OF THE TONE OF THE BASSOON. Seattle, Wash.: Berdon, 1965. 194 p.

A careful study of the acoustical aspects of the instrument, a glossary of technical terms, good bibliography.

Nederveen, Cornelis Johannes. ACOUSTICAL ASPECTS OF WOODWIND INSTRUMENTS. Amsterdam: Frits Knuf, 1969. 118 p.

Palmer, Harold. TEACHING TECHNIQUES OF THE WOODWINDS: A TEXTBOOK FOR THE INSTRUMENTAL TEACHER AND THE TEACHER IN TRAINING. Rockville Center, N.Y.: Belwin, 1962. 72 p.

Peters, Harry B., comp. THE LITERATURE OF THE WOODWIND QUINTET. Metuchen, N.J.: Scarecrow Press, 1971. 174 p.

Extensive listing of original compositions and arrangements.

Quantz, Johann Joachim. ON PLAYING THE FLUTE. Translated by Edward R. Reilly. Riverside, N.J.: Free Press, 1966. 365 p. Illus., music.

Rasmussen, Mary, and Mattran, Donald. A TEACHER'S GUIDE TO THE LITERATURE OF WOODWIND INSTRUMENTS. Durham, N.H.: Brass and Woodwind Quarterly, 1966. 226 p.

Rendall, Francis Geoffrey. THE CLARINET: SOME NOTES UPON ITS HISTORY AND CONSTRUCTION. London: E. Benn; New York: W.W. Norton and Co., 1971. 206 p. Music, photos.

Covers the development of the family of clarinets, including construction related acoustics. Includes lists of solo and ensemble music, method books, instrument makers (from 1700 on), and a bibliography.

Richmond, Stanley. CLARINET AND SAXOPHONE EXPERIENCE. New York: St. Martin's Press, 1972. 137 p. Illus., music.

Rockstro, R.S. A TREATISE ON THE FLUTE. 1928. Reprint. London: Musica Rara, 1967. 664 p.

Rothwell, Evelyn. OBOE TECHNIQUE. 2d ed. London and New York: Oxford University Press, 1962. 126 p.

Explains the techniques involved in achieving mastery of this instrument. Includes discussion of the English horn and oboe d'amore repertoire as well as repertoire for solo and ensemble performance.

Rowland-Jones, A. RECORDER TECHNIQUE. London and New York: Oxford University Press, 1959. 139 p.

Covers the historical development of the recorder, its repertoire, and performing technique.

Sawhill, Clarence, and McGarrity, Bertram. PLAYING AND TEACHING WOODWIND INSTRUMENTS. Englewood Cliffs, N.J.: Prentice-Hall, 1962. 134 p. Illus.

Spencer, William. THE ART OF BASSOON PLAYING. Reviewed by Frederick A. Mueller. Evanston, Ill.: Summy-Birchard, 1969. 72 p.

Stanton, Robert E. THE OBOE PLAYER'S ENCYCLOPEDIA. Enl. ed. Oneonta, N.Y.: Swift-Dorr Publications, 1974. 48 p. Paper.

Stubbins, William H. THE ART OF CLARINETISTRY. Ann Arbor, Mich.: Ann Arbor Publishers, 1965. 313 p.

Thurston, Frederick. CLARINET TECHNIQUE. 2d ed. London and New York: Oxford University Press, 1964. 92 p.

Concentrates on the technical aspects of performance. Includes guides for purchase and care of the instrument and a list of solo and ensemble repertoire.

Timm, Everett L. THE WOODWINDS: PERFORMANCE AND INSTRUCTIONAL TECHNIQUES. Boston: Allyn and Bacon, 1964. 211 p.

Voxman, Himie, and Merriman, Lyle, comps. WOODWIND ENSEMBLE MUSIC GUIDE. Evanston, Ill.: Instrumentalist Co., 1973. 280 p.

A comprehensive listing of compositions in print of instrumentation including one or more woodwinds. Includes catalogs of more than 200 publishers. Contains title, composer, arranger, editor, publisher, opus, key, date of composition, and instrumentation.

Warner, Thomas E. AN ANNOTATED BIBLIOGRAPHY OF WOODWIND INSTRUCTION BOOKS 1600-1830. Detroit Studies in Music Bibliography no. 11. Detroit: Information Coordinators, 1967. 138 p.

Comprehensive bibliography, arranged in chronological order, gives library or catalog locations, and reproduces original orthography of complete title page for located words.

Weerts, Richard. HOW TO DEVELOP AND MAINTAIN A SUCCESSFUL WOODWIND SECTION. West Nyack, N.Y.: Parker Publishing Co., 1972. 242 p.

Treats a wide range of problems and teaching methods. Numerous bibliographies.

_____, comp. ORIGINAL MANUSCRIPT MUSIC FOR WIND AND PERCUSSION INSTRUMENTS. Washington, D.C.: Music Educators National Conference, 1973. 42 p. Paper.

Contains more than 400 listings of graded solos, ensembles, and arrangements. Includes performance time, instrumentation, date of composition, available recordings, and location of publisher and/or composers.

Weston, Pamela. CLARINET VIRTUOSI OF THE PAST. London: Hale, 1971. 292 p.

Westphal, Frederick W. GUIDE TO TEACHING WOODWINDS. 2d ed. Dubuque, Iowa: William C. Brown Co., 1974. 328 p.

Whitwell, David. A NEW HISTORY OF WIND MUSIC. Evanston, Ill.: Instrumentalist Co., 1972. 80 p.

Wiesner, Glenn R., et al. ORTHODONTICS AND WIND INSTRUMENT PERFORMANCE. Washington, D.C.: Music Educators National Conference, 1973. 40 p. Paper.

Wilkins, Wayne. INDEX OF FLUTE MUSIC. Magnolia, Ark.: Music Register, 1974. 132 p.

See also "Chamber Music," below, this section.

Brasses

Corley, Robert, comp. BRASS PLAYERS' GUIDE TO THE LITERATURE 1973-74. North Easton, Mass.: Robert King Music Co., 1973. 63 p. Paper.

> A comprehensive survey of materials which are available for purchase in the United States.

Dale, Delbert A. TRUMPET TECHNIQUE. London: Oxford University Press, 1965. 93 p. Illus.

Everett, Thomas G. ANNOTATED GUIDE TO BASS TROMBONE LITERATURE. Nashville, Tenn.: Brass Press, 1973. 34 p.

Farkas, Philip. THE ART OF BRASS PLAYING. Bloomington, Ind.: Wind Music, 1962. 65 p. Illus., photos, paper.

_____. THE ART OF FRENCH HORN PLAYING. Evanston, Ill.: Summy-Birchard, 1956. 95 p. Illus., music, photos.

Fitzpatrick, Horace. THE HORN AND HORN PLAYING, AND THE AUSTRO-BOHEMIAN TRADITION FROM 1680-1830. London: Oxford University Press, 1970. 218 p. Music, illus.

Gregory, Robin. THE HORN: A COMPREHENSIVE GUIDE TO THE MODERN INSTRUMENT AND ITS MUSIC. Rev. ed. New York: Praeger, 1969. 410 p.

_____. THE TROMBONE: THE INSTRUMENT AND ITS MUSIC. New York: Praeger, 1973. 328 p.

Heim, Norman, comp. MUSIC AND TAPE RECORDINGS FILED IN THE NACWPI RESEARCH LIBRARY. College Park: University of Maryland, McKeldin Library, 1972. Unpaged. Paper.

> Alphabetical listing by composer of cataloged published and unpublished music and tapes in the National Association of College Wind and Percussion Instructors Library (about 1,000 items). Supplemental lists are issued periodically. For further details see "Pedagogical Guides and Reference Books," above, this section.

Heller, George N. ENSEMBLE MUSIC FOR WIND AND PERCUSSION INSTRUMENTS: A CATALOG. Washington, D.C.: Music Educators National Conference, 1970. 142 p.

Hunt, Norman J. BRASS ENSEMBLE METHOD FOR TEACHER EDUCATION. 2d ed. Dubuque, Iowa: William C. Brown Co., 1974. 145 p. Music, photos.

______. GUIDE TO TEACHING BRASS. Dubuque, Iowa: William C. Brown Co., 1968. 144 p. Music, photos.

The Instrumentalist Co., comp. BRASS ANTHOLOGY. Evanston, Ill.: 1969. 504 p. Illus., photos, tables.

A compendium of selected articles by leading authorities dealing with the principal aspects of brass instrument performance, which appeared in the INSTRUMENTALIST from 1946 through 1968.

INTERNATIONAL TROMBONE ASSOCIATION SOURCE LIBRARY. Catholic University of America, Washington, D.C. 20017. Dr. John R. Marcellus, Coordinator.

A repository of materials relating to the trombone--its history and literature. Includes manuscripts and published works commercial and private; records and tapes; theses not held by University Microfilms; papers or lists of literature held by other institutions, composers, performers, etc. Available on a limited loan basis.

Lowrey, Alvin L., comp. TRUMPET DISCOGRAPHY. 3 vols. in 1. Denver: National Trumpet Symposium, University of Denver School of Music, 1970. 109 p. Paper.

This three-volume series of recordings for the trumpet is one of the most complete references of its kind. Bibliography.

Mendez, Rafael. PRELUDE TO BRASS PLAYING. New York: Carl Fischer, 1961. 123 p. Music, photos.

Menke, Werner. HISTORY OF THE TRUMPET OF BACH AND HANDEL. 2d ed. Translated by Gerald Abraham. London: William Reeves Bookseller, 1934. 128 p.

Morley-Pegge, R. HORN TECHNIQUE. 2d ed. London: E. Benn, 1973. 239 p.

Morris, R. Winston. TUBA MUSIC GUIDE. Evanston, Ill.: Instrumentalist Co. 1973. 60 p. Paper.

An extensive annotated bibliography.

Mueller, Herbert C. LEARNING TO TEACH THROUGH PLAYING: A BRASS METHOD. Reading, Mass.: Addison-Wesley, 1968. 183 p.

Porter, Maurice. THE EMBOUCHURE. London: Boosey and Hawkes, 1967. 144 p. Illus.

Rasmussen, Mary. TEACHERS GUIDE TO THE LITERATURE OF BRASS INSTRUMENTS. Durham, N.H.: Appleyard, 1964. 84 p. Paper.

Schuller, Gunther. HORN TECHNIQUE. London and New York: Oxford University Press, 1962. 118 p. Illus., music.

Smithers, Don L. THE MUSIC AND HISTORY OF THE BAROQUE TRUMPET BEFORE 1721. Syracuse, N.Y.: Syracuse University Press, 1973. 304 p. Music, photos.

> Highly useful to music historians and music educators with a special interest in the repertory of trumpet music of the seventeenth century and the instruments which were used for performance of that music. Contains appendices that provide much information on the surviving sources of nearly all known music originally composed for the baroque trumpet.

Sweeney, Leslie. TEACHING TECHNIQUES FOR THE BRASSES. Rockville Center, N.Y.: Belwin, 1953. 56 p. Paper.

Weast, Robert. BRASS PERFORMANCE: AN ANALYTICAL TEXT OF THE PHYSICAL PROCESSES, PROBLEMS, AND TECHNIQUES OF BRASS. New York: McGinnis and Marx, 1961. 73 p. Photos, paper.

Wiesner, Glen R., et al. ORTHODONTICS AND WIND INSTRUMENT PERFORMANCE. Washington, D.C.: Music Educators National Conference, 1973. 40 p. Paper.

Winslow, Robert W., and Green, John E. PLAYING AND TEACHING BRASS INSTRUMENTS. Englewood Cliffs, N.J.: Prentice-Hall, 1961. 134 p. Music, photos, tables, paper.

Winter, James H. THE BRASS INSTRUMENTS: PERFORMANCE AND INSTRUCTIONAL TECHNIQUES. 3d ed. Boston: Allyn and Bacon, 1969. 184 p. Paper.

Wright, Frank, ed. BRASS TODAY. London: Bessen & Co., 1957. 126 p. Illus., photos, paper.

See also "Chamber Music," below, this section.

Percussion

Anthony, Dorothy Malone. THE WORLD OF BELLS. Des Moines, Iowa: Wallace-Homestead Book Co., 1971. Unpaged. Photos, paper.

A handbook for identifying bells from different eras, countries, and religions. Emphasis is on handbells.

Bartlett, Harry R., and Holloway, Ronald. GUIDE TO TEACHING PERCUSSION. 2d ed. Dubuque, Iowa: William C. Brown Co., 1971. 172 p. Paper.

_____. PERCUSSION ENSEMBLE METHOD. 2d ed. Dubuque, Iowa: William C. Brown Co., 1972. 184 p. Paper.

Bigelow, Arthur Lynds. THE ACOUSTICALLY BALANCED CARILLON: GRAPHICS AND THE DESIGN OF CARILLONS AND CARILLON BELLS. Princeton, N.J.: School of Engineering, Dept. of Graphics, 1961. 102 p. Photos, illus.

Although technical, this work is also intended for use by the layman and musician. Explains the tonal principles in bells.

_____. CARILLON: AN ACCOUNT OF THE CLASS OF 1892 BELLS AT PRINCETON UNIVERSITY WITH NOTES ON BELLS AND CARILLONS IN GENERAL. Princeton, N.J.: Princeton University Press, 1948. 75 p.

The author, a world renowned authority on carillons, provides an account of the origin and development of bells and carillons in general and the Princeton instrument specifically. Includes a list of carillons in the United States and Canada.

Blades, James. ORCHESTRAL PERCUSSION TECHNIQUE. London and New York: Oxford University Press, 1961. 85 p.

A description of the percussion instruments and their playing techniques. Includes a brief list of repertoire and a short discography.

_____. PERCUSSION INSTRUMENTS AND THEIR HISTORY. New York: Praeger, 1970. 509 p. Illus., music.

Extensive coverage of the use of percussion instruments through the ages. Numerous bibliographies.

Brindle, Reginald Smith. CONTEMPORARY PERCUSSION. London: Oxford University Press, 1970. 217 p. Music, photos.

Covers wide range of percussion instruments in general use, standard and unusual ones. Especially useful for its treatment of the orchestral use of these instruments. Bibliography and companion disc recording.

Buggert, Robert [W.]. TEACHING TECHNIQUES FOR THE PERCUSSION. Rockville Center, N.Y.: Belwin, 1960. 72 p.

Camp, John M.F. BELL RINGING: CHIMES, CARILLONS, HANDBELLS, THE WORLD OF THE BELL AND THE RINGER. New York: A.S. Barnes, 1974. 160 p. Illus., photos.

A guide to the art of bell ringing. Explains techniques and traditions. Bibliography.

_____. DISCOVERING BELLS AND BELLRINGING. Tring, Engl.: Shire, 1968. 46 p.

Carrington, John V. TALKING DRUMS OF AFRICA. 1949. Reprint. New York: Negro Universities Press, 1969. 96 p.

Coleman, Satis N. BELLS, THEIR HISTORY, LEGENDS, MAKING, AND USES. Chicago and New York: Rand McNally, 1928. 462 p. Illus., photos.

A survey of the history of bell making in all parts of the world. Suggestion for public school creative experiments are given. Bibliography.

Collins, Myron, and Green, John [E.]. PLAYING AND TEACHING PERCUSSION INSTRUMENTS. Englewood Cliffs, N.J.: Prentice-Hall, 1962. 134 p. Paper.

Combs, Michael F., comp. SOLO AND ENSEMBLE LITERATURE FOR PERCUSSION. Terre Haute, Ind.: Percussive Arts Society, 1972. 66 p.

THE GERHARDT MARIMBA XYLOPHONE COLLECTION. See entry in Appendix A for Library of Congress--The Music Division, under "District of Columbia."

Heim, Norman, comp. MUSIC AND TAPE RECORDINGS FILED IN THE NACWPI RESEARCH LIBRARY. College Park: University of Maryland, McKeldin Library, 1972. Unpaged. Paper.

Alphabetical listing by composer of cataloged published and unpublished music and tapes in the National Association of College Wind and Percussion Instructors Library (about 1,000 items). Supplemental lists are issued periodically. For further details see

See also "Pedagogical Guides and Reference Books," above, this section.

Heller, George N. ENSEMBLE MUSIC FOR WIND AND PERCUSSION INSTRUMENTS: A CATALOG. Washington, D.C.: Music Educators National Conference, 1970. 142 p.

Hong, Sherman, comp. PERCUSSION RESEARCH BULLETIN. Hattiesburg: University of Southern Mississippi, 1972. 7 p. Paper.

A bibliography of research studies in the field of percussion covering instruments, pedagogy, and literature. Bibliography of articles, books, and theses.

Mueller, Kenneth A. TEACHING TOTAL PERCUSSION. West Nyack, N.Y.: Parker Publishing Co., 1972. 220 p. Illus.

Music Educators National Conference. Contemporary Music Project. THE CONTEMPORARY MUSIC PROJECT LIBRARY. Vol. 1. Washington, D.C.: MENC, 1967-69. Unpaged.

Volume 1 of this series lists all works written for band, winds, and percussion/solos for the Composers in Public Schools Program during its ten-year period. Each work described provides name of composer, historical and technical data, and two representative score pages. For additional details of this project, see Contemporary Music Project (CMP) in Section 40: Contemporary Music.

Nketia, J.H. Kwabena. OUR DRUM AND DRUMMERS. Accra: Ghana Publishing House, 1968. 48 p.

Payson, A., and McKenzie, Jack. MUSIC EDUCATORS' GUIDE TO PERCUSSION. Rockville Center, N.Y.: Belwin, 1966. 128 p.

PERCUSSION RESEARCH COLLECTION.

A collection of percussion materials has been organized at the University of Southern Mississippi as a joint project of the university and the Percussive Arts Society. Photocopying of materials is available. For information write: Percussion Research Collection, Southern Station, Box 53, Hattiesburg, Mississippi 39401.

Percussive Arts Society. INTERNATIONAL PERCUSSION REFERENCE LIBRARY CATALOG. Tempe: Arizona State University, 1973. Unpaged.

A reference library of all compositions using percussion as the primary instrument. Compositions are available for perusal.

Reed, H. Owen, and Leach, Joel T. SCORING FOR PERCUSSION AND

THE INSTRUMENTS OF PERCUSSION. Englewood Cliffs, N.J.: Prentice-Hall, 1969. 150 p.

A practical guide to scoring for percussion.

Rice, William Gorham. CARILLON MUSIC AND SINGING TOWERS OF THE OLD WORLD AND THE NEW. New York: Dodd, Mead and Co., 1925. 397 p. Photos, illus.

The origin and history of carillons and the art of carillon playing.

Spohn, Charles [L.], and Tatgenhorst, John. THE PERCUSSION: PERFORMANCE AND INSTRUMENTAL TECHNIQUES. 2d ed. Boston: Allyn and Bacon, 1971. 169 p. Illus., music.

Taylor, Henry W. THE ART AND SCIENCE OF THE TIMPANI. Chester Springs, Pa.: Dufour Editions; London: John Baker, 1964. 76 p. Music, photos.

Weerts, Richard, comp. ORIGINAL MANUSCRIPT MUSIC FOR WIND AND PERCUSSION INSTRUMENTS. Washington, D.C.: Music Educators National Conference, 1973. 42 p.

Contains more than 400 listings of graded solos, ensembles, and arrangements. Includes performance time, instrumentation, date of composition, available recordings, and location of publisher and/or composer.

Westcott, Wendell. BELLS AND THEIR MUSIC WITH A RECORDING OF BELL SOUNDS. New York: G.P. Putnam's Sons, 1970. 99 p. Photos.

A history of bells throughout the world. Includes acoustic analyses, tuning, and carillon art.

Wilson, Wilfred G. CHANGE RINGING: THE ART AND SCIENCE OF CHANGE RINGING ON CHURCH AND HAND BELLS. New York: October House, 1965. 238 p. Illus., photos.

A comprehensive, authoritative textbook on the art of bell ringing. Includes conducting procedures. Bibliography.

See also "Chamber Music," below, this section.

CHAMBER MUSIC

Chazanoff, Daniel. "Early English Chamber Music for Strings: Performance Hints." MUSIC JOURNAL 24 (November 1966): 61-63.

A representative list of published three-, four-, five-, and six-part string works of early English composers. All listings include score and parts. Includes also a list of publishers and distributors of early English chamber music for strings.

Cobbett, Walter Willson, ed. COBBETT'S CYCLOPEDIC SURVEY OF CHAMBER MUSIC. 2d ed. 3 vols. London and New York: Oxford University Press, 1963. 1,437 p. Tables, music.

An in-depth study of European, British, and American chamber music. Includes articles and reviews on abstract subjects. Volumes 1 and 2 are photographic reprints of the original 1946 edition with a few additions, including marginal symbols. Volume 3 brings the survey up to date, covering the period since 1929. Bibliographies.

Donington, Robert. A PERFORMER'S GUIDE TO BAROQUE MUSIC. London: Faber, 1974. 320 p.

A comprehensive discussion of the important problems in performance of music of this era. Bibliography.

Garretson, Homer E. "An Annotated Bibliography of Written Material Pertinent to the Performance of Chamber Music for Stringed Instruments." Doctoral dissertation, University of Illinois, 1961. 91 p.

Heller, George N. ENSEMBLE MUSIC FOR WIND AND PERCUSSION INSTRUMENTS: A CATALOG. Washington, D.C.: Music Educators National Conference, 1970. 160 p.

Helm, Sanford M. CATALOG OF CHAMBER MUSIC FOR WIND INSTRUMENTS. 1952. Reprint. New York: Da Capo Press, 1969. 85 p.

Lists of chamber music for three to twelve instruments. Most items are original compositions or editions of originals. Some transcriptions. Bibliography.

Houser, Roy. CATALOGUE OF CHAMBER MUSIC FOR WOODWIND INSTRUMENTS. 1962. Reprint. New York: Da Capo Press, 1973. 159 p.

Hughes, Charles W. CHAMBER MUSIC IN AMERICAN SCHOOLS. Mt. Vernon, N.Y.: Charles Hughes, 1933. 202 p.

Traces the development of musical groups in the early American schools. Includes numerous lists of chamber works. Bibliography.

Kerman, Joseph. THE BEETHOVEN QUARTETS. New York: Alfred A.

Knopf Co., 1967. 386 p. Music, photos.

A critical study of Beethoven's sixteen string quartets. Includes other pertinent musical and nonmusical information. Bibliography.

Norton, M.D. Herter. THE ART OF STRING QUARTET PLAYING: PRACTICE, TECHNIQUE AND INTERPRETATION. New York: Simon and Schuster, 1962. 189 p.

Details the general principles of this type of ensemble performance. One of the few books on the subject.

Page, Athol. PLAYING STRING QUARTETS. Boston: Bruce Humphries, 1964. 131 p.

Useful guide to technique, interpretation, and historical background. Includes performance times of approximately 250 standard works.

Robertson, Alec. CHAMBER MUSIC. Baltimore, Md.: Penguin Books, 1960. 427 p. Music.

A compilation of analytical essays about selected chamber music works which range from duets to octets. Covers the period from the early eighteenth century to the present day.

Rowen, Ruth Halle. EARLY CHAMBER MUSIC. 1949. Reprint. New York: Da Capo Press, 1974. 188 p. Music.

Traces the evolution of instrumental chamber style from its initial period to its definitive classical form. Bibliography.

Rutan, Harold D. "An Annotated Bibliography of Written Material Pertinent to the Performance of Brass and Percussion Chamber Music." Doctoral dissertation, University of Illinois, 1960. 368 p.

Squire, Alan P. "An Annotated Bibliography of Written Material Pertinent to the Performance of Woodwind Chamber Music." Doctoral dissertation, University of Illinois, 1960. 130 p.

Ulrich, Homer. CHAMBER MUSIC. 2d ed. New York: Columbia University Press, 1966. 401 p.

A standard reference in the field of chamber music for a number of years, this second edition is greatly updated. Excellent bibliography.

ASSOCIATIONS

Academy of Wind and Percussion Arts (AWAPA), Box 2454, West Lafayette, Ind. 47906.

Accordian Teachers Guild International (ATG), 3132 South Lebanon Lane, Tempe, Ariz. 85282.

Publication: ATG BULLETIN. 10/year.

All American Association of Contest Judges, 1627 Lay Boulevard, Kalamazoo, Mich. 49001.

Publication: ON PARADE. Bimonthly.

Amateur Chamber Music Players, Inc. (ACMP), Box 547, Vienna, Va. 22180.

Publications: Directory. Annual.

Newsletter. Annual.

American Accordionists' Association (AAA), 165 West Tenth Street, New York, N.Y. 10014.

American Bandmasters Association (ABA), c/o Secretary, Lt. Col. William F. Santelman, 7414 Admiral Drive, Alexandria, Va. 22307.

Publication: JOURNAL OF BAND RESEARCH. Semiannual.

American Guild of English Handbell Ringers (AGEHR), 12001 River View Road, Washington, D.C. 20022.

Publications: OVERTONES. Quarterly.

Roster. Annual.

HANDBELL MUSIC.

American Harp Society (AHS), 6331 Quebec Drive, Hollywood, Calif. 90068.

Publication: AMERICAN HARP JOURNAL. Biennial.

American Old Time Fiddlers Association (AOTFA), 6141 Morrill Avenue, Lincoln, Neb. 68507.

Publication: AMERICAN FIDDLERS NEWS. 4/year.

American Recorder Society (ARS), 141 West 20th Street, New York, N.Y. 10011.

Publications: THE AMERICAN RECORDER. Quarterly.

INTERNATIONAL DIRECTORY OF MEMBERS. Annual.

American School Band Directors Association (ASBDA), 8215 Seward Street, Omaha, Nebraska 68114.

Publications: THE SCHOOL MUSICIAN, DIRECTOR AND TEACHER. Monthly.

Directory and Handbook. Annual.

The American Society for the Advancement of Violin Making, 408 South Lansdowne Avenue, Lansdowne, Pa. 19050.

Publication: NEWS BULLETIN. Quarterly.

American String Teachers Association (ASTA), 2596 Princeton Pike, Lawrenceville, N.J. 08648.

Publications: THE AMERICAN STRING TEACHER. Quarterly.

Numerous other publications for teachers.

American Symphony Orchestra League (ASOL), P.O. Box 66, Vienna, Va. 22180.

Publications: SYMPHONY NEWS. Bimonthly.

Numerous other publications related to orchestra matters, including information, handbooks, surveys.

Catgut Acoustical Society (CAS), c/o Mrs. Carleen Maley Hutchins, 112 Essex Avenue, Montclair, N.J. 07042.

Publication: Newsletter. Semiannual.

College Band Directors National Association (CBDNA), 59 Student Center, University of California, Berkeley, Calif. 94720.

Publication: Proceedings. Annual.

Fretted Instrument Guild of America (FIGA), One East Fordham Road, Bronx, N.Y. 10468.

Publications: FIGA NEWS. Bimonthly.

Directory of players with instruments played. Triennial.

Galpin Society, Rose Cottage, Bois Lane, Chesham Bois, Amersham, Bucks HP6 6BP, England.

Publication: GALPIN SOCIETY JOURNAL. Annual.

Guild of Carillonneurs in North America (GCNA), c/o Richard D. Gegner, 3718 Settle Road, Cincinnati, Ohio 45227.

Publications: RANDSCHRIFTEN (newsletter). Semiannual.

MUSIC BY SERIES OF COMPOSITIONS. Annual.

Bulletin. Annual.

International Clarinet Society (ICS), University of Denver, Denver, Colo. 80210.

International Confederation of Accordionists (ICA), Somerset House, Cranleigh, Surrey, England.

Publications: Newsletter. Bimonthly.

Bulletin. Annual.

International Double Reed Society (IDRS), c/o Dan Stolper, Michigan State University, Music Department, East Lansing, Mich. 48824.

Publication: TO THE WORLD'S OBOISTS. Quarterly.

International Horn Society (IHS), 337 Ridge Avenue, Elmhurst, Ill. 60126.

Publications: HORN CALL. 2/year.

Newsletter. 2 or 3/year.

Membership directory. Annual.

International Society of Bassists, University of Cincinnati College--Conservatory of Music, Cincinnati, Ohio 45221.

Publication: Newsletter. 3/year.

International Trombone Association (ITA), 1812 Truman Drive, Normal, Ill. 61761.

Publication: Journal. Annual.

International Trumpet Guild, 3444 North George Mason Drive, Arlington, Va. 22207.

Musical Box Society, International (MBSI), Box 202, Route 3, Morgantown, Ind. 46160.

Publications: MUSIC BOX SOCIETY BULLETIN. 3/year.

Newsletter. Bimonthly.

Directory. Biennial.

National Association of College Wind and Percussion Instructors (NACWPI), Division of Fine Arts, Northeast Missouri State University, Kirksville, Mo. 63501.

Publications: NACWPI JOURNAL. Quarterly.

MANUSCRIPT MUSIC CATALOG.

Membership directory. Annual.

LITTLE NIGHT MUSIC BOOKLET. Annual

National Association of Rudimental Drummers, Ludwig Drum Company, Chicago, Ill.

National Band Association (NBA), c/o Maxine Lefever, Box 2454, West Lafayette, Ind. 47906.

Publications: Directory. Annual.

THE INSTRUMENTALIST. Monthly.

SELECTIVE MUSIC LISTS FOR BAND.

DIRECTORY OF GUEST CONDUCTORS, ADJUDICATORS, CLINICIANS, AND SOLOISTS.

NEWSLETTER AND JOURNAL OF PROCEEDINGS. Quarterly.

National Catholic Bandmasters Association (NCBA), Quincy College Music Department, Quincy, Ill. 62301.

Publications: NATIONAL SCHOOL MUSICIAN. Monthly.

Newsletter. Monthly.

Membership list.

National Flute Association (NFA), c/o Linda Tauber, 3500 Milam Street, Apartment J205, Shreveport, La. 71109.

National School Orchestra Association (NSOA), c/o Lois Hobbs, 33 Sterling Lane, Smithtown, N.Y. 11787.

Publications: NSOA BULLETIN. 4/year.

THE INSTRUMENTALIST. 11/year.

Percussive Arts Society (PAS), 130 Carol Drive, Terre Haute, Ind. 47805.

Publications: PERCUSSIONIST. Quarterly.

PERCUSSIVE NOTES. 3/year.

The society, in cooperation with the University of Mississippi, also maintains a Percussion Research Collection at the University of Mississippi. For information write: Percussion Research Collection, Southern Station, Box 53, Hattiesburg, Mississippi 39401.

Society for Research and Promotion of Brass and Wind Music, Hochschule fur Musik and Darstellende Kuntz, Institut for Musikethnologie, Leunhardstrasse 15, 8010 Graz, Austria.

Publication: ALTA MUSICA

Society for Strings, 170 West 73d Street, New York, N.Y. 10023.

Society for the Preservation and Advancement of the Harmonica (SPAH), P.O. Box 865, Troy, Mich. 48084.

Publication: HARMONICA HAPPENINGS. Quarterly.

Society of the Classic Guitar (SCG), 409 East 50th Street, New York, N.Y. 10022.

Publications: GUITAR REVIEW. Irregular.

SCG BULLETIN. 3-4/year.

Suzuki Association of the Americas, P.O. Box 164, Mendham, N.J. 07945.

Publication: AMERICAN SUZUKI JOURNAL. Quarterly.

Tubists Universal Brotherhood Association, c/o Don C. Little, School of Music, North Texas State University, Denton, Tex. 76203.

United States Army, Navy and Air Force Bandsmen's Association, P.O. Box 1978, New Haven, Conn. 06521.

Publication: MUSICANA. Bimonthly.

United States of America School Band and Chorus, c/o Mr. Roy Martin, First Chair of America, Box 125, Greenwood, Miss. 38930.

Viola da Gamba Society of America (VdGSA), 3115 Laurel Avenue, Cheverly, Md. 20785.

Publications: CONSORT NEWS. Quarterly.

VdGSA NEWS. 3/year.

Journal (includes directory of gamba players). Annual.

Violoncello Society, 101 West 57th Street, New York, N.Y. 10019.

Women Band Directors National Association (WBDNA), 1736 Winchester Drive, Indianapolis, Ind. 46227.

Women's Association for Symphony Orchestras, 5100 Park Lane, Dallas, Tex. 75220.

Publication: HIGHLIGHTS. Annual.

World Saxophone Congress (WSC), c/o Frederick Hemke, School of Music, Northwestern University, Evanston, Ill. 60201.

Youth Symphony News, United States Youth Symphony Federation, 441 Washington Avenue, Palo Alto, Calif.

See also subsections on associations in part II: Music in Education.

Section 49

MUSICAL INSTRUMENTS—HISTORICAL REFERENCES

Bachmann, Alberto. AN ENCYCLOPEDIA OF THE VIOLIN. 1925. Reprint. New York: Da Capo Press, 1966. 470 p. Music, photos, paper.

Even though this is a 1925 work, it continues to be a standard reference work for performers and teachers of string instruments.

Baines, Anthony. EUROPEAN AND AMERICAN MUSICAL INSTRUMENTS. London: B.T. Batsford, 1966. 174 p. Illus., photos.

Virtually a pictorial museum. Especially useful as a reference tool to identify types and varieties of nonkeyboard instruments of Western society from the Renaissance onward.

_____, ed. MUSICAL INSTRUMENTS THROUGH THE AGES. New York: Walker and Co., 1976. 344 p. Music, illus., photos.

This work, commissioned by the Galpin Society, is a collection of articles written by expert musicologists. The approach of the book is historical, relating the history of each instrument or group of instruments to its music of the last four or five hundred years. There is also brief coverage of primitive and folk instruments. Electronic and mechanical instruments are omitted. Bibliography and glossary of terms.

_____. WOODWIND INSTRUMENTS AND THEIR HISTORY. Rev. ed. New York: W.W. Norton and Co., 1962. 384 p. Illus., music, photos.

Broad coverage of both the technical and historical aspects of these instruments. Bibliography.

Bate, Philip. THE FLUTE. New York: W.W. Norton and Co., 1969. 268 p. Illus.

Bibliography.

_____. THE TRUMPET AND TROMBONE: AN OUTLINE OF THEIR HISTORY,

DEVELOPMENT, AND CONSTRUCTION. New York: W.W. Norton and Co., 1966. 272 p. Illus., photos.

Berner, Alfred, et al., eds. PRESERVATION AND RESTORATION OF MUSICAL INSTRUMENTS: PROVISIONAL RECOMMENDATIONS. New York: Unipub; London: Evelyn, Adams, and Mackay, 1967. 77 p.

Suggestions for cleaning and preserving instruments against environmental hazards.

Bessaraboff, Nicholas. ANCIENT EUROPEAN MUSICAL INSTRUMENTS. Boston: Harvard University Press for the Museum of Fine Arts, 1941. 503 p. Illus., photos.

An elaborate catalog of musical instruments of the past based on the Leslie Lindsey Mason collection of musical instruments at the Museum of Fine Arts, Boston. A valuable research tool.

Boulton, Laura. MUSICAL INSTRUMENTS OF WORLD CULTURES. New York: Intercultural Arts Press, 1972. 89 p. Illus., photos.

Selected examples of instruments as related to various cultures.

Bowers, Q. David. ENCYCLOPEDIA OF AUTOMATIC MUSICAL INSTRUMENTS. Vestal, N.Y.: Vestal Press, 1972. 1,008 p. Illus.

An exhaustive source of information concerning the many types of music boxes, player-pianos, calliopes, coin-operated machines, parlor and field organs, etc. Includes a dictionary of special terms and an extensive index.

Bragard, Roger, and De Hen, Ferdinand J. MUSICAL INSTRUMENTS IN ART AND HISTORY. Translated by Bill Hopkins. New York: Viking Press, 1968. 281 p.

An encyclopedic work on musical instruments. Based primarily on the collection of instruments in the Brussells Instrumental Museum. Beautifully illustrated. Bibliography.

Buchner, Alexander. FOLK MUSIC INSTRUMENTS OF THE WORLD. New York: Crown, 1972. 292 p. Illus.

A study of the most primitive to more recent folk music instruments from around the world.

_____. MUSICAL INSTRUMENTS: AN ILLUSTRATED HISTORY. Rev. ed. New York: Crown, 1973. 292 p. Illus.

The 1956 edition revised to include jazz and electronic instruments.

Buetens, Stanley. METHOD FOR RENAISSANCE LUTE. Menlo Park, Calif.: Instruments Antiqua, 1969. 47 p.

California. University of. At Los Angeles. THE LACHMANN COLLECTION OF HISTORICAL INSTRUMENTS. Music Department, Schoenberg Hall. Los Angeles, Calif.

Carse, Adam. MUSICAL WIND INSTRUMENTS: A HISTORY OF THE WIND INSTRUMENTS USED IN EUROPEAN ORCHESTRAS AND WIND-BANDS FROM THE LATER MIDDLE AGES UP TO THE PRESENT TIME. 1939. Reprint. New York: Da Capo Press, 1965. 381 p. Illus., photos, paper.

Considered a standard reference book on this subject. Carse is a foremost authority. Bibliography.

Clemencie, Rene. OLD MUSICAL INSTRUMENTS. Translated by David Hermges. New York: Putnam; London: Weidenfeld and Nicolson, 1968. 120 p.

Copenhagen Musikhistorik Museum. FROM BONE PIPE AND CATTLE HORN TO FIDDLE AND PSALTERY: FOLK MUSIC INSTRUMENTS FROM DENMARK, FINLAND, ICELAND, NORWAY AND SWEDEN. Edited by Mette Muller. Copenhagen: 1972. 54 p.

Crane, Frederick. EXTANT MEDIEVAL MUSICAL INSTRUMENTS: A PROVISIONAL CATALOGUE BY TYPES. Iowa City: University of Iowa Press, 1972. 120 p. Illus.

A cataloged description of instruments preserved above the ground or uncovered in archaeological excavations. Covers the period from about A.D. 400 to approximately 1500. Signal instruments and noisemakers are included as well as traditionally defined musical instruments. Bibliography.

Crowhurst, Norman H. ELECTRONIC MUSICAL INSTRUMENTS. Blue Ridge Summit, Pa.: Tab Books, 1971. 168 p. Illus., photos.

A technical account of the working principles of these instruments.

Donington, Robert. THE INSTRUMENTS OF MUSIC. 3d ed. London: Methuen; New York: Barnes and Noble, 1970. 262 p.

Fox, Lilla Margaret. INSTRUMENTS OF POPULAR MUSIC: A HISTORY OF MUSICAL INSTRUMENTS. New York: Roy Publishers, 1968. 112 p.

Galpin, Francis W. OLD ENGLISH INSTRUMENTS OF MUSIC: THEIR HISTORY AND CHARACTER. 4th rev. ed. Revised by Thurston Dart. New

York: Harper and Row, 1965. 254 p. Illus.

Numerous illustrations and charts. In this edition spelling and date errors of earlier editions have been corrected in the light of research on instruments since 1945.

Geiringer, Karl. MUSICAL INSTRUMENTS: THEIR HISTORY IN WESTERN CULTURE FROM THE STONE AGE TO THE PRESENT. Translated by Bernard Miall. New York: Oxford University Press, 1945. 278 p. Photos.

Historical treatment of instruments showing the connection with the art and culture of the period. Bibliography.

Grunfeld, Frederic V. THE ART AND TIMES OF THE GUITAR. New York: Macmillan, 1969. 340 p. Illus., photos.

An illustrated history of guitars and guitarists. Bibliography.

Harrison, Frank [L.], and Rimmer, Joan. EUROPEAN MUSICAL INSTRUMENTS. New York: W.W. Norton and Co., 1964. 246 p. Photos.

An illustrated history of the development of European musical instruments from prehistoric times to the electronic instruments. Included is descriptive text on history, technical development, and use.

Headington, Christopher. THE ORCHESTRA AND ITS INSTRUMENTS. Cleveland, Ohio: World, 1967. 95 p.

Henley, William. UNIVERSAL DICTIONARY OF VIOLIN AND BOW MAKERS. 5 vols. Cyril Woodcock, managing ed. Brighton, Sussex: Amati, 1959-60.

Hoover, Cynthia A. MUSIC MACHINES--AMERICAN STYLE: A CATALOG OF THE EXPOSITION. Washington, D.C.: Smithsonian Institution Press, for the National Museum of History and Technology, 1971. 139 p.

Jalovec, Karel. ENCYCLOPEDIA OF VIOLIN MAKERS. 2 vols. London: Hamlyn, 1968. 881 p. Illus., music, photos.

Biographical details and comments on characteristics in the style of every known craftsman are given, together with illustrations of instruments by the most important makers, a bibliography, and a supplement describing the stringed instruments of the world.

Jenkins, Jean, ed. ETHNIC MUSICAL INSTRUMENTS: IDENTIFICATION-CONSERVATION. London: H. Evelyn for the International Council of Museums; New York: Unipub, 1970. 59 p. Illus.

Suggestions for identifying, cataloging, conserving, and restoring ethnic musical instruments.

Krishnaswami, S. MUSICAL INSTRUMENTS OF INDIA. Delhi: Government of India, Publications Division, 1965. 102 p. Photos.

Traces the evolution of the principal musical instruments of India. Many photographs.

Langwill, Lyndesay Graham. AN INDEX OF MUSICAL WIND-INSTRUMENT MAKERS. 3d ed., rev. Edinburgh: Lyndesay Langwill, 1972. 232 p. Illus.

An extensive reference book covering wind instrument makers, what they made, where, and when. Also describes their trademarks.

______. "Collections of Instruments in Europe and America." In GROVE'S DICTIONARY OF MUSIC AND MUSICIANS, edited by Eric Blom, 5th ed., vol. 4, pp. 509-15. London: Macmillan, 1954.

Leipp, Emile. THE VIOLIN: HISTORY, AESTHETICS, MANUFACTURE, AND ACOUSTICS. Toronto: University of Toronto Press, 1969. 126 p. Illus., photos.

An investigation of the instrument with emphasis on construction and acoustics. Bibliography.

Lichtenwanger, William, comp. A SURVEY OF MUSICAL INSTRUMENT COLLECTIONS IN THE UNITED STATES AND CANADA. Ann Arbor, Mich.: Music Library Association, 1974. 137 p.

Covers 572 collections. Includes locations, varieties of instruments contained in the collections, and loan arrangements. Bibliography.

Marcuse, Sibyl. MUSICAL INSTRUMENTS, A COMPREHENSIVE DICTIONARY. Garden City, N.Y.: Doubleday and Co., 1964. 608 p. Illus.

One of the most authoritative and complete reference books on musical instruments was written by Curt Sachs and published by Julius Bard in 1913 as REAL-LEXICON DER MUSIKINSTRUMENTE (see below). The Sachs work was revised, enlarged, and reprinted by Dover Publications in 1964. The present volume by Marcuse provides the English reader with a somewhat comparable source of information plus the advantage of research accomplished since Sachs's original work.

Moller, Max. THE VIOLIN MAKERS OF THE LOW COUNTRIES (BELGIUM AND HOLLAND). Amsterdam: M. Moller, 1955. 165 p.

Paetkau, David H. THE GROWTH OF INSTRUMENTAL MUSIC. New York: Vantage Press, 1962. 393 p.

Deals with the history and development of instruments and orchestration from primitive beginnings to the twentieth century. Bibliography.

Panum, Hortense. THE STRINGED INSTRUMENTS OF THE MIDDLE AGE. Rev. ed. Edited by Jeffrey Pulver. 1939. Reprint. New York: Da Capo Press, 1971. 511 p.

A veritable encyclopedia of stringed instruments of every conceivable origin and description. A detailed history of the medieval stringed instruments from earliest civilizations to more recent times.

Plenckers, Leo J. BRASS INSTRUMENTS: VOLUME I OF THE HAGUE MUNICIPAL MUSEUM CATALOGUE OF MUSICAL INSTRUMENTS. Amsterdam, Netherlands: Frits Knuf, 1969. 85 p. Paper.

This catalog describes the horns, trumpets, trombones, and all the other brass instruments of the museum collection, from the sixteenth-century "natural" instruments to the mechanized instruments from about 1900.

Robinson, Trevor. THE AMATEUR WIND INSTRUMENT MAKER. Boston: University of Massachusetts Press, 1973. 115 p.

Describes general and specialized techniques for making woodwind and brasswind instruments. Includes listings of museum collections of instruments, sources of materials, and general and specialized bibliographies.

Roda, Joseph. BOWS FOR MUSICAL INSTRUMENTS OF THE VIOLIN FAMILY. Chicago: W. Lewis and Sons, 1959. 335 p.

Sachs, Curt. THE HISTORY OF MUSICAL INSTRUMENTS. New York: W.W. Norton and Co., 1940. 505 p.

Covers the primitive and prehistoric epoch, antiquity, the middle ages, and the modern occident. Bibliography.

______. REAL-LEXIKON DER MUSIKINSTRUMENTE. New ed. Hildesheim, Germany: G. Olms Verlagsbuchhandlung; New York: Dover Publications, 1964. 451 p.

Considered by many as the most authoritative and comprehensive reference source on the subject. Originally published in 1913, the new edition contains 600 corrections and additions by Professor Sachs after the first publication, and 500 new entries in a supplement at the end of the volume. The introduction is in English; the main text is in German. (See Marcuse, Sibyl, above.)

Schlesinger, Kathleen. THE INSTRUMENTS OF THE MODERN ORCHESTRA AND EARLY RECORDS OF THE PRECURSORS OF THE VIOLIN FAMILY. London: William Reeves, 1969. 658 p.

Schwarts, Harry Wayne. THE STORY OF MUSICAL INSTRUMENTS FROM

SHEPHERD'S PIPE TO SYMPHONY. 1938. Reprint. Freeport, N.Y.: Books for Libraries Press, 1970. 365 p.

A well-written work for both layman and musician.

Smithers, Don L. THE MUSIC AND HISTORY OF THE BAROQUE TRUMPET BEFORE 1721. Syracuse, N.Y.: Syracuse University Press, 1973. 304 p. Music, photos.

Highly useful to music historians and music educators with a special interest in the repertory of trumpet music of the seventeenth century and the instruments which were used for performance of that music. Contains appendixes that provide much information on the surviving sources of nearly all known music originally composed for the baroque trumpet.

Stainer, Sir John. THE MUSIC OF THE BIBLE WITH SOME ACCOUNT OF THE DEVELOPMENT OF MODERN MUSICAL INSTRUMENTS FROM ANCIENT TYPES. 1914. Reprint. New York: Da Capo Press, 1970. 230 p.

An account of every musical instrument mentioned in the Bible, with discussions on what is known about their construction, origin, and uses.

Terry, Charles Sanford. BACH'S ORCHESTRA. London: Oxford University Press, 1932. 250 p. Illus.

A highly detailed account of the usage and characterization of musical instruments found in the works of Bach. One of the best sources in English on the subject.

Toronto Royal Ontario Museum. MUSICAL INSTRUMENTS IN THE ROYAL ONTARIO MUSEUM. Toronto: Ontario Museum, 1971. 96 p.

Winternitz, Emanuel. MUSICAL INSTRUMENTS AND THEIR SYMBOLISM IN WESTERN ART. New York: W.W. Norton and Co., 1967. 240 p. Photos.

A collection of scholarly essays that deal with interrelationships between musical instruments and visual art.

______. MUSICAL INSTRUMENTS OF THE WESTERN WORLD. New York: McGraw-Hill Book Co., 1967. 259 p. Illus., photos.

Primarily an illustrated reference work.

COLLECTION

METROPOLITAN MUSEUM OF ART, ANDRE MERTENS GALLERIES. New York, New York.

The Metropolitan Museum's Department of Musical Instruments holds nearly 4,000 instruments, about two-thirds of them of non-European origin. The department's nucleus is the Crosby Brown collection which came to the museum beginning in 1889. Other donors of large groups of instruments include Joseph Drexel (1889), Alice Getty (1943), the University of Pennsylvania (1953), and Burl Ives (1963). The collection is particularly famous for Western European materials, among them the oldest extant pianoforte (Bartolommeo Cristofori, 1720); the earliest undoubted Ruckers virginal (1581); a fine spinet made for Eleonora della Rovere (1540); and other important keyboard instruments including over thirty-five with plucked strings (harpsichords, spinets, virginals); oboes by Denner and Richters; violins by Stradivarius and Amati; recorders by Kynsecker, Oberlender, Gahn; and other important Renaissance and later winds and strings, many of them in playing condition. Among the greatest treasures are two medieval instruments, a crecelle, and the so-called Untermyer fiddle, actually a mandora.

About one-fifth of the collection is displayed in the Andre Mertens Galleries (1971). The department staff includes curatorial and restoration personnel, headed by Laurence Libin, associate curator in charge. Gallery concerts, lecture-demonstrations, technical drawings, and scholarly publications are offered on a regular basis. Requisitions are frequent, and a new catalog is in preparation. The collection is generally recognized as preeminent in the Western Hemisphere and is among the foremost collections in the world in quality and scope.

See also Section 1: Guides to Special Libraries and Collections, and appendix A: Supplemental Listing of Holdings in Certain Libraries as Revealed in a Recent Survey.

ASSOCIATIONS

American Musical Instrument Society, Seventeen Lincoln Avenue, Massapequa Park, N.Y. 11762.

Publications: Newsletter. 3/year.

Journal. Annual.

Membership roster. Annual.

AMERICAN MUSICAL INSTRUMENT MAKERS DIRECTORY.

Various scholarly papers relating to all aspects of early instruments.

American Society of Ancient Instruments (ASAI), 7445 Devon Street, Philadelphia, Pa. 19119.

Section 50

KEYBOARD MUSIC, INSTRUMENTS, AND PEDAGOGY

HISTORY, PERFORMANCE, AND PEDAGOGY

Adler, Kurt. THE ART OF ACCOMPANYING AND COACHING. Minneapolis: University of Minnesota Press, 1965. 260 p. Illus.

Broad coverage of procedures. Stresses human psychological factors of relationships as requisites to mastery in this field. Bibliography.

Caldwell, John. ENGLISH KEYBOARD MUSIC BEFORE THE NINETEENTH CENTURY. New York: Praeger, 1973. 328 p.

A comprehensive survey covering the sociological, technical, and musical development of keyboard works. Bibliography.

Christiani, Adolph F. THE PRINCIPLES OF EXPRESSION IN PIANOFORTE PLAYING. 1885. Reprint. New York: Da Capo Press, 1974. 303 p. Music.

A discussion of the mechanical means of expression, illustrated with selected music examples. A practical guide to interpretation of piano literature.

Clementi, Muzio. INTRODUCTION TO THE ART OF PLAYING ON THE PIANOFORTE. 1801. Reprint. New York: Da Capo Press, 1974. 63 p.

A reprint of one of the earliest keyboard methods written specifically for the pianoforte, with a new introduction by Sandra Rosenblum. Discussion of Clementi's use of ornamentation and other teaching devices.

Closon, Ernest. HISTORY OF THE PIANO. Edited and revised by Robin Golding. New York: St. Martin's Press, 1974. 154 p. Music, photos, illus.

Since it appeared first in French in 1944 this work has been translated, enlarged, and revised. It covers keyboard instruments from the clavichord, harpsichord, spinet, virginal, and piano. Describes the relationship between the instrument and the music written for it.

Edwards, Ruth. THE COMPLEAT MUSIC TEACHER. Los Altos, Calif.: Geron-X, 1970. 150 p.

Designed to help the beginning teacher. Includes suggestions in piano pedagogy for the young student as well as the adult beginner.

James, Philip. EARLY KEYBOARD INSTRUMENTS: FROM THEIR BEGINNING TO THE YEAR 1820. 1930. Reprint. New York: Harper and Row, 1970. 153 p. Illus.

The history of keyboard instruments to 1820, and a list of English makers of these instruments up to that time (excluding the organ). Bibliography and index.

Konowitz, Bert. MUSIC IMPROVISATION AS A CLASSROOM METHOD. New York: Alfred Publications, 1973. 92 p.

Step-by-step procedures for initiating improvisational skills in the classroom. Bibliography.

Last, Joan. INTERPRETATION FOR THE PIANO STUDENT. London and New York: Oxford University Press, 1960. 141 p. Music.

An analysis of the factors of fine piano performance. Primarily designed for teachers or students who have reached a moderate level of competence.

Lhévinne, Josef. BASIC PRINCIPLES IN PIANOFORTE PLAYING. 1924. Reprint. New York: Dover Publications, 1972. 48 p. Photos, music, paper.

A series of personal conferences with Lhévinne on the various aspects of piano artistry.

Matthay, Tobias. THE ACT OF TOUCH IN ALL ITS DIVERSITY: AN ANALYSIS AND SYNTHESIS OF PIANOFORTE TONE PRODUCTION. New York: Longmans, Green, 1924. 328 p. Illus.

A work of historical importance for teachers of the piano with an interest in early efforts to analyze how successful performers obtain certain musical effects.

_____. MUSICAL INTERPRETATION: ITS LAWS AND PRINCIPLES AND THEIR APPLICATION IN TEACHING AND PERFORMING. 1913. Reprint. Westport, Conn.: Greenwood Press, 1970. 163 p.

The principles of interpretation which are developed in this work have for many years received considerable attention by musicians in all branches of musical performance.

_____. THE VISIBLE AND INVISIBLE IN PIANOFORTE TECHNIQUE. London: Oxford University Press, 1947. 235 p. Music, photos.

A discussion of the physiological aspects of touch and technique as related to expressive musical performance.

Moldenhauer, Hans. DUO PIANISM. Chicago: Chicago Musical College Press, 1950. 400 p.

A discussion of the historical, sociological, and educational aspects of duo-pianism. Covers pedagogy and repertoire. Bibliography.

Newman, William S. THE PIANIST'S PROBLEMS: A MODERN APPROACH TO EFFICIENT PRACTICE AND MUSICIANLY PERFORMANCE. 3d ed. New York: Harper and Row, 1974. 208 p. Music, illus.

Treats various aspects of piano performance, including philosophy, musicianship, and technique.

Ortman, Otto. THE PHYSIOLOGICAL MECHANICS OF PIANO TECHNIQUE. New York: E.P. Dutton, 1962. 395 p. Illus.

One of the earliest major efforts to apply physiological principles to piano playing. As such, this is considered by many to be a classic reference work. Bibliography.

Pace, Robert. PIANO FOR CLASSROOM MUSIC. 2d ed. Englewood Cliffs, N.J.: Prentice-Hall, 1971. 123 p.

Combines the fundamentals of music, basic reading skills, repertoire, and piano techniques.

Robinson, Helene, and Jarvis, Richard L., eds. TEACHING PIANO IN CLASSROOM AND STUDIO. Washington, D.C.: Music Educators National Conference, 1967. 183 p.

Philosophy and practice of group instruction, with suggestions for course content and examples of teaching procedures. Lists recommended materials, equipment, and references.

Schonberg, Harold C. THE GREAT PIANISTS FROM MOZART TO THE PRESENT. New York: Simon and Schuster, 1966. 448 p. Illus.

This work traces the development of piano performance from the eighteenth to the twentieth century.

Slenczynska, Ruth. MUSIC AT YOUR FINGERTIPS: ADVICE FOR THE ARTIST AND AMATEUR ON PLAYING THE PIANO. 1968. Reprint. New York: Da Capo Press, 1974. 160 p.

A guide to piano performance, covering all aspects of pianistic technique. Includes repertoire lists for various levels of ability.

Sumner, William Leslie. THE PIANOFORTE. London: Macdonald, 1966. 221 p. Illus., photos.

A historical account of the mechanical and artistic development of the piano. Problems of technique are discussed and biographical information is given for representative composers and performers. Bibliography.

Wolff, Konrad. THE TEACHING OF ARTUR SCHNABEL: A GUIDE TO INTERPRETATION. New York: Praeger, 1972. 189 p. Illus.

Focus is on the works of Mozart, Beethoven, Schubert, Schumann, and Brahms. Useful for teachers and advanced students. Bibliography.

PIANO LITERATURE

Apel, Willi. THE HISTORY OF KEYBOARD MUSIC TO 1700. Translated by Hans Tichler. Bloomington: Indiana University Press, 1972. 800 p.

A meticulous chronological survey of music for the keyboard from the earliest manuscripts, dating from the fourteenth century to the end of the seventeenth century. Extensive bibliography.

Friskin, James, and Freundlich, Irwin. MUSIC FOR THE PIANO, A HANDBOOK OF CONCERT AND TEACHING MATERIAL FROM 1580 TO 1952. New York: Dover Publications, 1973. 448 p.

Hinson, Maurice. GUIDE TO THE PIANIST'S REPERTOIRE. Edited by Irving Freundlich. Bloomington: Indiana University Press, 1973. 880 p.

Extensive graded listings of solo works of more than 1,000 composers. Descriptions include available editions, difficulty, and character. Extensive bibliography.

Hutcheson, Ernest. THE LITERATURE OF THE PIANO: A GUIDE FOR AMATEUR AND STUDENT. 3d ed. Edited by Rudolph Ganz. New York: Alfred A. Knopf Co., 1964. 436 p. Music.

A guide to solo and ensemble music with suggestions for selection, interpretation, and performance. Historical background is included. Also, a list of works with annotations regarding editions. Bibliography.

Kirby, F.E. A SHORT HISTORY OF KEYBOARD MUSIC. New York: Free Press, 1966. 534 p. Music, illus.

This book attempts to provide an overview of the whole repertory of keyboard music from the historical standpoint. Highly useful two-part bibliography. Part 1 contains modern critical editions and facsimile reproductions of music and treatises important in the history of keyboard music. Part 2 presents the secondary literature.

Lubin, Ernest. THE PIANO DUET: A GUIDE FOR PIANISTS. New York: Grossman Publishers, 1970. 221 p. Photos, music.

Primarily a survey of the music composed expressly for the medium of the piano duet by master composers from Mozart to Debussy. The main body of the book is devoted to compositions of genuine musical interest and presently in print. An appendix discusses other works of historical interest but not necessarily available today.

Mathews, Denis, ed. KEYBOARD MUSIC. New York: Praeger, 1972. 386 p.

A collection of seven articles written by specialists in various areas of keyboard history and performance.

Rezits, Joseph, and Deatsman, Gerald. THE PIANIST'S RESOURCE GUIDE: PIANO MUSIC IN PRINT AND LITERATURE ON THE PIANISTIC ART. Park Ridge, Ill.: Pallma Music Corp., 1974. 993 p.

An extensive guide providing indexes on piano music in print; indexes on material about pianists, pianos, learning, teaching, technique, and ensemble playing; critical evaluations and a topical index. An updated edition is planned for 1976.

Rowley, Alec. FOUR HANDS, ONE PIANO: A LIST OF WORKS FOR DUET PLAYERS. London: Oxford University Press, 1940. 38 p.

A listing of music originally designed for duet performance and divided into the categories of the classics, the French school, English composers, educational etudes, and graded pieces, together with a list of publishers and alphabetical listing of composers.

Westerby, Herbert. THE HISTORY OF PIANOFORTE MUSIC. 1924. Reprint. New York: Da Capo Press, 1971. 407 p. Music, illus.

Covers the history of keyboard music from the sixteenth-century virginal music to 1924. Special emphasis on romantic and national styles of piano music. Includes lists of major editions, publishers, and journals. Bibliography.

PIANO TUNING AND SERVICING

Howe, Alfred H. SCIENTIFIC PIANO TUNING AND SERVICING. 3d ed. New York: Alfred H. Howe, 1955. 264 p. Illus., music.

A clearly defined work introducing the art of piano tuning. Bibliography.

Stevens, Floyd A. COMPLETE COURSE IN ELECTRONIC PIANO TUNING. Chicago: Nelson-Hall, 1974. 257 p. Illus.

Deals with basic techniques of tuning pianos by electronic means.

White, William Braid. PIANO TUNING AND ALLIED ARTS. 5th ed. Boston: Tuners Supply Co., 1953. 295 p. Illus., music.

A thorough treatment of the techniques of piano tuning. A work of long-standing acceptance. Bibliography.

HARPSICHORD AND CLAVICHORD

Bedford, Frances, and Conant, Robert. TWENTIETH-CENTURY HARPSICHORD MUSIC: A CLASSIFIED CATALOG. Hackensack, N.J.: Joseph Boonin, 1974. 95 p.

Boalch, Donald H. MAKERS OF THE HARPSICHORD AND CLAVICHORD, 1440 TO 1840. London: G. Ronald, 1956. 169 p.

Gillespie, John. FIVE CENTURIES OF KEYBOARD MUSIC: AN HISTORIC SURVEY OF MUSIC FOR HARPSICHORD AND PIANO. 1965. Reprint. New York: Dover Publications, 1972. 463 p.

Excellent resource and reference material concerning the development of keyboard music. Bibliography at the end of each section. Additional general bibliography closes the book.

Hubbard, Frank. THREE CENTURIES OF HARPSICHORD MAKING. Cambridge, Mass.: Harvard University Press, 1974. 369 p. Photos, illus.

Thorough treatment of the tradition of harpsichord making. Excellent bibliography on the subject plus a glossary.

Nurmi, Ruth. A PLAIN AND EASY INTRODUCTION TO THE HARPSICHORD. Albuquerque: University of New Mexico Press, 1974. 248 p. Music, illus.

A practical guide to understanding the instrument from the standpoint of its physical characteristics, tuning, and maintenance. Discusses various problems of performance.

Russell, Raymond. THE HARPSICHORD AND CLAVICHORD: AN INTRODUCTORY STUDY. 2d ed. New York: W.W. Norton and Co., 1973. 208 p. Photos.

An historical survey. Excellent bibliography.

Schott, Howard. PLAYING THE HARPSICHORD. New York: St. Martin's Press, 1971. 223 p.

An introductory text presenting the fundamentals of harpsichord playing. Includes a survey of the history, technique, and repertoire of the instrument. Bibliography.

ORGAN

Arnold, Corliss Richard. ORGAN LITERATURE: A COMPREHENSIVE SURVEY. Metuchen, N.J.: Scarecrow Press, 1973. 656 p.

A guide to the vast literature for the organ and its development. Extensive bibliographic material.

Edson, Jean Slater. ORGAN PRELUDES: AN INDEX TO COMPOSITIONS ON HYMN TUNES, CHORALES, PLAINSONG MELODIES, GREGORIAN TUNES, AND CAROLS. 2 vols. Metuchen, N.J.: Scarecrow Press, 1970.

Indexes and cross-indexes by composer, theme, and title of more than 3,000 hymn tunes, chorales, and so forth.

Geer, E. Harold. ORGAN REGISTRATION: IN THEORY AND PRACTICE. Glen Rock, N.J.: J. Fischer and Bros., 1957. 409 p. Illus., music.

Intensive treatment of organ registration. Bibliography.

Irwin, Stevens. DICTIONARY OF PIPE ORGAN STOPS. New York: G. Schirmer, 1962. 264 p.

Nardone, Thomas R., ed. ORGAN MUSIC IN PRINT. Philadelphia: Musicdata, 1975. 262 p.

Contains the complete organ music catalogs of more than 300 international music publishers. Entries are normally listed under title and composer, and may include the arranger, instrumentation, seasonal use, publisher, order number, and price in U.S. currency.

Ochse, Orpha. THE HISTORY OF THE ORGAN IN THE UNITED STATES. Bloomington: Indiana University Press, 1975. 512 p.

A well-documented account of the use and development of the organ in this country. Bibliography.

Sumner, William Leslie. THE ORGAN: ITS EVOLUTION, PRINCIPLES OF CONSTRUCTION AND USE. 3d ed. New York: Philosophical Library, 1962. 544 p.

The development of the organ from ancient times to the present. Comprehensive. Bibliography.

ASSOCIATIONS

American College of Musicians (ACM), 808 Rio Grande, Austin, Tex. 78701.

Publications: PIANO GUILD NOTES. Bimonthly.

SYLLABUS. Annual.

American Guild of Organists (AGO), 630 Fifth Avenue, New York, N.Y. 10020.

Publication: MUSIC/AGO--RCCO. Monthly.

American Lithuanian Roman Catholic Organist Alliance, c/o V. Mamaitis, 209 Clark Place, Elizabeth, N.J. 07206.

Publication: MUZIKOS ZINIOS [Music news]. Quarterly.

American Theatre Organ Society (ATOS), P.O. Box 1002, Middleburg, Va. 22117.

Publications: THEATRE ORGAN. Bimonthy.

Membership directory. Irregular.

International Pianists' Guild, c/o National Guild of Piano Teachers, 808 Rio Grande, Box 1807, Austin, Tex. 78767.

International Piano Guild, Box 1807, Austin, Tex. 78767.

Leschetizky Association (LA), 105 West 72d Street, New York, N.Y. 10023.

Publication: Newsletter. Quarterly.

National Association of Organ Teachers (NAOT), 7938 Bertram Avenue, Hammond, Ind. 46324.

Publications: THE ORGANIST MAGAZINE. Monthly.

THE TEACHER. Bimonthly.

ORGAN TEACHER ROSTER. Irregular.

National Guild of Piano Teachers (NGPT), 808 Rio Grande, Box 1807, Austin, Tex. 78767.

Publications: PIANO GUILD NOTES. Bimonthly.

Syllabus. Annual.

National Piano Foundation (NPF), c/o George M. Otto Associates, Inc., 435 North Michigan Avenue, Chicago, Ill. 60611.

National Society of Student Organists (NSSO), 7938 Bertram Avenue, Hammond, Ind. 46324.

Organ and Piano Teachers Association (OPTA), 436 Via Media, Palos Verdes Estates, Calif. 90274.

Publications: OPTA NEWSLETTER. Bimonthly.

MODERN KEYBOARD REVIEW. Bimonthly.

OPTA Membership directory. Annual.

Organ Historical Society (OHS), P.O. Box 209, Wilmington, Ohio 45177.

Publication: THE TRACKER. Quarterly.

Piano Technicians Guild, P.O. Box 1813, Seattle, Wash. 98111.

A nonprofit organization of professional piano technicians. Concerned with standards.

Publications: PIANO TECHNICIANS JOURNAL. 12/year.

Members bulletin. Monthly.

OFFICIAL DIRECTORY. Annual.

Section 51

MUSIC STRUCTURE, THEORY, AND COMPOSITION

NOTATION AND MANUSCRIPT WRITING

Boehm, Laszlo. MODERN MUSIC NOTATION. New York: G. Schirmer, 1961. 69 p. Music, illus., paper.

A handbook dealing with the practical problems of music notation as well as special symbols associated with particular instruments.

Cole, Hugo. SOUNDS AND SIGNS: ASPECTS OF MUSICAL NOTATION. New York: Oxford University Press, 1974. 162 p. Music, illus., paper.

An examination of the uses of musical notation in the Western world. Focus is on actual performance use, rather than on the ways notation should be interpreted. Twentieth-century music activities are included.

Donato, Anthony. PREPARING MUSIC MANUSCRIPT. Englewood Cliffs, N.J.: Prentice-Hall, 1963. 88 p. Music.

One of the very few existing guides to the writing of notation and layout procedures for the musical score.

Karkoschka, Erhard. NOTATION IN NEW MUSIC. Translated by Ruth Koenig. New York: Praeger, 1972. 183 p.

A compendium of information on methods of notation used to express the vocabulary (and various complex signs) found in the works of certain contemporary compositions.

Read, Gardner. MUSIC NOTATION: A MANUAL OF MODERN PRACTICE. 2d ed. Boston: Allyn and Bacon, 1969. 482 p. Music, illus.

One of the most complete text and reference sources available on the subject. Treats both the evolution of music notation as well as modern innovations. Bibliography.

Roemer, Clinton. THE ART OF MUSIC COPYING: THE PREPARATION OF MUSIC FOR PERFORMANCE. Sherman Oaks, Calif.: Roerick Music Co., 1973. 183 p. Illus., paper.

Provides much practical information concerning this important craft. One of the few references of this type.

Rosenthal, Carl A. PRACTICAL GUIDE TO MUSIC NOTATION FOR COMPOSERS, ARRANGERS AND EDITORS. New York: MCA Music Co., 1967. 86 p. Paper.

Deals with most problems encountered by those working with music copy.

HARMONY AND THEORY

Balkin, Alfred, and Taylor, Jack A. INVOLVEMENT WITH MUSIC: ESSENTIAL SKILLS AND CONCEPTS. Boston: Houghton Mifflin Co., 1975. 343 p. Music, paper.

Written as a programmed text suitable for teaching the fundamentals of music to nonmusic majors.

Barnes, Robert A. FUNDAMENTALS OF MUSIC: A PROGRAM FOR SELF-INSTRUCTION. New York: McGraw-Hill Book Co., 1964. 172 p.

A self-instruction program covering the elementary aspects of music, including rhythm; the keyboard; major and minor keys; intervals; and syllables. Intended to be accomplished in five hours.

Boatwright, Howard. INTRODUCTION TO THE THEORY OF MUSIC. New York: W.W. Norton and Co., 1956. 289 p. Illus., music.

A general introduction to the technical aspects of music. Intended to provide a sound foundation for more advanced subjects on theory.

Carlson, James C. MELODIC PERCEPTION: A PROGRAM FOR SELF-INSTRUCTION. New York: McGraw-Hill Book Co., 1965. 232 p.

A self-instruction program designed to develop ability to listen perceptively to melodic musical materials.

Chasteck, Winifred Knox. KEYBOARD SKILLS. Belmont, Calif.: Wadsworth Publishing Co., 1967. 215 p. Music, paper.

A functional approach to the development of keyboard skills through the study of particular chords in a wide range of accompaniment patterns. Glossary.

Christ, William, et al. MATERIALS AND STRUCTURE OF MUSIC. 2 vols. Englewood Cliffs, N.J.: Prentice-Hall, 1966, 1967. 485 p., 531 p.

Volume 1 presents basic music theory. Volume 2 develops the organization of materials presented in volume 1.

Cooper, Paul. PERSPECTIVES IN MUSIC THEORY: AN HISTORICAL-ANALYTICAL APPROACH. New York: Dodd, Mead and Co., 1973. 296 p. Music.

An integrated approach to music theory, presenting the theoretical concepts within the context of creating, performing, and analyzing. Traces similarities and differences of theoretical practices from the beginning of music writing, and guides the student in forming his own conceptions.

Dallin, Leon. FOUNDATIONS IN MUSIC THEORY. 2d ed. Belmont, Calif.: Wadsworth Publishing Co., 1967. 165 p. Music, illus., paper.

A combination text-workbook with programmed exercises. Presents the fundamentals of elementary music theory.

Fish, Arnold, and Lloyd, Norman. FUNDAMENTALS OF SIGHT SINGING AND EAR TRAINING. New York: Dodd, Mead and Co., 1964. 232 p.

A comprehensive program complete with exercises and examples for the development of skills in sight singing and ear training.

Forte, Allen. TONAL HARMONY IN CONCEPT AND PRACTICE. New York: Holt, Rinehart and Winston, 1962. 503 p. Illus., music.

Designed as a textbook for college harmony classes. Presents harmonic devices as related to melodic and rhythmic contexts. Stresses analysis and writing.

George, Graham. TONALITY OF MUSICAL STRUCTURE. New York: Praeger, 1970. 231 p. Illus., music.

Throughout the book the author makes the effort to avoid restating what has been written on the subject before, instead discussing mainly those musical structures in which tonality is of utmost importance and stressing the tonal aspect. Bibliography.

Goldman, Richard Franko. HARMONY IN WESTERN MUSIC. New York: W.W. Norton and Co., 1965. 242 p.

A study of the principles of tonal harmony from Bach through Wagner and Brahms. Presents the basic elements of harmony in the musical contexts that give them meaning. Part 2 of the text deals with the larger forms of harmonic organization, and with modulation and chromaticism.

Hanson, Howard. HARMONIC MATERIALS OF MUSIC. New York: Appleton-Century-Crofts, 1960. 381 p.

A guide to theoretical study that is not traditional. Stresses intervallic analyses and offers a fresh approach for figuring harmonic sounds.

Harder, Paul O. BASIC MATERIALS IN MUSIC THEORY: A PROGRAMMED COURSE. 2d ed. Boston: Allyn and Bacon, 1970. 255 p.

A step-by-step program for teaching the fundamentals of music.

_____. HARMONIC MATERIALS IN TONAL MUSIC: A PROGRAMMED COURSE. 2d ed. Boston: Allyn and Bacon, 1974. Part I, 341 p.; part II, 335 p. Paper.

A programmed text covering the techniques of musical composition from 1600 to 1900. Designed to permit great flexibility in use.

Herder, Ronald. TONAL/ATONAL. New York: Continuo Press, 1973. 209 p.

Describes what the author believes is a new learning procedure for acquiring a more complete understanding of tonality, chromaticism, and atonality.

Horacek, Leo, and Lifkoff, Gerald. PROGRAMED EAR TRAINING. 4 vols. New York: Harcourt Brace Jovanovich, 1970. Paper.

A series of four workbooks, each with an accompanying tape program, designed to provide the aural training necessary for the student's first two years of music theory. Instructor's manual available.

Knuth, Alice Snyder, and Knuth, William E. BASIC RESOURCES FOR LEARNING MUSIC. 2d ed. Belmont, Calif.: Wadsworth Publishing Co., 1973. 339 p.

An introduction to the fundamentals of music, with an emphasis on contemporary music. Provides in-depth instruction on the recorder, piano, ukelele, guitar, autoharp, and percussion instruments.

Landecker, Mildred N. CREATIVE MUSIC THEORY. Boston: Allyn and Bacon, 1972. 282 p.

Intended for use at the secondary school level. Includes material for keyboard experience, thematic and harmonic analysis, singing, and sight reading.

Lehmer, Isabel. KEYBOARD HARMONY. Vol. 1. Belmont, Calif.: Wadsworth Publishing Co., 1967. 232 p. Music, paper.

A compilation of materials for the development of an understanding of harmonic materials by means of the keyboard. Materials proceed in difficulty as the harmonic content increases in complexity.

Lewinsky, Edward E. TONALITY AND ATONALITY IN SIXTEENTH-CENTURY MUSIC. Los Angeles and Berkeley: University of California Press, 1961. 99 p. Music.

Traces similarities of sixteenth- and twentieth-century music. Bibliography.

Lieberman, Maurice. KEYBOARD HARMONY AND IMPROVISATION. 2 vols. New York: W.W. Norton and Co., 1957. 381 p. Music, paper.

Designed to provide the student with basic harmonic skills with practical applications. Resources developed in harmonic and melodic structure are integrated with exercises in improvisation throughout the text.

Martin, Gary M. BASIC CONCEPTS IN MUSIC. Belmont, Calif.: Wadsworth Publishing Co., 1966. 320 p. Paper.

An approach to programmed learning in music fundamentals designed to accommodate both fast and slow learners, beginning or more advanced students.

Mitchell, William J. ELEMENTARY HARMONY. 3d ed. Englewood Cliffs, N.J.: Prentice-Hall, 1965. 327 p.

Presents the essentials of elementary harmony in a well-organized fashion. A college text.

Murphy, Howard Ansley, and Stringham, Edwin John. CREATIVE HARMONY AND MUSICIANSHIP. Englewood Cliffs, N.J.: Prentice-Hall, 1951. 618 p. Music, illus.

The text is based on a sound philosophy for the teaching of learning theory and provides interrelated materials for a first-year college harmony, keyboard, ear training, and music reading course. Though written some years ago, this work continues to serve its purpose well.

Music Educators National Conference. Contemporary Music Project. COMPREHENSIVE MUSICIANSHIP: THE FOUNDATION OF COLLEGE EDUCATION IN MUSIC--A REPORT. Washington, D.C.: 1965. 88 p. Paper.

A report of a seminar sponsored by the Contemporary Music Project of the MENC in 1965. The forty music educators--including composers, theorists, musicologists, and performers--examined the state of musical training in American universities and colleges.

Olson, Robert G. MUSIC DICTATION: A STEREO-TAPED SERIES. Belmont, Calif.: Wadsworth Publishing Co., 1970. 100 p.

An organized system for learning to recognize the basic elements of music, allowing the students to progress at their own speed, and offering an opportunity to drill repeatedly on troublesome areas. The twenty-four stereo tapes and student manual offer diversified dictation examples for ear training practice and review during the first two years of a college music theory sequence.

Ottman, Robert W. ADVANCED HARMONY: THEORY AND PRACTICE. Englewood Cliffs, N.J.: Prentice-Hall, 1961. 267 p.

A companion volume to the author's ELEMENTARY HARMONY: THEORY AND PRACTICE (see below).

_____. ELEMENTARY HARMONY: THEORY AND PRACTICE. Englewood Cliffs, N.J.: Prentice-Hall, 1961. 286 p.

In addition to the theoretical presentation, a practical application is presented in each chapter. The latter includes written materials; ear training and reading; correlation with the author's MUSIC FOR SIGHT SINGING (Englewood Cliffs, N.J.: Prentice-Hall, 1956); and keyboard harmony.

Piston, Walter. HARMONY. 3d ed. New York: W.W. Norton and Co., 1962. 374 p. Music.

A sequential presentation of harmonic devices as seen in music of the various periods. Includes twentieth-century idioms.

Rameau, Jean-Phillipe. TREATISE ON HARMONY. Translated by Philip Gossett. New York: Dover Publications, 1970. 444 p.

A translation of the 1722 edition. Probably the first detailed explanation of the principles of diatonic harmonic theory which were to dominate music for almost two centuries. An important source book for music theorists.

Ratner, Leonard G. HARMONY: STRUCTURE AND STYLE. New York: McGraw-Hill Book Co., 1962. 336 p.

A nontechnical approach to harmony. The principles of the cadential formula, the sense of keys, statement and counter-statement, the two-voice structure, phrase and period structure, and the melodic role of ornamentation are primary features.

Riemann, Hugo. HISTORY OF MUSIC THEORY. 2 vols. Translated with commentary by Raymond Haggh. Lincoln: University of Nebraska Press, 1926. Reprint. New York: Da Capo Press, 1974. 431 p.

This monumental work which has been unavailable for some time (except in major library collections) is still one of the few basic references in the history of music theory. It was originally published in German in 1920. Includes an excellent bibliography.

Salzer, Felix. STRUCTURAL HEARING: TONAL COHERENCE IN MUSIC. 2 vols. 1952. Reprint. New York: Dover Publications, 1962. 667 p.

Extends the Schenker method to include modern, medieval, and Renaissance music.

Schenker, Heinrich. HARMONY. Edited and annotated by Oswald Jonas. Translated by Elisabeth M. Borgese. 1954. Reprint. Cambridge, Mass.: M.I.T. Press, 1973. 359 p.

Schillinger, Joseph. THE SCHILLINGER SYSTEM OF MUSIC COMPOSITION. 2 vols. Translated by Lyle Downing and Arnold Shaw. New York: Carl Fischer, 1946. 1,640 p.

An approach to the composition of music based on principles which are deeply rooted in modern physics, psychology, and mathematics.

Schoenberg, Arnold. STRUCTURAL FOUNDATIONS OF HARMONY. Rev. ed. Edited by Leonard Stein. New York: W.W. Norton and Co., 1969. 203 p.

Schoenberg's last completed theoretical work, representing his final thoughts on the subject of classical and romantic harmony.

Sessions, Roger. HARMONIC PRACTICE. New York: Harcourt, Brace & World, 1951. 441 p.

A sequential representation of the rudiments of music theory from primary triads to twentieth-century dissonances.

Shir-Cliff, Justine, et al. CHROMATIC HARMONY. New York: Free Press, 1965. 200 p.

A concise text dealing with chromaticism in terms of practices and procedures.

Siegmeister, Elie. HARMONY AND MELODY. 2 vols. Belmont, Calif.: Wadsworth Publishing Co., 1965.

A basic harmony text based on actual music drawn from a wide historical spectrum. Volume I: THE DIATONIC STYLE. 479 p. Volume II: MODULATION; CHROMATIC AND MODERN STYLES. 440 p. Student workbooks for each volume are available.

Terry, Charles Sanford. THE FOUR-PART CHORALES OF J.S. BACH. 1929. Reprint. New York: Oxford University Press, 1964. 537 p. Music.

Provides valuable information concerning sources, dates, and authorship. Includes metrical indexing of tunes, and chronological tables of melodies.

Williams, David Russell. A BIBLIOGRAPHY OF THE HISTORY OF MUSIC THEORY. 2d ed. Fairport, N.Y.: Rochester Music Publishers, 1971. 58 p.

Helpful, quick reference material. While not exhaustive, the bibliography is especially useful at the graduate level.

Winick, Steven. RHYTHM: AN ANNOTATED BIBLIOGRAPHY. Metuchen, N.J.: Scarecrow Press, 1974. 157 p.

A wide range of references organized into three parts. The first part deals with definition and explanations. The second part gives attention to perception and effects of training, and the third part is devoted to rhythmic instruction and materials.

Xenakis, Iannis. FORMALIZED MUSIC: THOUGHT AND MATHEMATICS IN COMPOSITION. Bloomington: Indiana University Press, 1971. 273 p. Illus., tables.

Presents the method of music composition using mathematics, computers, and various technological aids.

COUNTERPOINT

Atkisson, Harold F. BASIC COUNTERPOINT. New York: McGraw-Hill Book Co., 1956. 174 p.

Surveys counterpoint practice of the sixteenth, seventeenth, and eighteenth centuries.

Fux, Johann Joseph. THE STUDY OF COUNTERPOINT. Translated and edited by Alfred Mann. 1725. Reprint. New York: W.W. Norton and Co., 1943. 156 p.

The great eighteenth-century Austrian work which has been a major influence on the study of counterpoint for more than 200 years. Bibliography.

Kauder, Hugo. COUNTERPOINT: AN INTRODUCTION TO POLYPHONIC COMPOSITION. New York: Macmillan, 1960. 145 p. Music.

Presents the theoretical bases of counterpoint. Stresses individual development rather than imitation of examples.

Kennan, Kent. COUNTERPOINT. 2d ed. Englewood Cliffs, N.J.: Prentice-Hall, 1972. 289 p.

Content is based on eighteenth-century practice. Also available is a companion workbook. Bibliography.

Merritt, Arthur Tillman. SIXTEENTH-CENTURY POLYPHONY: A BASIS FOR THE STUDY OF COUNTERPOINT. 1939. Reprint. Cambridge, Mass.: Harvard University Press, 1967. 215 p. Music.

A systematic presentation of counterpoint from Gregorian chant to four-part counterpoint. Based mainly on the technique of vocal sacred music of the sixteenth century. Bibliography.

Piston, Walter. COUNTERPOINT. New York: W.W. Norton and Co., 1947. 235 p. Music.

A counterpoint textbook that has enjoyed long-term popularity.

Rubbra, Edmund. COUNTERPOINT: A SURVEY. London: Hutchinson University Library, 1960. 123 p. Music.

A study of the various types of counterpoint found in music from the early Middle Ages to the twentieth century. Includes a section on the teaching of counterpoint. Not intended as a text.

Rubio, P. Samuel. CLASSICAL POLYPHONY. Translated by Thomas Rive. Toronto: University of Toronto Press, 1972. 178 p. Music.

Procedures for analyzing and interpreting classical polyphony. Explains the notation and form. Bibliography.

Salzer, Felix, and Schachter, Carl. COUNTERPOINT IN COMPOSITION: THE STUDY OF VOICE LEADING. New York: McGraw-Hill Book Co., 1969. 576 p.

Presents counterpoint not only as a self-contained discipline, but also in its relation to other aspects of musical design.

Searle, Humphrey. TWENTIETH-CENTURY COUNTERPOINT: A GUIDE FOR STUDENTS. London: Ernest Benn, 1954. 158 p.

A detailed analysis of twentieth-century polyphonic devices of five leading contemporary composers. Some discussion of other modern composers' uses of counterpoint. Bibliography and discography.

FORM, STYLE, AND ANALYSIS

Berry, Wallace. FORM IN MUSIC: AN EXAMPLE OF TRADITIONAL

TECHNIQUES OF MUSICAL STRUCTURE AND THEIR APPLICATION IN HISTORICAL AND CONTEMPORARY STYLES. Englewood Cliffs, N.J.: Prentice-Hall, 1966. 472 p.

A text for advanced study of theory.

Cooper, Grosvenor, and Meyer, Leonard B. THE RHYTHMIC STRUCTURE OF MUSIC. Chicago: University of Chicago Press, 1960. 212 p. Music, illus.

A theoretical framework based essentially on a Gestalt approach, viewing rhythmic experience in terms of pattern perception or groupings and using the terms of prosody to identify them.

Crocker, Richard L. A HISTORY OF MUSICAL STYLE. New York: McGraw-Hill Book Co., 1966. 573 p.

An extensive and in-depth treatment of the subject.

Davie, Cedric Thorpe. MUSICAL STRUCTURE AND DESIGN. 1953. Reprint. New York: Dover Publications, 1966. 181 p.

A description of the various structural designs of musical styles with illustrations from music of the masters. Bibliographical references.

Fink, Michael. MUSIC ANALYSES: AN ANNOTATED BIBLIOGRAPHY. Los Alamitos, Calif.: Southeast Regional Laboratory for Educational Research and Development, 1972. 23 p.

Fontaine, Paul. BASIC FORMAL STRUCTURES IN MUSIC. New York: Meredith Publishing Co., 1967. 241 p.

Primarily a text for college-level students with some theory background.

Hutcheson, Jere T. MUSICAL FORM AND ANALYSIS: A PROGRAMMED COURSE. 2 vols. Boston: Allyn and Bacon, 1972.

Volume I: BASIC ELEMENTS IN MUSICAL FORM. 341 p.; volume II: THE LARGER STRUCTURAL UNITS. 335 p. A programmed text which presents musical structure in relation to the development of articulate and expressive performance practice.

Jones, George Thaddeus. SYMBOLS USED IN MUSIC ANALYSIS. Washington, D.C.: Catholic University of America, 1964. 384 p.

A research study supported by the Cooperative Research Program of the Office of Education concerned with symbolization for the analysis of tonal music. Concludes with a recommended standardized system. Bibliography.

Katz, Adele T. CHALLENGE TO MUSICAL TRADITION. 1945. Reprint. New York: Da Capo Press, 1972. 408 p.

A study of the concept of tonality in Western music from Bach to Schoenberg using Heinrich Schenker's method of musical analysis. Bibliography.

La Rue, John. GUIDELINES FOR STYLE ANALYSIS. New York: W.W. Norton and Co., 1970. 244 p.

A practical and methodical approach to the subject.

Leichtentritt, Hugo. MUSICAL FORM. Cambridge, Mass.: Harvard University Press, 1959. 467 p. Music.

Discussion of how the great masters of music have treated the matter of form. Includes analyses of selected masterpieces.

Macpherson, Stewart. FORM IN MUSIC: WITH SPECIAL REFERENCE TO THE DESIGN OF INSTRUMENTAL MUSIC. London: Joseph Williams; New York: Galaxy Music, 1930. 273 p. Music.

A discussion of design in instrumental music. Covers elementary principles and proceeds to the large symphonic forms.

Moore, Douglas. A GUIDE TO MUSIC STYLES: FROM MADRIGAL TO MODERN MUSIC. Rev. ed. New York: W.W. Norton and Co., 1962. 347 p. Music.

A straightforward and concise presentation of musical style and form by way of five major periods: the Renaissance, baroque, classic, romantic, and modern. Bibliography.

Newman, William S. THE SONATA IN THE BAROQUE ERA. Chapel Hill: University of North Carolina Press, 1959. 448 p.

A comprehensive, historical analysis of the sonata and its development in the baroque era. Bibliography.

_____. THE SONATA IN THE CLASSIC ERA. Chapel Hill: University of North Carolina Press, 1963. 897 p.

Covers the development of the sonata during the classic period. Forerunner of this volume is the author's book, THE SONATA IN THE BAROQUE ERA, above. Extensive bibliography.

Parrish, Carl, comp. and ed. A TREASURY OF EARLY MUSIC. New York: W.W. Norton and Co., 1958. 331 p.

An annotated collection of music illustrating the development of musical style from the early Middle Ages to the middle of the eighteenth century.

Rosen, Charles. THE CLASSICAL STYLE: HAYDN, MOZART, BEETHOVEN. New York: Viking Press, 1971. 467 p. Music.

An in-depth analysis of the meaning of classical style as revealed through the works of the three major figures of this period.

Salop, Arnold. STUDIES ON THE HISTORY OF MUSICAL STYLE. Detroit: Wayne State University Press, 1971. 345 p.

Provides important commentary for the aesthetician of music along with detailed discussion of specific works.

Szabolesi, Bence. A HISTORY OF MELODY. London: Barrie and Rockliff, 1965. 312 p. Illus., music.

A systematic history of melody.

Tovey, Sir Donald Francis. ESSAYS IN MUSICAL ANALYSIS. 7 vols. New York: Oxford University Press, 1935-44.

Volume 1: SYMPHONIES. 1935. 223 p.; volume 2: SYMPHONIES. 1935. 212 p.; volume 3: CONCERTOS. 1936. 226 p.; volume 4: ILLUSTRATIVE MUSIC. 1937. 176 p.; volume 5: VOCAL MUSIC. 1937. 256 p.; volume 6: SUPPLEMENTARY ESSAYS, GLOSSARY, INDEX. 1939. 118 p.; volume 7: CHAMBER MUSIC. 1944. 217 p.

Walton, Charles W. BASIC FORMS IN MUSIC. New York: Alfred Publishing Co., 1974. 218 p. Music.

A discussion of the structure of music, beginning with the primary units and proceeding to the larger orchestral forms. Representative examples from music literature are used for illustration and analysis. Focus is on listening.

______. MUSIC LITERATURE FOR ANALYSIS AND STUDY. Belmont, Calif.: Wadsworth Publishing Co., 1972. 329 p.

This source book follows the trend of using actual music as the basis for studying theory and musicianship. The material is applicable to the first several years of theory study and to various types of musicianship, music literature, and music history courses.

Ward, William R. EXAMPLES FOR THE STUDY OF MUSICAL STYLE. 3d ed. Dubuque, Iowa: William C. Brown Co., 1970. 471 p. Music.

Highly useful handbook concerning musical style covering the 200-year period following J.S. Bach.

COMPOSITION

Creston, Paul. PRINCIPLES OF RHYTHM. New York: Franco Columbo, 1964. 216 p.

An introduction to the study of rhythm from the seventeenth to the twentieth century. Primarily for students of composition. Bibliography.

Davison, Archibald. THE TECHNIQUE OF CHORAL COMPOSITION. Cambridge, Mass.: Harvard University Press, 1960. 206 p.

A practical guide for the beginning choral composer.

Dolan, Robert E[mmett]. MUSIC IN MODERN MEDIA. New York: G. Schirmer, 1967. 181 p.

A valuable source for individuals composing or arranging music for recording purposes.

Hindemith, Paul. THE CRAFT OF MUSICAL COMPOSITION. 2 vols. New York: Association Music Publishers; London: Schott and Co., 1941-42.

The basic principles of composition, based on the natural characteristics of tone. Book 1 (translated by Arthur Mendel, 1942), presents the underlying principles of this theory. Book 2 (translated by Otto Ortmann, 1941) is devoted to actual writing in two parts, presented in pedagogic order.

Lefkoff, Gerald, ed. COMPUTER APPLICATIONS IN MUSIC. Morgantown: West Virginia University Library, 1967. 105 p.

Consists of papers from the West Virginia University Conference entitled Computer Applications in Music.

Lindsay, Martin. TEACH YOURSELF SONGWRITING. Rev. ed. New York: Dover Publications, 1968. 160 p.

A handbook dealing with the popular song market and the technique of writing songs.

Manvell, Roger, and Huntley, John. THE TECHNIQUE OF FILM MUSIC. New York: Hastings House, 1957. 299 p. Photos, illus., music.

A comprehensive survey of the technique of composing music for films. Detailed analyses of selected scores is presented. Includes an index of British and American recordings of film music and a bibliography.

Nyman, Michael. EXPERIMENTAL MUSIC. New York: G. Schirmer, 1974. 154 p. Music, illus.

Developments in the experimental field of composition. Bibliography.

Reichardt, Jasia, ed. CYBERNETIC SERENDIPITY: THE COMPUTER AND THE ARTS. New York: Praeger, 1969. 101 p. Photos.

Explores the relationships between cybernetic devices and the parallel working methods of artists, composers, and poets.

Schoenberg, Arnold. FUNDAMENTALS OF MUSICAL COMPOSITION. Edited by Gerald Strang. New York: St. Martin's Press, 1967. 224 p.

Principles of thematic construction and development constitute the major focus of this work.

_____. MODELS FOR BEGINNERS IN COMPOSITION. New York: G. Schirmer, 1942. 45 p.

Emphasizes ear training, form, and the technique and logic of composition. Special stress on variation forms. Musical examples are given.

For electronic music see Section 41: Electronic Music, Musique Concrète, and and Computer Music.

ORCHESTRATION AND BAND SCORING

Bartolozzi, Bruno. NEW SOUNDS FOR WOODWIND. Translated by Reginald S[mith]. Brindle. New York and London: Oxford University Press, 1967. 78 p. Illus., music.

Proposes and explores new and different sounds which can be generated with conventional instruments and thereby extend tonal possibilities for composition.

Cacavas, John. MUSIC ARRANGING AND ORCHESTRATION. Melville, N.Y.: Belivin Mills Publishing Co., 1975.

Treats scoring techniques for strings, woodwinds, brasses, voices, marching bands, jazz ensembles, symphonic bands, and chamber ensembles.

Carse, Adam. THE HISTORY OF ORCHESTRATION. 1925. Reprint. New York: Dover Publications, 1964. 348 p.

Surveys the evolution of the orchestra from the Renaissance to the end of the nineteenth century.

Coerne, Louis Adolphe. THE EVOLUTION OF MODERN ORCHESTRATION. New York: Macmillan, 1908. 280 p. Music.

Traces the development of the orchestra and orchestration as related to the history of music. Analysis of selected orchestral sources.

Dolan, Robert Emmett. MUSIC IN MODERN MEDIA: TECHNIQUES IN TAPE, DISC, AND FILM RECORDING, MOTION PICTURE AND TELEVISION SCORING, AND ELECTRONIC MUSIC. New York: G. Schirmer, 1967. 181 p. Illus., music.

Details and explains the processes that produce the new sounds on disc, tape, and film recording; the techniques used in scoring music for documentary, cartoon, and feature motion pictures; music production methods in live, taped, and filmed television; and the relation of electronic music to these media.

Forsyth, Cecil. ORCHESTRATION. 2d ed. New York: Macmillan, 1949. 530 p. Music, photos.

Useful mainly as a reference for the use of instruments in pre-twentieth-century orchestration.

Hagen, Earle H. SCORING THE FILMS: A COMPLETE TEXT. New York: Criterion, 1971. 253 p. Illus., photos, music.

Designed to acquaint the musician with the techniques and background necessary for writing music for films.

Kennan, Kent. THE TECHNIQUE OF ORCHESTRATION. 2d ed. Englewood Cliffs, N.J.: Prentice-Hall, 1970. 364 p.

Progresses from a study of individual instruments through scoring for each section to scoring for orchestras. Also available is the author's ORCHESTRATION WORKBOOK (Englewood Cliffs, N.J.: Prentice-Hall, 1969. 92 p.) which provides exercises arranged in order to correspond with the orchestration text.

McKay, George F. CREATIVE ORCHESTRATION. Boston: Allyn and Bacon, 1963. 241 p. Photos, music.

A discussion of the principles of tonal relationships and the techniques of application which stress creativity. Bibliography.

Piston, Walter. ORCHESTRATION. New York: W.W. Norton and Co., 1955. 477 p. Music.

The subject is presented according to three divisions; namely, the instruments of the orchestra, an approach to the analysis of orchestra, an approach to the analysis of orchestration, and typical problems in orchestration.

Rauscher, Donald. ORCHESTRATION: SCORES AND SCORING. New York: Free Press, 1963. 340 p. Music.

Covers the basic elements of orchestration. Contains a considerable number of complete scores for illustration.

Read, Gardner. THESAURUS OF ORCHESTRAL DEVICES. New York: Pitman Publishing Corp., 1953. 631 p.

A lexicon of instrumentation. Excellent reference tool concerning orchestral techniques.

Reed, H. Owen, and Leach, Joel T. SCORING FOR PERCUSSION AND THE INSTRUMENTS OF PERCUSSION. Englewood Cliffs, N.J.: Prentice-Hall, 1969. 150 p.

A practical guide to scoring for percussion.

Rimsky-Korsakov, Nikolay. PRINCIPLES OF ORCHESTRATION. Translated by Edward Agate. 1922. Reprint, corrected. New York: Dover Publications, 1964. 333 p.

Fundamental principles as practiced by a foremost composer and orchestrator.

Rogers, Bernard. THE ART OF ORCHESTRATION: PRINCIPLES OF TONE COLOR IN MODERN SCORING. 1951. Reprint. Westport, Conn.: Greenwood, 1970. 198 p.

Deals with descriptions of instruments and their tone colors. Specific devices are illustrated. Bibliography.

Skinner, Frank. UNDERSCORE. New York: Criterion, 1960. 239 p.

A discussion of the technique of scoring music for motion pictures and television. All important aspects are included as well as a glossary of terms and a film footage table.

Wagner, Joseph. BAND SCORING: A COMPREHENSIVE MANUAL. New York: McGraw-Hill Book Co., 1960. 443 p.

A broad treatment of band scoring techniques.

______. ORCHESTRATION: A PRACTICAL HANDBOOK. New York: McGraw-Hill Book Co., 1959. 366 p.

Scope ranges from historical background and survey of each instrument of the orchestra to a detailed plan for scoring. Approach based on transfer of piano patterns to orchestral score.

Wright, Denis. SCORING FOR BRASS BAND. 4th ed. enl. London: John Baker, 1967. 121 p.

THE TEACHING OF MUSIC THEORY AND THE DEVELOPMENT OF MUSICIANSHIP

The Juilliard School of Music. THE JUILLIARD REPORT ON TEACHING THE LITERATURE AND MATERIALS OF MUSIC. New York: W.W. Norton and Co., 1953. 223 p.

A statement of the principles and practices which were employed in the special curriculum focusing on literature and materials of music which was inaugurated at the Juilliard School of Music in 1947.

Murphy, Howard A[nsley]. TEACHING MUSICIANSHIP: A MANUAL OF METHODS AND MATERIALS. New York: Coleman-Ross, 1950. 275 p. Music, illus.

Treats the development of musicianship through an understanding of musical structures. Bibliography.

Music Educators National Conference. Contemporary Music Project (CMP). CMP2--COMPREHENSIVE MUSICIANSHIP: THE FOUNDATION FOR COLLEGE EDUCATION IN MUSIC. Washington, D.C.: 1965. 88 p. Paper.

Summary of the recommendations for the improvement of music curricula formulated at the CMP Seminar on Comprehensive Musicianship held at Northwestern University in 1965.

_____. CMP4--CREATIVE PROJECTS IN MUSICIANSHIP. By Warren Benson. Washington, D.C.: 1967. 55 p. Paper.

A report of CMP pilot projects in teaching contemporary music at Ithaca College and Interlochen Arts Academy.

_____. CMP5--COMPREHENSIVE MUSICIANSHIP: AN ANTHOLOGY OF EVOLVING THOUGHT. Washington, D.C.: 1971. 119 p. Paper.

A discussion of the first ten years (1959-69) of the Contemporary Music Project, particularly as they relate to the development of comprehensive musicianship. Derived from articles and speeches by those closely associated with the project.

_____. CMP6--COMPREHENSIVE MUSICIANSHIP AND UNDERGRADUATE MUSIC CURRICULA. Washington, D.C.: 1971. 116 p. Paper.

A discussion of curricular implications of comprehensive musicianship as derived from thirty-two experimental college programs sponsored by the CMP under its Institute for Music in Contemporary Education.

Winick, Steven. RHYTHM: AN ANNOTATED BIBLIOGRAPHY. Metuchen, N.J.: Scarecrow Press, 1974. 157 p.

A wide range of references organized into three parts. The first part deals with definition and explanations. The second part gives attention to perception and effects of training; the third part is devoted to rhythmic instruction and materials.

INTERPRETATION

Dart, Thurston. THE INTERPRETATION OF MUSIC. 4th ed. London: Hutchinson University Library. 1967. 190 p. Music, illus.

A survey of some of the important problems involved in the performance of music written between 1350 and 1850.

Donington, Robert. THE INTERPRETATION OF EARLY MUSIC. 2d ed. London: Faber and Faber, 1965. 608 p. Music, tables, illus.

An in-depth analysis of those interpretative factors which are unique to the performance of early music. The emphasis is on baroque interpretation.

Keller, Hermann. PHRASING AND ARTICULATION: A CONTRIBUTION TO A RHETORIC OF MUSIC, WITH 152 MUSICAL EXAMPLES. New York: W.W. Norton and Co., 1973. 117 p. Music, paper.

A scholarly discussion of phrasing and articulation from the keyboard artist's point of view. Assumes familiarity with much music literature and a background in music history. Suggestions for musical research in significant areas of this subject are given. Bibliography.

Matthay, Tobias. MUSICAL INTERPRETATION: ITS LAWS AND PRINCIPLES AND THEIR APPLICATION IN TEACHING AND PERFORMING. 1913. Reprint. Westport, Conn.: Greenwood Press, 1970. 163 p.

The principles of interpretation which are developed in this work have for many years received considerable attention by musicians in all branches of musical performance.

Vinquist, Mary, and Zaslaw, Neal, eds. PERFORMANCE PRACTICE: A BIBLIOGRAPHY. New York: W.W. Norton and Co., 1971. 114 p.

Materials drawn from English, German, French, Italian, Spanish, and Dutch languages concerning the study of how early music was performed.

Wolff, Konrad. THE TEACHING OF ARTHUR SCHNABEL: A GUIDE TO INTERPRETATION. New York: Praeger, 1972. 189 p. Illus.

Focus is on the works of Mozart, Beethoven, Schubert, Schumann, and Brahms. Useful for teachers and advanced students. Bibliography.

ASSOCIATIONS

American Composers Alliance (ACA), 170 West 74th Street, New York, N.Y. 10023.

Publication: ACA BULLETIN. Quarterly.

American Society of Composers, Authors, and Publishers (ASCAP), One Lincoln Plaza, New York, N.Y. 10023.

American Society of Music Arrangers (ASMA), c/o Local 47, A.F. of M., 1777 Vine Street, Los Angeles, Calif. 90028.

Publication: THE SCORE. Irregular.

American Society of University Composers (ASUC), 250 West 57th Street, Room 626-27, New York, N.Y. 10019.

Publications: Newsletter. 3/year.

PROCEEDINGS OF THE AMERICAN SOCIETY OF UNIVERSITY COMPOSERS. Annual.

Journal of music scores. 1-3/year.

Composers Theatre, 25 West Nineteenth Street, New York, N.Y. 10011.

Publications: COMPOSERS AND CHOREOGRAPHERS: THE CCT REVIEW. 3-4/year.

Edvard Grieg Memorial Foundation, Ole Bulls plass 8, Bergen, Norway.

League of Composers, c/o American Music Center, 250 West 57th Street, Suite 626-27, New York, N.Y. 10019.

National Association of Composers, U.S.A., 133 West 69th Street, New York, N.Y. 10023.

Publication: ANNUAL BULLETIN.

Screen Composers' Association (SCA), 9250 Wilshire Boulevard, Beverly Hills, Calif. 90212.

Southeastern Composers' League (SCL), Music Department, University of Virginia, Charlottesville, Va. 22904.

Publications: SCL NEWSLETTER. 3/year.

CATALOG OF WORKS BY MEMBERS OF THE SOUTHEASTERN COMPOSERS LEAGUE.

Section 52
CONDUCTING

Aronowsky, Solomon. PERFORMING TIMES OF ORCHESTRAL WORKS. New York: De Graff, 1959. 802 p.

Bamberger, Carl, ed. THE CONDUCTOR'S ART. New York: McGraw-Hill Book Co., 1965. 322 p.

A compilation of twenty-six essays on conducting by the conductors themselves. Contains their ideas, theories, and beliefs.

Blackman, Charles. BEHIND THE BATON. New York: Charos Enterprises, 1964. 220 p.

A conductor's view of his art. Included are statements by forty other conductors and performers concerning the role of the conductor.

Bowles, Michael. THE ART OF CONDUCTING. Garden City, N.Y.: Doubleday and Co., 1959. 210 p.

A general analysis of this art and a discussion of the various problems encountered in conducting instrumental groups. Bibliography.

Boyd, Jack. REHEARSAL GUIDE FOR THE CHORAL CONDUCTOR. West Nyack, N.Y.: Parker Publishing Co., 1970. 254 p.

Detailed information on methods of planning rehearsals along logical and specific lines. Bibliography.

Daniels, David. ORCHESTRAL MUSIC: A SOURCE BOOK. Metuchen, N.J.: Scarecrow Press, 1972. 319 p.

Procedures for organizing rehearsals and planning programs. A special feature is the listing of instrumentation, timings, and publishers of more than 2,500 works.

Conducting

Davison, Archibald. CHORAL CONDUCTING. 1940. Reprint. Cambridge, Mass.: Harvard University Press, 1954. 73 p. Music.

An analysis of the important aspects of conducting all types of choral groups.

Decker, Harold A., and Herford, Julius, eds. CHORAL CONDUCTING: A SYMPOSIUM. New York: Appleton-Century-Crofts, 1973. 251 p. Music, illus.

A collection of articles dealing with performance techniques, literature, analysis, and research from the conductors' and musicologists' points of view. Bibliography.

Dolmetsch, Rudolph. THE ART OF ORCHESTRAL CONDUCTING. New York: Belwin, 1942. 46 p. Illus., music.

Discusses the art of baton technique, orchestral rehearsal procedures, program planning, and interpretation.

Ehmann, Wilhelm. CHORAL DIRECTING. Translated by George D. Siebe. Minneapolis, Minn.: Augsburg Publishing House, 1968. 214 p. Music.

Principles and methods for dealing with the various phases of choral training and conducting.

Ehret, Walter. THE CHORAL CONDUCTOR'S HANDBOOK. New York: Edward B. Marks, 1969. 55 p.

A discussion of the fundamentals of conducting. Suggestions for rehearsal procedures and program planning.

Eisenberg, Helen, and Eisenberg, Larry. HOW TO LEAD GROUP SINGING. New York: Associated Press, 1955. 62 p. Illus.

A practical, concise handbook for group leaders. Includes sections on repertoire.

Finn, William J. THE ART OF THE CHORAL CONDUCTOR. 2 vols. 1939. Reprint. Evanston, Ill.: Summy-Birchard, 1960. 594 p. Music, illus.

A reissue of a two-volume work which is considered by some to be a classic in its field. Its purpose is to establish principles and practices of choral technique. The treatment is comprehensive.

Fuchs, Peter Paul. THE PSYCHOLOGY OF CONDUCTING. New York: MCA Music, 1969. 145 p.

Explores the relationship between the conductor and other facets of the profession--based primarily on formal experiences, observations, and viewpoints expressed by ten leading individuals in the field.

Garretson, Robert L. CONDUCTING CHORAL MUSIC. 4th ed. Boston: Allyn and Bacon, 1975. 403 p. Illus., music.

Deals with techniques, practices, and problems. Seventy pages of source information on choral composers, octavo publications, collections of extended choral works, publishers, equipment, TV hand signals, etc. Bibliography.

Goldbeck, Frederick. THE PERFECT CONDUCTOR: AN INTRODUCTION TO HIS SKILL AND ART FOR MUSICIANS AND MUSIC LOVERS. London: Dennis Dobson, 1960. 187 p. Music, illus.

A narrative description of the various aspects of conducting as related to the score, the orchestra, the conductor, the baton, and the audience. Useful for musicians and laymen. Bibliography.

Green, Elizabeth A. [H.]. THE MODERN CONDUCTOR. 2d ed. Englewood Cliffs, N.J.: Prentice-Hall, 1969. 295 p. Illus.

Designed as a textbook, but highly useful as a reference work regarding conducting techniques. Bibliography.

Green, Elizabeth A.H., and Malko, Nicolai. THE CONDUCTOR AND HIS SCORE. Englewood Cliffs, N.J.: Prentice-Hall, 1975. 191 p. Music.

Discusses such important aspects of conducting as score study, interpretation, rehearsal techniques, and the teaching of conducting.

Grosbayne, Benjamin. TECHNIQUES OF MODERN ORCHESTRAL CONDUCTING. 2d ed. Cambridge, Mass.: Harvard University Press, 1973. 356 p.

A textbook which stresses the physical basis of conducting. Contains bibliography which is seriously outdated.

Holmes, Malcolm H. CONDUCTING AN AMATEUR ORCHESTRA. Cambridge, Mass.: Harvard University Press, 1951. 128 p. Music.

A handbook of orchestral procedure, from auditions to the public performance. Includes section on sources of orchestral repertoire. Bibliographical references.

Jacob, Gordon. HOW TO READ A SCORE. London and New York: Boosey and Hawkes, 1944. 67 p.

A handbook designed to give a working knowledge of score reading and related subjects. Bibliography.

Jones, Archie N. TECHNIQUE IN CHORAL CONDUCTING. New York: Carl Fischer, 1948. 136 p. Music, illus.

Covers the details involved in conducting choral groups, including baton technique, rehearsal procedure, and program planning. Bibliography and discography.

Kahn, Emil. ELEMENTS OF CONDUCTING. 2d ed. New York: Free Press, 1965. 244 p. Illus., music, paper.

Covers conducting technique, instrumentation, interpretation, and practical rehearsal matters.

McElheran, Brock. CONDUCTING TECHNIQUE: FOR BEGINNERS AND PROFESSIONALS. New York: Oxford University Press, 1966. 132 p. Music, illus.

A handbook for choral and instrumental conductors. Emphasis on baton technique.

Marple, Hugo D. THE BEGINNING CONDUCTOR. New York: McGraw-Hill Book Co., 1972. 317 p.

A student-oriented combination textbook-workbook dealing with basic techniques of conducting.

Moe, Daniel. PROBLEMS OF CONDUCTING. Minneapolis, Minn.: Augsburg Publishing House, 1968. 19 p.

Suggestions for dealing with conducting problems common to twentieth-century choral music.

Petters, Robert. PRINCIPLES OF CONDUCTING FOR MUSIC TEACHERS. Ann Arbor, Mich.: Campus Publications, 1969. 23 p.

Focuses on problems prevalent in the public school conducting profession.

Reddick, William J. THE STANDARD MUSICAL REPERTOIRE, WITH ACCURATE TIMINGS. 1947. Reprint. Westport, Conn.: Greenwood Press, 1970. 192 p.

A listing of performance timings of many works from the standard repertoire as performed by various professional artists. Movements are treated individually.

Rudolf, Max. THE GRAMMAR OF CONDUCTING: A PRACTICAL STUDY OF MODERN BATON TECHNIQUES. New York: G. Schirmer, 1950. 350 p. Music.

Presents a wide range of techniques, ranging from basics to the more advanced levels.

Saminsky, Lazare. ESSENTIALS OF CONDUCTING. London: Dennis Dobson, 1958. 64 p.

A concise description of the necessary qualifications of the choral and instrumental music director.

Scherchen, Hermann. HANDBOOK ON CONDUCTING. Translated by M.D. Calvocoressi. New York and London: Oxford University Press, 1933. 243 p.

A practical handbook and text for conducting.

Schonberg, Harold C. THE GREAT CONDUCTORS. New York: Simon and Schuster, 1967. 384 p. Photos.

A historical survey of those conductors who have greatly influenced the development of the art of conducting.

Stanton, Royal. THE DYNAMIC CHORAL CONDUCTOR. Delaware Water Gap, Pa.: Shawnee Press, 1971. 205 p. Illus., music.

An examination of the functions and attributes of the successful choral director. Bibliography.

Stoddard, Hope. SYMPHONY CONDUCTORS OF THE U.S.A. New York: Thomas Y. Crowell Co., 1957. 405 p.

Includes thirty-two full-length biographies and more than 400 short resumes of symphony conductors. Based on research and personal interviews.

Thomas, Kurt. THE CHORAL CONDUCTOR: THE TECHNIQUE OF CHORAL CONDUCTING IN THEORY AND PRACTICE. Translated by Alfred Mann and William H. Reese. New York: Association of Music Publishers, 1971. 91 p.

Deals with conducting techniques and problems encountered in choral work. Useful for beginners as well as advanced students. Bibliography.

Van Bodegraven, Paul, and Wilson, Harry Robert. THE SCHOOL MUSIC CONDUCTOR: PROBLEMS AND PRACTICES IN CHORAL AND INSTRUMENTAL CONDUCTING. Chicago: Hall & McCreary, 1942. 168 p.

Problems and practices in choral and instrumental conducting. Bibliography.

Van Hausen, Karl D. HANDBOOK OF CONDUCTING. Rev. ed. New York: Appleton-Century-Crofts, 1950. 99 p.

A discussion of the technical and psychological problems of this art. Specific illustrations are given from musical scores. Includes section on the problems of contemporary music. Bibliography.

Wooldridge, David. CONDUCTOR'S WORLD. New York: Praeger, 1970. 379 p.

Covers the musical and social history of the conductor's art from Weber to the present.

TIMINGS OF STANDARD ORCHESTRAL WORKS

See the following works, cited above: Aronowsky, Solomon. PERFORMING TIMES OF ORCHESTRAL WORKS; Daniels, David. ORCHESTRAL MUSIC: A SOURCE BOOK; and Reddick, William J. THE STANDARD MUSICAL REPERTOIRE WITH ACCURATE TIMINGS.

ASSOCIATIONS

American Bandmasters Association (ABA), 7414 Admiral Drive, Alexandria, Va. 22307.

Publication: JOURNAL OF BAND RESEARCH. Semiannual.

American Choral Directors Association (ACDA), c/o R. Wayne Hugoboom, 10616 Coquita Lane, Tampa, Fla. 33618.

Publication: CHORAL JOURNAL. Monthly.

American School Band Directors' Association (ASBDA), 8215 Seward Street, Omaha, Neb. 68114.

Publications: SCHOOL MUSICIAN, DIRECTOR AND TEACHER. 10/year.

Directory and handbook of the ASBDA. Annual.

American Symphony Orchestra League (ASOL), Symphony Hill, P.O. Box 66, Vienna, Va. 22180.

Publication: SYMPHONY NEWS. Bimonthly.

Association of Choral Conductors (ACC), 130 West 56th Street, New York, N.Y. 10019.

Publications: AMERICAN CHORAL REVIEW. Quarterly.

Research bulletins. 9/year.

College Band Directors National Association (CBDNA), 59 Student Center, University of California, Berkeley, Calif. 94720.

Publication: BOOK OF PROCEEDINGS. Biennial.

Koussevitzky Music Foundation, 30 West Sixtieth Street, New York, N.Y. 10023.

Publication: A catalog of its commissioned works.

National Association of Composers, U.S.A. 133 West 69th Street, New York, N.Y. 10023.

National Band Association (NBA), c/o M. Lefever, Box 2454, West Lafayette, Ind. 47906.

Publications: NEWSLETTER AND JOURNAL OF PROCEEDINGS. Quarterly.

NBA DIRECTORY. Annual.

SELECTED MUSIC LISTS FOR BAND (1969).

THE INSTRUMENTALIST. Monthly.

National Catholic Bandmasters' Association (NCBA), Quincy College Music Department. Quincy, Ill. 62301.

Publications: NATIONAL SCHOOL MUSICIAN. Monthly.

Newsletter. Monthly.

Membership list.

National School Orchestra Association, c/o Lois Hobbs, 33 Sterling Lane, Smithtown, N.Y. 11787.

Publications: NSDA BULLETIN. Quarterly.

THE INSTRUMENTALIST. 11/year.

United Choral Conductors Club of America, c/o Mozart Hall, 328 East 86th Street, New York, N.Y. 10028.

Section 53
ACOUSTICS

Backus, John. THE ACOUSTICAL FOUNDATIONS OF MUSIC. New York: W.W. Norton and Co., 1969. 312 p.

An extensive coverage of research in the areas of scientific knowledge that are relevant to music, including the physiological properties of sound; the ear and its perception of sounds; the effect of acoustical environment; the acoustical behavior of musical instruments; and the various applications of electronics and computers to the production, reproduction, and composition of music. Bibliography.

Barbour, J. Murray. TUNING AND TEMPERAMENT: A HISTORICAL SURVEY. East Lansing: Michigan State College Press, 1951. 228 p. Illus.

Discusses the various theories and varieties of tuning with criteria for evaluation. Bibliography.

Bartholomew, Wilmer T. ACOUSTICS OF MUSIC. New York: Prentice-Hall, 1942. 242 p. Music, illus.

Treats the foundational principles of acoustics and is written from the musician's standpoint. Extensive bibliography.

Benade, Arthur H. HORNS, STRINGS, AND HARMONY. New York: Doubleday and Co., 1960. 271 p. Illus.

While intended as an elementary approach to the subject of musical physics, this work is of value to the music educator who should have a practical knowledge of acoustics as related to performance and teaching. Bibliography.

Beranek, Leo L. MUSIC, ACOUSTICS, AND ORCHESTRATION. New York: John Wiley and Sons, 1962. 586 p.

An authoritative treatment of those factors which are important in acoustical planning for music. Includes reports on fifty-four important concert halls and opera houses of the world.

Berger, Melvin, and Clark, Frank. SCIENCE AND MUSIC. New York: Whittlesay House, McGraw-Hill Book Co., 1969. 176 p.

A book about musical acoustics. Especially suited to the junior high student.

Culver, Charles A. MUSICAL ACOUSTICS. Philadelphia: The Blakiston Co., 1941. 194 p. Photos, illus.

Presents the basic physical laws of acoustics as they relate to musical performance and enjoyment.

Gates, Everett. COMPARISON OF THE PYTHAGOREAN, JUST, MEAN-TONE, AND EQUALLY TEMPERED SCALES. Rochester, N.Y.: Eastman School of Music.

This well-designed chart reveals in detail the acoustical similarities and differences of the four important scale systems.

Hutchins, Carleen M., ed. MUSICAL ACOUSTICS, PART I: VIOLIN FAMILY COMPONENTS. Stroudsburg, Pa.: Dowden, Hutchinson and Ross, 1975. 478 p.

For description, see under "Strings" in Section 48: Instrumental Music.

Joseph, Jesse J. THE PHYSICS OF MUSICAL SOUND. Princeton, N.J.: Van Nostrand Co., 1967. 165 p. Paper.

Lloyd, L.S., and Boyle, Hugh. INTERVALS, SCALES AND TEMPERAMENTS. New York: St. Martin's Press, 1963. 246 p.

Treats the subject of intonation as related to intervals, scales, and just, meantone, and equal temperaments.

Lowery, H. THE BACKGROUND OF MUSIC. London: Hutchinson University Library, 1952. 200 p.

Discusses both the psychological and educational aspects of acoustics.

Murphy, O.J. "Measurements of Orchestral Pitch." JOURNAL OF THE ACOUSTICAL SOCIETY OF AMERICA 12 (January 1941): 395-98. Also published as Monograph B-1282 in the Bell Telephone Systems Technical Publications.

The results of 750 observations to determine if the standard frequency of 440 cycles for the note "A" in the treble clef, second space, is being adhered to in musical concerts.

Olson, Harry F. MODERN SOUND PRODUCTION. New York: Van Nostrand Reinhold Co., 1972. 335 p. Illus.

A detailed, technical exposition of significant elements, systems, principles, and techniques in modern sound production. Bibliography.

_____. MUSIC, PHYSICS, AND ENGINEERING. Rev. ed. New York: Dover Publications, 1967. 460 p.

Discusses nature of sound waves, musical notation, musical instruments, how the ear hears, elements of sound reproduction systems from the telephone to stereo sound systems, and electronic music.

Roederer, Juan G. INTRODUCTION TO THE PHYSICS AND PSYCHOPHYSICS OF MUSIC. London: English Universities Press; New York: Springer-Verlag, 1973. 161 p.

Deals with the physical systems and psychophysical processes that intervene in music. Some mathematical background is desirable. Bibliography.

Taylor, C.A. THE PHYSICS OF MUSICAL SOUNDS. London: English Universities Press, 1965. 208 p. (Distr. by Crane, Russak, and Co., New York.)

Deals with the relationship between physics and the production and perception of musical sounds. Bibliography and 45 rpm record.

ASSOCIATIONS

Acoustical Society of America, 335 East 45th Street, New York, N.Y. 10017.

Publication: JOURNAL OF THE ACOUSTICAL SOCIETY OF AMERICA. Monthly.

Audio Engineering Society, 60 East 42d Street, Room 929, New York, N.Y. 10017.

Publications: Journal. 10/year.

Directory of members. Biennial.

Part IV

SPECIAL USES OF MUSIC

While the principal function of music as one of the fine arts has always been to enhance man's aesthetic being, it also contributes to human welfare in various other ways. This part suggests sources of information which deal primarily with unique applications of music for the betterment of mankind.

Section 54

MUSIC AND THE PHYSICALLY AND MENTALLY HANDICAPPED

Alvin, Juliette. MUSIC FOR THE HANDICAPPED CHILD. London: Oxford University Press, 1965. 150 p.

Bailey, Philip. THEY CAN MAKE MUSIC. London: Oxford University Press, 1973. 143 p. Illus.

An account of experiences with exceptional children in British schools, hospitals, and clinics.

Coleman, Jack L., et al. MUSIC FOR EXCEPTIONAL CHILDREN. Evanston, Ill.: Summy-Birchard, 1964. 103 p. Photos, illus., music.

Focuses on instruments, songs, and recordings which can be used with exceptional children. A two-record album is available for use with the text.

Dobbs, J.P.B. THE SLOW LEARNER AND MUSIC. New York: Oxford University Press, 1967. 102 p. Paper.

Discusses the role of music in the education of mentally and physically handicapped children. While written with the British school system in mind, many of the procedures and suggestions are applicable elsewhere.

Egg, Maria. EDUCATING THE CHILD WHO IS DIFFERENT. New York: John Day Co., 1966. 192 p.

Deals with the education of the mentally retarded. Includes the music curriculum. Useful for parents and teachers.

Freeberg, William, and Lunan, Bert. RECREATION FOR THE HANDICAPPED: A BIBLIOGRAPHY. SUPPLEMENT I. ERIC No. ED 018 046. Washington, D.C.: Vocational Rehabilitation Administration, Department of Health, Education and Welfare, 1967. 27 p. Paper.

Contains more than 400 references arranged by categories. Music and drama activities are included, as well as information concerning the organization and administration of such programs.

Ginglend, David R., and Stiles, Winifred E. MUSIC ACTIVITIES FOR RETARDED CHILDREN. Nashville, Tenn.: Abingdon Press, 1965. 140 p. Music.

While the book consists largely of music, it contains many useful suggestions for teachers of retarded children. Introduction provides a basis for the use of music in such programs.

Graham, Richard M., comp. MUSIC FOR THE EXCEPTIONAL CHILD. Vienna, Va.: Music Educators National Conference, 1975. 251 p.

A collection of articles by well-qualified authors. Topics cover most of the important aspects of music and special education.

GUIDE TO PIANO LITERATURE FOR THE PARTIALLY SEEING. New York: American Foundation for the Blind, 1966. 16 p. Pamphlet.

A quick reference for music especially suitable for people with reduced vision. Considers note size, grade level, lighting, and placement of music.

Hardy, Richard E., and Cull, John G., eds. SOCIAL AND REHABILITATION SERVICES FOR THE BLIND. Springfield, Ill.: Charles C. Thomas, 1972. 403 p.

Although the focus of this book is not on music, it is a valuable reference for individuals engaged in this area of social and rehabilitation work. Includes history and philosophy of the agencies in the field; discussion of the psychological aspects of blindness; and the factors involved in rehabilitation services. Bibliographies.

HOW TO READ BRAILLE MUSIC NOTATION. Winnetka, Ill.: The Hadley School for the Blind.

A correspondence course, including braille music, audiotape, and discs.

Kirk, Samuel A. EDUCATING EXCEPTIONAL CHILDREN. 2d ed. Boston: Houghton Mifflin Co., 1972. 478 p.

The music educator who wishes to become involved in the field of special education will do well to first become familiar with basic concepts, definitions, and terms, as well as the characteristics of the individuals who are the focus of attention. For such an introduction to special education, this book is strongly recommended. Contains excellent bibliographies.

Library of Congress. Division for the Blind and Physically Handicapped. DIRECTORY OF LIBRARY RESOURCES FOR THE BLIND AND PHYSICALLY HANDICAPPED. 2d ed. Washington, D.C.: 1972. 24 p. Paper.

McLeish, John, and Higgs, Geoffrey. AN INQUIRY INTO THE MUSICAL CAPACITIES OF EDUCATIONALLY SUB-NORMAL CHILDREN. Cambridge, Engl: Cambridge Institute of Education, 1967. 12 p. Bibliography.

Malloy, Lawrence. ARTS AND THE HANDICAPPED. New York: Educational Facilities Laboratories, 1975. 79 p.

This report, sponsored cooperatively by the Educational Facilities Laboratory and the National Endowment for the Arts, describes various situations which are involved in developing facility, planning, and program solutions to the problem of arts for the handicapped. Included are sources for additional information on the use of the arts in handicapped programs.

Music Educators National Conference. MUSIC IN SPECIAL EDUCATION. Washington, D.C.: 1972. 64 p. Paper.

Originally published in the April 1972 issue of the MUSIC EDUCATORS JOURNAL. Treats some of the problems and solutions of teaching music to the handicapped, retarded, gifted, and emotionally disturbed children. Selected resources and bibliography.

New York. University of the State of. State Education Department. THE ROLE OF MUSIC IN THE SPECIAL EDUCATION OF HANDICAPPED CHILDREN. Albany, N.Y.: State Education Dept., 1971. 114 p.

Details the program of instructional units drawn up by various consultants and demonstrated at the 1971 New York State Conference on music and its use in the education of handicapped children.

Nye, Robert E., and Nye, Vernice T. MUSIC IN THE ELEMENTARY SCHOOL: AN ACTIVITIES APPROACH TO MUSIC METHODS AND MATERIALS. 3d ed. Englewood Cliffs, N.J.: Prentice-Hall, 1970. 660 p.

Treats a broad spectrum of trends, teaching techniques, media, and other aspects of music teaching by means of an activities approach. Includes a section on music for the disadvantaged and handicapped. Bibliography.

Riordan, Jennifer Talley. THEY CAN SING, TOO: RHYTHM FOR THE DEAF. Leavenworth, Kans.: Jericho Associates, 1971. 67 p. Music.

Designed specifically for use in teaching rhythm to young deaf children. Also useful with children in special education classes.

Robins, Ferris, and Robins, Jennet. EDUCATIONAL RHYTHMICS FOR MENTALLY AND PHYSICALLY HANDICAPPED CHILDREN. 2d ed. New York: Association Press, 1968. 239 p.

A method of practical application in remedial recreation.

Roucek, Joseph S. THE DIFFICULT CHILD. New York: Philosophical Library, 1964. 292 p.

Consists of sixteen articles by specialists. Deals with problems which may make a child difficult. One of the essays is entitled "Children with Difficulties in Musical Growth," by D.W. Jones. Bibliography.

Schattner, Regina. CREATIVE DRAMATICS FOR HANDICAPPED CHILDREN. ERIC No. ED 011 428. New York: John Day Co., 1967. 160 p.

Although the focus of this work is drama, music activities are also included with a bibliography and discography.

THE COUNCIL FOR EXCEPTIONAL CHILDREN (CEC) INFORMATION CENTER

The Council for Exceptional Children (CEC) established the information center in 1966. This center functions as the Clearinghouse on Exceptional Children in the Educational Resources Information Center (ERIC) program and also as a center in the Special Education Instructional Materials Center (IMC)--Regional Instructional Materials Center (RIMC) Network. The CEC center serves as a comprehensive source for information on research, instructional materials, programs, administration, teacher education, methods, and curricula in exceptional child education. In addition, the center has recently focused on the development of information analysis products, on user needs, and on evaluative studies. As an ERIC clearinghouse, the center abstracts and indexes documents for RESOURCES IN EDUCATION and indexes journal articles for announcement in CURRENT INDEX TO JOURNALS IN EDUCATION. (See "ERIC--Educational Resources Information Center" in Section 18: Information Services and Systems.)

The main purpose for establishing the IMC program was to improve the instruction of handicapped children through a more effective use of instructional methods, materials, and media. With the growing interest and concern about the role of music in this field, music educators will find the EXCEPTIONAL CHILD EDUCATION ABSTRACTS an important source for current information.

EXCEPTIONAL CHILD EDUCATION ABSTRACTS. Arlington, Va.: The Council for Exceptional Children, 1969-- . 4/year.

For abstracts available via computer see "Dialog Information Retrieval Service" in Section 18: Information Services and Systems.

Two other important publications distributed by the Council for Exceptional Children are:

EXCEPTIONAL CHILDREN. Reston, Va.: Council for Exceptional Children, 1934-- . 8/year.

Contains material on current trends, developments, and research in the field of special education.

TEACHING EXCEPTIONAL CHILDREN. Washington, D.C.: Council for Exceptional Children, 1968-- . Quarterly.

Designed primarily for teachers and deals with classroom activities.

ASSOCIATIONS

Alexander Graham Bell Association for the Deaf, 3417 Volta Place, N.W. Washington, D.C. 20007.

Publication: WORLD TRAVELER. 10/year.

THE VOLTA REVIEW. 9/year.

American Association of Workers for the Blind (AAWB), 1511 K Street, N.W., Suite 637, 15th and K Streets, Washington, D.C. 20005.

Publications: AAWB NEWS AND VIEWS. Bimonthly.

BLINDNESS. Annual.

Convention proceedings. Biennial.

American Association on Mental Deficiency (AAMD), 5201 Connecticut Avenue, N.W., Washington, D.C. 20015.

Publications: AMERICAN JOURNAL OF MENTAL DEFICIENCY. Bimonthly.

MENTAL RETARDATION. Bimonthly.

Directory of members. Biennial.

American Federation of Catholic Workers for the Blind and Visually Handicapped (AFCWBVH), 154 East 23d Street, New York, N.Y. 10010.

Publications: Proceedings of conferences.

Directory of member agencies.

American Foundation for the Blind (AFB), 15 West Sixteenth Street, New York, N.Y. 10011.

Publications: NEW OUTLOOK FOR THE BLIND. 10/year.

WASHINGTON REPORT. 6/year.

Newsletter. Quarterly.

DIRECTORY OF AGENCIES SERVING THE BLIND IN THE U.S. Biennial.

American Occupational Therapy Association, 6000 Executive Boulevard, Suite 200, Rockville, Md. 20852.

Publications: THE AMERICAN JOURNAL OF OCCUPATIONAL THERAPY.

EDUCATION NEWSPAPER.

Registry.

BULLETIN OF PRACTICE.

American Physical Therapy Association, 1156 Fifteenth Street, N.W., Washington, D.C. 20005.

Publications: PHYSICAL THERAPY. Monthly.

Newsletter.

American Printing House for the Blind (APH), 1839 Frankfort Avenue, P.O. Box 6085. Louisville, Ky. 40206.

Maintains an Instructional Materials Center for the Blind as part of ERIC (Educational Resources Information Center). Produces literature for the blind in all media-braille, talking books, large type, recordings, and so forth.

Publication: TANGIBLE APPARATUS.

The American Speech and Hearing Association, 9030 Old Georgetown Road, Bethesda, Md. 20014.

Publications: JOURNAL OF SPEECH AND HEARING DISORDERS. Quarterly.

JOURNAL OF SPEECH AND HEARING RESEARCH. Quarterly.

ASHA JOURNAL. Monthly.

LANGUAGE, SPEECH AND HEARING SERVICES IN SCHOOLS. Quarterly.

Directory. Annual.

Reports. Irregular.

Association for Children with Learning Disabilities, 5225 Grace Street, Pittsburgh, Pa. 15236.

Publications: ITEMS OF INTEREST. Monthly.

Conference papers. Annual.

Selected papers. Annual.

Association for Education of the Visually Handicapped (AEVH), 919 Walnut Street, Fourth floor, Philadelphia, Pa. 19107.

Publications: THE EDUCATION OF THE VISUALLY HANDICAPPED. Quarterly.

FOUNTAINHEAD (newsletter). Quarterly.

AEVH convention papers. Biennial.

Braille Institute of America (BIA), 741 North Vermont Avenue, Los Angeles, Calif. 90029.

Publications: BRAILLE MIRROR. Annual.

A child's music book, Braille Bible in King James version, a Braille calendar and cookbook.

Bureau of Education for the Handicapped, U.S. Office of Education, 400 Maryland Avenue, S.W., Washington, D.C. 20202.

Council for Exceptional Children, 1920 Association Drive, Reston, Va. 22091.

Publications: EXCEPTIONAL CHILDREN. 8/year.

Abstracts. Quarterly.

TEACHING EXCEPTIONAL CHILDREN. Quarterly.

Update. Quarterly.

Information Center--Recreation for the Handicapped, Outdoor Laboratory, Little Grassy, Southern Illinois University, Carbondale, Ill. 62901.

Publications: ICRH NEWSLETTER. Monthly.

RECREATION FOR THE HANDICAPPED, A BIBLIOGRAPHY. Annual.

Lighthouse Music School, (New York Association for the Blind), 111 East 59th Street, New York, N.Y.

Louis Braille Foundation for Blind Musicians (LBF), 112 East Nineteenth Street, New York, N.Y. 10003.

Braille transcription service.

The Music Foundation for the Visually Handicapped, P.O. Box 569, Ridgewood, N.J. 07451.

Provides free music instruction and instruments to visually handicapped residents of New Jersey.

The National Association for Creative Children and Adults, 8080 Springvalley Drive, Cincinnati, Ohio 45236.

Publications: CREATIVE CHILD AND ADULT QUARTERLY.

Quarterly.

Newsletter.

IT'S HAPPENING. Quarterly.

Annual proceedings.

Membership directory. Irregular.

National Association for Mental Health (NAMH), 1800 North Kent Street, Rosslyn, Va. 22209.

Publications: MENTAL HYGIENE. Quarterly.

REPORTER.

Pamphlets, leaflets, posters, and films.

National Association for Retarded Citizens (NARC), 2709 Avenue E East, Arlington, Tex. 76011.

Publication: MENTAL RETARDATION NEWS. 10/year.

National Association for the Visually Handicapped, 305 East 24th Street, New York, N.Y. 10010.

Specializes in large print materials (including music).

Publications: Bulletin. Annual.

CATALOG OF LARGE TYPE PUBLICATIONS.

National Association of the Deaf (NAD), 814 Tayer Avenue, Silver Spring, Md. 20910.

Publications: THE DEAF AMERICAN. Monthly.

Pamphlets and other educational materials.

National Braille Association (NBA), 85 Godwin Avenue, Midland Park, N.J. 07432.

Clearinghouse for hand produced braille materials.

Publications: Bulletin. 3/year.

BRAILLE BOOK BANK CATALOG. Biennial.

National Catholic Educational Association, One Dupont Circle, Suite 350, Washington, D.C. 20036.

Publications: SPECIAL EDUCATION NEWSLETTER. 3/year.

UPDATE. Monthly.

FORUM. 5/year.

NOTES. 5/year.

ALIVE. 4/year.

MOMENTUM. Quarterly.

PARISH COORDINATOR OF RELIGIOUS EDUCATION. Quarterly.

POLICY MAKER. Quarterly.

SEMINARY NEWSLETTER. Quarterly.

DATA BANK REPORT. Annual.

SUMMER PROGRAMS IN RELIGION. Annual.

The National Easter Seal Society for Crippled Children and Adults, 2023 West Ogden Avenue, Chicago, Ill. 60612.

Publications: REHABILITATION LITERATURE. Monthly.

EASTER SEAL COMMUNICATOR. 10/year.

National Society for Autistic Children (NSAC), 169 Tampa Avenue, Albany, N.Y. 12208.

Publications: NSAC NEWSLETTER. Bimonthly.

Proceedings. Annual.

NATIONAL DIRECTORY OF SERVICES AND PROGRAMS FOR AUTISTIC CHILDREN.

Occasional reprints, booklets, and pamphlets.

President's Committee on Mental Retardation, Room 2614, ROB #3, Seventh and D Streets, S.W., Washington, D.C. 20201.

Publications: PCMR MESSAGE. Bimonthly.

Annual report to the president.

Special reports.

Section 55

MUSIC IN THERAPY

Alvin, Juliette. MUSIC THERAPY. New York: Humanities Press, 1966. 174 p. Photos.

Historical background of music therapy from primitive uses to the twentieth century. Describes modern applications of music in medical treatment.

Berel, Marianne, comp. "Bibliography of Music Therapy." New York: United Cerebral Palsy Associations of New York State, 1969. 12 p. Mimeo.

Especially useful for researchers in the rehabilitation field--many references concerning the handicapped child.

Bright, Ruth. MUSIC IN GERIATRIC CARE. New York: St. Martin's Press, 1974. 116 p.

An up-to-date coverage of present practices concerning music in the care and rehabilitation of the aged, with suggestions for future applications.

Drinklage, H.A. "Music Therapy: A Selective Bibliography." In MUSIC THERAPY, 1958: EIGHTH BOOK OF PROCEEDINGS OF THE ASSOCIATION, by National Association of Music Therapy Journal, pp. 249-93. Cincinnati, Ohio: National Association of Music Therapy, 1958.

Farnsworth, Paul R. THE SOCIAL PSYCHOLOGY OF MUSIC. 2d ed. Ames: Iowa State University Press, 1969. 298 p.

Treats the sociopsychological variables associated with music. Extensive notes and references cited at end of each section.

Gaston, E. Thayer, ed. MUSIC IN THERAPY. New York: Macmillan, 1968. 490 p. Tables.

A comprehensive survey of theory, research, techniques, and clinical practice in music therapy. A source of importance for the music therapist. Excellent bibliographic references.

INDEX MEDICUS. Bethesda, Md.: National Library of Medicine. 1960-- . Monthly.

A compilation of citations to journal articles from the world's periodical biomedical literature. Includes medical applications involving music and music therapy. Annual cumulations issued by the American Medical Association under the title CUMULATED INDEX MEDICUS.

Licht, Sidney. MUSIC IN MEDICINE. Boston: New England Conservatory of Music, 1946. 132 p.

Deals with the therapeutic uses of music. Bibliography.

Music Research Foundation. MUSIC AND YOUR EMOTIONS: A PRACTICAL GUIDE TO MUSIC SELECTION ASSOCIATED WITH DESIRED EMOTIONAL RESPONSES. New York: Liveright, 1952. 128 p. Illus.

An introduction to the relationship of music to emotions. Includes reports on some scientific investigation of the effect of music on human emotions.

Nordoff, Paul, and Robbins, Clive. MUSIC THERAPY FOR HANDICAPPED CHILDREN: INVESTIGATIONS AND EXPERIENCES. Blauvelt, N.Y.: Rudolf Steiner Publications, 1965. 150 p.

A description of music therapy techniques which have been developed by the authors both here and abroad.

______. MUSIC THERAPY IN SPECIAL EDUCATION. New York: John Day Co., 1971. 253 p.

Explores a wide variety of musical applications for the benefit of handicapped children. Provides a basis for creating developmental experiences. Bibliography.

______. THERAPY IN MUSIC FOR HANDICAPPED CHILDREN. New York: St. Martin's Press, 1971. 144 p. Photos.

Descriptions of therapeutic applications.

O'Morrow, Gerald S., comp. ADMINISTRATION OF ACTIVITY THERAPY SERVICE. Springfield, Ill.: Charles C. Thomas, 1966. 419 p. Illus.

Basic principles and practices for the administrator or practitioner. of music therapy programs. Excellent bibliography.

Podolsky, Edward, ed. MUSIC THERAPY. New York: Philosophical Library,

1954. 335 p. Music, photos.

A collection of papers originally published in professional journals covering a wide range of topics related to therapeutic uses of music. Bibliography.

Priestley, Mary. MUSIC THERAPY IN ACTION. New York: St. Martin's Press, 1974. 274 p.

Schulliam, Dorothy, and Schoen, Max. MUSIC AND MEDICINE. 1948. Reprint. Freeport, N.Y.: Books for Libraries Press, 1971. 499 p.

Relationships between music and medicine. Especially useful for its historical treatment. Bibliography.

Soibelman, Doris. THERAPEUTIC AND INDUSTRIAL USES OF MUSIC: A REVIEW OF THE LITERATURE. New York: Columbia University Press, 1948. 274 p.

An evaluation of experiments in this field of endeavor. Extensive bibliography.

Washington State Library. MUSIC THE HEALER: A BIBLIOGRAPHY. Olympia, Wash.: Institutional Library Services Division, 1970. 30 p.

Includes bibliographies on all aspects of music therapy as related to geriatrics, emotionally disturbed children, medicine, and the handicapped, mentally ill, and mentally retarded.

See also Section 54: Music and the Physically and Mentally Handicapped.

ASSOCIATIONS

American Association for Music Therapy, c/o Department of Music and Music Education, Washington Square, New York University, New York, N.Y. 10003.

Membership is open to music therapists, students in all areas of music, and those who wish to support the development of music therapy. Responsible for creating new positions in many fine agencies and in special education programs in large school districts (primarily in the eastern United States).

Publications: Newsletter. 4/year.

Membership directory. Annual.

American Association for Rehabilitation Therapy (AART), P.O. Box 93, North Little Rock, Ark. 72116.

Publications: AMERICAN ARCHIVES OF REHABILITATION THERAPY. Quarterly.

REHABILITATION THERAPY BULLETIN. Quarterly.

REGISTRY OF MEDICAL REHABILITATION THERAPISTS AND SPECIALISTS. Annual.

American Corrective Therapy Association (ACTA) (formerly Association for Physical and Mental Rehabilitation), c/o Kirk Hodges, 6622 Spring Hollow, San Antonio, Tex. 78249.

Publications: AMERICAN CORRECTIVE THERAPY JOURNAL.

Chapter bulletins. Semiannual.

Presidential bulletin. Irregular.

American Dance Therapy Association, Suite 216E, 1000 Century Plaza, Columbus, Md. 21044.

Publications: Newsletter. Quarterly.

Conference proceedings. Annual.

Membership directory. Annual.

WRITINGS ON BODY MOVEMENT AND COMMUNICATION. Annual.

British Society for Music Therapy, London, England.

Publication: BRITISH JOURNAL OF MUSIC THERAPY. 3/year.

National Association for Music Therapy (NAMT), P.O. Box 610, Lawrence, Kans. 66044.

Promotes research and distributes information. Establishes qualifications and standards of training for music therapists; works to perfect programming techniques which aid treatment most effectively.

Publications: JOURNAL OF MUSIC THERAPY. Quarterly.

BOOK OF PROCEEDINGS. Annual.

Membership directory. Annual.

Section 56

MUSIC AND THE GIFTED

Fisher, Renee B. MUSICAL PRODIGIES: MASTERS AT AN EARLY AGE. New York: Association Press, 1973. 240 p. Illus.

A discussion of the gifted child, focusing mainly on the psychology of performance and its social implications. One section deals with the role of heredity and environment in educating the gifted child. Bibliography.

Gowan, John Curtis. ANNOTATED BIBLIOGRAPHY ON CREATIVITY AND GIFTEDNESS. Northridge, Calif.: San Fernando Valley State College Foundation, 1965. 197 p.

Hartshorn, William C., et al., eds. MUSIC FOR THE ACADEMICALLY TALENTED STUDENT IN THE SECONDARY SCHOOL. National Education Association Project on the Academically Talented Student and Music Educators National Conference, a Department of the National Education Association. Washington, D.C.: NEA, 1960. 127 p.

Discusses the basic functions of secondary music education, particularly for the academically talented student as distinguished from the musically talented student. Bibliography.

Los Angeles City Schools, Division of Instructional Services, Curriculum Branch. ENRICHMENT ACTIVITIES IN MUSIC FOR INTELLECTUALLY GIFTED PUPILS, ELEMENTARY SCHOOLS. Los Angeles, Calif.: 1962. 43 p. Paper.

A list of activities with suggested resources for stimulating the gifted child. Extensive bibliography.

Milliken, Russell A., and Epling, Christine Fraley. ANNOTATED BIBLIOGRAPHY FOR THE EDUCATION OF GIFTED CHILDREN. Athens: Ohio University Center for Educational Services, 1960. 35 p.

Includes general references as well as those for identification and teaching of the gifted; the role of parents, administration, and community.

Section 57
MUSIC AND RECREATION

Avedon, Elliott M. THERAPEUTIC RECREATION SERVICE: AN APPLIED BEHAVIORAL SCIENCE APPROACH. Englewood Cliffs, N.J.: Prentice-Hall, 1974. 254 p. Illus.

Identifies numerous musical activities which are appropriate for recreation programs. Bibliographic references.

Baird, Forrest J. MUSIC SKILLS FOR RECREATION LEADERS. Dubuque, Iowa: William C. Brown Co., 1963. 215 p.

Discusses recreational singing, instruments suitable for recreational purposes and how they are played, uses of rhythm in song and dance both for adults and children, and a rather detailed discussion of listening to music. A comprehensive index to materials is included, along with a bibliography.

Batcheller, John M., and Monsour, Sally. MUSIC IN RECREATION AND LEISURE. Dubuque, Iowa: William C. Brown Co., 1972. 135 p.

Appendixes include general sources on recreation and leisure, basic sources and references on the teaching of music, selected books about music for libraries and recreation centers, etc.

Carlson, Reynold Edgar, et al. RECREATION IN AMERICAN LIFE. 2d ed. Belmont, Calif.: Wadsworth Publishing Co., 1972. 552 p. Photos, illus.

Contains section on the role of music in recreation. Bibliographic references.

Freeberg, William, and Lunan, Bert. RECREATION FOR THE HANDICAPPED: A BIBLIOGRAPHY. SUPPLEMENT I. ERIC No. ED 018 046. Washington, D.C.: Vocational Rehabilitation Administration, Department of Health, Education and Welfare, 1967. 27 p.

Contains more than 400 references, arranged by categories. Music and drama activities are included, as well as information concerning the organization and administration of such programs.

Friedan, Betty. COMMUNITY RESOURCES POOL, SOUTH ORANGETOWN CENTRAL SCHOOL DISTRICT 1. ERIC No. ED 002 370. Orangeburg, N.Y.: South Orangetown School District 1, 1962. 11 p.

A description of a project which involved 250 elementary, junior, and senior high school students in Saturday seminars for sixteen weeks. The music program included composition, harp, and a variety of concerts. Community resource persons were utilized.

Kaplan, Max. MUSIC IN RECREATION: SOCIAL FOUNDATIONS AND PRACTICES. Champaign, Ill.: Stipes Publishers, 1955. 230 p. Illus., music.

A rather complete and effective guide for recreation leaders. Bibliography, film listings, discography.

Kraus, Richard Gordon. RECREATION AND LEISURE IN MODERN SOCIETY. New York: Appleton-Century-Crofts, 1971. 493 p. Illus.

Discusses the role of the arts in recreation and leisure. Bibliography.

_____. THERAPEUTIC RECREATION SERVICE: PRINCIPLES AND PRACTICES. Philadelphia: Saunders, 1973. 234 p. Illus.

Includes discussions concerning music in therapeutic recreation. Bibliography.

Leonhard, Charles. RECREATION THROUGH MUSIC. New York: Ronald Press, 1952. 160 p. Photos.

Deals extensively with the use of music in recreation programs. Bibliography and discography.

"Summer Music Camps and Summer Programs for Young Musicians--United States." In THE MUSICIAN'S GUIDE, pp. 337-58. New York: Music Information Service, 1972.

Listing includes those camps and programs which specialize in music and/or the performing arts, teen-age music programs on college campuses, and so forth. Arranged by state. Includes short description of programs and other pertinent information.

"Summer Music Camps, Clinics and Workshops--Addendum." INSTRUMENTALIST 29 (April 1975): 88-97.

ASSOCIATIONS

American Alliance for Health, Physical Education and Recreation (AAHPER),

1201 Sixteenth Street, N.W., Washington, D.C. 20036.

Publications: JOURNAL OF HEALTH, PHYSICAL EDUCATION, RECREATION. 9/year.

UPDATE. 9/year.

HEALTH EDUCATION. 6/year.

RESEARCH QUARTERLY.

American Music Conference, 150 East Huron Street, Chicago, Ill. 60611.

Cooperates with the National Recreation and Park Association in Planning music activities and prepares manuals for city recreational programs involving music.

National Recreation and Park Association (NRPA), 1601 North Kent Street, Arlington, Va. 22209.

Publications: PARKS AND RECREATION MAGAZINE. Monthly.

JOURNAL OF LEISURE RESEARCH. Quarterly.

THERAPEUTIC RECREATION JOURNAL. Quarterly.

GUIDE TO BOOKS ON PARKS. Annual.

PROCEEDINGS OF THE CONGRESS FOR RECREATION AND PARKS. Annual.

Books, pamphlets, management, aids, and newsletter.

Part V

TECHNOLOGY, MULTIMEDIA RESOURCES, AND EQUIPMENT

Section 58

TECHNOLOGY IN MUSIC EDUCATION

Allen, Dwight, and Ryan, Kevin. MICROTEACHING. Reading, Mass.: Addison-Wesley Publishing Co., 1969. 151 p.

A concise explanation of this technique of developing teaching skills. Highly useful for the preparation of teachers of music. Bibliography, references.

Boyce, William. HI-FI STEREO HANDBOOK. 4th ed. New York: Bobbs-Merrill Co., 1972. 400 p. Illus., photos.

A convenient reference source dealing with high fidelity sound systems.

Brown, James W., and Lewis, Richard B., eds. AV INSTRUCTIONAL TECHNOLOGY MANUAL FOR INDEPENDENT STUDY. 4th ed. New York: McGraw-Hill Book Co., 1973. 184 p. Illus.

A practical manual for self-instruction. Deals with the problems of choosing, using, and creating instructional materials. Includes instructions for the use and operation of audiovisual equipment.

Carpenter, Thomas H. TELEVISED MUSIC INSTRUCTION. Washington, D.C.: Music Educators National Conference, 1973. 222 p.

Delineates the development of televised music instruction; presents in-depth accounts of current programs; and describes lesson purpose, content, structure, and evaluation. Contributing authors discuss specific problems, issues, and directions. Bibliography.

Costello, Lawrence, and Gordon, George N. TEACH WITH TELEVISION: A GUIDE TO INSTRUCTIONAL TV. 2d ed. New York: Hastings House, 1965. 192 p. Illus.

A manual which describes how to produce and use instructional television most effectively at all educational levels.

Dale, Edgar. AUDIO-VISUAL METHODS IN TEACHING. 3d ed. New York: Holt, Rinehart and Winston, 1965. 534 p.

Suggests ways of using audiovisual instructional materials.

EDUCATIONAL PRODUCT REPORT. New York: Educational Product Information Exchange Institute (EPIE), 6/year.

Reports impartial evaluations of learning materials and equipment. Also issues EPIEgrams. 18/year.

Eickmann, Paul E., et al. TECHNOLOGY IN MUSIC TEACHING. Washington, D.C.: Music Educators National Conference, 1971. 155 p. Illus., tables, photos, music.

A systems approach to the use of instructional technology in the classroom. Provides practical guidance, and valuable references. Bibliography.

Erickson, Carlton W.H. FUNDAMENTALS OF TEACHING WITH AUDIO-VISUAL TECHNOLOGY. New York: Macmillan, 1965. 382 p.

Procedures for the utilization of instructional technology for the achievement of educational objectives.

Fantel, Hans. THE TRUE SOUND OF MUSIC. New York: E.P. Dutton, 1973. 237 p.

A practical guide to sound equipment for the home and school.

Goodwin, Arthur B. HANDBOOK OF AUDIO-VISUAL AIDS AND TECHNIQUES FOR TEACHING ELEMENTARY SCHOOL SUBJECTS. West Nyack, N.Y.: Parker Publishing Co., 1969. 224 p. Photos, illus.

Provides many practical suggestions for the elementary school teacher. Chapter 9, "Getting More from Audio-Visual Aids in Teaching Music," is devoted entirely to music teaching. Bibliography.

Kemp, Jerrold E. PLANNING AND PRODUCING AUDIOVISUAL MATERIALS. 3d ed. New York: Thomas Y. Crowell Co., 1975. 320 p.

Describes methods of preparing filmstrips, transparencies, graphics, sound recordings, movies, and television materials.

McLuhan, Marshall. UNDERSTANDING MEDIA: THE EXTENSIONS OF MAN. New York: McGraw-Hill Book Co., 1964. 318 p.

Minor, Ed, and Frye, Harvey R. TECHNIQUES FOR PRODUCING VISUAL

INSTRUCTIONAL MEDIA. New York: McGraw-Hill Book Co., 1970. 288 p.

Covers wide range of production techniques, from simple to complex. Includes bibliography and listing of sources for materials and equipment.

"Music Education." EDUCATIONAL TECHNOLOGY 11 (August 1971): entire issue.

The emphasis of the entire issue is on technological applications in music education.

Music Educators National Conference. "Technology In Music Teaching." MUSIC EDUCATORS JOURNAL 57 (January 1971): entire issue.

This important issue is devoted entirely to reviewing the state of art with a view to the future. Special consideration is given to programmed learning, films, television, the materials center, sound reproduction, synthesizers, computer-assisted instruction, research, and information storage and retrieval via computer.

New York. University of the State of. State Education Department. WORDS, SOUNDS, AND PICTURES ABOUT MUSIC. Albany, N.Y.: Bureau of Secondary Curriculum Development, 1970. 138 p. Photos.

A multimedia resource listing for teachers of music in grades seven to twelve.

SELECTION AND USE OF PROGRAMMED MATERIALS. Washington, D.C.: National Education Association. Filmstrip, 63 frames, color.

Features B.F. Skinner explaining the theory of programmed learning. Also presents descriptions of various teaching machines and materials with implications for education.

Sessions, Ken W. STEREO AND HI-FI PRINCIPLES AND PROJECTS. Blue Ridge Summit, Pa.: B/1 Tab Books, 1973. 620 p.

Skapiski, George J. FEASIBILITY OF PRODUCING SYNCHRONIZED VIDEO TAPES AS INSTRUCTIONAL AIDS IN THE STUDY OF MUSIC. Washington, D.C.: U.S. Office of Education, Bureau of Research, 1969. 83 p.

Sur, William Raymond, and Schuller, Charles Francis. "Music in the Visual Dimension." In MUSIC EDUCATION FOR TEEN-AGERS, 2d ed., pp. 405-39. New York: Harper and Row, 1966.

Describes the creation and use of many kinds of visuals for music teaching.

Zettl, Herbert. TELEVISION PRODUCTION HANDBOOK. 2d ed. Belmont,

Calif.: Wadsworth Publishing Co., 1969. 541 p. Illus.

A comprehensive discussion of the various elements involved in television production. The latest equipment is described and illustrated. Bibliography.

See also Section 41: Electronic Music, Musique Concrète, and Computer Music, and "Information Sources and Systems" in Section 17: Research Techniques.

Section 59
COMPUTER APPLICATIONS

Allvin, R.L. COMPUTER-ASSISTED MUSIC INSTRUCTION: A LOOK AT THE POTENTIAL. Los Gatos, Calif.: International Business Machines Corporation, Advanced Systems Developmental Division, 1968. 16 p.

A laboratory report. Describes the need for reconsidering the content and organization of music courses to take advantage of the potential of this kind of instructional technology. Includes some experiments. Bibliography.

American Musicological Society, Greater New York Chapter. MUSICOLOGY AND THE COMPUTER: MUSICOLOGY 1966-2000: A PRACTICAL PROGRAM: (Three Symposia). Edited by Barry S. Brook. New York: City University of New York Press, 1970. 275 p. Illus., music.

A compilation of papers by leading musicologists on the subject of computer applications to various aspects of music. In addition, it contains one of the finest bibliographies on the subject.

Bowles, Edmund A., ed. COMPUTERS IN HUMANISTIC RESEARCH: READINGS AND PERSPECTIVES. Englewood Cliffs, N.J.: Prentice-Hall, 1967. 288 p.

Forte, Allen. SNOBOL 3 PRIMER: AN INTRODUCTION TO THE COMPUTER PROGRAMMING LANGUAGE. Cambridge, Mass.: M.I.T. Press, 1967. 107 p. Illus., paper.

A practical approach to gaining computational experience for one who has not previously worked with computer machines. Procedural techniques are explained. Bibliography.

Hellwig, Jessica. INTRODUCTION TO COMPUTERS AND PROGRAMMING. New York: Columbia University Press, 1969. 215 p.

In view of the widespread use of computers in connection with the generation of musical ideas in contemporary composition, as well as for the treatment of research data, the music educator will find this text especially useful for developing an understanding of genera general principles.

Kostka, Stefan M. A BIBLIOGRAPHY OF COMPUTER APPLICATIONS IN MUSIC. Hackensack, N.J.: Joseph Boonin, 1974. 58 p.

Lefkoff, Gerald, ed. COMPUTER APPLICATIONS IN MUSIC. Morgantown: West Virginia University Library, 1967. 105 p.

Consists of papers from the West Virginia University Conference in 1966 entitled Computer Applications in Music.

Lincoln, Harry B. DEVELOPMENT OF COMPUTERIZED TECHNIQUES IN MUSIC RESEARCH WITH EMPHASIS ON THE THEMATIC INDEX. Washington, D.C.: U.S. Office of Education, Bureau of Research, 1968. Var. pag.

_______, ed. THE COMPUTER AND MUSIC. Ithaca, N.Y.: Cornell University Press, 1970. 354 p.

U.S. Office of Education. A STUDY OF COMPUTER TECHNIQUES FOR MUSIC RESEARCH. Washington, D.C.: 1970.

Note: Additional references for Computer-Assisted Music Instruction are contained in the following:

"Music Education." EDUCATIONAL TECHNOLOGY 11 (August 1971): entire issue.

Music Educators National Conference. "Technology In Music Teaching." MUSIC EDUCATORS JOURNAL 57 (January 1971): entire issue.

For description of the two items above, see Section 58: Technology in Music Education.

See also Section 41: Electronic Music, Musique Concrète, and Computer Music.

Section 60

COMPREHENSIVE GUIDES TO AUDIOVISUAL MATERIALS AND SERVICES

AUDIOVISUAL MARKET PLACE: A MULTIMEDIA GUIDE. Ann Arbor, Mich.: R.R. Bowker Co., 1966-- . Biennial.

A buying guide and source book of information on the entire audiovisual field. It provides company names, addresses, key personnel, and product lines for all active producers, distributors, and manufacturers of audiovisual learning materials and equipment. It includes a directory of national professional associations; a guide to educational television and radio stations, some of whose programs are available for loan, rent, or sale; a list of audiovisual dealers, contract production services and cataloging services; a bibliography of audiovisual reference works; and a calendar of exhibits and conferences.

EDUCATIONAL MEDIA CATALOGS ON MICROFICHE. New York: Olympic Media Information, 1975.

A collection of more than 300 different software catalogs describing many kinds of media for all school levels and in all subject areas.

EDUCATOR'S PURCHASING GUIDE (EPG). Philadelphia: North American Publishing Co., 1970-- . Annual.

A comprehensive compilation of educational product information. Includes all subjects and grade levels. Lists publishers, producers, and manufacturers of educational materials, equipment, and supplies for 12,000 product categories--more than 100,000 entries in the 1975 edition.

GUIDES TO EDUCATIONAL MEDIA: FILMS, FILMSTRIPS, KINESCOPES, PHONODISCS, PHOTOTAPES, PROGRAMMED INSTRUCTION MATERIALS, SLIDES, TRANSPARENCIES, VIDEOTAPES. 3d ed. Edited by Margaret Rufsvold and Carolyn Guss. Chicago: American Library Association, 1971. 116 p. Paper.

Covers generally available catalogs, indexes, and lists. Annotated.

Includes professional media associations and periodicals.

INDEX TO INSTRUCTIONAL MEDIA CATALOGS. New York: R.R. Bowker Co., 1974. 272 p.

Contains 30,000 entries detailing thirty-eight kinds of media in 149 subject areas, preschool through high school levels. Organized into a subject media index, products/services index, and a directory of companies.

NATIONAL AUDIOVISUAL CENTER. (National Archives and Records Service, General Services Administration.) Washington, D.C. 20409.

Since July 1969 the center has operated to furnish information about most federally produced audiovisual materials, lending and renting materials placed with the center by agencies, and selling materials approved for public sale by the producing agencies. Included are films produced by the Department of Health, Education and Welfare. One of the major subject areas covered by the center is education and culture. Catalogs are available.

NICEM INDEX TO PRODUCERS AND DISTRIBUTORS 1974-75. 4th ed. Los Angeles: National Information Center for Educational Media (NICEM), 1975.

Among the most comprehensive and up-to-date lists of producers and distributors. Contains 10,000 annotated entries.

A REFERENCE GUIDE TO AUDIOVISUAL INFORMATION. Compiled by James Limbacher. Ann Arbor, Mich.: R.R. Bowker Co., 1972. 197 p.

A comprehensive source of information concerning the audiovisual field. Includes 400 listings of reference works with bibliographic information.

See also Section 2: Directories--Comprehensive.

Section 61

PHONOGRAPH RECORDS AND AUDIO TAPES

GENERAL INDEXES, GUIDES, AND CATALOGS

AMERICAN RECORD GUIDE. New York: James Lyons, 1945-- . Monthly.

Reviews phonograph records and tapes.

Association for Recorded Sound Collection. A PRELIMINARY DIRECTORY OF SOUND RECORDINGS COLLECTIONS IN THE UNITED STATES AND CANADA. New York: New York Public Library, 1967. 157 p.

Alphabetical listing (by state) with Canada listed separately at the end. Gives name of the collection, address, name of curator or archivist, general subject of the collection, and general information.

BAND RECORD GUIDE. Evanston, Ill.: Instrumentalist Co., 1969. 102 p.

An index of recorded works for band.

Blanks, Harvey. THE GOLDEN ROAD. London: Angus and Robertson, 1968. 383 p.

An elaborate handbook for the collector of recorded classical music.

Clough, Frances F., and Cuming, G.J. THE WORLD'S ENCYCLOPEDIA OF RECORDED MUSIC. London: The London Gramophone Corp., 1952. 890 p. THIRD SUPPLEMENT: 1953-1955. 1957. 564 p.

For the most part, this work and its supplements bring Darrell's 1936 work up to date (to 1955). Includes every record of permanent music issued throughout the world.

Duckles, Vincent H[arris]. "Discographies." In his MUSIC REFERENCE AND RESEARCH MATERIALS: AN ANNOTATED BIBLIOGRAPHY, 3d ed., pp. 407-26. New York: Free Press, 1974.

Contains excellent guides for locating specialized record collections, such as ethnic music, early recordings, collectors' guides, and so forth.

HARRISON RECORD AND TAPE GUIDE TO 4-CHANNEL. New York: Weiss Publishing Co., 1974.

Complete listings of all 4-channel records and tapes.

HARRISON TAPE GUIDE. New York: Weiss Publishing Co., 1955-- . Bimonthly.

A comprehensive listing of prerecorded tape in all configurations--8-track, cassettes, open reels, quadrophonic (Q8), and quadrophonic reels.

Hemming, Roy. DISCOVERING MUSIC, WHERE TO START ON RECORDS AND TAPES, THE GREAT COMPOSERS AND THEIR WORKS, TODAY'S MAJOR RECORDING ARTISTS. New York: Four Winds Press, 1974. 379 p. Photos.

A guide to the selection of music recordings (disc and tapes). Considers the opinions of fifty outstanding musicians.

Library of Congress. MUSIC AND PHONORECORDS. A cumulative list of works represented by Library of Congress printed cards.

Cumulative for 1953-57 (Totowa, N.J.: Rowman and Littlefield Co., 1958. 1,049 p.); cumulative for 1958-62 (Totowa, N.J.: Rowman and Littlefield Co., 1963. 1,094 p.); cumulative for 1963-67 (Ann Arbor, Mich.: J.W. Edwards, 1969. 858 p.); cumulative annually (Washington, D.C.: Library of Congress, 1968-- .)

LIBRARY OF CONGRESS CATALOG--MUSIC AND PHONORECORDS. Washington, D.C.: Library of Congress, 1947-- . Quarterly.

An alphabetical master list of recordings and music reproduced from Library of Congress catalog cards. Comes in three quarterly editions and a cumulative annual. A subject index is included with each issue.

LIST-O-TAPES. Los Angeles, Calif.: Trade Service Publications, 1967-- . Weekly.

A weekly updating of available tape recordings.

NICEM INDEX TO EDUCATIONAL AUDIO TAPES 1974-75. 4th ed. Los Angeles: National Information Center for Educational Media (NICEM), 1974.

Among the most comprehensive and up-to-date sources for such materials. Contains 24,000 annotated entries.

NICEM INDEX TO EDUCATIONAL RECORDS 1974-75. 4th ed. Los Angeles: National Information Center for Educational Media (NICEM), 1974.

Among the most comprehensive and up-to-date sources for such materials. Contains 22,000 annotated entries.

PHONOLOG. Los Angeles: Trade Service Publications, 1948-- . Weekly.

Weekly updating of available recordings.

SCHOLASTICS 1974-75 AUDIO-VISUAL CATALOG FOR SCHOOLS AND LIBRARIES. New York: Scholastics Audio-Visual, 1969-- . Annual.

A comprehensive catalog of records--ethnic music collections, electronic music, folk songs for children, jazz anthologies, black literature, and so forth.

SCHWANN-1 RECORD AND TAPE GUIDE. Boston: W. Schwann, 1941-- . Monthly.

A comprehensive reference guide to recorded music (disc and tapes). A standard work. Convenient to use and easily located in libraries or at dealers in recorded music. Classical music listings include dates of composer and composition, language used in vocal music, and opus or thematic index numbers. Special section for electronic music.

THE SCHWANN-2 SEMI-ANNUAL SUPPLEMENT. Boston: W. Schwann, 1964-- . Semiannual.

Lists many records not in the above. Includes international pop and folk (including American Indian), and noncurrent popular, such as band, barbershop, Hawaiian, organ, and religious.

Other useful Schwann catalogs include:

SCHWANN CHILDREN'S RECORD AND TAPE GUIDE. Boston: W. Schwann, 1965-- . Annual.

SCHWANN ARTIST ISSUE. Boston: W. Schwann, 1953-- . Irregular.

Lists classical records cross-indexed by conductors, performers, and groups.

SCHWANN COUNTRY AND WESTERN TAPE AND RECORD CATALOG. Boston: W. Schwann, 1970. 100 p.

BASIC RECORD LIBRARY. Boston: W. Schwann, 1961-- . Irregular.

BASIC RECORD LIBRARY OF JAZZ. Boston: W. Schwann, 1974. 19 p.

Thiel, Jorn. INTERNATIONAL ANTHOLOGY OF RECORDED MUSIC. Vienna, Austria: Jugend und Volk, 1971. 208 p.

Discusses and evaluates some 3,000 long-playing records produced primarily in the United States and Europe. Includes a critical survey of major series as well as individual records.

REVIEWS—RECORDS AND TAPES

Consumers Reports. CONSUMERS UNION REVIEWS CLASSICAL RECORDINGS. Indianapolis, Ind.: Bobbs-Merrill Co., 1973. 376 p.

The main reviews in this book originally appeared in CONSUMER REPORTS magazine. Includes a section entitled "Basic Discography of Classical Music."

High Fidelity Magazine. RECORDS IN REVIEW. New York: Charles Scribner's Sons, 1955-- . Annual.

Covers all new long-playing classical and semiclassical releases.

Maleady, Antoinette O., comp. RECORD AND TAPE REVIEWS INDEX--1973. Metuchen, N.J.: Scarecrow Press, 1974. 683 p.

An important and convenient guide to reviews of records and tapes. Eighteen periodicals are indexed. The entries provide ample information to identify the review source and recording, the names of performers, and something of the reviewer's opinion.

Music Library Association. NOTES. Ann Arbor, Mich.: 1943-- . Quarterly.

Each issue of this journal contains a section entitled "Index to Record Reviews." Presents a cross-section of review citations that are indexed from criticisms found in leading periodicals.

POLART INDEX TO RECORD REVIEWS (INCLUDING TAPES). Detroit: Polart, 1960-- . Annual.

Covers reviews in fourteen American periodicals, keyed to the exact issue and page, giving length of review and whether the review makes a comparison with other recordings.

RECORD RATING SERVICE. Hudson, N.H.: 1966-- . Quarterly.

Classifies the general quality of recordings of serious and jazz music on disc and tape. Includes index of magazine recording reviews.

Additional sources for record and tape reviews are the music periodicals and professional journals which carry reviews as a regular feature. Some of the most prominent of these are listed here.

HIGH FIDELITY. New York: ABC Leisure Magazines, 1951-- . Monthly.

MUSIC EDUCATORS JOURNAL. Reston, Va.: MENC, Center for Educational Association, 1914-- . 9/year.

MUSIC JOURNAL. New York: Music Journal, 1943-- . Monthly.

MUSICAL QUARTERLY. New York: G. Schirmer, 1915-- . Quarterly.

NOTES. Ann Arbor, Mich.: Music Library Association, 1943-- . Quarterly.

OPERA NEWS. New York: Metropolitan Opera Guild, 1936-- . Monthly.

STEREO REVIEW. New York: Ziff-Davis Publishing Co., 1958-- . Monthly.

SPECIAL RECORD COLLECTIONS AND LISTINGS

Abraham, Gerald, general ed. THE HISTORY OF MUSIC IN SOUND. 10 vols. New York: Oxford University Press, 1953-59. Paper.

Designed as a companion reference to the NEW OXFORD HISTORY OF MUSIC. These ten handbooks list recordings with annotations. Volume I: ANCIENT AND ORIENTAL MUSIC. Edited by Egon Wellesz. 1957. 41 p.; volume II: EARLY MEDIEVAL MUSIC UP TO 1300. Edited by Dom Anselm Hughes. 1954. 69 p.; volume III: ARS NOVA AND THE RENAISSANCE. Edited by Dom Anselm Hughes. 1953. 82 p.; volume IV: THE AGE OF HUMANISM. Edited by [Sir] J[ack].A. Westrup. 1954. 71 p.; volume V: OPERA AND CHURCH MUSIC. Edited by [Sir] J[ack]. A. Westrup. 1954. 51 p.; volume VI: THE GROWTH OF INSTRUMENTAL MUSIC. Edited by [Sir] J[ack].A. Westrup. 1954. 51 p.; volume VII: THE SYMPHONIC OUTLOOK. Edited by Egon Wellesz. 1957. 63 p.; volume VIII: THE AGE OF BEETHOVEN. Edited by Gerald Abraham. 1958. 67 p.; volume X: MODERN MUSIC. Edited by Gerald Abraham. 1959. 63 p.

Bescoby-Chambers, John. THE ARCHIVES OF SOUND. Surrey, Engl.: The Oakwood Press, 1964. 153 p.

A guide to early sound recordings of violin, piano, player piano, and orchestral works. Includes a section of composers' interpretations of their own compositions and a short history of the recording industry. Bibliography.

Briegleb, Ann. DIRECTORY OF ETHNOMUSICOLOGICAL SOUND RECORDING COLLECTIONS IN THE UNITED STATES AND CANADA. Ann Arbor, Mich.: Society for Ethnomusicology, 1971. 45 p. Paper.

A useful guide to the location of ethnomusicological recordings. Includes descriptions of technical facilities, collection content, and geographical index.

Cohn, Arthur. THE COLLECTOR'S TWENTIETH-CENTURY MUSIC IN THE WESTERN HEMISPHERE. 1961. Reprint. New York: Da Capo Press, 1972. 256 p.

Discusses the recorded music of twenty-seven contemporary composers. Covers all releases up to May 1960.

Coover, James, and Colvig, Rieborn. MEDIEVAL AND RENAISSANCE MUSIC ON LONG-PLAYING RECORDS. Detroit: Information Coordinators, 1964. 122 p. SUPPLEMENT, 1962-1971. 1973. 258 p.

Index includes microgroove recordings issued in Great Britain, France, Germany, and the United States through 1959 devoted solely or mainly to medieval and Renaissance music. Edition published in 1964 includes 1960-61 supplement.

Harris, Kenn. OPERA RECORDINGS: A CRITICAL GUIDE. New York: Drake, 1973. 328 p.

Surveys the available complete recordings of seventy-six operas with comments and the author's evaluations.

Heim, Norman, comp. MUSIC AND TAPE RECORDINGS FILED IN THE NACWPI RESEARCH LIBRARY. College Park: University of Maryland, 1972. Unpaged.

Alphabetical lists by composer of cataloged published and unpublished music and tapes in the National Association of College Wind and Percussion Instructors Research Library (about 1,000 items). Supplemental lists are issued periodically. For details see "Pedagogical Guides and Reference Books--General" in Section 48: Instrumental Music.

Hickerson, Joseph C., comp. A LIST OF AMERICAN RECORD COMPANIES

SPECIALIZING IN FOLK MUSIC. Washington, D.C.: Library of Congress, 1972. 5 p. Paper.

International Institute for Comparative Music Studies and Documentation, comp. ORIENTAL MUSIC: A SELECTED DISCOGRAPHY. Occasional Publication no. 16. New York: Foreign Area Materials Center, University of the State of New York, State Education Department, and National Council of Associations for International Studies, 1971. 100 p.

International Library of African Music. THE SOUND OF AFRICA SERIES OF LONG PLAYING RECORDS CATALOGUE. Johannesburg, South Africa: 1963. 36 p. Paper.

A listing of recorded indigenous African music. Classified by language, types of song, and music and musical instruments. A set of indexed cards is also available.

Lawless, Ray M. FOLKSINGERS AND FOLKSONGS IN AMERICA. New York: Duell, Sloan, and Pearce, 1965. 750 p. Photos.

A handbook of biography, bibliography, and discography. Comprehensive and highly useful.

Library of Congress. Music Division. Archive of American Folk Song. CHECKLIST OF RECORDED SONGS IN THE ENGLISH LANGUAGE IN THE ARCHIVE OF AMERICAN FOLK SONG TO JULY, 1940. 3 vols. Washington, D.C.: Library of Congress, 1942.

_____. FOLK MUSIC: A CATALOG OF FOLK SONGS, BALLADS, DANCES, INSTRUMENTAL PIECES, AND FOLK TALES OF THE UNITED STATES AND LATIN AMERICA ON PHONOGRAPH RECORDS. Washington, D.C.: Government Printing Office, 1965. 107 p.

A sampling of folk music, most of which was recorded in its native environment and is available for purchase from the Library of Congress.

Merriam, Alan P. AFRICAN MUSIC ON L.P.--AN ANNOTATED DISCOGRAPHY. Evanston, Ill.: Northwestern University Press, 1970. 200 p.

Morgan, Wesley K., ed. HISTORICAL ANTHOLOGY OF MUSIC IN PERFORMANCE. Carbondale: Southern Illinois University Press.

A continuing systematic recording of the Davison-Apel HISTORICAL ANTHOLOGY OF MUSIC. Includes Late Medieval Music, Fifteenth-Century and Early Sixteenth-Century Music, part 1 and part 2; Late Sixteenth-Century Music, part 2 and part 3.

New York Library Association. Children and Young Adults Services Section. RECORDS AND CASSETTES FOR YOUNG ADULTS: A SELECTED LIST. New York: New York Library Association, 1972. 52 p. Paper.

Designed as a guide for starting a young adult record or cassette collection. Entries are annotated and listed by categories.

Princeton University Phonograph Record Library.

See under New Jersey in appendix A.

SCHWANN CHILDREN'S RECORD AND TAPE GUIDE. Boston: W. Schwann, 1965-- . Annual.

Convenient source for listings of children's records--folk music, introduction to classical music listening, kiddie, and so forth. This item is generally available at libraries and record dealers.

Smart, James A. THE SOUSA BAND: A DISCOGRAPHY. Washington, D.C.: Library of Congress, 1970. 123 p.

Accounts for the total recording history of the Sousa band.

Smolian, Steven. A HANDBOOK OF FILM, THEATER, AND TELEVISION MUSIC ON RECORD, 1948-1969. New York: The Record Undertaker, 1970. 128 p.

Society for Ethnomusicology, Committee on Ethnomusicology and Music Education. "Music in World Cultures: A Bibliography and Discography." MUSIC EDUCATORS JOURNAL 59 (October 1972): 134-35.

Stahl, Dorothy. A SELECTED DISCOGRAPHY OF SOLO SONG: A CUMULATION THROUGH 1971. Detroit Studies in Music Bibliography no. 24. Detroit: Information Coordinators, 1972. 137 p.

Arranged alphabetically by composer. Companion volume to earlier edition, A SELECTED DISCOGRAPHY OF SOLO SONG (Detroit Studies in Music Bibliography no. 13. Detroit: Information Coordinators, 1968). This volume cumulates, adding new entries and deleting those recordings no longer available.

Sublette, Ned, comp. A DISCOGRAPHY OF HISPANIC MUSIC IN THE FINE ART LIBRARY OF THE UNIVERSITY OF NEW MEXICO. Albuquerque: University of New Mexico, Fine Arts Library, 1973. 110 p.

UNESCO. AN ANTHOLOGY OF AFRICAN MUSIC. Prepared by the International Institute for Comparative Music Studies and Documentation. Wilhelmshöhe, Germany: Bärenreiter. 10 discs.

Provides wide coverage of the ancient musical cultures of Africa.

______. A MUSICAL ANTHOLOGY OF THE ORIENT. Prepared by the International Institute for Comparative Music Studies and Documentation. Wilhelmshöhe, Germany: Bärenreiter. 26 discs.

Provides wide coverage of the ancient musical cultures of the Near and Far East.

______. UNESCO ETHNIC MUSIC RECORDS. New York: Unipub, 1974. Pamphlet.

Includes a number of musical anthologies with commentaries edited by International Institute for Comparative Music Studies and Documentation.

UNESCO. Archives of Recorded Sound. A CATALOGUE OF RECORDED CLASSICAL AND TRADITIONAL INDIAN MUSIC. Paris: 1952. 235 p.

POPULAR MUSIC, JAZZ, AND ROCK RECORDINGS

Allen, Walter C. STUDIES IN JAZZ DISCOGRAPHY I. New Brunswick, N.J.: Institute of Jazz Studies, Rutgers University, 1971. 112 p.

Contains the edited proceedings of the first two annual conferences on discographical research in 1968 and 1969 and also the special conference on preservation and extension of the jazz heritage in 1969.

Delaunay, Charles. NEW HOT DISCOGRAPHY: THE STANDARD DICTIONARY OF RECORDED JAZZ. Edited by Walter E. Schaap and George Avakian. New York: Criterion, 1948. 608 p.

Harris, Rex, and Rust, Brian. RECORDED JAZZ. Hammondsville, Middlesex: Penguin Books, 1958. 256 p.

Includes biographical information and critical comments.

Jasen, David A. RECORDED RAGTIME 1897-1958. New York: Archon Books, 1973. 155 p.

Identifies all first issues of commercially released 78 rpm flat disc ragtime recordings throughout the world. Focus is on composition and the composer. Recording dates and composer data are given. Includes composer and performer indexes and bibliography.

Jepsen, J.G. JAZZ RECORDS: A DISCOGRAPHY. Holte, Denmark: Knudsen, 1966-- . Irregular.

Deals with recorded jazz from 1942 to 1969.

Langridge, Derek. YOUR JAZZ COLLECTION. Hamden, Conn.: Shoe String Press, 1970. 162 p.

Leadbitter, Mike, and Slaven, Neil. BLUES RECORDS, JANUARY 1943 TO DECEMBER 1966. London: Hanover Books, 1968. 381 p.

Includes artist and/or ensemble with discographies, instrumentation, and dates of recordings.

McCarthy, Albert, et al. JAZZ ON RECORD: A CRITICAL GUIDE TO THE FIRST 50 YEARS. New York: Oak Publications, 1968. 416 p.

A reference guide to recorded works of important artists in this field. Includes biographical data and some critical annotations.

Rohde, H. Kandy, ed. THE GOLD OF ROCK AND ROLL, 1955-1967. New York: Arbor House, 1970. 352 p.

Lists the ten most popular rock and roll recordings for each week during this period. Cataloged by title and artist.

Rust, Brian. JAZZ RECORDS, 1897-1942. 2 vols. London: Storyville Publications, 1970.

Alphabetical listing of performers and their recordings. Covers only American and British musicians.

Seidel, Richard, ed. THE BASIC RECORD LIBRARY OF JAZZ. Boston: W. Schwann, 1974. 20 p. Paper.

Contains listing of more than 250 jazz recordings with annotations. One section lists recommended jazz books and major jazz periodicals.

Williams, Martin. THE SMITHSONIAN COLLECTION OF CLASSIC JAZZ. Washington, D.C.: Smithsonian Institution; New York: W.W. Norton and Co., 1973.

UNIQUE PRACTICE AIDS

ACCOMPANIMENTS UNLIMITED, INC.

Taped piano accompaniments for certain instrumental solo works. List of works available from the producer--Accompaniments Unlimited, P.O. Box 5109, Grosse Pointe Branch, Mich. 48236.

MUSIC MINUS ONE.

Recorded chamber music with one instrument part missing, thus permitting the student to supply the needed part. List of recordings are available from the producer--Music Minus One, 43 West 61st Street, New York, N.Y. 10023.

COMPANIES SPECIALIZING IN RECORDS FOR MUSIC EDUCATION—PARTIAL LIST

NOTE: Catalogs or descriptive literature available on request.

BOWMAR RECORDS, INC., 622 Rodier Drive, Glendale, Calif. 91201.

CAPITOL RECORDS, EDUCATIONAL DEPARTMENT, Capitol Tower, 1750 North Vine Street, Hollywood, Calif. 90028.

COLUMBIA RECORDS, INC., Educational Department, 799 Seventh Avenue, New York, N.Y. 10019.

DECCA RECORDS (Division of MCA Inc.), 445 Park Avenue, New York, N.Y. 10007.

EDUCATIONAL RECORDS SALES, 157 Chambers Street, New York, N.Y. 10036.

FOLKWAYS/SCHOLASTIC RECORDS, 50 West 44th Street, New York, N.Y. 10036.

THE FRANSON CORPORATION, Institutional Trade Division, 100 Sixth Avenue, New York, N.Y. 10013.

KEYBOARD JR. PUBLICATIONS, INC., 1346 Chapel Street, New Haven, Conn. 06511.

MOTIVATION RECORDS (Division of Argosy Music Corporation), Mamaroneck, N.Y. 10543.

RCA VICTOR RECORD DIVISION, Educational Department, 155 East 24th Street, New York, N.Y. 10010.

RHYTHM-TIME RECORDS, P.O. Box 1106, Santa Barbara, Calif. 93102.

VOX PRODUCTIONS, INC., 211 East 43d Street, New York, N.Y. 10017.

Section 62

GUIDES TO FILMS AND FILMSTRIPS (GENERAL)

Audio-Visual Associates. INTERNATIONAL INDEX TO MULTI-MEDIA INFORMATION. Pasadena, Calif.: 1970-- . Quarterly.

An index to critical reviews on educational films.

Braun, Susan. CATALOG OF DANCE FILMS. New York: Dance Films Association, 1974. Unpaged.

Clark, Joan, ed. DIRECTORY OF FILM LIBRARIES IN NORTH AMERICA. New York: Film Library Information Council, 1971-- . Biennial.

EDUCATORS GUIDE TO FREE FILMS. Randolph, Wis.: Educators Progress Service, 1941-- . Annual.

Lists 4,371 educational, informational, and entertainment free-for-loan films.

EFLA EVALUATION CARDS. New York: Educational Film Library Association, 1946-- . Bimonthly.

Bimonthly evaluations of nontheatrical films in ready-to-file card catalog form. Since 1974 the film evaluations have been issued monthly in sheet form. Previously issued evaluations are available in book form as follows: FILM EVALUATION GUIDE: 1945-1965. 1965. 528 p.; SUPPLEMENT ONE: 1965-67. 1968. 157 p.; SUPPLEMENT TWO: 1967-71. 1972. 131 p.

International Music Centre, Vienna. FILMS FOR MUSIC EDUCATION AND OPERA FILMS. Paris: UNESCO, 1962. 114 p.

An international catalog of music films. The films are categorized with brief descriptions and indexed by countries and by composers.

NATIONAL AUDIO-VISUAL CENTER. See Section 60: Comprehensive Guides to Audiovisual Materials and Services.

NICEM INDEX TO 8MM MOTION CARTRIDGES 1974-75. 4th ed. Los Angeles: National Information Center for Educational Media (NICEM), 1974. 655 p.

Among the most comprehensive and up-to-date sources for such materials. Contains 22,000 annotated entries.

NICEM INDEX TO 16MM EDUCATIONAL FILMS 1974-75. 5th ed. 3 vols. Los Angeles: National Information Center for Educational Media (NICEM), 1975.

Among the most comprehensive and up-to-date sources for educational films. Contains 90,000 annotated entries.

NICEM INDEX TO 35MM FILMSTRIPS 1974-75. 5th ed. 2 vols. Los Angeles: National Information Center for Educational Media (NICEM), 1975.

Among the most comprehensive and up-to-date sources for such materials. Contains 52,000 annotated entries.

Shetler, Donald J. FILM GUIDE FOR MUSIC EDUCATORS. 2d ed. Washington, D.C.: Music Educators National Conference, 1968. 96 p. Paper.

An annotated listing of music films and filmstrips, kindergarten through graduate level. Describes content, grade level, and possible use. Index and bibliography.

UNESCO. CATALOGUE: TEN YEARS OF FILMS ON BALLET AND CLASSICAL DANCE. 1956-1965. Paris: 1968. 105 p.

A representative listing of films on ballet, classical, and modern dance. Covers the important stylistic movements within these three fields. Does not include videotapes.

Wisconsin Library Association. FILMS IN CHILDREN'S PROGRAMS. Madison, Wis.: 1972. 39 p.

A bibliography.

Section 63

COMPANIES OR SERVICES SPECIALIZING IN MUSIC EDUCATION FILMS

NOTE: The catalogs of film producers are highly useful for descriptions of film content. Normally catalogs and descriptive literature are available upon request. Previews are recommended.

ACI PRODUCTIONS, 16 West 46th Street, New York, N.Y. 10036.

AVIS FILMS, 2408 West Olice Avenue, Burbank, Calif. 91506.

BAILEY-FILM ASSOCIATES INC., 11559 Santa Monica Boulevard, Los Angeles, Calif. 90025.

BRANDON FILMS, 221 West 57th Street, New York, N.Y. 10019.

CAPITAL FILM SERVICE, 1001 Terminal Road, Lansing, Mich. 48906.

COLUMBIA BROADCASTING SYSTEM, 485 Madison Avenue, New York, N.Y. 10022.

CONTEMPORARY FILMS (Division of McGraw-Hill Book Co.), 330 West 42d Street, New York, N.Y. 10036.

CORONET FILMS, 65 East South Water Street, Coronet Building, Chicago, Ill. 60601.

WALT DISNEY PRODUCTIONS, Educational Film Division, 350 South Buena Vista Avenue, Burbank, Calif. 91503.

ENCYCLOPEDIA BRITANNICA EDUCATIONAL CORPORATION, 425 North Michigan Avenue, Chicago, Ill. 60611.

FILM ASSOCIATES, 11559 Santa Monica Boulevard, Los Angeles, Calif. 90025.

HOFFBERG PRODUCTIONS, INC., 321 West 44th Street, New York, N.Y. 10036.

Producers of Music Education Films

INDIANA UNIVERSITY, Audio-Visual Center, Bloomington, Ind. 47401.

INTERNATIONAL FILM BUREAU, 332 South Michigan Avenue, Chicago, Ill. 60604.

MCGRAW-HILL TEXT FILMS, 330 West 42d Street, New York, N.Y. 10018.

MODERN LEARNING AIDS, 1168 Commonwealth Avenue, Boston, Mass. 02134.

NATIONAL FILM BOARD OF CANADA, 680 Fifth Avenue, New York, N.Y. 10019.

NET FILM SERVICE INDIANA UNIVERSITY, Audio-Visual Center, Bloomington, Ind. 47401.

STERLING EDUCATIONAL FILMS, P.O. Box 8497, Universal City, Los Angeles, Calif. 90038.

STORYBOARD INC., 165 East 72d Street, New York, N.Y. 10021.

JOHN SUTHERLAND EDUCATIONAL FILMS, 201 North Occidental Boulevard, Los Angeles, Calif. 90026.

TEACHING FILM CUSTODIANS, 25 West 43d Street, New York, N.Y. 10036.

U.S. NATIONAL AUDIO-VISUAL CENTER, National Archives and Records Service, Washington, D.C. 20409.

Section 64
8mm CARTRIDGE FILM PRODUCERS AND DISTRIBUTORS

NOTE: Catalogs and descriptive literature available on request.

AVIS FILMS, 2408 West Olive Avenue, Burbank, Calif. 91506.

BAILEY FILM ASSOCIATES, 11559 Santa Monica Boulevard, Los Angeles, Calif. 90025.

EALING CORPORATION, 2225 Massachusetts Avenue, Cambridge, Mass. 02140.

INTERNATIONAL COMMUNICATION FILMS, 1371 Reynolds Avenue, Santa Ana, Calif. 92705.

UNIVERSAL EDUCATION AND VISUAL ARTS, 221 Park Avenue South, New York, N.Y. 10003.

Section 65

FILMSTRIP PRODUCERS AND DISTRIBUTORS

NOTE: Catalogs and descriptive literature available on request.

STANLEY BOWMAR CO., INC., 4 Broadway, Valhalla, N.Y. 10595.

CURRICULUM MATERIALS CORP., 1319 Vine Street, Philadelphia, Pa. 19100.

ENCYCLOPEDIA BRITANNICA EDUCATIONAL CORPORATION, 425 North Michigan Avenue, Chicago, Ill. 60611.

EYE GATE HOUSE, INC., 146-01 Archer Avenue, Jamaica, N.Y. 11435.

LEARNING ARTS, P.O. Box 917, Wichita, Kans. 67201.

WARREN SCHLOAT PRODUCTIONS, INC., Pleasantville, N.Y. 10570.

SOCIETY FOR VISUAL EDUCATION INC., 1345 Diversey Parkway, Chicago, Ill. 60614.

Section 66

VIDEO TAPES

NICEM INDEX TO EDUCATIONAL VIDEO TAPES 1974-75. 4th ed. Los Angeles: National Information Center for Education Media (NICEM), 1974. 380 p.

Among the most comprehensive and up-to-date sources for such materials. Contains 12,000 annotated entries.

OTHER SOURCES:

While there are scattered published lists of video tapes suitable for use in music education, one will do well to consult recent catalogs of producers and distributors of video tapes. Such companies can readily be located in the following NICEM index:

NICEM INDEX TO PRODUCERS AND DISTRIBUTORS 1974-75. 4th ed. Los Angeles: National Information Center for Educational Media (NICEM), 1975.

Contains 10,000 entries.

Section 67

SLIDES

NICEM INDEX TO EDUCATIONAL SLIDES 1974-75. 2d ed. Los Angeles: National Information Center for Educational Media (NICEM), 1974. 653 p.

Among the most comprehensive and up-to-date sources for such materials. Contains 18,000 annotated entries.

Section 68
OVERHEAD TRANSPARENCIES

INDEX

NICEM INDEX TO EDUCATIONAL OVERHEAD TRANSPARENCIES 1974-75. 4th ed. 2 vols. Los Angeles, Calif.: National Information Center for Educational Media (NICEM), 1974.

Among the most comprehensive and up-to-date sources for such materials. Contains 50,000 annotated entries.

PRODUCERS AND DISTRIBUTORS

NOTE: Catalogs and descriptive literature available on request.

STANLEY BOWMAR CO., INC., Valhalla, N.Y. 10595.

EDUCATIONAL AUDIO-VISUAL, 29 Marble Avenue, Pleasantville, N.Y. 10570.

EDUCATIONAL READING SERVICE, East 64 Midland Avenue, Paramus, N.J. 07652.

LEARNING ARTS, P.O. Box 917, Wichita, Kans. 67201.

TWEEDY TRANSPARENCIES, 208 Hollywood Boulevard, East Orange, N.J. 07018.

UNITED TRANSPARENCIES, INC., P.O. Box 688, Binghamton, N.Y. 13902.

VISUAL PRODUCTS DIVISION, 3M Center, Box 3344, St. Paul, Minn. 55101.

Section 69

SOURCES FOR EASY-TO-PLAY INSTRUMENTS AND MUSIC TEACHING AIDS —PARTIAL LIST

NOTE: Catalogs and descriptive literature are available on request.

CHILDREN'S MUSIC CENTER, 5373 West Pico Boulevard, Los Angeles, Calif. 90019.

EDUCATIONAL MUSIC BUREAU, INC., 434 South Wabash Avenue, Chicago, Ill. 60605.

GAMBLE HINGED MUSIC CO., INC., 312 South Wabash Avenue, Chicago, Ill. 60604.

HARGAIL MUSIC PRESS, 157 West 57th Street, New York, N.Y. 10019.

Recorders and recorder music.

KITCHING EDUCATIONAL (Division of Ludwig Drum Co.), 1728 North Damen Avenue, Chicago, Ill. 60647.

LYONS, 688 Industrial Drive, Elmhurst, Ill. 60126.

MAGNAMUSIC-BATON, INC., 6394 Delmar Boulevard, St. Louis, Mo. 63130.

Orff instruments and related materials.

NATIONAL AUTOHARP SALES COMPANY, P.O. Box 1120, University Station, Des Moines, Iowa 50311.

PERIPOLE INC., 51-17 Rockaway Beach Boulevard, Far Rockaway, Long Island, N.Y. 11691.

RHYTHM-BAND, INC., P.O. Box 126, Fort Worth, Tex. 76101.

TARG AND DINNER INC., 4100 West 40th Street, Chicago, Ill. 60632.

VIKING COMPANY, 113 South Edgemont Street, Los Angeles, Calif. 90004.

Distributors of Tone Educator Bells and Swiss Melodé Bells.

Section 70

MUSICAL INSTRUMENT MANUFACTURERS

THE AEOLIAN CORP., Washington and Commercial Streets, East Rochester, N.Y. 14445.

AEOLIAN-SKINNER ORGAN CO., INC., Pacella Park Drive, Randolph, Mass. 02368.

W.T. ARMSTRONG CO. (exclusive distributor: Norlin Music Co.), 7373 North Cicero Avenue, Lincolnwood, Ill. 60646.

ARTLEY, INC. (distributed by C.G. Conn), Nogales, Ariz. 85621. Marketing Offices: 616 Enterprise Drive, Oak Brook, Ill. 60521.

VINCENT BACH (division of the Magnavox Co.), Box 310, Elkhart, Ind. 46514.

BALDWIN PIANO & ORGAN CO., 1801 Gilbert Avenue, Cincinnati, Ohio 45202.

BENGE TRUMPETS, 1122 West Burbank Boulevard, Burbank, Calif. 91502.

E.K. BLESSING CO., 1301 West Beardsley Avenue, Elkhart, Ind. 46514.

BUESCHER BAND INSTRUMENTS (division of the Magnavox Co.), Box 310, Elkhart, Ind. 64514.

THE BUFFET-CRAMPON (distributed exclusively by Norlin Music Co.), 7373 North Cicero Avenue, Lincolnwood, Ill. 60646.

CHICKERING & SONS (division of Aeolian American Corp.), Washington & Commercial Streets, East Rochester, N.Y. 14445.

C.G. CONN, LTD., 616 Enterprise Drive, Oak Brook, Ill. 60521.

CUNDY-BETTONEY CO., Bradlee & Madison Streets, Boston, Mass. 02136.

J.C. DEAGAN, INC., 1770 West Berteau Avenue, Chicago, Ill. 60613.

THE ESTEY MUSICAL INSTRUMENT CORP., Harmony, Pa. 16037.

EVERETT PIANO CO., 900 Indiana Avenue, South Haven, Mich. 49090.

FRANK'S DRUM SHOP, 226 South Wabash Avenue, Chicago, Ill. 60604.

GEMEINHARDT CORP., 3200 South Nappanee, P.O. Box 788, Elkhart, Ind. 46514.

THE GETZEN CO., INC., 211 West Centralia Avenue, Elkhorn, Wis. 53121.

GIARDINELLI BAND INSTRUMENT CO., 1725 Broadway (55th Street), New York, N.Y. 10019.

GIBSON GUITARS (division of Norlin Music Co.), 7373 North Cicero Avenue, Lincolnwood, Ill. 60646.

GOODMAN DRUM CO., 141 Kneeland Avenue, Yonkers, N.Y. 10705.

GOYA GUITARS, INC., 53 West 23d Street, New York, N.Y. 10010.

FRED GRETSCH CO., 60 Broadway, Brooklyn, N.Y. 11211.

HAMMOND CORP., 4200 West Diversey Avenue, Chicago, Ill. 60639.

HARGAIL MUSIC, INC., 28 West 38th Street, New York, N.Y. 10018.

WM. S. HAYNES CO., 12 Piedmont Street, Boston, Mass. 02116.

M. HOHNER, INC., Andrews Road, P.O. Box 130, Hicksville, N.Y. 11802.

HOLTON (division of G. Leblanc Corp.), P.O. Box 459, Kenosha, Wis. 53141.

JENKINS MUSIC CO. (Jenco Musical Products), 1217 Walnut Street, Kansas City, Mo. 64142.

KAY MUSICAL INSTRUMENT CO., 2201 West Arthur Avenue, Elk Grove Village, Ill. 60007.

KIMBALL PIANO & ORGAN CO. (division of Jasper Corp.), Fifteenth and Cherry Streets, Jasper, Ind. 47546.

KING MUSICAL INSTRUMENTS, 33999 Curtis Boulevard, Eastlake, Ohio 44094.

KNABE (division of Aeolian Corp.), Washington and Commercial Streets, East Rochester, N.Y. 14445.

KOHLERT BAND INSTRUMENTS (W. German), Kohlert, Inc., Sole Importers, 14 Bixley Heath, Lynbrook, N.Y. 11563.

WILLIAM KRATT CO., 988 Johnson Place, Union, N.J. 07083.

LARILEE OBOE CO., 1700 Edwardsburg Road, Elkhart, Ind. 46514.

LATIN PERCUSSION, Box 88, Palisades Park, N.J. 07650.

G. LEBLANC CORP., 7019 30th Avenue, Kenosha, Wis. 53141.

LEEDY DRUM CO., 6633 North Milwaukee Avenue, Chicago, Ill. 60648.

LESHER WOODWIND CO., 1306 West Bristol Street, Elkhart, Ind. 46514.

WILLIAM LEWIS AND SON, 7373 North Cicero Avenue, Lincolnwood, Ill. 60646.

LINTON MFG. CO., 919 North Nappanee, Elkhart, Ind. 46514.

F. LOREE OF PARIS, 36-11 33d Street, Long Island City, N.Y. 11106.

LOWREY ORGAN CO. (CMI) (division of Norlin Music Co.), 7373 North Cicero Avenue, Lincolnwood, Ill. 60646.

LUDWIG INDUSTRIES, 1728 North Damen Avenue, Chicago, Ill. 60647.

LYON & HEALY, 243 South Wabash Avenue, Chicago, Ill. 60604.

MAGNUS ORGAN CORP., 1600 Edgar Road, Route 1, Linden, N.J. 07036.

MIRAFONE CORP., 8484 San Fernando Road, P.O. Box 909, Sun Valley, Calif. 91352.

MOENNING MUSIC CO. (importer of Gebrueder Moenning [German] instruments), 9427 East Las Tunas Drive, Temple City, Calif. 91780.

M.P. MOLLER, Church Organs, Hagerstown, Md. 21740.

MOOG (division of Norlin Music Co.), 7373 North Cicero Avenue, Lincolnwood, Ill. 60646.

MUSSER MARIMBAS, 505 East Shawmut Avenue, LaGrange, Ill. 60525.

NEUPERT HARPSICHORDS, c/o Magnamusic Distributors, Sharon, Conn. 06069.

F.E. OLDS & SONS, INC. (division of Norlin Music), 7373 North Cicero Avenue, Chicago, Ill. 60646.

PENZEL, MUELLER & CO., INC., 36-11 33d Street, Long Island City, N.Y. 11106.

POWELL FLUTES, 295 Huntington Street, Boston, Mass. 02115.

F.A. REYNOLDS (exclusive distributor: Norlin Music Co.), 7373 North Cicero Avenue, Lincolnwood, Ill. 60646.

ROGERS DRUMS (CBS), 1300 East Valencia Avenue, Fullerton, Calif. 92631.

SASSMAN HARPSICHORDS, Gregoire Harpsichord Shop, Charlemont, Mass. 01339.

SCHERL & ROTH, INC., 616 Enterprise Drive, Oak Brook, Ill. 60521.

SCHULMERICH CARILLONS, INC., 1809 Carillon Hill, Sellersville, Pa. 18960.

H. & A. SELMER INC. (division of the Magnavox Co.), Box 310, Elkhart, Ind. 46514.

Exclusive distributor in the United States for Besson automatic compensating harmony brasses, Premier percussion products, Symmetricut and Rico reeds, and Shastock mutes.

In addition to Selmer instruments, Selmer manufactures Vincent Bach brasses, Signet and Bundy woodwinds and brasses, and Buescher band instruments.

SLINGERLAND DRUM CO., 6633 North Milwaukee Avenue, Niles, Ill. 60648.

SOHMER & CO., INC., 31 West 57th Street, New York, N.Y. 10019.

STEINWAY & SONS, Steinway Place, Long Island City, N.Y. 11105.

STORY & CLARK PIANO CORP. (division of Norlin Music), 7373 North Cicero Avenue, Lincolnwood, Ill. 60646.

THOMAS ORGAN CO., Vox and Thomas Organs, 8345 Hayvenhurst, Sepulveda, Calif. 91343.

THE WURLITZER CO., 1700 Pleasant Street, De Kalb, Ill. 60115.

YAMAHA INTERNATIONAL CORP., 6600 Orangethorpe, Buena Park, Calif. 90054.

YORK MUSICAL INSTRUMENT CO., South 14 Bixley Heath, Lynbrook, N.Y. 11563.

AVEDIS ZILDJIAN CO., P.O. Box 198, Accord, Mass. 02018.

ZUCKERMANN HARPSICHORDS, INC., 115 Christopher Street, New York, N.Y. 10014.

Section 71

AUDIOVISUAL EQUIPMENT

THE AUDIO-VISUAL EQUIPMENT DIRECTORY, 1976-77. 22d ed. Fairfax, Va.: National Audio-Visual Association, 1976. 492 p. Photos.

An extensive listing of audiovisual equipment, complete with ordering information. Includes photos, specifications, manufacturer, and prices. Also provides helpful charts for screen size, film and tape running times, and numerous accessory items with their sources.

Also see Section 60: Comprehensive Guides to Audiovisual Materials and Services.

Section 72

PLATFORMS, SHELLS, STORAGE AND SOUND MODULES

NOTE: Catalogs and descriptive literature available on request.

HUMES & BERG MFG. CO., INC., 4801 Railroad Avenue, East Chicago, Ind. 46312.

Instrument lockers, risers, chairs, etc.

MIDWEST FOLDING PRODUCTS, 1414 South Western Avenue, Chicago, Ill. 60608.

Risers and platforms.

MITCHELL MFG. CO., 2740 South 34th Street, Milwaukee, Wis. 53246.

Risers and platforms.

S & H MFG. CO., 316 West Summit Street, Normal, Ill. 61761.

General music room equipment.

WALLACH & ASSOCIATES, INC., 5701 Euclid Avenue, Cleveland, Ohio 44103.

Storage and audiovisual cabinets of many kinds.

WENGER CORP., 575 Park Drive, Owatonna, Minn. 55060.

Sound modules, risers, etc.

Section 73
NONPRINT MEDIA—JOURNALS

AUDIO, North American Publishing Co., 401 North Broad Street, Philadelphia, Pa. 19130. Monthly.

AUDIO ENGINEERING SOCIETY JOURNAL, Room 929, 60 East 42d Street, New York, N.Y. 10017. Monthly.

AUDIOVISUAL INSTRUCTION, Association for Educational Communications and Technology, 1201 Sixteenth Street, N.W., Washington, D.C. 20036. 10/year.

EDUCATIONAL AND INDUSTRIAL TELEVISION, C.S. Tepfer Publishing Co., 607 Main Street, Ridgefield, Conn. 06877. Monthly.

EDUCATIONAL TECHNOLOGY, 140 Sylvan Avenue, Englewood Cliffs, N.J. 07632. Monthly.

HIGH FIDELITY/MUSICAL AMERICA, 165 West 46th Street, New York, N.Y. Monthly.

MEDIA AND METHODS, North American Publishing Co., 401 North Broad Street, Philadelphia, Pa. 19130. 9/year.

STEREO REVIEW, Ziff-Davis Publishing Co., One Park Avenue, New York, N.Y. 10016. Monthly.

Section 74

NONPRINT MEDIA—ASSOCIATIONS

Association for Educational Communications and Technology (AECT) (a department of the National Education Association), 1201 Sixteenth Street, N.W., Washington, D.C. 20036.

Publications: AUDIOVISUAL INSTRUCTION. 10/year.

Newsletter. Monthly.

AV COMMUNICATION REVIEW. Quarterly.

Membership directory. Annual.

Division of Education Technology, Bureau of Libraries and Educational Technology, U.S. Office of Education, 400 Maryland Avenue, S.W., Washington, D.C. 20202.

Educational Broadcasting Corporation, 356 West 58th Street, New York, N.Y. 10019.

Educational Film Library Association (EFLA), 17 West Sixtieth Street, New York, N.Y. 10023.

Publications: EVALUATIONS. 10/year.

SIGHTLINES. Quarterly.

ERIC Clearinghouse on Educational Media and Technology, Institute for Communication Research, Stanford, Calif. 94305.

Publication: Newsletter.

National Association of Educational Broadcasters, 1346 Connecticut Avenue, N.W., Washington, D.C. 20036.

Publications: EDUCATIONAL TELECOMMUNICATIONS REVIEW. Bimonthly.

Newsletter. Biweekly.

DIRECTORY AND YEARBOOK OF EDUCATIONAL BROADCASTING. Annual.

National Audio-Visual Association, 3150 Spring Street, Fairfax, Va. 22030.

Publications: NAVA NEWS. Semimonthly.

AUDIO-VISUAL EQUIPMENT DIRECTORY. Annual.

National Center for Audiotape, University of Colorado, Stadium Building, Boulder, Colo. 80309.

Publication: Catalog.

National Council on Jewish Audio-Visual Materials, 114 Fifth Avenue, New York, N.Y. 10011.

Publication: JEWISH AUDIO-VISUAL REVIEW. Annual.

National Education Association, 1201 Sixteenth Street, N.W., Washington, D.C. 20036.

Publications: REPORTER. 8/year.

TODAY'S EDUCATION. Quarterly.

Handbook. Annual.

Systems for Learning by Application of Technology to Education, P.O. Box 456, Westminster, Calif. 92683.

Publication: DAIRS AND SYSTEMS FOR INSTRUCTION NEWSLETTER.

APPENDIXES

Appendix A

SUPPLEMENTAL LISTING OF HOLDINGS IN CERTAIN LIBRARIES AS REVEALED IN A RECENT SURVEY

In the process of gathering information for this book a questionnaire was sent to a large number of libraries known to have music and music education holdings of considerable importance. These libraries were invited to describe their music collections as they saw fit. The responses received were summarized. While the coverage is far from complete, it does provide a considerable amount of information not previously available. The libraries are listed by state.

ARIZONA

THE UNIVERSITY OF ARIZONA, Music Collection, University Library, Tucson, Ariz. 85721

Contains special collections of regional material--including items (music and records) relating to Indians and Spanish-American music. A historical music textbook collection is being accumulated.

ARKANSAS

UNIVERSITY OF ARKANSAS, Fine Arts Library, Fayetteville, Ark. 72701

1. William Grant Still--scores on microfilm.

2. Collection of folk songs (vocal and instrumental) indigenous to the area and recorded by local performers.

CALIFORNIA

UNIVERSITY OF CALIFORNIA, BERKELEY, Music Library, Berkeley, Calif. 94720

A collection designed to support instruction and research in music history and musical composition. Outstanding collection of reference books in the music field, and an abundance of primary source materials for research, particularly in the fields of opera history, early instrumental music, and music theory. Included in the collection are the music reference libraries of the late Manfred Bukofszer and Alfred Einstein; also included are archives related to the life and works of Ernest Bloch, Alfred Hertz, and Albert Elkus. Important research resources are the Sigmund Romberg and the Harris D.H. Connick collections of opera scores. The Alfred Cortot Library, insofar as it pertains to opera, is also at Berkeley. Opera libretti are represented by a collection of some 5,000 items dating from 1600 to the early twentieth century. The Music Library holds some 3,000 manuscripts of early music, the largest body of which is a group of eighteenth-century string music by Giuseppe Tartini and his school at Padua. An important special collection is the Salz Collection of fine violins, violas, and bows, the gift of Ansley Salz of San Francisco.

UNIVERSITY OF CALIFORNIA, LOS ANGELES, Music Library, Schoenberg Hall, Los Angeles, Calif. 90024

1. Ernst Toch Archive--includes holographs, printed scores, recordings, correspondence, memorabilia.

2. Rudolf Friml Library of Music--holograph scores and sketches, recordings.

3. Alfred Newman Collection--film score recordings.

4. Meredith Willson Library, Stanley Ring Collection--popular American sheet music, 1850-present.

5. Orff-Schulwerk Collection.

6. Holograph film scores of Henry Mancini and Alex North.

7. Seventeenth-eighteenth-century Dutch song and psalm books.

8. Japanese contemporary music.

WILLIAM ANDREWS CLARK MEMORIAL LIBRARY, University of California, Los Angeles, 2520 Cimarron Street, Los Angeles, Calif. 90018

English music, 1640-1750 (manuscripts, early editions, especially Purcell, Handel); ballad opera, 1728-1810 (manuscripts, early editions, librettos).

JOHN EDWARDS MEMORIAL FOUNDATION, Folklore and Mythology Center, University of California, Los Angeles, Los Angeles, Calif. 90024

Country music (white country music from 1920s to the present); golden age of the American hillbilly; blues.

INSTITUTE OF ETHNOMUSICOLOGY ARCHIVE, Schoenberg Hall, University of California, Los Angeles, Los Angeles, Calif. 90024

Ethnomusicology (worldwide, with emphasis on the Orient, Southeast Asia, Africa, and the Balkans). Includes slides, tapes, discs, photographs, reprints, microfilm, motion picture films. Extensive collection of Oriental, Southeast Asian, African, Mexican, and Latin American instruments.

UNIVERSITY RESEARCH LIBRARY, Department of Special Collections, University of California, Los Angeles, Los Angeles, Calif. 90024

1. George Pullan Jackson Collection--nineteenth-century American hymnbooks.

2. Joseph C. Stone Collection--early American psalm books.

3. Lionel Barrymore Music Collection--manuscripts of his own works.

4. American, Irish, and English ballads (mostly texts).

5. Seventeenth-nineteenth-century dance.

6. American folk song (about 1,000 volumes of sheet music).

UNIVERSITY OF SOUTHERN CALIFORNIA, School of Music Library, Los Angeles, Calif. 90007

Ralph E. Rush Memorial Library for Research in Music Education (in progress).

FRANK V. DE BELLIS COLLECTION OF THE CALIFORNIA STATE UNIVERSITY AND COLLEGES, San Francisco State University, 1630 Holloway Avenue, San Francisco, Calif. 94132

The collection is devoted entirely to Italian subjects, authors, and composers. Holdings include about 5,000 titles of printed music (sixteenth-twentieth century), 500 pieces of manuscripts music (mostly eighteenth century), about 20,000 recordings (cylinder, acoustic, 78 rpm, 33 1/3 rpm), and about 1,000 volumes of sixteenth-twentieth-century editions of music literature.

SAN FRANCISCO CONSERVATORY OF MUSIC, 1201 Ortega Street, San Francisco, Calif. 94122

Some manuscripts and first editions of works of American composers, particularly Californian; materials pertaining to Ernest Bloch; ethnomusicology.

CONNECTICUT

YALE COLLECTION OF HISTORICAL SOUND RECORDINGS, Room 226, Sterling Memorial Library, New Haven, Conn. 06520

This collection, which includes the Collection of the Literature of the American Musical Theatre, contains about 60,000 recordings of musical and theatrical performances, literary readings, and political oratory, as well as extensive holdings of supplementary materials such as books, catalogs, and periodicals. Special holdings include the Witten Collection of early vocal recordings; the Capes-Openhym Collection of piano recordings; the Quincy Porter Collection of recordings; a large bequest of music, recordings, and other materials from the late Cole Porter; an extensive collection of materials donated by E.Y. Harburg; and a collection of recordings of the music of Charles E. Ives.

YALE UNIVERSITY COLLECTION OF MUSICAL INSTRUMENTS, 15 Hillhouse Avenue, New Haven, Conn. 06520

This major collection of instruments was founded in 1900 when Morris Steinert presented the major portion of his collection to the university. Around this nucleus of keyboard instruments the collection grew gradually until 1962 when the Belle Skinner Collection of Musical Instruments came to Yale. In 1962 the Emil Herrmann Collection of String Instruments was presented to the university. This collection documents the history of violin making, containing many examples by famous luthiers. In 1972 the major portion of the Albert Steinert Collection came on long-term loan to Yale from the Long Island School of Design. This collection, particularly rich in keyboard instruments, makes the Yale collection at present one of the foremost of the world with respect to keyboard instruments. Recent acquisition policy has been directed toward making the collection representative in the area of wind instruments as well.

DISTRICT OF COLUMBIA

LIBRARY OF CONGRESS--THE MUSIC DIVISION, Washington, D.C. 20540

The Library of Congress functions as the national library of the United States. The holdings in the Music Division offer the music educator a vast and unique resource that cannot be found at any other place in the world. Many of its services are also available through the interlibrary loan system. The collections of music and music literature assembled in the Library of Congress are remarkably diverse and comprehensive. The holdings include more than 4,000,000 pieces of music, some 300,000 books and pamphlets, and about 350,000 sound recordings. International in scope, and spanning many centuries, the collections are sufficiently rich and voluminous to provide a basis for the most penetrating research. Manuscript sources include autograph scores and letters by master composers and famous musicians from Bach to the present day. Numerous microfilm reproductions and facsimiles of rare and unique sources are available. The collection of music periodicals is probably unmatched anywhere in the world.

Every type of printed music is represented in the collections, from the classics to rock and roll. Books are available on all aspects of musical documentation, covering such diverse fields as history, biography, aesthetics, philosophy, psychology, and organology, to mention only a few. Pedagogical literature on file includes methods and studies for every instrument and voice, as well as manuals for the entire field of music education and textbooks on harmony, counterpoint, form and analysis, orchestration, and conducting.

The Music Division consists of an administrative section, a reference section, the Archive of Folk Song, and a recorded sound section. The division responds to inquiries from all areas of the United States and foreign countries. When circumstances permit, the inquirer is referred to adequate libraries near his home. If advisable, interlibrary loan may be suggested or, if appropriate, photoduplication may be arranged.

When an investigator needs special, individual service, the professional members of the Music Division staff are available for consultation in the division offices. Although the staff can provide guidance and suggestions, it is understandable, of course, that they cannot undertake such tasks as actual compilation of bibliographies for researchers, or selection of research topics. For additional descriptions of the offerings of the Music Division, the following booklets should be consulted:

THE MUSIC DIVISION: A GUIDE TO ITS COLLECTIONS AND SERVICES. Washington, D.C.: Library of Congress, (Request the latest edition; small charge.)

INFORMATION FOR READERS. Washington, D.C.: Library of Congress. (Free.)

LIBRARY OF CONGRESS PUBLICATIONS IN PRINT. Washington, D.C.: Library of Congress. An annual list of the various available catalogs in the field of music.

AUTOGRAPH MUSICAL SCORES AND AUTOGRAPH LETTERS IN THE WHITTALL FOUNDATION COLLECTION. Prepared by Edward N. Waters. Washington, D.C.: Library of Congress, Music Division, 1951. 18 p.

Listing, alphabetical by artist, of the autograph holdings in the Gertrude Clarke Whittall Foundation collection of musical scores and letters. Includes Bach, Beethoven, Brahms, Haydn (Joseph and Michael), Mendelssohn, Meyerbeer, Paganini, Reger, Schubert, Schumann, Schoenberg, Wagner, and Weber.

A vast collection of folklore and folk music material is readily available in the Music Division. The Archive of Folk Song maintains and administers a collection of recorded folk, primitive, and exotic music on cylinders, discs, magnetic tape, and wire, as well as numerous related manuscripts. Reference services are available for visitors and correspondents.

The archive includes sound recordings of more than 80,000 specimens of songs, chants, dances, tales, and the like from throughout the world. Primary attention has been focused on the native culture of the United States; the South, the Midwest, and the Far West are particularly well represented. The collections also include music of North American Indian tribes, the American Negro, and the early settlers and colonists. The musical traditions of Latin America and the Caribbean (in particular, Argentina, Brazil, Colombia, Guatemala, Haiti, Mexico, Puerto Rico, and Venezuela) and of the west coast of Africa south of the Sahara, the Congo region, and Morocco are covered in detail, as is music from the Far and Near East, particularly Korea, Japan, Iran, and Iraq.

Every effort is made to collect the music of peoples in all parts of the world so that the archive will be truly international in scope, service, and influence. The professional staff maintains close relations with academic institutions, scholars, and folklorists. It is the archive's policy to foster the collecting of music in neglected areas and to encourage the preservation and study of musical cultures outside the classical artistic tradition of Western society.

FOLK MUSIC, a printed catalog containing detailed information, is available from the Superintendent of Documents, Government Printing Office, Washington, D.C., 20402, for a small charge. Request the latest edition.

Also a useful booklet, FOLK RECORDINGS contains titles and contents of long-playing (33 1/3 rpm) folk records which have been selected from the Archive of Folk Song. The recordings listed in this catalog are issued for public sale by the Recorded Sound Section, Music Division, Library of Congress, Washington, D.C. 20540.

Under the system of interlibrary loans, the Library of Congress will lend certain books to other libraries for the use of investigators engaged in serious research. Requests for such loans must come from a library, not an individual.

Music (except in certain cases, such as unbound music, manuscripts, first editions, rare volumes, or parts for orchestral or chamber music works) is loaned on the same conditions as books. Musical scores may be loaned for reference and study only, not performance. Requests for loans should be directed to the Chief, Loan Division, Library of Congress, Washington, D.C. 20540.

The library will generally make photoduplicates of its materials which are available for research use. It performs such services for research, in lieu of loans of the material or in place of transcription. For information concerning the services, prices, conditions, and so forth, contact the Chief, Photoduplication Services, Library of Congress, Washington, D.C. 20540.

NATIONAL ARCHIVES, Eighth Street and Pennsylvania Avenue, N.W., Washington, D.C. 20408

While the National Archives does not contain holdings in music education as such, it does include the records of the extensive music activities of the Works Progress Administration (WPA) programs of the 1930s. Between 1933 and 1943, most intensively between 1935 and 1939, the government of the United States supported and subsidized, through its emergency relief agencies, an arts program that in material size and as an enterprise representing a distinctly cultural concern was unprecedented in the history of this or any other nation. Although all offical records are available in the National Archives, a rather comprehensive description is to be found in the following:

McDonald, William F. FEDERAL RELIEF ADMINISTRATION AND THE ARTS. Columbus: Ohio State University Press, 1969. 869 p. Bibliography.

FLORIDA

BELLM'S CARS AND MUSIC OF YESTERDAY, 5500 North Tamiami Trail, Sarasota, Fla. 33580

A unique collection of more than 1,000 mechanized music machines. Music boxes date from 1790 from many lands--nickelodeons, orchestrations, calliopes, hurdy-gurdies, band organs, dance organs, animated accordians, and various percussion instruments. All are restored and working.

ILLINOIS

CHICAGO PUBLIC LIBRARY, Music Department, 78 East Washington Street, Chicago, Ill. 60602

Includes a collection of some 6,000 "old pops" songs in their original sheet music covers, dating from 1830; popular songs of the United States. For reference use.

THE NEWBERRY LIBRARY, 60 West Walton Street, Chicago, Ill. 60610

A privately endowed library specializing in primary research materials in the humanities. A most valuable resource for the serious researcher in the humanities. The principal works in this collection (including music) are available in microfilm or photoduplication form from Micro-Photo Division, Bell and Howell Company, Old Mansfield Road, Wooster, Ohio 44691.

UNIVERSITY OF CHICAGO, Joseph Regenstein Library, Chicago, Ill. 60637

Fifty-thousand-volume collection of music and books on music for humanistic study, primarily in theory and history of music. Five thousand microfilms of original sources.

NORTHWESTERN UNIVERSITY, Music Library, 1810 Hinman Avenue, Evanston, Ill. 60201

Collection of music manuscripts including a portion of the Molkenhauer Archive. The emphasis is on twentieth-century composers. Collection of rare books and scores.

UNIVERSITY OF ILLINOIS AT URBANA-CHAMPAIGN, Music Library, Urbana, Ill. 61801

Consists of introductory, instructive, research, and reference materials. Special subject emphasis includes about 2,000 pre-1800 music manuscripts and editions of music on microfilm, with primary emphasis on Medieval and Renaissance vocal music, lute and keyboard music sources; 1,200 graduate music theses on microfilm, mainly in the field of music education and written since 1960; a special collection of 30,000 titles of American popular sheet music (1830-1950); the Rafael Joseffy collection of about 2,000 pieces of nineteenth-century piano music which includes extensive performance indications and markings by Joseffy; the Joseph Szigeti collection of about 700 items including published editions and manuscripts by various nineteenth-and twentieth-century composers mainly of violin and piano music; recordings of Szigeti performances; a special collection of 23,000 78 rpm recordings (1930-48) of vocal and instrumental art music and jazz; WGN radio station (Chicago) collection of orchestration (2,900 titles); University of Illinois School of Music concerts and programs from 1950 to date on about 2,500 reels of tape; current subscriptions to about seventy-five concert and program books issued annually by major colleges and universities in the United States. Current catalogs from about 800 music publishers, dealers, and record manufacturers are kept on file.

INDIANA

INDIANA UNIVERSITY, Music Library, Bloomington, Ind. 47401

1. The Apel Collection of Early Keyboard Music--scores. Virtually a comprehensive collection via photocopy of all keyboard music to 1700 in tablature.

2. Fritz Busch Collection--scores and phonorecords. Consists of annotated scores by the composer, with phonotapes of various performances.

3. Latin-American Collection--books, scores, phonorecords. Several thousand titles, with emphasis on concert music.

ARCHIVES OF TRADITIONAL MUSIC, Folklore Institute, Indiana University, Bloomington, Ind. 47401

One of the world's largest repositories of recorded musical and verbal forms which are, in the main, perpetuated by oral tradition rather than by writing or printing. In music this encompasses three general types: folk music, music of nonliterate societies, and oriental art music. A fourth general type, popular music, is also included, since it normally exhibits the same aspect of oral transmission. The holdings include some representation of the greater part of the world's cultural regions. The archives function as a public library of sound recordings. Duplicate copies of recordings can be secured for educational purposes only at the archives or by mail. In addition to the collections of phonorecordings, the archives maintain a specialized research library of books, periodicals, and memorabilia of interest to ethnomusicologists, folklorists, and discographers. The archives also house collections of motion picture film and microfilm.

BLACK MUSIC COLLECTION, Indiana University, Bloomington, Ind. 47401

Includes books, journals, scores, phonorecords. Collection is international in scope, including ethnic music as well as concert music; traditional music as well as music from various historic periods. Total number of titles is estimated at 7,000. Collection is still being developed. Interlibrary loans accepted. Scores are for reference purposes only, not performance without permission of composer or his agent. No photocopying of material not in the public domain.

KENTUCKY

UNIVERSITY OF KENTUCKY, Margaret I. King Library, Lexington, Ky. 40506

The Alfred Cortot Collection--263 early treatises, dealing primarily with music theory. Includes three incunabula and works from the sixteenth, seventeenth, and eighteenth centuries.

MAINE

THE MUSICAL WONDER HOUSE AND MUSIC MUSEUM, 18 High Street (Box 274), Wiscasset, Me. 04578

A unique collection of antique mechanical music instruments

including music boxes, both disc and cylinder types; early and rare barrel organs, pianos, automata, phonographs; automatic player pianos such as Ampico, Duo Art, and Welte. Also collections of rolls, discs for music boxes, and early recordings from the turn of the century.

MARYLAND

MUSIC EDUCATORS NATIONAL CONFERENCE HISTORICAL CENTER, McKeldin Library, University of Maryland, College Park, Md. 20742

For description see Music Educators National Conference under "Associations--General" in Section 24: Philosophical Foundations, Principles, and Practices.

MASSACHUSETTS

BOSTON PUBLIC LIBRARY, Copley Square, Boston, Mass. 02117

1. Allen A. Brown Music Library--approximately 30,000 books, scores, and manuscripts. Separate collection of 40,000 for circulation. Also available: clippings and pamphlets file, song file, publishers and dealers catalog file, first performance file, and obituary file.

2. Sound Archives--135,000 records, tapes, piano rolls, and so forth, dating from the inception of recording.

HARVARD MUSICAL ASSOCIATION, 57A Chestnut Street, Boston, Mass. 02108

Material relating to New England musicians in general, going back to the late eighteenth and early nineteenth centuries, with special emphasis on Boston--both books and music; exhaustive collection of piano-vocal opera scores; piano music for four and eight hands; definitive collection of Arthur Foote's works (both print and manuscript); Dwight's "Journal of Music."

WERNER JOSTEN LIBRARY, Center for the Performing Arts, Smith College, Northampton, Mass. 01060

1. Philip Hale Collection--rare first editions of early treatises on music.

2. The Einstein Collection--vocal and instrumental music of the fifteenth through the seventeenth centuries copied by Alfred Einstein in score from part-books in the libraries of Europe.

MICHIGAN

UNIVERSITY OF MICHIGAN, Stearns Collection of Musical Instruments, Ann Arbor, Mich. 48105

Contains about 18,000 instruments, most of which were collected in the last thirty years of the nineteenth century by Frederick Stearns. The collection is about equally divided between Western and exotic instruments. Also, instruments of Japan and Southeast Asia. Includes a Japanese gamelan in both the Slendro and Pelong scales.

MISSOURI

UNIVERSITY OF MISSOURI, Conservatory Library, 4420 Warwick Boulevard, Kansas City, Mo. 64111

Strong collection serves as curriculum and research support in the fields of music and music education for the university. Collection includes 64,151 volumes of books and music; 5,342 units of microforms; 10,688 records, tapes, etc.; twenty-eight linear feet of manuscripts; 259 items of realia. Warner Brothers Orchestral Library (on loan) contains 12,372 items. The library also has a special collection of American music in support of the Institute for Studies in American Music (established 1967).

INSTITUTE FOR STUDIES IN AMERICAN MUSIC, Conservatory of Music, University of Missouri, Kansas City, Mo. 64111

Among the several purposes of the institute is the establishment of archives and reference services, a center of resources and researches in American music, and the preparation of definitive bibliographies and discographies. Reference questions relating to the field of American music are solicited.

NEW JERSEY

PRINCETON UNIVERSITY, Phonograph Record Library, Princeton, N.J. 08540

A splendid record collection consisting almost entirely of Western art (or classical) music from Gregorian chant (about 600 A.D.) to the present time. There are over 6,000 monaural records, 3,000 stereo records, 12,000 78s, 500 tape recordings, and about 1,000 scores for use while listening. A unique feature of this collection is the effort to possess all important recordings of individual major works. There are, for example, eighteen recordings of Beethoven's Ninth Symphony--each with a different conductor--and twenty different performances of all six Brandenburg Concertos by Bach. This constitutes a rare research tool for investigators of interpretations, conductors, and so forth.

NEW MEXICO

UNIVERSITY OF NEW MEXICO, Fine Arts Library, Albuquerque, N.M. 87131

Archives of southwestern music includes tape recordings of American Indian, Mexican-American, and Anglo-American music indigenous to the Southwest.

NEW YORK

COLUMBIA UNIVERSITY, Music Department, Dodge Hall, 116th Street and Broadway, New York, N.Y. 10027

The collection includes many diverse and unique items of musical and musicological interest. A sampling of these holdings are listed here.

1. Wide range of books, dissertations, scores, microfilms, and so on.

2. A large collection of late eighteenth- and early nineteenth-century opera scores.

3. The Eric Hertzmann microfilm collection of Beethoven materials.

4. Many first and early editions of the opera, chamber music, symphonic literature, and keyboard scores of Haydn, Mozart, Beethoven, Schubert, Brahms, and others.

5. The Judah Joffe collection of 3,000 disc recordings and 100 cylinders, extending from the beginning of recorded music through the era of acoustical recordings.

6. Numerous other collections which are unique. For a description of these see: Seaton, Douglass. "Important Library Holdings at Forty-One North American Universities." CURRENT MUSICOLOGY 17 (1974): 7-68.

THE JUILLIARD SCHOOL, Lila Acheson Wallace Library, Lincoln Center Plaza, New York, N.Y. 10023

Extensive collection of librettos and piano-vocal scores of nineteenth-century operas. First and early published scores of many nineteenth-century orchestral and chamber works.

MANNES COLLEGE OF MUSIC, Library, 157 East 74th Street, New York, N.Y. 10021

Carlos Salzedo Collection of annotated scores, transcriptions, and original compositions for the harp. Leopold Mannes Collection of original manuscript compositions.

METROPOLITAN MUSEUM OF ART, ANDRE MERTENS GALLERIES, New York, N.Y. 10028

The Metropolitan Museum's Department of Musical Instruments holds nearly 4,000 instruments, about two-thirds of them of non-European origin. The department's nucleus is the Crosby Brown collection which came to the museum beginning in 1889. Other donors of large groups of instruments include Joseph Drexel (1889), Alice Getty (1943), University of Pennsylvania (1953), and Burl Ives (1963). The collection is particularly famous for Western European materials, among them the oldest extant pianoforte (Bartolommeo Cristofori, 1720), the earliest undoubted Ruckers virginal (1581), a fine spinet made for Eleonora della Rovere (1540), and other important keyboard instruments including more than thirty-five with plucked strings (harpsichords, spinets, virginals); oboes by Denner and Richters; violins by Stradivarius and Amati; recorders by Kynsecker, Oberlender, Gahn; and other important Renaissance and later winds and strings, many of them in playing condition. Among the greatest treasures are two medieval instruments, a crecelle and the so-called Untermyer fiddle, actually a mandora.

About one-fifth of the collection is displayed in the André Mertens Galleries (1971). The department staff includes curatorial and restoration personnel, headed by Laurence Libin, associate curator in charge. Gallery concerts, lecture-demonstrations, technical drawings, and scholarly publications are offered on a regular basis. Requisitions are frequent, and a new catalog is in preparation. The collection is generally recognized as preeminent in the Western Hemisphere and is among the foremost collections in the world in quality and scope.

THE NEW YORK PUBLIC LIBRARY, Music Division, 111 Amsterdam Avenue, New York, N.Y. 10023

The Music Division of the New York Public Library is located at the Library and Museum of the Performing Arts at Lincoln Center. It has great depth in nearly every area of the performing arts, and is intended primarily for the professional, advanced student, and specialist. The Music Division is one of the great scholarly collections for research in the world. In addition to the Main Reading Room, which contains an extensive music reference collection on open shelves and a number of special files, there is a Special Collections Reading Room. Three subsections of the division include the Rodgers and Hammerstein Archives of Recorded Sound, the Special Collections, and the Americana Collection. For additional information concerning the holdings of this library, see:

Campbell, Frank C. "The Music Division of the New York Public Library." FONTES ARTIS MUSICAE 16 (July-December 1969): 112-19.

Published works concerning the music collection:

The New York Public Library, Reference Department. MUSIC SUBJECT HEADINGS, AUTHORIZED FOR USE IN THE CATALOGS OF THE MUSIC DIVISION. Boston: G.K. Hall and Co., 1959.

______. DICTIONARY CATALOG OF THE MUSIC COLLECTION. 33 vols. Boston: G.K. Hall and Co., 1964. SUPPLEMENT. 1 vol.

Complete listings for the music collection in the research libraries of the New York Public Library.

GEORGE SHERMAN DICKINSON MUSIC LIBRARY, Vassar College, Poughkeepsie, N.Y. 12601

1. Acoustic recordings--acoustic and early electronic discs, cylinders, early playback machines, musical box with discs.

2. Gustav Cannreuther Collection--collection of older chamber music in parts.

3. Chittenden Collection--collected editions of piano music, from the library of Kate Chittenden.

4. Treasure Room--music and music literature, imprints prior to 1800, as well as facsimiles of early music.

5. Women composers--music composed by women; some early music.

6. Autograph file--rare letters by important composers.

7. Vassariana--recordings and literature relevant to the musical life of the college.

QUEENS BOROUGH PUBLIC LIBRARY, Art and Music Division, 18-11 Merrick Boulevard, Jamaica, Queens, N.Y. 11432

The Art and Music Division contains a selective collection of music curriculum guides for New York City and New York State.

UNIVERSITY OF ROCHESTER, Sibley Music Library, Eastman School, Rochester, N.Y. 14604

1. Krehbiel Collection--American folk music.

2. Pougin Collection--theatrical almanacs, journals, and primary sources pertaining to the French theater of the eighteenth and nineteenth centuries.

3. Gordon Collection--nineteenth-and twentieth-century chamber music, primarily for string instruments.

4. Olschki Collection--part books (sacred music of the early baroque of the Milanese School).

5. Carl Nielsen Collection--complete works in various editions.

6. Fr. Kuhlau Collection--complete works in various editions.

7. Percy Grainger Collection--manuscripts of Grainger's works.

8. Autograph Letter Collection--letters of composers from Handel through Hanson.

9. Autograph manuscripts of music by various composers including Debussy, Mendelssohn, Hanson, Brahms, Schubert, Rubinstein.

10. Archive of musical events in Rochester, 1923-present.

11. Early American songsters, eighteenth and nineteenth centuries.

SYRACUSE UNIVERSITY, Music Library, 2d Floor, Bird Library, Syracuse, N.Y. 13210

1. Liechtenstein music archives at Kromeriz, Czechoslovakia--microfilm copy of entire archive.

2. Mayer Wetherill Collection--nineteenth-century solo and ensemble music involving the violin.

3. Eighteenth-and nineteenth-century Italian libretto collection--1,356 items.

4. Composer's papers--Miklos Rozsa (musical manuscripts, personal papers); Franz Waxman (musical manuscripts, personal papers, recordings); Leo Sowerby (personal papers, little music).

NORTH CAROLINA

UNIVERSITY OF NORTH CAROLINA, Music Library, Hill Hall, Chapel Hill, N.C. 27514

A large research library of books, scores, recordings, microforms, and rare books--over 76,000 items. Supports research in musicology, and graduate and undergraduate performing degrees.

PETER MEMORIAL LIBRARY, Moravian Music Foundation, 20 Cascade Avenue, Winston-Salem, N.C. 27108

1. Johannes Herbst Collection--anthems and sacred songs of the Moravian Church in the eighteenth and early nineteenth centuries (manuscript).

2. Salem Congregation Collection--anthems and sacred songs of

the Moravian Church (manuscript).

3. Salem Collegium Musicum Collection--orchestral and chamber music in manuscript and printed editions from the eighteenth and nineteenth centuries.

4. The Twenty-sixth North Carolina Regiment Band Collection--Civil War band books, manuscript.

5. The Lowens Collection of American Music--sacred and secular printed music from the eighteenth and nineteenth centuries, including more than 1,000 tunebooks, dating back to 1755.

6. The Johanson Collection of Hymnology--hymnals and works on hymnology dating back to 1597.

7. The library also includes extensive holdings in Moravian Church history. The Bethlehem Congregation Collection, the Lititz Congregation Collection, the Nazareth Congregation Collection, and the Dover Congregation Collection--all manuscript anthems and sacred songs from the eighteenth and nineteenth centuries used in these congregations--all are under the administration of the Moravian Church, but are located in Bethlehem, Pennsylvania.

8. The Bethlehem Philharmonic Society Collection--manuscript and printed orchestral and chamber music from the eighteenth and nineteenth centuries are also located in Bethlehem, Pennsylvania.

OHIO

EMILIE AND KARL RIEMENSCHNEIDER MEMORIAL BACH LIBRARY, BALDWIN-WALLACE COLLEGE, Berea, Ohio 44017

Includes more than 500 books written about Bach, the Bach family, and the family's music, as well as fifteen manuscripts, and more than 2,000 separately published music pieces, including many rare editions. A catalog of the holdings, edited by Sylvia Kennedy, is available from Columbia University Press, 1960. 295 p.

OBERLIN CONSERVATORY LIBRARY, Oberlin College, Oberlin, Ohio 44074

The Mr. and Mrs. C.W. Best Collection of Autographs contains 110 items, most of which are holograph letters of noted composers.

PENNSYLVANIA

FREE LIBRARY OF PHILADELPHIA, Logan Square, Philadelphia, Pa. 19103

1. Music Department

a. Sheet Music Collection--150,000 pieces of popular sheet music, vocal and piano, primarily Americana since the revolution. Available for reference, either in person or by mail.

b. Drinker Library of Choral Music--700 titles in multiple copy, primarily baroque sacred music, many with orchestra parts. Bach cantatas, music by Schubert, Schumann, and others, are translated from the German by Henry Drinker into singable English. Available to choruses, choirs, community and festival groups upon payment of an annual subscription fee.

2. The Edwin A. Fleisher Collection of Orchestral Music--one of the largest and most complete collections of orchestral music in the world. Contains more than 12,000 compositions, each with conductor's score and complete set of parts.

CARNEGIE LIBRARY OF PITTSBURGH, 4400 Forbes Avenue, Pittsburgh, Pa. 15213

A circulating and reference-research collection, comprised of 76,000 volumes of music and books about music, and 19,250 records. Emphasis in lending collection is on practical editions of music since 1700. Reference collection includes 160 volumes of manuscripts; many early and first editions; monumental sets; historical anthologies; thematic catalogs; dictionaries, encyclopedias, etc., in English and foreign languages. Files of periodicals begin with the year 1722 and include a notable collection of nineteenth-century American music journals.

FOSTER HALL COLLECTION, University of Pittsburgh, Pittsburgh, Pa. 15260

A collection of material and information about the Pittsburgh composer, Stephen Collins Foster.

SOUTH DAKOTA

UNIVERSITY OF SOUTH DAKOTA, The Arne B. Larson Collection of Musical Instruments and Library, Vermillion, S.D. 57069

This is one of America's major collections of musical resource materials, including more than 2,500 antique musical instruments from all over the world, plus an extensive supporting library of books, music, periodicals, recordings, photographs, and related musical memorabilia. Strong representation of Western wind instrument development. The collection of nineteenth- and early twentieth-century music for wind instruments, as well as sheet music, is one of the most extensive in the country.

TEXAS

THE CROUCH MUSIC LIBRARY, Baylor University, Box 6307, Waco, Tex. 76706

1. Frances G. Spencer Collection of American Printed Music--about 30,000 items of printed music from the eighteenth, nineteenth, and twentieth centuries.

2. David Guion Collection--manuscripts and holographs.

3. Baylor Collection--some hardboards of the early nineteenth century, specializing in anthems, chamber music, and early Americana; also chamber music of the eighteenth century.

UTAH

BRIGHAM YOUNG UNIVERSITY, Library, Provo, Utah 84601

1. Josef Bonime Music Collection--a collection of manuscripts and published compositions of more than 25,000 items covering a variety of categories.

2. Capitol Records Manuscript Collection--the complete collection of all manuscripts composed or arranged for the recording of Capitol records through 1968, including scores and parts for symphony orchestras, stage bands, concert bands, choirs, and solo literature of classic, semiclassic, and popular genre.

3. Earl G. Vought Collection--a record collection consisting of 8,000 discs (78s and early LPs) including Gregorian chants, Bach cantatas, all the recorded symphonies of Haydn, all the masses of Haydn, all the symphonies and chamber music of Mozart, many of Mozart's operas and masses, and virtually all of the great works of Beethoven, Schubert, Schumann, Chopin, Brahms, and Wagner.

4. Collection of Ancient Instruments--the Lotta Van Buren collection of ancient instruments and music containing rare old instruments of the East and West, modern reproductions of ancient instruments, literature on ancient instruments, and a library of old instrument scores. Also included are a number of ancient costumes and pictures of interest. Especially noteworthy are three Arnold Dolmetsch keyboards, two clavichords, and a virginal, all signed by Dolmetsch.

VIRGINIA

AMERICAN SYMPHONY ORCHESTRA LEAGUE, P.O. Box 66, Vienna, Va. 32180

The league has an extensive collection of symphony orchestra concert programs dating back about fifteen years, more complete in recent years than earlier. These are available for research purposes, on appointment. Also, a collection of musical scores. Inquiries concerning accessibility of scores should be addressed to the league.

WASHINGTON

SEATTLE PUBLIC LIBRARY, Music Department, 4th and Madison, Seattle, Wash. 98104

KOMO Radio Music Library of 21,600 items of theatre orchestrations of the period 1900 to 1950; historical scrapbooks of Seattle musicians, Seattle Symphony Orchestra, Seattle Opera, and Seattle dancers; Seattle and Pacific Northwest composers' sheet music and manuscript collection, mainly popular songs from 1900 to date. Music holdings: 17,000 volumes; music literature: 15,000 discs.

WEST VIRGINIA

WEST VIRGINIA UNIVERSITY, West Virginia Collection, Library, Morgantown, W. Va. 26506.

Appalachian Folk Music Collection--a collection begun in 1971 of tape recordings of folk musicians in West Virginia and surrounding states, made by Thomas S. Brown. Indexes available.

CANADA

NATIONAL LIBRARY OF CANADA/BIBLIOTHEQUE NATIONALE DU CANADA, 395 Wellington Street, Ottawa, Ont. K1A 0N4, Canada

Specialty of the music division are items documenting Canada's musical history: printed, manuscript, and recorded music; books; periodicals; concert programs; personal papers; vertical files; pictures; and so forth. The Canadian concert programs are quite extensive for the period from 1970 and include a good sampling from the nineteenth century to 1970, including nearly complete sets for the major orchestras. The collection of manuscripts and papers includes those of two important Canadian composers of the first half of this century: Healey Willan (1880-1968), and Claude Champagne (1891-1965); also the papers of Alexis Contant, Hector Gratton, and Leo Smith, All Canadian composers. There are smaller files of manuscripts, correspondence, scrapbooks, and so on, of other Canadian musicians. The personal books and music of Percy Scholes and Healey Willan have been integrated into the general collections. Unique are Scholes's information files, including half a million clippings, extracts, letters, and brochures, and, 2,500 picture files. These files are non-Canadian in content.

METROPOLITAN TORONTO MUSIC LIBRARY, 559 Avenue Road, Toronto, Ont. M4V 2J7, Canada

A good collection in Canadian music, specializing in pre-1920 sheet music and programs. The collection is moderately strong in Canadian educational materials.

Appendix B
PERIODICALS

ACA BULLETIN
American Composers Alliance
170 West 74th Street,
New York, N.Y. 10023

ACCORDION AND GUITAR WORLD
20 Hessian Drive
Ridgefield, Conn. 06877

ACCORDION HORIZONS
American Accordionists Association, Inc.
244 West Fourth Street
New York, N.Y. 10014

ACTA MUSICOLOGICA
(Societe International de Musicologie)
15 CH 4000 Basel 15
Switzerland
(Text in English, French, and German)

ADAM, An International Quarterly
University of Rochester
Rochester, N.Y.

AFRICAN MUSIC
African Music Society
P.O. Box 138
Roodepoort, Transvaal, South Africa

AFTER DARK
10 Columbus Circle
New York, N.Y. 10019

AGMAZINE
American Guild of Musical Artists
1841 Broadway
New York, N.Y. 10023

ALL-AFRICA CHURCH MUSIC ASSOCIATION JOURNAL
All-Africa Church Music Association
Private Bag 636 E
Salisbury, Rhodesia

AMCA NEWSLETTER
Associated Male Choruses of America, Inc.
1338 Oakcrest Drive
Appleton, Wis. 54911

AMERICAN CHORAL FOUNDATION, INC. RESEARCH MEMORANDUM SERIES
American Choral Foundation, Inc.
130 West 56th Street
New York, N.Y. 10019

AMERICAN CHORAL REVIEW
Association of Choral Conductors
American Choral Foundation, Inc.
130 West 56th Street
New York, N.Y. 10019

*For additional information, i.e., name of editor, number of issues per year, type of contents, and so forth, see Section 7: Guides to Periodicals and Professional Journals.

AMERICAN EDUCATIONAL RESEARCH JOURNAL
American Educational Research Association
1201 Sixteenth Street, N.W.
Washington, D.C. 20036

AMERICAN HARP JOURNAL
American Harp Society
1117 Crestline Drive
Santa Barbara, Calif. 93105

AMERICAN MUSICAL DIGEST
M.I.T. Press
Cambridge, Mass. 02142

AMERICAN MUSICAL INSTRUMENT SOCIETY. JOURNAL
807 Walters Street, no. 72
P.O. Box 351
Lake Charles, La. 70601

AMERICAN MUSIC CENTER. NEWSLETTER
American Music Center
2109 Broadway, Suite 15-79
New York, N.Y. 10023

AMERICAN MUSICOLOGICAL SOCIETY. JOURNAL
American Musicological Society
William Byrd Press
2901 Byrdhill Road
Richmond, Va. 23205

AMERICAN MUSIC TEACHER
Music Teachers National Association
1831 Carew Tower
Cincinnati, Ohio 45202

AMERICAN OLD TIMES FIDDLERS NEWS
American Old Time Fiddlers Association
6141 Morrill Avenue
Lincoln, Neb. 68507

AMERICAN ORGANIST
Organ Interests, Inc.
1 Union Square
New York, N.Y. 10003
(Available in microfilm)

AMERICAN RECORDER
American Recorder Society, Inc.
141 West 120th Street
New York, N.Y. 10011

AMERICAN RECORD GUIDE
Box 319
Radio City Station
New York, N.Y. 10019

AMERICAN SOCIETY OF UNIVERSITY COMPOSERS, PROCEEDINGS
Columbia University
New York, N.Y. 10027

AMERICAN STRING TEACHER
American String Teachers Association
c/o Robert C. Marince
Lawrence Township Schools
2596 Princeton Pike
Trenton, N.J. 08638

AMERICAN SUZUKI JOURNAL
Suzuki Association of the Americas
P.O. Box 1340
Evanston, Ill. 60204

AMERICAN SYMPHONY ORCHESTRA LEAGUE. NEWSLETTER
American Symphony Orchestra League
Symphony Hill
Box 66
Vienna, Va. 22180

ARTI MUSICES
Institute of Musicology
Music Academy in Zagreb
Gunduliceva 6
Zagreb, Yugoslavia

ARTS IN SOCIETY
University Extension
University of Wisconsin
606 State Street
Madison, Wis. 53706

ARTS MANAGEMENT
408 West 57th Street
New York, N.Y. 10019

ASCAP TODAY
American Society of Composers, Authors, and Publishers
575 Madison Avenue
New York, N.Y. 10022

ASSOCIATION FOR RECORDED SOUND COLLECTIONS. JOURNAL
Rodgers and Hammerstein Archives of Recorded Sound
111 Amsterdam Avenue
New York, N.Y. 10023

ASSOCIATION OF COLLEGE AND UNIVERSITY CONCERT MANAGERS. BULLETIN
Association of College and University Concert Managers
College Printing and Typing Co.
2909 Syene Road
Madison, Wis. 53713

ATG BULLETIN
Accordian Teachers Guild, Inc.-- International
12626 West Creek Road
Minnetonka, Minn. 55343

AUSTRALIAN JOURNAL OF MUSIC EDUCATION
Australian Society for Music Education
Department of Music
University of Western Australia
Nedlands, Western Australia 6009
Australia

BACH
Riemenschneider Bach Institute
Baldwin-Wallace College
Berea, Ohio 44017

BAND JOURNAL
Ongaku No Tomo Sha Corp.
Kagurazaka 6-30, Shinjuku-ku
Tokyo, Japan
(Text in Japanese)

THE BASS SOUND POST
International Institute for the String Bass
382 Somerset Street
North Plainfield, N.J. 07060

BILLBOARD
165 West 46th Street
New York, N.Y. 10036

BOLETIN INTERAMERICANO DE MUSICA
Organization of American States
Department of Cultural Affairs, Music Division
Washington, D.C. 20006

BOOK REVIEW INDEX
Gale Research Co.
Book Tower
Detroit, Mich. 48226

BOSTON SYMPHONY ORCHESTRA PROGRAM BOOK/NOTES
Boston Symphony Orchestra
Program Office, Symphony Hall
Boston, Mass. 02115

BRASS AND WOODWIND QUARTERLY
Box 111
Durham, N.H. 03824

BRASS BULLETIN
P.O. Box 12
CH-1510 MOUDON
Switzerland

BRAVO
485 Lexington Avenue
New York, N.Y. 10017

BRITISH BANDSMAN
Bandsman's Press Ltd.
210 Strand
London, W.C. 2, Engl.

THE BRITISH CATALOGUE OF MUSIC
Council of the British National Bibliography
London, Engl.

BRITISH COLUMBIA MUSIC EDUCATOR
British Columbia Teachers Federation
2235 Burrard Street
Vancouver, B.C., Canada

BRITISH JOURNAL OF AESTHETICS
Thames and Hudson, Ltd.
44 Clockhouse Road
Farnborough, Hants, Engl.

BRITISH JOURNAL OF MUSIC THERAPY
British Society for Music Therapy
London, Engl.

BROADSIDE MAGAZINE
215 West 98th Street
New York, N.Y. 10025

THE CANADA MUSIC BOOK--LES CAHIERS CANADIENS DE MUSIQUE
Canadian Music Council
P.O. Box 156, Station E
Montreal 151, Que., Canada
(In English and French)

CANADIAN ASSOCIATION OF UNIVERSITY SCHOOLS OF MUSIC. JOURNAL
University of British Columbia
Department of Music
Vancouver, B.C., Canada
(Text in English and French)

CANADIAN COMPOSER/COMPOSITEUR CANADIEN
Creative Arts Co.
159 Bay Street
Toronto 116, Ont., Canada
(In English and French)

CANADIAN FEDERATION OF MUSIC TEACHERS ASSOCIATIONS. NEWS BULLETIN
Canadian Federation of Music Teachers Associations
297 Mandeville Street
Winnipeg, Man., Canada

CANADIAN MUSIC EDUCATOR
Canadian Music Educators Association
34 Cameron Road
St. Catherines, Ont., Canada

CENTRAL OPERA SERVICE BULLETIN
Central Opera Service
Lincoln Center, Metropolitan Opera
New York, N.Y. 10023

THE CHAUTAUQUAN
Chautauqua Institution
Chautauqua, N.Y. 14722

CHORAL AND ORGAN GUIDE
American Academy of Organ
Box 714
Mt. Vernon, N.Y. 10551

CHORAL JOURNAL
American Choral Directors Association
Box 17736
Tampa, Fla. 33612

CHORD AND DISCORD
P.O. Box 1171
Iowa City, Iowa 52240

CHURCH MUSIC (England)
Church Music Association
28 Ashley Place
London, W. 1, Engl.

CHURCH MUSIC (United States)
Concordia Publishing House
3558 South Jefferson Avenue
St. Louis, Mo. 63118

CHURCH MUSICIAN
Sunday School Board of the Southern Baptist Convention
127-Ninth Avenue, N.
Nashville, Tenn. 37203

CLAVIER
Instrumentalist Co.
1418 Lake Street
Evanston, Ill. 60204

CLOSE-UP
Country Music Association
700 Sixteenth Avenue, S.
Nashville, Tenn. 37203

COLLEGE BOARD REVIEW
College Entrance Examination Board
888 Seventh Avenue
New York, N.Y. 10019

COLLEGE MUSIC SYMPOSIUM
College Music Society, Inc.
c/o College of Arts and Sciences
Rutgers University
New Brunswick, N.J. 08903

COLLEGIUM MUSICUM: YALE UNIVERSITY
A-R Editions, Inc.
22 North Henry Street
Madison, Wis. 53703

COMPOSER (England)
Composers' Guild of Great Britain
10 Stratford Place
London, W. 1, Engl.

COMPOSER (United States)
Composers' Autograph Publications
Box 7103
Cleveland, Ohio 44128

COMPOSERS, AUTHORS, AND ARTISTS OF AMERICA
40-71 Elbertson Street
Elmhurst, N.Y. 11373

COMPOSIUM
Crystal Record Co.
P.O. Box 65661
Los Angeles, Calif. 90065

CONDUCTOR
National Association of Brass Band Conductors
W. Paxton & Co., Ltd.
36-38 Dean Street
London, W. 1, Engl.

CONSOLAIRE
World Library Publications
2145 Central Parkway
Cincinnati, Ohio 45214

COUNCIL FOR RESEARCH IN MUSIC EDUCATION. BULLETIN
Council for Research in Music Education
University of Illinois
College of Education, School of Music
Urbana, Ill. 61801

COUNTRY AND WESTERN EXPRESS
Country Music Enterprises
68 Golden House
Great Pulteney Street
London, W. 1, Engl.

COUNTRY AND WESTERN HIT PARADE
Charlton Building
Derby, Conn. 06418

COUNTRY AND WESTERN ROUND-ABOUT
21 Roseacres
Takeley, Dunmow
Essex, Engl.

COUNTRY AND WESTERN SPOT-LIGHT
Kelso, No. 1 R.D., Heriot
Otago, New Zealand

COUNTRY DANCE AND SONG
55 Christopher Street
New York, N.Y. 10014

COUNTRY SONG ROUNDUP
Charlton Publications, Inc.
Charlton Building
Derby, Conn. 06418

CREATIVE GUITAR INTERNATIONAL
Edinburg, Tex. 78539

CRICKET (United States)
Box 663
Newark, N.J. 07101

CULTURAL AFFAIRS
Associated Councils of the Arts
1564 Broadway
New York, N.Y. 10036

CULTURES (UNESCO)
Unipub, Inc.
650 First Avenue
New York, N.Y. 10016

CURRENT MUSICOLOGY
Columbia University
Department of Music
New York, N.Y. 10027

DANCE MAGAZINE
10 Columbus Circle
New York, N.Y. 10019

DANCE NEWS
119 West 57th Street
New York, N.Y. 10019

DANCE PERSPECTIVES
29 East Ninth Street
New York, N.Y. 10003

DIAPASON
434 South Wabash
Chicago, Ill. 60605

DIE REIHE
Theodore Presser Co.
Bryn Mawr, Pa. 19010

DISSERTATION ABSTRACTS, Section A: The Humanities and Social Sciences
University Microfilms
Ann Arbor, Mich. 48106

DOWN BEAT
Maher Publications, Inc.
222 West Adams Street
Chicago, Ill. 60606
(Available in microform)

DRUM CORPS NEWS
321 Revere Street
Revere, Mass. 02151

EARLY MUSIC
Oxford University Press
200 Madison Avenue
New York, N.Y. 10016

EASTERN REVIEW MAGAZINE
Box 495
Brooklyn, N.Y. 11201

EDUCATIONAL TECHNOLOGY
140 Sylvan Avenue
Englewood Cliffs, N.J. 07632

EDUCATION MUSICALE
Enseignement de la Musique en France
36 rue Pierre-Nicole
Paris (5e), France

ELECTRONIC MUSIC REVIEW
Trumansburg, N.Y. 14886

ENGLISH DANCE AND SONG
English Folk Dance and Song Society
Cecil Sharp House
2 Regents Park Road
London, N.W. 1, Engl.

ENTRACTE
29 br. Voltaire
Paris (11e), France

ETHNOMUSICOLOGY
Society for Ethnomusicology
Wesleyan University Press
Middletown, Conn. 06457

EURO PIANO
Verlag das Musikinstrument, Klueberstr
9, D-6000 Frankfurt am Main
West Germany
(Text in Danish, English, French, and German)

FIGA NEWS
Fretted Instrument Guild of America
2344 South Oakley Avenue
Chicago, Ill. 60608

THE FOLK DANCER
47-05 Fifth Street
New York, N.Y. 11101

THE FOLK HARP JOURNAL
P.O. Box 161
Mt. Laguna, Calif. 92048

THE FOLKLORE ENGLISH MONTHLY
172/22 Acharya, Jagadish Bose Road
Calcutta-14, India

FOLK STYLE
Country Music Enterprises
68 Golden House
Great Pulteney Street
London, W. 1, Engl.

FRETTS
P.O. Box 928
Santa Ana, Calif. 92701

GILBERT AND SULLIVAN JOURNAL
Gilbert and Sullivan Society
23 Burnside, Sawbridgeworth
Herts, Engl.

GOSPEL MUSIC SPEAK OUT
Box 253
Rockaway, N.J. 07866

GUILD-O-GRAM
American Guild of Music
815 Adair Avenue
Zanesville, Ohio 43701

GUITAR PLAYER MAGAZINE
348 North Santa Cruz Avenue
Los Gatos, Calif. 95030

GUITAR REVIEW
Society of the Classic Guitar
409 East 50th Street
New York, N.Y. 10022

THE GUITAR TEACHER
Sam Ulano, Editor
P.O. Box 1126, Radio City Station
New York, N.Y. 10010

HARMONICA HAPPENINGS
Society for the Preservation and Advancement of the Harmonica
Box 3006
Detroit, Mich. 48231

HARMONIZER
Society for the Preservation and Encouragement of Barber Shop Quartet Singing in America, Inc.
6315 Third Avenue
Kenosha, Wis. 53141

HARPSICHORD
International Harpsichord Society
Box 4323
Denver, Colo. 80204

THE HARRISON TAPE GUIDE
143 West 20th Street
New York, N.Y. 10011

HIGH FIDELITY/MUSICAL AMERICA
165 West 46th Street
New York, N.Y. 10036

HILLBILLY
Box 1
CH-4000 Basel 4, Switzerland
(Text in German)

HIP: The Jazz Record Digest
1973 Kennedy Drive
McLean, Va. 22101

HIT PARADER
Division Street
Derby, Conn. 06418

HORN CALL
International Horn Society
3007 North Farwell Avenue
Milwaukee, Wis. 53211

HUDEBNI VEDA
Institute of Musicology
Czechoslovakian Academy of Science
4, Prague 1, Czechoslovakia
(Text in Czech; summaries in English, German, and Russian)

HYMN
Hymn Society of America
475 Riverside Drive
New York, N.Y. 10027

HYMN SOCIETY OF GREAT BRITAIN AND IRELAND. BULLETIN
Hymn Society of Great Britain and Ireland
13a Linden Road
Newcastle upon Tyne NE3 4EY, Engl.

THE IAJRC JOURNAL
International Association of Jazz Record Collectors
106 Margaretta Court
Staten Island, N.Y. 10314

IMC NEWS
Intercollegiate Musical Council
437 Fifth Avenue
New York, N.Y. 10016

INCORPORATED SOCIETY OF ORGAN BUILDERS. JOURNAL
Incorporated Society of Organ Builders
Box No. 1, Ruislip
Middlesex, Engl.

INDIAN MUSIC JOURNAL
B-82, New Rajinder Nagar
New Delhi 5, India
(Text in English and Sanskrit; summaries in English)

INSTITUTE OF ETHNOMUSICOLOGY, SELECTED REPORTS
Institute of Ethnomusicology
University of California at Los Angeles
Los Angeles, Calif. 90024

INSTRUMENTALIST
Instrumentalist Co.
1418 Lake Street
Evanston, Ill. 60204
(Available in microfilm)

INTER-AMERICAN MUSIC BULLETIN
Organization of American States
Department of Cultural Affairs
Music Division
Washington, D.C. 20006

INTERNATIONAL FOLK MUSIC COUNCIL. BULLETIN
International Folk Music Council
Department of Music, Queen's University
Kingston, Ont., Canada
(Text in English; occasionally in French and German)

INTERNATIONAL MUSIC EDUCATOR. NEWSLETTER
International Society for Music Education
Uhlhornsweg 13, D-29, Oldenburg, Germany

INTERNATIONAL MUSICIAN
220 Mount Pleasant Avenue
Newark, N.J. 07104

INTERNATIONAL REVIEW OF THE AESTHETICS AND SOCIOLOGY OF MUSIC
Izdavacki zavod JAZU
Gundjliceva 24
4100 Zagreb, Yugoslavia

INTERNATIONAL SOCIETY FOR MUSIC EDUCATION--YEARBOOK
DK--3460 Birkrod
Carinaparken, 133 Denmark

INTERNATIONAL SOCIETY OF ORGANBUILDERS INFORMATION
International Society of Organbuilders
D-7128 Lauffen/Neckar
Postfach 234, West Germany
(In English and German)

INTERNATIONAL TROMBONE ASSOCIATION JOURNAL
c/o Larry Weed
School of Music
University of Southern Mississippi
Hattiesburg, Miss. 39401

INTERNATIONAL VIOLIN, GUITAR MAKERS AND MUSICIANS
4118 Mill Street
Miami, Ariz. 85539

JAZZ AND BLUES
Hanover Books Limited
London, Engl.

JAZZ FORUM
European Jazz Federation
Polish Jazz Society
Box 282
Ruthkowskiego 20, Warsaw, Poland
(Editions in English and Polish)

JAZZ HOT
14 rue Chaptal
Paris (9e), France

JAZZ JOURNAL
Novello & Co., Ltd.
The Cottage
27 Willow Vale
London, W. 12, Engl.

JAZZ NOTES
P.O. Box 55
Indianapolis, Ind. 46206

JAZZ REPORT MAGAZINE
Box 476
Ventura, Calif. 93001

JAZZ-RHYTHM & BLUES
11 Waverly Place
New York, N.Y. 10003
(Text in English, French, and German)

JAZZ TIMES
British Jazz Society
10 Southfield Gardens
Twickenham, Middlesex, Engl.

JEMF NEWSLETTER
John Edwards Memorial Foundation, Inc.
Folklore and Mythological Center
University of California
Los Angeles, Calif. 90024

JOURNAL MUSICAL FRANCAIS
126 rue des Rosiers
93-Saint-ouen, France

JOURNAL OF AESTHETIC EDUCATION
Bureau of Educational Research
College of Education
University of Illinois
Urbana, Ill. 61801

JOURNAL OF AESTHETICS AND ART CRITICISM
Wayne State University
Detroit, Mich. 48202

JOURNAL OF AMERICAN FOLKLORE
American Folklore Society, Inc.
University of Texas Press
Austin, Tex. 78712

JOURNAL OF BAND RESEARCH
American Bandmasters Association
University of Southern Florida
Tampa, Fla. 33620

JOURNAL OF CHURCH MUSIC
Fortress Press
2900 Queen Lane
Philadelphia, Pa. 19129

THE JOURNAL OF COUNTRY MUSIC
Country Music Foundation
700 Sixteenth Avenue, S.
Nashville, Tenn. 37203

JOURNAL OF JAZZ STUDIES
Transaction Periodicals Consortium
Rutgers University
New Brunswick, N.J. 08903

JOURNAL OF MUSIC THEORY
Yale University
New Haven, Conn. 06520

JOURNAL OF MUSIC THERAPY
National Association for Music Therapy
P.O. Box 610
Lawrence, Kans. 66044

JOURNAL OF POPULAR CULTURE
University Hall
Bowling Green University
Bowling Green, Ohio 43402

JOURNAL OF RESEARCH IN MUSIC EDUCATION
Society for Research in Music Education
Music Educators National Conference
Suite 601
8150 Leesburg Pike
Vienna, Va. 22810

JOURNAL OF THE ACOUSTICAL SOCIETY OF AMERICA
335 East 45th Street
New York, N.Y. 10017

JOURNAL OF THE AMERICAN MUSICOLOGICAL SOCIETY
c/o Editor, Department of Music
Cornell University
Ithaca, N.Y. 14850

JUILLIARD NEWS BULLETIN
Juilliard School
Lincoln Center Plaza
New York, N.Y. 10023

JUILLIARD REVIEW ANNUAL
Juilliard School of Music
Lincoln Center Plaza
New York, N.Y. 10023

JUNIOR KEYNOTES
National Federation of Music Clubs
600 South Michigan Avenue
Chicago, Ill. 60605

KLOK EN KIEPEL
Nederlandse Klokkenspel-Vereniging
Versterplein 8, Vught, Netherlands

KOUNTRY KORRAL
Box 8014
72008 Vaesteraas 8, Sweden

LISTENING POST
Bro-Dart, Inc.
1601 Memorial Avenue
Williamsport, Pa. 17701

LIST-O-TAPES
Trade Service Publications
2720 Beverly Boulevard
Los Angeles, Calif. 90057

LIVING BLUES
917 Dakin Street, Room 405
Chicago, Ill. 60613

MAGYAR ZENE/HUNGARIAN MUSIC
Kultura, Box 149
Budapest, Hungary

MAKING MUSIC
Rural Music Schools Association
Little Benslow Hills
Hitchen, Herts, Engl.

MANUALIERE
World Library Publications, Inc.
2145 Central Parkway
Cincinnati, Ohio 45214

MATRIX
7 Aynsley Road, Shelton
Stoke-on-Trent, Engl.

METRONOME: MODERN MUSIC AND ITS MAKERS
AMS Press, Inc.
56 East Thirteenth Street
New York, N.Y. 10003
(Available in microfilm)

METROPOLITAN OPERA PROGRAM
380 Madison Avenue
New York, N.Y. 10017

MICROCRITICA: ARTE-MUSICA-TEATRO-LITERATURA
Hornos 1110-2b
Buenos Aires, Argentina

MISCELLANEA MUSICOLOGICA: ADELAIDE STUDIES IN MUSICOLOGY
Libraries Board of South Australia
Adelaide, Australia

MISSOURI JOURNAL OF RESEARCH IN MUSIC EDUCATION
Missouri Music Education Association
Washington University
St. Louis, Mo. 63130

MODERN KEYBOARD REVIEW
436 Via Media
Palos Verdes Estates, Calif. 90274

MORAVIAN MUSIC FOUNDATION BULLETIN
Salem Station
Winston-Salem, N.C. 27108

MUSART
National Catholic Music Educators Association
4637 Eastern Avenue, N.E.
Washington, D.C. 20018

MUSIC
Distributed by Pergamon Press, Inc.
44-01 21st Street
Long Island City, N.Y. 11101

MUSICA (Netherlands)
P.O. Box 56
Hilversum, Netherlands

MUSICA (W. Germany)
Bärenreiter-Verlag Karl VoetterleKG
Heinrich-Schuetz-Allee 29-37
35 Kassel-Wilhelmshöhe, W. Germany

MUSICA DISCIPLINA: A Yearbook of the History of Music
American Institute of Musicology
P.O. Box 33655
Dallas, Tex. 75230

MUSICA E DISCHI
Corriere Internazionale della Musica
Via Carducci 8
Milan, Italy

MUSICAE SACRAE MINISTERIUM
Consociato Internationalis Musicae Sacrae
Piazza S. Agostino 20-A
00786 Rome, Italy
(Editions in English, French, German, Italian, and Spanish)

MUSIC/AGO-RCCO MAGAZINE
American Guild of Organists--Royal Canadian College of Organists
630 Fifth Avenue, Suite 2010
New York, N.Y. 10020

MUSICA JAZZ
Messaggerie Musicali
Galleria del Corso
I 20122 Milan, Italy

MUSICAL ARTICLE GUIDE
156 West Chelton Avenue
Philadelphia, Pa. 19144

MUSICAL BOX SOCIETY BULLETIN
19 Colony Drive
Summit, N.J. 07901

MUSICAL EVENTS
13 Heath Drive
Hampstead, London N.W.3, Engl.

MUSICAL MERCHANDISE REVIEW
437 Madison Avenue
New York, N.Y. 10022

MUSICAL NEWSLETTER
Musical Newsletter, Inc.
Box 250, Lenox Hill Station
New York, N.Y. 10021

MUSICAL OPINION
Musical Opinion, Ltd.
87 Wellington Street
Luton, Beds, Engl.

MUSICAL QUARTERLY
G. Schirmer, Inc.
4 East 49th Street
New York, N.Y. 10017

* British counterpart of the Music Educators Journal.

MUSICAL SALVATIONIST
Salvationist Publishing and Supplies, Ltd.
117-119 Judd Street
London, WC1H 9NN, Engl.

MUSICAL TIMES
Novello and Co., Ltd.
27 Soho Square
London, W.1, Engl.

MUSICANADA (English Edition)
Canadian Music Centre
33 Edward Street
Toronto 2, Ont., Canada

MUSIC AND LETTERS
Music and Letters, Ltd.
44 Conduit Street
London, W. 1R, ODE, Engl.

MUSIC AND MUSICIANS
Hansom Books
Artillery Mansions
75 Victoria Street
London, S.W. 1, Engl.

MUSICA UNIVERSITA
Istituzione Universitarie dei Concerti
Aula Magna Universita di Roma
Casella Postale 7181
Rome, Italy

MUSIC CLUBS MAGAZINE
National Federation of Music Clubs
Suite 1215
600 South Michigan Avenue
Chicago, Ill. 60605

MUSIC EDUCATORS JOURNAL
Music Educators National Conference
Suite 601
8150 Leesburg Pike
Vienna, Va. 22180

THE MUSIC FORUM
Columbia University Press
136 South Broadway
Irvington, N.Y. 10533

MUSICIAN OF THE SALVATION ARMY
Salvationist Publishing and Supplies Ltd.
117-119 Judd Street
London, WC1H 9NN, Engl.

THE MUSIC INDEX
1435-37 Randolph Street
Detroit, Mich. 48226

MUSIC INDUSTRY
Music Industry Publications
10a High Street
Tunbridge Wells, Kent, Engl.
(Text in English, German, and Italian)

MUSIC IN EDUCATION, INTERNATIONAL SOCIETY FOR EDUCATION
Novello and Co., Ltd.
1-3 Upper James Street
London, WIR4BP, Engl.

MUSIC JOURNAL
370 Lexington Avenue
New York, N.Y. 10017

MUSIC LEADER
Southern Baptist Convention
Sunday School Board
127 Ninth Avenue
Nashville, Tenn. 37203

MUSIC MINISTRY
Graded Press
201 Eighth Avenue
Nashville, Tenn. 37202

MUSIC POWER
Music Educators National Conference
Suite 601
8150 Leesburg Pike
Vienna, Va. 22180

MUSIC REVIEW
W. Heffer and Sons, Ltd.
104 Hills Road
Cambridge, Engl.

MUSIC TEACHER AND PIANO STUDENT
Evans Brothers, Ltd.
Montague House, Russell Square
London, W.C.1 Engl.

MUSIC TEMPO
King Enterprises
4136 Peak Street
Toledo, Ohio 43612

MUSIC TODAY NEWSLETTER
American Music Center, Inc.
2109 Broadway, Suite 15-79
New York, N.Y. 10023

MUSIC TRADES
Music Trades Corp.
P.O. Box 432
Englewood, N.J. 07631

MUSIC WORLD
Norlin Music Co.
7373 North Cicero Avenue
Lincolnwood, Ill. 60646

MUSIK IN DER SCHULE
Volk und Wissen Volkseigener
Verlag Berlin, Lindenstr
54a, 108 Berlin, E. Germany

MUSIK-INFORMATIONEN
Sigert-Verlag, GmbH, Ekbertstr
1433 Braunschweig, W. Germany

MUSIKINSTRUMENT
Verlag das Musikinstrument, Klueberstr
9, 6000 Frankfurt a.M., W. Germany
(Text in English, French, and German)

MUSIK OCH LJUDTEKNIK
Ljndtekniska Saellskapet, Fack 13
S-100 41 Stockholm 26, Sweden

MUSIK UND GESELLSCHAFT
Henschelverlag, Leipsiger Str. 26
108 Berlin, E. Germany

MUSIK UND GOTTESDIENST
Theologischer Verlag, Cramerstr
17, 8004 Zurich, Switzerland

MUZIEK MERCUUR
Dutch Association of Records Dealers
and Dealers in Music Instruments
P.O. Box 56
Hilversum, Netherlands

MUZIKA
Udruzenje Muzickih Pedagoga
Hrvatske
Socijalisticke Revolucije
17, Zagreb, Yugoslavia
(Text in Serbo-Croatian; summaries in
English)

NACWPI JOURNAL
National Association of College Wind
and Percussion Instructors
Simpson Publishing Co.
Kirksville, Mo. 63501

NAMM MUSIC RETAILER NEWS
National Association of Music
Merchants, Inc.
222 West Adams Street
Chicago, Ill. 60606

NAOT NOTES
National Association of Organ
Teachers, Inc.
7938 Bertram Avenue
Hammond, Ind. 46324

NATIONAL MUSIC COUNCIL
BULLETIN
National Music Council
2109 Broadway, Suite 15-79
New York, N.Y. 10023

NATS BULLETIN
National Association of Teachers of
Singing, Inc.
430 South Michigan Avenue
Chicago, Ill. 60605
(Available in microfilm)

NEW JERSEY MUSIC AND ARTS
Box 567
Chatham, N.J. 07928

NEW MUSICAL EXPRESS
IPC Magazines, Ltd.
112 Strand
London, W.C. 2, Engl.

THE NEW RECORDS
c/o H. Royer Smith Co.
Tenth and Walnut Streets
Philadelphia, Pa. 19107

THE NEW YORK REVIEW OF MUSIC
Susan Edelman, Editor
P.O. Box 1167, Ansonia Station
New York, N.Y. 10023

NOTES
Music Library Association
School of Music
University of Michigan
Ann Arbor, Mich. 48105

NUMUS-WEST
P.O. Box 146
Mercer Island, Wash. 98040

ONGAKU-GAKU/JOURNAL OF MUSICOLOGY
Tokyo University of Arts
Japanese Musicological Society
Department of Musicology
Veno Park, Daito-Ku
Tokyo 110, Japan
(Text in Japanese; summaries in English and German)

ON PARADE
All American Association of Contest Judges
518 Hicks Avenue
Plainwell, Mich. 49080

OPERA (England)
Seymour Press, Ltd.
334 Brixton Road
London, S.W. 9, Engl.

OPERA (Italy)
Editoriale Fenarete
Via Beruto 7
Milan, Italy
(Text mainly in Italian; some articles in English, French, German, and Spanish)

OPERA/CANADA
Canadian Opera Association
139 Adelaide Street W., Suite 517
Toronto 110, Ont., Canada
(Text mainly in English, occasionally in French)

OPERA JOURNAL
National Opera Association
University of Mississippi
University Extension
University, Miss. 38677

OPERA NEWS
Metropolitan Opera Guild, Inc.
1865 Broadway
New York, N.Y. 10023

THE ORGANIST MAGAZINE
8432 Telegraph Road
Department IM
Downey, Calif. 90240

ORGAN MUSIC EDUCATOR
Oregon Music Educators Association
337 West Riverside Drive
Roseburg, Ore. 97470

THE ORGAN YEARBOOK
Uitgeverij Frits Knuf
Postbox 20
2707 Buren
The Netherlands

OVERTURE
American Federation of Musicians (AFL-CIO)
Local 47, 817 North Vine Street
Los Angeles, Calif. 90038

PAN PIPES OF SIGMA ALPHA IOTA
George Banta Co., Inc.
Curtis Reed Plaza
Menasha, Wis. 54952

PERCUSSIONIST AND PERCUSSIVE NOTES
Percussive Arts Society
130 Carol Drive
Terre Haute, Ind. 47805

PERFORMING RIGHT
Performing Right Society, Ltd.
29-33 Berners Street
London, Engl.

PERSPECTIVES OF NEW MUSIC
Princeton University Press
Box 231
Princeton, N.J. 08540

PHILHARMONIC HALL PROGRAM AT LINCOLN CENTER
Saturday Review, Inc.
380 Madison Avenue
New York, N.Y. 10017

PHONOLOG
Trade Service Publications, Inc.
2720 Beverly Boulevard
Los Angeles, Calif. 90057

PIANO GUILD NOTES
National Guild of Piano Teachers
Box 1807
Austin, Tex. 78767

PIANO QUARTERLY
Piano Teachers Information Service
Box 707
Melville, N.Y. 11746

PIANO TECHNICIANS JOURNAL
Box 1813
Seattle, Wash. 98111

PIANO WORLD & TRADES REVIEW
Trade Papers (London) Ltd.
46 Chancery Lane
London, W.C. 2 1JB, Engl.
and:
Headinton Hill Hall
Oxford, OX3 OBW, Engl.

POLART INDEX TO RECORD REVIEWS (INCLUDING TAPES)
20115 Goulburn Avenue
Detroit, Mich. 48205

PTM
Piano Trade Publishing Co.
434 South Wabash Avenue
Chicago, Ill. 60605

QUARTERLY CHECKLIST OF MUSICOLOGY
American Bibliographic Service
P.O. Box 1141
Darien, Conn. 06820

RECORDED SOUND
British Institute of Recorded Sound
29 Exhibition Road
London, S.W. 7, Engl.

RECORDER AND MUSIC MAGAZINE
48 Great Marlborough Street
London, W.1, Engl.

RECORD RATING SERVICE
P.O. Box 67
Hudson, N.H. 03051

RECORD RESEARCH
65 Grand Avenue
Brooklyn, N.Y. 11205

RECORD RETAILER
Billboard Publications
7 Carnaby Street
London, WIV IPG, Engl.

RECORDS AND RECORDING
Hansom Books
Artillery Mansions
75 Victoria Street
London, S.W. 1, Engl.

RECORD WORLD
Record World Publishing Co., Inc.
1700 Broadway
New York, N.Y. 10019

RENAISSANCE QUARTERLY
(Formerly RENAISSANCE NEWS)
1161 Amsterdam Avenue
New York, N.Y. 10027

REVIEW OF EDUCATIONAL RESEARCH
American Educational Research Association
1126 Sixteenth Street, N.W.
Washington, D.C. 20036

REVISTA ITALIANA DI MUSICOLOGIA
Societa Italiana di Musicologia
Viuzzo del Possetto (Viale Europa)
50126 Florence, Italy

REVUE DE MUSICOLOGIE
Societe Francaise de Musicologie
28 F. Heugel
Depositaire Exclusif
2 Bis rue Vivienne
Paris (2e), France

RILM ABSTRACTS (Repertoire Internationale de la Litterature Musicale--International Repertory of Musical Literature)
c/o International RILM Center
City University of New York
33 West 42d Street
New York, N.Y. 10036

RINGING WORLD
Central Council of Church Bell Ringers
c/o Seven Corners Press
Onslow Street
Guildford, Surrey, Engl.

ROCK AND SOUL SONGS
Charlton Building
Derby, Conn. 06418

RPM WEEKLY
RPM Music Publications
1560 Bayview Avenue
Toronto 17, Ont., Canada

SACRED MUSIC
584 Lafond Avenue
St. Paul, Minn. 55103

(Replaces the former CAECILIA and the CATHOLIC CHOIRMASTER.)

SAENGER-ZEITUNG
Federation of Workers' Singing Societies of the USA
1729 Springfield Avenue
Maplewood, N.J. 07040
(Text in English and German)

SCHOLARS' GUIDE TO JOURNALS OF EDUCATION AND EDUCATIONAL PSYCHOLOGY
Box 1605
Madison, Wis. 53701

SCHOOL MUSICIAN DIRECTOR AND TEACHER
4 East Clinton Street
Joliet, Ill. 60434

SCHWANN RECORD AND TAPE GUIDE
137 Newberry Street
Boston, Mass. 02116

THE SCORE
American Society of Arrangers
224 West 49th Street
New York, N.Y. 10019

SELMER BANDWAGON
Selmer Division of the Magnavox Co.
Box 310
Elkhart, Ind. 46514

SEM NEWSLETTER
Society for Ethnomusicology
Trent University
Peterborough, Ont., Canada

SINGABOUT: JOURNAL OF AUSTRALIAN FOLKSONG
Bush Music Club
Box 433 Sydney, N.S.W. 2001
Australia

SING OUT
33 West 60th Street
New York, N.Y. 10023

SONG HITS
Charlton Publishing Co.
Division Street
Derby, Conn. 06418

SONGWRITER'S REVIEW
1697 Broadway
New York, N.Y. 10019

SONORUM SPECULUM
Donemus Foundation
Jacob Obrechtstraat 51
Amsterdam Z, Netherlands
(Text in English and German)

SOURCE, MUSIC OF THE AVANT GARDE
Composer Performer Edition
2101 22d Street
Sacramento, Calif. 95818

SPECULUM
1430 Massachusetts Avenue
Cambridge, Mass. 02138

STEREO REVIEW
One Park Avenue
New York, N.Y. 10016

STRAD
Lavender Publications, Ltd.
Borough Green
Sevenoaks, Kent, Engl.

STUDIA MUSICOLOGICA
Publishing House of the Hungarian Academy of Sciences
Alkotmany U. 21, Budapest 5, Hungary
(Text in English, French, German, Italian, or Russian)

STUDIES IN MUSIC
University Bookshop
Nedlands, Western Australia

STUDIES IN THE RENAISSANCE
1161 Amsterdam Avenue
New York, N.Y. 10027

STUDIES ON ORIENTAL MUSIC/ TOYO ONGAKU KENKYU
Japan Publications Trading Co., Ltd.
Box 5030, Tokyo International
Tokyo, Japan
(Text in Japanese; summaries in English)

SYMPHONY NEWS
American Symphony Orchestra League
Symphony Hill
P.O. Box 66
Vienna, Va. 22180

TEMPO (England)
Boosey & Hawkes, Inc.
Oceanside, N.Y. 11572
British address:
Boosey & Hawkes Music
Publishers Ltd.
295 Regent St.
London, W1A 1BR, Engl.

TO THE WORLD'S OBOISTS
(International Double Reed Society)
c/o Dan Stolper
Michigan State University, Music Department
East Lansing, Mich. 48824

TRACKER
Organ Historical Society, Inc.
250 East Market Street
York, Pa. 18702

TRIANGLE OF MU PHI EPSILON
Mu Phi Epsilon National Executive Office
1097 Arnott Way
Campbell, Calif. 95008

VARIETY
154 West 46th Street
New York, N.Y. 10036

WASHINGTON INTERNATIONAL ARTS LETTER
115 Fifth Street, S.E.
Washington, D.C. 20003

WELSH MUSIC
Guild for the Promotion of Welsh Music
10 Llanerch Path
Fairwater, CMBRAN Monmouthshire
NP4 4QN, Wales
(Text mainly in English, sometimes in Welsh)

WOODWIND WORLD--BRASS AND PERCUSSION
Swift-Dorr Publications, Inc.
17 Suncrest Terrace
Oneonta, N.Y. 13820

WOODWIND WORLD was established November 1957, reactivated June 1970. BRASS AND PERCUSSION was established January 1973. Combined with WOODWIND WORLD January 1975.

WORLD OF MUSIC
International Music Council--UNESCO
Box 3640
Weihergarten, D-65 Mainz
W. Germany
(Text in English, French, and German)

YOUTH SYMPHONY NEWS
United States Youth Symphony Federation
441 Washington Avenue
Palo Alto, Calif. 94301

INDEXES

AUTHOR INDEX

This index is alphabetized letter by letter. Numbers refer to page numbers. Indexed here are all authors, editors, compilers, and translators as well as organizations acting as corporate authors. Coauthors are listed individually. Authors whose names appear in different forms in the text are indexed using the fullest form of their name.

A

Abeles, Sally 225
Abraham, Gerald 179, 189, 316, 417
Ackerman, Paul 62, 64
Ades, Hawley 283
Adkins, Cecil 43
Adler, Kurt 283, 339
Adorno, Theodor W. 224
Agate, Edward 364
Albrecht, Otto E. 29
Alexander, Carter 49
Allen, Dwight 405
Allen, Larry D. 125, 233
Allen, Walter C. 421
Allen, Warren D. 191
Allvin, R.L. 409
Alvin, Juliette 383, 393
American Academy of Teachers of Singing 284
American Association of School Administrators 149
American Choral Directors Association, The 284, 292
American Council on Education 131
American Foundation for the Blind 384
American Institute for Research in Behavioral Sciences 141
American Music Conference 149
American Musicological Society, Greater New York Chapter 191, 409
American School Band Directors Association 299
American Society of Composers, Authors and Publishers 255
Ammer, Christine 71
Anderson, Simon V. 130
Anderson, Warren D. 83
Anderson, W.R. 186
Andress, Barbara L. 108
Andrews, Frances M. 125
Andrews, Gladys 109
Anthony, Dorothy Malone 318
Apel, Willi 71-72, 342
Applebaum, Sada 304
Applebaum, Samuel 304
Appleman, D. Ralph 284
Appleton, Jon H. 233
Appleton, Lewis 271
Arberg, Harold W. 91, 130, 149, 299
Arnold, Corliss Richard 345
Arnold, Godfrey E. 102, 287
Aronoff, Frances W. 107
Aronowsky, Solomon 369
Arvey, Verna 249
Ash, Lee 5

Author Index

Associated Councils of the Arts 9
Association for Childhood Education International 109
Association for Recorded Sound Collection 413
Association for Student Teaching 133
Aston, Peter 116
Atkisson, Harold F. 356
Austin, William W. 224
Avedon, Elliott M. 399
Ayre, Leslie 244

B

Bachmann, Alberto 331
Bachmann, Werner 304
Bacilly, Benigne de 284
Backus, John 377
Bailey, Ben Edward 99
Bailey, Eunice 107
Bailey, Philip 383
Baily, Leslie 245
Baines, Anthony 331
Baird, Forrest J. 399
Baird, Jo Ann 114
Baird, Peggy Flanagan 109
Baker, Theodore 72, 161
Balanchine, George 248
Balkin, Alfred 350
Bamberger, Carl 369
Barbour, J. Murray 377
Barish, Mort 13
Barlow, Harold 237
Barlow, Howard 29
Barlow, Wayne 167
Barnes, Robert A. 350
Barrett, Henry 304
Barry, Phillips 205
Bartholomew, Wilmer T. 377
Bartlett, Harry R. 318
Bartlett, Hazel 183
Bartolozzi, Bruno 311, 362
Barzun, Jacques 49, 213
Basart, Ann Phillips 168, 221
Batcheller, John M. 114, 399
Bate, Philip 331
Bauer, Marion 179
Beardsley, Monroe C. 161
Beaumont, Cyril W. 248
Becker, L.J. De. See De Becker, L.J.
Beckman, Frederick 123
Beckwith, Mary 120
Bedford, Frances 344
Beelke, Ralph 124
Beer, Alice S. 109
Behnke, Emile 284
Bekker, Paul 167
Belknap, Sara Yancey 237
Bellows, George Kent 216
Belz, Carl 261
Benade, Arthur H. 377
Benner, Charles L. 83
Bennett, Richard Rodney 225
Benson, Warren 222, 365
Bentley, Arnold 99
Benton, Rita 3, 49
Benzoor, N. 271
Beranek, Leo L. 377
Berel, Marianne 393
Berg, Richard C. 123
Berger, Kenneth 300
Berger, Melvin 125, 378
Berges, Ruth 240
Bergethon, Bjornar 109, 121
Berk, Lee 61
Berkowitz, Freda Pastor 29
Berlyne, D.E. 161
Berner, Alfred 332
Bernstein, Martin 167
Berry, Wallace 357
Bescoby-Chambers, John 418
Bessaraboff, Nicholas 332
Bessom, Malcolm E. 127, 149
Best, John W. 49
Besterman, Theodore 33
Biasini, Americole 107, 110
Bierley, Paul E. 300
Bigelow, Arthur Lynds 318
Binion, W.T., Jr. 302
Birge, Edward Bailey 83
Blacking, John 167
Blackman, Charles 369
Blades, James 318
Blanks, Harvey 413
Blesh, Rudi 257
Blom, Eric 3, 4, 16, 21, 72, 74, 335
Blomster, Wesley V. 224

Bloom, Benjamin S. 149
Bloom, Erie 3
Blum, Fred 33
Blume, Friederich 167, 179, 275
Boalch, Donald H. 344
Boardman, Eunice 109, 123
Boatwright, Howard 350
Bobri, Vladimir 305
Bockman, Guy Alan 168
Bodengraven, Paul Van. See Van Bodengraven, Paul
Boehm, Laszlo 349
Boelza, Igor Fedorovich 180
Bogsch, Arpad 61
Bohle, Bruce 76
Bond, R.W.I. 210
Bone, Philip James 305
Boney, Joan 133
Bonilla, Frank 141
Booth, Robert 141
Boretz, Benjamin 224
Borg, Walter R. 49
Borgese, Elisabeth M. 355
Bornoff, Jack 168, 224, 241
Borroff, Edith 180
Boulez, Pierre 224
Boulton, Laura 199, 332
Bowers, Q. David 332
Bowles, Edmund A. 409
Bowles, Michael 369
Bowman, David L. 141
Boyce, William 405
Boyd, Jack 284, 369
Boyden, David D. 305
Boyle, David 83
Boyle, Hugh 378
Brace, Michele 233
Bradshaw, Susan 224
Bragard, Roger 332
Brand, Erick D. 303
Brandel, Rose 199, 266
Braun, Susan 425
Breed, Paul F. 282
Briegleb, Ann 199, 418
Bright, Ruth 393
Brindle, Reginald Smith 311, 318, 362
Briscuso, Joseph J. 100
British Broadcasting Co. Music Library 281
Brocklehurst, J. Brian 83
Brockway, Wallace 237
Broder, Nathan 227
Brodnitz, Friederich S. 284
Brody, Elaine 241
Brook, Barry S. 30, 191, 409
Brooks, B. Marian 110
Brown, Calvin S. 168
Brown, Harry A. 110
Brown, Howard Mayer 180
Brown, James W. 405
Brown, Len 205
Browne, Lennox 284
Bruce, Violet Rose 249
Brummel, Leendert 3
Bruner, Jerome S. 84
Bryant, E.T. 72
Bryden, John R. 30, 275
Buchner, Alexander 203, 332
Buck, Percy C. 99
Buetens, Stanley 333
Buggert, Robert W. 168, 319
Bukofzer, Manfred F. 180, 191
Bull, Storm 221
Burgan, Arthur 303
Burgin, John Carroll 285
Burmeister, Clifton A. 50
Burney, Charles 180
Burnsworth, Charles C. 291
Buros, Oscar Krisen 99
Burrows, Raymond M. 30
Burton, Jack 243, 255
Bush, Alan 180
Busoni, Ferrucio 161
Butcher, Vada E. 266
Buttleman, Clifford V. 84, 213
Butts, Carrol M. 302

C

Cacavas, John 362
Cady, Henry L. 45
Caimi, Florentino 295
Caldwell, John 339
Calvocoressi, M.D. 373
Camden City Schools, New Jersey 142
Camp, John M.F. 319
Campbell, Frank G. 281
Campbell, Ronald F. 150
Campbell, Warren C. 101

Cannon, Beekman 180
Carabo-Cone, Madeleine 142
Carder, Polly 119
Carlson, Effie B. 221
Carlson, James C. 350
Carlson, Reynold Edgar 399
Carpenter, Nan Cooke 133
Carpenter, Thomas H. 405
Carrington, John V. 319
Carse, Adam 180, 333, 362
Carter, Henry H. 72
Caswell, Austin B. 284
Cellier, Francois Arsene 245
Central Midwest Regional Education Laboratory 107
Chao-Mei-Pa 199
Charbon, Marie H. 281
Charles, Sydney R. 17, 30
Charms, Desiree De. See De Charms, Desiree
Chase, Gilbert 213
Chasteck, Winifred Knox 350
Chavez, Carlos 168
Chazanoff, Daniel 321
Cheyette, Herbert 110
Cheyette, Irving 110
Chicorel, Marietta 13, 15
Childs, Barney 229
Chilton, John 257
Chipman, John H. 255
Choate, Robert A. 84, 123-24, 228
Chosky, Lois 118
Christ, William 351
Christiani, Adolph F. 339
Chujoy, Anatole 250
Claghorn, Charles Eugene 213
Clark, Frank 125, 378
Clark, Joan 425
Clarke, A. Mason 305
Clarke, Mary 248
Clayton, Peter 255
Clemencie, Rene 333
Clementi, Muzio 339
Clendenin, William R. 181
Closon, Ernest 339
Clough, Frances F. 413
CMP (Contemporary Music Project). See Music Educators National Conference. Contemporary Music Project
Cobbett, Walter Willson 322
Coerne, Louis Adolphe 363
Coffin, Berton 291
Cohen, Harold L. 142
Cohen, Selma Jeanne 248
Cohn, Arthur 221, 418
Coker, Wilson 161
Cole, Hugo 349
Coleman, Henry 175
Coleman, Jack L. 383
Coleman, Mina P. 161
Coleman, Satis N. 319
Collaer, Paul 200, 225
Colles, H.C. 186
Collier, Graham 257
Collier, Nina P. 142
Collins, Gertrude 305
Collins, Myron 319
Colorni, Evelina 285
Colvig, Rieborn 418
Colwell, Richard 84
Colwell, Ruth 84
Combs, Josiah 205
Combs, Michael F. 319
Conant, Robert 344
Cone, Edward T. 224
Consumers Reports 416
Contemporary Music Project. See Music Educators National Conference. Contemporary Music Project
Cook, Clifford 310
Cook, Harold E. 181
Cooke, Deryck 161, 168
Cooper, Grosvenor 358
Cooper, Irvin, 123, 125
Cooper, Lewis H. 311
Cooper, Martin 73, 187, 189
Cooper, Paul 351
Coover, James B. 73, 418
Cope, David 225
Copenhagen Musikhistorik Museum 333
Corey, Stephen 50
Corley, Robert 315
Costello, Lawrence 405
Cott, Jonathan 168
Council for Research in Music Education 84
Courlander, Harold 267

Cowell, Henry 213
Cowell, Sidney Robertson 207
Cox, John Harrington 205
Cox, Richard C. 150
Cox, Richard G. 285
Crane, Frederick 333
Creighton, James 305
Creston, Paul 361
Crews, Katherine 114
Crisp, Clement 248
Crocker, Richard L. 168, 358
Croft, Doreen J. 112
Crook, Elizabeth 110, 123, 124
Cross, Lowell M. 233
Cross, Milton 73, 238
Crowhurst, Norman H. 233, 333
Crystal Record Company 223
Csida, Joseph 64
Cudworth, Charles L. 3
Cull, John G. 384
Cullen, Marion E. 169
Culver, Charles A. 378
Cuming, G.J. 413
Cundiff, Hannah M. 85
Cuney-Hare, Maude 267
Curriculum Consultation Service 265
Curtis, Robert E. 64
Cushing, Helen Grant 281
Cutler, Bruce 62
Cutts, Norma E. 110
Cuyler, Louise 169
Czarnowski, Lucile K. 252
Czigany, Gyula 225

D

Daetz, Helen 57
Dahl, Ingolf 164
Dal, Erik 211
Dalby, John B. 297
Dalcroze, Emile. See Jaques-Dalcroze, Emile
Dale, Delbert A. 315
Dale, Edgar 406
Dalen, Deobold Van. See Van Dalen, Deobold
Dallin, Leon 169, 225, 351
Daniel, Ralph T. 72
Danielou, Alain 181
Daniels, Arthur 169
Daniels, David 297, 369
Daniels, Elva S. 114
Darnell, Josiah 120
Darrow, Gerald F. 285
Dart, Thurston 333, 366
Daugherty, D.H. 192
Davidson, Ake 181
Davie, Cedric Thorpe 358
Davies, B.N. Langdon 161
Davies, Hugh 233
Davies, J.G. 275
Davies, J.H. 17
Davis, Arthur Kyle, Jr. 205
Davis, Hazel 85
Davison, Archibald 285, 361, 370
D'Azevedo, Warren L. 267
Deane, Norma 304
Dean-Smith, Margaret 203, 204
Deatsman, Gerald 343
de Bacilly, Benigne. See Bacilly, Benigne de
De Becker, L.J. 73
Debussy, Claude 161
De Charms, Desiree 282
Decker, Harold A. 370
De Hen, Ferdinand J. 332
Deighton, Lee C. 79
De Lafontaine, Henry Cart. See Lafontaine, Henry Cart
Delaunay, Charles 421
De Lerma, Dominique-René 47, 213, 265, 267
De Long, Patrick D. 169
Denisoff, R. Serge 142, 205, 255
Dennis, Brian 225
Densmore, Frances 214
Dent, Frank L. 169
de Ramon y Rivera, I. Aretz. See Rivera, I. Aretz de Ramon y
Deri, Otto 225
De Smet, Robin 305
Deva, Bigamundre Chaitanya 200
Deveson, Richard 229
Dewey, John 162
De Yarman, Robert M. 100
De Young, Richard 285
Dichter, Harry 214
Diehl, Katharine S. 275
Diehl, Ned C. 295
Dimondstein, Geraldine 110

Dittmore, Edgar E. 101
Divenyi, Pierre L. 101
Dobbs, J.P.B. 383
Dolan, Robert Emmett 225, 361, 363
Doll, Ronald C. 150
Dolmetsch, Rudolph 370
Donato, Anthony 349
Donington, Robert 322, 333, 366
Dorf, Richard H. 234
Douglas, Alan L.M. 234
Douglas, Charles H. 113, 296
Douglas, Paul Marshall 312
Dove, Jack 3
Downing, Lyle 355
Downs, Robert B. 33
Drinker, Henry S. 291
Drinklage, H.A. 393
Drinkrow, John 244
Driver, Ann 111
Drummond, Andrew H. 242
DuBois, Charlotte 124
Duckles, Vincent Harris 21, 34, 192, 413
Duerksen, George L. 295
Duey, Philip A. 285
Dufourcq, Norbert 74
Dunstan, Ralph 73
Duvall, W. Clyde 300
Dwyer, Edward J. 282
Dwyer, Terence 169, 234, 246
Dykema, Peter W. 85, 127

E

Eaglefield-Hull, A. 73
Eagon, Angelo 214
Earhart, Will 85
East Chicago City School District, Indiana 142
Eaton, Quaintance 238, 246
Ebel, Robert L. 79
Edelson, Edward 127
Edmunds, John 215
Edson, Jean Slater 345
Educational Technology Publications 406
Educational Testing Service 103, 136
Edwards, Arthur C. 215, 305
Edwards, Ruth 340
Egg, Maria 383
Egger, E. 3
Ehmann, Wilhelm 370
Ehret, Walter 123, 370
Eickmann, Paul E. 406
Einstein, Alfred 162, 181, 182
Eisen, Jonathan 261
Eisenberg, Helen 370
Eisenberg, Larry 370
Eisenstein, Judith Kaplan 271
Eisler, Paul E. 182
Elam, Stanley 133
Elgar, Raymond 305
Ellinwood, Leonard 215, 276
Elliott, Kenneth 182
Elliott, Raymond 120
Ellison, Alfred 111
Elschek, Oskar 211
Engel, Carl 182
Engel, Lehman 246
England, Paul 238
English Folk Dance and Song Society 252
Epling, Christine Fraley 397
Epperson, Gordon 162
Erickson, Carlton W.H. 406
Eriksen, Mary Le Bow 117
Ernst, Carl D. 85
Ernst, David 234
Errante, F. Gerard 311
Eschman, Karl 226
Ethnomusicology, Society for. See Society for Ethnomusicology, Committee on Ethnomusicology and Music Education
Evans, Edward G., Jr. 174
Evans, Ken 111
Evenson, Flavis 115
Everett, Thomas G. 315
Eversole, James 174
Ewen, David 73, 169, 170, 215, 226, 238, 241, 244, 255

F

Fantel, Hans 406
Farga, Franz 306
Farish, Margaret K. 306
Farkas, Philip 315

Farnsworth, Paul R. 85, 99, 393
Feather, Leonard G. 257
Fellner, Rudolph 238
Ferguson, Donald N. 162, 170, 182
Field, Gladys S. 7, 21
Fields, Victor Alexander 285
Findlay, Elsa 119
Finell, Judith G. 223
Fink, Michael 358
Fink, Robert 162
Finkbeiner, Evelyn Robe 102, 287
Finkelstein, Sidney 170
Finn, William J. 370
Fish, Arnold 351
Fischer, Kurt Von. See Von Fischer, Kurt
Fisher, Miles Mark 267
Fisher, Renee B. 397
Fisher, William R. 124
Fiske, Roger 248
Fitzpatrick, Horace 315
Fixter, Deborah A. 136
Fontaine, Paul 358
Foote, Henry Wilder 276
Ford, Wyn K. 182
Forlano, George 145
Forsyth, Cecil 363
Forte, Allen 226, 351, 409
Foss, Roger V. 100
Foster, Donald L. 170
Foster, William 302
Fowler, Charles B. 129, 168
Fox, David J. 143
Fox, Lilla Margaret 333
Frankenstein, Alfred 170
Franklin, Erik 100
Fraser, Norman 210
Freeberg, William 383, 399
Freeburg, Roy E. 123
Freundlich, Irwin 342
Friedrich, Gary 205
Friskin, James 342
Fritz, Kenneth 134
Frye, Harvey R. 406
Fuchs, Peter Paul 370
Fuhr, Hayes M. 286
Fuld, James J. 182
Fullerton, Margaret 123
Fux, Johann Joseph 356

G

Gadan, Francis 248
Gaines, Joan 150
Galliard, J.E. 290
Gallup, Alice 123
Galpin, Francis W. 333
Gammond, Peter 255
Ganz, Rudolph 342
Gardiner, Julian 286
Gardner, Howard 85
Garland, Phyl 267
Garretson, Homer E. 322
Garretson, Robert L. 111, 371
Gary, Charles L. 85
Gaston, E. Thayer 393
Gates, Everett 378
Gayle, Addison, Jr. 267
Geer, E. Harold 345
Geerdes, Harold P. 150
Gehrkens, Karl L. 127
Geiringer, Karl 334
Gelineau, R. Phyllis 111, 121
Gentry, Linnell 205
George, Graham 351
Gerboth, Walter 17, 182
Giannaris, George 86
Gibbons, Irene 200
Gibson, Gordon 246
Gilbert, Cecile 252
Gilbert, Pia 250
Gilbert, Richard 311
Gillespie, James E. 311
Gillespie, John 171, 344
Gilliland, Dale V. 286
Gillis, Frank 44, 200, 203
Ginglend, David R. 384
Gingrich, Donald 114
Giteau, Cecile 5
Glasford, Irene S. 100
Gleason, Harold 217
Glenn, Mabelle 89
Glenn, Neal E. 122, 127, 133
Globus, Rodo S. 311
Gold, Cecil V. 311
Gold, Robert S. 257
Goldbeck, Frederick 371
Goldberg, Ira S. 271
Goldberg, Morton 61
Golding, Robin 339

Goldman, Bernard 50
Goldman, Richard Franko 300, 351
Goldovsky, Boris 246
Golin, Sanford 143, 268
Gombosi, Marilyn 276
Good, Carter V. 79
Goodwin, Arthur B. 406
Gordon, Boelzner 215
Gordon, Edwin 100, 101, 144
Gordon, George N. 405
Gordon, Roderick Dean 44, 45
Gossett, Philip 354
Gowan, John Curtis 397
Gradenwitz, Peter 271
Graf, Herbert 238, 242
Graff, Henry F. 49
Graham, Floyd Freeman 150
Graham, Richard M. 384
Grant, Gail 248
Grant, W. Parks 73
Gray, Vera 111
Great Cities Program for School Improvement 143
Green, Elizabeth A.H. 306, 371
Green, John E. 317, 319
Green, Stanley 244
Greenberg, Marvin 111
Greene, John S. 10
Greer, R. Douglas 101, 102
Gregor, Carl 258
Gregory, Julia 183
Gregory, Robin 315
Greyser, Stephen A. 63
Griffin, Louise 143
Griffith, Celeste 309
Grodner, Murray 306
Grosbayne, Benjamin 371
Grout, Donald Jay 183, 241
Grunfeld, Frederic V. 306, 334
Guss, Carolyn 411
Guterman, Norbert 164
Gutsch, Kenneth U. 101

H

Haberman, Martin 250
Hagen, Earle H. 363
Haggh, Raymond 355
Haggin, Bernard H. 171
Hagopian, Viola L. 183
Hale, Leslie William 286
Hall, Doreen 119
Hall, Douglas Kent 261
Hall, James B. 162
Hall, Mary 57
Hansen, Peter S. 183, 227
Hanson, Howard 352
Harder, Paul O. 227, 352
Hardwick, John Michael Drinkrow 245
Hardy, Richard E. 384
Harewood, George Henry (Earl of Harewood) 238
Hargens, C.W. 282, 286
Harman, Alec 183
Harris, Daniel 292
Harris, Ernest E. 307
Harris, Kenn 239, 418
Harris, Rex 421
Harrison, Frank L. 77, 192, 334
Hart, Philip 297
Hartley, Harry J. 151
Hartley, Katherine 14
Hartley, Kenneth R. 276
Hartley, Ruth E. 144
Hartnoll, Phyllis 171
Hartog, John F. 144
Hartshorn, William C. 123, 128, 397
Harvard University. Graduate School of Education 144
Hausen, Karl D. Van. See Van Hausen, Karl D.
Hausman, Ruth L. 215
Hawkins, Sir John 183
Haydon, Glen 192
Hayes, Elizabeth 128
Hays, William 183
Haywood, Charles 203, 206
Headington, Christopher 334
Heaton, Wallace 282, 286
Heger, Theodore E. 184
Heim, Norman 296, 311, 315, 319, 418
Heine, Richard W. 303
Helbig, Otto H. 215
Heller, George N. 311, 316, 320, 322
Hellwig, Jessica 409
Helm, Sanford M. 322

Hemming, Roy 171, 414
Hemphill, Paul 206
Hen, Ferdinand J. De. See De Hen, Ferdinand J.
Hendrickson, Clarence V. 296
Henley, William 334
Henry, Nelson B. 89, 92
Henthoff, Nat 258
Herbert-Caesari, Edgar F. 286
Herder, Ronald 352
Herford, Julius 370
Hermann, Edward J. 123, 151
Hermeges, David 333
Hernon, Peter 41
Herter, M.D. 179, 189
Hertzberg, Alvin 111
Herzog, George 206
Heskes, Irene 271-72
Hess, Robert P. 112
H.E.W. See U.S. Department of Health, Education, and Welfare
Heyer, Anna Harriet 34
Hickerson, Joseph C. 204, 206-7, 258, 418
Hickok, Dorothy 112
Higgs, Geoffrey 385
Hill, George R. 34
Hill, John D. 101, 144
Hill, Thomas H. 128, 130
Hiller, Lejaren A., Jr. 234
Hilton, Louis B. 37, 312
Hindemith, Paul 361
Hindley, Geoffrey 74
Hinson, Maurice 342
Hinz, Marian C. 144
Historical Records Survey, District of Columbia 216
Hitchcock, H. Wiley 184, 216
Hixon, Donald L. 216
Hodeir, Andre 258
Hodgson, Percival 306
Hoffer, Charles R. 128, 171
Hoffman, Mary E. 109
Hoggard, Lara 123
Holden, Frances 287
Holloway, Ronald 318
Holmes, Malcolm H. 371
Holz, Emil A. 300
Hong, Sherman 320
Hood, Mantle 200
Hood, Marguerite V. 112
Hoover, Cynthia A. 334
Hopkins, Bill 332
Hopkins, Jerry 261
Horacek, Leo 352
Horn, Robert 58
Horner, V. 86
Horst, Louis 250
Horton, John 112
Horzoll, Eugene 174
Hotteterre, Jacques 312
House, Robert W. 87, 151, 296
Houser, Roy 322
Howard, John Tasker 216
Howe, Alfred H. 344
Howe, Hubert S. 234
Howerton, George 287
Howes, Frank 162
Hubbard, Frank 344
Huber, Louis H. 247
Hughes, Anselm. See Hughes, Dom Anselm
Hughes, Charles W. 322
Hughes, David G. 30, 184, 275
Hughes, Dom Anselm 179, 189, 276, 417
Hughes, Gervase 244
Hughes, William O. 121, 125
Humphrey, Doris 250
Humphreys, Louise 112
Hunt, Norman J. 316
Huntley, John 361
Huntley, Leston 63
Huray, Peter Le. See Le Huray, Peter
Hurd, Michael 239
Husmann, Heinrich Von. See Von Husmann, Heinrich
Hutcheson, Ernest 342
Hutcheson, Jere T. 358
Hutchings, Arthur J. 184
Hutchins, Carleen M. 306, 378
Hymovitz, Leon 144

I

Illing, Robert 74
Imig, Warner 123
Ingram, Madeline D. 287
Institute of International Education 65

Instrumentalist, The 300, 312, 316
International Association of Universities. See UNESCO. International Association of Universities
International Directory of Music Education. See UNESCO. International Society for Music Education
International Education, Institute of. See Institute of International Education
International Institute for Comparative Music Studies and Documentation, The 419
International Library of African Music 419
International Music Centre, Vienna 425
International Music Council 298
International Society for Music Education 86
Intravaia, Lawrence J. 301
Irwin, Stevens 345
Isaacson, Leonard M. 234
Ives, Charles 162

J

Jackson, Richard 216
Jacob, Gordon 371
Jacobi, Roger E. 300
Jacobs, Arthur 13, 74, 184, 239, 291
Jacobus, Lee A. 173
Jalovec, Karel 306, 334
James, Philip 340
Janson, H.W. 172, 184
Jaques-Dalcroze, Emile 86, 119
Jarvis, Richard L. 341
Jasen, David A. 258, 421
Jass Enterprises 61
Jeffers, Edmund V. 134
Jenkins, Jean 200, 334
Jennings, John W. 288
Jensen, Clayne R. 112, 252
Jensen, Mary Bee 112, 252
Jepsen, J.G. 421
Jipson, Wayne R. 128
John, Malcolm 126
John, Robert W. 113, 121, 296
Johnson, Harold Earle 242
Johnson, Harry A. 266
Jonas, Oswald 355
Jones, Archie N. 86, 371
Jones, George Thaddeus 358
Jones, Harry Earl 282
Jones, Le Roi 268
Joseph, Jesse J. 378
Joyce, Mary 250
Judd, F.C. 234
Juilliard School of Music, The 113, 365
Julian, John 276

K

Kagen, Sergius 292
Kahn, Emil 372
Kaiman, Bernard D. 115, 253
Kallin, Anna 229, 230
Kaplan, Barbara 123-24
Kaplan, Max 86, 121
Karkoschka, Erhard 349
Karp, Theodore 74
Karpeles, Maud 211
Katayen, Lelia 74
Katz, Adele T. 359
Katz, Bernard 268
Kauder, Hugo 356
Kaufmann, Walter 185
Kay, Ernest 77
Keil, Charles 268
Keller, Hermann 366
Keller, Michael A. 21
Kemp, Jerrold E. 406
Kendall, John D. 310
Kennan, Kent 357, 363
Kennedy, Peter 211
Kennington, Donald 258
Kerman, Joseph 172, 184, 322
King, A. Hyatt 21
Kinkle, Roger D. 256
Kirby, F.E. 343
Kirk, Samuel A. 384
Kjelson, Lee 123, 287
Klaus, Kenneth B. 185
Klein, Bernard 7
Kline, Peter 245
Klotman, Robert H. 151, 307
Knapp, J. Merrill 239

Knocker, Edith 307
Knodel, Arthur 164
Knuth, Alice Snyder 352
Knuth, William E. 352
Kochel, Ludwig Ritter von 31
Koenig, Ruth 349
Kofsky, Frank 145, 268
Kohanski, Dorothy D. 145
Kohrs, Karl 238
Kolodin, Irving 242
Konowitz, Bert 340
Kostka, Stefan M. 410
Kowall, Bonnie C. 86, 92
Kragen, Kenneth 134
Krasilovsky, M. William 64
Kraus, Egon 87, 151
Krehbiel, Henry Edward 268
Kreitler, Hans 101, 162
Kreitler, Shumalith 101, 162
Krishnaswami, S. 335
Krohn, Ernst C. 185, 192
Kroll, Oscar 312
Krone, Beatrice Perham 123
Krone, Max T. 287
Kruger, Chaddie B. 58
Krummel, D.W. 185
Kruzas, Anthony T. 4
Kuernsteiner, Karl 125
Kuhn, Wolfgang E. 296, 307
Kunst, Jaap 200
Kutsch, K.J. 282

L

Labuta, Joseph A. 151, 301
Lacy, Gene M. 298
Lafontaine, Henry Cart 181
Lamb, Gordon H. 287
Lamb, Norman 307
Land, Lois Rhea 113
Landeck, Beatrice 107, 123
Landecker, Mildred N. 352
Landis, Beth 85, 119, 123
Landon, Grelun 209
Landon, Joseph W. 113, 151
Landor, R.A. 87
Landsman, Jerome 307
Lang, Paul Henry 185, 216, 227
Langridge, Derek 422
Langwill, Lyndesay Graham 4, 312, 335
Lann, Jack H. 77
Larsen, Egon 306
Larson, William S. 44
La Rue, John 359
Lasker, Henry 129
Lasocki, David 312
Last, Joan 340
Laufe, Abe 244
Lawless, Ray M. 207, 419
Lawrence, Robert 249
Layton, Robert 229
Leach, Joel T. 320, 364
Leadbitter, Mike 422
Leblanc, Albert 297
Lee, Jack 302
Lefkoff, Gerald 361, 410
Lehman, Paul R. 102, 312
Lehmann, Lotte 287
Lehmer, Isabel 353
Le Huray, Peter 277
Leichtentritt, Hugo 185, 359
Leigh, Robert 282
Leipp, Emile 307, 335
Leonard, Neil 258
Leonhard, Charles 87, 123
Lerma, Dominique-René De. See De Lerma, Dominique-René
Lesure, Francais 35
Letz, Hans 307
Lewanski, Richard C. 4
Lewine, Richard 256
Lewinsky, Edward E. 353
Lewis, Marianna 58
Lewis, Richard B. 405
Lhevinne, Joseph 340
Library Association 16
Library of Congress 4, 414
Library of Congress. Copyright Office 61
Library of Congress. Division for the Blind and Physically Handicapped 385
Library of Congress. General Reference and Bibliography Division 216
Library of Congress. Music Division 204
Library of Congress. Music Division. Archive of American Folk Song 207, 419

Licht, Sidney 394
Lichtenwanger, William 335
Lieberman, Maurice 353
Liess, Andreas 119
Lifkoff, Gerald 352
Limbacher, James 412
Lincoln, Harry B. 131, 235, 410
Lindsay, Martin 361
Lindsey, Margaret 134
Linker, Robert White 185
Lins, L. Joseph 63
Livingston, James A. 87
Lloyd, A.L. 204, 211
Lloyd, L.S. 378
Lloyd, Norman 74, 351
Locke, Alain 268
Lockhart, Aileene 250
Lockspeiser, Edward 172
Loewenberg, Alfred 241
Loft, Abraham 307
Lohman, Maurice A. 145
Lomax, Alan 204, 207
Lomax, John 207
Long, Charles M. 145
Long, John H. 172
Long, Maureen W. 4
Long, Patrick D. De See De Long, Patrick D.
Longstreet, Stephen 258
Longyear, Rey M. 184
Loon, Hendrick Willem Van. See Van Loon, Hendrick Willem
Lorenz, Denis 5
Los Angeles City Schools 397
Lovell, John R. 269
Lowens, Irving 217
Lowery, H. 378
Lowrey, Alvin L. 316
Lubbock, Mark H. 244
Lubin, Ernest 343
Luchsinger, Richard 102, 287
Ludin, Robert W. 102
Luening, Otto 123, 235
Lunan, Bert 383, 399
Lutolf, Max 36
Lynn Farnol Group 72

M

Macak, Ivan 211
McCall, Adeline 124
McCarthy, Albert 258, 422
McCray, James 287
McDonald, William F. 152
McElheran, Brock 372
McGarrity, Bertram 313
McGehee, Thomasine C. 172
McGrath, Earl J. 136
MacGregor, Beatrix 111
Machlis, Joseph 172
McKay, George F. 363
MacKeigan, Helaine 4
McKenzie, Duncan 126
McKenzie, Jack 320
MacKenzie, Norman 134
McKinney, Howard D. 186
McLeish, John 385
McLuhan, Marshall 406
McMillan, L. Eileen 123
Macmillan Information Division 10
McMullen, Roy 87
Macpherson, Stewart 359
Madsen, Charles A., Jr. 102
Madson, Charles H. 50
Madson, Clifford K. 50, 102
Mahoney, Margaret 134
Maillard, Robert 248
Maleady, Antoinette O. 416
Malko, Nikolai 371
Malloy, Lawrence 385
Malm, William P. 184
Malone, Bill C. 208
Manchester, P.W. 250
Mangler, Joyce Ellen 208
Mann, Alfred 356, 373
Manners, Ande 118
Manvell, Roger 361
Mara, Thalia 249
Marco, Guy A. 17
Marcouiller, Don R. 302
Marcuse, Sibyl 335
Markel, Roberta 87
Markewich, Reese 259
Marks, Martin 103, 308
Marple, Hugo D. 126, 173, 372
Marquis, George Welton 227
Marrocco, W. Thomas 215, 217
Marsh, Mary Val 113, 124, 126
Martin, F. David 173
Martin, Gary M. 353

Martindale, Don 176
Marvel, Lorene M. 113
Marx, Henry 228
Mason, Bernard S. 253
Mason, Daniel Gregory 173
Mason, Francis 248
Mason, Henry L. 277
Matesky, Ralph 307
Mathews, Denis 343
Mathews, Max V. 235
Mathews, Paul W. 121
Mattfeld, Julius 243, 256
Matthay, Tobias 340-41, 366
Mattran, Donald 312
Maynard, Olga 114
Meisel, Tobie Garth 250
Mellers, Wilfrid Howard 173, 256
Melly, George 256
Meltzer, Richard 261
MENC. See Music Educators National Conference
Mendez, Rafael 316
Menke, Werner 316
Mercer, Frank 180
Mercer, Jack 301
Merriam, Alan P. 44, 200, 203, 259, 419
Merriman, Lyle 314
Merritt, Arthur Tillman 357
Meske, Eunice Boardman 152
Meyer, Leonard B. 173, 358
Miall, Bernard 334
Miller, William Hugh 173
Milliken, Russel A. 397
Mills, Elizabeth 310
Millsaps, Daniel 58
Minor, Ed 406
Mitchell, Anne G. 224
Mitchell, Donald 227
Mitchell, Ronald E. 239
Mitchell, William J. 353
Mixter, Keith E. 34, 50, 192
Modlinger, Roy 144
Moe, Daniel 288, 372
Mohatt, James L. 101
Moldenhauer, Hans 341
Mole, Michaela M. 13
Moles, Abraham 163
Moller, Max 335
Monsour, Sally 114, 126, 399
Moore, Chauncey O. 208
Moore, Douglas 359
Moore, Ethel 208
Moore, Frank Ledlie 239, 245
Moore, Isabel 134
Moore, June 298
Moore, Randall S. 50
Morgan, Hazel B. 50, 87, 91-92
Morgan, Wesley K. 419
Morgenstern, Sam 29, 237
Morley-Pegge, R. 316
Morris, R. Winston 316
Morrison, Theodore 277
Moseley, Nicholas 110
Moses, Harry E. 129
Mozart, Leopold 307
Mueller, Frederick A. 313
Mueller, Herbert C. 317
Mueller, John H. 298
Mueller, Kate 298
Mueller, Kenneth A. 320
Muller, Mette 333
Mulligan, Mary Ann 114
Murphy, Howard Ansley 353, 365
Murphy, O.J. 298, 378
Murphy, Sister Therese Cecile 310
Murray, Ruth Lovell 115
Mursell, James L. 88-89, 102, 121
Music Educators National Conference (MENC) 10, 41, 63, 65, 89, 103, 152, 292, 407
Music Educators National Conference (MENC). Commission on Teacher Education 134-35
Music Educators National Conference (MENC). Committee on Contemporary Music 135, 223
Music Educators National Conference (MENC). Contemporary Music Project 135, 221, 282, 298, 301, 320, 353, 365
Music Educators National Conference (MENC). Elementary Commission 115
Music Educators National Conference (MENC). Music in American Life Commission on Music in the Senior High School 129
Music Educators National Confer-

ence (MENC). National Commission on Instruction 108, 152
Music Industry Council 63
Music Library Association 152
Music Publishers' Association of the United States, Inc. 61
Music Publishers' Protective Association, Inc. 61
Music Research Foundation 103, 394
Music Teachers National Association, The 92
Mussulman, Joseph A. 89, 217
Mutschler, Marla 308
Myers, Louise Kifer 115
Myers, Rollo 227
Mynatt, Constance V. 115, 253

N

Nabokov, Nicolas 229, 230
Nadeau, Roland 173
Nallin, Walter E. 174
Nanry, Charles 259
Nardone, Thomas R. 282, 345
Nathan, M. Montagu 186
National Association of Secondary School Principals 130, 152
National Association of State Directors of Teacher Education and Certification 135
National Council of State Supervisors of Music 152, 153
National Society for the Study of Education 89
Neckritz, Benjamin 145
Nederveen, Cornelis Johannes 312
Neidig, Kenneth L. 153, 288
Nelson, Sheila M. 308
Nemussurei, Mihali 309
Nettl, Bruno 184, 201, 204, 208
Nettl, Paul 174, 186, 250
Neumann, Frederick 308
Newcomb, Stanley 302
Newman, Bernard 65
Newman, Elizabeth 115
Newman, William S. 341, 359
New York. University of the State of. State Education Department 385, 407
New York City Foundation Center 58
New York Library Association Children and Young Adults Services Section 420
New York State Commission on Cultural Resources 153
New York State Education Department 146
Nite, Norman N. 261
Nketia, J.H. Kwabena 269, 320
Nordholm, Harriet 121, 123
Nordoff, Paul 394
Norton, M.D. Herter 167, 323
Nulman, Macy 272
Nurmi, Ruth 344
Nye, Robert E. 115-16, 120, 121, 146, 385
Nye, Vernice T. 116, 120, 146, 385
Nyman, Michael 361

O

Ochse, Orpha 345
Office of Education, U.S. See U.S. Office of Education
Oliver, Paul 259
Olson, Harry F. 379
Olson, Robert G. 354
O'Morrow, Gerald S. 394
Opsahl, Julian E. 303
Orrey, Leslie 241
Ortman, Otto 341
Osborn, Wendell L. 103
Ottman, Robert W. 354
Otto, Richard A. 301

P

Pace, Robert L. 122, 341
Paetkau, David H. 335
Page, Athol 323
Pair, Mary Wilson 9
Palisca, Claude V. 153, 184
Palmer, Harold 312
Palmer, King 247
Panum, Hortense 336
Parker, De Witt H. 163
Parks, Edna D. 277
Parrish, Carl 76, 193, 359
Parry, C. Hubert H. 186
Parry, Hildegarde W. 307
Partch, Harry 228

Pauly, Reinhard G. 184, 239
Pavlakis, Christopher 8, 22, 59, 132
Paynter, John 116
Payson, A. 320
Pearsall, Ronald 186
Pegram, Wayne F. 301
Pellegrino, Ronald 235
Percival, John 249, 251
Percival, Rachel 111
Percussive Arts Society 320
Perera, Ronald C. 233
Perle, George 228
Perry, Margaret 126
Persichetti, Vincent 228
Peters, Harold B. 312
Peterson, Paul W. 288
Petters, Robert 372
Peyser, Ethel 179
Peyser, Joan 228
Pfautsch, Lloyd 288
Phelps, Roger P. 50, 59
Philips, Thomas 246
Pichierri, Louis 208
Picken, Laurence 211
Picker, Martin 167
Pierce, Anne E. 122
Pilpel, Harriet 61
Pisk, Paul A. 188
Piston, Walter 354, 357, 363
Pitts, Lilla Belle 90
Pittsburgh Public Schools, Pennsylvania 146
Pizer, Russell A. 301
Pleasants, Henry 239
Plenckers, Leo J. 336
Podolsky, Edward 394
Pogonowski, Lee 110
Poladian, Sirvart 245
Pollack, Barbara 250
Polmar, Mary 114
Polnauer, Frederick F. 103, 308
Porter, Evelyn 116, 251
Porter, Keyes 215
Porter, Maurice 317
Potter, Ralph K. 288
Pottle, Ralph R. 297
Prall, D.W. 163
Pratt, Waldo Selden 74
Price, Steven D. 208
Priestley, Mary 395
Pruett, James W. 193
Pulver, Jeffrey 75, 336

Q

Quantz, Johann Joachim 312

R

Rachow, Louis 14
Rader, Melvin 163
Raebeck, Lois 116, 120
Raffe, W.G. 251
Rafferty, Sadie 187
Raikin, Bruno 306
Rainbow, Bernard 116
Rameau, Jean-Phillipe 354
Rasmussen, Mary 312, 317
Rathbone, Charles H. 117
Ratner, Leonard G. 174, 354
Rauchhaupt, Ursula von 174
Rauscher, Donald 364
Raynor, Henry 186
Read, Gardner 349, 364
Read, Sir Herbert Edward 75
Reaney, Gilbert 35
Reddick, William J. 372
Redmond, Bessie C. 30
Reed, H. Owen 320, 364
Reeder, Barbara 223, 266
Rees, Robert A. 63
Reese, Gustave 186, 187
Reese, William H. 373
Regelski, Thomas A. 90
Reich, Willi 230
Reichardt, Jasia 362
Reid, Cornelius 288
Reilly, Edward R. 312
Reimer, Bennett 90, 124, 163, 174
Reiss, Alvin H. 63
Rendall, Francis Geoffrey 313
Renna, Albert A. 123
Rensch, Roslyn 308
Reynolds, Jane L. 122
Reynolds, William Jensen 277
Rezits, Joseph 343
Rhea, Raymond 123
Rhode, H. Kandy 422
Rice, William C. 287

Rice, William Gorham 321
Rich, Maria F. 59, 240, 243, 247
Richards, Mary Helen 120
Richards, Stanley 244
Richey, Robert W. 65
Richmond, Stanley 313
Riedel, Johannes 259
Riehm, Diethard 312
Riemann, Hugo 354
Riemens, Leo 282
Rimmer, Frederick 182
Rimmer, Joan 334
Rimsky-Korsakov, Nikolay 364
Rinderer, Leo 117
Rinehart, Carroll 124
Riordan, Jennifer Talley 385
Ritter, Frederic Louis 217
Rive, Thomas 357
Rivera, I. Aretz de Ramon y 210
Roach, Hildred 269
Robbins, Clive 394
Roberts, John Storm 269
Roberts, Kenneth 292
Robertson, Alec 187, 323
Robertson, J.M. 153
Robins, Ferris 386
Robins, Jennet 386
Robinson, Helene 341
Robinson, Trevor 336
Rockefeller Brothers' Fund, Special Studies Project 217
Rockstro, R.S. 313
Roda, Joseph 336
Roe, Paul F. 289
Roederer, Juan G. 379
Roemer, Clinton 350
Rogers, A. Robert 90
Rogers, Bernard 364
Rogers, Elizabeth 179
Rolland, Paul 308
Rose, Al 259
Rose, Arnold 289
Rose, Hanna Toby 146
Rosen, Charles 360
Rosenberg, Bruce A. 208
Rosenthal, Carl A. 350
Rosenthal, Harold 240, 242
Rosenwald, Hans 229
Rosewall, Richard 289
Ross, Anne 240, 242
Ross, Jerrold 112
Ross, Ted 64
Rossi, Nick 187, 228
Rostand, Claude 228
Rothenberg, Stanley 61
Rothmuller, Aron Marks 272
Rothrock, Carson 299
Rothwell, Evelyn 313
Roucek, Joseph S. 386
Routley, Erik 228, 277
Rowen, Ruth Halle 323
Rowland-Jones, A. 313
Rowley, Alec 343
Roxon, Lillian 262
Rubbra, Edmund 357
Rubio, P. Samuel 357
Rublowsky, John 269
Rudolph, Max 372
Rufsvold, Margaret 411
Runes, Dagobert 75
Runkle, Aleta 117
Rush, Ralph E. 307
Rushmore, Robert 289
Russcol, Herbert 235
Russell, Carroll 250
Russell, Joan 251
Russell, Raymond 345
Russel-Smith, Geoffry 120
Russo, William 259
Rust, Brian 421, 422
Rutan, Harold D. 323
Ruth, Diane 135
Ryan, Kevin 405

S

Sablosky, Irving L. 217
Sacher, Jack 75, 174
Sachs, Curt 187, 251, 336
Sadie, Stanley 239
Saerchinger, Cesar 162
Sainsbury, John S. 75
Salop, Arnold 360
Saltonstall, Cecilia Drinker 299
Salzer, Felix 355, 357
Salzman, Eric 184, 229
Saminsky, Lazare 372
Sample, Mabel Warkentin 289
Sandved, K.B. 75
Sargent, Sir Malcolm 187

Savage, Edith 124
Sawhill, Clarence 313
Sax, Gilbert 51
Schachter, Carl 357
Schafer, William J. 259
Schattner, Regina 386
Schenker, Heinrich 355
Scherchen, Hermann 373
Schillinger, Joseph 355
Schiotz, Askel 289
Schlager, Karlheinz 36
Schlesinger, Kathleen 336
Schleuter, Stanley L. 100
Schmidt, Lloyd 153
Schnabel, Arthur 163
Schnapper, Edith B. 193
Schneider, Edwin H. 45, 51
Schoen, Max 103, 175, 395
Schoenberg, Arnold 355, 362
Schoep, Arthur 292
Scholes, Percy A. 75-76
Scholl, Sharon 187
Schonberg, Bessie 251
Schonberg, Harold C. 341, 373
Schoolcraft, Ralph Newman 14, 237
Schott, Howard 345
Schrickel, Harry G. 75
Schubert, Inez 117
Schuller, Charles Francis 130, 407
Schuller, Gunther 260, 317
Schulliam, Dorothy 395
Schultz, E.J. 112
Schwadron, Abraham A. 163
Schwarts, Harry Wayne 336
Schwartz, Elliott S. 229, 235
Schwartz, H.W. 301
Schwartz, Paul 175
Sear, Walter 236
Searle, Humphrey 229, 249, 357
Searle, Townley 245
Sears, M.E. 283
Seashore, Carl E. 100, 101, 104
Seaton, Douglass 5
Seay, Albert 184
Sedoris, Robert D. 51
Seidel, Richard 260, 422
Selhorst, Eugene J. 188
Seltsam, William H. 243
Seltzer, George 299
Sendrey, Alfred 272
Serposs, Emile 123
Sessions, Ken W. 407
Sessions, Roger 355
Shapiro, Elliot 214
Shapiro, Nat 256
Sharp, Cecil 208
Sharp, Harold S. 247
Sharp, Marjorie Z. 247
Shaw, Arnold 355
Shaw, Martin 175
Sheehy, Emma D. 117
Sheehy, Eugene 16
Shemel, Sidney 64
Shetler, Donald J. 426
Shir-Cliff, Justine 355
Short, Craig R. 10
Shumsky, Abraham 51
Shuter, Rosamund 104
Sidnell, Robert 154
Siebe, George D. 370
Siegel, Jane A. 101
Siegmeister, Ellie 355
Silberman, Charles E. 117
Silverman, Ronald 124
Silvey, H.M. 47
Simon, Alfred 256
Simon, George T. 256
Simon, Henry W. 240, 242
Singleton, Ira C. 130
Skapiski, George J. 407
Skinner, Frank 364
Slaven, Neil 422
Slenczynska, Ruth 342
Sloane, Irving 303, 309
Slocum, Robert B. 76
Slonimsky, Nicolas 72, 175, 229
Smart, James A. 420
Smet, Robin De. See De Smet, Robin
Smith, Charles T. 164
Smith, G. Jean 299
Smith, Hannah Coffin 299
Smith, James A. 112
Smith, Robert B. 122
Smith, William James 76
Smithers, Don L. 317, 337
Smolian, Steven 420
Snyder, Alice M. 123
Snyder, Keith D. 154
Society for Ethnomusicology, Com-

mittee on Ethnomusicology and Music Education 420
Soibelman, Doris 395
Sollinger, Charles 309
Solow, Linda 34
Sonneck, Oscar G. 217-18, 243
Sorrell, Walter 164
Souchon, Edmond 259
Southern, Eileen 269
Sparks, Edgar H. 278
Spencer, William 313
Spiess, Lincoln Bruce 193
Spohn, Charles L. 303, 321
Springer, George H. 303
Squire, Alan P. 323
Squire, Russell N. 90
Stahl, Dorothy 420
Stainer, Sir John 278, 337
Stambler, Irwin 209, 256
Standifer, James A. 123, 124, 223, 266
Stanley, Douglas 289
Stanton, Hazel 101
Stanton, Robert E. 313
Stanton, Royal 373
Starr, William J. 168
Steane, J.B. 283, 290
Stearns, Jean 251
Stearns, Marshall W. 251, 260
Stein, Leonard 355
Steiner, Frances 121
Steinhoff, Carl R. 146
Stephan, Rudolf 75
Sternfeld, Frederick William 187-88, 189
Stevens, Denis W. 74, 278
Stevens, Denise 187
Stevens, Floyd A. 344
Stevens, H.S. 272
Stevenson, Robert Murrell 188, 193, 278
Stevenson, Ronald 188
Stewart, Rex 260
Stigand, Isobella 309
Stiles, Winifred E. 384
Stockmann, Erich 211
Stoddard, Hope 373
Stoll, Dennis Gray 14
Stone, Edward F. 111
Stoutamire, Albert 218
Stover, Edwin L. 136
Straeten, Edmund Sebastian Joseph van der 309
Strang, Gerald 362
Strange, Allen 236
Stravinsky, Igor 164
Stringham, Edwin John 175, 353
Strobel, Heinrich 229
Strunk, Oliver 188
Stubbins, William H. 313
Stuckenschmidt, H.H. 229
Sublette, Ned 420
Sumner, William Leslie 342, 346
Sunderman, Lloyd F. 90, 290
Sur, William Raymond 124, 130, 407
Surian, Elvidio 241
Suzuki, Shinichi 91, 310
Swalin, Benjamin F. 309
Swan, Alfred J. 130, 175
Swanson, Bessie R. 118
Swanson, Frederick J. 126
Sweeney, Leslie 317
Swift, Frederic Fay 136
Szabo, Helga 120
Szabolesi, Bence 360
Szende, Otto 309
Szmodis, I. 309

T

Tanner, Paul O.W. 260
Tatgenhorst, John 321
Taubman, Howard 175
Taubman, Joseph 62
Taylor, C.A. 379
Taylor, Henry W. 321
Taylor, Jack A. 350
Taylor, Jed H. 283
Telberg, Val 74
Tellstrom, A. Theodore 91
Terry, Charles Sanford 337, 356
Terry, Walter 249, 251
Tesson, William 173
Thackray, R. 118
Thayer, Robert W. 101
Thea, Lois 133
Thiel, Jorn 416
Thomas, Edrie 176

Thomas, Kurt 373
Thompson, Helen M. 128, 130
Thompson, Kenneth 223
Thompson, Oscar 76
Thompson, Randall 136
Thompson, Verne W. 188
Thomson, Francis Coombs 132
Thomson, Virgil 230
Thurston, Frederick 313
Tichler, Hans 342
Tiede, Clayton H. 304
Timm, Everett L. 314
Timmerman, Maurine 309
Tinctores, Johannes 76
Tolbert, Mary R. 124
Toplansky, Howard 311
Toronto Royal Ontario Museum 337
Torossian, Aram 164
Tortolano, William 292
Tosi, Pietro Francesco 290
Tovey, Sir Donald Francis 360
Towers, John 240
Tracey, Hugh 266, 270
Troth, Eugene W. 123
Trythall, Gilbert 236
Tumbusch, Tom 244
Turetzky, Bertram 309
Turfery, Cossar 247
Turner, Margery J. 252
Turner, Roland 59
Turrentine, Edgar M. 133
Tuthill, Burnet Corwin 136

U

Ulanov, Berry 162, 260
Ulehla, Ludmila 230
Ulrich, Homer 176, 188, 293, 323
UNESCO (United Nations Educational, Scientific and Cultural Organization) 5, 14, 34, 91, 201, 224, 249, 420-21, 426
UNESCO. Archives of Recorded Sound 421
UNESCO. International Association of Universities 134
UNESCO. International Society for Music Education 10
United Nations Educational, Scientific and Cultural Organization. See UNESCO
U.S. Congress. House. Committee on the Judiciary 218
U.S. Department of Health, Education, and Welfare. 16, 154
U.S. Department of Health, Education, and Welfare. Arts and Humanities Program 91, 130, 299
U.S. Office of Education 410
University of the State of New York. See New York. University of the State of
Unks, N. 150
Upton, William T. 218
Uris, Dorothy 290

V

Van Bodegraven, Paul 373
Van Dalen, Deobold 51
van der Straeten, Edmund Sebastian Joseph. See Straeten, Edmund Sebastian Joseph van der
Van Hausen, Karl D. 373
Van Loon, Hendrick Willem 164
Van Waesberghe, Joseph Smits 36
Vaughan, Mary Ann 113
Veinstein, Andre 5
Vetterl, Karel 204, 211
Vincent, John 230
Vinquist, Mary 366
Vinton, John 224
Vogel, Eric S. 236
Volbach, Walther Richard 247
Von Fischer, Kurt 36
Von Husmann, Heinrich 36
von Kochel, Ludwig Ritter. See Kochel, Ludwig Ritter von
von Rauchhaupt, Ursula. See Rauchhaupt, Ursula von
von Wasielewski, Wilhelm Joseph. See Wasielewski, Wilhelm Joseph von
Von Westerman, Gerhart 242
Voorhees, Anna Tipton 176
Voxman, Himie 314

W

Wachsmann, Klaus P. 189, 210
Wadsworth, Barry J. 118

Waesberghe, Joseph Smits Van. See Van Waesberghe, Joseph Smits
Wager, Willis Joseph 62, 136, 190
Wagner, Joseph 364
Wagner, Lavern 169
Walker, Alan 176
Walker, David S. 124
Wallace, William 104
Wallaschek, Richard 189
Walls, Howard 62
Walter, Don C. 176
Walton, Charles W. 360
Walton, Ortez 270
Ward, Eric 143
Ward, John Owen 65, 75-76
Ward, William R. 360
Warnack, John 240
Warner, Thomas E. 314
Washington State Library 395
Wasielewski, Wilhelm Joseph von 309
Wassell, Albert W. 309
Watanabe, Ruth 34, 51, 193
Watson, Corine 76
Watson, Jack M. 76
Watters, Lorrain 123
Weast, Robert 317
Webb, Lois N. 85, 150
Weber, Max 176
Webern, Anton 230
Webster, John C. 101
Wechsberg, Joseph 309
Weerts, Richard 302, 314, 321
Weichlein, William J. 22
Weidemann, Charles Conrad 118
Weidensee, Victor 297
Weinstock, Herbert 237
Weisshaar, Otto H. 304
Wellesz, Egon 179, 189, 417
Wells, Thomas 236
Wersen, Louis G. 123
Wertman, Charles H. 309
Westcott, Wendell 321
Westerby, Herbert 343
Westerman, Gerhart Von. See Von Westerman, Gerhart
Westervelt, Esther Manning 136
Westinghouse Learning Corporation 17
Weston, Pamela 314
Westphal, Frederick W. 314
Westrup, Sir Jack A. 72, 77, 179, 189, 417
Weyland, Rudolph H. 154
Whalon, Marion K. 17
Wheeler, Lawrence 116, 120
Whipple, Guy M. 92
Whitburn, Joel 257
White, Davidson 266
White, Edward A. 204
White, Newman I. 209
White, Sylvia 187
White, William Braid 344
Whitlock, John B. 122
Whitlock, Weldon 290
Whitwell, David 302, 314
Whybrew, William E. 104
Wichita Unified School District #259, Kansas 147
Wienandt, Elwyn A. 278
Wiesner, Glenn R. 314, 317
Wilder, Alec 218
Wilder, Robert D. 230
Wilgus, D.K. 205, 209
Wilkins, Wayne 310, 315
Williams, David Russell 356
Williams, Lois G. 176
Williams, Martin 260, 422
Williamson, Audrey 246
Willingham, Warren W. 132
Willis, John 252
Willis, Vera G. 118
Willman, Fred 114
Willoughby, David 222
Wilson, G.B.L. 249
Wilson, Harry Robert 123, 290, 373
Wilson, Wilfred G. 321
Winchell, Constance M. 16
Winick, Steven 356, 366
Wink, Richard L. 176
Winold, Allen 177
Winsel, Regnier 290
Winslow, Robert W. 317
Winter, James H. 317
Winternitz, Emanuel 74, 337
Wiora, Walter 189
Wisconsin Library Association 426
Wisler, Gene C. 122
Wolf, Arthur S. 20
Wolfe, Irving 123, 137
Wolfe, Richard J. 218

Wolff, Konrad 342, 367
Wolfson, Arthur M. 272
Wolman, Benjamin B. 79
Wood, Sarah P. 149
Wooldridge, David 374
Worner, Karl H. 190
Worrel, John W. 64
Wright, Al G. 302, 303
Wright, Denis 365
Wright, Frank 317
Wrightstone, J. Wayne 147
Wynar, Bohdan S. 16

X

Xenakis, Iannis 356

Y

Yarman, Robert M. De. See De Yarman, Robert M.
Yates, J.V. 77
Yates, Peter 230
Yerbury, Grace D. 218
Young, Margaret Labash 5
Young, Percy M. 293
Young, Richard De. See De Young, Richard
Young, Robert H. 278
Young, William T. 108, 147
Youngsberg, Harold 123

Z

Zaslaw, Neal 366
Zettl, Herbert 407
Zhito, Lee 62, 64
Zimmerman, Marilyn P. 118
Zuckerkandl, Victor 164, 177
Zumbrunn, Karen Lee Fanta 147

TITLE INDEX

This index is alphabetized letter by letter. Numbers refer to page numbers. Lengthy titles are frequently shortened but are not altered otherwise. Indexed here are titles to all books, pamphlets, collections, series, articles, journals, and publications of associations.

A

AAMOA Resource Papers 265
Abstracts in Anthropology 27, 199
"Accountability" 84
Accountability and Objectives for Music Education 87
Acoustical Aspects of Woodwind Instruments 312
Acoustical Foundations of Music, The 377
Acoustically Balanced Carillon, The 318
Acoustical Society of America Journal 27, 39
Acoustics of Music 377
Acta Musicologica 43, 190, 194, 198
Action Research to Improve School Practices 50
Action Research Way of Learning, The 51
Act of Touch in All its Diversity, The 340
Administering the Elementary Band 301
Administration in Music Education 151
Administration of Activity Therapy Service 394
Advanced Harmony 354
Aesthetic Analysis 163
Aesthetics: Dimension for Music Education 163
Aesthetics: Problems in the Philosophy of Criticism 161
Aesthetics of Rock, The 261
African Music 201, 270
African Music on L.P. 419
Afro-American Folksongs 268
Afternoon Remedial and Enrichment Program, Buffalo 141
After School Centers Project 144
After-School Tutorial and Special Potential Development in I.S. 201-Manhattan 145
Age of Beethoven (Record Supplement), The 179, 417
Age of Enlightenment, The 189
Age of Humanism, The 189
Age of Humanism (Record Supplement), The 179, 417
Age of Rock: Sounds of the American Cultural Revolution, The 261
Age of Rock 2: Sights and Sounds of Cultural Revolution, The 261
Amateur Wind Instrument Maker, The 336
American Bibliography 216

Title Index

American Choral Review 293, 294, 374
American Colleges and Universities 131
American Composers on American Music 213
American Educational Research Journal 39
American Fiddlers News 324
American Folklore: A Bibliography of Major Works 206
American Folksong and Folk Lore, a Regional Bibliography 207
American Harp Journal 324
American Journal of Mental Deficiency 387
American Journal of Occupational Therapy 388
American Library Resources: A Bibliographical Guide 33
American Music 217
American Musical Instrument Makers Directory 197, 338
American Music: From Storyville to Woodstock 259
American Music Handbook, The 8, 22, 59, 132
American Musicological Society Journal 190, 194, 197
American Music Teacher, The 38, 96, 156
American Opera Librettos 242
American Popular Song 218
American Popular Songs from the Revolutionary War to the Present 255
American Recorder 324
American Record Guide 413
American Reference Books Annual 16, 19
American String Teacher 325
American Suzuki Journal 328
American Symphony Orchestra, The 298
America's Music 213
Anatomy of Musical Criticism, An 176
Anatomy of Voice, The 290
Ancient and Oriental Music 189
Ancient and Oriental Music (Record Supplement) 179, 417
Ancient European Musical Instruments 332
Anglo-American Folksong Scholarship Since 1898 209
Annals of Opera, 1597-1940 241
Annotated Bibliography for the Education of Gifted Children 397
Annotated Bibliography of New Publications in the Performing Arts 14
Annotated Bibliography of the Professional Education of Teachers 134
Annotated Bibliography of Woodwind Instruction Books 1600-1830, An 314
Annotated Bibliography of Written Material Pertinent to the Performance of Brass and Percussion Chamber Music, An 323
Annotated Bibliography of Written Material Pertinent to the Performance of Chamber Music for Stringed Instruments, An 322
Annotated Bibliography of Written Material Pertinent to the Performance of Woodwind Chamber Music, An 323
Annotated Bibliography on Creativity and Giftedness 397
Annotated Catalog of American Violin Music Composed Between 1947-1961 307
Annotated Guide to Brass Trombone Literature 315
Annual Bibliography of European Ethnomusicology 211
Annual Register of Grant Support 57
Anthem in England and America, The 278
Anthology of African Music, An 421
Anthropology of Music, The 200
Approaches to Public Relations for the Music Educator 150
Archives of Sound, The 418
Ars Nova and the Renaissance 189
Ars Nova and the Renaissance (Record Supplement) 179, 417
Art, Affluence and Alienation 87
Art and Music in the Humanities 169
Art and Science of the Timpani, The 321
Art and Times of the Guitar, The 306, 334

Art as Experience 162
Arti Musices 194
Artistic Choral Singing 290
Artistic Singing 290
Art of Accompanying and Coaching, The 339
Art of Bassoon Playing, The 313
Art of Brass Playing, The 315
Art of Clarinetistry, The 313
Art of Conducting, The 369
Art of French Horn Playing, The 315
Art of Making Dances, The 250
Art of Music, The 180
Art of Music Copying, The 350
Art of Music Engraving and Processing, The 64
Art of Orchestral Conducting, The 370
Art of Orchestration, The 364
Art of Ragtime, The 259
Art of Sound, The 174
Art of String Quartet Playing, The 323
Art of the Choral Conductor, The 370
Arts, The 164
Arts and Human Development, The 85
Arts and the Handicapped 385
Arts and the Schools 153
Arts at the Grass Roots, The 62
Arts Management Handbook, The 63
Arts on Campus, The 134
ASBDA Curriculum Guide, The 299
ASCAP Biographical Dictionary of Composers, Authors and Publishers, The 72
Asian Music 202
Audio-Visual Equipment Directory, The 445
Audio-Visual Market Place, The 411
Audio-Visual Methods in Teaching 406
AV Instructional Technology Manual for Independent Study 405
Awards for Singers 59

B

Bach 194
Bach's Orchestra 337
Background of Music, The 378
Backgrounds and Approaches to Junior High Music 126
Backgrounds and Traditions of Opera, The 240
Bagpipe Music Index 310
Baker's Biographical Dictionary of Musicians 72
Balanchine's New Complete Stories of the Great Ballets 248
Ballads and Folksongs of the Southwest 208
Ballet: An Illustrated History, The 248
Ballet Companion, The 249
Ballet Music 248
Ballet Music: An Introduction 249
Band Director's Brain Bank 301
Band Encyclopedia 300
Band Instrument Repair Manual 303
Band Music Guide 300
Band Pagentry 302
Band Record Guide 413
Band Scoring 364
Bands of America 301
Bands of the World 302
Baroque Concerto, The 184
Baroque Music 184
Basic Choral Concepts 288
Basic Concepts in Music 353
Basic Concepts in Music Education 89
Basic Counterpoint 356
Basic Formal Structures in Music 358
Basic Forms in Music 360
Basic Materials in Music Therapy 352
Basic Music: Functional Musicianship for the Non-Music Major 121
Basic Principles in Pianoforte Playing 340
Basic Record Library 416
Basic Record Library of Jazz 260, 416, 422
Basic Resources for Learning Music 352
Basic String Repairs 303
Bassoon and Contrabassoon, The 312
Beethoven Encyclopedia 174
Beethoven Quartets, The 322
Beginning Conductor, The 372
Beginning Electronic Music in the Classroom 125, 233
Beginning Folk Dancing 112, 252

Behind the Baton 369
Bel Canto 288
Bel Canto for the Twentieth Century 290
Bel Canto in its Golden Age 285
Bell Ringing 319
Bells and Their Music with a Recording of Bell Sounds 321
Bells, Their History, Legends, Making and Uses 319
Bibliographic Index 23, 33
Bibliography for String Teachers 309
Bibliography of Books for Children 109
Bibliography of Computer Applications in Music, A 410
Bibliography of Early Secular American Music, A 217
Bibliography of Electronic Music, A 233
Bibliography of Hammered and Plucked (Appalachian or Mountain) Dulcimers and Related Instruments, A 206
Bibliography of Instrumental Music of Jewish Interest 271
Bibliography of Jazz, A 259
Bibliography of Jazz and Pop Tunes Sharing the Chord Progressions of Other Compositions. See New Expanded Bibliography of Jazz Compositions Based on the Chord Progressions of Standard Tunes, The
Bibliography of Jewish Music 272
Bibliography of Jewish Periodicals 271
Bibliography of Jewish Vocal Music 271
Bibliography of Music Therapy 393
"Bibliography of Negro and African Music" 266
Bibliography of North American Folklore and Folksong, A 206
Bibliography of Periodical Literature in Musicology and Allied Fields, A 192
Bibliography of Publications Relating to the Archive of Folk Song, A 204
Bibliography of Research Studies in Music Education, 1932-1948 44
Bibliography of Research Studies in Music Education, 1949-1956 44
Bibliography of Sir William Schwenck Gilbert with Bibliographical Adventures in the Gilbert and Sullivan Operas, A 245
Bibliography of the Blues, A 258
Bibliography of the History of Music Theory, A 356
Bibliography of Theses and Dissertations in Sacred Music 276
Bibliotheca Bolduaniana: A Renaissance Music Bibliography 185
Big Bands, The 256
Bio-Bibliographical Dictionary of Twelve-Tone and Serial Composers, A 221
Bio-Bibliographic Index of Musicians in the United States of America Since Colonial Times 215
Biographical Dictionaries and Related Works: An International Bibliography
Biographical Dictionary of American Music 213
Biographical Dictionary of English Music, A 75
Biographical Dictionary of Fiddlers, A 305
Biographical Index of Musicians in the the United States of America Since Colonial Times 216
Biography Index 23
Bio-Mechanics 100
"Bio-Mechanics, A New Approach to Music Education" 103, 308
Black Aesthetic, The 267
Black American Music 269
"Black Music: A Bibliographic Essay" 265
Black Music in America 269
Black Music in Our Culture 267
Black Music of Two Worlds 269
Black Nationalism and the Revolution in Music 145, 268
Black's Dictionary of Music and Musicians 73
Black Song 269
Blue Book of Broadway Musicals, The 243

Blue Book of Tin Pan Alley, The 255
Blues People 267
Blues Records, January 1943 to December 1966 422
Book of World-Famous Music, The 182
Book Review Digest 19
Book Review Index 19
Books in Print 1976 15
Boulez on Music Today 224
Bowker Serials Bibliography Supplement 21
Bows for Musical Instruments of the Violin Family 336
Braille Book Bank Catalog 390
Braille Mirror 389
Brass Anthology 316
Brass Ensemble Method for Teacher Education 316
Brass Instruments: Performance and Instructional Techniques, The 317
Brass Instruments: Volume I of the Hague Municipal Museum Catalogue 336
Brass Performance 317
Brass Players' Guide to the Literature 315
Brass Today 317
Breitkopf Thematic Catalogue, The 30
Bridge to 20th Century Music 227
Bringing Opera to Life 247
British Catalogue of Music, The 194
British Humanities Index 23
British Union Catalogue of Early Music Printed Before the Year 1801 193
Broadway's Greatest Musicals 244
Bruckner Society of America. See Chord and Discord
Building a Superior School Band Library 301
Building Instructional Programs in Music Education 154
Bulletin of the Folk-Song Society of the Northeast 205
Business and Law of Music, The 62
Business of Music, The 61
"Buyer's Guide" 296

C

California Journal of Educational Research 39
Cantus Firmus in Mass and Motet 278
Careers in Music (Music Educators National Conference) 65
Careers in Music (National Association of Music Executives in State Universities) 138
Careers in Music (Ward) 65
Carillon 318
Carillon Music and Singing Towers of the Old World and the New 321
Carl Orff 119
Catalog of Chamber Music for Wind Instruments 322
Catalog of Dance Films 425
Catalog of Folklore and Folk Songs 203
Catalog of Published Concert Music by American Composers 214
Catalog of the Johannes Herbst Collection 276
Catalogue: Ten Years of Films of Ballet and Classical Dance, 1956-1965 249, 426
Catalogue of Chamber Music for Woodwind Instruments 322
Catalogue of Early Books on Music 183
Catalogue of Music for Small Orchestra 299
Catalogue of Recorded Classical and Traditional Indian Music, A 421
Census of Autograph Music Manuscripts of European Composers in American Libraries, A 29
Challenge to Musical Tradition 359
Chamber Music (Robertson) 323
Chamber Music (Ulrich) 323
Chamber Music in American Schools 322
Change Ringing 321
Changing Forms for Modern Music 226
Charles Edward Ives, 1874-1954: A Bibliography of His Music 213
Chautauqua 277
Checklist of American Music Periodicals 1850-1900, A 22

Checklist of Music Bibliographies and Indexes in Progress and Unpublished, A 314
Checklist of Recorded Songs in the English Language in the Archive of American Folk Song to July 1940 207, 419
Checklist of Twentieth Century Choral Music for Male Voices, A 292
Checklist of Writings on 18th Century French and Italian Opera 241
Chicorel Bibliography to Books on Music and Musicians 15
Chicorel Bibliography to the Performing Arts 13
Child Development 39
Child Development Abstracts and Bibliography 27
Children and Dance and Music 114
Children and Music 107
Children Discover Music and Dance 117
Children's Books in Print 15, 110
Children's Music 120
Children's Song Index 281
Chippewa Music 214
Choctaw Music 214
Choral Arranging 283
Choral Conducting 370
Choral Conducting: A Symposium 370
Choral Conductor 373
Choral Conductor's Handbook, The 370
Choral Directing 370
Choral Director's Guide 288
Choral Journal 293, 374
Choral Music 291
Choral Music Education 289
Choral Music for Women's Voices 291
Choral Music in Print 282
Choral Music of the Church 278
Choral Techniques 287
Choral Tradition, The 293
Chord and Discord 194, 197
Choreographic Music 249
Chorus and its Conductor, The 287
Chromatic Harmony 355
Chronological Thematic Catalogue of Works by Wolfgang Amadeus Mozart. See Chronologisch-Thematisches Verzeichnis Samtlicher-Tonwerke Wolfgang Amadé Mozart
Chronologisch-Thematisches Verzeichnis Samtlicher-Tonwerke Wolfgang Amadé Mozart (Chronological Thematic Catalogue of Works by Wolfgang Amadeus Mozart) 31
CIJE. See Current Index to Journals in Education
Clarinet: Its History, Literature, and Great Masters, The 312
Clarinet: Some Notes Upon its History and Construction, The 312
Clarinet and Saxophone Experience 313
Clarinetists' Solo Repertoire, The 311
Clarinet Performing Practices and Teaching in the United States and Canada 311
Clarinet Technique 313
Clarinet Virtuosi of the Past 314
Classical Polyphony 357
Classical Style, The 360
Classic Guitar Construction 309
Classroom Music Enrichment Units 114
Clearance of Rights in Musical Compositions 61
Close-Up 210, 262
Cobbett's Cyclopedic Survey of Chamber Music 322
Codification of African Music and Textbook Project 266
"Collections of Instruments in Europe and America" 4, 335
Collector's Twentieth-Century Music in the Western Hemisphere, The 418
College Blue Book, The 10, 131
College Catalog Collection (Microfiche) 131
College Music 136
College Music Symposium 138, 155, 194
College Programs for High School Students 127
Commentary Upon the Art of Proper Singing, A 284

Communication and the Arts 44
Community Resources Pool, South Orangetown Central School District 1 400
Comparison of the Pythagorean, Just, Mean-tone, and Equally Tempered Scales 378
Compleat Music Teacher, The 340
Complete Book of Ballets 248
Complete Book of Classical Music, The 169
Complete Book of Light Opera 244
Complete Book of the American Musical Theater 244
Complete Course in Electronic Piano Tuning 344
Complete Encyclopedia of Popular Music and Jazz, The 1900-1950 256
Complete Report of the First International Music Industry Conference, The 62
Composer and Nation 170
Composers for the American Musical Theatre 244
Composers of Operetta 244
Composers of Tomorrow's Music 226
Composers of Yesterday. See Great Composers, 1300-1900: A Biographical and Critical Guide
Composers Since 1900: A Biographical and Critical Guide 226
Composing with Tape Recorders 234
Composium Annual Index of Contemporary Compositions 1975 223
Comprehensive Catalog of Available Literature for the Double Bass 306
Comprehensive Dissertation Index 43
Comprehensive Musicianship: An Anthology of Evolving Thought 222, 365
Comprehensive Musicianship: The Foundation for College Education in Music 222, 365
Comprehensive Musicianship: The Foundation of College Education in Music 135, 353
Comprehensive Musicianship and Undergraduate Music Curricula 222, 365
Comprehensive Music Programs 85
Computer and Music, The 235, 410
Computer Applications in Music 361, 410
Computer-Assisted Music Instruction 409
Computers in Humanistic Research 409
Concepts for a Musical Foundation 84
Concerto Themes 40
Concise Biographical Dictionary of Singers, A 282
Concise Dictionary of Music, A 76
Concise Encylopedia of Jewish Music 272
Concise Encyclopedia of Music and Musicians, The 73
Concise History of Opera, A 241
Concise Introduction to Music Listening, A 171
Concise Introduction to Teaching Elementary Music, A 121
Concise Oxford Dictionary of Music, The 75
Concise Oxford Dictionary of Opera 240
Conducting an Amateur Orchestra 371
Conducting Choral Music 371
Conducting Technique 372
Conductor and His Score, The 371
Conductor's Art, The 369
Conductor's Manual of Choral Literature, The 287
Conductor's World 374
Conn Chord 38
Constructing Classroom Tests in Music 99
Consumers Union Reviews Classical Recordings 416
Contemporary Composers on Contemporary Music 229
Contemporary Contrabass, The 309
Contemporary Harmony 230
Contemporary Hungarian Composers 225
Contemporary Music: A Suggested List for High Schools and Colleges 129, 135, 222
Contemporary Music and Music Cultures 226
Contemporary Music for Schools 222
Contemporary Music in Europe 227

Contemporary Music Performance Directory, The 223
Contemporary Music Project Library, The 282
Contemporary Music Project Library, Volume 1, The 301, 320
Contemporary Music Project Library, Volume 2, The 298
Contemporary Percussion 318
Contemporary Tone Structrue 226
Copyright for Musical Compositions 61
Copyright Guide, A 61
Copyright Handbook for Fine and Applied Arts 62
Corpus Mensurabilis Musicae 190, 196
Corpus of Early Keyboard Music 190, 196
Corpus Scriptorum De Musica 190, 196
Council for Research in Music Education Bulletin 37
Counterpoint (Kennan) 357
Counterpoint (Piston) 357
Counterpoint: An Introduction to Polyphonic Composition 356
Counterpoint: A Survey 357
Counterpoint in Composition 357
Country Music U.S.A. 208
Courses of Study 153
Cowboy Songs and other Frontier Ballads 207
Craft of Musical Composition, The 361
Craft of Music Teaching in the Elementary School, The 117
Creative Child and Adult Quarterly 390
Creative Dramatics for Handicapped Children 386
Creative Harmony and Musicianship 353
Creative Music in Education 118
Creative Music Theory 352
Creative Orchestration 363
Creative Projects in Musicianship 222, 365
Creative Rhythmic Movement for Children 109
Creative Singing 111
Creative Teaching of Music in the Elementary School 112
Critical Annotated Bibliography of Periodicals, A 281
Crowell's Handbook of Gilbert and Sullivan 245
Crowell's Handbook of World Opera 239
Culturally Disadvantaged 141
Cultural Policy and Arts Administration 63
Cumulative Book Index 15
Current Index to Journals in Education (CIJE) 23, 54, 148
Current Issues in Music Education 51
Current Musicology 195
Curriculum Improvement 150
Cybernetic Serendipity 362
Cyclopaedic Dictionary of Music, A 73

D

Dance 250
Dance and Dance Drama in Education 249
Dance Composition and Production for High Schools and Colleges 128
Dance Encyclopedia, The 251
Dance in America, The 251
Dance in Classical Music, The 250
Dance in Elementary Education 115
Dances and Stories of the American Indian 253
Dance Scope 253
Dance World 252
David Ewen Introduces Modern Music 170, 226
Deaf American, The 390
Decade of Music, A 171
Demonstration and Teacher Training Programs for Teachers of Disadvantaged Pupils in Non-Public Schools 144
Detroit Studies in Music Bibliography. See Selected Discography of Solo Song, A
Developing and Administering a Comprehensive High School Music Program 129

Developing Individual Skills for the High School Band 302
Developing Skills in Proposal Writing 57
Development and Practice of Electronic Music, The 233
Development of a Music Curriculum for Young Children 110
Development of Computer-Assisted Instruction in Instrumental Music 295
Development of Computerized Techniques in Music Research with Emphasis on the Thematic Index 410
Development of Materials for a One-Year Course in African Music for the General Undergraduate Student 266
Diatonic Modes in Modern Music, The 230
Dictionary-Catalog of Operas and Operettas 240
Dictionary of Ballet, A 249
Dictionary of Behavioral Science 79
Dictionary of Christian Worship, A 275
Dictionary of Contemporary Music 224
Dictionary of Education 79
Dictionary of Hymnology, A 276
Dictionary of Middle English Musical Terms, A 72
Dictionary of Modern Ballet 248
Dictionary of Modern Music and Musicians, A 73
Dictionary of Music 74
Dictionary of Musical Terms (Baker) 72
Dictionary of Musical Terms (Tinctores) 76
Dictionary of Musical Terms in Four Languages, A 76
Dictionary of Musical Themes, A 29
Dictionary of Musicians from the Earliest Times, A 75
Dictionary of Opera and Song Themes, A 29, 237
Dictionary of Pipe Organ Stops 345
Dictionary of Popular Music 255
Dictionary of the Dance 251
Dictionary of Twentieth-Century Composers: 1911-1971, A 223
Dictionary of Vocal Themes, A. See Dictionary of Opera and Song Themes, A
Difficult Child, The 386
Directory of American Contemporary Opera 243
Directory of Ethnomusicological Sound Recording Collections in the United States and Canada 199, 418
Directory of Film Libraries in North America 425
Directory of Foreign Contemporary Opera 240
Directory of Institutions and Organizations Concerned Wholly or in Part with Folk Music 210
"Directory of Known Youth Orchestras (In the U.S.)" 299
Directory of Library Resources for the Blind and Physically Handicapped 385
Directory of Music Faculties in Colleges and Universities--U.S. and Canada 10, 131, 138, 155
Directory of Music Research Libraries 3, 49
Directory of National Arts Organizations 9
Directory of Nationally Certified Teachers 156
Directory of Opera Companies and Workshops in the U.S. and Canada 243
Directory of Opera Producing Organizations in the United States and Canada 243
Directory of Performing Ensembles 219, 231
Directory of Publishing Opportunities 63, 64
Directory of Scholarly and Research Publishing Opportunities, The. See Directory of Publishing Opportunities
Directory of Sets and Costumes for Rent, Opera Companies and Other Sources 247
Directory of Special Libraries and Information Centers 5

"Directory of Summer Music Camps, Clinics, and Workshops" 150
Directory of the Music Industry 61
"Discographies" 413
Discography of Hispanic Music in the Fine Art Library of the University of New Mexico, A 420
"Discovering and Stimulating Culturally Deprived Talented Youth" 147
Discovering Bells and Bellringing 319
Discovering Music Together 123
Discovering Music, Where to Start on Records and Tapes 171, 414
Discovering Music with Young Children 107
Discovery in the Urban Sprawl 144
Disopaedia of the Violin, The 305
Dissertation Abstracts International 27, 44, 195
"Doctoral Dissertations in Music and Music Education" 45
Doctoral Dissertations in Music and Music Education, 1957-1963 44
Doctoral Dissertations in Music and Music Education, 1963-1967 44
Doctoral Dissertations in Music and Music Education, 1968-1971 45
Doctoral Dissertations in Musicology 43
Doctoral Research Series, The 148
Documentary Report of the Tanglewood Symposium 84
Drake Guide to Gilbert and Sullivan, The 245
Duality of Vision, The 164
Duo Pianism 341
Dynamic Choral Conductor, The 373

E

Early American Imprints 216
Early American Sheet Music, its Lure and its Lore, 1768-1889 214
Early Chamber Music 323
Early Concert-Life in America. 218
"Early English Chamber Music for Strings: Performance Hints" 321
Early English Hymns 277
Early Keyboard Instruments 340
Early Medieval Music up to 1300 189
Early Medievàl Music up to 1300 (Record Supplement) 179, 417
Early Music 195
Early Opera in America 243
East Chicago Junior Police 142
Eastern School Music Herald 94
Eclectic Curriculum in American Music Education 119
Ecrits Imprimes Concernant La Musique 35
Educating Exceptional Children 384
Educating the Child Who is Different 383
Educating the Disadvantaged Child 146
Educational Administration Abstracts 27, 151
Educational Leadership 155
Educational Media Catalogs on Microfiche 411
Educational Planning--Programming--Budgeting 150
Educational Product Report 406
Educational Research 49
Educational Rhythmics for Mentally and Physically Handicapped Children 386
Education Associations 9
Education Books and Audiovisuals Catalog 130, 153
Education Directory--Elementary and Secondary Education 9, 132
Education Directory--Higher Education 9
Education for Musical Growth 88
Education Index 19, 23
Education of Everychild, The 87
Education of the Visually Handicapped 389
Educator 262
Educators Guide to Free Films 425
Educators Purchasing Guide (EPG) 411
Educator's World 7
Effective Methods for Building the High School Band 301
Effects of a Listening Program in Contemporary Music Upon the Appreciation by Junior High School Students 147
Effects of Music 175
EFLA (Educational Film Library Association) Evaluation Cards 425

Eingeldruke vor 1800 36
Electronic Music 235
Electronic Music: A Listener's Guide 235
Electronic Music: Systems, Techniques, and Controls 236
Electronic Musical Instrument Manual, The 234
Electronic Musical Instruments (Crowhurst) 233, 333
Electronic Musical Instruments (Dorf) 234
Electronic Music and Musique Concrete 234
Electronic Music for the Seventies 234
Electronic Music for Young People 114
Electronic Music Studio Manual, An 235
Electronic Music Synthesis 234
Elementary Harmony 353
Elementary Harmony: Theory and Practice 354
Elements of Conducting 372
Elements of Musical Understanding 177
El-Hi Textbooks in Print 15, 150
Embouchure, The 317
Empirical Foundations of Education Research 51
Encyclopedia of Associations 9
Encyclopedia of Automatic Musical Instruments 332
Encyclopedia of Concert Music 73
Encyclopedia of Country and Western Music, The 205
Encyclopedia of Education, The 79
Encyclopedia of Educational Research 79
Encyclopedia of Folk, Country, and Western Music 209
Encyclopedia of Jazz 257
Encyclopedia of Jazz in the Sixties, The 257
Encyclopedia of Popular Music 256
Encyclopedia of the Arts (Read) 75
Encyclopedia of the Arts (Runes & Schrickel) 75
·Encyclopedia of Theatre Music 256
Encyclopedia of the Violin, An 331
Encyclopedia of Violin Makers 334
English Folk Songs from the Southern Appalachians 208
English Keyboard Music Before the Nineteenth Century 339
Enjoyment of Music, The 172
Enrichment Activities in Music for Intellectually Gifted Pupils, Elementary Schools 397
Ensemble Music for Wind and Percussion Instruments 311, 316, 320, 322
EPG. See Educator's Purchasing Guide
Equal Opportunity Review, The 148
ESEA Title I, Evaluation Report, Wichita Program for Educationally Deprived Children, September 1968-August 1969 147
ESEA Title I Projects Evaluation Report, 1967 146
Essays Before a Sonata 161
Essays in Musical Analysis 360
Essays on Music and History in Africa 189
Essentials of Bassoon Techniques 311
Essentials of Conducting 372
Essentials of Teaching Elementary School Music 116, 120
Ethnic Musical Instruments 200, 334
Ethnomusicologist, The 200
Ethnomusicology (Kunst) 200
Ethnomusicology (Society for Ethnomusicology) 190, 195, 202
Ethnomusicology and Folk Music: An International Bibliography of Dissertations and Theses 45, 200, 203
Ethos and Education in Greek Music 83
Eurhythmics, Art and Education 119
European and American Musical Instruments 331
European Composers Today 226
European Musical Instruments 334
Evaluation and Synthesis of Research Studies Relating to Music Education 45
Evaluation of Music Teaching and Learning, The 84
Everyman's Dictionary of Music 72

Evolution of African Music and its Function in the Present Day, The 270
Evolution of Modern Orchestration, The 363
Evolution of the Art of Music, The 186
Examples for the Study of Musical Style 360
Exceptional Child Education Abstracts 27, 51, 386
Exceptional Children 387, 389
Expansion of the After School Study Centers for Disadvantaged Public and Non-Public School Pupils, The 145
Experience of Music, The 174
Experiences in Music 121
Experimental Dance 251
Experimental Music 361
Experimental Music: Composition with an Electronic Computer 234
Experimental Music in Schools 225
Experimental Research in Music 50
Experimental Research in Music--Workbook in Design and Statistical Texts 50
Experimental Research in the Psychology of Music: 6 101
Experimental Research in the Psychology of Music: 7 101
Experimental Research in the Psychology of Music: 8 100
Experimental Research in the Psychology of Music: 9 100
Experiments in Musical Creativity 222
Explaining Music 173
Explore and Discover Music 113, 126
Exploring Music 123
Exploring the Arts with Children 110
Exploring Twentieth-Century Music 225
Extant Medieval Musical Instruments 333

F

Facing the Music in Urban Education 145
Favorite Operas by German and Russian Composers 238
Favorite Operas by Italian and French Composers 238
Feasibility of Producing Synchronized Video Tapes as Instructional Aids in the Study of Music 407
Federal Relief Administration and the Arts 152
Fifty Favorite Operas. See Favorite Operas by German and Russian Composers
Film Evaluation Guide 425
Film Guide for Music Educators 426
Films for Music Education and Opera Films 425
Films in Children's Programs 426
Films on Traditional Music 211
First Steps in Teaching Creative Dance 250
Fischer Lexikon. See Music A to Z
Five Centuries of Keyboard Music 344
Five Sense Store, The 107
Flute, The 331
Folk and Traditional Music of the Western Continent 184, 204
Folk Dance Teaching Cues 252
Folk Dancing for Students and Teachers 115, 253
Folk Directory, 1971 252
Folk Music 207, 419
Folk Music Instruments of the World 203, 332
Folksingers and Folksongs in America 207, 419
Folk Song in England 204
Folk Songs du Midi des Etats-Unis. See Folk Songs of the Southern United States
Folk Songs of Europe 211
Folk Songs of the Americas 211
Folk Songs of the South 205
Folk Songs of the Southern United States 205
Folk-Songs of Virginia 205
Folksongs of Virginia: A Checklist, The 208
Folk Songs of the World 203
Folk Song Style and Culture 204
Fontes Artis Musicae 6

Formalized Music 356
Form in Music: An Example of Traditional Techniques of Musical Structure and their Application in Historical and Contemporary Style 357
Form in Music: With Special Reference to the Design of Instrumental Music 359
Foundation Directory, The 58
Foundations and Frontiers of Music Education 86
Foundations and Principles of Music Education 87
Foundations Grants Index, The 58
Foundations in Music Theory 351
Foundations of Music 167
Four Ages of Music, The 189
Four Decades of Choral Training 285
Four Hands, One Piano: A List of Works for Duet Players 343
Four-Part Chorales of J.S. Bach, The 356
Frank C. Brown Collection of North Carolina Folklore, The 209
Free Voice, The 288
French Music Today 228
From Bone Pipe and Cattle Horn to Fiddle and Psaltery 333
Fundamentals of Choral Expression 286
Fundamentals of Music 350
Fundamentals of Musical Composition 362
Fundamentals of Sight Singing and Ear Training 351
Fundamentals of Teaching with Audio-Visual Technology 406

G

General Bibliography for Music Research 34, 192
General History of Music, A 180
General History of the Science and Practice of Music, A 183
General Index to Modern Musical Literature in the English Language, A 16
Genesis of a Music 228
Gerhardt Marimba Xylophone Collection, The 319
German and Austrian Violin-Makers 306
Gilbert and Sullivan and Their Operas 245
Gilbert and Sullivan Book, The 245
Gilbert and Sullivan Companion, The 244
Gilbert and Sullivan Opera 246
Glory of the Violin, The 309
Golden Encyclopedia of Music, The 74
Golden Guitars 209
Golden Road, The 413
Gold of Rock and Roll, 1955-1967, The 422
Grammar of Conducting, The 372
Grand Tradition, The 283, 290
Grants and Aid to Individuals in the Arts 58
Grants Register, The 59
Great Cities Research Council Educational Communications Project 143
Great Composers, 1300-1900: A Biographical and Critical Guide 170
Great Conductors, The 373
Great Day Coming 142, 205
Greatness in Music 162
Great Pianists from Mozart to the Present, The 341
Great Singers from the Dawn of Opera to Our Own Time, The 239
Grove's Dictionary of Music and Musicians 74
Growing with Music 123
Growth of Instrumental Music, The 335
Growth of Instrumental Music (Record Supplement), The 179, 417
Guidance in Voice Education 286
Guide for the Beginning Choral Director 284
Guidelines for Junior College Music Programs 139
Guidelines for Style Analysis 359
Guidelines in Music Education 153

Guides to Educational Media 411
Guide to Accountability in Music Instruction 151
Guide to Aesthetics, A 164
Guide to American Educational Directories 7
Guide to Braodway Musical Theatre 245
Guide to Effective Music Supervision, A 154
Guide to English Folk Song Collections 1826-1952, A 203
Guide to Federal Assistance for Education, The 58
Guide to Good Singing and Speech, A 286
Guide to Grants, Loans, and Other Types of Government Assistance Available to Students and Educational Institutions 57
Guide to Music Styles, A 359
Guide to National Bibliographic Information Centers 5, 34
Guide to Piano Literature for the Partially Seeing 384
Guide to Reference Books 16
Guide to Reference Material 16
Guide to Research in Music Education, A 50
Guide to Student Teaching in Music, A 133
Guide to Teaching Brass 316
Guide to Teaching Percussion 318
Guide to Teaching Strings, A 307
Guide to Teaching Woodwinds 314
Guide to the Performing Arts, 1967 237
Guide to the Performing Arts--1968 14
Guide to the Pianist's Repertoire 342
Guide to the Study of the United States of America, A 216
Guide to Union Catalogues and International Loan Centers 3
Guitar and Mandolin: Biographies of Celebrated Players and Composers, The 305
Guitar in the Classroom 309
Guitar Repair 303
Guitar Review 328
Guitar Years 209

H

Hague Gemeentemuseum Catalogue of the Music Library, The 281
Handbook for Music Teachers 116
Handbook of American Operatic Premieres, 1731-1962, A 243
Handbook of Audio-Visual Aids and Techniques for Teaching Elementary School Subjects 406
Handbook of Conducting 373
Handbook of Film, Theatre, and Television Music on Record, A 420
Handbook of International Study for U.S. Nationals 57
Handbook of Jazz, A 260
Handbook of Music and Music Literature in Sets and Series, A 17, 30
Handbook of Music Terms 73
Handbook of Singing 289
Handbook of Soviet Musicians 180
Handbook on Conducting 373
Handschriften Mit Mehrstimmiger Musik, Des 14., 15. und 16. Jahrhunderts 36
Harmonica Happenings 328
Harmonic Materials in Tonal Music 352
Harmonic Materials of Music 352
Harmonic Practice 355
Harmonic Structure of the Tone of the Bassoon, The 312
Harmonizer 294
Harmony (Piston) 354
Harmony (Schenker) 355
Harmony: Structure and Style 354
Harmony and Melody 355
Harmony in Western Music 351
Harp, The 308
Harper's Dictionary of Music 71
Harpischord and Clavichord, The 345
Harrison Record and Tape Guide to 4-Channel 414
Harrison Tape Guide 414
Harvard Brief Dictionary of Music, The 72
Harvard Dictionary of Music 71

Hawaii: Music in its History 215
Hearing Music with Understanding 175
He Dreams What is Going on Inside His Head 168
Heritage of Music: The Music of the Jewish People 271
Hi-Fi Stereo Handbook 405
Highlights 329
High School Band Director's Handbook, The 300
High School Marching Band, The 302
Historical Anthology of Music in Performance 419
Historical Musicology 193
Historical Sets, Collected Editions, and Monuments of Music 34
Historic Contribution of Russian Jewry to Jewish Music, The 272
History and Encyclopedia of Country, Western, and Gospel Music, A 205
History of American Church Music, The 276
History of Art and Music, A 172, 184
History of European Music, A 184
History of Jazz 260
History of Keyboard Music to 1700, The 342
History of Melody, A 360
History of Modern Music, A 225
History of Music (Worner) 190
History of Music, A (Robertson and Stevens) 187
History of Music: An Index to the Literature Available in a Selected Group of Musicological Publications, The 185, 192
History of Musical Instruments, The 336
History of Musical Style, A 358
History of Musical Thought, A 182
History of Music and Musical Style, A 188
History of Music in Sound, The 179, 417
History of Music in the U.S. Armed Forces during World War II, A 215
History of Music Theory 354
History of Orchestration, The 362
History of Pianoforte Music, The 343
History of Public School Music in the United States 83
History of Russian Music 186
History of Scottish Music, A 182
History of the Organ in the United States, The 345
History of the Piano 339
History of the Trumpet of Bach and Handel 316
History of the Violin, The 309
History of Violin Playing from its Origins to 1761 and its Relationship to the Violin and Violin Music, The 305
History of Western Music, A 183
History of Western Music: Short Edition, A 183
Hit Tunes 255
Horn, The 315
Horn and Horn Playing, and the Austro-Bohemian Tradition from 1680-1830, The 315
Horn Call 326
Horn, Strings, and Harmony 377
Horn Technique (Morley-Pegge) 316
Horn Technique (Schuller) 317
How Musical is Man? 167
How to Arrange and Rehearse Football Band Shows 302
How to Develop and Maintain a Successful Woodwind Section 314
How to Lead Group Singing 370
How to Locate Educational Information and Data 49
How to Read a Score 371
How to Read Braille Music Notation 384
How to Teach Music to Beginners 115
How to Write Learning Activity Packages for Music Education 113
Humanities: A Selective Guide to Information Sources, The 90
Humanities Index 24
Humanities Through the Arts, The 173
Human Values in Music Education 88
Hymns and Tunes: An Index 275
Hymn Tunes of Lowell Mason: A Bibliography 277

I

"Important Library Holdings at Forty-One North American Universities" 4
Improved Educational Services in Selected Special Service Elementary and Junior High Schools 146
Improvement of Self Image; Public Law 89-10 144
Improving and Extending the Junior High School Orchestra Repertory 298
Index Medicus 24, 394
Index of English Songs, An 204
Index of Flute Music 315
Index of Gregorian Chant, An 30, 275
Index of Musical Wind-Instruments, An 335
Index of Violin Music (Strings) 310
Index to American Doctoral Dissertations 45
Index to Biographies of Contemporary Composers 221
Index to Book Reviews in the Humanities, An 19
Index to Characters in the Performing Arts, Part II--Operas and Musical Productions 19
Index to Graduate Degrees in Music, U.S. and Canada 131
Index to Instructional Media Catalogs 412
Index to Musical Festschriften and Similar Publications, An 17
Index to Song Books 282
Index to Symphonic Program Notes in Books 176
Index to Top-Hit Tunes, 1900-1950 255
Individualized Instruction in Music 152
Information on Music 17
Information Theory and Esthetic Perception 163
Inquiry into the Musical Capacities of Educationally Sub-Normal Children, An 385
Inside Jazz 257
Institute of Ethnomusicology, Selected Reports 195
Instructional Objectives in Music 83
Instrumentalist, The 327, 375
Instrumentalists' Handy Reference Manual 296
Instrumental Music: Principles and Methods of Instruction 296
Instrumental Music for Today's Schools 296
Instrumental Music in the Public Schools 297
Instrumental Music Printed before 1600 180
Instruments of Music, The 333
Instruments of Popular Music 333
Instruments of the Modern Orchestra and Early Records of the Precursors of the Violin Family, The 336
Integrating Music with Other Studies 114
Interdisciplinary Index of Studies in Physics, Medicine, and Music Related to the Human Voice, An 282, 286
International Anthology of Recorded Music 416
International Catalogue of Published Records of Folk Music 211
International Catalogue of Recorded Folk Music 211
International Cyclopedia of Music and Musicians, The 76
International Directory of Music Education Institutions 10, 14
International Electronic Music Catalog. See Repertoire International des Musiques Electroacoustiques
International Equivalences in Access to Higher Education 133
International Folk Dance at a Glance 252
International Index to Multi-Media Information 425
International Inventory of Musical Sources. See RISM
International Jazz Bibliography: Jazz Books from 1919-1968 258
International Listing of Teaching Aids in Music 151

International Music Educator, The. See International Society for Music Education Yearbook
International Musician 65
International Percussion Reference Library Catalog 320
International Repertory of Musical Literature. See RILM Abstracts
International Society for Music Education Yearbook 37
International Who's Who in Music and Musicians' Directory 77
International Who's Who 1973-74 77
Inter Nos 294
Internships in Teacher Education 133
Interpretation for the Piano Student 340
Interpretation of Early Music, The 366
Interpretation of Music, The 366
Interpreting Music through Movement 112
Intervals, Scales, and Temperaments 378
Introduction to Advanced Study in Music Education 133
Introduction to Computers and Programming 409
Introduction to Educational Administration 150
Introduction to Folk Music in the United States, An 208
Introduction to Indian Music, An 200
Introduction to Library Resources for Music Research, An 50
Introduction to Music, An 167
Introduction to Musical History, An 189
Introduction to Music Appreciation 173
Introduction to Music Education 90
Introduction to Musicology 192
Introduction to Music Research 35, 51, 193
Introduction to the Art of Playing on the Pianoforte 339
Introduction to the Physics and Psychophysics of Music 379
Introduction to the Theory of Music 350
Introduction to Twentieth Century Music, An 183, 227
Invitation to Listening 176
Involvement with Music 350
IRCD Bulletin, The 148
Italian Ars Nova Music 183

J

Jass Guide to Public Domain Music 61
Jazz: New Perspective 258
Jazz and the White Americans 258
Jazz Composition and Orchestration 259
Jazz Dance 251
Jazz Lexicon, A 257
Jazz Masters of the 30's 260
Jazz on Record 422
Jazz Records 421
Jazz Records, 1897-1942 422
Jewish Music Notes 273
Jewish Music Programs 271
John Philip Sousa: A Descriptive Catalogue of His Works 300
John Philip Sousa: American Phenomenon 300
Journal of Abnormal Psychology 39
Journal of Aesthetics and Art Criticism 195
Journal of American Folklore 210
Journal of Band Research 324, 374
Journal of Country Music 262
Journal of Educational Psychology 39
Journal of Educational Research 39
Journal of Experimental Education 40
Journal of Experimental Psychology 40
Journal of Jazz Studies 263
Journal of Music Therapy 396
Journal of Personality and Social Psychology 40
Journal of Research in Music Education 37, 95, 155
Journal of Teacher Education 40, 137, 154
Journal of the Acoustical Society of America 379
Juilliard Repertory Library 113
Juilliard Report on Teaching the Literature and Materials of Music, The 365
Junior High School General Music 125

Junior High School Music Handbook, A 126
Junior Keynotes 96

K

Keep Your Voice Healthy 284
Keyboard Harmony 353
Keyboard Harmony and Improvisation 353
Keyboard Music 343
Keyboard Skills 350
The King's Musick 181
Know Your Synthesizer 236
Kobbe's Complete Opera Book 238
Kodaly Concept of Music Education, The 120
Kodaly Method, The 118

L

La Musique, Les Hommes, Les Instruments, Les Oeuvres 74
Language of Modern Music, The 227
Language of Music, The 161, 168
Language of the Ballet, The 249
Language of the Music Business, A Handbook of its Customs, Practices, and Procedures, The 63
Larousse Encyclopedia of Music 74
Law of Copyright Under the Universal Convention, The 61
Leadership for Learning in Music Education 151
Leading Children's Choirs 289
Learning and Teaching Music 120
Learning Directory 17
Learning Music: Musicianship for the Elementary Classroom Teacher 121
Learning Music Through Rhythm 112
Learning to Teach Through Playing: A Brass Method 317
Learning to Teach Through Playing: String Techniques and Pedagogy 307
Learning to Teach through Playing, a Woodwind Method 312
Lecture-Performance, The 169
Legal Protection for the Creative Musician 61
Legal Protection of Literature, Art and Music 61
Lexicon of Musical Invective 175
Liberal Education and Music 136
Liberation of Sound: An Introduction to Electronic Music, The 235
"Libraries and Collections" 3
Library Journal Book Review, The 20
Library of Congress Catalog--Music and Phonorecords 414
Listen 172
Listen: A Guide to the Pleasures of Music 173
Listener's Guide to Musical Understanding 169
Listening to Music 168
Listening to Music Creatively 175
List of American Record Companies Specializing in Folk Music, A 204, 418
List of Folklore and Folk Music Archives and Related Collections in the United States and Canada, A 206
List-o-Tapes 414
"Lists of Music Periodicals" 21
Literature and Materials Guide for Instrumental Music 295
Literature of Jazz: A Critical Guide, The 258
Literature of the Piano, The 342
Literature of the Woodwind Quintet, The 312
Liturgical Terms for Music Students 276
Living Musicians 215
Looking at the Double Bass 305

M

McColvin and Reeves' Music Libraries 3
Magic of Music, The 123
Magic of Opera, The 239
Maintenance and Repair of Band Instruments 303
Makers of the Harpsichord and Clavichord, 1440 to 1840 344
Making Music Your Own 123
Man and His Music 183
Mandan and Hidatsu Music 214

Man, Mind and Music 162
Manual of Music Librarianship 152
Manual of Television Opera Production, A 246
Manuscripts of Polyphonic Music (c. 1320-1400) 35
Manuscripts of Polyphonic Music: 11th-Early 14th Centuries 35
Marching Band, The 303
Marching for Marching Bands 302
Masters' Abstracts 47
Masters' Theses in Education 47
Masterworks of the Orchestral Repertoire 170
Materials and Structure of Music 351
Meaning and Teaching of Music, The 85
Measurement and Evaluation in Music 104
Measurement of Musical Talent 101
"Measurements of Orchestral Pitch" 298, 378
Measuring the Contribution of the Arts in the Education of Disadvantaged Children 142
Medieval and Renaissance Music on Long-Playing Records 418
Melodic Perception: A Program for Self-Instruction 350
Memorable Days in Music 169
Men and Music in Western Culture 176
Menominee Music 214
Mental Hygiene 390
Mental Retardation 387
Mental Warmups for the Choral Director 288
Method for Renaissance Lute 333
Methods of Establishing Equivalence between Degrees and Diplomas 134
Metropolitan Opera Annals 243
Metropolitan Opera 1883-1966, The 242
Microfiche Reprint Series 18
Microteaching 405
Mikis Theodorakis 86
Millions for the Arts 58
Milton Cross New Encyclopedia of the Great Composers and Their Music, The 73
Miracle of the Met, The 238
Miscellanea Musicologica 195
Missouri Journal of Research in Music Education 37
MMPC Interaction: Early Childhood Curriculum 107
Models for Beginners in Composition 362
Modern Age, The 189
Modern Arts: An Outline, The 170
Modern Ballet 249
Modern Book of Esthetics, A 163
Modern Conductor, The 371
Modern Culture and the Arts 162
Modern Dance Forms in Relation to the Other Modern Arts 250
Modern Dance in Education 251
Modern French Music 227
Modern Guide to Symphonic Music, A 170
Modern Marching Band Techniques 302
Modern Music (Record Supplement) 179, 417
Modern Music Notation 349
Modern Researcher, The 49
Modern Sound Production 379
Monsieur Croche the Dilettante Hater 161
More About this Music Business 61
More Stories of the Great Operas 238
More Than Singing 287
Mort's Guide to Festivals, Feasts, Fairs and Fiestas 13
Motion Study and Violin Bowing 306
Multimedia Materials for Afro-American Studies 266
Music (Bryant) 72
Music (Daniels and Wagner) 169
Music (Horton) 112
Music: A Design for Listening 176
Music: Black, White, and Blue 28
Music: History and Theory 181
Music: Materials for Teaching 110
Music: The Listener's Art 174

Musicache 18
Music, Acoustics, and Orchestration 377
Music Activities for Retarded Children 384
Musica Disciplina 190, 195, 197
Musical Ability in Children and its Measurement 99
Musical Acoustics 378
Musical Acoustics, Part I: Violin Family Components 306, 378
Musical America: Annual Directory of the Performing Arts 13
Musical Anthology of the Orient 421
Musical Characteristics in Children 118
Musical Director's Guide to Musical Literature (for Voices and Instruments), The 130
Musical Experience, The 171
Musical Form 359
Musical Form: A Consideration of Music and Its Ways, The 174
Musical Growth in the Elementary School 109
Musicalia: Sources of Information 17
Musical Instruments: An Illustrated History 332
Musical Instruments: Their History in Western Culture 334
Musical Instruments, a Comprehensive Dictionary 335
Musical Instruments and Their Symbolism in Western Art 337
Musical Instruments in Art and History 332
Musical Instruments in the Royal Ontario Museum 337
Musical Instruments of India 335
Musical Instruments of the Western World 337
Musical Instruments of World Cultures 199, 332
Musical Instruments Through the Ages 331
Musical Interpretation 340, 366
Musical Lexicography 73
Musical Merchandise Review 38
Musical Production, The 247
Musical Quarterly, The 38, 195, 417
Musical Structure and Design 358
Musical Symbol, The 162
Musical Thought 168
Musical Wind Instruments 333
Musicana 328
Music Analyses: An Annotated Bibliography 358
Music and Aesthetics 161
Music and Art in the Public Schools 85
Music and Drama 33
Music and History of the Baroque Trumpet Before 1721, The 317, 337
Music and Letters 195
Music and Literature 168
Music and Meaning 161
Music and Medicine 395
Music and Movement 111
Music and Musicians in Early America 217
Music and Painting 172
Music and Perceptual-Motor Development 114
Music and Phonorecords 414
Music and Reason 164
Music and Society 173
Music and Tape Recordings Filed in the NACWPI Research Library 296, 311, 315, 319, 418
Music and Technology 224
Music and the Classroom Teacher 88, 121
Music and the Culture of Man 187
Music and the Line of Most Resistance 163
Music and the Reformation in England: 1549-1660 277
Music and the Theatre 239
Music and the Twentieth Century Media 168, 224
Music and Young Children 107
Music and Your Emotions 103, 394
Music, an Overview 89
Music Arranging and Orchestration 362
Music Article Guide 24
Music as Metaphor 162
Music A. to Z. 75
Music at Your Fingertips 342

Music Before the Classic Era 188
Music Books for the Elementary School Library 109
Music Bulletin 94
Music Cataloging Bulletin 6, 96
Music Code of Ethics 63
Music Cultures of the Pacific, the Near East, and Asia 184
Music Curriculum Guides 149
Music Curriculum in a Changing World, The 90
Music Dictation 354
Music Director's Complete Handbook of Forms 153
Music Drama in Schools 126
"Music Education" 407
Music Education: A Handbook for Music Teaching in the Elementary Grades 117
Music Education: Psychology and Method 100
Music Education: The Background of Research and Opinion 86
Music Education for Teenagers 130
Music Education in Action 86
Music Education in the Elementary School 110
Music Education in the Modern World 86
Music Education Principles and Programs 88
Music Education Source Book I 91
Music Educators' Guide to Percussion 320
Music Educators Journal, The 38, 95, 155, 417
Music Educators Journal Index 24
Music Educators National Conference and the Star Spangled Banner 213
Music Essentials 122
Music Faculty 104
Music Festivals of the World 14
Music for Elementary School Children 115
Music for Exceptional Children 383
Music Form and Analysis: A Programmed Course 358
Music for the Academically Talented Student in the Secondary School 128, 397
Music for the Exceptional Child 384
Music for the General College Student 134
Music for the Handicapped Child 383
Music for the Modern Dance 250
Music for the Piano 342
Music for the Violin and Viola 307
Music for the Voice 292
Music for Today: Elementary School Methods 117
Music Forum, The 195
Music from the Middle Ages to the Renaissance 187
Music Fundamentals for the Classroom Teacher 122
Music Handbook 122
Music Handbook for the Elementary School 111
Music, History, and Ideas 185
Musicians and Libraries in the United Kingdom 4
Musician's Guide, The 7, 21
Musician's Guide to Copyright and Publishing, A 62
Musician's Handbook of Foreign Terms 71
Musicianship for the Classroom Teacher 121
Musicianship for the Elementary Teacher 122
Music Improvisation as a Classroom Method 340
Music in America (Marrocco and Gleason) 217
Music in America (Ritter) 217
Music in American Education: Past and Present 91
Music in American Education: Source Book Number 2 87, 92
Music in American Life 213
Music in American Schools 88
Music in Ancient Israel 272
Music in Childhood Education 111
Music Index, The 24
Music Industry Council Guide for Music Educators, The 63
Music in Early America: A Bibliography 216
Music in Early Childhood (Batcheller) 114

Music in Early Childhood (Music Educators National Conference) 108
Music in Education 91
Music in England Before 1800: A Select Bibliography 182
Music in Europe and the United States 180
Music in General Education 85
Music in Geriatric Care 393
Music in Higher Education, 1973-74 138, 156
Music in History 186
Music in Medicine 394
Music in Modern Media 225, 361, 363
Music in New Hampshire 208
Music in Open Education (Monsour) 114
Music in Open Education (Music Educators National Conference) 115
Music in Opera 241
Music in Our Life 123
Music in Our Schools 153
Music in Our Times 123
Music in Recreation 400
Music in Recreation and Leisure 399
Music in Secondary Education, Resource Book 129
Music in Secondary Schools 130
Music in Special Education 385
Music in the Baroque Era 180
Music in the Child's Education 122
Music in the Classic Period 184
Music in the Cultured Generation 217
Music in the Education of Children 118
Music in the Elementary School: An Activities Approach 116, 146, 385
Music in the Junior College 136
Music in the Medieval and Renaissance Universities 133
Music in the Medieval World 184
Music in the Middle Ages 186
Music in the Modern Age 188
Music in Therapy 393
Music in the Renaissance 187
Music in the Romantic Era 181
Music in the School Curriculum 149
Music in the Senior High School 129
Music in the Sticks and Stones 118
Music in the Twentieth Century 224
Music in the United States 215
Music in the United States: A Historical Introduction 184, 216
"Music in the Visual Dimension" 407
Music in Today's Classroom 113
Music in Western Civilization 185
Music in World Cultures 201
"Music in World Cultures: A Bibliography and Discography" 420
Music Journal 38, 417
Music Lessons You Can Teach 122
Music Literature for Analysis and Study 360
Music Machines--American Style 334
Music Monographs in Series 33
Music, Movement and Mime for Children 111
Music Notation 349
Music of Acoma, Isleta, Cochiti, and Zuni Pueblos 214
Music of Africa, The 269
Music of Black Americans, The 269
Music of Central Africa, The 199, 266
Music of East and Southeast Asia 182
Music of Israel, The 271
Music of Our Time 228
Music of the Americas 200
Music of the Bible with Some Account of the Development of Modern Musical Instruments from Ancient Types, The 278, 337
Music of the Classic Period 184
Music of the Indians of British Columbia 214
Music of the Jews, The 272
Music of the Minnesinger and Early Meistersinger 185
Music of the Most Ancient Nations 182
Music of the North American Indian 214
Music of the Old South 218
Music of the Western Nations 185
Musicological Studies and Documents 190, 196
Musicology 192

Musicology and the Computer 191, 409
Music, Physics, and Engineering 379
Music Power 155
Music Prodigies 397
Music Project Library: Works for Brass, Winds and Percussion/Solos 223
Music Project Library: Works for Chorus and Voice 223
Music Project Library: Works for Orchestra and String Instruments 223
Music/Record Career Handbook, The 64
Music Reference and Research Materials 34, 192
Music Research Handbook 50
Music Resource Guide for Primary Grades 113
Music Revolution, The 149
"Music Serials in Microform and Reprint Editions" 21
Music Since 1900 229
Music Skills for Recreation Leaders 399
Music Teaching in the Junior High and Middle School 126
Music Tempo 38
Music, the Arts, and Ideas 173
Music Theatre in a Changing Society 241
Music the Healer: A Bibliography 395
Music Therapy (Alvin) 393
Music Therapy (Podolsky) 394
"Music Therapy: A Selective Bibliography" 393
Music Therapy for Handicapped Children 394
Music Therapy in Action 395
Music Therapy in Special Education 394
Music Through the Ages 179
Music Through the Centuries 187
Music Through the Dance: A Handbook 116, 251
Music Trades Magazine 38
Music with Children 111
Music World 38
Music Yearbook, The 113
Musiktidning 293
Musique Concrete 234

N

NAMM Music Retailer News 67
Nashville Sound, The 206
NASM, the First Forty Years 136
National Anthems 174
National Anthems of the World 175
National Directory for the Performing Arts and Civic Centers, The 13
National Directory for the Performing Arts/Educational, The 14
National Faculty Directory 131
National School Musician 375
National Society for Study in Education, The Thirty-fifth Yearbook 92
National Society for Study in Education, The Fifty-seventh Yearbook 92
National Union Catalog of Manuscript Collection, 1959-1962, Index, The 4
Natural Singing and Expressive Conducting 288
Negro and His Music, The 268
Negro Folk Music, U.S.A. 267
Negro in the U.S.: A List of Significant Books Selected From a Compilation by the N.Y. Public Library, The 265
Negro Musicians and Their Music 267
Negro Slave Songs 267
New Approaches to Music in the Elementary School 116
New College Encyclopedia of Music, The 77
New Dance 252
New Dictionary of Music, A 74
New Dimensions in Music: Sound, Beat, and Feeling 123
New Dimensions in Music: Sound, Shape, and Symbol 124
New Dimensions in Music Education 90

New Directions in Music 225
New Encyclopedia of Music and Musicians, The 74
New Encyclopedia of the Opera, The 238
New Expanded Bibliography of Jazz Compositions Based on the Chord Progressions of Standard Tunes, The 259
New History of Wind Music, A 302, 314
New Hot Discography: The Standard Dictionary of Recorded Jazz 421
New Music, The 228
New Objectives for Cultural Enrichment Programs 142
New Orleans Jazz 259
New Outlook for the Blind 387
New Oxford History of Music, The 189
New Sounds for Woodwind 311, 362
New World of Electronic Music, The 236
New York Times Guide to Continuing Education in America, The 132
New York Times Guide to Listening Pleasure, The 175
New York Times Index 20
NICEM Index to Educational Audio Tapes 1974-75 414
NICEM Index to Educational Overhead Transparencies 1974-75 437
NICEM Index to Educational Records 1974-75 415
NICEM Index to Educational Slides 1974-75 435
NICEM Index to Educational Video Tapes 1974-75 433
NICEM Index to 8mm Motion Cartridges 1974-75 426
NICEM Index to Producers and Distributors 1974-75 412, 433
NICEM Index to 16mm Educational Films 1974-75 426
NICEM Index to 35mm Filmstrips 1974-75 426
NIMAC Manual--Managing Interscholastic Music Activities 152
Nineteenth-Century Romanticism in Music 184
1973 Folk Music Festivals, Fiddlers' Conventions, and Related Events in the United States and Canada 206
1973-1974 American Library Directory, 29th Edition 4
Nootka and Quileute Music 214
North American Folklore and Folk Music Serial Publications 207
North American Folklore and Folksong Societies and Fiddlers' Associations 207
Northern Indian Music 181
Northern Ute Music 214
Notation in New Music 349
Notation of Medieval Music, The 193
Notes 5, 20, 95, 196, 416, 417
Nurtured by Love 91, 310

O

Objective Measurement in Instrumental Music Performance 101
Objective Psychology of Music, An 102
Oboe Player's Encyclopedia, The 313
Oboe Technique 313
Observations on the Florid Song 290
Official Directory of Music Education Leadership 155
"Official Directory--Registry of Music Education Leadership" 10, 41
Old as the Hills: The Story of Bluegrass Music 208
Old English Instruments of Music 333
Old Musical Instruments 333
One Hundred Years of Music in America 216
On Parade 324
On Playing the Flute 312
Open Classroom Reader, The 117
Open Education 117
Opera: A Modern Guide 239
Opera: Dead or Alive 239
Opera: Its Story Told through the Lives and Works of its Foremost Composers 241
Opera: Origins and Sidelights. See Backgrounds and Traditions of Opera, The

Opera and Church Music (Record Supplement) 179, 417
Opera and its Future in America, The 238
Opera Directory, The 240
Opera for the People 242
Opera Guide 242
Opera in Your School 246
Opera News 417
Opera Production 246
Opera Recordings 239, 418
Opera Repertory U.S.A. 243
Operas on American Subjects 242
Opera Themes and Plots 238
Operetta Book, The 244
Orchestra, The 167
Orchestra and its Instruments, The 334
Orchestra from Beethoven to Berlioz, The 180
Orchestral Music: A Source Book 297, 369
Orchestral Music: Its Story Told through the Lives and Works of its Foremost Composers 170
Orchestral Percussion Technique 318
Orchestra News 38
Orchestration (Forsyth) 363
Orchestration (Piston) 363
Orchestration: A Practical Handbook 364
Orchestration: Scores and Scoring 364
Orchestration Workbook 363
Orff and Kodaly Adapted for the Elementary School 120
Orff Echo 92
Organ: Its Evolution, Principles of Construction and Use, The 346
Organist Magazine, The 346
Organization, Administration, and Presentation of Symphony Orchestra Youth Concert Activities for Music Educational Purposes in Selected Cities, The 128
Organizing and Developing the High School Orchestra 298
Organizing the Instrumental Music Library 297
Organ Literature: A Comprehensive Survey 345
Organ Music in Print 345
Organ Preludes: An Index 345
Organ Registration 345
Oriental Music: A Selected Discography 419
Original Manuscript Music for Wind and Percussion Instruments 314, 321
Original Music for Men's Voices: A Selected Bibliography 292
Origins of Bowing and the Development of Bowed Instruments up to the Thirteenth Century, The 304
Orpheus in the New World: The Symphony Orchestra as an American Cultural Institution 297
Orthodontics and Wind Instrument Performance 314, 317
Our American Music 216
Our Drum and Drummers 320
Outline of Music, The 187
Oxford Companion to Music 76

P

Pan Book of Opera, The. See Opera: A Modern Guide
Papago Music 214
Papers of the International Seminar on Experimental Research in Music Education 99, 103
Parents' and Teachers' Guide to Music Education 87
Parent's Guide to Music Lessons, A 118
Passaic, N.J. Report on ESEA Title I Summer Program 145
Pastoral Music 96, 156
Path to New Music, The 230
Pawnee Music 214
People and Music 172
Percussion: Performance and Instrumental Technique, The 321
Percussion Ensemble Method 318
Percussion Instruments and their History 318
Percussionist 327

Percussion Research Bulletin 320
Percussive Notes 327
Perfect Conductor, The 371
"Performance-based Teacher Education: What is the State of the Art?" 133
Performance Practice: A Bibliography 366
Performer's Guide to Baroque Music, A 322
Performing Arts, The 217
Performing Arts Books in Print: An Annotated Bibliography 237
Performing Arts Libraries and Museums of the World 5
Performing Arts Management and Law 62
Performing Arts Research: A Guide to Information Sources 17
Performing for Others 114
Performing Times of Orchestral Works 369
Pergamon Dictionary of Musicians and Music 74
"Periodicals" 21
Perspectives in Music Education 86, 92
Perspectives in Musicology 191
Perspectives in Music Theory 351
Perspectives on Contemporary Music Theory 224
Philosophies of Music History 191
Philosophy of Modern Music 224
Philosophy of Music Education, A 90
Phonetics and Diction in Singing 283
Phonolog 415
Phrasing and Articulation 366
Physical Therapy 388
Physics of Musical Sound, The 378
Physics of Musical Sounds, The 379
Physiological Mechanics of Piano Technique, The 341
Physiology of Violin Playing, The 309
Piaget's Theory of Cognitive Development 118
Pianist's Problems, The 341
Pianist's Resource Guide, The 343
Piano Duet: A Guide for Pianists, The 343
Piano for Classroom Music 341
Pianoforte, The 342
Piano Guild Notes 96, 346, 347
Piano Technician's Journal 38, 67, 347
Piano Tuning and Allied Arts 344
Pitch Pipe 294
Place of Musicology in American Institutions of Higher Learning, The 191
Plain and Easy Introduction to the Harpsichord, A 344
Planning and Equipping Educational Music Facilities 150
Planning and Producing Audio-Visual Materials 406
Planning and Producing the Musical Show 246
Planning for Junior High School General Music 125
Playing and Teaching Brass Instruments 317
Playing and Teaching Percussion Instruments 319
Playing and Teaching Stringed Instruments 307
Playing and Teaching Woodwind Instruments 313
Playing Social and Recreational Instruments 113, 296
Playing String Quartets 323
Playing the Harpsichord 345
Poetics of Music in the Form of Six Lessons 164
Poets in Song 272
Pollart Index to Record Reviews (Including Tapes) 416
Popular American Composers from Revolutionary Times to the Present 215
Popular Music: An Annotated Index of American Popular Songs 256
Popular Titles and Subtitles of Musical Compositions 29
Post-Baccalaureate Grants and Awards in Music 58, 135
Practical Band and Instrument Repair Manual, The 304
Practical Guidelines for Developing the High School Band 301

Practical Guide to Music Notation for Composers, Arrangers and Editors 350
Practical Suggestions for Young Teachers 136
Precision Marching 303
Preliminary Checklist of Research on the Classic Symphony and Concerto to the time of Beethoven, A 34
Preliminary Directory of Sound Recordings Collections in the United States and Canada, A 413
Prelude to Brass Playing 316
Prentice-Hall History of Music Series, The 184
Preparing for a Career in Education 65
Preparing Music Manuscript 349
Present State of Music Education in the World, The 87
Preservation and Restoration of Musical Instruments 332
Preventive Maintenance of Musical Instruments 304
Primitive Music 189
Principles and Practices of Electronic Music 236
Principles and Problems of Music Education 90
Principles of Aesthetics, The 163
Principles of Conducting for Music Teachers 372
Principles of Expression in Pianoforte Playing, The 339
Principles of Musical Education 89
Principles of Orchestration 364
Principles of Rhythm 361
Principles of the Flute, Recorder, and Oboe 312
Private Foundations and Business Corporations Active in Arts/Humanities/Education 58
Problems of Conducting 372
Problems of Opera Production 247
Proceedings of the Music Teachers National Association 92
Process of Education, The 84
Producing Opera for America 242
Producing Opera in the College 247
Professional Symphony Orchestra in the United States, The 299
Programmed Ear Training 352
Program to Excite Potential 145
Project to Develop a Curriculum for Disadvantaged Students in the Intermediate School, A 145
Pronouncing Pocket Manual for Musical Terms 72
Proposed Standards for State Approval of Teacher Education 135
Protestant Church Music 275
Protestant Church Music in America 278
Providing for Individual Differences in the Elementary School 110
Psychological Abstracts 27, 54
Psychological Review 40
Psychology of Conducting, The 370
Psychology of Music, (Mursell) The 89, 102
Psychology of Music, (Seashore) 104
Psychology of Music: A Survey for Teacher and Musician, The 103
Psychology of Musical Ability, The 104
Psychology of Musical Talent, The 104
Psychology of Musicians 99
Psychology of Music Teaching, The 100
Psychology of School Music Teaching, The 89
Psychology of the Arts 101, 162
Psychology of the Vibrato in Voice and Instrument 101
PTG Official Directory 67
PTM Magazine 38
Public Relations in Music Education 150
Published Music for the Viola da Gamba and Other Viols 305

Q

Quantitative and Qualitative Effects of Revised Selection and Training Procedures in the Education of Teachers of the Culturally Disadvantaged 141
Quarterly Checklist of Musicology 196
Quartets of Beethoven, The 173

R

Ragas of North India, The 185
Ragtimer, The 262
Rare Works on Microfiche 181
Rational and Social Foundations of Music, The 176
Rationale for a Culturally Based Program of Action Against Poverty Among New York Puerto Ricans 141
Readers Guide to Periodical Literature 24
Reading and Writing in the Arts 50
Readings in Black American Music 269
Real Jazz Old and New, The 258
Real-Lexikon der Musikinstrumente 336
Recent Publications on Folklore Archives and Archiving in North America, 1969-1971 207
Recommended Standards and Evaluative Criteria for the Identification of Music Teachers 135
Record and Tape Reviews Index 416
Recorded Jazz 421
Recorded Ragtime 1897-1958 258, 421
Recorder Technique 313
Record Rating Service 417
Records and Cassettes for Young Adults 420
Records in Review 416
Recreation and Leisure in Modern Society 400
Recreation For the Handicapped: A Bibliography 383, 399
Recreation in American Life 399
Recreation through Music 400
Recueils Imprimes XVI-XVII Siecles 35
Recueils Imprimes, XVIII Siecle 35
Reed Trio: An American Bibliography of Original Published Works, The 311
Reference Guide to Audiovisual Information, A 412
Reference Materials in Ethnomusicology 201
Reflections on Afro-American Music 265
Rehearsal Guide for the Choral Conductor 284, 369
Relating the Arts 114
Renaissance and Baroque Music 167, 179
Renaissance and Baroque Musical Sources in the Americas 193
Renaissance Quarterly 196
Répertoire Internationale de la Litterature Musicale. See RILM Abstracts
Répertoire International des Musiques Electroacoustiques (International Electronic Music Catalog) 233
Répertoire International des Sources Musicales. See RISM
Research in Education (Best) 49
Research in Education (ERIC). See Resources in Education
Research in Music Behavior 102
Research in Music Education 51
Research in Primitive and Folk Music in the United States 206
Resources in Education (RIE) 27, 54, 148
Response to Music 83
Resumé of Materials, Suggestions, and References Gathered During the Shippensburg Conference on the Education of the Migrant Child 144
Review of Educational Research 40
Revista Italian Di Musicologia 196
Revolt into Style: The Pop Arts 256
Revue De Musicologia 196
Rhode Island Music and Musicians 1733-1850 208
Rhythm: An Annotated Bibliography 356, 366
Rhythm and Movement: Applications of Dalcroze Eurhythmics 119
Rhythm and Tempo 187
Rhythmic Structure of Music, The 358
Rhythm, Music and Education 86
RIE. See Resources in Education
RILM Abstracts (Répertoire Internationale de la Litterature Musicale [International Repertory of Musical Literature]) 28, 34, 193

Rise of Music in the Ancient World East and West, The 187
RISM (Répertoire International des Sources Musicales [International Inventory of Musical Sources]) 35-36, 193
Rock 261
Rock Encyclopedia 262
Rock On: The Illustrated Encyclopedia of Rock 261
Rock Story, The 261
Role of Music in the Special Education of Handicapped Children, The 385
Romanticism (Record Supplement) 179, 417
Romantic Period in Music, The 185
Rudiments of the Flute, Recorder, and Oboe 312
Russian-English Dictionary of Musical Terms 74
Russian Music and its Source in Chant and Folk Songs 175

S

Sacred Music 278
Saenger-Zeitung 294
Schillinger System of Music Composition, The 355
Scholar's Guide to Journals of Education and Educational Psychology 63
Scholarships and Fellowships for Foreign Study--A Selected Bibliography 65
Scholarships, Fellowships and Loans News Service 59
Scholastics 1974-75 Audio-Visual Catalog for Schools and Libraries 415
School Administrator, The 155
School and Amateur Orchestras 297
School Music 94
School Music Administration and Supervision 154
School Music Administrator and Supervisor, The 151
School Music Conductor, The 373
School Music Handbook 85
School Musician, Director and Teacher 325, 374
School Music Program, The 89, 152
School Music Teaching: Its Theory and Practice. See New Dimensions in Music Education
School Musician, Director and Teacher 38
School Personnel Research and Evaluation Services 103, 136
Schools and Symphony Orchestras: A Summary of Selected Youth Concert Activities 91, 130, 299
Schools are for Children 111
Schwann Artist Issue 415
Schwann Children's Record and Tape Guide 415, 420
Schwann Country and Western Tape and Record Catalog 415
Schwann-1 Record and Tape Guide 415
Schwann-2 Semi-annual Supplement, The 415
Science and Music 125, 378
Science and Sensations of Vocal Tone, The 286
Science of Vocal Pedagogy, The 284
Science of Voice, The 289
Scientific Piano Tuning and Servicing 343
Score, The 367
Scored for Listening: A Guide to Music 168
Scoring for Brass Band 365
Scoring for Films 363
Scoring for Percussion and the Instruments of Percussion 320, 364
Search for Musical Understanding, The 168
Secondary School Music 127
Secondary School Music Program from Classroom to Concert Hall, The 127
Secondary School Vocal Music Program, The 128
Second Line 262
Secular Music in America 1801-1825: A Bibliography 218
Segovia Technique, The 305

Select Bibliography of European Folk Music, A 204, 211
Selected and Annotated Bibliography of Studies Concerning the Taxonomy of Educational Objectives, A 150
Selected Bibliography of Published Choral Music by Black Composers 266
Selected Discography of Solo Songs, A 420
"Selected Readings on Electronic Music" 233
Selection and Use of Programmed Materials 407
Selective Bibliography of Works on Music Testing, A 102
Selective Clarinet Bibliography, A 311
Selective List of Master's Theses in Musicology, A 47
Selective Music Lists, 1971: Band, Orchestra, and String Orchestra 297
Selective Music Lists, 1972: Instrumental Solos and Ensembles 297
Selective Music Lists-1974: Vocal Solos and Ensembles 292
Self-Esteem and Goals of Indigent Children, The 143, 268
Selmer Bandwagon 38
Seminar on the Role of the Arts in Meeting the Social And Educational Needs of the Disadvantaged, A 146
Seminole Music 214
SEM Newsletter 196
Sense of Music, The 177
Senso-Motor Study and its Application to Violin Playing 103, 308
Serial Composition and Atonality 228
Serial Music: A Classified Bibliography 221
Shaker Music 181
Shakespeare in Music 171
Shakespeare's Use of Music: A Study of the Music and Its Performance in the Original Production of Seven Comedies 172
Shakespeare's Use of Music: The Final Comedies 172
Shakespeare's Use of Music: The Histories and Tragedies 172
Shining Trumpets: A History of Jazz 257
Short History of Keyboard Music, A 343
Short History of Music, A 182
Short History of Music in America, A 216
Short History of Opera, A 241
Short History of Western Music, A 184
Show Band 303
Silver Burdett Music 124
Simon's Directory of Theatrical Materials, Services and Information 247
Sing a Song of Social Significance 255
Singer and His Art, The 289
Singer and the Voice, The 289
Singer's Art, The 285
Singers in New York 282
Singer's Italian 285
Singer's Manual of German and French Diction, The 285
Singer's Repertoire 291
Singing Voice, The 289
Sir Arthur Sullivan: An Index to the Texts of his Vocal Works 245
Sixteenth-Century Polyphony 357
Sketch of a New Esthetic of Music 161
Slow Learner and Music, The 383
Smithsonian Collection of Classic Jazz, The 260, 422
SNOBOL 3 Primer 409
Social and Rehabilitation Services for the Blind 384
Social History of Music, A 186
Social Implications of Early Negro Music in the United States, The 267
Social Psychology of Music, The 85, 99, 393
Social Science Index 24
Societé Internationale de Musicologie. See Acta Musicologica
Sociological Abstracts 28
Solo and Ensemble Literature for Percussion 319
Solos for Unaccompanied Clarinet: An Annotated Bibliography 311

Some Twentieth Century American Composers: A Selective Bibliography 215
Sonata in the Baroque Era, The 359
Sonata in the Classic Era, The 359
Song Catalogue 281
Song in American from Early Times to about 1850 218
Song Index 283
Songs in Action 111
Songs in Collections: An Index 282
Sound and Silence: Classroom Projects in Creative Music 116
Sound and Symbol Vol. 1: Music and the External World 164
Sound and Symbol Vol. 2: Man the Musician 164
Sound Exploration and Discovery 114
Sound of Africa Series of Long Playing Record Catalogue, The 419
Sound of Soul, The 267
Sounds and Signs 349
Source Book for Higher Education, The 132
Source Book of African and Afro-American Materials for Music Educators 223, 266
Source Readings in Music History 188
Sources of Information on Funds for Education 57
Sousa Band: A Discography, The 420
So You Have to Teach Your Own Music? 120
Spectrum of Music 124
Speculum 196
Speculum: An Index of Musically Related Articles and Book Reviews 20
Standard Education Almanac 10
Standard Musical Repertoire, with Accurate Timings, The 372
Star Spangled Banner: Hearings before Subcommittee, The 218
State Certification of Music Teachers 137
State Education Journal Index 25, 41
"State Publications: A Bibliographic Guide for Reference Collections" 41
State Supervision of Music 156
Stereo and Hi-Fi Principles and Projects 407
Stereo Review 417
Story of Dance Music, The 186, 250
Story of Jazz, The 260
Story of Musical Instruments from Shepherd's Pipe to Symphony, The 336
Story of Rock, The 261
Story of the Blues, The 259
Stravinsky 229
Stravinsky and the Dance 248
String Class Publications in the United States 309
Stringed Instruments of the Middle Ages, The 336
String Ensemble Method 305
String Music in Print 306
Strings, Performance and Instructional Techniques, The 307
Structural Foundations of Harmony 355
Structural Hearing 355
Structure of Atonal Music, The 226
Studia Musicologica 196
Studies in Jazz Discography I 421
Studies in Medieval and Renaissance Music 180
Studies in Music 196
Studies in Music Literature 188
Studies in Musicology 193
Studies in the New Experimental Aesthetics 161
Studies in the Renaissance 196
Studies on the History of Musical Style 360
Study of Computer Techniques for Music Research 410
Study of Counterpoint, The 356
Study of Jazz, A 260
Study of Music in the Elementary School 115
Study of Remedial Procedures for Improving the Level of Musical Attainment Among Preschool Disadvantaged 108, 147
"Study of the Musical Achievement of Culturally Deprived Children and Culturally Advantaged Children at the Elementary School Level, A" 144

Study to Explore New Methods of Identifying and Measuring Musical Talent, A 103
Subject Catalog of the Department (HEW) Library 16, 154
Subject Collections 14
Subject Collections in European Libraries, A Directory and Bibliographical Guide 4
Subject Guide to Books in Print 16
"Subsidization of Research in Music" 59
Successful College Concerts 134
Summer Musical Talent Showcase for Disadvantaged High School Students 143
"Summer Music Camps and Summer Programs for Young Musicians - United States" 400
"Summer Music Camps, Clinics and Workshops - Addendum" 400
Summer 1967 Elementary School Programs for Disadvantaged Pupils in Poverty Areas in New York City 143
Summer Program in Music and Art for Disadvantaged Pupils in Public and Non-Public Schools 146
Supervising Music in Elementary School 151
Supervising the Successful School Music Program 149
Supervisor's Service Bulletin 94
Survey of Choral Music, A 293
Survey of Christian Hymnology, A 277
Survey of Musical Instrument Collections in the United States and Canada, A 335
Suzuki Concept, The 310
Suzuki Education in Action 310
Suzuki Violin Method in American Music Education, The 310
Symbols Used in Music Analysis 58
Symphonic Music: Its Evolution Since the Renaissance 176
Symphonic Music, 1880-1954 298
Symphonic Outlook (Record Supplement), The 179, 417
Symphony (Cuyler), The 169
Symphony (Rauchhaupt), The 174
Symphony Conductors of the U.S.A. 373
Symphony News 325, 374
Symphony Themes 30

T

Talent, Education and Suzuki. See The Suzuki Violin Method in American Music Education
Talking Drums of Africa 319
Tanglewood Symposium 89
Taxonomy for Behavioral Objectives in Music, A 153
Taxonomy of Educational Objectives 149
Teacher Education and Music 135
Teacher Education in Music 135
Teachers Guide to the Literature of Brass Instruments 317
Teacher's Guide to the Literature of Woodwind Instruments, A 312
Teacher's Manual, Orff-Schulwerk for Children 119
Teachers of Young Children 112
Teaching and Administration of High School Music, The 127
Teaching and Learning: An Introduction to New Methods and Resources in Higher Education 134
Teaching Band Instruments to Beginners 300
Teaching Children Music in the Elementary School 115
Teaching Creative Music in Today's Secondary School 129
Teaching Exceptional Children 387, 389
Teaching Instrumental Music 295
Teaching Junior High School Music 125
Teaching Music 109
Teaching Musical Appreciation 169
Teaching Music Appreciation Through Listening Skill Training 176
Teaching Music Creatively in the Elementary School 110
Teaching Musicianship 365
Teaching Musicianship in the High School Band 301

Teaching Music in the Secondary School 128
Teaching Music in Today's Secondary Schools 127
Teaching of Action in String Playing, The 308
Teaching of Arthur Schnabel, The 342, 367
Teaching Performing Groups 83
Teaching Piano in Classroom and Studio 341
Teaching Rhythm and Using Classroom Instruments 112
Teaching Singing 285
Teaching Stringed Instruments in Classes 306
Teaching Techniques for the Brasses 317
Teaching Techniques for the Percussion 319
Teaching Techniques of the Woodwind 312
Teaching Total Percussion 320
Teach with Television 405
Teach Yourself Songwriting 361
Technical Manual and Dictionary of Classical Ballet 248
Technique and Style in Choral Singing 287
Technique in Choral Conducting 371
Technique of Choral Composition, The 285, 361
Technique of Electronic Music, The 236
Technique of Film Music, The 361
Technique of Orchestration, The 363
Techniques for Producing Visual Instructional Media 407
Techniques of Modern Orchestral Conducting 371
Techniques of Twentieth Century Composition 225
Technology in Music Teaching 406
"Technology in Music Teaching" 407
Technology of Computer Music, The 235
Televised Music Instruction 405
Television Production Handbook 407
Ten Great Musicals of the American Theatre 244
Terminology in the Field of Singing 284
Tests and Measurement in Music 102
Tests in Print: A Comprehensive Bibliography 99
Teton Sioux Music 214
Texts of the Choral Works of Johann Sebastian Bach in English Translation 291
Theatre Books in Print. See Performing Arts Books in Print: An Annotated Bibliography
Theatre Organ 346
Theatre Student: Gilbert and Sullivan Production, The 245
Thematic Catalogues in Music: An Annotated Bibliography 30
Theory and Method in Ethnomusicology 201
Theory of Music, The 36
Therapeutic and Industrial Uses of Music 395
Therapeutic Recreation Service: An Applied Behavioral Science Approach 399
Therapeutic Recreation Service: Principles and Practices 400
Therapy in Music for Handicapped Children 394
There's Music in Children 117
Thesaurus of Orchestral Devices 364
They Can Make Music 383
They Can Sing, Too: Rhythm for the Deaf 385
This is Music 124
Three Centuries of American Hymnody 276
Three Centuries of Harpsichord Making 344
Three Classics in the Aesthetics of Music 161
Three-Year Longitudinal Predictive Validity Study of the Musical Aptitude Profile, A 101
Threshold to Music 120
Title I ESEA 1966-67 Projects of the Camden City Board of Education 142
Title I Projects and Others, Espanola Valley Pilot Program Research 142

Tonal/Atonal 352
Tonal Harmony in Concept and Practice 351
Tonality and Atonality in Sixteenth-Century Music 353
Tonality of Musical Structure 351
Top Pop Records 1955-1970 257
To Sing in English 290
Total Body Technique of Violin Playing 308
To the World's Oboists 326
Toward an Aesthetic Education 163
Traditional Artist in African Societies, The 267
Training the Boy's Changing Voice 126
Training the High School Orchestra 299
Training the Singing Voice 285
Treasury of Early Music, A 359
Treatise on Harmony 354
Treatise on the Flute, A 313
Treatise on the Fundamental Principles of Violin Playing [Versuch Einer Grundlichen Violinschule], A 307
Tri-M Notes 93
Trombone, The 315
Tropen-und Sequenzenhandschriften 36
True Sound of Music, The 406
Trumpet and Trombone, The 331
Trumpet Discography 316
Trumpet Technique 315
Tuba Music Guide 316
Tudor Church Music 278
Tuning and Temperament 377
Tuning the School Band and Orchestra 297
Twentieth-Century Church Music 228, 277
Twentieth Century Composers, Volume I--American Music Since 1910 230
Twentieth Century Composers, Volume II: Germany and Central Europe 229
Twentieth Century Composers, Volume III: Britain, Scandinavia, and the Netherlands 229
Twentieth Century Counterpoint: A Guide 357
Twentieth Century Harmony 228
Twentieth-Century Harpsichord Music: A Classified Catalog 344
Twentieth Century Music (Myers) 227
Twentieth Century Music (Stuckenschmidt) 229
Twentieth-Century Music (Wilder)
Twentieth-Century Music (Yates) 230
Twentieth-Century Music: An Introduction 184, 229
Twentieth-Century Music Idioms 227
Twentieth-Century Music in Western Europe 221
Twentieth-Century Views of Music History 183
Twenty-Seven Major American Symphony Orchestras 298
Twilight of the Gods: The Music of the Beatles 256
Two Brothers 272

U

Ulrich's International Periodicals Directory 22
Underscore 364
Understanding Educational Research 51
Understanding Media 406
Understanding of Music, The 171
UNESCO Ethnic Music Records 421
United States Music: Sources of Bibliography and Collective Biography 216
"U.S. Musical Contests, Awards, Grants, Fellowships and Honors" 59
Universal Dictionary of Violin and Bow Makers 334
Universality of Music, The 162
"Upward Bound - War on Talent Waste at Indiana University" 147
Urban Blues 268
Urban Disadvantaged Series, The 148
Uses of Music, The 89
Using Media in the Music Program 114
Using Music with Headstart Children 143

V

Variety 256
Versuch Einer Grundlichen Violinchule. See Treatise on the Fundamental Principles of Violin Playing, A
Victor Book of Ballets and Ballet Music, The 249
Victor Book of the Opera, The 240, 242
Victorian Popular Music 186
Viola: Complete Guide for Teachers and Students, The 304
Violin, The 307, 335
Violin and Keyboard: The Duo Repertoire 307
Violin and Viola, The 308
Violin Concerto, The 309
Violin Left Hand Techniques 308
Violin Makers of the Low Countries, The 335
Violins and Violinists 306
Violin Teaching in Class 305
Violoncello and its History, The 309
Visible and Invisible in Pianoforte Technique, The 341
Visible Speech 288
Vocal and Instrumental Music in Print 283
Vocal Pedagogy: A Summary of Courses Offered 286
Vocal Technique for Children and Youth 287
Voice, Song and Speech 284
Voice-Speech-Language 102, 287
Volta Review, The 387

W

Washington International Arts Letter 59
Webster's Biographical Dictionary 76
Western Music 188
Who's Who in America 77
Who's Who in Music and Musicians International 77
Who's Who in the Arts 77
Who's Who in the World 77
Who's Who of Jazz 257
Wichita Program for Educationally Deprived Children 147
Will Earhart 84
Wind Band, The 300
With the Artists: World Famous String Players Discuss Their Art 304
Women's Higher and Continuing Education, A 136
Woodwind Anthology (Globus) 312
Woodwind Anthology, The (Instrumentalist) 311
Woodwind Ensemble Music Guide 314
Woodwind Instruments and Their History 331
Woodwinds, The 314
Word-by-Word Translations of Songs and Arias, Part I: German and French 291
Word-by-Word Translations of Songs and Arias, Part II: Italian 292
Words, Sounds and Pictures about Music 407
World Chronology of Music History 182
World History of the Dance 251
World of Bells, The 318
World of Learning 11
World of Music, The 93, 173
World of Music: An Illustrated Encyclopedia, The 75
World of Musical Comedy, The 244
World of Opera, The 237
World of Twentieth-Century Music, The 226
World's Encyclopedia of Recorded Music, The 413
Worlds of Jazz, The 258
World Traveler 387

Y

Yearbook of Higher Education 132
Yellow Book: A Brief Sketch of the History of Chinese Music, The 199
You Can Teach Music 121
Young Person's Guide to the Opera 239
Your Future in Music 64
Your Future in the High Fidelity Industry 65
Your Jazz Collection 422
Youth Music 129
Yuman and Yaqui Music 214

SUBJECT INDEX

This index is alphabetized letter by letter. Underlined numbers represent main entries. Indexed here are the major areas in music and music education as well as selected associations, individuals important in the field, and important sources of information relating to music and education.

A

Abstracting journals 27-28, 44, 53-54
Academically talented students and music. See Talent
Accompaniments, recorded 422
Accompanying. See Keyboard music, instruments, and pedagogy
Accountability in music education 84, 87, 151. See also Music education
Accreditation. See Certification of music teachers
Acoustics 377-79
  associations 379
  orchestral 298
  sound spectograph 288
  strings 306
  tuning instruments 297
  woodwinds 312
Action research. See Research
Administration and supervision of music education 149-57
  associations 154-57
  courses of study 16, 153
  forms 153
  journal abstracts 27
  NASM curriculum
  See also music education; Specific subject areas and school levels.
Aesthetics and music 107, 153, 161-65
  associations 165
  journals 165
  See also Appreciation and understanding of music; Philosophical foundations, principles, and practices; Arts and music
African music 189, 199, 201, 266, 269, 319
  artists 267
  central Africa 266
  phonograph records 419
  source material 223
  UNESCO records 421
  See also Black culture
Afro-American music. See African music; Black culture
American Bandmasters Association Research Center 95
American music 213-19
  associations 219
  bands 301
  catalog 214
  early concert life 218
  folk music 205-9
  history 184
  survey of the performing arts 217

Subject Index

American String Teachers Association 95, 325
Analysis. See Form, style, and analysis
Anthropology and music
  abstracts 199
  journal abstracts 27
  See also Ethnomusicology; Musicology
Appalachian folk music 208
Appreciation and understanding of music 167-77
  psychological aspects 101-2
  See also Philosophical foundations, principles, and practices; Aesthetics and music; History of music; Arts and music
Aristotle 187
Armed forces, music in. See U.S. Armed Forces, music in
Ars Nova 183, 189, 193
Artist managers 13, 14
Arts and music
  administration of programs 62, 63
  cybernetics 362
  for the disadvantaged 146
  general education 85, 87, 101, 110, 134, 153
  in general music 101, 153
  for the handicapped 385
  open classroom 112
  painting 172
  See also Aesthetics and music; Appreciation and understanding of music; History of music; Humanities
Arts in education. See Arts and music
Art songs. See Songs
Asian music 182
Associations (by subject)
  acoustics 379
  administration and supervision of music education 154-57
  aesthetics 165
  American music 219
  black culture 270
  business aspects of music 65-67
  chamber music 324
  choral music 293-94
  composition and theory 367-68
  comprehensive listings 7-14
  conducting 374-75
  contemporary music 230-31
  conventions 7-8
  dance 253-54
  ethnomusicology 201-2
  festival and concert managers 65-66
  fiddlers' 206
  folk music and folklore 209-11
  handicapped 387-91
  higher education 137-39
  history of music 190
  instrumental music 324-29
  instruments (historical) 338
  Jewish music 272-73
  keyboard music and instruments 346-47
  libraries 5-6
  music education (general) 92-97
  musicology 196-98
  music therapy 395-96
  nonprint media 451-52
  opera 253-54
  popular music 262-63
  recreation and music 400-401
  religious music 278-80
  special education 387-91
  state (MENC) 10
  for students 93, 96
  teacher education 137-39
Associations, directories and encyclopedias of 7-14
Audio tapes. See Phonograph records and audio tapes
Audiovisual technology
  equipment 405, 411, 445
  materials and instruction 152, 405-8, 411-12
  teaching applications 114, 405-8
  See also Films and filmstrips
Awards. See Scholarships and fellowships

B

Ballet 248-49
  books in print 237
  films 425-26
  See also Dance; Festivals

Band
administration and pedagogy 295-303
contemporary literature 301
elementary 300, 301
encyclopedia 300
literature guide 300
marching 302-3
record guide 413
scoring 362-65
wind band 300
See also Instrumental music
Beatles 256
Beethoven
encyclopedia 174
quartets 322-23
Behavior modification 102
Bel canto. See Choral and vocal music
Bells. See Instrumental music, percussion
Biblical references to music 337
Bibliographical sources
guides 33-36
indexes 23-25
information centers 36
in progress and unpublished 35
See also Indexing journals; Specific subject areas
Biographical indexes. See Indexing journals
Biography. See Dictionaries and encyclopedias of education; Dictionaries and encyclopedias of music
Bio-mechanics 100, 103, 308
Black culture 265-70
associations 270
black nationalism 145
elementary school programs 143
folk music 267
slave songs 267
See also African music
Blind, music for the. See Special education
Bluegrass music 208
Blues. See Jazz
Book reviews 19-20, 23-25
Books and literature, guides to 15-18
Braille music. See Special education
Brasses. See Instrumental music
British music
folk music journals 211
popular music 256
Union catalog, early music 193
Business aspects of music 61-67
associations 65-67
careers 64-65
copyright and legal matters 61-62
engraving 64
music industry 62-67
publishing 64

C

Cantatas (themes) 29
Cantus firmus 278
Careers in music 64-65, 136, 282
See also Business aspects of music
Carrilons. See Instrumental music, percussion
Catalogs. See Thematic indexes and catalogs; Specific subject areas
Ceremonial music 89
Certification of music teachers 135, 137, 139
See also Higher education and teacher education, music in
Certification standards for piano Teachers. See Music Teachers National Association
Chamber Music 173, 321-23
themes 29
Chant. See Gregorian chant
Chautauqua 277
Childhood education, music in. See Early childhood education, music in; Elementary school music
China and music 199
Choral and vocal music 281-94
administration 289
associations 293-94
bel canto 285, 288, 290
children's song index 281
chorales of Bach 356
choral music in print, catalog 282
composition 361
conducting 287-88, 369-75
contemporary choral music 282, 292

indexes and catalogs 281-83
interpretation 287
journals 293-94
medical aspects 282, 284, 286-87
New York opportunities 282
ornamentation 290
pedagogy 283-93
physiological aspects 282, 284-90
repertory 291-93
sacred music in print, catalog 282
secondary school music 128
secular music in print, catalog 282
song books, index 282
themes 29
university courses 286
vibrato studies 101
vocal terminology, dictionary 284
youth vocal development 287
See also Careers in music; Religious music; Junior high and middle school music; For school choral programs consult specific school level
Church music. See Religious music
Civic centers 13, 14
Classroom instruments. See Instrumental music, easy-to-play instruments
Classroom teacher, music and the 88, 120-22
Clavichord. See Keyboard music, instruments, and pedagogy
Code of ethics, music 63
Cognitive learning 118, 149, 150. See also Music education
College and university information 10
Competitions (music). See Festivals
Composition 361-62
associations 367-68
choral 285, 361
computer applications 234, 235, 356, 361, 362, 410
experimental 361
film music 361
jazz 259
masses and motets 278
in secondary schools 129
See also Music structure, theory, and composition; Electronic music, music concrete, and computer music
Computer applications 191, 200, 234, 235, 356, 361, 362, 409-10
research services 53-55
See also Section 41: Electronic music, music concrete, and computer music
Concerto
research on 34
themes 29, 30
Concrete, music 233-35
Conducting 369-75
associations 374-75
choral 284, 287, 288
rehearsal guides 284
timings 369, 372
Conservatories. See Higher education
Contemporary music 221-31
associations 230-31
band 301
choral music 282, 292
church music 228
computers 361
dictionaries 221-24
experimental 361
in inner city "deprived" schools 147
media, use of 225
notation 349
performance directory 223
polyphonic devices 357
recordings 418
schools 129, 222, 223
See also American music; Electronic music, music concrete, and computer music
Contemporary Music Project (CMP) 221-23
Continuing education 132
women's 136-37
Copyright information. See Business aspects of music
Council for Exceptional Children 386
Counterpoint 356-57
Courses of study. See Administration and supervision of music education
Criticism 176
Curriculum guides and sources. See

Administration and supervision of music education; State journals and other publications; Specific subject areas; Individual school levels
Cybernetic devices and the arts 362

D

Dalcroze eurhythmics. See Dance
Dance 250-54
associations 253-54
books in print 237
Dalcroze eurhythmics 107, 118-20
directories 13, 14
films 426
folk dance teaching 112
folk dancing 115, 252-53
history 186
in the secondary school 128
See also Ballet; Elementary school music
Datrix II 44, 53
Deaf, music for the. See Special education
Department of Health, Education and Welfare, subject catalog of. See U.S. Department of Health, Education and Welfare, subject catalog of.
Dialog Information Retrieval Service 53
Dictation, music 354
See also Music structure, theory, and composition
Dictionaries and encyclopedias of education 79
Dictionaries and encyclopedias of music 71-77
opera 29
musical themes 29
song themes 29
See also specific subject matter areas
Direct Access to Reference Information. See Datrix II
Directories
comprehensive listings 7-8
organizations and institutions 9-11
See also specific areas of interest, e.g. Dance
Disadvantaged. See Urban education and the culturally disadvantaged
Dissertaions and theses 43-47
American, index to 45
ethnomusicology 44, 200
folk music 200
sacred music 276
theses 47
Drama and music in schools 33, 126

E

Early childhood education, music in 107-8
books in print 15
journal abstracts 27
records 420
song index 281
vocal development 287
Early music
books 183
catalog 193
Ear training. See Music structure, theory, and composition
Easy-to-play instruments. See Instrumental music, easy-to-play
Education, music in 85
Educational Resources Information Center (ERIC) 53
ERIC Document Reproduction Service 54
Electronic music, music concrete, and computer music 233-36
classroom activities 233
computer applications 409-10
instruments 233, 234, 333
junior high level 125
scoring 363
for young people 114
See also Contemporary music
Elementary classroom teacher 120-22
Elementary music book series 122-24
Elementary school music 109-24
children's vocal development 287
classroom teacher 120-22
music book series 122-24
See also Early childhood education, music in
English music 182, 203, 204

anthem development 278
church music 277
See also Religious music
Engraving. See Business aspects of music; music education
Equipment guides 411-12
ERIC. See Educational Resources Information Center
Eskimos and music 200
Ethnic music 189
instruments 200, 331-38
See also Phonograph records and audio tapes; Ethnomusicology
Ethnomusicology 199-202
associations 201-2
central African music 266
dissertations 43-47
folk music 44
recordings 418, 420
See also Musicology; Folk music and folklore
Eurhythmics. See Dalcroze
European composers, manuscripts in American libraries 29
Evaluation in music education. See Music education
Exceptional children, music for. See Special education
Experimental research. See Research

F

Faculties, Music. See Higher education and teacher education, music in
Federal aid programs 57-59
Fellowships. See Scholarships and fellowships
Festivals 7, 8, 10, 13, 14
folk music 206
foreign 7-8
Film music
composition 361
scoring 363, 364
Films and filmstrips
companies 427-28
directories and guides 425-26
8mm cartridge producers 429
filmstrip producers 431
folklore 211
free 425
NICEM 8mm index 426
NICEM filmstrip index 426
NICEM 16mm index 426
reviews and evaluations 425-26
Filmstrips. See Films and filmstrips
Fine arts. See Arts and music
Folk music and folklore 203-11
Appalachian 208
associations 209-11
bluegrass 208
festivals 206
films 211
Hawaii 215
instruments 331-38
New Hampshire 208
North Carolina 209
recordings 203, 207, 210, 418-20
Rhode Island 208
Virginia 205, 208
See also Dance
Foreign study 10, 11, 57, 65. See also Higher education and teacher education, music in
Forms for music administration 153
Form, style, and analysis 357-60
Sonata themes 29
See also Music structure, theory, and analysis
Foundations. See Grant support programs
Fraternities 69
Funding agencies. See Grant support programs

G

General music series 16, 122-24
General music textbooks 16
Geriatric uses of music. See Special Education, music therapy
Gifted, music for the. See Special education
Gilbert and Sullivan 245-46. See also Operettas
Grant support programs 57-59, 78
See also Scholarships and fellowships
Gregorian chant
textual incipits index 275
thematic index 30, 275

Guitar. See Instrumental music

H

Handicapped and music, the. See Special education
Harmony. See Music structure, theory, and composition
Harp. See Instrumental music
Harpsichord. See Keyboard music, instruments, and pedagogy
Hawaiian music 215
Headstart programs 143
Hebrew music. See Jewish music
HEW. See U.S. Department of Health, Education and Welfare
Hi-fidelity industry 65
Hi-fidelity systems 405, 407
Higher education and teacher education, music in 131-39
- accreditation 9-10
- associations 137-39
- certification of teachers 135, 137, 139
- contemporary music 135
- degrees 9-11
- directories 7-11
- facilities for performing arts 13-14
- facts and statistics 9-11
- faculties, directories of 10, 11
- foreign study 10
- institutional information 13, 14, 131-33
- international music institutions 13, 14
- internships 133
- junior college music 136
  - NASM curriculum 138
- medieval and renaissance universities 133
- music curriculum 353
- performance-based 133
- student teaching 133
- teacher education programs 135
- teacher examinations 136
- women in 136-37

History of Music 179-90
- associations 190
- See also Appreciation and understanding of music; Musicology; Ethnomusiocology

Honor societies 70
Humanities 168, 170, 172, 173
- book reviews 19
- index 24. See also Indexing journals
- information sources 90
- See also Music education; Arts and music; Aesthetics and music

Hymnology. See Religious music

I

Improvisation 340, 353
Indexes
- American doctoral dissertations 45
- in progress and unpublished 35
- See also Thematic indexes and catalogs; specific subject areas

Indexing journals 23-25
Indian music 181, 185, 200
- records 421

Indian (American) music 200, 214
Industrial uses of music 395
Industry and music 7-8, 62-64
Information centers (bibliographic) 36
Information services and systems 53-55
Information theory 163
Institutional information 9-11
Instrumental music 295-347
- associations 324-29, 338
- band 295-303
- brasses 315-18
- buyers' guides 295
- chamber music 321-23
- computer-assisted instruction 295
- conducting 369-75
- ethnic 331-38
- instruments
  - Biblical 278, 337
  - collections of 4, 10, 331-38
  - easy-to-play 111, 113, 118, 296, 439
  - electronic 333
  - ethnic 200
  - folk 331-38
  - guitar 209
  - historical references 331-38
  - manufacturers 7, 8, 334, 335, 441-44

repair and maintenance 303-4, 332
rhythm band 439
Jewish 271
library administration 297
orchestra 297-99
orchestral music analyses 170
pedagogical guides 295-304
percussion 318-21
percussion scoring 320, 364
performance measurement 101
platforms, shells, storage and sound modules 447
recorders 439
reference books 295-97
strings 304-10
acoustics 378
physiological studies 103
techniques 304-21
tuning 297, 298, 377
vibrato studies 101
woodwinds 310-15
recordings 311
scoring for 362
See also Careers in music; Conducting; Orchestration; Band, scoring; Physiological aspects of music
International Association of Music Libraries 6
International directories. See Associations
International Society for Music Education 155
international status 86, 87
yearbook 37
International Trombone Association 316
Interpretation 287, 366-67
See also Keyboard music, instruments, and pedagogy
Interscholastic activities 152
Israel, music of. See Jewish music

J

Jaques-Dalcroze. See Dalcroze eurhythmics
Jazz 257-60
Bibliography 258-59
black nationalism 268
composition 259
orchestration 259
records 260
Smithsonian Jazz Collection 260
See also Popular music; Phonograph records and audio tapes
Jewish Music 271-73
associations 272-73
encyclopedia 272
periodicals bibliography 271
Journals
aesthetics and music 165
music, education research 37-38
nonprint media 449
psychology of music 104-5
research in allied fields 39-40
Junior college music. See Higher education and teacher education, music in
Junior high and middle school music 125-26

K

Keyboard harmony. See Music structure, theory, and composition
Keyboard music, instruments, and pedagogy 339-47
accompanying 339
associations 346
clavichord 344-45
harpsichord 344-45
history, performance, pedagogy 339-42
improvisation 340, 353
organ 345-46
organ music in print 345
piano certification standards 96
piano literature 342-44
four-hand 343
piano tuning and servicing 344
piano tuning trade journals 38
See also Music Teachers National Association
Kochel catalog 31
Kodaly, principles of 118-20

L

Leadership 151
Leadership, registry of music education 41
Legal matters in music. See Business aspects of music and music education
Leisure, music and. See Special education
Libraries and collections
directories 3-11
foreign
Canada 3, 4
Europe 3, 4
France 3
Italy 3
Portugal 3
Spain 3
United Kingdom 4
music research 3, 49, 50
See also Appendix A
Library, music
administration 297
associations 5-6
librarianship 152
Literature, musical, voices and instruments combined 130

M

Manhattanville Music Curriculum Program 107
Manuscripts
collections 4, 29
European composers in American literature 29
polyphonic music 35
Manuscript writing 349-50
Marching band. See Band, marching
Mason, Lowell 277
Masters' theses 47
Medical aspects of music
voice 282, 286-87
See also Special Education, music therapy
MENC. See Music Educators National Conference
Metropolitan Opera 238, 243
Microfiche, music on 17-18, 181
media catalogs on 411
music serials 21
rare works 181
Microfilm, music serials 21
Microteaching 405
Middle schools. See Junior high and middle school music
Minority groups and music. See Urban education and the culturally disadvantaged
Monographs 33
Monuments. See Sets and series 30
Moog synthesizers 235
Moravian music 276
Mozart, Wolfgang 31
MTNA. See Music Teachers National Association
Mursell, James L. 88-89
Museums 5, 10, 11
Musicals. See Opera
Musical talent 94-105
Music book series 122-24
Music concrete, computer applications 409-10
Music councils and arts programs, organization of 62
Music education
accountability 84
administration evaluation 83-85
associations and their publications 92-97
British and American compared 86
British primary schools and music 112
cognitive learning 118, 149, 150
comprehensive programs. 90, 129, 153
history and trends 83-92
institutions 7-8
international status 86, 87, 91, 93
music book series 122-24
objectives
philosophical foundations, principles, practices 83-92
planning and equipping facilities 150
standards (MENC) 89
See also Administration and supervision of music education

Music Educators National Conference 93–95
- associated organizations 94
- directory 10, 41
- historical center 94–95
- publications 10
- state organizations 10, 94
- student membership 94

Musicianship
- interpretation 366–67
- teaching of 365–66

Music Industry Council 63
Music, instrumental. See Instrumental Music
Music Library Association (MLA) 5
Musicology 191–97
- associations 196–98
- dissertations 43–47
- journals 194–96
- masters' theses 47

Music structure, theory, and composition 349–68
- associations 367–68
- band scoring 362–65
- composition 361–62
- counterpoint 356–57
- form, style, and analysis 357–60
- harmony and theory 350–56
- interpretation 366–67
- keyboard harmony 353
- Latin treatises 35
- notation and manuscript writing 349–50
- orchestration 362–64
- polyphonic music 35
- teaching methods 365–66
- See also Bibliographical sources

Music Teachers National Association 96

N

NACWPI. See National Association of College Wind and Percussion Instructors
NASM. See National Association of Schools of Music
National anthems 174, 175, 213, 218
National Association of College Wind and Percussion Instructors (NACWPI) 95, 315, 319
- recordings 418
- research library 296, 311

National Association of Schools of Music (NASM) 96, 136, 138–39
- NASM curriculum 138

National Audiovisual Center 412
National Council for the Arts 59
National Endowment for the Arts 59
National Information Center for Educational Media. See NICEM Indexes
National Music Council 97
National Society for Study in Education 92
New Hampshire and music 208
New York City Opera 242
NICEM Indexes (National Information Center for Educational Media)
- audio tapes 414
- 8mm motion picture cartridges 426
- overhead transparencies 437
- producers and distributors 412
- records (educational) 415
- 16mm educational films 426
- slides 435
- 35mm filmstrips 426
- video tapes 433

North Carolina folklore 209
Notation, music 349–50
- medieval 193

O

Ohio State University School of Music Information System 54–55
Open classroom 111–12, 114, 115, 117
Open education. See Open classroom
Opera 237–48
- American 242–43
- associations 253–54
- books in print 237
- companies and workshops 243

dictionary--catalog 240
directories 13, 14
foreign contemporary 240
history 240-42
light opera and musicals 243-46
Metropolitan Opera 238, 243
New York City Opera 242
production guides 246-47
recordings 239, 418
stage direction 246
television productions 246
themes 29
See also Films and filmstrips; Festivals
Operettas 243-46
books in print 237
dictionary--catalog 240
Oratorios, themes 29
Orchestra 297-99
American symphony 297, 298, 299
conductors (USA) 373
literature, contemporary 299
literature for small orchestras 299
pitch measurements 378
scores 30
themes 29
tuning 298
youth 90
youth concerts 128, 130, 299
youth directory 299
See also Instrumental music
Orchestration 362-64
acoustics 377
jazz 259
scoring for percussion 320, 364
Orff, principles of 118-20
Organ. See Keyboard music, instruments, and pedagogy
Organizations
directories 9-11
See also Associations
Oriental music, discography 419, 420
Ornamentation, vocal 290
Orthodontics and instrument performance 314
Overhead transparencies 437

P

Painting. See Arts and music
Parents' guides 87, 107, 118
People-to-People Music Committee 97
Percussion. See Instrumental music, percussion
Performing arts
artist managers 13, 14
directories 13, 14
Performing rights. See Business aspects of music; Music education
Periodicals and professional journals
abstracting and services 22
British folk music 210
educational, index to 54
guides to 7, 8, 10, 13, 14, 21-25
indexing journals 23-25
information for writers 63
Jewish (bibliography) 271
medical indexes 24
musicology 194-96
out-of-print music education journals 94
performing arts index 14
reprint editions, list of 21
research (allied fields) 39-40
research (music education) 37 38
serials in microform 21
state publications 41
Yiddish 271
See also appendix B for alphabetical listing
Philosophical foundations, principles, and practices 83-92. See also Music education
Phonograph records and audio tapes 413-23
band 420
brasses 315
encyclopedias 413-23
ethnomusicological 199
festivals 13
folk music 207, 211
guides to 171
Harrison Record and Tape Guides 414
history of music 179
international catalog of folk music 211
jazz 260, 421, 422
NICEM record index 415

NICEM tape index 414
opera recording guides 239
operatic singing analyzed 283
percussion 319, 321
popular 257
recording companies 423
reviews 416-17
Schwann catalogs 415, 416, 420
Smithsonian Jazz Collection 260
Sousa discography 420
special collections 417-22
trombone 316
trumpet 316
woodwinds 311
Physical aspects of music. See Acoustics
Physiological aspects of music
brasses 317
orthodontics 314
piano 341
string playing 306, 308, 309
voice 282, 284-90
Piaget's theory 118
Piano
See Keyboard music, instruments, and pedagogy
Piano tuning and servicing. See Keyboard music, instruments, and pedagogy
Planning and equipping music facilities. See Music education; Administration and supervision of music education
Plato 187
Polyphonic music, manuscripts 35
Polyphony. See Counterpoint
Popular music 255-57
associations 262-63
index 256
jazz, Smithsonian Jazz Collection 260
titles 29
See also Phonograph records and audio tapes
Primitive music 189
Professional journals. See Periodicals and professional journals
Programmed instruction 16, 84
See also Technology in music education
Program notes 30, 176
Proposal writing 57
Psychological aspects of music 89 99-105, 118
abstracts 27
journals 104-5
psychophysics of music 379
Public relations 150
Public school music. See Music education
Public school music history 83
Public school systems directories 9
Publishers, listing of 7, 8, 13, 64
Publishing. See Business aspects of music; Music education

R

Recorder. See Instrumental music
Records. See Phonograph records and audio tapes
Recreation. See Special education
Rehearsals. See Conducting
Religious Music 89, 275-80
associations 278-80
contemporary 228
dissertations and theses 276
Gregorian chant 275
instruments (Biblical) 278
journals 278-80
liturgical dictionary 276
Moravian 276
sacred music in print, catalog 282
Tudor 278
twentieth century 277
See also Jewish music
Repair of instruments. See Instrumental music, repair and maintenance
Research
action 50, 51
bibliographic sources 33-36
computer applications 409-10
evaluation 45
experimental 50, 99-101
grants, funding 57-59
institutions 11
journals
allied fields 39-40, 53-54
music education 37-38

See also Periodicals and professional journals; Lists of associations and their publications at the end of each section
libraries 3-6
performing arts 17
proposal writing 57
suggestions for improvement 51
techniques 49-51
vocal 282, 284, 286-87
See also appendix A; Psychological aspects of music; Physiological aspects of music
Retrieval information services. See In-services and systems
Rhode Island and music 208
Rhythm 86, 11, 112, 114, 119, 187, 361
bibliography 356, 366
Dalcroze 107
for the deaf 385
Rhythm band instruments, teaching aids 439
Rock music 261-62
See also Popular music; Phonograph records and audio tapes
Russia and music 175, 180, 186

S

Sacred music. See Religious music
Scale systems 378
Scheduling 151
Schenker theory method 355
Schillinger system of composition 355
Scholarships and fellowships 7, 8, 10, 14, 57-59, 78
foreign study 65
Schwann Record and Tape Guides 415, 416, 420
Science and music
junior high 125
See also Acoustics
Score reading. See Conducting
Scores (Symphonic) 30
Seashore, Carl E. 100
Secondary school music 127-30
Serials in microform. See Periodicals and professional journals
Sets and series 17, 30, 34
Shaker music 180
Shakespeare and music 171, 172
Sight singing. See Music structure, theory, and composition
Singers
awards for 59
biographical dictionary 282
care of voice 284
interpretations of 283
in New York 282
opera 239
opportunities 282
See also Choral and vocal music
Slides (35mm) index 435
Smithsonian Jazz Collection 260
Social psychology of music 85, 393
Sonata. See Form, style, and analysis
Songs 282-94
slave 267
themes 29
Song writing. See Composition
Sororities 69-70
Soundproof modules 447
Sousa, John Philip 300
catalog 300
discography 420
Spanish music discography 420
Special education
associations 387-91, 395-96, 400-401
the blind and music 383-87
music therapy 393-96
exceptional children 383-86
computer data bnak 53
the gifted and music 128, 397
the handicapped and music, the 383-91
instructional materials center 386
music therapy 393-96
recreation and music 383, 399-401
Staging 13
Standards for music programs 152
State journals and other publications 25, 41
Stereo sound systems. See Hi-fidelity systems
String instruction and performance. See Instrumental music

Student organizations 93, 94, 96
See also Fraternities; Sororities; Honor Societies
Summer programs and camps 10-11, 14, 150, 400
for the disadvantaged 146
See also Urban education and the culturally disadvantaged
Supervision. See Administration and supervision of music education
Suzuki talent education 91, 310
Symphonic themes 29, 30
Symphony orchestra. See Orchestra
Symphony research 34
Synthesizers 235, 236

T

Talent 99-104
of the academically gifted 128
of the gifted 397
Tanglewood symposium, reports 84, 89
Teacher education. See Higher education and teacher education, music in
Technology in music education 405-8
Teenagers, music for 130
Television and music instruction 405-8
scoring for 363, 364
stations 411
video tape guides 411-12, 433
Terms, musical. See Dictionaries and encyclopedias
Tests and measurements 99-104
music teacher 136
Textbooks
elementary and secondary 15-16
MENC collection 94-95
Theatre music. See Popular music
Thematic indexes and catalogs 29-31
Theory, music. See Music structure, theory, and composition
Therapy and music. See Special education, music therapy
Theses. See Masters' theses
Trade journals 38
Tudor church music 278
Tuning 377
Twentieth century music 183, 184, 215

U

UNESCO record anthologies 421
Union Catalogs 3, 4
United Kingdom's musicians and activities 13
U.S. Armed Forces, Music in 215
U.S. Department of Health, Education and Welfare, subject catalog of 154
Urban education and culturally disadvantaged 108, 141-48
ERIC clearinghouse 148
Great Cities Program 143
teacher training 144

V

Victorian music 186
Video tapes. See Television and music instruction
Viola. See Instrumental music
Virginia and music 205, 208
Visible speech 288
Vocal music. See Choral and vocal music
Voice. See Choral and vocal music

W

Wallenstein Collection of Music 95
Wind band. See Band
Women in continuing education 136-37
Woodwinds. See Instrumental music
Works Progress Administration (WPA) 152
WPA. See Works Progress Administration

Y

Yearbooks and source books 91-92
Young Audiences, Inc. 97
Youth concerts. See Orchestra
Youth orchestra. See Orchestra